Just One Evil Act

ALSO BY

ELIZABETH GEORGE

FICTION

A Great Deliverance

Payment in Blood

Well-Schooled in Murder

A Suitable Vengeance

For the Sake of Elena

Missing Joseph

Playing for the Ashes

In the Presence of the Enemy

Deception on His Mind

In Pursuit of the Proper Sinner

A Traitor to Memory

I, Richard

A Place of Hiding

With No One as Witness

What Came Before He Shot Her

Careless in Red

This Body of Death

Believing the Lie

YOUNG ADULT

The Edge of Nowhere

NONFICTION

Write Away: One Novelist's Approach
to Fiction and the Writing Life

ANTHOLOGY

A Moment on the Edge: 100 Years of
Crime Stories by Women

Two of the Deadliest: New Tales of Lust, Greed, and
Murder from Outstanding Women of Mystery

ELIZABETH GEORGE

Just One Evil Act

DUTTON

DUTTON
Published by the Penguin Group
Penguin Group (USA) LLC
375 Hudson Street
New York, New York 10014

USA | Canada | UK | Ireland | Australia | New Zealand | India | South Africa | China
penguin.com.
A Penguin Random House Company

REGISTERED TRADEMARK—MARCA REGISTRADA

LIBRARY OF CONGRESS CATALOGING-IN-PUBLICATION DATA
George, Elizabeth, 1949–
Just one evil act / Elizabeth George.
pages   cm.
ISBN 978-0-525-95296-1
1. Havers, Barbara (Fictitious character)—Fiction. 2. Lynley, Thomas (Fictitious character)—Fiction. 3. Women detectives—England—Fiction. 4. Kidnapping—Investigation—Fiction. 5. London (England)—Fiction. 6. Mystery fiction. I. Title.
PS3557.E478J87   2013
813'.54—dc23   2012049712

Printed in the United States of America
1   3   5   7   9   10   8   6   4   2

Set in Bembo Std
Designed by Amy Hill

To Susan Berner
wonderful friend,
outstanding role model,
and
twenty-five years
superlative reader

Just One Evil Act

The world is still deceived with ornament.
In law, what plea so tainted and corrupt
But, being season'd with a gracious voice,
Obscures the show of evil?

THE MERCHANT OF VENICE

15 NOVEMBER

S itting on a plastic chair inside Brompton Hall among a crowd of two hundred shouting individuals—all dressed in what had to be called alternative garb—was the last thing Thomas Lynley had ever expected to find himself doing. Edgy music was blasting from speakers the size of a tower block on Miami Beach. A food stall was doing a very brisk business in hot dogs, popcorn, lager, and soft drinks. A female announcer was periodically shrieking above the din to call out scores and name penalties. And ten helmeted women on roller skates were racing round a flat ring delineated with tape on the concrete floor.

It was supposed to be an exhibition match only: something to educate the populace in the finer points of women's flat track roller derby. But it was a case of tell-that-to-the-players, for the women engaged in the bout were deadly serious.

They had intriguing names. All of them were printed, along with suitably menacing photos, in the programmes that had been distributed as spectators took their seats. Lynley had chuckled as he'd read each nom de guerre. Vigour Mortis. The Grim Rita. Grievous Bodily Charm.

He was there because of one of the women, Kickarse Electra. She skated not with the local team—London's the Electric Magic—but rather with the team from Bristol, a savage-looking group of females who went by the alliterative collective Boadicea's Broads. Her actual name was Daidre Trahair, she was a large animal veterinarian employed at Bristol's zoo, and she had no idea that Lynley was among the howling mass of spectators. He wasn't sure if he was going to keep matters that way. He was, at this point, operating strictly by feel.

He had a companion with him, having lacked the courage to venture into this unknown world on his own. Charlie Denton had accepted his invitation to be enlightened, educated, and entertained at Earls Court Exhibition Centre, and at this moment, he was milling among the crowd at the snack stall.

He'd made the declaration of "It's on me, m'lord . . . sir," with that final word a hasty correction that one would think by now he'd not even have to make. For he'd been seven years in Lynley's employ, and when he wasn't addressing his passion for the stage through auditions for various theatrical events in Greater London, he served as manservant, cook, housekeeper, aide-de-camp, and general factotum in Lynley's life. He'd so far managed Fortinbras in a north London production, but the West End north London was not. So he soldiered on in his double life, determinedly believing that his Big Break was only round the next corner.

Now, he was amused. Lynley could see that in Denton's face as he made his way back across Brompton Hall to the array of chairs among which Lynley sat. He carried a cardboard food tray with him.

"Nachos," Denton said as Lynley frowned down at something that looked like orange lava erupting from a mountain of fried tortilla. "Your dog's got mustard, onions, and relish. The ketchup looked iffy so I gave it a pass, but the lager's nice. Have at it, sir."

Denton said all this with a twinkle in his eye, although Lynley reckoned it could have been just the light shining on the lenses of his round-framed spectacles. He was daring Lynley to refuse the offered repast and instead come forth as he really was. He was also entertained by the sight of his employer sitting chummily next to a bloke whose potbelly overhung his baggy jeans and whose dreadlocks fell the length of his back. Lynley and Denton had come to depend upon this individual. His name was Steve-o, and what he didn't know about women's flat track roller derby did not, apparently, bear knowing at all.

He was attached to Flaming Aggro, he'd told them happily. Plus, his sister Soob was a member of the cheering squad. This latter group of individuals had taken up a position whose disturbing proximity to Lynley added to the general cacophony surrounding him. They wore black from head to toe with embellishments of hot pink in the form of tutus, hair decorations, knee socks, shoes, or waistcoats, and they had so far spent most of their time screaming "Break 'em, baby!" and shaking pink and silver pompoms.

"Great sport, innit?" Steve-o kept saying as the Electric Magic piled the points onto the scoreboard. "It's tha' Deadly Deedee-light does most of the scoring. Long 's she don't rack up the penalties, we're in, mate." And then onto his feet he leapt, shouting, "Do it, Aggro!" as his girlfriend swept by in the midst of the pack.

Lynley was loath to tell Steve-o that he was a supporter of Boadicea's Broads. It was a matter of chance that he and Denton had placed themselves among the Electric Magic fans. The Boadicea's Broads crowd was on the other side of the taped-off ring, being led into a frenzy of synchronised shouting by their own squad of cheerleaders who, like those supporting the Electric Magic, were dressed in black but with touches of red. They appeared to have more experience in the arena of cheerleading. They executed vague dance moves with accompanying leg kicks that were most impressive.

It was the sort of event that should have appalled Lynley. Had his father been there—doubtless dressed to the nines with one or two touches of ermine and red velvet lest someone doubt his position in society—he would have lasted less than five minutes. The sight of the women on roller skates might have given him a coronary, and listening to Steve-o drop his *t*'s and ignore his *h*'s would have made the poor man's blood run cold. But Lynley's father was long in his grave, and Lynley himself had spent most of the evening grinning so much that his cheeks were actually beginning to hurt.

He'd learned far more than he'd ever have imagined possible upon having made the decision to accept the invitation that had been printed on a handbill he'd found among his post a few days earlier.

He'd discovered they were meant to keep their eyes on the jammer, identified by the star cap that stretched across her helmet. This wasn't a permanent position for a skater, as the star cap was passed round among the women. But the jammer was the team's scoring position, and the ultimate scoring came during a power jam when the opposing team's jammer had to sit in the penalty box. He'd learned the purpose of the pack and, thanks to Steve-o, what it meant when the lead jammer rose from her crouched position to place her hands on her hips. He was still rather vague on the purpose of the pivot—although he knew who she was by the striped cap she wore stretched over her helmet—but he was definitely getting the idea that roller derby was a sport of strategy as well as skill.

Mostly, he'd kept his eyes on Kickarse Electra throughout the match-up between London and Bristol. She, he discovered, was quite a jammer. She skated aggressively, like a woman to the roller skates born. Lynley wouldn't have thought it possible of the quiet, thoughtful veterinarian he'd met seven months earlier on the coast of Cornwall. He knew she was practically unbeatable at darts. But this . . . ? He never would have guessed it.

His pleasure in the wild sport had been interrupted only once, in the middle of a power jam. He'd felt his mobile vibrate in his pocket, and he'd dug it out to see who was ringing him. His first thought was that the Met was calling him back to work. For the caller was his usual partner, Detective Sergeant Barbara Havers. Still, she was ringing from her home phone and not from her mobile so perhaps, he thought, he was in luck and nothing had occurred that wanted his attention.

He'd answered, but he'd not been able to hear her. The noise was far too intense. He'd shouted that he would ring her back as soon as he was able to do so, and he'd shoved the mobile back into his pocket and forgotten about the matter.

The Electric Magic won the bout twenty minutes later. The two groups of skaters congratulated each other. Athletes mingled with spectators then, cheerleaders mingled with athletes, referees mingled with each other. No one was in a hurry to leave, which was all to the good since Lynley intended to do a little mingling himself.

He turned to Denton. "I'm not sir."

Denton said, "Pardon?"

"We're here as friends. Make it school chums. You can do that, can't you?"

"What, me? Eton?"

"It's well within your skill set, Charlie. And call me either Thomas or Tommy. It doesn't matter which."

Denton's round eyes got even rounder behind his spectacles. He said, "You want me to . . . I'll probably choke if I try to say it."

"Charlie, you're an actor, yes?" Lynley said. "This is your BAFTA moment. I'm not your employer, you're not my employee. We're going to talk to someone, and you're going to pose as my friend. It's . . ." He sought the correct term. "It's improv."

Charlie's face brightened. "C'n I do the Voice?"

"If you must. Come with me."

Together, then, they approached Kickarse Electra. She was in conversation with London's Leaning Tower of Lisa, an impressive Amazonian who stood at least six feet five inches tall in her roller skates. She would have been an imposing presence anywhere, and she was particularly striking next to Kickarse Electra, who, even in her skates, was some seven inches shorter.

Leaning Tower of Lisa first saw Lynley and Denton. She said, "You two look like trouble of the very best kind. I claim the smaller one." And she rolled over to Denton and put her arm round his shoulders. She kissed his temple. He became the colour of pomegranate seeds.

Daidre Trahair turned. She'd taken off her helmet and she'd raised a pair of plastic goggles to the top of her head. They now held back wisps of her sandy hair, which had escaped from the French braid that contained it. She was wearing her spectacles beneath her goggles, but they were badly smudged. She could see through them perfectly well, though, a fact Lynley ascertained by the colour that her skin took on when she looked at him. He could only just see this colour through her makeup, however. Like the other skaters, she was heavily painted, with an emphasis on glitter and lightning bolts.

"My God," she said.

"I've been called worse." He held up the handbill advertising this event. "We thought to take up the offer. Brilliant, by the way. We quite enjoyed it."

Leaning Tower of Lisa said, "This your first?"

"It is," Lynley told her. And then to Daidre, "You're far more skilled than you let on when we first met. You do this as well as you throw darts, I see."

Daidre's colour deepened. Leaning Tower of Lisa said to her, "You *know* these blokes?"

Daidre said inarticulately, "Him. I know him."

Lynley extended his hand to the other skater. "Thomas Lynley," he told her. "You've got your arm round my friend Charlie Denton."

"Charlie, is it?" Leaning Tower said. "He's awfully sweet-looking. Are you sweet in character as well as in looks, Charlie?"

"I believe he is," Lynley told her.

"Does he like big women, then?"

"I expect he takes them as they come."

"He doesn't talk much, does he?"

"You might be an overpowering presence."

"Isn't that always the case?" Leaning Tower released Denton with a laugh and another solid kiss on his temple. "You change your mind, you know where to find me," she said to him as she rolled away to join her mates.

Daidre Trahair had apparently used the duration of this exchange to come to her wits. She said, "Thomas. You're the last person I would have thought to see at a roller derby match." Then she turned to Denton and extended her hand, saying, "Charlie, I'm Daidre Trahair. How'd you like the match?" She offered this question to them both.

"I'd no idea women could be so ruthless," Lynley said.

"There's Lady Macbeth," Denton pointed out.

"There is that."

Lynley's mobile vibrated in his pocket. He took it out and gave it a glance as before. As before, the caller was Barbara Havers. He let it go to message as Daidre said, "Work?" Before he could reply, she added, "You *are* back at it, aren't you?"

"I am," he told her. "But not tonight. Tonight Charlie and I would like you to join us for a postgame . . . whatever. If you've a mind for it."

"Oh." She looked from him to the milling skaters. She said, "It's only that . . . the team usually go out. It's rather a tradition. Would you like to join us? Apparently this group"—with a nod at the Electric Magic—"go to Famous Three Kings on North End Road. Everyone's invited. It'll be a bit of a crowd scene."

"Ah," Lynley said. "I was rather hoping—*we* were hoping—for something more conducive to conversation. Can you possibly break with this tradition for once?"

She said regretfully, "I do wish . . . It's only that we've come by coach, you see. It would be rather difficult. I have to return to Bristol."

"Tonight?"

"Well, no. We're in a hotel for the night."

"We can take you there whenever you're ready," he offered. And when she still hesitated, he added, "We're actually quite harmless, Charlie and I."

Daidre looked from him to Denton and back to him. She fingered back some of the hair that had come undone from the braid. She said, "I'm afraid I have nothing special . . . I mean, we don't generally dress for going out."

"We shall find a place entirely suitable for whatever state of dishabille you demonstrate," Lynley told her. "Do say yes, Daidre," he added in a quiet voice.

Perhaps it was the use of her name. Perhaps it was the change in his tone. She thought for a moment and then said all right. But she would have to change and perhaps she ought to get rid of the glitter and the lightning bolts as well?

"I find them rather compelling," Lynley told her. "What about you, Charlie?"

"It all makes a certain statement," Denton said.

Daidre laughed. "Don't tell me what that statement is. I'll be a few minutes. Where shall I meet you?"

"We'll be just outside. I'll pull my car round the front."

"How will I know . . . ?"

"Oh, you'll know," Denton told her.

CHELSEA
LONDON

"I see what he meant" were Daidre's first words to Lynley when he got out of the car at her approach. "What is this exactly? How old is it?"

"Healey Elliott," he told her. He opened the door for her. "Nineteen forty-eight."

"Love of his life," Denton added from the back as she slid within. "I'm hoping he leaves it to me in his will."

"Small chance of that," Lynley told him. "I plan to outlive you by several decades." He pulled away from the building and headed towards the car park's exit.

"How do you two know each other?" Daidre asked.

Lynley didn't reply till they were on Brompton Road, motoring past the cemetery. "School together" was what he said.

"With my older brother," Denton added.

Daidre glanced over her shoulder at him, then looked at Lynley. Her eyebrows drew together as she said, "I see," and Lynley had a feeling that she saw more than he really wanted her to.

He said, "He's ten years older than Charlie," and with a glance at the rearview mirror, "That's right, isn't it?"

"Close enough," Denton said. "But listen, Tom, would you mind if I begged off all this? It's been a deucedly long day and if you'll drop me in Sloane Square, I can walk the rest of the way. Early hours at the bank tomorrow. Board meeting. Chairman all in a dither about a Chinese acquisition. You know."

Deucedly? Lynley mouthed. *Tom? Bank? Board meeting?* He half expected Denton to lean forward and give him a wink-wink, nudge-nudge next. He said, "You're sure, Charlie?"

"Couldn't be more so. Long day for me today, longer one tomorrow." To Daidre he added, "Blasted worst employer on earth. Duty calls and all that."

She said, "Of course. And what about you, Thomas? It's late and if you'd rather—"

"I'd rather spend an hour or so with you," he said. "Sloane Square it is, Charlie. You're sure about the walk?"

"Brilliant night for it," Denton said. He said nothing more—thank God, Lynley thought—till they reached Sloane Square, where Lynley dropped him in front of Peter Jones. Then it was, "Cheerio, then," to which Lynley rolled his eyes. He reckoned he was lucky Denton hadn't added "Pip-pip" to his farewell. He was definitely going to have to speak to him. The Voice was bad enough. The vocabulary was worse.

"He's rather sweet," Daidre said as Denton crossed over into the square and made for the Venus fountain in its centre. From there it was a short stroll to Lynley's home in Eaton Terrace. Denton seemed to bounce as he walked. He was, Lynley reckoned, entertained by his own performance.

"*Sweet* wouldn't quite be my word of choice," Lynley said to Daidre. "He's a lodger with me, actually. It's a favour to his brother."

Their own destination wasn't far from Sloane Square. A wine bar on Wilbraham Place stood three doors away from a pricey boutique on the corner. The only table available was one by the door, which wasn't what he would have wished for considering the cold, but it would have to do.

They ordered wine. Something to eat? Lynley offered Daidre. She demurred. He said he would do likewise. There was, he told her, something to be said for the staying power of nachos and hot dogs.

She laughed and fingered the stem of a single rose that was vased on the table. She had the hands one would expect of a doctor, he thought. Her nails were clipped short, to the end of her fingers, and her fingers were strong-looking and not at all slender. He knew what she would call them. Peasant hands, she would say. Or gypsy hands. Or tin-streamer hands. But not the hands one would expect of an aristo, which she most definitely was not.

Suddenly it seemed there was nothing to say after all the time that had passed since last they'd met. He looked at her. She looked at him. He said, "Well," and then he thought what an idiot he was. He had wanted to see her again and here she was and the only thing he could think of was to tell her that he never could quite make out if her eyes were hazel or brown or green. His own were brown, very dark brown at complete contrast to his hair, which was blond in the height of summer but which now, in mid-autumn, was washed-out brown.

She smiled at him and said, "You're looking quite well, Thomas. Very different from the night you and I met."

How true that was, he realised. For the night they'd met was the night he'd broken into her cottage, the only structure on Polcare Cove in Cornwall where an eighteen-year-old cliff climber had fallen to his death. Lynley had been looking for a phone. Daidre had been arriving for a few days' respite from her job. He remembered her outrage at finding him there inside her cottage. He remembered how quickly that outrage had changed to concern for him from something she had read upon his face.

He said, "I *am* well. Good days and bad days, of course. But most of them are good now."

"I'm glad of it," she said.

They fell into silence again. There were things that could have been said. Such as, "And you, Daidre? And what about your parents?" But he couldn't say them, for she had two sets of parents and it would be cruel to force her to talk about one of them. He'd never met her adoptive parents. Her natural parents, on the other hand, he'd seen: at their ramshackle caravan by a stream in Cornwall. Her mother had been dying but hoping for a miracle. She may have passed at this point, but he knew better than to ask.

She said suddenly, "So how long have you been back?"

"At work?" he said. "Since the summer."

"And how do you find it?"

"Difficult at first," he replied. "But of course, it would be."

"Of course," she said.

Because of Helen went unsaid between them. Helen his wife, a victim of murder, and her husband, a detective employed by the Met. The facts of Helen didn't bear thinking about, much less commenting upon. Daidre wouldn't go near that topic of conversation. Nor would he.

He said, "And yours?"

She frowned, obviously not knowing what he was referring to. Then she said, "Oh! My job. It's quite fine. We have two of our female gorillas pregnant and a third not, so we're watching that. We're hoping it won't cause a problem."

"Would it? Normally?"

"The third one lost a baby. Failure to thrive. So things could develop because of that."

"Sounds sad," he said. "Failure to thrive."

"It is, rather."

They were silent again. He finally said, "Your name was on the handbill. Your skating name. I saw it. Have you skated in London prior to this?"

"I have," she said.

"I see." He twirled his wineglass and watched the wine. "I do wish you'd phoned me. You have my card still, don't you?"

"I do," she told him, "and I could have phoned but . . . It's just that it felt . . ."

"Oh, I know how it felt," he said. "Same as before, I daresay."

She gazed at him. "My sort don't say 'I daresay,' you see."

"Ah," he said.

She took a sip of wine. She looked at the glass and not at him. He thought of how different she was, how completely different to Helen. Daidre hadn't Helen's insouciant wit and carefree nature. But there was something compelling about her. Perhaps, he thought, it was everything that she kept hidden from people.

He said, "Daidre," as she said, "Thomas."

He let her go first. "Perhaps you might drive me to my hotel?" she said.

BAYSWATER
LONDON

Lynley wasn't stupid. He knew that driving her to her hotel meant exactly that. It was one of the things he liked about Daidre Trahair. She said exactly what she meant.

She directed him to Sussex Gardens, which lay to the north of Hyde Park in the midst of Bayswater. It was a busy thoroughfare, heavily trafficked both day and night, lined with hotels differentiated one from the other only by their names. These were displayed on the hideous plastic signs that had become so prevalent all over London.

Cheap and lit from within, they were a depressing statement about the decline of individual neighbourhoods. These particular signs identified the sort of hotels that dwelled in the land between essentially all right and utterly horrible, with ubiquitous dingy white sheer curtains at the windows and ill-lit entries with brass fixtures in need of polishing. When Lynley pulled the Healey Elliott up to Daidre's hotel—which was called the Holly—he reckoned he knew which end of the spectrum between all right and horrible the place actually lay.

He cleared his throat.

She said, "Not exactly up to your standards, I expect. But it's a bed, it's only for the night, there's an en suite bathroom, and the expense for the team is minimal. So . . . you know."

He turned to look at her. She was backlit from a streetlamp near the car, and there was a nimbus of light round her hair, putting him in mind of Renaissance paintings of martyred saints. Only the palm leaf was missing from her hand. He said, "I rather hate to leave you here, Daidre."

"It's a bit grim, but I'll survive. Believe me, this is far better than the last place we stayed. An entire cut above, it is."

"That's not actually what I meant," he said. "At least not altogether."

"I suppose I knew that."

"What time do you leave in the morning?"

"Half past eight. Although we never quite manage to get off on time. Heavy partying the night before. I'm probably the first one back."

"I've a spare room in my house," he told her. "Why not sleep there? You could have breakfast with me, and I'd have you back here in time to ride with your teammates to Bristol."

"Thomas . . ."

"Charlie does the breakfasts, by the way. He's an exceptional cook."

She let this one rest there for a minute before she said, "He's your man, isn't he?"

"What on earth do you mean?"

"Thomas . . ."

He looked away. On the pavement a short distance from them, a girl and boy began to have an argument. They'd been holding hands, but she tossed his away like the wrapper from a takeaway burger.

Daidre said, "No one says *deucedly* any longer. At least not this side of a costume drama."

Lynley sighed. "He does get carried away."

"So is he your man?"

"Oh no. He's definitely his own man. I've been trying to rein him in for years, but he enjoys acting the role of servant. I think he believes it's extraordinarily good training. He's probably right."

"So he's not a servant?"

"Lord no. I mean, yes and no. He's an actor, or at least he would be if he had things his way. In the meantime, he works for me. I've no trouble with him going to auditions. He has no trouble with my failing to show up for a dinner he's slaved over for hours in the afternoon."

"Sounds like you fit hand in glove."

"More like foot in sock. Or perhaps sockless foot in shoe." Lynley looked away from the arguing couple who were now shaking their mobile phones at each other. He turned to Daidre. "So he'll be there in the house, Daidre. He'll act as chaperone. And, as I said, we'd have a chance to talk over breakfast. And during the ride back here. Although, of course, I could pop you into a taxi should you prefer that."

"Why?"

"A taxi?"

"You know what I mean."

"It's just that . . . things seem unfinished between us. Or perhaps unsettled. Or merely uneasy. Frankly, I'm not sure what it is, but I expect you feel it as much as I do."

She seemed to think about this for a moment, and from her silence Lynley took hope. But then she shook her head slowly and put her hand on the door handle. "I don't think so," she said. "And besides . . ."

"Besides?"

"Water off a duck's back. That's how I'd put it, Thomas. But I'm not a duck and things don't work that way for me."

"I don't understand."

"You do," she said. "You know that you do." She leaned over and kissed him on the cheek. "I won't lie, though. It was completely lovely to see you again. Thank you. I hope you enjoyed the match."

Before he could reply, she got out of the car. She hurried into the hotel. She did not look back.

BAYSWATER
LONDON

He was still sitting there in front of the hotel in his car when his mobile rang. He was still feeling the pressure of her lips against his cheek and the sudden warmth of her hand on his arm. So deep was he into his thoughts that the mobile's ringing startled him. He realised at its sound that he'd not phoned Barbara Havers back as he'd said he would. He glanced at his watch.

It was one a.m. Couldn't be Havers, he thought. And in the way that the mind will go spontaneously from one thought to another, in the time it took to fish the mobile from his pocket, he thought of his mother, he thought of his brother, he thought of his sister, he thought of emergencies and how they generally did occur in the middle of the night because no one made a friendly call at this hour.

By the time he had the mobile out, he'd decided it had to be a disaster in Cornwall, where his family home was, a heretofore unknown Mrs. Danvers in their employ having set the place alight. But then he saw it was Havers ringing again. He said into the phone hastily, "Barbara. I am so sorry."

"Bloody hell," she cried. "Why didn't you ring back? I've been sitting here. And he's alone over there. And I don't know what to do or what to tell him because the worst of it is that there's sod all *anyone* can do to help and I know it and I lied to him and said we'd do something and I need your *help*. Because there has to be something—"

"Barbara." She sounded completely undone. It was so unlike her to babble like this that Lynley knew something was badly wrong. "*Barbara*. Slow down. What's happened?"

The story she told came out in disjointed pieces. Lynley was able to pick up very few details because she was speaking so fast. Her voice was odd. She'd either been weeping—which hardly seemed likely—or she'd been drinking. The latter made little sense, however, considering the urgency of the story she had to tell. Lynley put together what he could, just the salient details:

The daughter of her neighbour and friend Taymullah Azhar was missing. Azhar, a science professor at University College London, had come home from work to find the family flat stripped of nearly all possessions belonging to his nine-year-old daughter as well as to her mother. Only the child's school uniform remained, along with a stuffed animal and her laptop, all of this lying on her bed.

"Everything else is gone," Havers said. "I found Azhar sitting on my front step when I got home. She'd rung me, too, Angelina had done, sometime during the day. There was a message on my phone. Could I look in on him this evening? she'd asked me. 'Hari's going to be upset,' she said. Oh yes, too right. Except he's not upset. He's destroyed. He's wrecked, I don't know what to do or to say, and Angelina even made Hadiyyah leave that giraffe behind and we *both* know why because it meant a time when he'd taken her to the seaside and he'd won it for her and when someone took it off her on the pleasure pier—"

"Barbara." Lynley spoke firmly. "*Barbara.*"

She breathed in raggedly. "Sir?"

"I'm on my way."

CHALK FARM

LONDON

Barbara Havers lived in north London, not far from Camden Lock Market. At one in the morning, getting there was merely a matter of knowing the route, as there was virtually no traffic. She lived in Eton Villas, where parking one's car depended upon very good luck. There was none of that at an hour when the residents of the area were all tucked up into their beds, though, so Lynley made do with blocking the driveway.

Barbara's digs sat behind a conversion, a yellow Edwardian villa done into flats at some point during the late twentieth century. She herself occupied a structure behind it, a wood-framed building that had once done duty as God only knew what. It had a tiny fireplace, which suggested it had always been used as some sort of living space, but its size suggested that only a single occupant had ever lived there, and one needing very little room.

Lynley cast a glance at the ground-floor flat inside the conversion as he made his way along the paved path towards the back of the villa. This was, he knew, the home occupied by Barbara's friend Taymullah Azhar, and the lights within it were still blazing out onto the terrace in front of the flat's French windows. He assumed from his conversation with Barbara that she'd been inside her own digs when he'd spoken to her, though, and when he got behind the villa, he saw the lights were on inside her bungalow as well.

He knocked quietly. He heard a chair scraping against the floor. The door swung open.

He was unprepared for the sight of her. He said, "God in heaven. What have you done?"

He thought in terms of ancient rites of mourning in which women chopped off their hair and poured ashes upon the stubble that remained. She'd done the first, but she'd skipped the second. There were, however, ashes aplenty on the small table in what went for the kitchen. She'd sat there for hours, it seemed to Lynley, and in a glass dish that had served as her ashtray, the remains of at least twenty cigarettes lay crushed, spilling burnt offerings everywhere.

Barbara looked ravaged by emotion. She smelled like the inside of a fireplace. She was wearing an ancient chenille dressing gown in a hideous shade of mushy-peas green, and her sockless feet were tucked into her red high-top trainers.

She said, "I left him over there. I said I'd be back but I haven't been able to. I didn't know what to tell him. I thought if you came . . . Why didn't you ring me? Couldn't you tell . . . Bloody hell, sir, where the hell . . . Why didn't you . . . ?"

"I'm so sorry," he said. "I couldn't hear you on my mobile. I was . . . It doesn't matter. Tell me what happened."

Lynley took her arm and guided her to the table. He took away the glass dish of cigarette dog ends as well as an unopened packet of Play-ers and a box of kitchen matches. He put all of this on the worktop of her kitchen area, where he also set the kettle to boil. He rustled in a cupboard and came up with two bags of PG Tips as well as some ar-tificial sweetener, and he excavated through a sink filled with un-washed crockery till he discovered two mugs. He washed them, dried them, and went to the small refrigerator. Its contents were as appalling as he'd expected they would be, heavily given to takeaway food cartons and to-be-heated ready-made meals, but among all of this he found a pint of milk. He brought it out as the kettle clicked off.

Throughout everything, Havers was silent. This was completely un-characteristic of her. In all the time he'd known the detective sergeant, she'd never been without a comment to toss in his direction, particularly in a situation like this one in which he was not only making tea but actually giving some thought to toast as well. It rather unnerved him, this silence of hers.

He brought the tea to the table. He placed a mug in front of her. There was another sitting near to where the cigarettes had been, and he removed this. It was cold, a skin of someone's indifference to it floating on its surface.

Havers said, "That was his. I did the same thing. What is it about tea and our bloody society?"

"It's something to do," Lynley told her.

"When in doubt, make tea," she said. "I could do with a whiskey. Or gin. Gin would be nice."

"Have you any?"

"'Course not. I don't want to be one of those old ladies who sip gin from five o'clock in the afternoon till they're comatose."

"You're not an old lady."

"Believe me, it's out there."

Lynley smiled. Her remark was a slight improvement. He pulled the other chair out from the table and joined her. "Tell me."

Havers spoke of a woman called Angelina Upman, the apparent mother of Taymullah Azhar's daughter. Lynley himself had met both Azhar and the girl Hadiyyah, and he'd known that the mother of this child had been out of the picture for some time prior to Barbara's purchase of the leasehold on her bungalow. But he'd not been told that Angelina Upman had waltzed back into the lives of Azhar and Hadiyyah the previous July, and he'd never learned that not only were Azhar and the mother of his child not married but also that Azhar's name was not on the birth certificate of the girl.

Other details came pouring forth, and Lynley tried to keep up with them. It hadn't been due to the fashion of the times that Azhar and Angelina Upman had remained unmarried. Rather, there had been no marriage possible between them because Azhar had left his legal wife for Angelina, and this was a woman he'd refused to divorce. With her, he had two other children. Where they all lived was something Barbara didn't know.

What she did know was that Angelina had seduced Azhar and Hadiyyah into believing she'd returned to take her rightful place in their lives. She needed to obtain their trust, Barbara said, so that she could lay her plans and execute them.

"That's why she came back," Barbara told him. "To get everyone's trust. Mine included. I've been a bloody idiot most of my life. But this one . . . I've sodding outdone myself."

"Why did you never tell me any of this?" Lynley asked.

"Which part?" Havers asked. "Because the bloody idiot part I would've expected you already knew."

"The part about Angelina," he said. "The part about Azhar's wife, the other children, the divorce or lack thereof. All of that. Any of that. Why didn't you tell me? Because you certainly must have felt . . ." He could say no more. Havers had never spoken of her feelings either for Azhar or for his young daughter, and Lynley had never asked. It had seemed more respectful to say nothing when the truth, he admitted, was that saying nothing had just been the easier thing to do.

"I'm sorry," he said.

"Yeah. Well, you were occupied anyway. You know."

He knew she was talking about his affair with their superior officer at the Met. He'd been discreet. So had Isabelle. But Havers was no fool, she hadn't been born recently, and she was nothing if not acutely percipient when it came to him.

He said, "Yes. Well. That's over, Barbara."

"I know."

"Ah. Right. I expect you do."

Havers turned her tea mug in her hands. Lynley saw it bore a caricature of the Duchess of Cornwall, helmet-haired and square-smiled. Unconsciously, she covered this caricature with her hand as if in apology to the unfortunate woman. She said, "I didn't know what to tell him, sir. I came home from work and I found him sitting on my front step. He'd been there hours, I think. I took him back to his flat once he'd told me what happened—that she'd taken off and that Hadiyyah was with her—and I had a look round and I swear to God, when I saw she'd taken everything with her, I didn't know what to do."

Lynley considered the situation. It was more than difficult and Havers knew this, which was why she'd been immobilised. He said, "Take me to his flat, Barbara. Put on some clothes and take me to his flat."

She nodded. She went to the wardrobe and rooted around for some clothes, which she clutched to her chest. She started to head towards the bathroom, but she stopped. She said to him, "Ta for not mentioning the hair, sir."

Lynley looked at her shorn and ruined head. "Ah, yes," he said. "Get dressed, Sergeant."

CHALK FARM
LONDON

Barbara Havers felt appreciably better now that Lynley had arrived. She knew she should have been able to do something to take hold of the reins of the situation, but Azhar's grief had undone her. He was a self-contained man and had always been so in the nearly two years that she had known him. As such, he'd played his cards so close that most of the time she could have sworn he had no cards at all. To see him broken by what his lover had done and to know that she herself should have recognised from their first meeting that something was up with Angelina Upman and with all of Angelina Upman's overtures of friendship towards her . . . This was enough to break Barbara as well.

Like most people, she'd seen only what she wanted to see in Angelina Upman, and she'd ignored everything from red flags to speed bumps. Meantime, Angelina had seduced Azhar back to her bed. She'd seduced her daughter into abject devotion. She'd seduced Barbara into unwitting conspiracy through garnering her cooperative silence about everything having to do with Angelina herself. And this—her disappearance with her daughter in tow—was the result.

Barbara got dressed in the bathroom. In the mirror she saw how terrible she looked, especially her hair. Her head bore great bald patches in spots, and in other spots the remains of what had been an expensive Knightsbridge hairstyle sprang out of her scalp like so many weeds waiting to be pulled from a garden. The only answer to what she'd done to herself was going to be to shave her head completely, but she didn't have time to do that just then. She came out of the bathroom and rooted for a ski cap in her chest of drawers. She put this on and together she and Lynley returned to the front of the house.

Everything was as she'd left it in Azhar's flat. The only difference was that instead of sitting staring at nothing, Azhar was walking aimlessly through the rooms. When, hollow-eyed, he looked in their direction, Barbara said to him, "Azhar, I've brought DI Lynley from the Met."

He'd just emerged from Hadiyyah's bedroom. He was clutching the little girl's stuffed giraffe to his chest. He said to Lynley, "She's taken her."

"Barbara's told me."

"There's nothing to be done."

Barbara said, "There's always something to be done. We're going to find her, Azhar."

She felt Lynley shoot her a look. It told her that she was making promises that neither he nor she could keep. But that was not how Barbara saw the situation. If they couldn't help this man, she thought, then what was the point of being cops?

Lynley said, "May we sit?"

Azhar said yes, yes, of course, and they went into the sitting room. It was still fresh from Angelina's redecoration of it. Barbara saw it now as she should have seen it when Angelina unveiled it to her: like something from a magazine, perfectly put together but otherwise devoid of anyone's personality.

Azhar said as they sat, "I telephoned her parents once you left."

"Where are they?" she asked.

"Dulwich. They wished not to speak to me, of course. I am the ruination of one of their two children. So they will not contaminate themselves through any effort to be of assistance."

"Lovely couple," Barbara noted.

"They know nothing," Azhar said.

"Can you be sure of that?" Lynley asked.

"From what they said and who they are, yes. They know nothing about Angelina and, what's more, they do not want to know. They said she made her bed a decade ago and if she doesn't like the smell of the sheets, it's not down to them to do anything about that."

"There's another child, though?" Lynley said, and when Azhar looked confused and Barbara asked, "What?" he clarified with, "You said you were the ruination of one of their two children. Who is the other and might Angelina be with this person?"

"Bathsheba," Azhar said. "Angelina's sister. I know only her name but have never met her."

"Might Angelina and Hadiyyah be with her?"

"They have no love for each other as I gather these things," Azhar said. "So I doubt it."

"No love for each other according to Angelina?" Barbara asked sharply. The implication was clear to both Lynley and Azhar.

"When people are desperate," Lynley said to the man, "when they plan something like this—because it *would* have taken some planning, Azhar—old grudges are often put to rest. Did you ring the sister? Do you have the number?"

"I know only her name. Bathsheba Ward. I know nothing else. I'm sorry."

"Not a problem," Barbara said. "Bathsheba Ward gives us something to start with. It gives us a place to—"

"Barbara, you are being kind," Azhar said. "As are you"—this to Lynley—"to come here in the dead of night. But I know the reality of my situation."

Barbara said hotly, "I told you we'll find her, Azhar. We *will*."

Azhar observed her with his calm, dark eyes. He looked at Lynley. His expression acted as acknowledgement of something Barbara didn't want to admit and certainly didn't want him to have to face.

Lynley said, "Barbara's told me there's no divorce involved between you and Angelina."

"As we were not married, there is no divorce. And because there was no divorce between me and my wife—my legal wife—Angelina did not identify me as Hadiyyah's father. Which was, of course, her right. I accepted this as one of the outcomes of not divorcing Nafeeza."

"Where is Nafeeza?" he asked.

"Ilford. Nafeeza and the children live with my parents."

"Could Angelina have gone to them?"

"She has no idea where they live, what their names are, anything about them."

"Could they have come here, then? Could they have tracked her down, perhaps? Could they have wooed her out there?"

"For what purpose?"

"Perhaps to harm her?"

Barbara could see how this was entirely possible. She said, "Azhar, that could be it. She could have been taken. This could look like something it isn't at all. They could have come for her and taken Hadiyyah as well. They could have packed everything. They could have forced her to make that call to me."

"Did she sound like someone under duress in the phone message, Barbara?" Lynley asked her.

Of course, she had not. She'd sounded just as she'd always sounded, which was perfectly pleasant and completely open to friendship. "She could have been acting," Barbara said, although even she could hear how desperate she sounded. "She fooled me for months. She fooled Azhar. She fooled her own daughter. But maybe she wasn't fooling at all. Maybe she never intended to leave. Maybe they came for her out of the blue and they've taken her somewhere and she had to leave that message and they forced her to sound—"

"You can't have it both ways," Lynley said, although his voice was kind.

"He is right," Azhar said. "If she was forced to make a phone call, if she was taken from here—she and Hadiyyah—against her will, she would have said something in that phone call to you. She would have left a sign. There would be some indication, but there is not. There is nothing. And what she did leave—Hadiyyah's school uniform, her laptop, that little giraffe—this was to tell me that they are not returning." His eyes grew red-rimmed.

Barbara swung to Lynley. He was, she had long known, the most compassionate cop on the force and quite possibly the most compassionate man she'd ever met. But she could see upon his face that what he felt—beyond sympathy for Azhar—was knowledge of the truth in front of them. She said to him, "Sir. *Sir.*"

He said, "Aside from checking with the families, Barbara . . . She's the mother. She's broken no law. There's no divorce with a judge's decree and a custody ruling that she's defying."

"A private enquiry, then," Barbara said. "If we can do nothing, then a private detective can."

"Where am I to find such a person?" Azhar asked her.

"I can be that person," Barbara told him.

16 NOVEMBER

Absolutely not" was how Acting Detective Superintendent Isabelle Ardery greeted Barbara's request for time off. She went on from this to demand an immediate explanation for the headgear Barbara happened to be wearing. This was a knitted cap of the sort skiers wore, complete with pompom on the top. On the fashion side of things, it scored a zero. On the police side of things, it was into negative numbers. For prior to its ruin, Barbara's hair had been cut and styled upon the strongest recommendation of the acting detective superintendent herself, and since her strongest recommendation was first cousin to an order, Barbara had complied. Thus, its ruin smacked of defiance, which was exactly how Isabelle Ardery was going to see it.

"Take off that hat," Ardery said.

"As to time off, guv . . ."

"I'd like to remind you that you've just had time off," the superintendent snapped. "How many days were you at the beck and call of Inspector Lynley while he was on his little sojourn up in Cumbria?"

Barbara couldn't deny this. She had just finished assisting Lynley in a private endeavour in which he'd been engaged. He'd been tapped by Assistant Commissioner Sir David Hillier for a hush-hush matter near Lake Windermere, and Isabelle Ardery had discovered Barbara's involvement in the matter. She'd not been pleased. Thus, she was going to embrace the idea of Detective Sergeant Havers having more time off to engage in an extracurricular round of policing with all the enthusiasm of a woman being asked to dance the Viennese waltz with a porcupine.

"Take off the hat," Isabelle repeated. "Now."

Barbara knew that way would lead to a very dark place. So she said, "Guv, this is an emergency. This is personal. This is family."

"What part of your family would 'this' be? As I understand matters, you have one member to your family, Sergeant, and she's in a nursing home in Greenford. You can't be saying your mother wants some policing done for her, can you?"

"It's not a nursing home. It's a private residence."

"Is there a carer present? And does she require care?"

"Of course there is and of course she does," Barbara told her. "Obviously, you know that."

"So the policing matter involving your mother is what, exactly?"

"All right." Barbara sighed. "So it's not my mother."

"You said a family matter?"

"All right. It's not my family either. It's a friend, and he's in trouble."

"As are you. Now am I going to have to ask you again to remove that ridiculous hat?"

There was nothing for it. Barbara pulled the ski cap from her head.

Isabelle stared. She raised a hand as if to ward off an apocalyptic vision. "What," she said tersely, "am I to make of this? A momentary slip of the scissors leading to a fatal disaster? Or an unspoken message to your superior officer, in this case that officer being me?"

"Guv, that's not on," Barbara said. "And it's not why I've come to talk to you."

"That's obvious enough. But it's what *I* wish to talk about. And we're back to our previous manner of dress as well, I see. Let me ask again: What sort of message are you sending me, Sergeant? Because the one I'm getting has to do with your future as a traffic warden in the Shetland Islands."

"You know you can't make an issue of this," Barbara told her. "My hair, my clothes. What difference do they make if I'm doing the job?"

"That's just it, isn't it?" Isabelle countered. "*If* you're doing the job. Which, as it happens, you haven't been doing. Which, as it happens, you've just walked in here proposing *not* to do for a few more days or perhaps weeks. While, I expect, you plan to continue collecting your wages in order to keep the only member of your family ensconced in the care home into which she's been placed. Now what is it *exactly* that you want, Sergeant? To continue to be employed and to be paid for being employed or to chase round aiding some nonexistent member of your family in an objective about which, by the way, you are being remarkably closemouthed."

They were face-to-face across the acting superintendent's desk. Outside her office, the buzz of activity rose and fell. Conversations were going on up and down the corridor. The occasional hush among Barbara's fellow officers told her that sound of her argument with Superintendent Ardery was being heard. More gossip for the water cooler, she thought. DS Havers has blotted her copybook again.

She said, "Look, guv, a friend of mine has lost his kid. She's been taken by her mother—"

"So she's hardly lost, is she? And if she's been taken against a ruling of the court, then this 'friend' of yours can ring up his solicitor or his local nick or anyone else who comes to mind because it is *not* your job to swan round the country assisting people in distress unless you are ordered to do so by your commanding officer. Have I made myself clear, Sergeant Havers?"

Barbara was silent. She was also steaming. Her brain was racing with what she *wanted* to say, which was along the lines of "What's twisting your knickers, you bloody cow?" But she knew where a remark like that could get her. The Shetland Islands would seem like paradise compared to where she'd end up. She said reluctantly, "I s'pose you have."

"Good," Isabelle told her. "Now get back to work. And work consists of a meeting you have with the CPS. You can speak to Dorothea about it. She's set it up."

VICTORIA
LONDON

Dorothea Harriman was not only the departmental secretary but also the fashion plate upon whose image Barbara had been supposed to model her makeover. But from the first Barbara had failed to see how Dee Harriman managed to be so gorgeously done up on her paltry

Met salary. She'd declared more than once that it was just a matter of knowing one's colours—whatever that meant—and knowing how to accessorise. Plus, she'd revealed, it did help to keep a record of where the best consignment shops were. Anyone could do it, Detective Sergeant Havers. Really. I could teach you if you like.

Barbara didn't like. She reckoned that Dee Harriman spent every free moment hiking up and down each high street in the capital, prowling for clothes. Who the bloody hell wanted to live like that?

Upon seeing Barbara on her way into Isabelle Ardery's office, Dorothea had been kind enough not to say a word about her head and the ski cap covering it. She'd been an ardent admirer of the cut and the highlights that Barbara had received at the hands of a Knightsbridge stylist. But after wailing "Detective Sergeant Havers!" she'd seemed to read on Barbara's face that the road to interpersonal hell was going to be paved with any questions she might ask about what Barbara had done to herself.

She'd come to whatever terms she needed to come to with regard to Barbara's appearance when Barbara stopped at her desk. She'd obviously overheard the row in the superintendent's office, and she was ready with the information that Isabelle had said she would hand over.

She was supposed to ring the number on this message, Harriman told Barbara. That clerk from the CPS that she'd been meeting with when she skipped out to help Detective Inspector Lynley up in Cumbria . . . ? He was waiting to take up business again. Those witness statements needed going over. The detective sergeant remembered, surely?

Barbara nodded because, of course, she did. The Crown Prosecutor was a Silk with chambers in Middle Temple. She would, she told Harriman, make the call and get on to this business without delay.

"Sorry." Harriman tilted her head towards Isabelle's office. "She's not altogether herself today. Don't know why, exactly."

Barbara did. God only knew how many times a week Isabelle Ardery and Thomas Lynley had been doing their mutual knicker-trawling. But with that at an end, she wagered things round the Yard were going to get tense.

She went to her desk and plopped into its chair. She looked at the phone number Dee Harriman had handed to her. She picked up the handset of the phone and was about to punch in the number when she heard her name spoken—a simple "Barb"—and she looked up to see her fellow detective sergeant Winston Nkata towering over her. He was fingering the long scar on his cheek, the one that marked his formative years spent ganging on the streets of Brixton. He was, as always, impeccably groomed, a man who looked like someone who did his shopping with Harriman hovering at his side. Barbara wondered if he removed his shirt every half hour or so for a spot of pressing in a back room somewhere. Not an inch was wrinkled, not a seam was rucked.

"I had to ask." His voice was soft, his accent a blend of his background, with its Caribbean and its African history.

"What?"

"DI Lynley. He told me . . . your . . . the difference. I 'spect you know what I mean. No big deal to me, 'course, but I reckoned something happened, so I asked him. Plus"—with a tilt of his head towards Isabelle's office—"there was that."

"Oh. Right." He was talking about her hair. Well, everyone was going to be doing that, either to her face or behind her back. At least Winston, as always, was courteous enough to talk to her directly.

"Inspector told me what's going on," he said. " 'Bout Hadiyyah and her mum. Look, I know she's . . . how you feel about her and all that, Barb. I reckoned the guv wasn't going to go for your wanting more time off, so . . ." He slipped a torn bit of a daily calendar towards her. It was one of those desk calendars that had upon it an inspirational saying. This one was "To make God laugh, tell Her your plans," which, Barbara decided, fitted the situation quite well. On this slip of calendar Winston's copperplate handwriting had unfurled a name, Dwayne Doughty, along with an address on the Roman Road in Bow and a telephone number. Barbara read this and looked up. "Private detective," Winston told her.

"Where'd you find a private detective so quick?"

"Where everything gets found: the Internet, Barb. Section on his site from satisfied customers and all the rest. He may've put 'em there himself, but he's worth looking into."

"You knew she'd lock me to my desk, didn't you?" Barbara said shrewdly.

"Figgered, is all," he told her. Kindly, once again, he made no exact mention of what Barbara had done to her appearance.

19 NOVEMBER

Barbara Havers laboured at the job of metaphorically keeping her nose clean at work for the next two days. This meant several meetings with the clerk at the CPS, during which the only pleasurable moment came from once being taken by the Crown Prosecutor for lunch in the impressive dining hall of Middle Temple. The lunch might have been nicer had the Silk not wished to discuss the case in minute detail, but in a situation in which beggars couldn't be et cetera, Barbara did her best to add sparkle and wit to a conversation that actually made her want to bury her head in her mash and commit suicide by carbohydrate inhalation. It was the kind of employment she particularly despised, and she reckoned that Superintendent Ardery was forcing her into it because this was her only way of taking revenge upon Barbara for what she had done to herself.

She'd had to shave the rest of her head. There was nothing else for it, as the hairstyle could not have been saved. What remained was stubble that left her looking vaguely like a cross between a neo-Nazi and a female boxer. She kept it covered with a selection of knitted caps, on which she'd stocked up at the Berwick Street market.

There were actually two cases ongoing to which she could have been assigned, had Ardery chosen to do so. DI Philip Hale was heading one; DI Lynley was heading the other. But until Isabelle Ardery had reached the conclusion that Barbara had been punished enough for her transgressions, Barbara knew that she was stuck with the clerk from the CPS and the witness statements that the Crown Prosecutor was intent upon verifying.

They finished early in the afternoon two days after Barbara's confrontation with the superintendent. She saw her chance in this, so she took it. She rang up Azhar at University College London and she told him she was heading his way. Where are you? she wanted to know. Having a conference with four graduate students in the lab, he told her. Wait for me there, she said. I've come up with something.

The lab proved easy enough to find. It was a place of white coats, computers, fume cupboards, and biohazard signs, complete with impressive microscopes, petri dishes, boxes of slides, glass-fronted cabinets, refrigerators, stools, work stations, and other, more mysterious furnishings. When Barbara joined Taymullah Azhar there, he introduced her politely to the students. Their names were lost to her almost as soon as Azhar said them, mostly because of Azhar himself.

Barbara had seen him daily since Hadiyyah's disappearance. She'd taken him food, but she could tell he had eaten very little of it. Now he was looking worse than ever, mostly from lack of sleep, she decided. Obviously, he was maintaining himself on a diet of cigarettes and coffee. So was she.

She asked him how soon he could get away from the lab. She added that she'd come up with the name of someone who could probably help them. He's a private detective, she told him. Hearing this, Azhar told Barbara he could leave at once.

On their way to Bow, Barbara told Azhar what she had managed to learn about the man towards whose office they were heading. Despite the affirmations of putative "satisfied customers," she'd done some digging about him, and it hadn't been tough, considering the sort of nonsense people advertised about themselves these days on the Internet. She knew Dwayne Doughty was fifty-two years old. She knew he played weekend rugby. She knew he'd been married twenty-six years and was the father of two. Considering the photos he'd posted on his Facebook page, she'd concluded it was a matter of pride to him that each generation of his family had done better than the last. His progenitors had excavated a living from the coal mines of Wigan. His children were graduates of redbrick universities. The way things were going for the Doughty clan, his grandchildren— if he had any off his kids—would take firsts at either Oxford or Cambridge. They were, in short, an ambitious family.

The building that housed Doughty's office, however, didn't suggest ambition. It sat above an establishment called Bedlovers Bedding and Towels, which was closed at the moment and sheltered by a faded blue metal drop-down security door in need of having its rust seen to. Bedlovers itself was housed in a narrow building, bookshelved between the Money Shop and Bangla Halal Grocers.

Oddly, virtually no one was out and about. Two Muslim men in traditional garb were exiting a building some thirty yards down the street, but that was it. Most of the shops were closed. It was a far cry from central London, where the pavements seemed packed both day and night.

They gained access to Dwayne Doughty's office through a door to the left of Bedlovers. It was unlocked, and it opened to a staircase at the foot of which was a square of speckled lino with a welcome mat upon it.

Above stairs, there were two offices only. One bore a sign reading *Knock First Please*. The other, apparently with no need of knocking, bore a request that asked enterers not to let the cat out. They chose *Knock First Please* as being more likely. They did so and a man's voice called, "S'okay. Enter," with an accent that suggested the Doughtys had left Wigan for the East End many decades ago.

Barbara had already told Azhar that she wouldn't be identifying herself as someone from the Met. Doughty might get the wrong idea, like this was a sting operation. They didn't want that.

Doughty was in the middle of attempting to upload photos into a digital picture frame of the sort that altered images every ten seconds or so. He had the directions spread out on his desk along with cords, his camera, and the frame itself. He was squinting at the brochure of directions, one fist clenched and the other ready to crumple the directions into a ball.

He looked up at them and said, "Written by some Chinese bloke with a bloody sadistic streak, this is. I don't know why I bother."

"I hear you," Barbara said.

Even had she not known Doughty played amateur rugby, his nose would have told her as much. It looked as if it had been broken multiple times and his NHS doctor had finally thrown up his hands in defeat and said, "Let it do what it will." It was certainly doing that. It headed off in one direction and then swerved in another, giving his face such an odd asymmetry that it was impossible to move one's gaze from it. Everything else about the man was average: medium build, medium-brown hair, medium weight. Aside from his nose, he was the kind of man one wouldn't notice on the street. But the nose made him unforgettable.

"Miss Havers, I take it?" He rose. Medium height as well, Barbara thought. He added, "And this is the friend you spoke of?"

Azhar crossed the room and extended his hand. "Taymullah Azhar," he said.

"Is it mister?"

"Just Azhar."

Hari, Barbara thought out of nowhere. Angelina called him Hari.

"And this is about a missing child?" Doughty said. "Your child?"

"It is."

"Sit, then." Doughty indicated a chair in front of his desk. There was another, mismatched to the first, at the window—as if its use was for spying on action in the street—and Doughty placed it next to the first, carefully matching one's angle to the other's.

Barbara glanced round the office as he did this. She'd half expected the place to be in the best tradition of private eyes from nearly a century of gumshoe novels. But this office looked like something inhabited by a military officer with its olive-green desk, olive-green metal filing cabinets, and olive-green bookshelves. These contained a matching set of books, neat stacks of periodicals, and university graduation photos of both of his children. There was also—on his desk—a photo of a woman near Doughty's own age, presumably his wife.

Everything was neatly in its place, from the maps of Greater London and the UK pinned to bulletin boards on the wall to the in-and-out boxes on the desk, to the holder for mail and the holder for business cards. Aside from the photos, there was nothing in the room suggestive of decoration beyond a dusty artificial plant atop one of the filing cabinets.

Together, Barbara and Azhar went over the details for Dwayne Doughty. He took notes and Barbara was reassured when he asked good, sharp questions. These gave evidence to the fact that he knew the law. Unfortunately, these also gave evidence to the fact that there was very little that he could do.

Barbara was able to tell him something more than Azhar had been able to reveal to Lynley and to her when they'd met with him on the night of his daughter's disappearance. In what little spare time Isabelle Ardery had been allowing her, she'd managed to locate Bathsheba Ward, the sister of Angelina Upman.

"She's in Hoxton," Barbara told Doughty, and she gave him the address, which he took down in block letters, all upper case. "Married to a bloke called Hugo Ward. Two kids, but they're his, not hers. I had her on the blower, and she pretty much confirmed everything already known about Angelina and her family. The whole lot of them broke off communications about ten years ago when Angelina got together with Azhar. She claims to have no clue where she is and even less interest in finding out. Some sort of digging might be in order there. Bathsheba could be lying."

Doughty nodded as he wrote. "Rest of the family?"

"The Upmans are in Dulwich," Barbara said. She felt Azhar's gaze on her, and she said, "I phoned one evening. Just to see if they'd had any word. Nothing. Except Bathsheba seemed to be telling the truth: no love lost."

"Spoke to them at length, did you?" Doughty asked, his eyes narrowing in on Barbara speculatively.

"The dad. Not at length. Just to ask where Angelina was. Old school chum looking for her. That sort of thing. He hadn't a clue and was happy to announce it. He could've been covering for her, but he didn't seem the type to go to that much trouble."

Doughty gave Azhar his attention, then. He turned to a fresh page in the legal pad on which he'd been taking down the details Barbara had given him. He used the same block printing to put *DAD* at the top of the page. Barbara hadn't seen what he'd put at the top of her own. He said to Azhar, "Give me every name that you can think of associated with Angelina Upman. I don't care who it is, where it comes from, or when she might have known this person. Then we'll do the same for your daughter. Let's see what we can come up with."

BOW
LONDON

Dwayne Doughty stood at the window once the woman and man had left. He waited till they departed the building that housed his office. He watched them walk towards the arch at the corner that announced one was entering the precinct of the Roman Road. They disappeared round the corner to the left. For good measure, he waited another thirty seconds. Then he left his office and went next door.

He didn't worry about letting the cat out. There was no cat, the sign merely a device to keep people from entering precipitately. He went inside, where a woman was sitting at a bank of three computer monitors. She was wearing a set of earphones, and she was watching a replay of the meeting Doughty had just had. He said nothing until the replay ended with a shaking of hands and with the woman—Barbara Havers—looking round his office a second time.

He said, "What d'you reckon, Em?"

Emily watched him, on replay, walking to the window and keeping himself from view. She reached for a plastic bag of carrot sticks and crunched one of them between her teeth. "Cop," she said. "She could be someone from his local nick, but I'd go higher. One of the special groups. Whatever they're called. SO and a number. I can't keep up with the changes they keep making at the Met."

"What about the other?"

"He seems legit. Just what you'd expect from someone with a daughter who's gone missing but is with the mother. The mother doesn't mean the kid harm, and the dad knows this. So you get despair from him but not that frantic sense of *now* when someone's scared to death a pervert has the kid."

"So?" Doughty said, interested as always to see how her twenty-six-year-old mind would take the case.

She leaned back in her chair. She yawned and energetically went at her scalp. She wore her hair in a mannish style and she dressed like a man as well. She was, in fact, often mistaken for a man and the extracurricular pursuits she chose were more manly than womanly in nature: trick skiing, snowboarding, cliff climbing, windsurfing, mountain biking. She was Doughty's second right hand, the best tracer in the business, an even better blagger, a woman who could run twelve miles in the morning with a forty-pound pack on her back and still show up to work on time.

"I'd say normal course of action," Em told him. "But step lightly, watch our backs, and skate on the right side of the law." She shoved herself away from the monitors and got to her feet. "How'd I do?"

"I agree with everything you said," he told her.

30 NOVEMBER

It was eleven days later when a phone call from the private investigator took Barbara and Azhar back to Dwayne Doughty's office. In the intervening time, he'd made the journey to Chalk Farm to have a look at Azhar's flat. He'd prowled round the place, examining what little there was to examine. He'd given Hadiyyah's school uniform a look, and he'd asked Azhar why the little girl's stuffed giraffe might have been left behind when nearly everything else belonging to her was gone. He'd nodded thoughtfully at whatever implications there were in Azhar's having won a different giraffe for Hadiyyah only to have it taken from her by a group of yobs on a pleasure pier, and he'd removed Hadiyyah's laptop from the premises, saying it bore further examination by someone he employed.

Now they sat in his office, in the same two chairs they'd occupied before. It was early evening.

Doughty had been personally to see Bathsheba Ward, the sister. Unfortunately, he had little more to report than what Barbara had been able to unearth herself. Added to her information they now knew that Bathsheba had a furniture design business called WARD in Islington. "Posh shop and all that," Doughty said. "Lots of dosh involved, and evidently it comes from the husband." Twenty-three years older than Bathsheba, he told them, Hugo Ward had left his first wife and two children six months after he'd offered his umbrella to Bathsheba Upman while she was trying to hail a cab on Regent Street. "Love at first sight," the private investigator said with a dismissive wave, to which he added after a moment's thought, "No offence intended. Wasn't thinking about you and yours," to Azhar.

"No offence taken," Azhar said quietly.

What Barbara thought was that pinching married men looked to be a family hobby. Interesting that both sisters had gone the same route.

"Got nothing much more from this Bathsheba other than lip-curling when it came to questions about the sister," Doughty told them. "No love lost. She gave me fifteen minutes of what she called her 'valuable time,' but it took less than ten. She's either the best liar I've come across in twenty years or she doesn't know a thing about Angelina's whereabouts."

"Nothing else, then?" Barbara said.

"Not a dust mote."

"What about Hadiyyah's laptop?"

"Superficially it looks wiped clean."

"'Superficially'?"

"Computer delving . . . ? These things take time. A certain delicacy . . . knowledge of a few sophisticated programmes? It's not a case of presto. If it were, we'd have no need of experts. So keep your fingers crossed on that score. The hard drive's wiped, but there was a reason, and we may still find it."

Azhar took a manila folder from his briefcase. He had received Angelina's credit card billing, he said. Perhaps there was something in it that could be of help? He handed it over to Doughty, who put on a pair of the sort of cheap magnifying spectacles one could buy at Boots. He glanced at it and said, "This Dorchester bit could be something. Not enough for a room, but—"

"Afternoon tea," Barbara said. "Angelina took me. Hadiyyah as well. It's for earlier this month, isn't it?"

Doughty nodded. He read further on the credit card billing and named the salon where Barbara had received her ill-fated hair makeover.

She explained that that would be where Angelina herself had her hair done by a high-end stylist called Dusty, and Doughty made a note of this, indicating that Dusty would need talking to since Angelina might have altered her hair colour and style prior to her disappearance. Several other entries turned out to be boutiques in the Primrose Hill area, but there were no entries at all after the one for the hair salon, which indicated that Angelina Upman had probably ceased using the card at that point, knowing that to use it would be to leave a trail.

"Could be she's got another card altogether. Could be she's going by another name," Doughty told them. "She might have arranged for a new passport or identity card. If she's done that, she's probably gone the route most people go: using names they can easily get the paperwork on. D'you happen to know her mother's maiden name?"

"I do not." Azhar sounded regretful. There was, after all, so much he did not know about the woman who'd borne his child. "Perhaps, however, I can ring and ask one of her parents . . . ?"

"I c'n get it," Barbara said. It would be a simple enough matter coming from the police, after all.

Doughty said, "No. Let me work on that end of things." He placed the credit card bill in a folder on which Barbara could see was printed *Upman/Azhar* along with the year. He removed the magnifying reading specs, and he leaned towards them, his gaze going from Azhar to Barbara to Azhar once more. "Got to ask this, and no offence is intended. Did you give her a reason to run off? Let me put it this way. You two seem close. You seem like friends, but in my experience when men and women seem friendly, there's more going on. There's probably a fancy term for whatever you two really are to each other, but I don't know what it is. I guess what I'm asking is, did you two get up to something you shouldn't've and did she walk in on it, find out about it, accost you over it, or what have you?"

Barbara felt her face go red. Azhar was the one to answer the question. "Of course we did not. Barbara is as much Angelina's friend as she is mine. She is close to Hadiyyah as well."

"Angelina knew there was nothing between you two?"

Barbara wanted to say, "Just look at me, you idiot," in response to this, but she found herself uncharacteristically reluctant to speak her mind. Instead she heard Azhar say, "Of course she knew that there could not have been . . ." And *then* what she wanted to say was "Why?" But of course, she knew the answer to that.

"Right. Well. Just asking," Doughty said. "This sort of thing? No stone left unturned, and no bedsheet unrumpled if you know what I mean."

He was adept with the clichés, Barbara thought. She had to give the private investigator that much.

He went on. "Aside from that laptop, what's left is your own family," he told Azhar. "Getting rid of your daughter and her mother in order to persuade you to return to the wife you left."

"That would be impossible," Azhar said.

"Which part of it? The getting rid part or the returning part?"

"Either part. We have not spoken for years."

"Speaking, mate, isn't always required."

"Nonetheless, I have no wish for them to be brought into this."

Barbara looked at Azhar then, for the first time since Doughty had brought up the question of their relationship. She said, "She might have found them, Azhar. She might have tracked them down. She did talk to me about them, one afternoon. She said Hadiyyah would love to meet them. If she *did* find them, if certain arrangements were made . . . It has to be checked out."

"It does not have to be checked out." Azhar's voice was steely.

Doughty raised and lowered his hands at this. He said, "That leaves us with the laptop and the mother's maiden name, then. And I've got to tell you, that last probably isn't going to get us far." He reached in a drawer and brought out a business card, which he handed over to Azhar. "You ring me in a couple of days, and I'll tell you where we've got with everything. Like I said, it probably won't be far, but there's always the slim chance we'll come up with something. Even if we do, though . . . You know the real problem here is you've no rights to anything, yes?"

"Believe me, that knowledge is engraved on my heart," Azhar told him.

BOW

LONDON

Doughty went through the same ritual as the first time, once Taymul-lah Azhar and his companion had left. He found Em Cass in her usual position, watching part of the video feed of Doughty's meeting with the two others. She was wearing a vintage man's three-piece suit on this day, and she'd loosened the necktie although the waistcoat was still formally buttoned. On a coat rack in a corner, she'd hung a man's overcoat and fedora. A black umbrella was tightly furled beneath this.

To look at Em, which Doughty had to admit that he rather enjoyed doing, one would never guess that her hobby was pulling men in clubs for anonymous sex. It was her practice to time how long it took from the first meaningful glance to the deed itself. So far her record was thirteen minutes. She had been trying to better it for the past two months.

Doughty had spent considerable energy in an attempt to talk to her about this risky behaviour. Her response to his attempts was always the same: She pooh-poohed it. *His* response to *her* response was always the same as well: "Oh, I'm on board now. You're twenty-six. I'd for-gotten that makes you immortal."

Now he said to her, "What d'we have, then?"

Em said, "She's covered her tracks well enough. We need that maiden name. The Scotland Yard woman could've got it easily enough. Why'd you not want her to?"

"Because she doesn't know we know she's the Met. And . . . other reasons. A feeling I have."

"You and your feelings," Em said.

"Beyond that, I reckon getting the mother's maiden would hardly be a problem for you. How're we getting on with the kid's laptop?"

"I've been beavering, but much as I hate to say it, I think it's time to call in Bryan."

"I thought you said never again."

"I did. It'd be a blessing if you'd find someone else, Dwayne."

"He's the best there is."

"There's got to be a second best out there." She rolled her chair away from her desk and absentmindedly picked up her keys. There were only three—house, car, office—and it was her habit to twirl them on their ring when she was thinking. Now she didn't twirl them, though. Instead, she studied the fob on the ring with them: Tweety Bird with a facial expression saying this was one canary who didn't suffer fools. She said, "What it is . . ."

"Yeah?" Doughty encouraged her. Em thoughtful was out of the ordinary. She was generally an action female, not a contemplative one. She finally said, "I saw that card trick, Dwayne. What're you up to?"

Doughty smiled. "You never cease to amaze. No wonder Bryan wants a romp with you."

"Please. He puts me off my work, he does."

"I thought you liked men wanting to give you a length."

"Some men. A bloke like Bryan Smythe . . ." She shuddered and tossed Tweety Bird back on the desk. "Give him an inch—which is probably all he has anyway—and stalking's going to be his next career choice. I don't like men making what they want so obvious."

"I'm going to make a note of that." He pretended to do so on his palm. " 'Bry, try subterfuge.' " And then, nodding at her telephone, "I'll let you get on with it, then. Mother's maiden name first. How long d'you expect that'll take?"

"Give me ten minutes."

"Have at it, then." He headed for the door and had his hand on the knob before she spoke again. She said his name. He turned. "Say what?"

"You didn't answer the question. Good diversion with Bryan, but you have to know it didn't work."

"What question was that?" he asked her, putting on his all-innocence expression for her.

She laughed. "Please. Whatever you're up to, or how much you're planning to charge the poor bloke for it, can I suggest we keep it all legal for once?"

"On my honour," he told her solemnly.

"Oh, *that's* reassuring," she replied.

17 DECEMBER

SOHO AND CHALK FARM
LONDON

Barbara Havers was in her third hour of dragging herself into shops in Oxford Street when she wondered whether it would have been wiser to shoot Bing Crosby before he could have recorded it or to shoot the person who composed "The Little Drummer Boy" before he had a chance to dream it up. She reckoned the latter would have been the better choice. If not Bing, then someone else would have ended up crooning a-rum-pa-pum-pum at least once an hour from the first of November until the twenty-fourth of December.

The damn song had been accosting her from the moment she'd got off the Underground at Tottenham Court Road. There she'd been greeted by a busker singing the carol into a microphone at the bottom of the escalator, and the same bloody song had been blaring inside Accessorize, outside Starbucks, and at the entry to Boots. The blind violin player who'd been fiddling for the past few decades in front of Selfridges was also sawing through the sentimental ditty. It was like a form of Chinese water torture.

She was doing her Christmas shopping. With one member of what went for family to buy for, this was generally a simple matter usually conducted via catalogue and telephone. Her mother's needs were simple, her wants practically nonexistent. She spent her days watching videos featuring Laurence Olivier—the younger the version of that actor the better—and when she wasn't doing that, she was engaged in whatever craft her carer had going that day for the lodgers in her home in Greenford. This was a woman called Florence Magentry—Mrs. Flo to those who engaged her services—and she, too, was someone for whom Barbara was shopping. Generally, Barbara would have been looking for a gift for her neighbours as well, especially Hadiyyah. But still there had been no word of her whereabouts, and every day that passed made hope of finding her that much more distant.

Barbara tried not to think about Hadiyyah. The private investigator Doughty was working away on the problem of the little girl's whereabouts, she told herself. When there was word, she would be the first to hear it from Azhar.

She was shopping for him as well. She wanted something that might cheer him up, however briefly. He'd become more and more silent in the weeks that had passed since Hadiyyah's disappearance with her mother, and he'd begun staying away from his flat as much as possible. Barbara couldn't blame him for this. What else was the man to do? There *was* nothing else unless he wanted to set out after Hadiyyah on his own. And then, where would he even look? The world was vast and Angelina Upman had planned her flight from Chalk Farm in such a way as to leave no trace of herself behind.

Barbara had tried to stay positive about Dwayne Doughty's being able to locate Hadiyyah and her mother. But here in Oxford Street what came sweeping back to her was the memory of the last time she'd been in this part of town. Summer and under orders from Isabelle Ardery to do something about her lack of fashion sense, she and Hadiyyah had come here together to purchase some sort of preliminary building block for a new wardrobe. They'd managed a few items and they'd had a good many laughs, and all of that was gone from her life now. Barbara was, as a result, as depressed as Azhar, but she felt she had far less right to the feeling. Hadiyyah wasn't, after all, *her* daughter although she often felt like something just as important.

A-rum-pa-pum-pum had tormented Barbara at least seven more times before she found what she was looking for to give to Azhar.

Near Bond Street, a group of stalls brightly decorated with fairy lights were offering everything from flowers to hats. Among these, one merchant was selling board games. Among the games was one called Cranium. Barbara picked it up. A game for the brain? she wondered. A game about the brain? A brain being necessary to play the game? Whatever in a basket, Barbara decided. Certainly, it was just the thing for a professor of microbiology. She plunked down her money and made her escape. She was heading back for the tube station when her mobile rang.

She flipped it open without checking the number. It didn't much matter to her who was ringing. She was on rota, and in any other circumstances she would have been steeling herself against the possibility that she was being called back to work. But these days, she wasn't minding work. It was providing her an escape.

As it was, though, Azhar and not the Met was ringing her. Barbara heard his voice with a rush of pleasure. He could see her car sitting in the driveway, he said. Would she mind if he joined her for a moment's conversation?

Damn but she was in Oxford Street, she told him. She was on her way home, though. Was it . . . Had he heard . . . Was there something she should . . . ?

He said he would wait for her. He himself was at home, having just spoken to Mr. Doughty.

"And?" Barbara said.

"We shall speak." His tone told her the news wouldn't be good.

She made decent time back to Eton Villas, a miracle considering she had to use the miserable Northern Line. She was carrying her purchases in the direction of her bungalow when Azhar came out of the ground-floor flat. He walked across to her and politely took two of her shopping bags. She said ta, and she tried to sound cheerful in keeping with the holiday season, but she could see from his face that the conclusion she'd drawn from his tone of voice on the mobile had been correct.

She said to him, "So what d'you want to drink, then, tea or gin? I've got both. It's a little early for gin but what the hell. If we're owed, we're owed."

He offered her a smile. "Ah. If only Islam allowed me to drink."

"There's always cheating," she told him. "But I don't want to be the one to corrupt you. Tea, then. Strong. I'll throw in a teacake and let me tell you, I don't do that for just anyone."

"You are far too good to me, Barbara," he said, but his smile was rote. He'd always been the most courteous of men.

Inside her small bungalow, Barbara lit the electric fire in the tiny fireplace and removed her coat, her scarf, and her gloves. She was of two minds about her knitted cap, though. Her hair had begun to grow out, but she still looked like someone who'd had recent chemo. Azhar had, from the first, been far too decent to mention the wreck she'd made of her hair. She reckoned he wasn't about to change course now and query her on the topic of head shaving. So she thought, what the hell, and she tossed the cap along with everything else on the daybed.

She busied herself with making the tea and popping teacakes beneath the grill in her oven. The fact that she had butter for these and milk for the tea actually made her feel like a domestic goddess. She'd even spent the morning prior to her shopping spree putting her hovel into some kind of order. This allowed Azhar to sit at her table and even gaze into the kitchen area without being assaulted by the sight of her knickers drying on a line above the kitchen sink.

He didn't bring her into the picture of his phone call to her till she had a pot of tea on the table, along with mugs, teacakes, and all the et ceteras. Then, maddeningly, he began with small talk about her Christmas shopping, her mother's health, and Inspector Lynley having to face his first Christmas after the death of his wife. Finally, he told her he'd been to Bow at Dwayne Doughty's invitation. At first he'd thought the news would be good. He reckoned that Doughty had wished to demonstrate in person how far his skills as a private investigator had taken him. But things turned out quite differently.

"He merely wished to settle the account," Azhar said quietly. "Payment in person was preferable to awaiting a cheque by post during the Christmas season, evidently."

"But what did he tell you? Anything?" Barbara also wanted to ask why Azhar hadn't included her on this journey to the detective's office. But she shook herself mentally and ordered her psyche to get a grip because, for God's sake, this man's daughter was missing and whether he took Barbara Havers with him to learn if she'd been found was hardly as important as her being found in the first place.

Azhar said, "He'd got the maiden name of Angelina's mother. Ruth-Jane Squire. But that was as far as he was able to go because there was no indication through any of his sources that Angelina had used the name for anything: new passport, driving licence, forged birth certificate, or whatever else one might need a false name for."

"And that was it?" Barbara asked. "Azhar, that doesn't make sense. These blokes—private investigators—skate round the law all the time. They look through people's rubbish, they hack into phones, they hack into their email accounts, they intercept their post, they use blaggers to—"

"Blaggers?"

"Some bugger on the payroll who's willing to pretend he's whoever he needs to be to get information: ring up Angelina's GP and act like you're her social worker or whatever and can you tell me if it's true she's been infected with syphilis, sir?"

He looked startled. "The point of this being . . . ?"

"The point of this being that people talk if you act like you've got a reason to ask them questions. Blaggers play on sounding more official than officials. So I'd've thought Doughty had a score of them available."

"He has an associate," Azhar told her. "A woman. But her part was to investigate airlines, taxis, minicabs, trains, and the Underground. She discovered nothing."

"She was there? With Doughty? She made a report to you?"

"He had her report. I did not meet her." Azhar frowned. "Was this somehow important? That I meet her?" He picked up his teacake, examined it, put it back on the plate. "I see that I should have taken you with me. You would have thought of this. I am . . . I was anxious, Barbara. When he rang me and said that we needed to meet as soon as we could, that he did not wish to speak to me of his news by telephone . . ." Azhar glanced away, and Barbara could see a heaviness settle upon him. "I thought he had her. I thought I would walk into his office and there she would be and perhaps even Angelina with her so that all of us could talk together and come to an agreement." He looked back at her. "It was foolish of me, but everything about me has been foolish for many years now."

"Don't say that," Barbara said. "Life happens, Azhar. We do things. We make decisions, they lead to consequences, and that's how it is."

"This is, of course, true," he told her. "But my first decision was both thoughtless and irrational. I saw her, you see. From across the room, I saw her."

"Angelina?" Barbara felt a leap of her heart, that indication of pure excitement coursing through her body. "*Where?*"

"There were other places to sit that day in the food hall. I chose her table."

"Oh. When you met her," Barbara said.

"When I met her," he agreed. "I saw her and I made that decision to ask if I might join her although I had no right to make it." He paused, either to consider his words carefully or to consider how saying them would affect his friendship with Barbara. "I decided then and there upon an affair with her. It was—I was—so very full of my . . . my ego. And so very stupid."

Barbara wasn't sure how to respond to this because she wasn't sure how she felt about the information. It was no business of hers how the affair that had produced Hadiyyah had begun, she told herself. But just because something was in the past and not her business did not mean she was immune from speculating and from drawing conclusions. She just didn't like her speculations. She liked even less her conclusions. And she disliked herself most of all because both of these—speculations and conclusions—had to do with her, with Barbara Havers, with thinking about what it might be like to be such a woman as Angelina Upman whom a man like Azhar looked upon and made decisions about, the sort of decisions that brought worlds to an end.

"I'm sorry about all of it," Barbara said. "Not about Hadiyyah, though. I don't expect you're sorry about her either."

"Of course I am not," he said.

"So where do things stand? You paid Doughty for his time and efforts and now what?"

"He tells me that she will surface eventually. He tells me that in anticipation of this, it would be wise for me now to pay a call upon

Angelina's parents. He says that she will turn to them at some point in time because people rarely cut themselves off from their families permanently when there is no longer a reason to do so."

"That reason being you, you mean?"

"He says that if Angelina being dead to them was predicated from the first on her affair with me and on my refusal to marry her once she was carrying my child, then I should go to the parents and I must declare my desire to marry her and all will be forgiven."

Barbara shook her head. "What in God's name is he basing *that* advice on? A ouija board?"

"Her sister. He points out that, as far as the parents are concerned, there's no she's-dead-to-us about Bathsheba despite her having done the same as Angelina: having had an affair with a married man. He claims the reason is that the man in question married Bathsheba. His conclusion is that my own declaration of an intention to marry her will position the parents to tell me whatever they know about her disappearance. Whether they know something now or learn something in the future."

"What makes Doughty think they might know something now?"

"Because no one disappears without a trace," Azhar said. "The fact that Angelina appears to have done so indicates someone helped her do it."

"Her parents?"

"The way Mr. Doughty put it was this: They're the sort of people who turn a blind eye to adultery as long as adultery leads to the altar. He said I must use that fact. He said I must get used to using people."

He looked at her, half of a sad smile on his face and his eyes so tired that Barbara wanted to put her arms round the poor bloke and rock him to sleep. Using people wasn't large in Azhar's skill set, even in a situation in which he desperately wanted the return of his child. She wasn't sure how he was going to manage it.

She said, "So. What's the plan, then?"

"To go to Dulwich and speak to her parents."

"Let me go with you, then."

His entire face softened. "That, my friend Barbara, is what I so hoped that you might say."

19 DECEMBER

Barbara Havers had never been to Dulwich before she went there in the company of Azhar, but the moment she clapped eyes on the place, she reckoned it was the part of town to which she ought to be aspiring. Far south of the river in the Borough of Southwark, Dulwich bore no resemblance to that part of the inner city at all. It was the embodiment of the term *leafy suburb*, although the trees that seemed to line every street were leafless now. Still, they grew the sort of branches that indicated the deep shade they would provide in summer and the rich colours they would offer in autumn, and they stood near pavements that were wide, spotless, and utterly devoid of the remains of chewing gum that polka-dotted the pavements in central London.

Houses in this part of the world were distinguished: large, brick, and pricey. Shops on the high street ran the gamut from ladies' boutiques to actual "grooming establishments" for men. Primary schools were housed in well-kept Victorian buildings, and Dulwich Park, Dulwich College, and Dulwich Picture Gallery all spoke of an environment in which the upper middle class mingled over cocktails and sent their children into the world with educations courtesy of nothing less than excessively costly boarding schools.

Fish out of water did not do justice to how Barbara felt as she drove her ancient Mini through the streets of this place. With Azhar manning the A–Z in the passenger seat, she only hoped that when they finally found where the Upmans lived, she would have a bit of luck and discover that their home didn't make her feel so much like a recent arrival from a war-torn country, her car a donation from a well-meaning Christian organisation.

She had no luck in this matter. The house that matched Azhar's quiet "This appears to be the place, Barbara" sat on the corner of Frank Dixon Close. It was neo-Georgian in style: perfectly balanced, large, brick, trimmed in white, with freshly painted black gutters, rainheads, and downspouts. A neatly trimmed and weedless lawn fronted it, broken into two sections by a flagstone path leading to the front door. On either side of this, garden lights illuminated flower-beds. Inside the house itself, a faux candle stood in every window as acknowledgement of the holiday season.

Barbara parked, and she and Azhar stared at the place. She finally said, "Looks like someone's not hurting for lolly," and she gazed round at the neighbourhood. Every house that she could see in the street suggested buckets of cash had been spent upon it. If nothing else, Frank Dixon Close was a burglar's wet dream.

When they knocked on the door, no one came to answer. They excavated for a bell and found it beneath a swag of holiday holly. They had more success when they pressed upon this, for within the house a voice called out, "Humphrey, can you get that, darling?" In short order a succession of deadlocks went from bolted to un-, the door swung open, and Barbara and Azhar were looking at the father of Angelina Upman.

Azhar had told her that Humphrey Upman was managing director of a bank and his wife was a child psychologist. What he hadn't mentioned was the fact that the man was a racist, but that became clear in very short order. His expression gave him away. It was of the order of "there goes the neighbourhood," all flared nostrils and pursed lips, and he moved sharply to block the doorway lest Azhar launch himself inside the house with a gunny sack at the ready to clear the place of the family silver.

When he said, "And you want . . . ?" however, it was also clear that he knew quite well who Azhar was, even if he was still in the dark as to Barbara's identity.

She took up the reins by bringing out her warrant card. "Conversation is what we want, Mr. Upman," she told him as he scrutinised her identification.

"What would the Metropolitan police have to do with me?" He handed the ID back, but he made no move to open the door any wider than the width of his own body.

"Let us inside and I'll be happy to tell you," Barbara replied.

He considered this and said, "He remains out here," in reference to Azhar.

"A bloody fascinating imperative, that, but it's not the best start to our conversation."

"I have nothing at all to say to him."

"That's good since you're not required to."

Barbara was wondering how much longer she was going to have to keep up the repartee with the man when, from behind him, his wife said, "Humphrey? What's . . ." Her voice dropped off when she looked over her husband's shoulder and saw Azhar.

Azhar said to her, "Angelina has disappeared. She's been gone for a month. We are trying—"

"We've been made very much aware that she's gone," Humphrey Upman cut in. "Let me say this so that you both will understand it perfectly: If our daughter were dead—if our daughter *is* dead—it could not matter less at this point."

Barbara wanted to ask the man if he'd always been filled with such paternal goodwill, but she didn't have the opportunity. His wife said, "Let them in, Humphrey," to which he replied without a glance in her direction, "Filth has no place in this house."

Barbara thought of the expression as it was used by villains, but she knew Upman wasn't making reference to her. It was Azhar he intended to insult.

She said, "Mr. Upman, if you say another word in that direction—"

His wife interrupted. "If you're concerned about contamination, Humphrey, then take yourself to another room. Let. Them. In."

Upman waited just long enough to suggest that his wife would be paying later for her remarks. Then he turned on his heel and left her to swing open the door and allow them entrance. She led the way into a living room, beautifully decorated but without a sign of personal taste other than that of an interior designer. It looked out upon the back garden of the property, and through its French windows, landscaping lights illuminated paths, a fountain, statuary, dormant flowerbeds, and lawn.

In a corner of the room, a Christmas tree stood. It was yet to be decorated, but the fact that they'd interrupted Ruth-Jane Upman in the midst of handling this holiday chore was evident by a string of lights that had been spread on the floor and a box of ornaments sitting on the hearth of a fireplace.

She offered neither one of them a seat. Their stay was, obviously, not meant to be long. She said, "Have you reason to believe my daughter is dead?" No emotion accompanied this question.

Barbara said, "You've not heard from her?"

"Of course not. When she took up with this man"—a cursory glance at Azhar—"we ended our relationship with her. She would not see reason. So we would not see her." She addressed Azhar then with, "Has she left you at last? Well, really, what else would you actually expect?"

"She has left me before," Azhar said with some dignity. "We have come to see you because it is my earnest wish to—"

"Has she indeed? *Has* she left you once before? And yet you didn't dash over here then—whenever it was—to enquire about her. What brings you now?"

"She has my daughter."

"Which one would that be?" And then, reading something upon Azhar's face, Ruth-Jane Upman added, "Yes, Mr. Azhar. We know all about you. When it comes to you, Humphrey did the homework and I graded every one of the papers."

Barbara said impatiently, "Angelina has taken Hadiyyah with her. I expect you know which one of Azhar's daughters Hadiyyah is."

"I assume she's the . . . one . . . Angelina gave birth to."

"She's also the *one*," Barbara said, "who probably misses her dad."

"Be that as it may, I have no interest in her. Nor have I interest in Angelina. Nor have I, frankly, interest in you. Neither her father nor I have any idea where she is, where she might be going, or where she might end up in the future. Is there anything else? Because I'd like to finish decorating my Christmas tree, if you don't mind."

"Has she contacted you?"

"I believe I just said—"

"What you said," Barbara interrupted, "was that you have no idea where she is, where she's going, or where she might end up. What you didn't say was whether you've spoken to her. During which conversation, we can both assume, she wouldn't necessarily have to say where she is."

Ruth-Jane said nothing to this. Barbara thought, Bingo. But what she also thought was that there was no way in hell that Angelina Upman's mother was going to give them a thing to go on. She might have spoken to Angelina at some point; she might have been the recipient of a telephone message, a text message, a letter, a card, or whatever else of the "I've left him, Mum" variety. But, no matter the case, she wasn't about to admit that to Barbara.

"Azhar wants to know where his daughter is," Barbara told Angelina's mother quietly. "You can understand that, can't you?"

She seemed completely indifferent. "Whether I understand or not makes no difference to anything. My answer remains the same. I've had no personal contact with Angelina."

Barbara brought her card from the pocket of her jacket. She held it out to the woman. She said, "I'd like you to ring me if you hear from her. It being Christmastime, you may well do."

"You might like me to do that," Ruth-Jane Upman said. "But granting your wishes isn't one of my powers."

Barbara laid her card on a table nearby. She said, "You think about that, Mrs. Upman."

Azhar looked as if he wanted to make some sort of appeal, but Barbara tilted her head towards the doorway. There was no point to further discussion with the woman. She might let them know if she heard from Angelina. She might not do so. It was not in their hands to bend her will to theirs.

They headed for the door. In the corridor leading to it, the walls bore pictures, three of them black-and-white shots of a spontaneous nature. Barbara paused to look at them. They were all, she saw, of the same subjects: two girls. In one they were at the seaside building a sand castle, in another they rode a merry-go-round with one of them on the high pony and the other on a low one, in the last they stood holding out carrots to a mare and her adorable foal. What was interesting was not the expert nature of the photographs, however. Nor was it notable how they'd been framed and mounted. What would cause any viewer to stop and give the pictures a thorough study was the girls themselves.

They would be Angelina and Bathsheba, Barbara reckoned. She wondered why no one had ever mentioned that the girls were perfectly identical twins.

20 DECEMBER

ISLINGTON
LONDON

It seemed to Barbara that there was a final possibility to be explored. She did so on her lunch hour the very next day, and she didn't tell Azhar she was going to do it. He was dispirited enough. To him, writing out a cheque to pay Dwayne Doughty was the same as saying, "Case closed." To her, perhaps the case *was* closed in Doughty's eyes, but till she'd worked every possible angle that she could think of, she couldn't accept that Hadiyyah and her mother were permanently gone.

Barbara had been keeping her nose remarkably clean at New Scotland Yard. There was nothing she could do about the wreck she'd made of her hair, but she'd decided it behooved her to slither onto the better side of Acting Detective Superintendent Ardery, so her manner of dress had been for days if not impeccable then at least not worthy of note. She'd worn tights, and she'd polished her brogues. At Ardery's command, she'd even begun working on a case with DI John Stewart without complaint, although most of the time what she wanted to do was crush out a burning fag on his face. As for fags, she'd refrained from smoking in the Met stairwells as well. She was on the border of making herself ill with her own wonderfulness, so she knew it was time to do a little something on the side.

She went to WARD. She had the home address of Angelina's sister, but she reckoned Bathsheba would greet her appearance on the doorstep in a fashion not dissimilar from her parents. Going at her in her own workplace at least would give Barbara the advantage of surprise.

WARD was on Liverpool Road, conveniently close to the Business Design Centre. It was one of those achingly trendy establishments, so uncrowded with its products as to make Barbara wonder if it was, perhaps, a front for money laundering instead of what it purported to be, which was a showroom for the furniture designed by its eponymous owner. The woman herself was within. Barbara had ascertained as much with a phone call and an appointment made earlier in the day. She knew better than to make it known to Bathsheba Ward that her putative customer was actually a police officer. Instead, she offered her an airy explanation along the lines of "I've heard so much about you."

In advance she'd done a bit of homework on the woman. She'd managed this while ostensibly entering a report into HOLMES for DI Stewart, who'd decided he'd play out his personal dislike of her by giving her an assignment which should have gone to a civilian typist. Instead of grousing, arguing, or banging about the incident room making her displeasure known, she'd said, "Right. Will do, sir," and she'd offered him what passed for a congenial smile when his eyes narrowed at her quick cooperation. Thus, she'd had time to delve into Bathsheba Ward née Upman, so when she walked into the showroom she knew that Bathsheba had eschewed university for design school after having failed to make it as a professional model because of her height and after also having failed to find her place in the cutthroat world of fashion design. With furniture, however, she'd been wildly successful: awards aplenty along with photos of the pieces which had won them. The crowning glory of a young career had been the acquisition of one of her pieces by the V&A and another by the Museum of London. These two events were especially memorialised in Bathsheba's office by plaques and exquisitely preserved articles from glossy magazines.

Bathsheba herself was rather unnerving, Barbara found. Her resemblance to her sister was so startling that Barbara first concluded that the two women could have impersonated each other. With a closer look, however, Barbara saw that Bathsheba was the mirror image of Angelina: identifying physical marks upon each of them had been reversed, with a beauty mark at the edge of Bathsheba's left eye which, on Angelina, was on the right, and the same situation with a dimple. Bathsheba also had none of Angelina's light sprinkling of freckles, but this would have been owing to keeping herself out of the sun.

She also had none of Angelina's warmth, although, Barbara reckoned, that warmth had just been a ruse to ease Barbara into not noticing the myriad ways in which Angelina had been, from the first, planning her escape with Hadiyyah. Chances were very good that both women were, by nature, as sly as anacondas hiding hungrily behind one's sofa. She made a mental note to take care, to keep her eyes open and her wits in ready-for-anything mode.

As things turned out, she needn't have worried. Once Barbara let it be known that she was there under false pretences, that this really wasn't about purchasing a £25,000 focal point for a state-of-the-art flat along the river in Wapping, Bathsheba Ward was less than pleased and didn't try to hide it.

"I've been contacted already about this matter," she said. They were at a conference table in her office where, in advance of their meeting, she'd spread out photographs of some of her work in situ. It was dead gorgeous and Barbara told her as much before she dropped the unfortunate bomb of her real reason for this call upon the furniture designer's valuable time. "That private detective person . . . the one my sister's whatever-he-is hired to find her . . . ? I told him I have no idea where Angelina is or with whom she might currently be cohabitating because, believe me, she *will* be cohabitating with someone. She might have moved in next door to me, and I wouldn't know. I haven't seen her in years."

"Expect you'd recognise her, though," Barbara said sardonically.

"Being identical twins doesn't extend to having identical thoughts, Sergeant . . ." She looked at Barbara's card, which she held in manicured fingers. As she'd spoken, she'd moved to her desk upon which sat photographs of a beaky-faced man who was, presumably, her husband, along with photographs of two young adults—one with a toddler in arms—who were, also presumably, her stepchildren from that beaky husband's first marriage. ". . . Havers," Bathsheba finished, reading Barbara's surname from the card. The card itself she tossed on the desk.

"She's managed to disappear without leaving a trail," Barbara told her. "All her belongings're gone, and so far we've not been able to trace how she got her gear to wherever she got it, along with Hadiyyah's."

"Perhaps she got her 'gear' "—Bathsheba made the word sound like *cow dung*—"over to Oxfam, deposited it there, and waved farewell to it. She'd hardly leave a trail of shipping slips if she'd done that, wouldn't you say?"

"A possibility," Barbara admitted. "But so is having someone's assistance, along the lines of she-doesn't-ship-it-but-someone-else-does. We've also not been able to find any means of her leaving Chalk Farm. Public transport, taxi, minicab. It's like she beamed herself out of the place. Or someone else did the beaming for her."

"Well, that wouldn't be me," Bathsheba said. "And if you've tracked no one else who helped her, perhaps you ought to be thinking something a little more ominous than you've been thinking."

"Such as?"

Bathsheba pushed her chair away from her desk. Both the desk and the chair were her own pieces: sleek and modern with gorgeous bits of various unnameable woods worked into them. She herself was sleek and modern as well, with the same long and light hair as her sister, with a fashion sense that accentuated everything about her that was trim and lithe. She looked like someone who spent hours sweating in the company of a personal trainer. Even her earlobes looked as if they'd been given marching orders as to what kind of workout would keep them as youthful and vigorous as possible. She said, "I do wonder if you or that man—the detective man—might have given thought to Angelina and her daughter having been disposed of."

It took a moment for Barbara to work out what Bathsheba meant, so casually had the remark been made. "You mean murdered? By whom, exactly? There wasn't a single sign of violence in the flat, and she'd left a message on my answer machine that didn't sound like someone was forcing her into pretending she was doing a runner while in reality holding a knife to her throat."

Bathsheba raised her well-developed shoulders. "I have no explanation for that message, obviously. But I do wonder . . . Everyone seems so intent upon believing him, you see."

"Who?"

Bathsheba's eyes—blue and large like her sister's—opened wider. "Surely you don't need me to spell out . . . ?"

"Are you talking about Azhar? Doing what? Murdering Angelina and Hadiyyah—his own daughter, for God's sake—and then putting on a BAFTA-worthy performance of grief for the past five weeks? What'd he do with their bodies, in your vision of how things happened?"

"Buried them, I'd suppose." She smiled ghoulishly. "You do see how it could have been, I hope. None of us—her family—have seen Angelina in years. We wouldn't know from Adam or Eve if she went missing. All I'm suggesting is what might be possible."

"All you're suggesting is something ludicrous. Have you *met* Azhar?"

"Once. Long ago. Angelina brought him to a wine bar to show him off. She was like that, my sister. Always wanting me to know what she'd managed to accomplish, what made her absolutely unique. To be frank, she hated being a twin as much as I did. Our parents shoved twinship down our throats. I daresay even today they're not entirely sure of our names. To them, we were always 'the twins.' Sometimes we got lucky and became 'the girls.'"

Barbara hadn't missed the past tense, and she pointed this out. Any implication made no difference to Bathsheba Ward. She said in turn that she hadn't seen her sister since a day in a South Kensington Starbucks where they'd met in order that Angelina might triumphantly announce her pregnancy ten years earlier.

"There was no further point after that," Bathsheba said. "My sister would have trotted out that child or the fact of that child every time we spoke."

"No kids of your own?" Barbara asked shrewdly.

"Two, as you can see from the pictures." She indicated the frames on her desks.

"Look a bit old to be yours."

"Children don't necessarily need to be . . . how do they put it? . . . the fruit of one's own loins."

Barbara wondered if women had loins. She also wondered what the bloody hell "loins" were when it came to *Homo sapiens*. But she recognised the inherent uselessness of leading their conversation in that direction. The only topic remaining to them was Bathsheba's reference to her sister fleeing Azhar into the arms of another man. Did Bathsheba have anything she wished to offer on that front? Barbara asked. Did Bathsheba know, for example, that Angelina had left Azhar once before, spending a year away from both him and Hadiyyah in a location that they had referred to as Canada but that might, in reality, have been anywhere on the planet?

"I'm not surprised" was Bathsheba's airy reply.

"Why not?"

"I assume things between her and whatever-his-name-is became a little too tame for Angelina. So if you're looking for her now and you've convinced yourself that he didn't harm them, then look among men who are different from Angelina, in the way whatever-his-name-is is different."

Barbara wanted to grab Bathsheba by the throat and recite *Taymullah Azhar* into her face, forcing her to say the name till she was clear on the fact that he was actually a human being and not some sort of unmentionable social disease. But really, what would have been the point? Bathsheba would only have found another way to indicate her distaste for Azhar, probably choosing his ethnicity or his religion as likely areas for her aversion. Barbara also wanted to point out to her that Mr. Beaky Face didn't look like such a prize if it came to that. At least her sister has chosen a handsome man, she wanted to sneer. But instead, she politely said, "Azhar. Your sister calls him Hari. That should be easy to remember, eh?"

"Azhar. Hari. Whatever you like. My point is that Angelina was always interested only in men who were—who are—different from her."

"In what way?"

"In any way. Different from her makes her distinct. She's spent her life trying to be just that: distinct. I don't blame her for that. Our parents expected us to be close. Devoted, capable of reading each other's mind, whatever you like. We were dressed identically and forced into each other's company from the day we were born. 'Celebrate your twinship' was how my mother put it. 'Other people would kill to have an identical twin.' "

Barbara wondered if other people would also kill because they had an identical twin. The street of Angelina's potential murder ran in both directions, after all. If Azhar had supposedly disposed of his lover and their daughter, why could Bathsheba Ward not have done the same thing to her sister and niece? Stranger things had happened in the great city of London.

"You sound fairly unworried about her," Barbara said. "About your niece as well."

Bathsheba smiled with perfect insincerity. "You seem intent upon the fact that Angelina's alive. I'm merely accepting your judgement. As to my niece, I don't know the child. And none of us intend to get to know her."

BOW
LONDON

Dwayne Doughty was the *next* final stone because, Barbara had to admit, she couldn't take no and if there was the slightest chance that she didn't have to take no, she was going to go for that chance like Ophelia being tossed a rope from a bridge on the off chance she was having second thoughts as she floated by. So at day's end, she drove to Bow.

The area hadn't improved since she'd last seen it, although there were more people along the pavements. In the Roman Road, the Roman Café and Kebab was doing a bang-up business, and the halal grocer appeared to be bagging goods as fast as housewives in chādors managed to fling them in the vicinity of the till. The money store was closing for the day, but the door that led to Dwayne Doughty's office was still unlocked, so Barbara helped herself. She entered and at the top of the stairs, she met Doughty in conversation with an androgynous being who turned out to be Em Cass, the woman Azhar had said Doughty employed. Em Cass and Doughty exchanged what looked to Barbara like a wary glance when they clocked Barbara's presence. They acted a wee bit like guilty lovers, which Barbara supposed they might well have been. Until Doughty made it clear that his companion was a woman by calling her Emily, Barbara reckoned he was the sort of man who liked a bit of boy flesh on the side. Turned out she was wrong on all fronts. They'd been discussing a triathlon along with the intentions of some bloke called Bryan to accompany Em with stopwatch, mineral water, and power bars. Doughty was finding this amusing. Em Cass was not.

They were leaving for the day, Doughty told Barbara. He did wish she'd rung first for an appointment. As it was, he needed to be off and so did Em.

Barbara said, "Yeah. Sorry. Should have but I was in the area and thought I'd take a chance. Just five minutes of your time?"

They both looked supremely doubtful about all of it: from being in the area to five minutes of their time. One wasn't generally in the area of the Roman Road, and nothing they did took only five minutes unless it was to endorse a client's cheque, which could be accomplished in far less time.

"Five minutes?" Barbara repeated. "I swear." She brought out her chequebook. A dead moth fell out of it. Not a good sign, but Doughty overlooked this. "I'll pay, of course."

"This is about . . . ?"

"Same as before."

They exchanged another look. Barbara wondered again. Private eyes were notorious for all sorts of skulduggery. They were also known for providing the fruits of their labour to various tabloids round the capital. If Doughty or his assistant had been into this game, Barbara wondered was there something they didn't want her to know.

Doughty sighed and said, "Five minutes." He opened the office and ushered her inside.

Barbara said, "What about . . . ?" in reference to his employee.

"Triathlon training is triathlon training," he told her. "You'll have to make do with me."

"What's she do for you exactly?" Barbara followed him into his office as Emily Cass powered down the stairs.

"Emily? This and that with the computer. Research. Phone calls. Tying loose ends. The occasional interview."

"What about blagging?"

He looked cagey enough at this to suggest that Emily Cass had talents extending beyond those related to swimming, biking, and running marathons.

Barbara said, "Look. I've talked to Azhar. I know what you told him. No trace left. Completely disappeared. But no one disappears without leaving some sort of trail, and I don't see how Angelina Upman managed to do it."

"Nor do I," he said frankly. "But such is the case. It happens."

"Her alone maybe. All right. On a stretch. She takes off with no one noticing or, for that matter, no one much caring. But that's not the situation here. Someone cares. And she's not alone. She's got a nine-year-old with her—and this is a kid who's bloody close to her dad, by the way—so even if Angelina doesn't want to be found, at some point Hadiyyah's going to start talking about Dad and where he is and why they're not sending him a bloody postcard."

Doughty nodded but then he said, "Children are told all sorts of things about their parents in this kind of situation. I expect you know that."

"Such as?"

"Such as 'Dad and I are divorcing' or 'Dad's dropped dead in his office this morning' or anything for that matter. Point is, she's done a successful runner, I've told the professor as much, and if there's more to be done, I don't know what it is and he'll need someone else to do it."

"He told me you managed the last name. Angelina's mother. Ruth-Jane Squire."

"Hardly a difficult feat. He probably could have managed that much himself."

"In possession of that and other details—addresses, birthdates, and whatnot—you and I both know that a blagger can go miles: banks, credit cards, postal boxes, mobile phone records, landline records, passports, driving licences. But you still say there was no trail?"

"That's exactly what I'm saying," Doughty told her. "I might not like it, the professor certainly doesn't like it, and you might not like it, but that's how it is."

"Who's Bryan, then?"

"Who?"

"I heard Emily mention Bryan. Is he your blagger?"

"Miss . . . Havers, is it?"

"Excellent memory, mate."

"Bryan is my tech expert. He did the more detailed work on the laptop from the little girl's room."

"And?"

"The result's the same. The child used it. The mother did not. Which is to say there was nothing on it that could have been deemed remotely suspicious."

"Then why did someone wipe it clean?"

"Perhaps to muddy the waters, to make it look as if there was something on it that needed to be removed. But there wasn't. Now." Doughty had been sitting but he got to his feet and his intention was clear: Farewells were in order and hers was the job of making them. "You've had your five minutes. I've a wife at home and a dinner to eat, and if you've a wish for a longer natter with me, it's going to have to take place at another time."

Barbara eyed him. There had to be something else, if not here then elsewhere. But aside from sliding burning slivers of bamboo beneath Dwayne Doughty's fingernails, she reckoned she'd got all she could from the man. She took a Biro from her bag and opened her chequebook.

At this, Doughty held up his hand. "Please. It's on the house," he said.

15 APRIL

He decided that the encounter between them could happen most easily in a *mercato*. There were enough of them in and around Lucca, and the best took place inside the colossal wall that encircled the oldest part of the town. Piazza San Michele's *mercato* was a now-and-then occurrence, mad with Lucchese from neighbourhoods beyond the wall who wandered in through one of the great gates for a day of browsing through stalls selling everything from scarves to wheels of cheese. But Piazza San Michele was also the central point of the walled city, making an escape from the place fraught with problems. That left him with a choice between either the *mercato* in Corso Giuseppe Garibaldi not more than a stone's throw from escape through Porta San Pietro, or the decided insanity of the *mercato* that stretched the distance from Porta Elisa to Porta San Jacopo.

When he thought about these latter two *mercati*, his final decision had to do with the atmosphere and with what sort of people tended to frequent each of them. Corso Giuseppe Garibaldi attracted tourists, along with a more well-heeled kind of shopper, and its offerings appealed to those with ready cash to hand over for its delicacies. Because of this, he found that the family did not shop often in this place. So he was left with the other.

This other *mercato* stretched along the narrow, curving lane of Passeggiata delle Mura Urbane, which backed right up to the looming mass of the city's wall. Frequenters of the place had to elbow between one another, and in doing so they had to avoid stepping on barking dogs and encountering beggars at the same time as they attempted to make their demands of *lo venderebbe a meno?* heard above the din of conversations, arguments, musicians playing for a handout, and people shouting into their mobile phones. Indeed, the more he thought about it, the more he realised that this *mercato* in Passeggiata delle Mura Urbane was actually perfect. Anything could happen unnoticed in the place, and it had the additional advantage of being quite close to the home on Via Santa Gemma Galgani, where every Saturday the family met for lunch. On nice days, such as this one, that lunch was served in the garden just a portion of which he'd been able to glimpse from the street.

It was to this place—to this house and garden—that everyone would assume at first that the child had gone. It was a natural conclusion for people to reach, and he could easily imagine how things would play out. Papà would turn round and see she wasn't immediately within sight, but he would actually think nothing of it. For the house was close, and in that house standing within its beautiful garden lived a boy just the age of the child. She called him Cugino Gugli, which she pronounced *Goo-lee* because her Italian was limited and she could not yet say Guglielmo. But the boy did not seem to mind since he could not pronounce her name either, and anyway their bond was of *calcio* only. And one did not need a real language for bonding over *calcio*. One only needed the willingness to kick a football towards a goal.

She wouldn't fear him when he approached her. She didn't know him, but she would have been taught that the strangers to fear were the ones with lost animals in need of finding, the ones with kittens in a box—just behind that parked car, *cara bambina*—the ones who gave off the stench of lust and longing, the ill-dressed, the foul-breathed, the unbathed, the ones with something to show you or give you or a special place to take you where a very special treat was waiting for you . . . But he was none of this, and he had none of this. What he did have was his looks—*la faccia d'un angelo*, as his mamma liked to say—along with a message. Plus, he was to say a single word and that word was going to seal the deal. It was a word he'd never heard before in any of the three languages he spoke, but he'd been told it would convince the child of the veracity of the tale he would tell her. Hearing it, she would understand him perfectly. This was why he— and not someone else—had been chosen for the job at hand.

Because he was good at his job, he'd taken time to gather the information he needed to carry off the assignment. Most families, he knew, kept to routines. It made life easier for them. So a month of careful watching, surreptitious following, and copious note-taking had told him what was required of him. Once he'd been given the date for action, he was ready.

They would park their Lancia outside the city wall, in the *parcheggio* near Piazzale Don Aldo Mei. From there, they would part ways for two hours. Mamma would head towards Via della Cittadella, where the yoga studio was. Papà and Bambina would stroll towards and through Porta Elisa. Mamma's walk was the longer one, but she carried only her yoga mat and she liked the exercise. Papà and Bambina each carried one *borsa della spesa*, indicating that at the end of their time in the *mercato*, they'd be burdened with their purchases within those bags.

At this point, he knew them all so well that he could have described the likely clothes that Mamma would wear and he could have named the colours of the *borse* that Papà and Bambina would carry. His would be green and made of webbing. Hers would be orange and of solid material. They were nothing if not creatures of habit.

On the day set for everything to happen, he established himself in the *parcheggio* early. This was his eighth time following the family, and he was assured that nothing was going to disrupt their normal routine. He was in no hurry. For when the job was done, it had to be done perfectly and in such a way that several hours would pass before anyone had the slightest idea that something might be wrong.

He'd left his own vehicle in the *parcheggio* in Viale Guglielmo Marconi. He'd arrived several hours before the *mercato* opened in order to capture a parking bay that gave him quick access to the exit. He'd bought a large piece of *focaccia alle cipolle* on his way to Piazzale Don Aldo Mei. After he ate, he chewed on breath mints to rid his mouth of the scent of the onions. He took a *pianta stradale* from the shoulder bag he carried, and he unfolded this on the boot of a car, ostensibly looking for a route. He would be just another tourist in Lucca to anyone who saw him.

The family arrived ten minutes behind schedule, but he didn't consider this a problem. They parted as always just inside the gate, with Mamma walking off to her yoga experience and Papà and Bambina heading inside the tourist office where there was a WC. They were innately practical people as well as being utterly consistent. First things first and besides, there were no toilets once one began to wander through the *mercato*.

He lingered outside, across the street, waiting for them. It was a glorious day, sunny but not yet blazing hot the way it would be in three months' time. Trees on the top of the great wall behind him bore new, freshly unfurling leaves, and these were shading the *mercato* at the moment, rustling in a soft breeze as well. As the morning continued, the sun would fall brightly on the stalls that lined the lane. As the day grew older, the bright light would move from the merchants onto the ancient buildings across from them.

He lit a cigarette and smoked with great pleasure. He'd nearly finished when Papà and Bambina left the tourist office and set off into the *mercato*.

He followed them. In the times he'd spent tailing them from Porta Elisa to Porta San Jacopo, he'd come to know where and when they would stop, and he'd been careful about selecting the point at which he knew the time would have arrived for him to act. For just within the city wall at Porta San Jacopo, the far end of the *mercato*—a musician played. Here Bambina always stopped to listen, with a two-euro coin in her hand to offer the man at some point during his performance. She waited for Papà to join her there. But today that was not going to happen. She would be gone when Papà finally arrived.

The *mercato* was, as always, crowded. He remained unnoticed. Where Papà and Bambina stopped, he stopped, too. They bought fruit and a selection of vegetables. Then, Papà bought fresh pasta while Bambina danced over to the kitchen goods and sang out, "She wanted a potato peeler." He himself chose a cheese grater and then it was on to the scarves. They were cheap but colourful, and Bambina always tried new ways of tying one round her pretty little neck. On and on it went, with an extended stay at Tutti per 1 Euro, where everything from buckets to hair ornaments was sold. An examination of shoes neatly arranged in rows and available for trying on if one's feet were clean led to intimate apparel for *le donne* and from that to sunglasses and leather *cinture*. Papà tried on one of these, weaving it into the loops of his faded blue jeans. He shook his head and handed it back. By the time he had done so, Bambina had already gone on ahead.

It was where the severed head of a pig announced the stall of the *macellaio* and his display of meats that Bambina skipped onward towards Porta San Jacopo. At this point, he knew, things would follow an unbreaking pattern, so he removed the five-euro note that he had folded carefully into his pocket.

The musician was where he always stood, some twenty yards from Porta San Jacopo. The man was, as usual, gathering a crowd as he played Italian folksongs on his accordion. He had a dancing poodle as a companion, and he accompanied his music and the dog by singing into a microphone clipped onto the collar of his blue shirt. It was the same shirt he wore every week, tattered along the cuffs.

He waited through two songs. Then he saw his moment. Bambina dodged forward to put her customary two-euro coin in the collection basket, and he moved forward for the moment when she would return to the other listeners.

"*Scusa*," he said to her once she'd rejoined the crowd and stood in front of him. "*Per favore, glielo puoi dare . . . ?*" He nodded at his hand. The five-euro note was folded neatly in half. It lay across a greeting card that he had removed from his jacket pocket.

She frowned. A tiny part of her lip was sucked into her mouth. She looked up at him.

He indicated the collection basket with a tilt of his head. "*Per favore*," he repeated with a smile. And then, "*Anche . . . leggi questo. Non importa ma . . .*" He let the rest hang there, with another smile. The card he handed her had no envelope. It would be easy enough to open and to read the message within, as he'd asked her to do.

And then he added what he knew would convince her. It was a

single word and her eyes widened in surprise. At that point he went on in English, the words formed in such a way that their derivation was something she would not fail to recognise:

"I shall be happy to wait on the other side of Porta San Jacopo. You have absolutely nothing to fear."

17 APRIL

T he day had been bloody odd. Barbara Havers was long used to still waters when it came to Lynley, but even she had been surprised that his depths had somehow managed to hide from her the fact that he had been seeing someone. *If* it could actually be called seeing someone. For it appeared his social life post the Isabelle Ardery entanglement consisted of regular attendance at a sporting event she had never heard of.

He'd insisted that she had to see it. An experience she was unlikely to forget, was how he'd put it. She'd avoided the dubious thrill of this attempt to broaden her social sphere for as long as she could. Ultimately, though, she'd caved in to his insistence. Thus, she'd found herself at a daylong roller derby elimination tournament in which the victors turned out to be a group of extremely athletic women from Birmingham who looked as if eating small children was their other extracurricular activity of choice.

During the event, Lynley had explained all the fine points of the sport—such as they were—to Barbara. He'd named the positions, the responsibilities of the players, the penalties, and the points. He'd talked about the pack and the objective that the pack had in relation to the jammer. And along with everyone else—including her, it had to be said—he'd leapt to his feet in protest when someone got an elbow to the face and a penalty was not called.

After several hours, she reached the point of wondering what the hell this entire experience was all about and she also reached the point of considering that Lynley might have brought her to witness the spectacle as a potential outlet for her aggressions. But then, it transpired that at the end of God only knew which bout it was, because at that point she had lost count, they were approached by a skater with lightning bolts painted on her cheeks, fire-red lipstick on her mouth, and glitter rising from her eyelids to her eyebrows. This vision of athleticism had removed her helmet, said, "How nice to see you again, Sergeant Havers," and Barbara found herself looking upon Daidre Trahair. At which point things became remarkably clearer.

At first Barbara thought she was meant to play the duenna. She reckoned Lynley needed someone whose presence would soothe the veterinarian into accepting a dinner invitation. But then it turned out that Lynley had been seeing Daidre Trahair regularly since first running into her the previous November. That was where he had been on the night he'd failed to return her phone call. First at a roller derby match and then out for drinks although, from the look of things, matters hadn't got too much further than that between them lo these many months that had passed, a point that Lynley made clear as they waited for the skaters at the end of the tournament.

Daidre Trahair came to join them. What happened next was, apparently, what had happened each of the times she and Lynley had met. She invited him—and Barbara—to attend a postgame celebration, which would take place in a pub called Famous Three Kings. Lynley demurred and instead invited her—and Barbara—out for an early dinner. Daidre claimed she was hardly dressed for a meal. Lynley—and Barbara twigged that this was the new bit in their routine—said that wouldn't matter as he'd laid on something at his home. If Daidre—and Barbara, of course—would dance attendance there, he would be only too pleased to drive Daidre to her hotel afterwards.

Clever man. Barbara decided not to be offended by his use of her. She only hoped he hadn't cooked the food himself or they were in for a meal they would long remember, and for all the wrong reasons.

Daidre hesitated. She looked from Lynley to Barbara. An Amazonian woman approached and asked them all if they were coming to tipple a few at the pub where someone called McQueen was waiting to challenge Daidre at darts again. Her moment of escape was at hand, but Daidre didn't grasp at it. She said—her gaze flickering to the woman and then back to Lynley—that she would have to beg off. Her friends, she said, were insisting . . . if Lisa would make her excuses? Lisa tossed a knowing look Lynley's way. Right, she said. Stay safe, not sorry.

Barbara wondered if she was supposed to leg it, now that Daidre's presence in Lynley's home was assured, but he made it clear that she was to do nothing of the sort. Besides, she'd left her Mini blocking his garage in a mews round the corner from his digs, so one way or another she was going to have to get to it in order to scarper.

On the way to Belgravia, they made polite conversation in the manner of their countrymen: They talked about the weather. After that, Daidre and Lynley went on to speak of gorillas, for a reason that Barbara couldn't suss out. Some female gorilla was happily pregnant. On the other hand, something was wrong with the right front foot of one of the elephants. Negotiations were ongoing for a visit from some pandas, and Berlin Zoo still wished to get its hands on a polar bear cub born early last year. Was that difficult, Lynley wanted to know, breeding polar bears in captivity? It was always difficult breeding in captivity, Daidre told him. Then she fell silent, as if she'd accidentally spoken a double entendre.

At Lynley's house, they parked in the mews. Since Barbara had to move her car to allow Lynley access to his garage, she made noises as if to leave them then. Lynley said, "Don't be ridiculous, Barbara. I know you're dying for a meal," and he shot her a look whose meaning she couldn't fail to read: She was not to desert him in his hour of need.

Barbara hadn't a clue how she was supposed to facilitate matters for Lynley. She knew Daidre Trahair's background. She knew how unlikely it was that the veterinarian would allow things—whatever they were at present—to progress with Lynley. Through no fault of his own, the poor bloke had a title, an ancestral line stretching back to the Domesday Book, and a gargantuan family pile in Cornwall. Sitting at a table laid out with sixteen pieces of silver cutlery, he would know innately which fork to use when and why there were additional spoons and whatevers at the top of his plate, along with those on each side of it. For her part, Daidre's family probably still ate with knives and their fingers. The niceties of life where she was from did not extend to place settings of heirloom china and a line of wineglasses to the right of one's dinner plate.

Luckily, Lynley had thought of all this, Barbara saw. Inside the house and laid out in the dining room—although it was a bit of a problem that the bloke actually *had* a dining room—were three settings of plain white crockery, and the cutlery had handles that looked like Bakelite. Probably purchased for this exact moment, Barbara thought sardonically. She'd seen his regular stuff. It hadn't been purchased at the local Conran Shop.

The meal itself was simple. Anyone could have put it together, and although Barbara would have laid easy money on that *anyone* not being Thomas Lynley, she went along with the pretence that he'd actually stood over a hob stirring the soup and had worn an apron over his bespoke suit while he tossed the salad. Even followed a recipe to make the quiche, she decided. What he'd actually done, of course, was hoof it down to Partridges on the King's Road. If Daidre knew this, though, she didn't let on.

"Where's Charlie?" Barbara asked as she and Daidre stood uselessly by with wineglasses clasped in their hands as Lynley went to and from the kitchen.

Charlie Denton had decamped to Hampstead for the day, Lynley told them, attending a matinee production of *The Iceman Cometh*. But "Back any time now," he assured them heartily. Daidre was not to feel ill at ease that he might leap upon her should Barbara leave them.

Which was what she did as soon as she could. Lynley was guiding them into the drawing room for postprandial drinks when Barbara decided that she'd done her duty by her superior officer and it was time to go home. Early hours yet, she declared airily, but there you had it. There was something about roller derby, you know. She was knackered.

She saw Daidre wandering to the table between the two front windows. On it stood a silver-framed picture of Lynley and his wife on their wedding day. Barbara glanced at him and wondered why he hadn't removed it prior to bringing Daidre into his home. He'd thought of everything, but he hadn't thought of this.

Daidre picked up the picture as anyone might have done. Barbara and Lynley exchanged a look. Before Daidre could turn and mention the picture—the obvious comment being one about how lovely a woman Helen Lynley had been—Barbara said expansively, "So I'll say an early good-night, sir. And thanks for the meal. Got to dash before I become a pumpkin." She added, "Or whatever," when she realised that her Mini would turn into the pumpkin and not herself. She'd never been good with allusions to fairy tales.

Daidre said, "I should go as well, Thomas. Perhaps Barbara can drop me at my hotel?"

Another look between Lynley and Barbara, but he jumped in before she had to come up with the reason on her own. "Nonsense," he said. "I'm happy to drive you. Whenever you're ready."

"Take him up on that," Barbara told her. "It'd take me till morning to clear the takeaway cartons from the passenger seat of my heap."

That said, she got herself out of the town house. The last thing she saw was Lynley pouring brandy into two crystal balloons. Whoops on that one, she thought. He should have used teacups or something. Supper within a bona fide dining room had been bad enough.

She quite liked the vet, but she wondered about Lynley's pursuit of her. There was definitely a kind of tension between them. It just didn't seem sexual to Barbara.

No matter, she thought. It wasn't her affair. As long as Lynley didn't ensnare himself with Isabelle Ardery again, anyone else was fine by her. For his time with Isabelle had constituted the malodorous dead elephant. She was that happy the rotting corpse of it had finally been removed from the room.

She was thinking of nothing in particular when she saw the panda car in front of the yellow Edwardian villa when she arrived home. It was double-parked in the street next to an ancient Saab, and in the evening light, most of the inhabitants of the building behind which Barbara's tiny bungalow sat stood along the driveway in clusters, as if waiting to see someone brought outside in handcuffs. Barbara parked hastily and illegally. She got out and heard someone saying, "Don't know . . . Didn't hear a thing till the cops showed up," and she made fast time to join the onlookers.

"What's going on?" She addressed her question to Mrs. Silver, who lived in a flat on the second floor of the house. She was wearing, as always, one of her pinafore aprons and an accompanying turban, and she was chewing nervously on what looked like a tongue depressor bearing chocolate stains.

"She's phoned the police," Mrs. Silver said. "Or someone has. Maybe he did it. There was shouting at first. All of us heard it. Both of them. Another man as well. Not an English speaker, him. He was shouting in I-don't-know-what language. I couldn't tell. Well, it's my hearing, isn't it? But it doesn't matter. They must have been heard all the way to Chalk Farm Road."

This was shorthand for something. What it was Barbara didn't know. She looked round to see who else was in the crowd, but what she noticed was who wasn't there. And then her gaze went to the villa itself, where every light appeared inside of the ground-floor flat and the French windows were standing open.

Her throat got tight. She murmured, "Is Azhar . . . ? Has something . . . ?"

Mrs. Silver turned to her. She read something on Barbara's face. She said, "She's come back, Barbara. She's not alone. Something's happened and she's brought the police to sort it out."

CHALK FARM
LONDON

"She" could have only one meaning. Angelina Upman had returned. Barbara dug in her chaotic shoulder bag and brought out her warrant card. It was the one thing that would gain her access to Azhar's flat, no matter who was in charge inside.

She worked her way through the rest of her neighbours. She entered the picket gate and crossed the lawn. The shouting became intelligible as she approached the French windows. It was easy to recognise Angelina's voice.

"Make him tell you!" She was screaming at someone. "It's Pakistan! He's put her there. She's with his family. You're a monster! To do this to your own *daughter*."

And then Azhar's voice, in a panic, "How can you say . . . ?"

Then a foreigner, a heavy accent, "Why you no make to arrest this man?"

Barbara entered to a scene in which everyone seemed frozen into position: Two uniformed constables had placed themselves between Taymullah Azhar and Angelina Upman. Her face looked painted with the mascara that had raccooned her eyes, and her features were pinched. The man with her was handsome, looking like someone who could pose for the sculpture of an athlete. His hair was curly and thick, his shoulders broad, his chest like a trunk. His fists were clenched as if he would punch Azhar could he only reach him. One of the constables was preventing this, holding him back as Azhar and Angelina shouted at each other.

Azhar was the first to see Barbara. His face had been worn for months, but now it looked worse. He'd been running on empty since their final conversation with Dwayne Doughty, taking on more graduate students, attending every conference that would take him as far from Chalk Farm as he could get. He'd returned from another one—this time in Berlin— only the night before, stopping by her bungalow to ask if there had been anything . . . any message . . . any word . . . ? It was his regular question upon returning. Her answer had always been the same.

Angelina turned when she saw Azhar's expression alter. So did the man with her. In doing so, he fully exposed his face. It had a port wine birthmark like the mark upon Cain, extending from his right ear onto his cheek. It was the only thing that marred his beauty.

The constable holding back this man spoke. "Madam, you'll have to leave."

Barbara flipped him her warrant card. "DS Havers," she said. "I live in the back. What's happened? C'n I help?"

"It's Hadiyyah" was all that Azhar managed to say.

"He's taken my child," Angelina cried. "He's kidnapped Hadiyyah. He has her somewhere. Do you understand? Oh, of course you do. You've bloody well helped him, haven't you?"

Barbara tried to take this in. Helped who do what? was what she wondered.

"Tell me where she is!" Angelina shouted. "You goddamn bloody well tell me where she is!"

"Angelina, what happened?" Barbara asked. "Listen to me. I don't know what's going on."

The story came from all directions. When the constables understood that Barbara was a friend of the family and not there from the Met, they attempted to escort her from the premises, but at that point both Angelina and Azhar wanted her to stay, each for their own reasons, although those reasons went unspoken other than Angelina crying, "She needs to bloody hear this, she does," and Azhar saying, "Barbara knows my daughter very well."

"Your daughter, your daughter," Angelina snarled. "You're *no* father to a child you would treat like this."

She'd been taken from a market in Lucca, Italy, Barbara discovered. This had happened two days previously. She'd been there with Lorenzo—the man in the flat with Angelina and obviously, to Barbara, Angelina's new lover—as they had done their weekly shop. She was to wait where she always waited, where a musician played, but she hadn't been there when Lorenzo arrived and he hadn't thought to search for her.

"Why not?" Barbara asked.

"What difference does it make?" Angelina demanded. "We know what happened. We know who took her. She would never walk off with a stranger, anywhere. And no one could possibly have carried her off in the middle of a market in front of hundreds of people. She would have screamed. She would have fought. You've taken her, Hari, and as God is my witness, I'm going to—"

"*Cara,*" Lorenzo said, "*non devi.*" He moved to her. "*La troveremo,*" he said. "*Te lo prometto.*" At this she began to weep. Azhar took a step towards her.

"Angelina," he said, "you must listen to me. So much depends—"

"I don't believe you!" she cried.

"Did you phone the police in Lucca?" Barbara asked her.

"Of course I phoned them! What do you think I am? I phoned

them, they came, they searched, they're still searching. And what are they finding? *Nothing.* A nine-year-old gone without a trace. And *he* has her. Because no one else could have taken her. Make him tell me where she *is*." This last she directed to the constables. They looked to Barbara as if for some sort of help.

What Barbara wanted to say was, "He supposedly took her like *you* took her? Like *you* told Azhar where she was?" But instead she turned to Angelina's companion. "Tell me exactly what happened," she said. "Why didn't you look for her when she wasn't where you expected her to be?"

"Are you accusing *him*?" Angelina cried.

"If Hadiyyah's missing—"

"*If*? What d'you think this is?"

"Angelina, please," Barbara said. "If Hadiyyah's missing, there's no time to waste. I need to know what happened from start to finish." And to Lorenzo, "Why didn't you look for her at once?"

"Because of my sister," he said. And when Angelina protested the fact that he was even replying when they all knew who'd taken her daughter, he said, "*Per favore, cara,*" in a gentle voice. "*Vorrei dire qualcosa, va bene?*" Then, in the limited English he possessed, he explained. "My sister live near this *mercato*. There we go always after, to her house. When Hadiyyah I miss from this place, I think she go there. To play."

"Why would you think that?" Barbara asked.

"*Mio nipote . . .*" He looked to Angelina for help.

"His nephew is there," she said. "Hadiyyah and the boy play together."

Across the room Azhar closed his eyes. "All these months," he said. And for the first time since his child had gone missing, Barbara saw the man's lips struggle with the effort not to weep.

"I finish with making shop," Lorenzo said. "I think I see Hadiyyah when I go to the house."

"She knew how to get there?" Barbara asked.

"There she go many times to play, *sì*. Angelina come to the *mercato* then, and—"

"From where?"

"Piazzale—"

"I mean what was she doing? What were you doing, Angelina?"

"Are you now accusing *me*—"

"Of course not. Where were you? What did you see? How long were you gone?"

She was doing her yoga, as it turned out. She went regularly to a class in the town.

"She come to the *mercato*, we meet like always, we go to my sister. Hadiyyah is not there."

They'd thought at first she'd become lost somewhere in the large market. Or, perhaps, she'd become distracted on her way to the musician and now was back there in the market waiting for them in her usual place near Porta San Jacopo. They returned, this time with Lorenzo's sister and her husband, and the four of them had begun to search.

They searched the market. They extended the search outside the city wall, where the rest of Lucca—the modern part of the town— spread out in all directions. They walked the top of the huge wall itself with its *baluardi*, the great ramparts from which defences were long ago maintained. On these were now planted trees and lawns, and among them were places children could play. But Hadiyyah had been nowhere on the wall, nor had she been just beneath it at the playground near Porta San Donato, so close to her school as to be a natural destination for a little girl tired of waiting for her parents.

Barbara looked at Azhar when the word *parents* was spoken. He looked as if he'd taken a blow.

At that point they began to think the unthinkable and had phoned the police. But Angelina had also phoned Azhar. Gone for a few days from University College, she'd learned. Not answering his mobile, she'd then discovered. Not answering his landline here in Chalk Farm, either. And that was when she knew what had actually happened.

"Angelina," Azhar said desperately, "I was at a conference."

"Where?" she demanded.

"Germany. Berlin."

"You can prove that, sir?" the constable asked.

"Of course I can prove it. It was four days long. There were many sessions. I delivered a paper and also attended—"

"You left Berlin long enough to take her, didn't you?" Angelina said. "That would have been simple. That's what you did. Where is she, Hari? What have you done with her? Where have you taken her?"

"You must listen," Azhar said, and then to her companion whom he had otherwise ignored, "You must ask her to listen. I could not find you once you left me, Angelina. I tried. Yes, I tried. I hired someone many months ago. But there was no trail. Please listen to me."

"Madam," the constable said, "this is a matter to be handled at the source, not here. The Italian police need to instigate a wider search, beyond Lucca. They'll also be able to make sure that his attendance at this conference—"

"Do you know how easily he could have made it for himself to leave that bloody conference?" Angelina said. "He's taken her from Italy, don't you see? She might be in Germany. Why in God's name won't you listen to me?"

"How could I have taken her?" Azhar countered. He shot Barbara an agonised look.

She said, "Angelina, her passport. Her papers. *Think.* You took everything with you. I was here. I checked. Azhar came for me the night you left him. He couldn't have taken her from Italy without documents of some kind."

"Then you're part of this," Angelina declared. "You've helped him, haven't you? You'd know how to get a false passport for her. Identity cards. Everything you need." And saying this, she began to weep. "I want my daughter," she cried. "I want my little girl."

"On my life, I do not have her, Angelina," Azhar said brokenly. "We must go to Italy at once to find her."

ILFORD
GREATER LONDON

Neither Angelina nor her lover—a bloke whose name turned out to be Lorenzo Mura—was about to consider a return to Italy until whatever stones they'd decided needed to be turned over were turned over. Barbara learned this within a quarter hour's conversation with them.

No matter what Azhar produced in an attempt to convince his former lover that he'd been exactly where he said he'd been, no amount of paperwork—from the conference in Berlin, from the hotel in which he'd stayed, from the flight he'd taken to get there, from the restaurants in which he'd eaten—was going to persuade Angelina that time was of the essence in a kidnapping case and that time needed to be spent in Italy and not in a shouting match in Chalk Farm.

She wanted to go to Ilford, she announced. When she said this, Azhar looked so appalled that Barbara thought he might sick up on the floor. She herself said, "*Ilford?* What in God's name has Ilford got to do with anything?" and Azhar answered with four words that spoke volumes, "My wife and parents."

Barbara said to Angelina, "You think he's got Hadiyyah stowed with his parents? Come on, Angelina. Have some sense. We need to—"

"Shut up!" she screamed. The two constables tried to intervene, but before they could stop her, she had gone for Azhar. "You'd do *anything!*" she cried.

Barbara grabbed her and pulled her away, and when Angelina swung on her next, she said, "All right. Ilford. We're going to Ilford."

"Barbara, we cannot . . ." Azhar's voice was a separate agony from everything else.

"We're going to have to," Barbara told him.

The local constables, at this point, were only too happy to leave the matter in the hands of the Metropolitan police. They faded out of the flat, and the one favour they did before departing the property altogether was to disperse the neighbours. Thus, when Barbara and her companions left Azhar's flat and headed for his car, they were able to do so in a relatively inconspicuous manner.

They rode to Ilford in silence. Barbara could hear Lorenzo murmuring something to Angelina as they went along, but he did his murmuring in Italian, and he might as well have been speaking Martian.

Azhar kept his gaze on the road and a strangling grip upon the steering wheel. From his rapid and shallow breathing, Barbara had an idea of the degree to which he was wrestling with everything going on.

Azhar's family turned out to live directly off Green Lane, just round the corner from an establishment called Ushan's Fruit and Veg.

It was a street of terrace houses like so many other similar streets in the city where the now-lit streetlamps shone on homes distinguished only by the nature of their patch of front garden. Unlike areas closer to the centre of town, however, this particular street wasn't lined with cars. They would be an expense most families daren't take on.

"Which one?" Angelina said, as Azhar stopped the car midway down the street.

Lorenzo opened the car door and helped her out. He kept his hand on the small of her back. Azhar indicated the house by going to the door. When he rang the bell, a teenage boy was the one to answer. It was a terrible moment. Barbara saw the anguish of it in the very immobility of Azhar's face. She knew he was looking at his son. She also knew he hadn't seen him in a decade.

That the boy hadn't a clue who this group of people was was obvious enough. He said, "Yeah?" and used the heel of his hand to move his floppy hair from his forehead. Barbara saw Azhar make a gesture as if to touch the boy, but he stopped himself short of doing so. Then he said, "Sayyid. I am your father. Will you tell these people with me that no child has been brought to this house?"

The boy's lips parted. He seemed to tear his gaze from Azhar, and he directed it to Barbara and then to Angelina. When he finally spoke, it was clear he'd been well schooled in the family history. "Which of them is the whore?" he asked.

Azhar said, "Sayyid. Please do as I say. Tell these people that no child of nine years old—a little girl—has been brought to this house."

"Sayyid?" A woman's voice, then. She spoke from behind the boy, sounding as if she was in another room. "Who is there, Sayyid?"

He made no reply. He locked eyes with his father, as if challenging him to identify himself to the wife he'd deserted. When he didn't respond, footsteps approached and Sayyid stepped away from the door. Azhar and his wife stood face-to-face. Without looking at her son, she said, "Sayyid, go to your room."

Barbara had expected the traditional dress of *shalwar kameez*. She'd expected the scarf. What she hadn't expected was how beautiful Azhar's wife was because she'd thought—perhaps like most people, she reckoned—that Azhar would have left an ordinary kind of woman in order to take up life with an extraordinary one. Men being men, she'd reckoned, they'd trade up, not down, not even across. But this woman far outclassed Angelina in the beauty department: dark, sloe-eyed, with cheekbones to kill for, a sensuous mouth, an elegant long neck, and perfect skin.

Azhar said, "Nafeeza."

Nafeeza said, "What brings you here?"

Angelina was the one to answer. "We want to search the house."

"Please, Angelina," Azhar said quietly. "Surely you can see . . ." And then to his wife, "Nafeeza, my apologies for this. I would not . . . If you would please tell these people that my daughter is not here."

She wasn't a tall woman, but she brought herself up to her full height, and when she did this, the suggestion made was one of strength running through her body. She said, "Your daughter is upstairs in her room. She is doing her school prep. She's a very fine student."

"I am pleased to hear that. You must be . . . She will be a source of . . . But I do not speak of . . ."

"You know who he's talking about," Angelina said.

Barbara took out her police ID. She could barely stand the amount of pain that seemed to be rolling off Azhar. She said to his wife, "C'n we come in, Mrs. . . ." And to her dismay she realised she hadn't a clue what to call her. She switched to, "Madam, if we c'n come in. We've a missing child we're looking for."

"And you think this child is within my house?"

"No. Not exactly."

Nafeeza looked them over, each of them, one at a time, and she took her time doing it. Then she stepped back from the door. They entered the house and filled a narrow corridor that was already filled by a stairway, boots, coats, rucksacks, hockey sticks, and football equipment. They crowded into a small lounge to the right.

There, they saw that Sayyid hadn't gone to his room. He was in the lounge, on the edge of the sofa, elbows on his thighs and hands dangling between his knees. Above him on the wall a large picture featured thousands of people on pilgrimage to Mecca. There were no other pictures or decorations aside from two small school photographs in frames on a table. Azhar went to these and picked them up. His gaze upon them was hungry. Nafeeza crossed the room and removed them from his hand. She placed them facedown on the table.

She said to him, "There is no child here, aside from mine."

"I want to look," Angelina said.

"You must tell her that I speak the truth, husband," Nafeeza said. "You must explain to her that I have no reason to lie about this. Whatever has happened, it is nothing to do with me or with my children."

"So *she's* the one?" Sayyid put in. "She's the whore?"

"Sayyid," his mother said.

"I am sorry, Nafeeza," Azhar said to her. "For this. For what it was. For who I was."

"*Sorry?*" This from Sayyid. "You c'n bloody talk to Mum about *sorry*? You're a piece of shit and don't think *we* think anything else. If you plan to—"

"Enough!" his mother said. "You will wait in your room, Sayyid."

"While this one"—with a sneer towards Angelina—"goes through our house looking for her bastard brat?"

Azhar looked at his son. "You may not say—"

"You, wanker, don't tell me what to do." And with that, he leapt to his feet, pushed his way through all of them, and left the room. His footsteps did not go up the stairs, however, but rather into the corridor, where they could hear him making a telephone call. He spoke in Urdu. This seemed to mean something to both Azhar and Nafeeza, Barbara saw, because Azhar's wife said to him, "It will not be long," and he said again, "I am so sorry."

"You do not know sorrow." Nafeeza then spoke to the rest of them, her gaze going from one face to the other. Her voice contained perfect dignity. "The only children in this house are the children from my own body, got off this man and abandoned by him."

Barbara said to Azhar in a low voice, "Who's the kid ringing?"

"My father," Azhar told her.

What she thought at this was, Hot bloody hell. What she knew was that things were about to get worse. She said to Angelina, "We're wasting time. You can see Hadiyyah isn't here. You can tell, for God's sake. Can't you see these people wouldn't do him a favour any more than your family would do you one?"

"You're in love with him," Angelina snapped. "You've been from the first. I no more trust you than I'd trust a snake." Then she said to Lorenzo, "You check above and I'll—"

Sayyid was back in the room in a flash. He threw himself at Lorenzo, shouting, "Get out of our house! Get out! Get out!"

Lorenzo batted him away like a fly. Azhar took a step forward. Barbara grabbed his arm. Things were going in a very bad direction, and the last thing they needed was one of these people making a call to the local cops.

"You listen to me," she said, her tone sharp. "You have a choice here, Angelina. Either you believe what Nafeeza's telling you, or you conduct a search and explain yourself to the cops when they get here. Because if I was Nafeeza, I'd be on the blower the minute Mr. Universe here put his big toe on the stairs. You're wasting time. We're wasting time. So for God's sake think. Azhar was in Germany. He's shown you that. He wasn't in Italy and he had no idea that *you* were. So you can continue to raise holy hell, or we can all get on a plane and get back to Italy and lean on the cops there to find Hadiyyah. I suggest you decide. *Now*."

"I won't believe till—"

"For God's bloody sake! What's wrong with you?"

"You may search." Nafeeza spoke quietly. She indicated Barbara. "Only you," she said.

"Is that good enough for you?" Barbara asked Angelina.

"How do I know that you aren't part of this? That you and he together haven't—"

"Because I'm a bloody cop, because I love your daughter, because if you can't see that the last thing either of us would do—me *or* Azhar—is what you've done to him by hiding her away somewhere and denying her access to one of her own parents, because if that's what you really think has happened . . . He's not *like* you, all right? I'm not like you. And you goddamn know that. So if you don't stay in this room while I look through the house to prove Hadiyyah isn't here, I'm going to ring the cops myself and have them out here on a domestic disturbance. Am I being clear enough for you?"

Lorenzo murmured to Angelina in Italian. He put his hand gently on the back of her neck. "All right," she said.

Barbara made for the stairs. It was not a major project to search the house because there was so little of it. Three floors comprised its interior, with bedrooms, bathrooms, a kitchen, little else. Barbara startled Azhar's other daughter in the midst of her school prep, but she was the only living creature above stairs.

She returned to the others. She said, "Nothing. All right? Let's leave. Now."

Angelina's eyes grew bright with tears, and it came to Barbara how deeply she'd been hoping that—despite the ludicrous nature of what she'd decided had happened to her child—Hadiyyah would indeed be in the house. For a moment, Barbara felt sympathy for her. But she stamped on the feeling. Azhar was who mattered. And he was minutes away from a confrontation with his father. She knew they had to get him out of the neighbourhood before that occurred.

They had no luck. They were leaving the house when two men in traditional dress came storming down the street from the direction of Green Lane. One of them carried a shovel and the other a hoe. It wasn't a case for Sherlock to read their intentions.

"Get in the car," she said to Azhar. "Do it. *Now*."

He didn't budge. The men were shouting in Urdu as they tore towards them. The taller had to be Azhar's father, Barbara figured, because his face was transfixed by rage. The other—his companion—was much the same age, perhaps a partner in administering retribution.

"*La macchina, la macchina.*" This from Lorenzo to Angelina. He opened the car door and bundled her inside. Barbara half expected him to follow her and lock the doors, but he didn't do so. He seemed to be a bloke who liked to mix things up. He might have had no love for Azhar. But when it came to a street fight? *No problema.*

Between the Urdu being shouted by the older men and the Italian being shouted by Lorenzo, Barbara had no idea who was accusing whom of what. But the target of the Pakistani men was clearly Azhar, and she didn't intend him to get hurt. The older men came in swinging their tools. She pushed Azhar out of the way. She yelled, "Police!" at the top of her lungs. This didn't impress. Lorenzo swung.

She reckoned he was swearing in Italian. He didn't sound pleasant as he chose his words. He was good with his fists and better with his feet and, farm implements or not, the potential assailants were on the ground before they knew what had hit them. But they didn't remain there. They threw themselves back into the fray as Sayyid came roaring out of the house. Then an older woman and two other men debouched from the house next door as Sayyid barreled into his father and drove his fist into Azhar's throat.

Someone screamed. Barbara thought it might have been herself except she had her mobile phone in her hand and was punching in the nines to bring the local rozzers. Clearly, her declaration of identity wasn't going to stop this lot.

Azhar's father got to him. He pulled Sayyid off and fell upon him himself. Lorenzo went after the man only to be jumped by the former hoe wielder. The older woman pounced upon Azhar and his father, screaming what sounded to Barbara like a name as she pulled and dragged and did what she could to put an end to things. Barbara did the same to the bloke on Lorenzo. Nafeeza came out of the house and grabbed Sayyid. But three more teenage boys came into the street with cricket bats and two women began to shout imprecations from the pavement on the opposite side.

It took the police to break everything up. Two panda cars and four uniformed constables handled things. It was down to Barbara that no one ended up arrested, although all of them ended up explaining themselves in the local nick. She offered her identification once they got there. She said it was a family dispute. Azhar's father spat, "He is not family," but the cops brought in an officer who spoke good Urdu and he gave everyone a chance to say what needed to be said on the matter. The end of it all was time wasted, anguish caused, horrors visited upon everyone, and nothing learned. They rode back to Chalk Farm in near silence.

Azhar didn't speak. Angelina only wept.

18 APRIL

Y ou've gone quite mad" was how Isabelle Ardery dealt with
Barbara's request. She added to this, "Get back to work, Sergeant, and let's not talk of this again."

"You know they need a liaison officer" was how Barbara countered
her superior officer's command.

"I know nothing of the sort," Ardery told her. "And I have no intention of sending you or anyone else barging into a foreign investigation."

She'd been finishing up with someone on the phone when Barbara
had entered her office. Planning an extended celebration, no doubt.
The announcement had descended from on high thirty minutes earlier in the person of Assistant Commissioner Sir David Hillier gracing
their side of New Scotland Yard's two tower blocks with his florid-
faced presence. He'd imparted upon the assembly of officers the news
that *Acting* had been dropped—permanently—from the *Detective Superintendent* that until that precise moment had preceded Isabelle Ardery's name. Kudos all around and let flow the champers. Whatever
hoops she'd needed to jump through for the past nine months, Isabelle
Ardery had apparently managed to catapult herself through them.

Azhar had left early that morning, accompanying Angelina Upman
and Lorenzo Mura to Lucca, Italy. Barbara had been determined to

follow hard upon their heels. She had it all worked out—how this would happen—and she had just concluded presenting the matter to the superintendent.

It had seemed perfectly logical to her. A British national had disappeared upon foreign soil. A British national may well have been kidnapped. When a crime such as this occurred, a liaison officer was generally assigned to breach the cultural, linguistic, investigatory, and legal gaps between the two countries involved. Barbara wished to be that officer. She knew the family, and all that was needed was Detective Superintendent Ardery's okay on the matter, and off she could go.

Ardery didn't see things that way. She heard Barbara out, taking in the entire subject, beginning with Hadiyyah's November disappearance in the company of her mother and ending with her current disappearance from a crowded market in Italy. She listened without asking questions other than to clarify names, locations, and relationships, and when Barbara concluded and waited for the logical "of course you must go to Tuscany at once" that she believed would be coming on the verbal wings of a hundred angels, Ardery pointed out what she called "a few salient details that the sergeant had apparently overlooked."

First among them was the fact that the British embassy was not involved in this matter. No one had rung them or paid a call upon them or sent them a telegram, email, fax, or smoke signal, and without the involvement of the embassy—diplomats pouring oil on potentially troubled waters in advance of the Met's incursion into someone else's patch—they did not barge round like bulls among the Belleek attempting an investigation where they were not wanted.

Second, the superintendent pointed out, the purpose of the liaison officer was to liaise, which, as they both knew, meant to keep the family in the UK apprised of everything relative to the investigation that was occurring on foreign soil. But the parents of the child were in Italy, no? Or at least on their way to Italy, according to the sergeant's own words. Indeed, the mother of the child *lived* in Italy, no? Somewhere in Lucca? Outside of Lucca? In the vicinity of Lucca? And with an Italian national, yes? So she had no reason to request a liaison officer. Hence, there was no case to present as to the need of sending

Detective Sergeant Barbara Havers into Tuscany to be of assistance in whatever was going on.

"What's going on," Barbara said, "is the disappearance of a nine-year-old girl. A nine-year-old *British* girl. No one saw it happen, and *whatever* it was that happened, it happened in the middle of a market. A crowded market with hundreds of witnesses who apparently saw nothing."

"As of yet," Ardery said. "They can't all have been talked to at this point. How long has the child been gone?"

"What difference does it make?"

"I wouldn't think I'd need to explain that to you."

"Bloody hell, you know the first twenty-four hours are crucial. And now it's been more than forty-eight."

"And I assure you, the Italian police know that as well."

"They're telling Angelina—"

"Sergeant." Isabelle's voice had been firm but not unsympathetic despite her words. Now, however, it had an edge. "I've told you the facts. You seem to think I have power in this matter when I don't. When a foreign country—"

"What part of this don't you bloody understand?" Barbara cut in. "She's been snatched in public. She might be dead by now."

"She might well be. And if that's the case—"

"Listen to yourself!" Barbara shrieked. "This is a kid we're talking about. A kid I know. And you're declaring 'she might well be' like you're talking about a cake left too long in the oven. It might well be burnt. The cheese might well be mouldy. The milk might well be sour."

Isabelle surged to her feet. "You damn well control yourself," she said. "You're too involved by half. Even *if* the embassy rang up and said the Met's presence was wanted at once, you'd be the last officer I'd consider sending. You've no objectivity at all, and if you don't understand that objectivity above everything else is crucial when it comes to a crime, then you need to get back to wherever you learned your policing skills and learn them again."

"And what if something like this happened to one of your boys?" Barbara demanded. "Just how objective would you manage to be?"

"You've gone quite mad" was the conclusion to it all, plus the order to get back to work.

Barbara stormed from Ardery's office. For the moment, she couldn't even recall what the work was that she was supposed to get back to. She flung herself in the direction of her desk, where her computer's screen attempted to remind her, but she could think of nothing and would be good for nothing unless and until she got herself to Italy.

LUCCA

TUSCANY

Chief Inspector Salvatore Lo Bianco had an evening ritual that he adhered to as often as he was able to be at home for dinner. With a cup of *caffè corretto* in his hand, he climbed to the very top of the tower in which he and his mamma lived, and there in the perfectly square rooftop garden he drank in peace and watched the sunset. He enjoyed sunsets and how they caressed the ancient buildings of his city. But more than sunsets, he enjoyed the time away from his mamma. At seventy-six years old and in possession of a very bad hip, she no longer climbed to the top of Torre Lo Bianco, the tower that had been his family home for generations. The last two flights of stairs were narrow and metal, and a misstep on them would finish her off. Salvatore didn't want to endanger his mamma even though he hated living with her as much as she loved having him at home once again.

Having her Salvatore at home meant she'd been right, and his mamma loved being right more than she loved being content or even being in a state of grace. She'd worn black since the day he'd brought home the Swedish girl he'd met eighteen years earlier in Piazza Grande, and to this maddening choice of telegraphing her displeasure— she'd even worn black to their wedding—she had now taken to carrying rosary beads every moment of the day, and she'd been fingering them piously since the evening he'd revealed that he and Birgit were divorcing. He was supposed to think that his mamma was praying for Birgit to come to her senses and ask her husband to return to the family home in Borgo Giannotti, just beyond the city wall. But the truth of the matter was that she was fulfilling her promise to the Virgin: Bring an end to this blasphemous marriage of my son to *quella puttana straniera*, and I will spend the rest of my life honouring you with a daily rosary. Or five. Or six. Salvatore didn't know how many rosaries were actually involved, but he imagined there were plenty of them. He wanted to point out to her that the Catholic Church didn't recognise divorce, but there was a part of him—good son that he was—that simply didn't want to spoil her fun.

Salvatore took his *caffè* to one side of the tower garden and spent a moment inspecting his tomato plants. Already they were showing their fruit, which would ripen beautifully here so high above the city. He looked from them in the direction of Borgo Giannotti. He had things on his mind and one of them was Birgit.

His mother had been right, of course. Birgit had been a mistake on every front. Opposites might indeed attract, but their kind of attraction had cooled with a rather disturbing speed. He should have known early on that this was going to be the case when he'd brought her home to meet his mamma and her reaction to his mamma's devotion to him—she'd only that day washed, starched, and perfectly ironed his fifteen dress shirts—had been along the lines of "So you have a penis. So what, Salvatore?" instead of understanding the importance of the male child in an Italian family where extending the family line and name was paramount to everyone in it. He'd thought this amusing at first, Birgit's lack of understanding about this element of his culture. He'd thought the clashes of Italian and Swedish traditions and beliefs would become minimal over time. He'd been wrong. At least she hadn't decamped to Stockholm with their two children once he and she had parted, and for this Salvatore was grateful.

Second on his mind was the matter of this missing child. This missing *British* child. It was bad enough that she was foreign. That she was British made it worse. Shades of Perugia and Portugal were all over the situation. Salvatore knew not a soul would blame him for not wanting this circumstance in Lucca to turn in a direction similar to those. Tabloid reporters everywhere, international tabloid reporters at that, television news encampments right outside the *questura*, hysterical parents, official demands, embassy phone calls, jurisdictional jockeying among the various police forces. Things hadn't got to that point yet, but Salvatore knew that they could.

He was mightily worried. Three days after the girl's disappearance and the only leads they'd come up with were from a half-drunk accordion player who performed on market days near Porta San Jacopo and a well-known young drug addict who on these same days knelt directly in the pathway of the shoppers entering the *mercato* with a sign on his chest reading, *Ho fame*, as if with the hope that this declaration of hunger would delude passersby who might otherwise rightly suspect he intended to use whatever euros he managed to collect to purchase whatever it was he was actually intending to ingest. From the accordion player, Salvatore had learned that the child in question was present every market Saturday to listen to him play. *La Bella Piccola*, as he called her, always gave him two euros. But on this day, she had given him seven. First she had given him the coin. Then she had placed a five-euro note into his basket. He thought this note had been handed to her by someone standing near her. Who was this? the accordion player had been asked. He didn't know. In the crowd, he explained, there were always many people. Along with his dancing poodle, he smiled and nodded and did his best to entertain them. But the only ones he truly noticed were those who give him a little money for his music. Which was why, of course, he knew *la Bella Piccola* by appearance if not by name. Because, as he had already said, she always gives me money, *Ispettore*. He said this last with an expression indicating he knew quite well that Salvatore Lo Bianco would rather part with a finger than drop a coin into someone's basket.

When asked if there was anything at all unusual that he noticed about the girl that day, the accordion player first said there was nothing. But after a pause for thought he admitted that a dark-haired man *might* have given her the five-euro note, as such a man had been standing behind her. But, for that matter, an ageing woman with crepe-skinned breasts that hung to her waist might have done so as well. She'd been standing right next to the girl. In either case, all he could tell the *ispettore* by way of description was dark hair for the one and pendulous breasts for the other, which applied to eighty percent of the population. Indeed, the woman could have been Salvatore's own mother.

The kneeling young drug addict added a bit to this. From this man—a hapless youth called Carlo Casparia, the disgrace of his long-suffering Padovan family—Salvatore had learned that the girl had passed right by him. Although he was facing outward—away from Porta San Jacopo so that he could greet the entering shoppers with his spurious declaration of hunger—Carlo knew it was the same child whose picture was now posted on walls and doors and in windows round the town. For she'd paused and looked around as if she'd been seeking someone, and when she saw *Ho fame* on his sign, she'd skipped back to him and had given him the banana she had been carrying. Then she'd walked on. From there, she'd simply vanished. Into thin air, as things turned out. There were no other leads.

Once the mother of the child had made it apparent through various means of hysteria that the child wasn't a runaway, that she wasn't playing with friends somewhere, that they—the mamma and her lover—had searched the area, that every corner had been poked and every loose stone had been overturned, Salvatore had rounded up the usual suspects. He'd ordered them brought to the *questura*, and there on Viale Cavour, he'd grilled eight sex offenders, six suspected paedophiles, a recidivist thief awaiting trial, and a priest about whom Salvatore had had suspicions for years. Nothing had come of this, but the local paper had the story now. It wasn't big yet—it had not, thank God, gone either provincial or national—but it would if he didn't come up with this child soon.

He took a final sip of his *caffè corretto*. He turned from the sight of the sunset and headed for the rooftop opening that would take him back down to his mamma. His mobile rang, and he glanced at the number. He groaned when he saw it and considered what to do.

He could let the call go to voice mail, but he knew there was little point to that. The caller would continue to ring him four times an hour all through the night. He gave a moment's thought to tossing the mobile over the tower's edge to break in the narrow street below, but instead he answered.

"*Pronto*," he sighed.

He heard what he expected to hear. "Come to Barga, Topo. It's time you and I had a little talk."

BARGA

TUSCANY

It was only natural that Piero Fanucci could not possibly live in a town convenient to Lucca. That would have made everyone's life easier, and *il Pubblico Ministero* was not a man interested in making anyone's life easier, least of all the policemen who did his bidding. He liked to live in the Tuscan hills. Thus he lived in the Tuscan hills. If someone he wished to converse with concerning an investigation had to sweat an hour's drive on an April evening to get to him, that was simply how things were.

At least *il Pubblico Ministero* didn't live in the old part of Barga. Getting to him, then, would have meant a climb up endless stairs and a negotiation of the maze of passageways that led in the direction of the Duomo, high on the top of the hill. Instead, thank God, Fanucci lived along the road from Gallicano. It was a dangerous series of switchbacks climbing at a hair-raising angle from a village in the valley, but at least one could get there by car.

When Salvatore arrived, he knew that *il Pubblico Ministero* would be alone. His wife would be travelling to the home of one of their six children, which was how she had navigated her marriage to Fanucci since those children had become old enough to marry and to purchase homes of their own. His occasional lover—a long-suffering woman from Gallicano who cleaned and cooked and obeyed a single word from Fanucci, *resta*, by taking herself to his bedroom once she'd finished her solitary dinner in his kitchen and had done the washing up after his solitary dinner in the dining room—would also have departed. Fanucci would be with his only true love, among the cymbidiums he tenderly babied in a manner he might have applied, but did not, to his family. Salvatore would be meant to admire whichever of the orchids was currently in bloom. Until he had done so, and at a length and with the level of sincerity *il Pubblico Ministero* required, he would not be told the reason that he had been summoned to Barga.

Salvatore parked in front of Fanucci's house, a stout and square terracotta-coloured villa that stood in a plot of expensively maintained gardens behind a wrought-iron gate. This was, as always, locked, but a code admitted him.

He didn't bother with the house. Instead, he walked around to the back of the villa where a terrace overlooked a steep drop to the valley and the hillsides opposite, into which dozens of Tuscan villages were tucked. Lights were coming on in those villages now. In another hour, they would provide a scattering of sequins on the cape of night.

At the far corner of the terrace rose the roof of the orchid house, which stood on the lawn below. Steps led down to this lawn, and a gravel path edged it. Salvatore followed this to the grape arbour that provided shade for a seating area. A table and chairs stood here, on the table a bottle of grappa, two glasses, and a plate of the kind of *biscotti* that Fanucci favoured. *Il Pubblico Ministero* himself was not seated here, however. As Salvatore had anticipated, he was within the orchid house awaiting compliments. Salvatore mentally readied himself and entered.

Fanucci was in the midst of spraying the leaves of a dozen or more of his plants. These stood on a potting shelf that ran along one side of the orchid house. They were spindly in that way of orchids, tied to thin bamboo poles to keep them upright, each offering a single spine of blooms that Fanucci was tenderly keeping away from the spray. He had his spectacles on the tip of his nose and a hand-rolled cigarette between his lips. His gut hung over the *cintura* that cinched his trousers.

Fanucci didn't look up from what he was doing. He didn't speak. This gave Salvatore time to evaluate his superior in an effort to know what to expect from him during their encounter. For Fanucci was notoriously volatile, *il drago* to some and *il vulcano* to others.

He was also the ugliest man Salvatore had ever seen, deeply swarthy like the *contadini* in Basilicata, the land of his birth; cursed with warts that exploded from his face like something only San Rocco could cure; in possession of a sixth finger on his right hand which he waved about in conversation, all the better to read upon the faces of those to whom he spoke the level of their aversion for him. His appearance had been a torment in his impoverished youth, but he'd learned to use it. At an age and of a level of success at which he now could have done something to normalise his looks, he refused to do so. They served him well.

Salvatore said, "Beautiful as always, *Magistrato*. What do you call this one?" and he gestured to a bloom whose fuchsia petals bore flecks of yellow that eased into the interior of the flower like spots of sunlight banishing the night.

Fanucci glanced briefly at the orchid. He dislodged ash from his cigarette down the front of a white shirt already spotted by olive oil and tomato sauce, no concern to Fanucci who would not, of course, have to wash the garment. He said, "It does nothing, that. One flower a season. It belongs in the garbage. You know nothing of flowers, Topo. I keep thinking you will learn, but you're hopeless." He set down his sprayer. He drew in on his cigarette and coughed. It was a deep and wet cough and his breath wheezed in his chest. Smoking was suicide for the man, but he persisted. There were many officers in both the *polizia di stato* and the *carabinieri* who hoped he would succeed in his efforts. "How's your mamma?" Fanucci asked him.

"Same as always," Salvatore said.

"That woman's a saint."

"So she would have me believe."

Salvatore strolled to the end of the potting shelf, admiring the flowers as he went. The air inside the orchid house was fragrant with the scent of fine potting soil. Salvatore thought how he would have liked to feel it—rich, loamy, and crumbling—within his hands. There was an honesty about this soil that he liked. It was what it was, and it did what it did.

Fanucci finished his nightly babying of his orchids and stepped out of the orchid house. Salvatore followed. At the table, he poured two glasses of grappa. Salvatore would have preferred San Pellegrino, but he accepted the grappa as he was meant to do. He said no to the offer of the *biscotti*, however. He slapped his hands on his stomach and made noises to suggest his mamma's fine cooking was doing him in, although he was, as always, scrupulously careful about his weight.

He waited for Fanucci to get around to the purpose of this evening's command appearance in Barga. He knew better than to suggest that *il Pubblico Ministero* might want to reveal the significance of this encounter and not waste his time with social niceties or anything else. Fanucci would play out this meeting in whatever way he'd decided to play it out. There was no point to pushing the man. He was as immovable as a boulder. So Salvatore asked after the man's wife, after his children, after his grandchildren. They talked of the wet spring they'd had and the promise of a long and hot summer. They spoke about a ridiculous dispute among the *vigili urbani* and the *polizia postale*. They considered how to manage the crowds for an upcoming battle of the bands that would occur in Lucca's Piazza Grande.

Finally, when Salvatore was beginning to despair of getting away from *il Pubblico Ministero* before midnight, Fanucci brought forth the reason for his request of Salvatore's presence. He removed from the seat of one of the other chairs a folded newspaper. He said, "And now we must talk of this, Topo," and he unfolded it to reveal the headline.

With sinking spirits, Salvatore saw that Fanucci had got his hands on an early copy of tomorrow's edition of *Prima Voce*, the leading newspaper that covered the entire province. *Da Tre Giorni Scomparsa* introduced the subject of the number-one story, and below it was a picture of the British girl. She was a pretty creature, which gave the story its importance. What promised more coverage in the days to come, however, was her connection to the Mura family.

Seeing this, Salvatore understood at once why he had been called to Barga. When he'd informed *il Pubblico Ministero* about the situation with the missing English girl, he hadn't mentioned the Muras. He'd known that, just like the paper, Fanucci would have been all over this, putting his fingers where Salvatore didn't want them. For the Muras were an ancient Lucchese family, silk merchants and landowners of old, whose influence had begun two centuries before Napoleon's un-fortunate sister was given control of the town. As such, the Muras could cause trouble for any investigation. They hadn't done so yet, but their silence in this matter was something upon which no wise man would want to depend.

"You made no mention of the Mura family, Topo," Fanucci said. His voice was friendly—mere idle curiosity this was—but Salvatore was not deceived by its tone. "Why is this so, my friend?"

"I did not think to, *Magistrato*," Salvatore told him. "This child is not a Mura, nor is her mamma. Mamma and one of the Mura sons are lovers, *certo*—"

"And you think this means . . . what, Topo? That he wishes the child not be found? That he hired someone to kidnap her and get her out of the way of his life with her mamma?"

"Not at all. But I have until this moment been concentrating my efforts on those likely to have abducted the girl. As Mura himself was not one of my suspects—"

"And your others have told you what, Salvatore? Do you keep other things from me as you have kept the Mura family's involvement with this child a secret?"

"It was not a secret, as I have said."

"And when they phone me demanding answers—these Muras—asking for updates, wanting names of suspects and details of the investigation and I do not even know their connection to this girl . . . what then, Topo?"

Salvatore had no answer for this. His objective had been to keep *il Pubblico Ministero* as much at a distance from this case as he could. Fanucci was an inveterate meddler. Knowing what to tell him and when to tell him was an art that Salvatore had still not perfected. He said, "*Mi dispiace*, Piero. I was not thinking. This sort of lapse"—he indicated the copy of *Prima Voce*—"it will not happen again."

"To make sure of this, Topo . . . ," Fanucci said and then made a pretence of considering his disciplinary options when Salvatore knew quite well that he had chosen one and planned it out in advance. "You shall give me daily reports, I think."

Salvatore had to protest. "But so often there is nothing new to tell. And then other days, there is so little time in which to fashion a report."

"Ah, but you will manage it, won't you? Because, Salvatore, I do not wish to learn anything more about this investigation by dipping my nose into *Prima Voce. Capisci*, Topo?"

What choice did he have? None at all. "*Capisco, Magistrato*," he said.

"*Bene*. Now. We go over this case together, you and I. You tell me everything. Every detail."

"Now, Piero?" Salvatore asked, for truly the hour was growing late.

"Now, my friend. For now that your wife has left you, what else have you to do, eh?"

19 APRIL

She was a sinner. She was a woman who had promised God the gift of her person if He would grant her a single prayer. He had done so, and now she was here, in the simple handmade cotton of summer and the rough wool of winter, where she had been for nearly ten years. She kept her breasts bound tightly against temptation. The thorns of the rose bushes within her care she tediously removed from stems of the plants, and these she fixed within the undergarments she wore. The resulting pain was constant, but it was required. For one did not pray for a sin, be cursed with its granting, and then go untouched to the end of one's days.

She lived simply. Above the barn into which she herded goats for milking, her rooms were small and plain. A bedroom furnished with a single hard bed, a chest, and a prie-dieu with a crucifix above it, and the rest of her lodgings merely a kitchen and a tiny bath. But her needs were few. Chickens, a vegetable garden, and fruit trees provided food. The occasional fish, flour, bread, cow's milk, and *formaggio* came from the villa, and this she received in exchange for the care that she took of the villa's grounds. For its inhabitants never left the place. No matter the season or the weather, there they remained within the walls of Villa Rivelli. And so she had lived, year after year.

She wanted to believe that God's grace would come upon her at some time. But as the years passed, it had begun to seem that a different truth lay at the heart of the matter: Sometimes our temporal suffering is not enough. Nor will it ever be.

He had said to her, "God's will isn't something we can anticipate when we pray, Domenica. *Capisci?*" And she had nodded. For how could she not understand this simple tenet of her faith when his eyes spoke of the sin she'd committed, not only against God and against her family but against him most of all?

She had reached to touch him then, only wanting to curve her hand on the warm flesh of his cheek and to feel the plane of a cheekbone that gave his face its handsome structure. But his lips formed a sneer of distaste, so she dropped her hand to her side and lowered her eyes. Sinner and sinned against. This was who they were to each other. He would never forgive her. She could not blame him.

Then he had brought the child to her. The girl had skipped between the great gates of the Villa Rivelli, and her astonishment at the wonder of the place was ablaze upon her pretty face. She was dark like Domenica herself, with eyes the colour of *caffè*, skin the colour of *noci*, and hair a *cascata castana*: waves of darkness shot through with red in the sunlight, falling to her waist and asking for fingers to caress it and hands to brush it and someone—like Domenica—to tame it beneath the springtime sun.

The child had darted first to the great fountain that shot rainbows into the crystalline air. It was a large circular pool on the lawn, midway between the great villa gates and the loggia that gave way to the enormous front doors. She had dashed next to the loggia itself, where the ancient sculptures in their curved embrasures still shockingly represented the antique Roman gods. She cried out a word that Domenica—from the window of her lodging above the barn—could not understand in the distance between them. She turned in a whirl of her beautiful hair and called out in the direction from which she'd come.

Domenica had seen him, then. He'd walked onto the grounds in that way of his that she'd known from the time of their shared adolescence. He struts, said her girlfriends. He is danger incarnate, said her aunts. He is our nephew and we give him shelter as we must, said her father. So it had begun. And when he walked between the gates of Villa Rivelli with his smoky gaze fixed on the child ahead of him, Domenica's heart had leapt high in her chest and the thorns of her garments had dug in deeply and she had known not only what she wanted—what she *still* wanted—but also what was meant to be. Almost ten years of punishment at her own hands, and had God forgiven? Was this her sign?

"This you must do for me" had not been spoken from the mouth of God, but how did God really speak unless it was through his servants?

The child had skipped to him and had looked up and had spoken, and in the distance Domenica had watched him tenderly cup the girl's head and nod and touch her forehead. And then with his hand on her shoulder, he'd turned her from the enormous villa and he'd gently guided her on the path of amber *sassolini* and walked its curve to the old camellia hedge where an arch gave way to an expanse of beaten earth upon which the stone barn rose. Seeing him with the child like this, Domenica had felt the first stirring of hope.

From within, she had heard their footsteps on the stairs. She'd gone to meet them. The door was open, for the day was warm, and streamers of brightly coloured plastic kept the flies without and the fragrance of baking bread within. When she'd parted the streamers, she'd looked upon them both: the man and child. He stood with his hands upon her shoulders. She stood with an upturned face lit with anticipation.

"*Aspettami qui,*" he had said. He was speaking to the child, and she nodded to indicate she understood. "*Tornerò,*" he added. She was to wait in this place. He would return.

"*Quando?*" she asked. "*Perché Lei ha detto—*"

"*Presto,*" he said. He gestured then to Domenica, silent before them with bowed head and heart a beating boulder within her chest. "Suor Domenica Giustina," he said although his tone was not one of respect. "*Rimarrai qui alle cure della suora, sì? Capisci, carina?*" And the child had nodded. She understood. She would remain here with Sister Domenica Giustina, to whom she had just been introduced.

Domenica did not know the child's name. She was not given it and she dared not ask, for she was not worthy of the information yet. So she called her Carina, and the child accepted this graciously.

Now, she and the child were among the vegetables, nascent in April but soon to produce. They were weeding in the pleasant warmth of the day. They hummed separate tunes and periodically glanced up at each other and smiled.

Carina had been there less than a week, but it seemed that she had been with Domenica always. She spoke little. Although Domenica often heard her among the goats, chatting to them, she communicated only in words or phrases or simple sentences to Domenica. Many times Domenica did not understand her at all. Many times Carina did not understand Domenica. But they worked in harmony, and they ate in harmony, and when the day ended they slept in harmony as well.

Only in prayer did they differ. Carina did not kneel before the crucifix. Nor did she use her beads although Domenica had pressed into her hands a rosary carved from the pits of cherries. She'd hung it round her neck in a sacrilegious *collana* that Domenica had removed hastily and pressed back into her hands with the tiny crucifix nested among the beads, with the corpus facing upward so that she could see and not be mistaken about its use. But when she still did not use it for prayer, when she could neither mouth the words nor their responses at Domenica's side in their morning, noontime, and evening devotions, she understood that Carina lacked the one thing necessary to eternal life. This was a sign from God.

Domenica rose from kneeling among the burgeoning peppers. She pressed her hands into the small of her back, and the thorns questioned her with the pain of their injection into her flesh. Surely, they asked, it was time for their removal now that Carina's presence suggested that she had been forgiven by God? But no, she decided. Not yet. There was work to be done.

Carina rose also. She looked at the cloudless sky, not fierce as it would be in summer but pleasant and warm. Behind her, clothing hung on a line to dry: the garments of the little girl she was. She'd brought nothing with her aside from what she'd had on her back, so now she wore the white linen of an angel, and through it her child's form was like a wraith with the spindly legs of a foal and the matchstick arms of a sapling tree. Domenica had fashioned two such garments for her. When winter arrived, she would fashion more.

She gestured to Carina. *Vieni,* she said. Come with me. She left the garden and waited to see that the child shut its gate behind her and checked—as she had seen Domenica do—to ensure that its latch was fixed.

Domenica led Carina to the arched opening in the camellia hedge that gave them admittance to the immediate area around the villa. The child loved this place and, as long as Domenica could watch her, she spent two hours each day exploring it. She loved the *peschiera* with its hungry goldfish that Domenica allowed her to feed. She danced round the fish pool's rectangular length, and at its western end, she perched on the wall that overlooked the perfect pathways and parterres of the *giardino* below. Once, Domenica had taken her there, among the flowers in their precise arrangements, and they'd stolen a look at the Grotta dei Venti, its cavelike shelter of shells and mortar exhaling cool air onto them, seeming like the breath of the lichenous statues that stood on pedestals within.

Today, though, she took her to another place, not of the grounds but of the villa itself. For on its eastern side, steps led down to a pair of great green doors and within these doors lay the cellars of the villa, vast and mysterious and disused for the past one hundred years. Time was the cellars housed wine, and the ancient barrels and casks spoke of this use. There were dozens of them, dust-covered and bound to one another by the webs of a century's spiders. Among them, the terracotta urns that once held olive oil were black with mould and the wooden presses that had created that oil bore the rust of disuse upon their gears and a fine down of grime along the metal courses and the spout from which *l'oro di Lucca* had once seeped with delicious abundance.

There was much to explore in the cellar: vaulted ceilings where the black mould grew, uneven floors of stone and tiles, ladders balanced against huge casks, enormous sieves lying in a forgotten pile, a fireplace with the ashes of long-ago fires still dormant within it. The smells were rich and varied. The sounds were hushed: just the cries of the birds outside, the sound of a goat bleating, the rhythm of water dripping, and above them the faintest vocal music as if the angels of heaven were singing.

"*Senti, Carina,*" Domenica whispered, a finger at her lips.

The child did so. When she caught the disembodied singing, she said, "*Angeli? Siamo in cielo?*"

Domenica smiled to think that this place could ever be mistaken for heaven. She said, "*Non angeli, Carina. Ma quasi, quasi.*"

"*Allora fantasmi?*"

And Domenica smiled. There were no ghosts here. But she said, "*Forse. Questo luogo è molto antico. Forse qui ci sono fantasmi.*"

She had never seen one, though. For if ghosts wandered the cellars of the Villa Rivelli, they did not haunt her. Only her conscience did that.

She allowed Carina some moments to discover that this place held no danger to her. Then she beckoned her to follow. There was more within these dim, damp rooms, and its promise was Domenica's salvation.

There was faint light. It came from windows at the villa's base. They were obscured by shrubbery and filthy with having been ignored so long, but enough light came through them to see the passages that led from one vaulted room to another.

The one she sought was deep within the cellar, and their footsteps echoed against the cool walls as they made their way to it. It was entirely different from the rest, lined with barrels but having a harlequin floor, and in this floor's centre lay a marble pool. From this spot had come the sound of water that they'd heard. It bubbled up from a spring beneath the villa, and it filled the pool and drained from this to a hole in the floor from which it trickled outside to go on its way.

Three marble steps descended into the pool. Along its sides, green mould grew. Its bottom was black. The grout that held the marble in place was dark with mildew, and the air in the room was pungent.

But it was the pool itself that was important to Domenica. She'd never been in it. She'd avoided it because of the mould and the mildew and whatever else might have been living within the water. Now, though, she knew. The word of almighty God had told her.

She gestured to the pool. She removed her sandals. She motioned for the child to do the same. Then she lifted her gown over her head and she laid it carefully on the floor. Just as carefully, she descended the slick marble steps and she entered the pool. She turned back to Carina and gestured again. *Fai così*, her movements said.

But Carina's eyes were wide. She remained immobile.

"*Non avere paura*," Domenica told her. There was nothing to fear in this place.

Carina swung around. Domenica thought she might wish the comfort of privacy to remove the cotton shift she wore, so she hid her face in her hands. But instead of the sound of clothes being removed, there were racing footsteps against the floor as the child retreated.

Domenica lowered her hands swiftly. No one was there except herself, slime on her legs from the water of the pool as she mounted the steps to climb out of it. She looked down to make sure of her footing. She then saw what the child had seen.

Her tightly bound breasts were bleeding. Blood from the swaddling she used on the rest of her body was beginning to drip down her legs. What a sight she had presented to a child who did not know of her sin! She would have to explain in some form or another.

For it was crucial that Carina have no fear.

HOLBORN
LONDON

Barbara Havers had developed a snout among the members of the fourth estate. With him she had a back-scratch sort of relationship that she'd taken care to nurture. Sometimes he provided her with information. Sometimes she did the same for him. Mutual snoutship, as she liked to think of it, was rather unusual in her line of work. But moments arose when a journalist could be useful, and after her conversation with Superintendent Isabelle Ardery, Barbara reckoned she was at such a moment.

The last time she'd met her snout, it had cost her a bundle. Foolishly, she'd suggested lunch and he'd been more than happy to oblige her. She'd ended up having to pay for the lout's roast beef, Yorkshire pud, and all the et ceteras in exchange for a single name from the bloke.

She wasn't about to make that mistake twice as she could hardly put "gathering information from a tabloid journalist" down on a convenient expense account. So she made arrangements to meet her snout at the Watts Memorial. This worked out fine because the journalist was covering a trial at the Old Bailey anyway.

It had begun to rain as she'd left the Yard. The downpour increased as she wended her way to Postman's Park. She found shelter under the green-tiled roof that preserved the Watts Memorial from the ravages of both time and London's weather, and she lit up a fag beneath a particular memorial celebrating an act of equine heroism in Hyde Park: a runaway carriage in 1869 and the requisite damsel in distress. The death involved was to her rescuer, one William Drake. Alas, Barbara thought, they didn't make men the way they used to.

And they certainly didn't make them like Mitchell Corsico. When he appeared from the direction of the Royal Courts of Justice, he was garbed as usual, like an American cowboy. Barbara wondered, also as usual, how he got away with the get-up. Obviously, one's manner of dress at *The Source* was not nearly as important as one's manner of gathering information for the scurrilous tabloid.

She had that in spades, and she intended to give it to Corsico. One way or another, a fire was going to be lit beneath Superintendent Ardery's Pilates-maintained bum, and Barbara reckoned she'd come up with that way. She'd brought with her photographs that she'd snared from Azhar's flat that morning. There was one of him. There was one of Hadiyyah. There was one of Angelina Upman. Best of all, there was one of the three of them together making at happy families in the distant past.

Corsico spied her. He clomped through puddles in his pointy-toed boots and beneath the memorial's roof he removed his Stetson. Barbara half expected him to say, "Howdy, ma'am," at this, but it turned out he merely wished to remove the excess water from it, which he did. She received most of it against her legs. Good thing, she decided, that she was in trousers. Still, she brushed the water off and eyed him. He said sorry and dropped onto the bench at her side.

"So?" he said.

"Kidnapping."

"And I should be gobsmacked by this information because . . . ?"

"Kidnapped in Italy."

"And kidnapped in Italy should send me scurrying for my laptop and an Internet connection why . . . ?"

"The victim's British."

Corsico gave her a look. "Okay. I'm moderately interested."

"She's nine years old."

"I'm getting intrigued."

"She's bright, personable, and pretty."

"Aren't they always?"

"Not like this." Barbara brought out the first photo, the one of Hadiyyah. Corsico was no fool. He clocked at once that she was mixed race, and one eyebrow rose to indicate Barbara was to proceed with the titillation of his brain cells. She handed over the photo of Angelina Upman, then the one of Azhar, then the happy family together with Hadiyyah in a pushchair at two years old. Everyone, thank God, was suitably attractive.

The Source, Barbara knew as one of its devoted readers, was never going to go front page with anyone—kidnapped, dead, or otherwise—unless that person had a certain look. Hardened criminals with mugs like three-day-old roadkill made the front page if they were arrested for a crime that had taken the tabloid's fancy. But an ugly kid kidnapped? An ugly woman murdered? A grief-stricken father or husband with a face like a salmon? Not going to happen.

"Kid could be dead," Barbara pointed out, although she despised herself for having to use the word *kid* to refer to Hadiyyah, not to mention *dead*. But Corsico couldn't be made to know her interest in the case. If he twigged, she knew he'd not cooperate. He'd see at once that he was being used and, story or not, he would walk away. "Kid could be in a Bangkok cathouse," she added. "Kid could be sold to someone with a cellar in the Belgian countryside. Kid could be in the US by now. Who the hell knows . . . because *we* bloody well don't."

The *we* got him as she'd hope it might. The *we* meant more was in the offing. The *we* meant there was a chance for *The Source* to lead a charge against the Met, and both of them knew that when it came to news, leading charges against the Met was a close second to having a salacious scoop on a Member of Parliament or a picture of an inebriated naked prince clutching at the crown jewels as someone snapped away with a mobile's camera.

But still he was cautious, Mitchell Corsico. Caution in moments like these had got him where he was today, with a page-one by-line two or three times each week and every other tabloid in the country willing to offer him six figures to start digging up dirt. So he said, careful to sound noncommittal, "Why's no other paper got this tale, then?"

"Because none of them have the whole story, Mitch."

"Sordid, is it?" He meant *sordid enough*, of course.

"Oh, I think it's right up your alley," she told him.

21 APRIL

Dorothea Harriman was the one who gave the word that Detective Superintendent Ardery had been called over to Tower Block. *Sent for* was the actual term she used. When Barbara heard this from the departmental secretary as she herself was depositing coins into one of the vending machines to score a Fanta, she knew that the assistant commissioner was the likeliest person to have given the order for Ardery to make haste to Tower Block. This probably wasn't good for the super, but Barbara was no mourner for that news. If she was condemned to continue working with DI Stewart as a bloody typist till Ardery saw fit to assign her elsewhere, then whatever Ardery had to suffer was fine by her.

It didn't occur to Barbara that Sir David Hillier's request for the detective superintendent might have to do with her and her machinations on the Mitchell Corsico front. She'd been ringing Corsico practically hourly since their meeting at Postman's Park, and as far as she'd been able to gather, "working on it" was the extent to which he'd gone.

She was at the point of gnashing her teeth with impatience to see something happen. She had heard only single words from Azhar since he'd left with Angelina and her lover. But it was always the same word,

"Nothing," and the sound of his voice was like a lump of ice in her throat, freezing off words of comfort that she might have said to him.

That something was about to happen became clear the moment Isabelle Ardery returned from Tower Block. She barked, "*Sergeant* Havers, into my office at once," and added, "Inspector Lynley, you as well," in a voice only slightly less hostile. Murmurs rose from the rest of the officers bent to various tasks. Only DI Stewart looked pleased. Any dressing-down that was delivered to Barbara Havers had always been fine with him.

Barbara shot Lynley a what's-going-on look. He shook his head in an I-don't-know. He led the way to Ardery's office and stepped aside to let Barbara enter first. He did the honours with the door at Ardery's request.

The superintendent had thrown something on her desk. That something was a tabloid. That tabloid was *The Source*. The day of reckoning for the Met had arrived—not bad, Barbara thought, as Mitch had managed it within forty-eight hours—and finally something was going to be done about the matter of a British child's disappearance in Italy.

Mitch had done a fine job, from what Barbara could see. *UK Schoolgirl Kidnap!* comprised a three-inch headline, *Mitchell Corsico* comprised the by-line, and a photograph of Hadiyyah looking utterly winsome took up half the page. There was an inset of an aerial photo as well. Top of a huge wall, a paroxysm of European cobbled streets, the tops of market stalls, masses of people . . . The hold-up in the story, Barbara reckoned, had had to do with getting a decent shot of the place from which Hadiyyah had disappeared. She angled closer to see if the story made a jump from page one and, if so, where. Page three! She wanted to crow when she saw it. This signalled to one and all that the story was going to have significant legs. Those legs would have feet, those feet would be in metal-toed Doc Martens, and those Doc Martens would be stamping all over the Met from now till the kidnapping of Hadiyyah Khalidah was resolved. Hillier would have known that the moment the press office got the tabloid to him hot off the metaphorical presses. Which was, naturally, what Isabelle Ardery wished to discuss with Detective Sergeant—"And believe me, I'd kick you down to filing clerk if I could"—Barbara Havers.

She gathered up the tabloid, threw it at Barbara, and told her to regale herself, Inspector Lynley, and Ardery as well with an oral reading of what she'd "clearly been determined to see publicised."

Barbara said, "Guv, I didn't—"

"Your jelly-covered fingers are all over this, Sergeant," Ardery said. "Do *not* presume to believe that I'm quite so stupid."

"Guv," Lynley said, and his tone spoke of an attempt at appeasement.

She said sharply to him, "I want you to hear this as well. You need to be entirely up-to-date and *completely* in the picture, Thomas."

Barbara felt her first niggle of discomfort at this. It presaged something she didn't want to consider. She cooperated with Ardery's command to read the story aloud. When she reached each significant point—and there were many—Ardery had her stop and repeat it.

So what they all came to learn and hear repeated was that no British police were involved in the search for a missing English child snatched from a market in Lucca, Italy; that no British police had been sent to Tuscany to be of assistance to the Italian coppers; that no British police had been assigned to liaise with the desperate family of the kidnap victim here in the UK or in Italy either. There were hints aplenty as to why this state of affairs *was* this state of affairs: The girl in question was a mixed-race child; as a result this was not a crime destined to be heavily investigated in either country, where foreigners—particularly those with origins in the Middle East—were looked upon daily with more and more suspicion and equal distaste. Bradford was given as an example of this. So was the condition of the housing estates in "the worst of our inner cities." Mosques were attacked; women in chādors or headscarves were harassed; young dark-skinned men were chased down and frisked for weapons or bombs . . . Tsk, tsk, tsk, declared the tabloid piously. What *was* the world coming to?

Corsico had included every possible detail that might juice up the story and produce follow-ups via the sorts of hush-hush phone calls that had long been every tabloid's bread and butter in London: the father's position as a professor of microbiology at University College; the maternal grandparents' upper-middle-class status as denizens of Dulwich; the maternal aunt's career as an award-winning designer of furniture; the mother's late-autumn disappearance with the now-missing child into regions heretofore unknown but now suspected to have been Tuscany all along; the unwillingness of all parties to comment upon anything that had occurred. All of this begged for someone with inside information on any person whose name appeared in the story to ring *The Source* and spill beans of the reputation-ruining kind. This would happen in due course, naturally. It always did.

Assistant Commissioner Hillier had, it seemed, called Isabelle onto his Wilton carpet for a proper caning, and she was bound and determined to pass the joy on to Barbara. The AC had done his homework in advance as well. So what he'd known when Ardery had entered his office was that the story was true from start to finish, with the possible embellishment of the women in chādors. No police from the UK were involved, not even the coppers in north London where the girl's father apparently lived. Had she, Isabelle, heard from the Camden police at all in this matter? No, of course not. Well, get on it, then. Because the press office wants something to report in the morning and it had better be of the nature of someone's being assigned to this.

What Barbara knew was that Isabelle Ardery could not prove that Barbara herself was behind the story. Every person in the department despised Mitchell Corsico from the time he'd been embedded with them during an investigation of serial killings. No one wanted to touch him with a barge pole, which was what made him so useful to Barbara.

She laid the paper carefully back on Ardery's desk. She said just as carefully, "Seems to me it was bound to come out, guv."

"Oh, is that how you see it?" Ardery was standing at the bank of windows with her arms crossed beneath her breasts, and it came to Barbara how tall she was—more than six feet when she had her shoes on—and how she used her height to intimidate. Her posture was a straight edge and, as she was dressed in a pencil skirt and a fine silk blouse, it was no large problem for Barbara to see the shape she was in. This shape was also meant to intimidate, so Barbara decided not to be intimidated. The woman had, after all, a fatal flaw and he was standing there in the office with them.

She glanced at Lynley. He was looking sombre. He said, "It's not a good situation any way you look at it, guv."

"It's not a 'good situation' because the sergeant here has made it so."

"Guv, how can you possibly say—"

Barbara's protest was cut off abruptly when Ardery said, "You're assigned to it. You're leaving for Italy tomorrow. You're given leave to make your preparations." She wasn't, however, looking at Barbara when she made the declaration.

Barbara said, "But I know the family, guv! And the inspector's already dealing with an investigation. You can't send him—"

"Are you questioning me?" Ardery snapped. "Are you actually *presuming* that the result of this"—with gesture at the tabloid—"would be some sort of imprimatur on my part, including a blessing as you skip off to Italy, on some all-expenses-paid jaunt? Do you actually think I'm so easily manipulated, Sergeant?"

"I'm not saying . . . I'm only—"

"Barbara." Lynley's voice was quiet. It served as both warning and solace, and clearly the superintendent heard this as well because she said, "Do not *dare* to take her side in this matter, Thomas. You know as well as I that she's behind this story, and the fact that she's not at this moment filing memos at a nick on the Isle of Dogs is owing only to a lack of proof that she and this . . . this Corsico person are inside each other's pocket."

"I'm not taking anyone's side," Lynley said calmly.

"And don't you take that infuriating tone with me," she snapped. "You're thinking appeasement, and I won't be appeased. I want this Italy thing handled, I want it finished, and I want you back here at work in London before I know you're missing. Is that clear?"

Barbara saw a muscle work in Lynley's jaw. Definitely, this wasn't the tone of the pillow talk he and Ardery had once engaged in. He said, "You do know I'm working on—"

"It's been reassigned to John Stewart."

"But he's already working on another case," Barbara protested.

"And he has your capable assistance, doesn't he, Sergeant?" Ardery said. "So you'll be rather busy from this moment on. Now, get out of this office and get your next assignment from him because at this point he has enough to keep you occupied and out of trouble indefinitely. For which, by the way, you ought to get down on your knees and thank God. So leave us. And don't let me catch sight of you doing *anything* but seeing to what DI Stewart decides you're actually capable of doing."

Barbara opened her mouth to protest. Lynley shot her a look. It wasn't the least bit friendly, for like it or not, the deed was done. At her machinations, he was going to Italy. At her machinations, she was going nowhere.

BELGRAVIA
LONDON

Lynley waited until he got home to ring Daidre Trahair. He found the vet still at the Bristol Zoo, discussing with a team of assistants the problems attendant to anaesthetising an ageing male lion for the purpose of removing three of his teeth.

"He's eighteen," she told Lynley. "In lion years . . . Well, one must consider the condition of his heart and his lungs. It's always delicate when you anaesthetise an animal that large anyway."

"I suppose you can't just ask him to say 'Ah' and administer novocaine," Lynley commented.

"One would wish," she said. Then, "Unfortunately, I'm set to do this on Wednesday, Thomas. So I'm afraid I'll not be in London again this month."

Lynley wasn't happy with this news as her bimonthly roller derby matches had become more an anticipated event than an amusing diversion in the last few months. Still, he said, "As to that . . ." And he gave her his news. He was off to Italy as a result of Barbara Havers's fruitless effort to insert herself into a Tuscan investigation. "I'll be setting off in the morning. So please forge ahead with your feline dental work with complete impunity."

"Ah." There was a pause. In the background he could hear a man's voice call out, "You coming with us, Dai, or meeting us there?"

She said to him in reply, "Hang on. I'll be along in a moment," and then into the phone to Lynley, "You'll be gone a while, then?"

"I've no idea, actually." He waited for a disappointed "Oh, I see" upon which he could hang one or two hopes. Instead she said, "What sort of investigation is it?"

"Kidnapping," he said. "A nine-year-old British girl."

"That's dreadful."

"Barbara knows the family."

"Lord. No wonder she wanted to go."

Lynley didn't really want to hear any justification for Barbara Havers's behaviour, especially as he was the one who appeared to be paying the price for it. He said, "Perhaps. Nonetheless, I could have done without being sent over to mediate between the parents and the Italian police."

"Will that be your job?"

"It's likely."

"Should I wish you good luck? I'm not sure of the proper form."

"It hardly matters," but what he wanted to say was, "You might tell me you'll miss me," although he had an idea this might not be the case.

"When do you leave for Italy, then?"

"As soon as I can arrange the details. Or Charlie can, actually. He's working on it now."

"Ah. I see. Well." Still there was no disappointment in her words or her tone, despite his wish to hear this from her. He tried to come up with a reason for this that avoided the cold reality of her simply *not* being disappointed at all.

He said, "Daidre . . ." and then wasn't sure where else to go with the conversation.

She said, "Hmm?"

"I suppose I should let you be off, then. Sounds as if you've got something on this afternoon."

"Darts tournament," she said. "After work. Down the local pub. Well, not local to my home but local to the zoo."

Her home was a place he had not seen. He tried to make nothing of this, but he knew better than to do so. "You plan to scour the floor with your opponents, I daresay. I recall how wily you are when it comes to darts."

"You fell into my scheme," she replied lightly. "As I recall, you and I had a bet, with the loser doing the washing up after dinner. No worries in this instance, though. There's no washing up to be done and my opponent knows we're evenly matched."

He wanted to ask who her opponent was, but he couldn't bring himself to be so pathetic. So he said, "I hope to see you when I'm back from Italy."

"Do ring me when you return."

That was that. He rang off and stood looking at the phone. He was in the drawing room of his home in Eaton Terrace, a formal room with pale-green walls and creamy woodwork, with a gilt-framed portrait of his paternal great-grandmother hanging above the fireplace. Dressed in white in an impressionistic rose garden, she stood in profile, a study in Edwardian lace and Edwardian good manners, and she seemed to gaze into a distance that she wished to encourage him to see. Look elsewhere, Thomas, she was saying to him.

He sighed. On a table between the two windows that looked out into Eaton Terrace, his wedding picture with Helen still stood in a silver frame. In it she laughed at his side among a small group of their friends. He picked it up and saw that in it, rapt and lucky, he gazed upon her.

He set the picture down and turned from it. Denton, he saw, was in the doorway.

Their gazes met, held, and then Charlie looked away. He said lightly, "Got your gear out. Few things that you'll need but you better check through it. I looked up the weather. It'll be warm. Printed your boarding pass. Gatwick to Pisa. You've a car at the airport."

"Thank you, Charlie," Lynley said. He headed in the direction of the stairs.

"Anything . . ." Denton hesitated.

"Anything?" Lynley said.

Denton's gaze flicked over to the table where Helen's picture was, then back to Lynley. "Anything I should set about while you're gone?"

Lynley knew what Charlie Denton meant. He knew what he thought. It was the same thing everyone thought, but it was also the one thing he himself could not yet bear to address.

He said lightly, "Not that I can think of, Charlie. Just carry on as usual." It was, of course, what they both did best.

BOW

LONDON

The private detective was Barbara's only hope once Isabelle Ardery handed the case over to Lynley. Barbara was burning over this and burning over her failure to anticipate what Ardery's move would be once the story hit *The Source*, but she knew there was no point in crying over the milk on the floor. The only point was Hadiyyah. Lynley would do what he could to help find her, within the parameters of Italian law and British-Italian police diplomacy. But both of these items were going to hobble him, and to expect Barbara to remain in London at the beck and call of John Stewart without doing *something* to assist in the search for the girl was lunacy on the superintendent's part.

So she went to the only place she reckoned help was available, and that was back to Dwayne Doughty and his androgynous assistant Em Cass. She phoned in advance this time. She made a regular appointment for the end of that day. Doughty didn't sound like a man who was going to start laying down the palm fronds in welcome, so she made sure to add the fact that she wished him to have his retainer figured out in advance as she intended to hire him.

He'd begun with, "Terribly sorry and all that, but I don't know that I have the time—"

She countered with, "Double the retainer," which had convinced him to have another think on the topic.

They met not in his office this time but not too far away at a rather trendy pub called the Morgan Arms in Coborn Road. There were tables outside, and at them pub-going smokers hunched in the cool evening air. Barbara would have joined them, but she found that Em Cass was the clean-living type. Apparently passive smoking and success in triathlons did not mix.

They went inside. Barbara took out her chequebook. Doughty said, "Let's keep the cart and the horse in their respective positions," before he went to the bar and ordered drinks. He came back with a pint of Guinness for himself, an ale for Barbara, a virtuous mineral water for Em, and a thoughtful four bags of crisps. These he tossed on the table

that Barbara had chosen, in a far corner, conveniently distant from a
hen party on the other side of the pub, eight women who appeared
determined to build up a significant head of prematrimonial steam.

Barbara had no preamble to offer the private detective and his assistant. She said only, "Hadiyyah's been kidnapped."

Doughty opened the crisps, one packet at a time. He spilled them
onto a napkin that he'd unfolded upon the table. He said, "This is
news because . . . ?"

"I don't mean originally," Barbara told him. "I don't mean by her
mum. I mean now. A few days ago. She was in Italy and she's been
kidnapped." She sketched in the details: Lucca, the market, Hadiyyah's
disappearance, Angelina Upman, Lorenzo Mura, and their arrival in
Chalk Farm. She left out the bits about Ilford and the brouhaha with
Azhar's legal family. Mostly, she didn't want to think about them.

"Angelina thinks Azhar took her. That's why she came to London.
She thinks he found her in Tuscany, took her, and has her stowed
somewhere."

"And she thinks this why?"

"Because no one saw anything. There was a crowd of people—it
was in the middle of a market—and no one saw Hadiyyah get snatched.
So Angelina thinks Hadiyyah wasn't snatched. She thinks Azhar knew
she'd be in the market. She thinks he waited there. She thinks Hadiyyah saw him and went with him. At least that's what I suspect she
thinks since mostly she was just screaming."

"The child?"

"Angelina. 'You've taken her, where is she, where have you put
her, I want her back,' et cetera, et cetera."

"And no one saw a thing?"

"Apparently not."

"These same people in the market, then, also didn't witness what
would have been, I expect, quite a reunion between a nine-year-old
and the father she hasn't seen in five months? I mean, had Mr. Azhar
taken her."

"You're getting the point," Barbara said. "I like that about you."

"How was he supposed to have managed all this?" Doughty asked.

"No clue, but Angelina wasn't thinking straight. She was in a panic—who wouldn't be?—and all she wanted was Hadiyyah back. The Italian coppers haven't made much progress in finding her."

Doughty nodded. Em Cass took a sip of her mineral water. Barbara downed some ale and a handful of crisps. Not salt-and-vinegar—her favourite—but they would do. She was suddenly ravenous.

Doughty shifted his weight in his chair and looked to the windows that gave a view of the people at the tables outside on the pavement. He said, as he inspected them, "Let me ask you this, Miss Havers. How can you be sure the professor *didn't* take his daughter? I've been in the midst of these sorts of disputes in the past, and be assured about one thing: When it comes to marital breakups and children—"

"This isn't a marriage."

"We can forego the niceties. They've been, for all intents and purposes, man and wife, no? So when it comes to relationship breakups in which children are involved, anything can happen and it usually does."

"How is he supposed to have snatched her? And what was he supposed to be thinking? That he could grab Hadiyyah, bring her back to London, and not find Angelina on his doorstep the very next day? And how was he supposed to have found her in the first place?"

Em Cass spoke. "He could have hired an Italian detective, Miss Havers, much the same way he hired Dwayne. If he somehow found out on his own that Angelina had gone to Italy . . . or if he suspected it . . . Like Dwayne says, in this kind of situation, anything can happen."

"Right. Whatever. Okay. Let's say somehow Azhar sussed out she was in Italy. Let's say that he then unearthed an Italian private detective. Let's even say that detective—God only knows how . . . perhaps going door-to-door all over the bleeding country—actually found Hadiyyah and reported this to him. That doesn't change the fact that Azhar was in Germany when Hadiyyah was taken. He was at a conference and there're going to be a few hundred people, not to mention a hotel and an airline, who can confirm that."

Doughty looked interested at last. "Now that's a very nice detail. That's something checkable and you can rely upon the coppers checking it. The Italians . . . Let's face it. The country looks disorganised as hell to an outsider, but I expect they know what they're doing when it comes to mounting an investigation, don't you?"

The fact was Barbara didn't at all have that expectation of the Italian police. She barely had that expectation of their own police. So she said, "Brilliant. Yes. Whatever in a teacup. But I need your help, Mr. Doughty, no matter what the Italian rozzers are up to."

Doughty shot a look at Em Cass. Neither of them said, "What kind of help?" This wasn't a good sign, but Barbara forged on.

"Look. I know this kid. I know her dad. I need to do something. You get that, yes?"

"Perfectly understandable," Doughty said.

"What about the UK police, then?" Em Cass fixed her gaze on Barbara, and the blandness of her expression told the tale that Barbara would have preferred to go unspoken.

There was a little silence among them. Across the room, the hen party was heating up. The bride-to-be had mounted the banquette and was squashing her face against the window. She was shouting, "This's my las' chance, lads!" with her veil askew and the red *L* on her back descending to her arse as if it and not she were embarking on matrimony.

"The Met's sent a DI over to liaise," Barbara said. "He's called DI Lynley. He's going over today."

"Intriguing that you should be in possession of this bit of knowledge." Doughty munched on his crisps. He looked at Em Cass. They both looked steadily at Barbara.

She downed some ale. "All right. I could have given you some other name—called myself Julie Blue-eyes or whatever—and I didn't," she pointed out. "I knew it would take you less than five minutes to suss out I'm a cop. That has to count for something."

"I half expect you to say 'trust me' next," Em Cass said dryly.

"I *am* saying that! I'm not here with a wire in my knickers to play-act desperation and catch you doing something you shouldn't. I *know* you lot cross over the line now and then, and I don't bloody care. Fact is, I want you to cross the line if you need to. I need to find this kid, and I'm asking for your help because my colleague—the DI?—he's not going to do what you lot can do because he won't have the resources over there to do it. He's also not going to be keen on breaking any laws. That's not who he is." Implying, of course, that breaking laws *was* who she was so she'd not be saying word one about any law-breaking that Doughty and Em Cass did.

Nonetheless, Doughty said, "You'll need someone else. We don't break—"

"What I'm saying is I don't care if you break laws or not, Mr. Doughty. Spy on anyone you need to spy on. Go through their rubbish. Hack into their mobiles and their Internet accounts. Take over their email. Pretend to be their mothers. Pretend to be *them*. I've given you more than one angle to pursue and I need you pursuing it. Please."

They didn't ask why she wasn't pursuing it herself, so Barbara didn't have to tell them the unpalatable truth: that once again and through her own fault, her job was on the line. With Ardery watching her and John Stewart throwing work at her and two cases now his responsibility, her ability to do anything other than keep her nose on the grindstone of her regular employment was not only severely curtailed; it was also virtually nonexistent. Employing Doughty and his assistant was at least something she could do. This meant, at least, that she wouldn't have to wait for word from Lynley, who probably wasn't going to keep her in the picture anyway because, she knew, he was displeased with her, because she was the reason he'd been sent out of the country at all.

Doughty sighed. He said, "Emily?" and seemed to defer to his assistant.

She said, "We've nothing pressing on at the moment. Just the divorce case and that bloke claiming compensation for the back injury. I suppose there're a few things we can check. This Germany business would top the list."

"Azhar didn't—"

"Hang on." Doughty pointed a meaningful finger at Barbara. "For starters, you'd be keeping an open mind about everything, Miss . . . Oh, nonsense. May I call you what you are? Detective Sergeant, isn't it, Em?"

"Is," Em acknowledged.

"So you'd be wise to prepare yourself for anything, Detective Sergeant. Question is, are you ready for that?"

"For anything?" Barbara clarified.

Doughty nodded.

"Absolutely," she said.

BOW

LONDON

They walked out of the pub together, but on the pavement they went their separate ways. Dwayne Doughty and Em Cass watched the ill-dressed detective heading towards the Roman Road. When she was out of sight, he and Em ducked back into the pub. This was completely at Emily's urging.

"This is a bad idea," she said. "We don't work for cops, Dwayne. That's a road to a place we don't want to go."

He didn't entirely disagree with her. But she wasn't seeing the complete equation. "Checking an alibi in Berlin . . . Child's play, Emily. And one wants the child to be found, wouldn't you agree?"

"That can't be in our hands. There're all sorts of limitations on what we can do, and with Scotland Yard breathing down our neck—"

"She admitted her position there. She could have lied. That indicates something."

"It indicates bollocks. She knew we'd check on her the moment she gave her name when she first came to see us with the professor. She's not stupid, Dwayne."

"But she *is* desperate."

"So she's in love with him. So she's in love with the girl."

"And love, as we know, is quite wonderfully blind."

"No. *You* are. You haven't asked for my vote on the matter, but you're going to get it. I say no. I say we tell her ta-ta and we wish you the best but there's nothing we can do to help you. Because that's the truth. There's nothing, Dwayne."

He considered her. Emily rarely spoke with passion. She was far too cool a customer for that. She didn't command the kingly salary he paid her because she was a woman who ever got caught up in the emotion of the moment. But she was passionate about this, which told him the extent to which she was also worried about it.

"Really, there's nothing to be concerned about," he told her. "And this allows us to keep our eyes on the ball. Our job remains what it's always been: information providers. Whether we provide the information for the coppers or for Joe Ordinary off the street, it's no matter to us. What people do with what we give them is their business, not ours, once we hand it over."

"Do you actually think anyone's likely to believe that?"

He eyed her and smiled his long, slow smile. "Come along, Em. Where's the trouble in this? I'm happy to listen if you care to point it out."

"I have. The Metropolitan police. That woman: Sergeant Havers."

"Who, as you yourself have said, has come to us driven by love. And love, as I myself pointed out, is wonderfully—"

"Blind. All right. Brilliant." Emily stepped back outside, positioning herself downwind of the smokers. "Where do you want to begin?" she asked Doughty dully. She wasn't happy, but she was a pro. And she, like him, had bills to pay.

"Thank you, Emily," he said. "We do this German business as arranged. But in advance and for safety's sake, we do phone records. A very clean sweep."

"What about computers?"

He gave her a look. "Going deep with computers means we bring in Bryan."

She rolled her eyes. "Give me notice so I can vacate the office."

"I will do. But really, you should just submit to him, Em. Things would go much more swimmingly if you did."

"You mean he'd do as I say when *you* need him to do it."

"There are worse things than having a man like Bryan Smythe under your thumb."

"Yes, but all the worse things have to do with having a man like Bryan Smythe under my thumb." She made a moue of distaste. "Heartless seduction in the name of holding our secrets close? That's just not on."

"You'd prefer the alternative?"

"We don't know the alternative."

"But we can guess."

Em looked beyond him into the pub. He glanced in the same direction. The hen party was forming a conga line. There was no music playing, but this, apparently, wasn't putting the slightest damper on their pleasure. They began rumbaing in the general direction of the exit, shouts and giggles and stumbles their accompaniment.

"God," Em Cass sighed. "Why are women such fools?"

"We're all fools" was Doughty's rejoinder. "But it's only in hindsight that we see it."

22 APRIL

O pposite the *giardino* and at the far end of the *peschiera*, a low
wall edged the top of a hillside, still green and lush from
winter's rainfall. This hillside fell away to reveal distant
villages that shimmered in the warm spring sunshine, and a road
twisted up to them from the alluvial plain far below. This road was
something equally visible, and because of this, Sister Domenica Giustina saw him coming from a great distance.

She and Carina had gone to feed the fish that shot through the
waters of the *peschiera* like bits of orange flame, and they'd backed
away from the pond's edge to watch the fish gobbling at the food with
their greedy mouths. When this was finished, Sister Domenica Giustina had turned the child to admire the view. *"Che bella vista, nevvero?"*
she had murmured, and she'd begun to name the villages for Carina.
Solemnly, Carina repeated each name. She was changed from that
earlier day in the cellar. She was more hesitant, more watchful, perhaps
more worried. But that could not be helped, Domenica decided. Some
things took precedence over others.

That was when she saw the car flashing rapidly in and out of the
trees far below, climbing ever higher on its way to the villa. She recognised it even at this great distance, for it was bright red and its top was

down and she would, of course, have known the driver anywhere on earth. His coming, though, represented danger. For bringing Carina to her also meant he could take her away. He'd done so before, had he not?

"*Vieni, vieni,*" she said to the child. And lest Carina misunderstand her, she clasped her hand and scooted her along the narrow terrace and down the path. They went across the wide lawn at the back of the villa. They hurried in the direction of the cellars.

Above on the building, the thick curtains on one of the windows twitched. Sister Domenica Giustina saw this, but what was inside the villa was no worry to her. What was outside the villa presented the danger.

She could tell Carina was not happy to descend to the cellars once again. Sister Domenica Giustina had not attempted another time to bring her to the murky pool within this place, but she could tell the child was afraid that she might. There was nothing to fear in that pool, but she had no way to explain to Carina why this was the case. And now she had no intention of taking her to that part of the cellars at all. She merely wanted her to remain near the first of the old wine casks.

"*Veramente, non c'è nulla da temere qui,*" she murmured. Spiders, perhaps, but they were harmless. If one feared anything, one should fear the devil.

Thankfully, Carina understood at least something of what Sister Domenica Giustina said, and she seemed relieved when she apparently realised that Sister Domenica Giustina's intentions were to take her no farther into the cellars than the second room. She hunkered between two of the ancient wine casks there, her knees pressed into the dusty floor. Still, she said in a whisper, "*Non chiuda la porta. Per favore, Suor Domenica.*"

She could do that much for the child, of course. There was no need to close the door as long as Carina could promise to be silent as a mouse.

Carina made that promise. "*Aspetterai qui?*" Sister Domenica Giustina asked.

Carina nodded. Yes, of course. She would wait.

By the time he arrived, Sister Domenica Giustina was among her vegetables. She heard the car first, its engine purring and its tyres rolling sonorously over the *sassolini*. She heard its engine stop, its door open and then close, and then in a moment his footsteps as he mounted the stairs to the small habitation above the barn. He called her name. She rose from the dirt, carefully wiping her hands on a rag that hung from her waist. Above, she heard two doors slam and then his footsteps coming down the stairs. Then the garden gate creaked and she lowered her head. Domenica, humble. Domenica, subservient to any wish that he might have.

"*Dov'è la bambina?*" he asked. "*Perché non sta nel granaio?*"

She said nothing. She heard him cross the garden, and she saw his feet when he stopped before her. She told herself that she had to be strong. He would not remove Carina from her care, despite the child's not remaining above the barn as he had instructed.

"*Mi senti?*" he said. "*Domenica, mi senti?*"

She nodded, for she was not deaf and this he knew. She said to him, "*La porterai via di nuovo.*"

"*Di nuovo?*" he repeated, incredulous. Why, he seemed to be asking, would he *ever* remove the child from her care?

"*Lei è mia,*" she said.

She looked up then. He was watching her. On his face, it seemed a calculation of her words was being made. Knowledge appeared to be breaking over him, and he seemed to confirm this when he put his hand on the back of her neck, said, "*Cara, cara,*" and drew her closer.

The heat of his hand on her flesh was like a brand that marked her forever his. She felt it throughout her body, even to her blood.

"*Cara, cara, cara,*" he murmured. "*Non me la riprenderò più, mai più.*" He lowered his mouth to hers. His tongue probed and caressed. Then he lifted the linen shift she wore.

"*L'hai nascosta?*" he said against her mouth. "*Perché non sta nel granaio? Te l'ho detto, no? 'La bambina deve rimanere dentro il granaio.' Non ti ricordi? Cara, cara?*"

But how could she have kept Carina hidden within the cold stone barn as he had demanded she do? Domenica wondered. She was a child, and a child must be free.

He rained tender kisses against her neck. His fingers touched her. First here. Then there. And the flames seemed to eat at her flesh as he lowered her gently to the ground. On the ground, he entered her and he moved within her with mesmerising rhythm. She could not abhor it.

"*La bambina,*" he murmured into her ear. "*Capisci? L'ho ritornata, tesoro. Non me la riprenderò. Allora. Dov'è? Dov'è? Dov'è?*" And with each thrust, he said the words, Where is she? I brought her back to you, my treasure.

Domenica received him. She allowed the mantle of sensations to cover her until they peaked at their completion. She did not think.

Afterwards, he lay panting in her arms. But only for an instant before he rose. He adjusted his clothing. He looked down upon her, and she saw his lip move in a twist that did not speak of love. "*Copriti,*" he said between his teeth. "*Dio mio. Copriti.*"

She lowered her linen shift in compliance. She looked up at the sky. Its blue was unbroken by a single cloud. The sun shone in it, like God's grace falling upon her face.

"*Mi senti? Mi senti?*"

No, she *hadn't* been listening. She hadn't been there. She'd been in the arms of her beloved but now—

He jerked her upright. "*Domenica, dov'è la bambina?*" He barked the words.

She scrambled to her feet. She looked to the earth where, between the rows of fresh young lettuces, the mark of her body flattened the dirt. She gazed at this in confusion. "*Che cos'è successo?*" she murmured, and she looked at him. She said insistently, "*Roberto. Che cos'è successo qui?*"

"*Pazza,*" he responded. "*Sei sempre stata pazza.*"

From this, she knew that something had indeed occurred between them. She could feel it in her body, and she could smell it in the air. They'd mated in the dirt like animals, and she'd stained her soul yet another time.

He asked again where the little girl was, and Sister Domenica Giustina felt the pain of this question like a sword piercing her side to take the last of her blood. She said to him, "*Mi hai portato via la bambina già una volta. Non ti permetterò di farlo di nuovo.*"

She repeated herself, insistently this time: He'd taken the child away from her once. He would not do so again.

He lit a cigarette. He tossed the match to one side. He smoked and said, "How can you trust me so little, Domenica? I was young. So were you. We are older now. You have her somewhere. You must take me to her."

"What will you do?"

"I mean no harm. I want to know she is well. I have clothing for her. Come. I'll show you. It's in the car."

"If it is, you may leave it and go your way."

"*Cara*," he murmured. "This I cannot do." He glanced beyond them where through the magnificent camellia hedge the villa loomed, silent but watchful. "You do not wish me to remain here," he said. "That would not be good for either of us."

She understood what he was threatening. He would remain. There would be trouble unless she produced the child.

"Show me the clothing," she said.

"That is my wish." He opened the gate and held it for her. As she passed him, he smiled. His fingers lightly touched her neck, and she shuddered at the feeling of his flesh upon her own.

At the car, she saw the bags on the floor. There were two of them. He had not lied. Clothing was folded neatly within them. It was a little girl's clothing, used but still serviceable.

She looked at him. He said, "I seek her comfort, Domenica. You must learn to trust me again."

She nodded abruptly. She turned from the car. She said, "*Vieni.*"

She led him through the camellia hedge. At the cellar steps, however, she paused. She looked at her cousin. He smiled, and it was a smile she knew well. Nothing to fear, it said. Innocent, it proclaimed. She had only to believe as she once had done.

She descended. He followed. "*Carina*," she called quietly. "*Vieni qui. Va tutto bene, Carina*," and as if in answer, she heard the patter of the little girl's feet as she emerged from her hiding place among the casks in the second room.

She skipped out to them. The light was dim, but in it Sister Domenica Giustina could see the cobwebs in the child's dark hair. Her knees were marked from the filthy floor, and her shift bore the soil of generations of the cellar's disuse.

Her face lit up when she saw who was with Sister Domenica Giustina, and completely unafraid, she danced over to him.

She spoke in English, saying, "Yes! Yes! Have you come to fetch me? Do I get to go home?"

LUCCA
TUSCANY

Being called to the office of *il Pubblico Ministero* was only slightly less infuriating than having to make the drive to his home in Barga. The second was an insult and designed to be one. The first was merely *un'eritema*, like an itch on the skin that cannot be scratched. Thus, Salvatore Lo Bianco knew he should have been at least moderately grateful that Fanucci hadn't waited until evening to direct his appearance once again into the ministerial presence among his cymbidiums. But he was not. For he'd made his daily reports as he'd been instructed, and still Piero edged closer and closer to becoming an intrusive presence in the investigation. Piero was not a stupid man, but his mind was like a prison cell: closed, locked, and with no one in possession of the key.

As a magistrate, Piero knew that the power within an investigation was his, and he liked to play with it. It was he who assigned the lead officer to a case. Thus someone assigned could just as easily be unassigned, and everyone knew it. So when he made a request for one's presence, one had to comply. Or one had to face the consequences of failing to do so.

So Salvatore took himself to Palazzo Ducale, where Piero Fanucci had a suite of offices as impressive as local revenues could make them. He walked, as the way wasn't long, for the *palazzo* stood in Piazza Grande, where a gaggle of tourists gathered near the central statue of the town's beloved Maria Luisa di Borbone. There they snapped pictures, learned the history associated with the loathsome Elisa Bonaparte, who'd been condemned by her brother to rule in this

Italian backwater, and they watched a colourful carousel on the piazza's south side take laughing children on a trip to nowhere.

Salvatore watched this, also. He took a moment to consider what he wanted to impart to the magistrate. A piece of information had fallen into his lap from a most unexpected source: Salvatore's own daughter. For she was enrolled in the Scuola Elementare Statale Dante Alighieri here in Lucca. And so, as it happened, was the missing child.

This wasn't unusual. Children from the area surrounding Lucca often came into town for their education. What was unusual was the amount of information that Bianca had actually managed to glean from the girl.

He hadn't told Bianca that Hadiyyah Upman was missing. He hadn't wished to frighten his child. But he also hadn't been able to prevent her from seeing the flyers that were being posted around the town, and she'd recognised her little schoolmate. Recognising her, she'd told her mother of their acquaintance. Birgit, praise God, had informed Salvatore.

Over a casual but indifferent gelato purchased from the only café on Lucca's great wall, Salvatore had probed carefully for details. His daughter, it turned out, had assumed that Lorenzo Mura was Hadiyyah's father, not understanding at first that had that been the case, the child's Italian probably would have been much better. Hadiyyah had revealed to her that her father was, instead, in London. A professor, she'd said proudly, at a university. She and her mummy were in Italy visiting Mummy's friend Lorenzo. Dad had intended to come for Christmas, but then he'd had too much work and was supposed to be there at Easter instead. But things had come up once again for him because he was so terribly busy . . . Here's a picture of him. He's a scientist. He sends me emails and I write to him and p'rhaps he can come for summer hols . . .

"D'you think her dad came to take her home to London?" Bianca had asked Salvatore, her great dark eyes reflecting a worry that an eight-year-old's eyes should never reflect.

"Possibly, *cara*," Salvatore had said. "Possibly indeed."

The question now was whether he was going to share this information with Piero Fanucci. It would, he decided, all depend on how his meeting with the magistrate went.

Fanucci's secretary was the first person Salvatore encountered when he climbed the great staircase. A long-suffering seventy-year-old, she reminded Salvatore of his own mother. Instead of black, though, she always wore red. She dyed her hair the colour of coal, and she possessed an unattractive moustache that—in the years he had known her—she'd never bothered to remove. She'd maintained her position in the magistrate's office because she was completely unappealing to Piero, so he hadn't once molested her. Had she been even marginally attractive to *il Pubblico Ministero*, she would not have lasted six months, as Fanucci's career was littered with the spiritual and psychological corpses of the women who'd been victimised by him.

Once inside the office suite, Salvatore learned that a wait for the magistrate would be necessary. For a junior prosecutor had been taken into the presence in advance of Salvatore's appearance, he was told. That meant someone was being dressed down. Salvatore sighed and took up a magazine. He flipped through it, noted which closeted homosexual American celebrity was currently attaching himself to a conveniently stupid supermodel twenty years his junior, and tossed this *rivista idiota* to one side. After five minutes he requested that Fanucci's secretary let the magistrate know that he was waiting.

She looked shocked. Did he truly want to chance an eruption of *il vulcano?* she asked. He did, he assured her.

But it turned out that interrupting Fanucci was not necessary. A pale-to-the-gills young man emerged from the magistrate's office and scuttled on his way. Salvatore strode in, unannounced and not wishing it otherwise.

Piero eyed him. His facial warts were pale excrescences against skin inflamed by whatever had gone on between him and his underling. Apparently deciding to say nothing about Salvatore's unheralded entrance into his office, he gave a sharp and wordless nod to a television on one of his office bookshelves, and he clicked it on without preliminaries.

It was a recording of a broadcast, made that morning by England's BBC. Salvatore spoke very little English and was thus unable to follow the rapid-fire conversation between the two presenters. They were engaged in a strange discussion about UK newspapers, it seemed, and one at a time they held them up to the camera.

Salvatore saw quickly that no translation of this broadcast was actually going to be necessary. Piero stopped the recording when the presenters reached the front page of a particular tabloid. *The Source*, it was called. It had the story.

This, he knew, was not a good development. One tabloid meant many. Many meant the possible incursion of British reporters into Lucca.

Fanucci clicked the recording off. He indicated that Salvatore was to take a seat. Piero himself remained standing because standing was power, and power, Salvatore thought, could be demonstrated in so many ways.

"What more have you learned from this street beggar of yours?" Fanucci asked. He meant the poor drug addict, him of the *Ho fame* sign. Salvatore had brought the youth once into the *questura* for a formal interrogation, but Fanucci was pressing for another. This would be, he'd instructed Salvatore, a more serious one, a lengthier one, one designed to "encourage" the unfortunate's memory . . . such as it was.

Salvatore had been avoiding this. While Fanucci believed drug addicts capable of anything to support their habit, Salvatore did not. In the case of this particular drug addict, Carlo Casparia had been occupying that same spot at the entrance to Porta San Jacopo for the past six years without incident, a disgrace to his family but a menace to no one but himself.

He said, "Piero, there is nothing more to be learned from this man Carlo. Believe me, his brain is too addled to have planned a kidnapping."

"Planned?" Fanucci repeated. "Topo, why do you say this was planned? He saw her, and he took her."

And then? Salvatore thought. He produced an expression on his face that he hoped projected that question without having to ask it directly.

"It could be," Fanucci said, "that we have a crime of opportunity, my friend. Can you not see that? He has told you that he saw the child, no? He was not so brain-addled that he forgot that. So why this one

child in his memory, Topo? Why not another? Why did Carlo remember a child at all?"

"She gave him food, *Magistrato*. A banana."

"Bah! What she gave him was a promise."

"*Come?*"

"The promise of money. Must I spell it out for you what happens
once he takes the child?"

"There has been no demand for ransom."

"Why should there be ransom when so many other opportunities
exist to make money off an innocent girl?" Fanucci counted them off
on the fingers of his six-fingered hand. "She is bundled into the back
of a car and bundled out of the country, Topo. She is sold into the sex
trade somewhere. She is made into a household slave. She is handed
over to a paedophile with a clever basement into which she is stuffed.
She is given to a satanic worship group for sacrifice. She is made a rich
Arab's plaything."

"All of which, Piero, would beg for planning, no?"

"None of which, Topo, we will ever learn until you question Carlo
again. You must see to this without delay. I wish to read it in your
next report to me. Tell me how else you intend to spend your time,
little man, if not with this and in this direction?"

In answer to the insulting question, Salvatore first asked his blood
to cool. Then he chose a significant detail that had arisen from the
posters and handbills round the central part of town. He'd received
two phone calls from two hotels in Lucca, one within the city's wall
and one from Arancio, not far from the road to Montecatini. A man
had come by, in possession of a picture of the missing child in the
company of a nice-looking woman, presumably her mother. The
man had been looking for them, and he'd left a card with the hotel
receptionists. Unfortunately, the card in both cases had been tossed
away.

Fanucci swore at the stupidity of women. Salvatore didn't bother
to tell him that in both cases the receptionists had been men. What
he did tell him was that this individual had been seeking the girl at
least a month earlier or perhaps six weeks. That, he said, was the limit
of what they knew.

"Who was this man?" Fanucci demanded. "What did he look like, at least?"

Salvatore shook his head. Trying to get a local receptionist to remember what someone looked like a month or six weeks or eight weeks after having seen the individual only once and probably for less than a minute . . . ? He extended his hands, palms up, empty. It could have been anyone, *Magistrato*.

"And this is all you know? This is all you have?" Fanucci demanded.

"With regard to this person seeking the woman and the girl, *purtroppo*, it is," Salvatore lied. And when Fanucci would have begun a tedious lecture about Salvatore's general incompetence or a diatribe ending with a threat to replace him, Salvatore threw the magistrate a bone.

He shared the fact of the emails that had gone from the child Hadiyyah and her father. "He's here in Lucca now," Salvatore said. "This is something that must be explored."

"A London father who writes emails to his daughter residing in Italy?" Fanucci scoffed. "How is this important?"

"There are broken promises about visits he intended to make here," Salvatore said. "Broken visits, broken hearts, and runaway children. It is a possibility that must be explored." He looked at his watch. "I meet with these people—the parents together—in forty minutes."

"After which you'll report . . . "

"*Sempre*," Salvatore said. He would report something, he told himself. Just enough to keep *il Pubblico Ministero* satisfied that things were moving along under his idiotic direction. "So, my friend, if there is nothing else . . . ?" He got to his feet.

"As it happens, we are not finished," Fanucci said. A smile touched his mouth without touching his eyes. Power still lay within his hands, and Salvatore saw he'd been outmanoeuvred again.

He sat. He looked as unruffled as he could. "*E allora?*" he said.

"The British embassy has phoned," Fanucci told him. There was a tinge of pleasure in the tone he used, and Salvatore knew at once that the infuriating man had saved the best for last. He said nothing in reply. It was the least he could do to attain revenge. "The English police are sending a Scotland Yard detective." Piero jerked his head at the television, at the recording they'd watched. "It seems they have no choice after the publicity."

Salvatore swore. This was not a development he'd anticipated. Nor was it a development he liked.

"He'll stay out of the way," Fanucci told him. "His purpose, I'm told, will be to liaise between the investigation and the girl's mother."

Salvatore swore again. Not only would he now have to attend to the demands of *il Pubblico Ministero* but he'd also have to do the same for a Scotland Yard officer. More exasperating calls upon his time.

"Who is this officer?" he asked in resignation.

"Thomas Lynley is his name. That's all I know. Except for one detail you should keep in mind." Fanucci paused for dramatic effect and, as their encounter had gone on quite long enough, Salvatore played along with him for once.

"What's the detail?" he asked wearily.

"He speaks Italian," Fanucci said.

"How well?"

"Well enough, I understand. *Stai attento, Topo.*"

LUCCA
TUSCANY

Salvatore chose Café di Simo as their meeting place. In other circumstances, he might have met the parents of the missing child in the *questura*, but his preference generally was to save the *questura* for purposes of intimidation. He wished to see the parents as much at ease as he could possibly make them, and requiring them to come to the *questura* with its hustle, bustle, and inescapable police presence would not effect the degree of calm he wanted in them. Café di Simo, on the other hand, was rich in history, atmosphere, and delectable items from its *pasticceria*. It spoke not of suspicion but of comfort: a *cappuccino* or *caffè macchiato* for each of them, a plate of *cantucci* to be shared among all of them, and a quiet chat in the soothing side room with its panelled walls, small tables, and bright white floor.

They did not come together, the mother and the father. She arrived alone, without her partner Lorenzo Mura, and the professor arrived three minutes later. Salvatore placed the order for their drinks at the bar and, *piatto di biscotti* in hand, led them to the back of the café, where a doorway gave onto the interior room and where, conveniently, no one else was sitting at present. Salvatore intended to keep things that way.

"Signor Mura?" was how he politely asked about the signora's partner. Odd, he thought, that Mura was not with her. In their earlier meetings, he'd hovered about like the woman's guardian angel.

"*Verrà*," she said. He would be coming. She added, "*Sta giocando a calcio*," with a sad little smile. Obviously, Angelina Upman knew how it looked that her lover was off at a football match instead of at her side. She added, "*Lo aiuta*," as if to clarify.

Salvatore wondered at this. It didn't seem likely that football—either played or watched or coached—would do much to help anyone in the situation, as she claimed. But perhaps an hour or two of the sport took Mura's mind off things. Or perhaps it merely got him away from his partner's understandable, unceasing, and probably frenzied worry about her daughter.

She did not, however, appear frenzied now. She appeared deadened. She looked quite ill. The girl's father—the Pakistani from London—did not look much better. Both of them were raw nerve endings and twisted stomachs. And who could blame them?

He noted how the professor held out a chair for the signora before taking a seat himself. He noted how the signora's hands shook when she put the *zucchero* into her espresso. He noted how the professor offered her the plate of *biscotti* although Salvatore had gently pushed it in his own direction. He noted the signora's use of *Hari* in speaking to the father of her child. He noted the father wince when he heard her use this name.

Every detail of every interaction between these two people was important to Salvatore. He had not spent twenty years of his life as a policeman only to escape knowing that family came under suspicion first when tragedy fell upon a member of it.

Using a combination of his wretched English and the signora's moderately decent Italian, Salvatore brought them as up-to-date as he wished them to be. The airports had all been checked, he told them. So had the train stations. So had the buses. The net of their search for the child had been cast and was still in place: not only in Lucca but outward into the surrounding towns. So far, *purtroppo*, there was nothing to report.

He waited for the signora to make a slow translation for the father of her child. Her serviceable Italian got the main points across to the dark-skinned man.

"None of this is as . . . as simple as it used to be," he said when she was finished. "Before EU, the borders were, of course, a different thing. Now?" He made a what-you-will gesture, not to show indifference but rather to indicate the difficulties they faced. "It has been a good thing for criminals, this lack of strong borders. Here in Italy"— with an apologetic smile—"with EU we gain a system of money that is no longer mad, eh? But as for everything else, as for policing . . . tracing movements is much more difficult now. And if the motorway is used to access the border . . . These things can be checked, but it takes much time."

"And the ports?" The child's father asked the question. The mother translated, unnecessarily in this case.

"Ports are being checked." He didn't tell them what anyone with a basic knowledge of geography knew. How many ports and accessible beaches were there in a narrow country with a coastline of thousands of kilometres? If someone had smuggled the child out of Italy via the sea, she was lost to them. "But there is a chance—every chance—that your Hadiyyah is still in Italy," he told them. "Possibly she is still in the province. This is how you must think, please."

The signora's eyes shone with tears, but she blinked quickly and did not shed them. She said, "How many days is it usually, Inspector, before . . . something . . . some kind of clue? . . . is found." She did not, of course, wish to say "before a body is found." None of them wished to say that despite all of them probably thinking it.

He explained to her as best he could the complexity of the area in which they lived. Not only were the Tuscan hills nearby, but beyond them the Apuan Alps rose like threats. Within both these places were hundreds of villages, hamlets, villas, farms, cottages, retreats, caves, churches, convents, monasteries, and grottoes. The child could be literally anywhere, he told them. Until they had a sighting, a clue, a memory shaken from someone's busy life, they were playing a waiting game.

Angelina Upman's tears fell then. She accompanied them with not the slightest drama. They merely leaked out of her eyes and down her cheeks, and she did nothing to blot them away. The professor moved his chair closer to hers. He put his hand on her arm.

Salvatore told them about Carlo Casparia to give them a small hope to hold on to. The drug addict had been questioned and would be questioned again, he said. They were still trying to excavate something from the wasteland that was his brain. At first he had seemed a possible candidate to have orchestrated an abduction, Salvatore explained. But as there was no ransom demanded by anyone . . . ? He paused questioningly.

"*Sì*, no ransom," Angelina Upman affirmed in a whisper.

. . . Then they had to assume he was not involved. He could, of course, have taken the child and handed her over to someone else for payment. But this suggested a degree of planning and an ability to go unnoticed in the *mercato* that did not seem possible for Carlo. He was as well known as the accordion player to whom their daughter had given money. Had he led the child off somewhere, one of the *venditori* would have seen this.

Into this explanation that Salvatore was giving, Lorenzo Mura finally arrived. He deposited an athletic bag on the floor and brought a chair to the table. His eyes took in the proximity of the London professor to the signora. His glance lingered on the other man's hand, still on the signora's arm. Taymullah Azhar removed it, but he did not change the position of his chair. Mura said, "*Cara*," to Angelina Upman and kissed the top of her head.

Salvatore did not like the fact that Mura's practice, coaching, or game of *calcio* had taken precedence over this meeting. Thus, he merely went on. Should Lorenzo Mura wish to be updated at this point, someone else was going to have to do it. He said, "So this, you see, would have been out of character in Carlo. We seek someone for whom the taking of a child is *in* character. This has led us to the paedophiles we have under surveillance and to those we suspect of being paedophiles."

"So?" Lorenzo was the one to ask the question. He did it abruptly, the way one would expect of someone from such a distinguished family. They would assume the police would jump to their bidding in the manner in which the police had done during the years of their immense wealth. Salvatore did not like this, but he understood it. Nonetheless, he did not intend to be cowed.

He ignored Mura's question and said to the parents of the missing girl, "As it happens, my daughter is acquainted with your Hadiyyah, although I did not know this until my Bianca saw the posters in town. They attend the Dante Alighieri school together. They have, it seems, spoken many times since your daughter joined Bianca's class. She told me something that has caused me to wonder if perhaps it is not an abduction that we are looking upon."

The parents said nothing. Mura frowned. They were, clearly, all thinking the same thing. If the police weren't considering the child's disappearance an abduction, then the police were considering it a runaway. Or a murder. There was no other alternative.

"Your little one told my Bianca much about you," Salvatore said, this time to the professor alone. He waited patiently for the signora to translate. "She said that you had written in emails that you would visit her at Christmas and then at Easter."

The professor's strangled cry stopped Salvatore from going on. The signora raised a hand to her mouth. Mura looked from his lover to the father of her child, his eyes narrowing in speculation, as the professor said, "I did not . . . Emails?" and the situation became immediately more complex.

Salvatore said, "*Sì*. You wrote no emails to Hadiyyah?"

The professor, stricken, said, "I did not know . . . When Angelina left me, there was no word where they had gone. I had no way to . . . Her laptop was left behind. I had no idea . . ." He spoke with such difficulty that Salvatore knew every word he said was the absolute truth. "Angelina . . ." The professor looked at her. "Angelina . . ." It seemed the only thing he could say.

"I had to." She breathed the words rather than said them. "Hari. You would have . . . I didn't know how else . . . If she'd had no word from you, she would have wanted . . . She would have wondered. She adores you and it was the only way . . ."

Salvatore sat back in his chair and examined the signora. His English was just good enough to pick up the gist. He examined the professor. He looked at Mura. He could see that Mura was in the dark about this matter, but he—Salvatore—was quickly putting together pieces that he did not like. "There were no real emails," he clarified. "These emails that Hadiyyah received . . . You wrote them, Signora?"

She shook her head. She lowered it so her face was partially obscured by her hair, and she said, "My sister. I told her what to say."

"Bathsheba?" the professor asked. "*Bathsheba* wrote emails, Angelina? Pretending? And yet when we spoke to her . . . when we spoke to your parents . . . all of them said . . ." One of his two hands clenched into a fist. "Hadiyyah believed the emails, didn't she? You set the address to be authentically English. So she would have no doubt, no questions," he finally said. "So she would think I wrote to her, making promises that I did not keep."

"Hari, I'm *sorry*." The signora's tears fell copiously now. A broken story came from her lips. This story was about her sister, the aversion she felt—and the family felt—for this man from Pakistan, her willingness to assist Angelina in escaping and hiding away from him, the communication between the two women, how everything from last November until this moment had come to pass, except, of course, the abduction of the child.

The signora's head was in her hands as she spoke. "I'm so sorry" was her conclusion.

The professor looked at her long. To Salvatore, it seemed that he went inside himself to find some inner quality that would allow him to bring forth what, in the same position, Salvatore could not possibly have produced. "It's done, Angelina," the professor said. He spoke with astounding dignity. "I cannot pretend to understand. I never will understand. Your hatred of me? This . . . what you have done . . . Hadiyyah's safety is what is important now."

"I *don't* hate you!" the signora wept. "It's that you don't understand me, that you never understood me, that I tried and tried and couldn't make you see—"

The professor put his hand on her arm once again. "Perhaps we failed each other," he said. "But that is of no importance now. Only Hadiyyah. Angelina, hear me. Only Hadiyyah."

Sudden movement from Lorenzo Mura caused Salvatore to glance his way. The man's port wine birthmark would always make the rest of his skin look pale by comparison, but Salvatore did not miss the angry flush that climbed from his neck and the muscle in his jaw that moved as he ground his teeth together. He leaned forward quickly. Just as quickly—perhaps sensing Salvatore's gaze upon him—he returned to his original position. Salvatore noted this. There were things about this man, he thought, that bore looking into as well.

He said to the parents, "You will want to know that the British police have become involved in this matter. A Scotland Yard detective arrives today."

"Barbara Havers?" The professor said the name in such hope that Salvatore was loath to disappoint him.

"It is a man," he said. "Thomas Lynley is his name."

The professor touched his former partner's shoulder. He left it there. "I know this man, Angelina," he said. "He will help find Hadiyyah. This is very good news."

Salvatore doubted that. He thought it best to tell them that the detective's purpose would only be to keep them informed of what was happening with the investigation. But before he had a chance to say this, Lorenzo Mura was on his feet.

"*Andiamo*," he said abruptly to Angelina, jerking her chair away from the table. He nodded a farewell to Salvatore. The professor he ignored altogether.

LUCCA
TUSCANY

Lynley made the drive from Pisa to Lucca with no trouble, well prepared by Charlie Denton with directions, Internet maps, satellite depictions of the town, and car parks marked with mighty red *P*'s both inside and outside of the city's huge wall. Charlie had gone so far as to indicate the location of the *questura* as well, and on the satellite photo he'd pointed out with arrows the Roman amphitheatre where Lynley would find his *pensione*. He'd booked himself into the same B & B that Taymullah Azhar was using. This, he reckoned, would simplify matters when he needed to speak to the London professor.

He'd been to Italy innumerable times—in childhood, adolescence, and as an adult—but somehow he'd never been to Lucca. So he was unprepared for the sight of the perfectly kept wall that had long protected the town's medieval interior, both from marauders and from the occasional floods that its position on the alluvial plain of the River Serchio exposed it to. In many ways Lucca resembled numerous towns and villages he'd seen in Tuscany from his childhood on: with their narrow cobbled streets, their piazzas dominated by churches, and their fountains bubbling with fresh spring water. But in three ways it was different: in its number of churches, its remaining towers, and most of all its distinguishing wall.

He had to drive around this wall twice before he found the car park Denton had identified as being closest to the amphitheatre, so he was able to take in the towering trees upon it, as well as the statues, the military bulwarks, the parks, and the people on bikes, on roller-blades, in running clothes, and guiding pushchairs. A police car drove at a snail's pace through them. Another stood parked above one of the many gates that gave access into the oldest part of the town.

He himself gained entrance through Porta Santa Maria. There he parked, and from there it was a short walk only to reach Piazza dell' Anfiteatro, an ovoid marking upon the campestral landscape of the town. Lynley had to walk half the circumference of the repurposed amphitheatre to find one of the tunnel-like *gallerie* that allowed him access to the interior of the place, and once within its precinct, he paused and blinked in the bright sunlight that fell upon the yellow and white buildings inside and upon the stones that constituted the foundation of the piazza. Here there were tourist shops, cafés, apartments, and *pensioni*. His own was called Pensione Giardino although he suspected the garden of its name comprised only the impressive display of cacti, succulents, and shrubbery arranged in terracotta pots on various surfaces in front of the establishment.

It took a brief few minutes for Lynley to acquaint himself with the proprietor of the place. She was a young, heavily pregnant woman who introduced herself breathlessly as Cristina Grazia Vallera before she handed him his key, pointed out a claustrophobic breakfast room, and gave him the hours of *colazione*. That taken care of, she disappeared towards the back of the building, from which the crying of a small child emanated along with the welcome scent of baking bread, leaving him to find his room on his own.

He had no difficulty with this. He climbed the stairs, saw there were four rooms only, and located his at the front of the building, number three. It was warm within, so he opened the metal shutters over the window, then the window itself. He looked out at the piazza below him, where, at its centre, a group of students had positioned themselves in a large circle, facing outward. They were each sketching their own views of the piazza as their teacher moved among them. Thus, he saw Taymullah Azhar the moment the London man came through the *galleria* and headed for the *pensione*.

Lynley watched his progress. He had nothing with him but his devastation, and Lynley knew this feeling, its every nuance. He watched—one step back from the window—until Azhar disappeared beneath him into their shared accommodation.

Lynley removed his jacket and placed his suitcase upon the bed. In a moment, he heard footsteps on the tiles in the corridor, so he went to the door. When he opened it, Azhar was at the door to his own room, which was next to Lynley's. He glanced over—as one would do—and Lynley was struck, even in the dim light of the corridor, by how contained the man was, even in his wretchedness.

"The chief inspector told us you were coming," Taymullah Azhar said to Lynley, walking over to shake his hand. "I am, Inspector Lynley, so very grateful that you are here. I know how busy a man you are."

"Barbara wanted to be sent," Lynley told him. "Our guv wouldn't allow it."

"I know she must walk a very fine line in all of this." Azhar used a thin hand to indicate the *pensione*, but Lynley knew he meant the situation of Hadiyyah's disappearance. He also knew that the "she" in Azhar's remarks did not refer to Isabelle Ardery.

"She does," he told the London professor.

"I wish she would not. To have her on my conscience . . . what might happen to her . . . to her employment with the police . . . I do not wish this," Azhar said frankly.

"Let go of that burden," Lynley said. "Over a long acquaintance, I've found that Barbara goes her own way in matters that are important to her. Frankly? I wish she wouldn't. Her heart's always in the right place, but her wisdom—especially her political wisdom—often takes an ill-advised back seat to her heart."

"This I have come to understand."

Lynley explained to Azhar what his own position in the investigation would be as long as he remained in Lucca. He was in all respects an outsider, and how much he would be able to assist the Italian police was going to depend entirely upon them and upon the public minister. This man—a magistrate—directed the investigation, Lynley told Azhar. That was how Italian policing was structured.

"My job is to be a conduit for information." Lynley went on to tell Azhar how it had come about that the Metropolitan police had decided to send a liaison officer to Lucca at all: because of *The Source* and what appeared to be Barbara Havers's leaking information to that rag. "This has made her less than popular with Superintendent Ardery, as you can imagine. Nothing can be proved, of course, as to whether she actually gave them the story. But I have to say that I'm hoping my presence here will also keep Barbara out of any further trouble in London."

Azhar took this in, quiet for a moment. "I will hope . . ." But he did not conclude the thought. Instead, he said, "The tabloids here are following the story, as well. I myself do what I can to keep it alive. Because with the tabloids involved . . ." He shrugged sadly.

"I understand," Lynley told him. Pressure upon the police was pressure upon the police. No matter where it came from, it produced results.

Azhar went on to tell him that he was also carrying handbills to the nearby towns and villages. Rather than endure the agony of waiting for word of anything, he instead had been going out each day and posting these handbills in an ever-widening circumference around Lucca. He brought them from his room and handed one to Lynley. Mostly it comprised a large and very good picture of the little girl, with her name and the word *MISSING* written in Italian, German, English, and French beneath the photo along with a phone number that Lynley took to be that of the police.

Lynley was struck by the innocence of Hadiyyah's expression in the handbill's photograph and by how much of a child she still was. In the way of the modern world, children were growing up at a younger and younger age, so Hadiyyah could have looked like a miniature Bollywood film star despite her age. Instead, though, the photo showed a little girl with plaited hair tied off in small bows. She wore a crisp school uniform, and she had lively brown eyes and an impish grin. She looked quite small for a nine-year-old, which Azhar confirmed that indeed she was. This meant, of course, that she could have been mistaken for a younger child. Excellent pickings for a paedophile, Lynley thought grimly.

"This immediate area is not so difficult to canvass with the pictures," Azhar said as Lynley gave the handbill back to him. "But as I move farther away from Lucca and as the towns rise up into the hills . . . Things are more difficult then."

From his room's chest of drawers, he took a map. He explained that he was about to set out for the rest of the day to continue canvassing the area with Hadiyyah's picture. If Inspector Lynley had the time, he would show him where he had gone so far. Lynley nodded and they descended the stairs. They went out into the piazza, where, across from the *pensione*, a café offered a handful of small tables and, more important, shade. There they sat and ordered Coca-Cola, after which Azhar opened his map.

Lynley saw that he'd circled the towns he'd so far visited, and although he himself was familiar with the Tuscan landscape, he allowed

Azhar to explain the difficulties he was encountering just going from one point to another in the nearby hills. Lynley could tell Azhar's mere act of speaking about what he was doing acted to assuage what had to be tremendous anxiety, so he nodded, looked over the map with him, and noted how assiduous Azhar was being in his search for his daughter.

Finally, though, the London professor ran out of words. So he said what he no doubt had been trying to avoid saying from the first. "It's been a week, Inspector." And when Lynley said nothing but merely nodded, Azhar went on. "What do you think? Please tell me the truth. I know how reluctant you might be, but I wish to hear it."

Lynley did Azhar the honour of believing that he meant what he said. He looked away from him for a moment, seeing the students at work on their drawings around the piazza, noting the ubiquitous green, shuttered windows protecting interiors of Italian apartments from the sun. A dog barked from somewhere within one of these apartments. From another the sound of piano music drifted. Lynley thought of how to approach the truth. There seemed no other way but to tell it directly.

"This is different from the kidnapping of a very small child," he said quietly to Hadiyyah's father. "A toddler snatched from a pushchair or a baby from its pram? That kind of kidnapping with no request for ransom suggests an intention to keep the child or to pass her along for a purpose that doesn't involve harming her. An illegal 'adoption' perhaps, effected by money. Or just handing the child over to relatives desperate for a little one of their own. But to take a child Hadiyyah's age—nine years old—suggests something else."

Azhar asked no questions. His hands, folded on his map, gripped each other tightly. "There has," he said quietly, "been no sign of . . . There has been no indication . . ."

No body was what he meant. "Which is a very good sign." Lynley did not add how easily hidden in the Tuscan hills or in the Apuan Alps beyond them a body could be. Instead he said, "From this, we can conclude she's well. Perhaps frightened, but well. We can also conclude that if someone's intention is to pass Hadiyyah along to someone else, she would have to be hidden away for a time first."

"Why is this?"

Lynley sipped his Coke and poured more from the can into the glass where three ice cubes did their limited best to keep it cold. He said, "It's not likely a nine-year-old is going to forget her parents, is it? So she has to be held for a period of time until she becomes docile, used to her captivity, and reconciled to it and to her situation. She's in a foreign country; her ability to speak the language is, perhaps, limited. Within time and in order to survive, she needs to learn to see her captors as her saviours. She needs to learn to depend upon them. But all of this works to our benefit. It puts time on our side and not on theirs."

"Yet if she is not to be handed to another family for purposes of adoption," Azhar pointed out, "then I do not see—"

Lynley cut him off quickly, to spare him speculations. "She's young enough to be schooled in any number of things a child might be wanted for, but the point isn't what those things are so much as it's she's alive and must be kept safe and well." He didn't add the more horrifying kind of scenario that was possible in this situation of Hadiyyah's potential imprisonment, however. He didn't point out that she was the perfect age to be held prisoner for a paedophile's pleasure: in a basement, in a house with a carefully hidden and even more carefully soundproofed room, in a cellar, in an abandoned building high in the hills. For someone to have taken her so successfully from a market in the middle of the day, someone had to have prepared the abduction. Preparation for abduction also indicated preparation for use. Nothing could have been left to chance. So while time was on their side, the truth of the matter was that circumstances were not.

Yet there was one hope which could be to their benefit, and it came from Hadiyyah herself. For not everyone behaved as human psychology otherwise indicated she would behave. And there was a relatively simple way to ascertain if Hadiyyah was, potentially, among those people who acted differently from what might otherwise be expected of them in similar circumstances.

"May I ask," Lynley said, "how likely is it that Hadiyyah would fight her situation?"

"What do you mean?"

"Children are often extremely resourceful. Might she raise a ruckus at an opportune moment? Might she draw attention to herself in some way?"

"In what way?"

"Behaving other than she's told to behave. Trying to escape her captivity. Throwing herself into an attack on her captors. Producing a convenient tantrum. Setting a fire. Slashing a vehicle's tyres. Anything other than being docile." Anything other, Lynley didn't add, than being a little girl.

Azhar seemed to go within himself to find a reply. Church bells rang somewhere in the town, joined by other church bells echoing off the narrow Lucchese streets. A flock of pigeons circled overhead, domesticated homing birds by the close formation they kept in the sky.

Azhar cleared his throat. "None of those things," he said to Lynley. "She has not been brought up to be a trouble to anyone. I have—God forgive me—been very careful about that."

Lynley nodded. It was, unfortunately, the way of the world. So often little girls—no matter their culture—were taught by their parents and by society to be pliant and sweet. It was little boys who were taught to use their wits and their fists.

"Inspector Lo Bianco," Azhar added, "seems to feel there is . . . despite a week . . . there is hope . . . ?"

"And I agree," Lynley said. But what he didn't point out to the other man was that, with no word from kidnappers or anyone else, the hope he was clinging to was fading ever faster.

VICTORIA
LONDON

Barbara Havers put it off as long as possible. Indeed, she tried to restrain herself altogether. But by early afternoon she could no longer wait for her first report from DI Lynley. So she rang his mobile.

She knew he was unhappy with her. Any other officer would have kissed her feet for having bulldogged the circumstances of Hadiyyah's disappearance in such a way that he ended up getting sent to Italy as a liaison officer for the girl's family. But Lynley had other matters on his mind that went far beyond travelling to Italy at the expense of the Met. He had roller derby matches to attend and Daidre Trahair to . . . to *whatever* he was attempting to do with the large animal vet.

When Lynley answered with a single word—"Barbara"—she said in a rush, "I know you're cheesed off. I'm bloody sorry, sir. You've got things on your . . . on your mind or whatever and I've put a spanner and I know that."

He said, "Ah. As I suspected."

She said, "I'm not admitting to anything. But how could anyone who knows her—and her dad and her mum—not want to do something? You see that, don't you?"

"Does it actually matter what I see?"

"I'm sorry. But things'll wait, won't it? She'll wait, won't she?"

There was silence. Then he said in that maddening, well-bred fashion of his, " 'Things'? 'She'?"

Barbara realised she was heading in the absolutely wrong direction. She said hastily, "Never mind. Not my business at all. Can't think why I even said . . . except I'm worn out with worry and I can see it's best that you're there and I'm here and if I only knew how—"

"Barbara."

"Yeah? What? I mean I know I'm babbling and it's only because I know you're cheesed off and you've a right to be because I bollocksed things properly this time but it was only because—"

"*Barbara.*" He waited on his end for her silence. Then he said, "There's nothing to report. When there is, I'll ring you."

"Is he . . . ? Are they . . . ?"

"I've not met Angelina Upman. I've spoken to Azhar. He's as well as he can be, under the circumstances."

"What's next? Who d'you talk to? Where d'you go? Are the cops there handling things? Are they letting you—"

"Do my job?" he interrupted pointedly. "Such as it is, yes. And, believe me, it's going to be limited. Now is there anything else?"

"S'pose not," she said.

"Then we'll speak later," he told her and rang off, leaving her to wonder if he actually meant it.

She shoved her mobile in her bag. She'd made the call from the Met canteen, where the only option to keep her nerves in check had been consuming a muffin the size of Gibraltar. She'd gobbled it down like a stray dog keeping a handout secret from the rest of the pack. She'd washed it on its way with huge gulps of tepid coffee. When this didn't work to calm her savage breast—she *should* have tried music, she admitted—then she'd given in to phoning Italy. But there was no satisfaction available from Lynley, she realised. So she faced either eating a second muffin or coming up with something else to soothe herself.

She hadn't heard from Dwayne Doughty. She told herself that the reason for this had to do with her having employed him for less than twenty-four hours. But a voice within her demanded to know how long it could possibly take for the man to make certain Taymullah Azhar had indeed been in Berlin during the time his daughter had gone missing from Lucca. She herself could have done it in an hour or two of tracing his movements and confirming all reports of his presence. And she would have done it, using the Met's resources, had she wished to risk another blot on her copybook. But with Superintendent Ardery's eyes upon her and DI Stewart doubtless making daily reports on the level of her cooperation as part of his team, she had to be careful. Whatever she did, she had to do it on her time and without the resources of the Met.

Luckily her mobile phone wasn't one of the Met's resources. She couldn't be faulted for using it while taking a break. Nor, she reckoned, could she be faulted for using it while making a visit to the ladies' in order to answer a pressing call from nature.

She went there next. Carefully, she checked to see all the stalls were empty. She punched in Mitchell Corsico's number.

"Brilliant job" was what she told him when he barked his greeting with a harried "Corsico," designed to illustrate how busy a man he was down there in the journalistic gutters.

"Who's this?" he asked.

"Postman's Park," she told him. "Watts Memorial. I wore fuchsia, you wore Stetson. Are you going to Italy?"

"I wish."

"What? The story's not big enough for you lot?"

"Well, she isn't dead, is she?"

"Bloody hell! You lot are a sodding group of—"

"Save it. It's not me making this decision. What d'you think? I have that kind of power? So unless you've got something more to give me . . . I mean aside from the Ilford end of things, which the higher-ups are beginning to like for a few more front pages."

Barbara went icy. "What Ilford business? What're you on about, Mitch?"

"What I'm 'on about' is the other dimensions of the story. What I'm 'on about' is your convenient failure to mention your own involvement in what's going on."

"What the hell? What kind of involvement?"

"The kind that ended up with you in a street brawl with Professor Azhar's parents. Let me tell you, mate, this whole 'abandoned second family in Ilford' part of the story has given it legs over here."

Barbara's iciness rendered her nearly incapable of rational thought. All she was able to say in reply to this was "You can't go that way. There's a kid. Her life's on the line. You have to—"

"That," Corsico told her, "would be your part of the equation. My part is the story. My part is readership. So while the kidnapping of a cute kid sells papers—you won't get an argument from me on that score—the kidnapping of a cute kid whose dad has a secret second family willing to talk—"

"They're not a secret. And they won't be willing."

"Tell that to the kid. Sayyid."

Barbara thought frantically. She had to keep him from thrusting upon Azhar the humiliation of a public exposé of his tortuous personal life. She could only imagine how it would play out in *The Source* should Mitchell Corsico score an interview with Azhar's son. It was unthinkable that this might happen, not only because of Azhar himself but also because of Hadiyyah. Focus needed to be maintained on her, on her abduction, on the search, on the Italians themselves, on *whatever* was going on in Italy.

She said, "All right. I see your point. But there's something you might want to know about our end of things. I mean the Met's end of things."

"And that would be what?"

"That would be DI Lynley." She hated to do it, but she had no other choice that she could see. "DI Lynley's gone over. He's the liaison officer."

Silence at Mitchell Corsico's end. Barbara could almost hear the wheels turning in his mind. He'd been angling for an interview with the inspector since the moment Lynley's wife had been murdered on the front steps of their home. Pregnant, just returned from shopping, looking for her keys to unlock her front door. Accosted by a kid with a gun who'd shot her for the fun of it and rendered her brain-dead. With the inspector left in the position of having to decide to take her off the machines keeping their baby alive. If Corsico wanted a story that would go the distance, Lynley was the story. Both of them knew it.

She said, "The press office here'll be making the announcement, but you can make it in advance, if you want. And you know what this means, I expect. He'll be liaising with the parents, but he'll have to talk to the press and answer their questions. The press means you. And answering questions means an interview. *The* interview, Mitch."

"I see where you're heading. I won't lie about it, Barb. Lynley's a bloody decent angle and he always will be. But the fish I'm frying—"

"Lynley *is* the story." Barbara heard her voice rise with impatience and urgency. "Mention Lynley's name to your higher-ups and you're on the next plane to Italy." Which, she added, was where she needed him: pursuing the story there, feeding details to his editor here, whipping up in the UK reading public a frenzy about what was being done to find an appealing little British girl.

"And I will," Corsico said. "No worries on that score. But first things first, and the first is the kid."

"That's what I'm trying to—"

"I don't mean the kid Hadiyyah," he cut in. "I mean the other. Sayyid."

"Mitch, don't—"

"Thanks for the tip on Lynley, though." He ended the call.

VICTORIA
LONDON

Barbara cursed and headed for the door. She had to stop Corsico from getting to Azhar's family in Ilford, and there weren't a lot of options jumping into her mind on how to do this. She reckoned Nafeeza would remain mute on all matters concerning her husband. But his son, Sayyid, was a wild card in the family deck.

She swung the door open, her mind febrile. She walked directly into Winston Nkata. The black man didn't pretend he was just passing by. Instead, he jerked his head towards the interior of the ladies' toilet. In case she was dim on his intentions, he stepped past her, grabbing her arm on the way inside.

She said, "Whoops. You lost? Gents is just down the corridor, Winnie."

Nkata was not amused. She could tell by the manner in which his enunciation altered from careful Africa-via-the-Caribbean to South-Brixton-on-the-street.

He said in a harsh whisper, "You gone off your nut? Bloody lucky Stewart tole me to follow you, innit. Someone else 'n you back in uniform tomorrow."

She decided that playing dumb was her best course. She said, "What? Win, what're you talking about?"

"I'm talkin 'bout your job," he said. "I'm talkin 'bout losin it. They find out you made yourself a snout for *The Source* 'n you back in uniform. Worse, you done. You finished, innit. And don't be so thick to think there i'n't people in the department'd be happy as hell to see that happen, Barb."

She went for offended. "A *snout*?" she hissed. "That's what you think? I'm a snout for *The Source*? I'm not a snout. Not theirs and not anyone's."

"That so? You just gave them DI Lynley. I heard you, Barb. Now you goin to tell me you gave up Lynley to someone other than that same bloke wrote the story 'bout Hadiyyah? You think I'm stupid enough to go for that? You're on the phone with Corsico, Barb, and one look at your mobile records's goin to show that. Not to mention your bank account, innit."

"*What?*" Now she *was* offended. "You think I'm taking money to do this?"

"I don' know why the hell you're doin it. I don't care why the hell you're doin it. And you bes' believe me when I say no one else's goin to care 'bout the why of it either."

"Look, Winnie. You and I both know that someone's got to keep this story alive. That's the only way *The Source* is going to send a reporter over to Italy. And only a British reporter in Italy is going to keep the pressure on the Met so that Lynley stays in place till this gets resolved. Plus a British reporter raises the stakes for the Italian reporters to keep the pressure on the Italian police. That's how it works. Pressure gets results and you know that."

"What I know," he said, and he was calmer now, so he was back to the gentle Caribbean from his mother that had always so influenced his way of talking, "is that no one's goin to take your side, Barb. This comes out, and you're on your own. You got to know that. You got no one here."

"Oh, thanks very much, Winston. It's always good to know who one's friends are."

"I mean no one with the power to step in," Winston said.

He meant Lynley, of course. For Lynley was the only officer who would risk stepping onto the pitch if it came down to having to defend the wicket of Barbara's ill-conceived decision to involve *The Source*. And he was the only officer to do this not so much because he was devoted to Barbara as because he didn't need his employment at the Met so he didn't care about alienating their superiors.

"So you see," Winston said, apparently reading realisation on Barbara's face. "You're walkin on the wrong side in this, Barb. That bloke Corsico? He'd throw your mum under a bus 'f it meant a story. He'd throw his own mum 'f that'd help."

"That can't matter," Barbara told him. "And I c'n handle Corsico, Winston." She tried to move past him to get to the door. He stopped her easily enough since he towered above her.

"No one 'handles' a tabloid, Barb. You don't know that now, you learn it soon enough."

ILFORD

GREATER LONDON

There were not a lot of avenues available to Barbara when it came to the chess game of managing what Mitchell Corsico wrote about. But in the case of his intention to talk to the boy Sayyid there appeared to be only one. She phoned Azhar. She reached him on a bad connection in the hills of Tuscany. They did not speak long. From him she learned what she already knew: that Lynley had arrived and that he and the inspector had spoken prior to Azhar's making his way into the hills to continue posting pictures of Hadiyyah in the villages to the north of Lucca.

"Sayyid's comprehensive?" Azhar said when she asked the name of the school. "Why do you need this, Barbara?"

She hated to tell him, but she didn't see the alternative: *The Source* was considering the boy as just that, a source for the kind of "human interest" story so beloved to its readers.

Azhar gave her the name of the school at once. "For his own sake . . ." His voice was urgent. "You know what the tabloid will make of him, Barbara."

She knew well. She knew because she read the bloody rag herself. It was like mental candyfloss and she'd been addicted to the stuff for years. She thanked Azhar and told him she would keep him in the picture of what happened with his son.

The more difficult project was getting away from the Met. She couldn't risk waiting for the end of her workday. Knowing Corsico, by the time that arrived, he would already have buttonholed the boy and given him the outlet he was looking for to unload his grievances against his father. She had to leave Victoria, and she had to do it now. She merely needed a decent excuse. Her mum provided it.

Barbara went to DI Stewart. On the whiteboard, he was jotting brief notations about the day's actions. She didn't bother to look for her own. She knew Stewart. No matter her expertise in anything, he'd keep her there in the building and under his thumb transcribing reports, just to drive her as mad as possible.

"Sir," she said, although the word felt like a rock on her tongue. "I've just had a call from Greenford." She tried to sound anxiety-ridden about it, which wasn't too far from the truth. She *was* anxious. Just not about her mum.

Stewart didn't look away from the whiteboard. He was, it appeared, giving crucial attention to the legibility of his cursive. "Have you indeed?" he said in a tone that demonstrated the extent of his ennui when it came to all things Barbara Havers. She wanted to bite his ears off.

"My mum's taken a fall. She's in casualty, sir. I'm going to need to—"

"Where, exactly?"

"In the home where she—"

"I mean casualty, Sergeant. Which hospital? Where is she?"

Barbara knew the game on that one. If she named a hospital, he'd ring the casualty department and make sure her mother was there. She said, "Don't know yet, sir. I was planning to ring from the car."

"Ring whom?"

"Lady who runs the home. She phoned me after nine-nine-nine. She didn't know yet where they were going to take her."

DI Stewart seemed to measure this on his potential-for-bollocks meter. He looked at her. "I'll want to know," he said. "The department will, of course, wish to send flowers."

"Let you know soon 's I find out," she told him. She grabbed her shoulder bag, said, "Ta, sir," and avoided looking at Winston Nkata. He avoided looking at her as well. He didn't need a potential-for-bollocks meter. But at least he said nothing. He would be her friend in this one matter.

It was a long drive to Ilford, but she made it before the end of the school day. She found the secondary comprehensive, and she had a quick look round the immediate area to make sure Mitchell Corsico wasn't hiding in a wheelie bin ready to spring out the moment he saw her. The coast appeared relatively clear aside from an ancient woman pushing a nicked shopping trolley along the pavement, so Barbara sprinted inside the building. Her Metropolitan Police ID got her into the head teacher's office with virtually no delay.

She told the head teacher—a woman with the unfortunate name of Mrs. Ida Croak, if her desk's nameplate was to be believed—the truth. A tabloid journalist was on his way to attempt an interview with one of her pupils on the topic of his father's desertion of the family for another woman. She gave Sayyid's name. She added, "It's a smear piece that this bloke has in mind. You know what I mean, I expect: something pretending to be a human interest story while all the time dragging everyone through the mud. I want to stop it from happening, for Sayyid's own sake, for his mum's sake, and for the family's sake."

The head teacher looked appropriately concerned but also, it had to be admitted, appropriately confused by Barbara's advent to her office. She asked the reasonable question. "Why are the Metropolitan police involved?"

That was, of course, the crux of the matter. Certainly, the Met had no love for *The Source*, but sending officers out to stop stories from being gathered was hardly within its purview. She said, "It's a personal favour to the family. You c'n ring Sayyid's mum and ask her if she'd like me to carry the boy past the journalist and bring him home to keep him from getting accosted."

"The journalist's *here*?" She said it as if the Grim Reaper was waiting outside the front doors, scythe at the ready.

"He will be. I didn't see him on my way in, but I expect he'll show up at any moment. He knows I mean to stop him if I can."

Mrs. Croak hadn't climbed to her position as head teacher for nothing. She said, "I'll need to phone," and she asked Barbara to wait outside her office.

Barbara knew that this could also mean Mrs. Croak was phoning the Met as well, checking up on the validity of her warrant card as if she'd come with the intention of snatching Sayyid in order to have her way with him. She could only pray this wasn't the case. All she needed was Mrs. Croak being rung through to John Stewart or, worse, to Superintendent Ardery. Her nerves were on edge till the head teacher emerged from her office and motioned Barbara to rejoin her within.

"The mother's on her way," she said. "She doesn't drive, so she's bringing the boy's grandfather. They'll take him home at once."

Barbara's head filled with a mental *Oh no!*, like the thought balloon of the cartoon character she felt she was fast becoming. Her intention had been to warn Sayyid not to talk to the tabloids—to any tabloids—but after her previous encounter with Azhar's father, she knew very well that *he* might turn out to be a most cooperative interviewee only too happy to rubbish Azhar from London to Lahore and back again. She was going to have to reason with him as best she could. That, she knew, was going to be dicey since the last time she'd encountered the man was in the midst of a brawl in front of his own home.

Barbara said, "D'you mind if I wait, then? I'd like a word . . ."

Of course, the sergeant could do as she wished, Mrs. Croak told her. If she wouldn't mind waiting elsewhere, however . . . as one's schedule was quite busy . . . as one would want to have a private word with Sayyid's mother upon her arrival . . .

Barbara minded not in the least. Her intention was to grab Nafeeza and paint a proper picture for her about Mitch Corsico's intentions just in case Mrs. Croak hadn't done so. She had to be made to understand that, no matter how appealing it might sound to unburden oneself and one's grievances in a public forum, *The Source* could not that forum be. "No tabloid journalist is your friend," she would say.

So she waited outside. Thus she was in position when Nafeeza and Azhar's father showed up. Thus she was in position when Mitch Corsico showed up as well.

Luckily Nafeeza arrived at the school first. She and Azhar's father came hustling towards the main doors, and they saw Barbara simultaneously. Nafeeza said with great dignity, "Thank you, Sergeant. We are in your debt," and Azhar's father nodded at her.

"Don't let anyone get to him," Barbara said as they went inside. "It'll turn out bad. Try to explain this to him."

"We understand. We will."

Then they were gone. Then Corsico arrived.

Barbara saw him take up a lurking position across the street from the school at a newsagent's shop. He clocked her at once, cocked his ridiculous Stetson at her, and crossed his arms on his chest beneath the digital camera that hung round his neck. His expression said that she'd checked his king but shouldn't feel exactly triumphant about it.

Barbara looked away from him. All she needed to do was to get Sayyid, his mum, and his granddad to their car. All she needed to do was to have a word with the boy in order to underscore the dangers he faced if he gave in to his inclination to abuse his dad in the press. The fact that Sayyid wouldn't see the opportunity as dangerous had to be dealt with. Barbara doubted that it was going to be enough for his mum and his grandfather merely to instruct him to hold his tongue.

After ten minutes of waiting, the main door to the comprehensive opened once again. Barbara had been lingering near the pavement, at the side of an urn planted with a sad-looking holly bush. She came forward as the three others approached. In her peripheral vision, she saw Corsico take a step into the quiet street.

She said quickly, "Nafeeza, the reporter's just there in the cowboy get-up. He's got a camera. Sayyid, that's who you need to keep clear of. He means to—"

"You!" Sayyid snarled. And to his mother, "You didn't say that his whore . . . You didn't *tell* me that his whore was the one—"

"Sayyid!" his mother said. "This woman is not your father's—"

"You're so bloody stupid! Both of you are stupid!"

His grandfather grabbed onto him and said something in Urdu. He began to strong-arm him towards a battered Golf.

"I'll talk to whoever I want to talk to!" Sayyid declared. "You," to Barbara, "you fucking whore. You keep away from me. Keep away from us. Go back to my father's bed and suck his cock like you want to."

Nafeeza slapped him so hard his head snapped to one side. He began to shout. "I'll talk to anyone I want! I'll tell the truth. About her. About him. About what they do when they're alone because I know, I know, I know what he's like and what she's like and—"

His grandfather punched him. He began to roar in Urdu. Over his roaring, Nafeeza cried out and grabbed onto him. He shook her off and hit Sayyid again. Blood spurted from the boy's nose to speckle the front of his neat white shirt.

"Bloody hell," Barbara said. She dashed forward to free the teenager from his grandfather's clutches.

Dog's dinner was what she thought about the mess. What Corsico thought she reckoned she'd be seeing sooner or later on the front page of *The Source*.

LUCCA

TUSCANY

Lynley went to the *questura* once he and Taymullah Azhar parted at Pensione Giardino. This police building sat outside the city wall, not far from Porta San Pietro, an easy walk from anywhere within the medieval centre of the town. The colour of apricots, it was an imposing Romanesque building given to sobriety and solidity, located a short distance from the train station. Police and other judicial officials came and went from it, and while Lynley's entrance garnered him curious looks, he was taken quickly enough to Chief Inspector Salvatore Lo Bianco's office.

Salvatore Lo Bianco had been brought fully into the picture about Lynley's assignment to the case, he discovered. Clearly, the Italian wasn't pleased about this. A stiff smile of welcome indicated where he stood on the matter of a Scotland Yard copper showing up on his patch, but he was far too polite to let anything other than perfectly—and rather cool—good manners indicate his displeasure.

He was quite a small man, Lynley topping him by at least ten inches. His salt-and-pepper hair was thinning at the crown, and he was swarthy of complexion with the scars of adolescent acne pitting his cheeks. But he was a man who'd obviously learned to make the most of his physical assets, for he was trim, athletic-looking, and beautifully suited. His hands looked as if they were manicured weekly.

"*Piacere,*" he said to Lynley, although Lynley doubted the other man was at all pleased to make his acquaintance and he couldn't blame him. "*Parla italiano, sì?*"

Lynley said yes, as long as the person speaking to him didn't talk like someone describing the action at a horse race. To this, Lo Bianco smiled. He gestured to a chair.

He offered *caffè . . . macchiato? americano?* Lynley demurred. He then offered *tè caldo.* After all, Lynley was a mad Englishman, *no?,* and everyone knew the English drank tea by the gallon. Lynley smiled and said he required nothing. He went on to tell Lo Bianco he'd met Taymullah Azhar at the *pensione* where they both were staying. He had yet to meet with the missing girl's mother. He hoped the chief inspector would facilitate that.

Lo Bianco nodded. He eyed Lynley and seemed to take the measure of him. Lynley hadn't failed to note that while he was seated, Lo Bianco had remained standing. He wasn't bothered by this. He was in foreign territory in more ways than one, and both of them knew it.

"This thing that you do," Lo Bianco said in Italian from in front of a filing cabinet where he had positioned himself. "This liaison with the family. It suggests to us—especially to the public minister, I must tell you—that the British police think we do not work well here in Italy. As police, I mean."

Lynley hastened to reassure the chief inspector. His presence, he told him, was largely a political move on the part of the Met. The UK tabloids had begun to cover the story of the little girl's disappearance. In particular, a rather base tabloid—if the chief inspector knew what he meant—was giving the Met a proper caning about the matter. Tabloids in general were not so much interested in the regulations of policing between countries as they were in stirring up trouble. To avoid this, he had been sent to Italy, but it was not his intention to get in Chief Inspector Lo Bianco's way. If he could be of assistance, of course, he would be happy to offer himself in the investigation. But the chief inspector should be assured that his sole purpose was to serve the family in whatever way he could.

"As it happens, I'm acquainted with the child's father," he said. He didn't add that one of his colleagues was more than merely acquainted with Taymullah Azhar.

Lo Bianco watched him closely as he spoke. He nodded and seemed appeased by all of this. He said knowingly, "Ah, your UK tabloids," in a fashion that indicated Italy did not itself suffer from the same sort of gutter journalism that went on in England, but then he relented and said, "Here, too," and he went to his desk, where, from a briefcase, he brought out a paper called *Prima Voce*. Its front page, Lynley saw, bore the headline *Dov'è la bambina?* It also featured a picture of a man kneeling in the street somewhere in Lucca, his head bent and a hand-lettered sign reading *Ho fame* in his hands. For a crazy moment, Lynley thought this was a form of strange Italian punishment akin to being held in the stocks for public ridicule. But the man turned out to be the only person of interest the police had come up with: an inveterate

drug user called Carlo Casparia who had seen Hadiyyah on the morning of her disappearance. He'd been in for questioning twice, the
second time at the request of *il Pubblico Ministero* himself. This man,
Piero Fanucci, had become convinced that Carlo was involved in the
child's disappearance.

"*Perché?*"

"At first because of the drugs themselves and his need to purchase
more. Now because he has not been in the *mercato* to beg since the
girl disappeared." Lo Bianco produced a philosophical expression. "*Il
Pubblico Ministero?* He thinks this is an indication of guilt."

"And you?"

Lo Bianco smiled, seeming pleased at having been read by his fellow detective. "I think Carlo does not wish to be further harassed by
the police and, until this matter is settled, will not return to the *mercato* where he can be easily picked up for more questions. But you see,
it is an important matter to the *magistrato*—and to the public—that
progress be made. And this questioning of Carlo, it looks like progress.
You will see that for yourself, I think."

What he meant by this last statement became clear when Lo Bianco
suggested Lynley meet the public minister. He was in Piazza
Napoleone—"Piazza Grande, we call it," he said—which was not far,
but they would drive. "The privilege of the police," he said, for few
vehicles were allowed within the city's wall, where most people either
walked, rode bicycles, or took the tiny buses that scooted along with
virtually no sound.

In Piazza Grande, they entered an enormous *palazzo* converted—
like the vast majority of such buildings in Italy—into a use far removed
from its original one. They climbed a wide stairway to the offices of
Piero Fanucci. They were shown into his office without ado by a
secretary whose surprised "*Di nuovo, Salvatore?*" indicated this was not
Lo Bianco's first visit to the magistrate that day.

Piero Fanucci, the public minister in charge of the investigation
and, as was customary in Italy, the man who would ultimately prosecute the case, did not look up from the work upon which he was
intent when Lo Bianco and Lynley entered. Lynley recognised this
move for what it was, and when Lo Bianco shot him a look, he lifted

one shoulder an inch. It was not necessary, this gesture told Lo Bianco, that he be welcomed to Italy with open arms.

"*Magistrato*," Lo Bianco said, "this is the Scotland Yard officer, Thomas Lynley."

Fanucci made a noise somewhere between his nose and his throat. He shuffled papers. He signed two documents. He punched a button on his phone and barked at his secretary. In a moment she entered and removed from in front of him several manila folders, replacing them with others. He began to look through them. Lo Bianco bristled.

"*Basta, Piero*," Lo Bianco said. "*Sono occupato, eh?*"

At this declaration, Piero Fanucci looked up. Clearly, he was not in a mood to care particularly about how busy the chief inspector might be. He said, "*Anch'io, Topo*," and in response Lynley saw the chief inspector's jaw set, either at being called "mouse" by the public minister or at the man's lack of cooperation. Then Fanucci directed his gaze at Lynley. He was ugly beyond measure, and he spoke without the slightest attempt to ensure that Lynley understood his Italian, which was heavily accented, dropping endings off the words in the manner of the southern part of the country. Lynley picked up the gist more by the man's tone than anything else. Either because he felt it or because he found it useful, outrage was what Fanucci projected.

"So the British police believe we need a liaison with the missing girl's family," he said, more or less. "This is absurd. We are keeping the family fully informed. We have a suspect. It is a matter of one or two more interrogations before he directs us to this child."

Lynley said, as he had said to Lo Bianco, "It's merely a matter of public pressure in England, generated by our press. The relationship between our police and our journalists is an uneasy one, Signor Fanucci. Mistakes have been made in the past: unsafe convictions, overturned imprisonments based on poor investigations, revelations of officers selling information . . . Oftentimes when the tabloids speak, the higher-ups react. That's the case here, I'm afraid."

Fanucci steepled his fingers beneath his chin. He had, Lynley saw, an adventitious finger on his right hand. It was hard not to look at, considering the position in which the public minister—doubtless deliberately—had placed them. "We have not that situation here," Fanucci declared. "Our journalists do not determine our movements."

"You're very lucky in this," Lynley said with all seriousness. "Were that only the case at home."

Fanucci scrutinised Lynley, taking in everything from the cut of his clothes to the cut of his hair to the adolescent scar that marred his upper lip. "You will, I hope, remain out of our way in this matter," he said. "We do things differently here in Italy. Here *il Pubblico Ministero* from the first involves himself in the investigation. He does not depend solely upon the police to present him with a case tied in ribbons."

Lynley didn't comment on the oddity of a system that, on the surface, appeared to have no checks and balances. He merely told the public minister that he understood how things proceeded and, if necessary, he would make certain that the parents of the missing girl also understood since they would, perforce, be used to a rather different system of law and justice.

"Good." Fanucci waved his hand in an off-with-you-then motion that gave the advantage to his sixth finger. They were being dismissed but not before he said to Lo Bianco, "What more do you have on this business of the hotels, Topo?"

"Nothing as yet," Lo Bianco said.

"Get something today," Fanucci instructed him.

"*Centamente*" was Lo Bianco's evenly spoken reply, but once again that tightening of his jaw demonstrated how he felt about being so directed. He made no further remarks until they were out of the *palazzo* and standing in the enormous piazza. Chestnut trees newly in leaf lined two sides of this, and in its centre a group of boys were elbowing each other, shouting to one another as they kicked a football in the direction of a carousel.

Lynley said to him, "Interesting gentleman, *il Pubblico Ministero*."

Lo Bianco snorted. "He is who he is."

"May I ask: What did he mean about the hotels?"

Lo Bianco shot him a look but then explained: a stranger coming to enquire about this same missing girl and her mother.

"Before her disappearance or after?" Lynley asked.

"Before." It was, Lo Bianco told him, six or eight weeks earlier. When the girl disappeared and her photo was shown in the newspapers and on posters round Lucca, a few hotels and *pensioni* reported a man who had been seeking either her or her mother. He had, Lo Bianco said, pictures of them both. The receptionists and the *pensioni* owners all agreed upon that. They all, interestingly enough, agreed upon the man himself. Indeed, they remembered him quite clearly and were able to provide Lo Bianco with an adequate description of the fellow.

"From eight weeks ago?" Lynley asked. "Why are their memories so clear?"

"Because of who it was who came to ask about this child."

"You know? They knew?"

"Not his name, of course. They did not know his name. But his description? That would not be so easy to forget. His name is Michelangelo Di Massimo, and he comes from Pisa."

"Why was someone from Pisa looking for Hadiyyah and her mother?" Lynley asked, more of himself than of Lo Bianco.

"That is a most interesting question, no?" Lo Bianco said. "I am working on an answer to it. When I have it, then it will be time to have some words with Signor Di Massimo. Until then, I know where he is." Lo Bianco shot him a look, shot another look at the *palazzo* behind them, and smiled briefly.

Lynley read in both the smile and those glances something that told him much about the man. "You haven't told Signor Fanucci this, have you?" he said. "Why not?"

"Because the *magistrato* would have him dragged from Pisa to our *questura*. He would grill him for six or seven hours, a day, three days, four. He would threaten him, not feed him, give him no water, give him no sleep, and then ask him to 'imagine, if he would' how this abduction of the child occurred. And then he would charge him based on what it was he 'imagined.'"

"Charge him with what?" Lynley asked.

"*Chissà?*" he said. Who knows. "Anything to keep the journalists supplied with details showing the case is well in hand. Despite his words to you, this is often his way." He began walking towards the police car and he said over his shoulder to Lynley, "Would you like to have a look at this man, this Michelangelo Di Massimo, *Ispettore*?"

"I would indeed," Lynley told him.

PISA
TUSCANY

Lynley hadn't known that catching a glimpse of Michelangelo Di Massimo was going to involve a lengthy drive to Pisa. When it became obvious by their entrance onto the *autostrada* that this was the case, he wondered about Lo Bianco's motives.

Lo Bianco took them to a playing field on the north side of *il centro*. There, a training session of football was going on. At least three dozen men were on the field, engaged in dribbling towards a goal.

At the edge of the field, Lo Bianco stopped the police car. He got out, as did Lynley, but he did not approach the players. Instead, he leaned against the car and removed from his jacket pocket a packet of cigarettes. He offered one to Lynley, to which Lynley demurred. He took one himself, keeping his gaze fixed on the players on the field as he lit up. He watched the action, but said nothing at all. Clearly, he was waiting for some sort of reaction from Lynley, something that would indicate that the English policeman had passed a test which had nothing at all to do with his knowledge of the rules of football.

Lynley gave his own attention to the field and the players upon it. In the way of many things Italian, on the surface the practice session appeared to be a largely disorganised affair. But as he watched, matters began to take on more clarity, especially when he noted a single individual who appeared to be attempting to direct a lot of the action.

This man was difficult not to notice. For his hair was bleached to a colour somewhere on the spectrum between yellow and orange, and it presented a stark contrast to the rest of him, upon which black hair grew like a pelt. Chest, back, arms, and legs. A five o'clock shadow that doubtless appeared at one in the afternoon. Given this and the general swarthiness of his complexion, it was hardly credible that he'd bleached the hair on his head, but this fact certainly went a long way to explain why several hotels and *pensioni* had remembered him as the person who'd come asking about Hadiyyah and her mother.

Lynley said, "Ah. I see. Michelangelo Di Massimo, no?"

"*Ecco l'uomo,*" Lo Bianco acknowledged. This said, he jerked his head at the police car. They began the journey back to Lucca.

Lynley wondered why the chief inspector had gone to this trouble of driving all the way to Pisa. Surely, a brief search on a computer at the *questura* would have produced an adequate photo of Di Massimo. That Lo Bianco had chosen not to use the Internet for this purpose suggested that there was more than one reason he wished Lynley to see Di Massimo in person and that reason had only partly to do with having an opportunity to observe the startling contrast between the hair on his body and the hair on his head.

Things became clear when their route back to Lucca did not take them at once to the *questura* but rather to the boulevard that followed the course of Lucca's great wall on the outside of it. From this *viale*, they accessed another street that led out of the town and, as it turned out, gave them access to a lane leading into the Parco Fluviale. This was a long but rather narrow community park—a place for walking, running, cycling—that followed the course of the River Serchio. Perhaps a quarter of a mile along the way, an area of gravel offered parking for no more than three cars, with two picnic tables sitting beneath great holm oaks and a tiny skateboard park just beyond. There was an open space of grass as well, largely triangular in shape and marked on its boundaries by juvenile poplars. In this small *campo*, a group of young boys round ten years old were kicking footballs towards temporary goalposts.

Here in the gravel area, Lo Bianco stopped his car. He gazed out at this makeshift practice field. Lynley followed his gaze and saw that among the children, a man stood to one side, dressed in athletic clothes, a whistle round his neck. This he blew upon and then he shouted. He stopped the action. He started it once again.

Rather than merely watch what was happening on the playing field, however, this time Lo Bianco honked the car's horn twice before opening his door. The man on the field looked in their direction. He said something to the boys and then jogged across to the police car as Lo Bianco and Lynley got out of it.

He, too, was a man whose appearance would be difficult to forget, Lynley noted. Not because of his hair, however, but because of a port wine birthmark on his face. It wasn't overly large, comprising an area of flesh from his ear into his cheek the approximate size and shape of a child's fist, but it was enough to make him remarkable, especially as the birthmark marred what otherwise would have been a startlingly handsome face.

"*Salve.*" He nodded at Lo Bianco. "*Che cos'è successo?*" He sounded anxious as he no doubt would be. The sudden appearance of the police at his football practice session would indicate to him that something had occurred.

But Lo Bianco shook his head. He introduced the man to Lynley. This was Lorenzo Mura, Lynley discovered. He recognised the name as being that of the lover of Angelina Upman.

Lo Bianco made very quick work of telling Mura that Lynley spoke Italian fairly well, which of course could have been code for "watch what you say in front of him." He went on to explain Lynley's purpose in being sent to Italy, which, apparently, he'd already revealed to Mura. "The liaison officer we have been expecting" was how he put it. "He will want to meet Signora Upman as soon as possible."

Mura didn't seem over the moon about either the prospect of Lynley's meeting Angelina or the fact of Lynley's assignment as a liaison between the parents of the child—which, of course, would include Taymullah Azhar—and the police. He gave a curt nod and stood waiting for more. When more did not come, he said in English to Lynley, "She has been not well. She remains so. You will make a care in your actions with her, yes? This man, to her he causes grief and upset."

Lynley glanced at Lo Bianco, at first thinking that "this man" referred to the chief inspector and whatever his investigation was doing to provoke even more anxiety in a woman who had already suffered her only child abducted. But when Mura continued, Lynley saw he wasn't speaking of his fellow officer but rather of Taymullah Azhar, for he said, "It was not my wish he come to Italy. He is of the past."

"Yet doubtless deeply worried about his child," Lynley said.

"*Forse*," Lorenzo Mura muttered, either in reference to Azhar's paternity or to his putative concern.

Mura said to Lo Bianco, "*Devo ritornare . . .*" with a glance afterwards at the children waiting for him on the field.

"*Vada*," Lo Bianco said and watched Mura jog back to the players.

Mura called for a ball to be kicked in his direction and expertly dribbled it in the direction of the goal while the boys tried to block him. They failed at this and the goalie also failed to block the ball as it soared into the net. Clearly, when it came to football, Lorenzo Mura knew what he was about.

Lynley also knew, then, why he and Lo Bianco had first gone to Pisa for a glimpse of Michelangelo Di Massimo. He said to the chief inspector, "Ah. I see."

"Interesting, no?" Lo Bianco said. "Our Lorenzo, he plays football for a team here in Lucca as well as gives this private coaching to boys. Me, I find this fascinating." He reached in his jacket and brought out his cigarettes again. "There's a connection, Inspector," he said as he politely offered them to Lynley. "Me, I intend to find it."

FATTORIA DI SANTA ZITA
TUSCANY

Salvatore had been prepared to dislike this British policeman. He knew that the British police held their counterparts in Italy in low esteem. There were reasons for this. They began with what was seen by many as the police failure to control the Camorra in Naples and the Mafia in Palermo. They continued, more locally, with the decades in which *il Mostro di Firenze* had managed to murder young lovers without being apprehended. They reached an international apex, however, with the absolute hash that had been made of the murder of a young British student in Perugia. Indeed, as a result the UK police saw the Mediterraneans as indolent, stupid, and eminently bribable. So when Salvatore had first been told that a British policeman would arrive and, perhaps, monitor his investigation into the disappearance of this little English girl, he had expected to feel upon himself the evaluative eyes of Inspector Lynley's constant speculation, leading to his equally constant assessments and judgement. Instead, however, Salvatore was seeing that either the man was doing no assessing or judging at the moment—which was hardly likely—or he was capable of masking any conclusions he was drawing, whether they be premature or not. Reluctantly, Salvatore liked this about Lynley. He also liked that the Englishman's questions were intelligent, his ability to listen was impressive, and his talent for putting facts together quickly was worthy of note. These three characteristics alone nearly made Salvatore forgive the UK officer for being many centimetres taller than he and dressing in an elegantly rumpled and casual manner that suggested mounds of money and self-confidence.

When they left the *calcio* practice, they also left the immediate environs of Lucca, heading in the direction of the nearby hills. It was not a long drive to reach the ancient summer home of the Mura family, for the Tuscan hills began to undulate across the landscape not far north of the Parco Fluviale. Salvatore drove them up into these hills. At this time of year, the land was lush with midspring's abundant vegetation. Trees bore new leaves the colour of limes, and along the verges wildflowers grew.

The road shot in and out of the sunlight of late afternoon. When they had followed it for some nine kilometres, they reached the dirt lane into Fattoria di Santa Zita, marked by a sign that announced the place and also showed upon it the various functions of the farm by means of depictions of grapes, olive branches hung with fruit, and both a donkey and a cow looking more like those who'd watched over the birth of Jesus than the everyday farm animals that were raised on the Mura land.

Salvatore glanced at Lynley as they rumbled down the lane towards the farm buildings whose terracotta roofs were visible through the trees. He could see the Englishman taking in the environment and evaluating it.

He said, "The Muras, *Ispettore*, they are an ancient family here in Lucca. They were merchants of silk, very rich, and this place in the hills was their summer home. It has been theirs—the summer home of the Mura family—for . . . I would say three hundred years, perhaps?

The older brother of Lorenzo did not wish to have it pass to him. He lives in Milano and practises psychiatry there and for him this place was a burden. The sister of Lorenzo lives within the city wall of Lucca and she, too, found the old place a burden. So it fell to Lorenzo to keep it, to sell it, or to make something of it . . ." Salvatore indicated the land and its emerging buildings. "You will see," he said. "I think it is not so much different in your own country with these ancient places."

They swung past a barn that Lorenzo had converted into a winery and tasting room. Here, he bottled both the complex Chianti and the simpler Sangiovese for which the *fattoria* was known. Beyond it, a farmhouse was undergoing reconstruction for its future as an accommodation for travellers interested in staying in an *agriturismo*. And then, beyond this, two rusting gates stood open in an enormous and wildly overgrown hedge. Salvatore drove through these gates, a route that took them up to the villa that had long been part of the Mura family's history. This building, too, was undergoing work. Scaffolding was being constructed on its sides.

He allowed Lynley a moment to take the villa in, idling the police car on the gravel driveway that swept up to the structure. It was an impressive sight, especially if one did not look too closely at all the spots in which the poor place was about to crumble into pieces. Two sets of stairs—perfectly proportioned on the front of the building—led up to a loggia where a jumble of outdoor furniture stood scattered about as if someone kept moving it to follow the sunlight. A door—its panels painted in faded depictions of the *cinghiali* that roamed the hills—was set at the precise centre of the loggia, and on either side of it old sculptures depicted the seasons in human form, with *Inverno*, unfortunately, having lost his poor head and the basket of flowers carried by *Primavera* having been chopped in half at some time in the past. There were three floors to the villa and a cellar as well, and there were rows of windows, all of them shuttered.

After a moment of looking all this over, Inspector Lynley nodded. He glanced at Salvatore and said, "As you said, in England, we have places not unlike this: old distinguished homes belonging to old, distinguished families. They are at once a burden and a privilege. It is easy to understand why Signor Mura would wish to save this place."

Salvatore took the inspector at his word. He himself knew there were great houses aplenty in Lynley's country. Whether Lynley himself actually understood the passion of the Italians for their family homes . . . ? That was another matter, of course.

He drove them along the lawn on the gravel that encircled it. He parked near the steps up to the first floor of the place. Between these two sets of stairs, wisteria grew abundantly on the front of the building, nearly hiding another doorway, this one leading into the *piano terra* of the home. As they got out of the car, this smaller doorway opened, and Angelina Upman came out from what Salvatore knew was the part of the house where the kitchen and the other quotidian rooms were situated. She looked far worse than she had looked earlier that day. Lorenzo had not been exaggerating the truth of the matter. She was very thin, and beneath her eyes the flesh looked bruised.

At once, she became emotional at the sight of the English policeman. Her eyes altered from dull to luminous with tears. She said in English, "Thank you, thank you for coming, Inspector Lynley." To Salvatore she said in Italian, "I must speak English with this man, for my own Italian is not quite . . . It will be easier for me. You understand why I must speak English, Chief Inspector?"

"*Certo*," Salvatore said. His own English was somewhat serviceable, as she knew. If they spoke slowly, he would be able to follow what they said.

"*Grazie*," she said to him. "Please come inside."

So they entered into the bowels of the place where the light was dim and the atmosphere sombre. It was odd to Salvatore that she had chosen to lead them here. The *soggiorno* on the *primo piano* would have been more pleasant. The loggia outside also would have been welcoming. But she seemed to prefer the darkness and the shadows, which would make her less easy to read, of course.

Another interesting detail, Salvatore thought. Indeed, in this matter of the missing child, there were interesting details aplenty.

FATTORIA DI SANTA ZITA
TUSCANY

Angelina took them into a cavernous kitchen within the villa, a room that was hovering between centuries. It was outfitted with both the conveniences of a cooker and refrigerator and the curiosities of an enormous wood-burning oven, a vast fireplace, and a large stone sink in which one could bathe two Alsatians simultaneously. At the room's centre, a scarred table held a pile of newspapers, magazines, daily crockery, and faded kitchen linens, and at this table Lynley and Lo Bianco sat while Angelina brought to them a bottle of the wine produced there on the farm, along with cheese, fruit, Italian meats, and some freshly baked bread. She poured them each a glass of Chianti but had none herself, choosing water instead.

When she sat, she took up one of the linen table napkins and held it like a form of talisman. She repeated what she had said upon greeting Lynley: "Thank you so much for coming, Inspector."

"It's mostly Barbara's doing," Lynley told her. "Frankly, she may have gone a bit too far this time to get her way in matters, but that remains to be seen. Hadiyyah's quite important to her."

Angelina pressed her lips together for a moment. "I did a terrible thing. I know that. But what I can't accept is that this—what's happened to Hadiyyah—is to be my punishment. Because if that's the case . . ." Her fingers tightened on the piece of linen she held.

Lo Bianco made a noise in his throat that seemed to indicate his understanding of the concept: that there was always a connection between the forms of temporal punishment one suffered and the crimes of the heart one committed against other people. To Lynley's way of thinking, this was a less than useful way of looking at what had happened.

He said, "I'd try not to think like that. It's normal—believe me, I do understand—but it's not helpful." He smiled at her kindly and added, " 'That way madness lies' is a good way to put it. Madness—clouded thinking, if you will—isn't useful to anyone just now."

"It's been a week," she said. "Can you tell me what it means that it's been a week without a sign or a word? There's been no request for a ransom and Renzo's family would pay. I know they would. And people *are* kidnapped for ransoms in this country. All over the world they're kidnapped for ransoms. Aren't they? Isn't it true? I've been trying to discover how many children are kidnapped in Italy every year. See—" Here she dug into the pile of newspapers and magazines and brought out information she'd printed from the Internet. "I've been looking and searching and trying to see how long it usually is before kidnappers . . . before there's something to tell the parents . . ." She fell into silence. In this silence, tears tracked down her cheeks.

Lynley glanced at Lo Bianco. As police they both knew that Angelina was grasping at straws, that in this day kidnapping for ransom was far less likely than kidnapping for sale, for sex, for sick recreational murder, especially when it came to the disappearance of a child. Lo Bianco's fingers rose and fell against the base of his wineglass. It was a gesture saying, Tell her what you will at this point as it is important only to give her a moment's peace of mind.

"I wouldn't disagree," Lynley told her carefully. "But the more important point now is to go back and consider what happened on the day she disappeared: where you were, where Signor Mura was, where Hadiyyah was, who was around her, who might have seen something but as of yet not come forward because they're not even aware that they did see something . . ."

"We were all doing what we always do," Angelina murmured numbly.

"Which is, you see, an important detail," Lynley reassured her. "It tells the police that, if you're creatures of habit, someone could have seen this over time and planned how and where to abduct her. It tells the police that, perhaps, this was no crime of opportunity but something considered from every angle. It also explains why no one might have noticed anything because what would have been taken into account by Hadiyyah's abductor would be exactly that: how to carry this child off without anyone noticing."

Angelina pressed the table napkin beneath her eyes. She nodded and said, "I see that. I do," and she rapidly told Lynley how they'd organised the day on which Hadiyyah had disappeared: She had gone to her yoga class, Lorenzo and Hadiyyah had gone into the street

market, Hadiyyah had skipped ahead as always to look at the colourful stalls and eventually to listen to the accordion player, and it was
there that they all would meet to walk to the home of Lorenzo's sister
for lunch. They did this without variation on their market day in
Lucca. Anyone who knew them—or who watched them and waited
for an opportunity—would have learned this.

Lynley nodded. He'd heard most of this already from Lo Bianco,
but he could see that it gave Angelina a sense of hope being kept alive
to give him the information. Across the table from him, Lo Bianco
listened to this repetition of details with apparent patience. When
Angelina was finished, he said to Lynley, "*Con permesso . . . ?*" and
leaned forward to ask a few questions of his own. He did so in somewhat battered English.

"I ask a question not to ask before, signora. How was Hadiyyah
with Signor Mura? All this time away from her papà. How was she
with your lover?"

"She was fine with Lorenzo," Angelina said. "She likes Lorenzo."

"This you are certain?" Lo Bianco said.

"Of course I am," Angelina told him. "Making certain . . . It was
one of the reasons . . ." She gave a glance to Lynley, then looked back
at Lo Bianco. "That's one of the reasons my sister created the emails.
I thought if Hadiyyah heard from Hari, if she thought at first that this
was just a visit we were making to Italy, if over time she came to
believe her father wasn't going to come for her . . ."

"Emails?" Lynley asked.

Lo Bianco quickly explained in Italian: that Angelina's sister had
manufactured emails putatively from the little girl's father. In these
he promised to come to Italy. In these he broke those promises.

"Was she able to access his email account in some way?" Lynley
asked.

"She created a new account for him, through a friend of hers at
University College," Angelina told him. "I told my sister what to say
in the emails. She said it." Angelina turned to Lo Bianco. "So Hadiyyah had no reason to dislike Lorenzo, to think that he was going to
stand in place of her father and to realise from this that her life was
permanently altered. I made sure of that."

"Still, there could be . . . It could be the daughter and Signor Mura . . ." Lo Bianco seemed to search for the word.

"Friction?" Lynley said. "There might have been friction between them?"

"There was no friction," Angelina said. "There is no friction."

"And Signor Mura, he likes your Hadiyyah?"

Angelina's jaw loosened. If she could have gone paler than she already was, she would have done so. Lynley could see her taking in Lo Bianco's question and drawing a conclusion from it. She said, "Renzo loves Hadiyyah. He would do nothing to harm her, if that's what you're thinking. Everything he's done, everything I've done, it's all been *because* of Hadiyyah. I wanted her back, I was so unhappy, I'd left Hari to be with Renzo here but I couldn't do it without Hadiyyah, so I returned to Hari for those few months and waited and waited and Lorenzo waited, and it was all for Hadiyyah, because of Hadiyyah, so you can't say Lorenzo . . ."

Lo Bianco produced the Italian version of tsk, tsk, tsk. Lynley tried to follow Angelina's story. She'd woven, it seemed, quite a web of deceit to engineer her new life in Italy. This brought up a point of interest for him, one that might have implications from the past that reached into the present.

"When did you meet Signor Mura?" he asked her. "How did you meet him?"

She'd met him in London, she said. She'd been without an umbrella on a day with sudden rain, so she'd ducked for protection into Starbucks.

Lo Bianco made a noise of moderate disgust at this, and Lynley glanced at him. It was Starbucks, however, that was apparently garnering the Italian man's disapproval and not the fact of Angelina Upman's meeting someone inside the place.

The coffee house was crowded with other people having the same idea. Angelina purchased a cappuccino for herself and was drinking it on her feet by the window when Lorenzo entered with the same idea in mind: to get out of the rain. They began to chat, as people sometimes do, she explained. He'd come to London for three days' holiday and the weather was maddening to him. In Tuscany at this time of year, he said, the sun is out, the days are warm, the flowers are blooming . . . You should come to Tuscany and see for yourself, he told her.

She could see that he looked for a wedding ring on her in that casual way that unattached people sometimes do when they meet one another. She did the same to him. She didn't tell him about Azhar, about Hadiyyah, or about . . . other things. At the end of their time in the Starbucks when the rain had ceased, he handed her his card and said that if she ever came to Tuscany, she was to ring him and he would show her its beauties. And so, eventually, that was what she did. After a row with Hari . . . another row with Hari . . . always the nighttime rows with Hari, spoken in fierce whispers so that Hadiyyah wouldn't know there were difficulties between her mother and father . . .

" 'Other things'?" was Lynley's question at the end of her story. In his peripheral vision, he saw Lo Bianco's sharp nod of approval.

"What?" she asked.

"You said that at that first meeting you didn't tell Signor Mura about Hadiyyah, Azhar, or other things. I'm wondering what those other things were?"

Clearly, she didn't want to go further, as her gaze moved away from Lynley and dropped to the table and the computer printouts upon it. She made a poor show of inauthentic concentration upon Lynley's question. He finally said to her, "Every detail *is* important, you know," and waited in silence. Lo Bianco did likewise. Water dripped in the enormous kitchen sink, and a clock ticked loudly. And she finally spoke.

"At that time, I didn't tell Lorenzo about my lover," she said.

Lo Bianco released a nearly silent whistle of air. Lynley glanced at him. *Le donne, le donne,* his expression said. *Le cose che fanno.*

"D'you mean another man?" Lynley clarified. "Other than Azhar."

Yes, she said. One of the teachers at the dancing school where she took classes. A choreographer and an instructor. At the time of her meeting Lorenzo Mura, this man had been her lover for some years. When she left Azhar to take up life with Lorenzo, she also left this man.

"His name?" Lynley asked.

"He's in London, Inspector Lynley. He's not Italian. He doesn't know Italy. He doesn't know where I am. I simply . . . I mean I should have told him something. I should have told him anything. But I simply . . . stopped seeing him."

"That wouldn't have prevented him from trying to find you," Lynley pointed out. "After several years as your lover—"

"It wasn't serious," she said hastily. "It was fun, a release, excitement. Between us, there was never any plan to be together permanently."

"In your head," Lo Bianco pointed out. "*Ma forse . . .*" This was true. Perhaps in the head of her lover an entirely different idea existed. "He was married?"

"Yes. So he wouldn't have expected me to hang about in his life and when I left him—"

"It works not in that way," Lo Bianco told her. "There are men, for them marriage equals not a thing."

"I do need his name, Angelina," Lynley told her. "The chief inspector's right. While your previous lover could be completely uninvolved with what's happened here in Italy, the fact of him in your life means that he needs to be eliminated from the enquiry. If he's still in London, Barbara can handle this. But it has to be done."

"Esteban Castro," she finally said.

"He's from Spain?"

"Mexico City," she said. "His wife is English. Another dancer."

"You were also . . ." Lo Bianco searched for the word, but Lynley was fairly certain where he was heading, so he cut in, saying, "You were acquainted with her?"

Angelina dropped her gaze again. "She was a friend."

Before either Lynley or Lo Bianco could comment on these facts or ask further questions, Lorenzo Mura arrived at Fattoria di Santa Zita and entered as the others had done: through the ground-floor door that brought him along the dark passage and into the kitchen. He dropped an athletic bag on the tiles and came to the table. He kissed Angelina and asked what was going on among them. Clearly, he was fully capable of reading the atmosphere in the room. "*Che cos'è successo?*" he demanded.

Neither of the detectives spoke. It was, Lynley felt, for Angelina to tell her current lover—or not to tell him—of the subject they'd been discussing. She said to them, "Lorenzo knows about Esteban Castro. We have no secrets from each other."

Lynley doubted that. Everyone had secrets. He was beginning to conclude that Angelina's had deposited her into the position she occupied at the moment: mother of a missing child. He said, "And Taymullah Azhar?"

"What about Hari?" she asked.

"Sometimes relationships are open," Lynley said. "Did he know about your other lover?"

"Please don't tell Hari," she said quickly.

With a grunt, Lorenzo pulled a chair from the table. He sat, grabbed a glass, and poured himself some wine. He tossed it back—no thoughtful sipping and evaluating here—and cut a wedge of cheese and a hunk of bread. He said fiercely, "Why do you protect this man?"

"Because I've dropped an explosive into his life and that's *enough*. I won't have him hurt more."

"*Merda.*" Lorenzo shook his head. "This makes no sense, this . . . this care you have for this man."

"We have a child together," Angelina said. "When you have a child with someone, it changes things between you. That's how things are."

"*Così dici.*" Mura's voice was gentler when he said this, but still he didn't appear to be convinced that having had a child by Taymullah Azhar was significant enough a reason for Angelina to wish not to devastate the man further. And perhaps, Lynley thought, it was not enough reason. Perhaps had Azhar ended his marriage instead of merely leaving his wife, things would have been much different for Angelina Upman. And, perhaps, Lorenzo Mura knew this. No matter the situation at present or in the future, a connection existed and would always exist between Angelina and the Pakistani man. And Mura would have to come to terms with that.

LUCCA
TUSCANY

It was later than usual when Salvatore made his evening climb to the top of the tower. Mamma had had what she'd decided was an altercation in the *macelleria* while doing her shopping for this night's dinner, and that altercation—apparently with a tourist woman who did not understand that when Signora Lo Bianco entered the shop, everyone else stepped back out of respect for her age—had to be discussed from every angle.

"*Sì, sì,*" Salvatore murmured throughout this recitation of the woes of Mamma's day. He shook his head and looked appropriately outraged, and at the first opportunity, he climbed to the roof to enjoy his nightly *caffè corretto*, the sight of evening falling upon his city with its citizens taking their daily *passeggiata* arm in arm in the streets, and, most important, the silence that went with all of this, high above everything.

The silence did not last long, however. Into it, his mobile phone rang. He took it from his pocket, saw the caller, and cursed. If this involved another drive to Barga, he would refuse.

"So?" the *magistrato* barked at Salvatore's *pronto*. "*Mi dica, Topo.*"

Salvatore knew what Fanucci wished to be told: everything that had occurred with this police detective from England. He told the public minister what he felt was sufficient to satisfy him. He added the new intriguing detail of Signora Upman's additional lover in London: Esteban Castro. She either liked them foreign or she liked them hot-blooded, he told Fanucci.

"*Puttana*" was Fanucci's evaluation of her.

Well, times have changed, was what Salvatore wanted to say to Fanucci. Women were not necessarily loose because they took lovers. But, indeed, were he to say this to Fanucci, the truth was that he'd be doing so only to arouse the man's ire. For he himself did not believe that it was the way of the world today for women to string along more than one lover at a time, married or otherwise. That Angelina Upman, perhaps, made a habit of doing so was a curious new bit of information about her. Salvatore was more than willing to share this information with Fanucci because, if nothing else, it spared him from having to go in the direction of Michelangelo Di Massimo and his bleached yellow hair.

"So, he chases her? This Esteban Castro?" Fanucci said. "He follows her to Lucca. He plans his revenge. She leaves him for another and he does not accept this and he plans how to show her suffering equal to what she has caused him, *vero?*"

The idea was ludicrous, but what difference did that make? At least it wasn't additional nonsense about the Casparia youth. Salvatore murmured, "*Forse, forse, Piero.*" But they must move with caution, he said. They would see soon enough because this English detective would phone London and see about tracking down this lover of Angelina Upman. He would be useful that way, Ispettore Lynley.

There was silence as Fanucci evaluated this. Salvatore heard in the background someone speaking to Fanucci. A woman's voice. It would not be his wife but rather the long-suffering housekeeper. *Vai*, Fanucci barked at her, his way of lovingly telling her that her performance between the sheets of his bed would not be necessary on this evening.

Then, into the phone, the *magistrato* announced the main reason for his call to Salvatore: a special report for the *telegiornale* had been arranged. He, Fanucci, had made these arrangements. They would film this report at the home of the missing girl's mother, and it would end with an appeal from this child's parents: We love our precious little one and we want her back. Please, please return her to us.

If the mamma wept, that would be useful, Fanucci told him. Television cameras liked weeping women in situations when children went missing, no?

And when would this television filming occur? Salvatore enquired.

Two days hence, Fanucci told him. He himself and not Salvatore would do the speaking for the Italian police.

"*Certo, certo,*" Salvatore murmured with a sly smile at Fanucci's eternal self-importance. The presence on television screens throughout Italy of Piero Fanucci would, of course, strike fear into the hearts of all malefactors.

23 APRIL

Mitchell Corsico had wasted no time. He had a reputation as a reporter who didn't let grass grow, and this alacrity, combined with a nose for scandal, did not desert him just because Barbara had thwarted him at the secondary comprehensive that Taymullah Azhar's son Sayyid attended. When Barbara caught sight of the front page of *The Source* the next day, she saw that out of what Corsico had witnessed in front of Sayyid's school he had managed to create a stop-the-presses moment. *Missing Girl Has Love Rat Dad* was the headline that announced the sordid tale. Beneath this, several pictures of the deserted family offered evidence to accompany the story.

Barbara didn't see red when her gaze fell upon this latest edition of *The Source*. She saw black: in the form of her vision going absolutely dark for a moment so that, in front of her local newsagent, she had a terrible instant of thinking she might well faint directly onto the chewing gum–studded pavement of Chalk Farm Road. How Corsico had managed to get his hands on the material displayed on the front page of the tabloid hovered between mystery and miracle to her. What she reckoned, though, was that the reporter had followed Azhar's family directly to their home and employed one of several strong-arm techniques to get someone to talk.

These were easy enough for Barbara to envision: Corsico having a few words with neighbours and gathering information that way; Corsico shoving his card through the post slot in the door of Nafeeza's home, telling her through this slender opening that it was a case of talk-to-me-or-let-your-neighbours-do-the-talking-for-you. He could even have found a friend of Sayyid and in this way got a message to the boy: Meet me at the pub the park the local cinema the corner grocery the railway station the bus stop. We can talk there. Here's your chance to tell the full story. At the end of the day, what did it matter how he had put his sticky hands on the information? For the nasty tale was in the tabloid now, and the nasty tale named names.

Barbara rang Corsico. "What the bloody hell are you up to?" she demanded without preamble.

He didn't enquire who was ringing his mobile. Obviously, he knew because his reply was "I thought this is what you wanted, Sergeant."

"Do *not* use my rank on the phone," she hissed. "Where the hell are you?"

"In bed, actually. Having a lie-in. And what's the problem? Don't want anyone to know that you and I are each other's new best friend?"

Barbara let that one go. "The story isn't about Azhar. The story is about the Italian police and how they're handling—or not handling or refusing to handle or *whatever*—Hadiyyah's disappearance. It was about the Met not sending an officer to assist. Then it was supposed to be about the Met sending a certain, particular, you-want-a-story-on-him officer over to assist. And *then* it was about you getting your fat arse over to Italy to keep the pressure on. I gave you all the details you needed and all the bloody hell you had to do was to use them in a story and to follow them—and not something else, mind you—to the next story. You knew this, Mitchell."

He yawned loudly. Barbara wanted to dive into her mobile and beam herself into the louse's bedroom, all the better to smack him silly. He said, "What I *knew*, as you put, is that you wanted a story. What I *know* is that you've got your story. Several, in fact, with more on the way. I've got some interesting pictures of yesterday's scuffle with . . . I take it that was Granddad?"

"You need to back off," she told him, although the idea of pictures made her momentarily dizzy. "You need to sodding back off, Mitchell. These people in Ilford are *not* the story. A missing English girl in Italy is. There's plenty of information on that and I'll get it to you as it comes in and in the bloody meantime—"

"Uh, *Sergeant* . . . ?" Corsico cut in. "You don't tell me what the story is. You don't tell me where the story is. I follow information wherever it leads and just now the information is leading to a house in Ilford and a very unhappy teenage boy."

So he *had* got to Sayyid, Barbara thought bitterly. Who bloody knew where he'd go next?

"You're using that kid to—"

"He needed to vent. I let him vent. I needed a story. He gave me a story. This is a reciprocal relationship Sayyid and I have. Mutually beneficial. Just like yours and mine."

"You and I have no relationship."

"But we do. And it's growing every day."

Barbara felt someone tapping skeletal fingers on her spine. "Exactly what is that supposed to mean?"

"For now it means I'm following a story. You might not love the direction it's heading in. You might want to direct its course a bit. You might need to give me more information in order to do that and when you give me that information—"

"*If*, not when."

"*When*," he repeated, "you give me that information, I'll be happy to take a look at it or have a listen to it and I'll decide if it constitutes a train I can climb on. That's how it works."

"How it works—" she began, but he cut in.

"You don't get to decide that, Barb. At first you did, but now you don't. Like I said, our relationship is growing. Changing. Developing. This could be a marriage made in heaven. If we both play our cards right," he added.

The skeletal fingers felt as if they would close on her neck and choke off her breath. She said, "Watch yourself, Mitchell. Because I swear to God, if you're threatening me, you're going to be bloody sorry about it."

"Threatening you?" Corsico laughed with a complete lack of humour. "That would *never* happen, Barb." Then he rang off, leaving Barbara standing in Chalk Farm Road with a copy of *The Source*'s latest edition in one hand, her mobile phone in the other, cars whizzing by as drivers made their way to work, and pedestrians pushing past her as they made their way to the Underground station.

She knew she ought to join the latter group. She had barely enough time to get to work in order to avoid the baleful eye and meticulous note-taking of DI John Stewart. But she needed an immediate injection of caffeine and pastry into her body in order to be able to cope— let alone think—so she decided that DI Stewart and the assignment he would doubtless give her that day—more transcription please, Sergeant, as we're having *such* a time keeping up with the action reports coming in every hour—would have to wait. She ducked into a recently opened establishment called Cuppa Joe Etc. She purchased a latte and an et cetera, which in this case was a chocolate croissant. God knew she was owed both, after the conversation with Corsico.

When her mobile chimed the opening lines of "Peggy Sue" two bites into the chocolate croissant and three gulps of latte later, Barbara hoped it was Corsico having a change of mind rather than a change of heart since the bloke apparently didn't own a heart. But it turned out to be Lynley. Barbara's insides did flip-flops at the possibilities attendant to a phone call from him.

She answered with, "Good news?"

"I'm afraid not."

"Oh God. No."

"No, no," Lynley said hastily. "Neither good nor bad news. Just some intriguing information that wants checking out."

He told her of his meeting with Azhar and his subsequent meeting with Angelina Upman. He told her of the existence of yet another married lover of Angelina's—in addition to Azhar, this one also in London—being left for Lorenzo Mura.

"D'you mean she was having it off with this bloke while she and Azhar . . . I mean after she had Hadiyyah by Azhar and . . . I mean once Azhar had left his wife . . . I mean . . . Hell, I don't bloody know what I mean."

Yes, Lynley said to it all. This man was a fellow dancer and choreographer in London with whom Angelina had been involved at the time she met Lorenzo Mura. And at *that* time, she also was the lover of Azhar and the mother of his child. The bloke was called Esteban Castro, and according to Angelina Upman, she merely disappeared from his life, giving him no word why. One day she was there in his bed, the next day she was gone, having left him—and Azhar—for Mura. His wife was a friend of hers as well. So both of these people would need to be checked out. For perhaps during the brief four months of Angelina's putative return to Azhar, she'd taken up with Castro again as well, only to leave him another time.

"But Barbara," Lynley told her, "this must be done on your own time, not on the Met's time."

"But the guv'll let me get onto this if you ask her, won't she?" Barbara said. After all, Lynley and Isabelle Ardery hadn't parted enemies from their own affair. They were both professionals, after all. DI Lynley had been sent to Italy on a case. If he rang and asked her in his most pear-shaped of I've-gone-to-Eton tones—

"I did ring her," he said. "I asked her if she might lend me you to look into this end of things in London. She won't allow it, Barbara."

"Because you asked for me," Barbara said bitterly. " 'F you'd asked for Winston, she'd be all over herself to cooperate. We both know that."

"We didn't go in that direction," he said. "I could have asked for Winston but I assumed you'd prefer to do this, no matter when it had to be done."

There was truth in that. Barbara knew she ought to be grateful to Lynley for having recognised how important it was to her to be kept in the loop of what was going on. So she said, "I s'pose. Thanks, sir."

He said wryly, "Don't overwhelm me with your gratitude, Sergeant. I'm not certain I could bear it."

She had to smile. "I'm tap-dancing on the tabletop here. If you could only see."

"Where are you?"

She told him.

"You're going to be late into work," he said. "Barbara, at some point you have to stop giving Isabelle ammunition."

"That's what Winston's been saying, more or less."

"And he's correct. Having a professional death wish isn't the best of ideas."

"Right," she said. "Whatever. Point taken. Anything else?" She was about to ask him how things were going in the direction of Daidre Trahair, but she knew there was little point in this since Lynley wouldn't tell her. There were lines between them that nothing on earth could make the bloke cross.

"There is," he said. "Bathsheba Ward." He went on to tell her about the emails that Bathsheba had apparently written at the request of her twin sister, emails purportedly from Taymullah Azhar from University College to his daughter in Italy.

"That bloody cow lied to me!" Barbara cried in outrage. "She knew all along where Angelina was!"

"It appears that way," Lynley told her. "So there's a chance she might know something more about what's going on now."

Barbara considered this but she couldn't come up with a way that Bathsheba Ward might be involved in Hadiyyah's disappearance, much less a reason for it. Unless Angelina herself was involved.

She said, "How's Angelina coping, then?"

"Distraught, as you might imagine. Not well physically either, it seems."

"What about Azhar?"

"Equally so, although far more self-contained."

"That sounds like him. I wonder how he's holding it together. He's been going through hell since last November."

Lynley told her what the Pakistani man was doing with the hand-bills of his daughter throughout the town and into the villages that surrounded it. "I think it's giving him a purpose, more than anything else," Lynley concluded. "To have to sit and wait while your child is missing . . . That's intolerable for any parent."

"Yes. Well. Intolerable describes how it's been for Azhar."

"As to that . . ." Lynley hesitated on his end of the conversation.

"What?" Barbara asked, feeling trepidation.

"I know you're close to him but I do have to ask this. Do we know where he was when Hadiyyah disappeared?"

"At a conference in Berlin."

"Are we certain of that?"

"Bloody hell, sir, you can't think—"

"Barbara. Just as everything having to do with Angelina wants looking into, so does everything having to do with Azhar. And with everyone else remotely connected to what's going on here, so obviously that means Bathsheba Ward as well. Because something *is* going on here, Barbara. A child doesn't disappear from the middle of a crowded marketplace with no one knowing a thing about it, with no one seeing anything unusual, with no one—"

"All right, all right," Barbara said, and she told him about Dwayne Doughty in Bow and to what end she was employing him. They were in the process of eliminating Azhar as a suspect in his daughter's disappearance. She'd put him onto Esteban Castro next, the man's wife, and Bathsheba Ward as well, but only if she couldn't get to these others on her own because she vastly preferred to have her own fingers on the pulse of an enquiry and not be relying on someone else's.

"Sometimes we have to rely on others" was Lynley's concluding remark.

Barbara wanted to scoff, but she didn't. The fact was that of all the officers whom she knew at the Met, relying on others was a characteristic that applied to Lynley least of all.

VICTORIA
LONDON

Barbara passed the day being at the completely cooperative, borderline unctuous, and therefore highly suspect beck and call of DI John Stewart and making sure that Superintendent Ardery saw her obediently, if maddeningly, entering the reports of other officers into the Met's computer system as if she were a civilian typist and not what she was: a trained officer of the police. She noted that, once or twice, Isabelle Ardery paused in passing from one area to another: observing her, observing Stewart, narrowing her eyes, and frowning as if she disapproved of the cut of Barbara's hair, which, of course, she did.

Barbara took a few moments here and there to do a little exploring via the World Wide Web. She discovered the whereabouts of Esteban Castro, currently dancing in a West End revival of *Fiddler on the Roof*—was there dancing in *Fiddler on the Roof*? she wondered—as well as teaching dance classes at his own studio in the company of his wife. He was dark-skinned, brooding, smouldering, cropped of hair, heavy-lidded of eye. His publicity pictures showed him in various dancing guises, various poses, and various costumes. He seemed to have the posture and the musculature that went with ballet and the loose body attitude that went with jazz and modern dance. Looking at his pictures, Barbara could see his appeal to a woman looking for excitement . . . or whatever Angelina Upman had been looking for because who the hell knew? She was turning out to be quite the cipher.

There were references to Esteban's wife, so Barbara followed the trail to her. Another dancer, she saw. Royal Ballet. Not within shouting distance of prima ballerina but someone had to dance in the chorus, no? One couldn't exactly have the numero uno swan without the rest of the flock milling round in the back wondering what all the hoo-ha with the hunter was about. She was called Dahlia Rourke— what the hell kind of name was Dahlia? Barbara wondered—and she was pretty in the rather severe and bony way that went with ballet: all cheekbones, scarily visible collar bones, thin wrists, and very little in the hips, all the better to be hoisted around by some bloke in need of a more serious codpiece. She'd be on the scrawny side when it came to playing at the two-backed beast, so perhaps this had driven poor smouldering Esteban into the arms of Angelina. Except, Barbara thought, Angelina herself would probably be no cushion of comfort when it came to the plunge and groan of the clutch and grope. Perhaps Esteban merely liked them skeletal.

She jotted a few notes and printed a few pictures. She also did some additional looking into Bathsheba Ward. She had a feeling that garnering the slippery cow's cooperation in anything having to do with Hadiyyah, Angelina, and Azhar was going to be a business requiring careful planning and more than a little arm twisting. But in the case of Bathsheba, the arm twisting was going to have to be subtle or it was going to have to threaten her business.

Barbara was considering all of the information she'd gathered when her mobile made its timeless declaration of love to Peggy Sue. It was Dwayne Doughty, reporting back on his investigation into the whereabouts of Taymullah Azhar when Hadiyyah had been snatched from the *mercato* in Lucca.

"Got you on speaker, if you don't mind," Doughty told her. "Em's here as well." He went on to tell her that every detail was on the up-and-up. Azhar had indeed been in Berlin. He had indeed attended the conference. He sat in on talks and panel discussions, and he presented two papers as well. The only way he could have also got to Italy and snatched his daughter would have been to have the ability to be in two places at once or to have an identical twin that no one knew about. This last bit was of the ha-ha-ha-we-know-how-unlikely-that-scenario-is variety. But it did bring into the picture something that Barbara wanted to make sure Dwayne Doughty knew.

"Talking of identical twins," she said. She gave him the new information about Bathsheba Ward: that she'd apparently known all along where her sister was, that she'd written emails to Hadiyyah in the guise of her father.

"That explains a few minor details we've dug up at our end," Doughty said. "It seems our Bathsheba trotted off to *bell'Italia* herself last November round the same time the fair Angelina did her runner. Fascinating point, if you ask me."

"Got it in a bucket," Barbara told him. For if, from the first, Bathsheba had been part of Angelina's planned escape from London, how terribly difficult would it have been for Angelina to use her sister's passport for her travel, thereby covering the tracks of her own movements as she made her escape?

"Our Bathsheba's cage needs a bit of rattling," Doughty said. "The question is, dear Sergeant, which of us is best able to do it?"

BOW

LONDON

When Dwayne Doughty rang off, he waited for Em Cass's inevitable commentary, which was not long in coming. They were in her office—the better to record the conversation with Sergeant Havers—and Em removed her earphones after checking the quality of the recording. She set them on the table with its bank of monitors. Today she was wearing a fawn-coloured man's three-piece suit cut perfectly to fit her. She complemented it with two-toned shoes—tan and navy—which would have looked all wrong had she not chosen a necktie to balance the ensemble. She dressed like a man better than most men did, Doughty had to admit. No bloke on earth could beat Em Cass in a dinner jacket, that was certain.

She said to him, "We shouldn't've got involved in this mess, Dwayne. You know it, I know it, and every day we know it better. Soon's I saw her with the professor, soon's I reckoned she was a cop, soon's I traced her to the Met . . ."

"Hush," Dwayne told her. "Things are in motion and other things are being handled."

As if in demonstration of this latter fact, a knock sounded on the door and it opened. Bryan Smythe slipped into Em Cass's office. Doughty saw Em roll her desk chair away from the monitors as if this would distance her from the computer wizard. Before he could welcome the sex-starved bloke, Em said, "You said you'd warn me, Dwayne."

"The situation's slightly altered," Doughty said. "I think you've been making that very point." And to Bryan with a glance at his watch, "You're early. And we're meant to be meeting in my office, not here."

Bryan blushed unattractively. He was not, alas, a being whose flesh took on rosy hues with any degree of complement to the rest of him. "Knocked over there," he said in apparent reference to Doughty's own office. "Heard you over here so . . ."

"You should've waited over there," Em told him.

Bryan looked at her. "I wouldn't've seen you, then," he said frankly.

Doughty groaned. The man knew nothing about playing women, about the chat, about anything to do with males and females and how they actually managed to end up in a horizontal position—or, in Em's case, in any position—exchanging bodily fluids with each other. Doughty did wish that Em Cass would give the poor sod one decent go, though. A mercy bonk wouldn't kill her, and it might allow Bryan to see that a chasm always existed between one's dreams and the reality of those dreams coming true.

"And," Bryan went on, "wasn't the point *not* to use the phones from now on?"

"We all need disposable mobiles, then," Emily said shortly. "Use once, toss it, buy another. That way this sort of encounter"—she made the words equate to *this visitation of the plague*—"wouldn't need to happen."

"Let's not get hasty," Doughty said. "We're not rolling in dosh here, Emily. We can't be dashing out to buy disposable mobiles right and left."

"Yes, we can. Bill it to that slag from the Met." Em swung round in her chair, her back to them. She pretended to tie her shoe.

Doughty hazarded an evaluative look at Bryan. The young man wasn't a permanent employee and they needed his amazing expertise. It was one thing for Emily Cass not to want to bed him. He couldn't blame her for that. But to insult and estrange him to a degree that he ended up leaving them high and dry . . . ? That couldn't be allowed.

He said meaningfully to his assistant, "Bryan's completely right, Emily. So let's all get through this intriguing moment of each other's company without permanent damage, yes?" He didn't wait to have her cooperation. He said to Bryan, "Where are we?"

"Phone records all have been dealt with," Bryan said. "Going out, coming in. But it's been expensive, more than I thought. Three blokes were involved in it by the time I was finished, and their rates're going up."

"We'll have to absorb the cost. There's no way around that that I can see. What else?"

"Still going after the rest. It takes a delicate hand and a lot of help from insiders. They're available, but the money involved . . . ?"

"I thought it would be simple."

"Might've been. But you should've talked to me first. Before, not after. Laying trails? Far easier than erasing them."

"You're supposed to be an expert, Bryan. I pay you what I pay you to be the best." Doughty heard Emily's derisive guffaw. He frowned at her. She didn't need to make the situation worse.

"I am the best but that means I have the kind of contacts you need in all the places you need them. It doesn't mean I'm Superman."

"Well, you need to *become* Superman. And you need to do it now."

Emily, obviously, could take no more, for she burst out with "This is just great. It's all made in heaven. I *told* you this was something we needed to stay away from. Now I'm telling you again. Why won't you believe me?"

"We're in the process of making ourselves as clean as newborns," Doughty said. "That's what this meeting is all about."

"Have you ever *seen* a newborn?" Emily demanded.

"Point taken," Doughty said. "Bad analogy. Given time, I'll think of another."

"Wonderful," she said. "You don't *have* time, Dwayne. And it's your thinking that got us into this position."

SOHO
LONDON

Esteban Castro's dance studio was situated next to a car park at the midway point between Leicester Square and what went for China-town. Barbara Havers found it without much difficulty directly after work. Getting to it was more of a challenge, however. It was on the top floor of a six-storey building sans lift, and as she huffed and puffed her way up the stairs to the sound of postmodern music growing ever louder, Barbara gave serious thought to eliminating smoking from her life. Fortunately, as she liked to think of it, she'd recovered her sanity, if not her breath, by the time she got to the translucent half-glass door of Castro-Rourke Dance. So she dismissed the idea of committing herself to tobacco abstinence as the product of a moment's mere idle thought.

She entered the dance establishment and found herself in a small lobby replete with posters. These featured both Dahlia Rourke in tutu mode, adopting various exotic positions suggestive of contortion, and Esteban Castro in every mode imaginable: from tight-clad and leaping through the air, to arse-pointed-outward and arm flung upward in a flamenco stance. Other than the decorative posters, the lobby had nothing else in it but a counter on which were spread brochures for various dancing classes. These appeared to run the gamut from ballroom to ballet.

There was no one in the lobby. From the noise level, though, it seemed that dancing classes were happening on both sides of it, where closed doors led to other rooms. The noise comprised the postmodern music she'd heard on the stairway, which stopped and started and stopped in one of the rooms—broken by a shout of "No, no, no! Does that actually feel to you like a toad experiencing delight and surprise?"—and loud commands of *royale! royale!*, which came from the other. The *no*s were spoken by a man, presumably Esteban Castro, so Barbara went for that door and swung it open. No one to announce her? Not a problem, she thought.

The room she entered was a good-size space with mirrored walls, ballet barres, a row of folding chairs along one side, and a pile of garments—costumes perhaps?—in one corner. In the middle on the smooth hardwood floor stood the man himself, and facing him at the far end of the room were six dancers—male and female—in various leotards, legwarmers, and ballet shoes. They looked abashed, impatient, irritated, weary. When Castro told them to "resume the starting position and *feel* it this time," no one looked exactly thrilled by the idea. "He likes the motorcar," Castro snapped at them, "and *you've* got a plan, all right? Now for God's sake, *you* be a toad and *you* be five foxes so we can get out of here before midnight."

Two of the dancers had clocked Barbara at the doorway, and one of them said, "Steve," to Castro and jerked his head in her direction.

Castro swung round, took in Barbara, and said, "Class doesn't start till seven."

"I'm not—" she began.

"And I hope you've brought other shoes," he added. "Doing the foxtrot in those? Not going to happen." He was, of course, referring to her high-top trainers. He hadn't yet got a clear glimpse of the rest of her clothing, or he would no doubt have pointed out that draw-string trousers and a tee-shirt reading *Celebrating 600 Years of the Bubonic Plague* weren't exactly foxtrot material either.

Barbara said to him, "I'm not here for a class. You're Mr. Castro? I need a word."

He said, "Obviously, I'm in the middle of something."

"Got that in a bucket. So am I." She heaved her shoulder bag around and dug inside it for her warrant card. She crossed the room to him and let him have as much of a look as he wanted.

After a moment he said, "What's this about?"

"Angelina Upman."

His gaze rose from her warrant card to her face. "What about her? I haven't seen her in ages. Has something happened to her?"

"Funny you'd go there first," she noted.

"Where else am I supposed to go when the cops show up?" He didn't, apparently, require an answer to this. Instead, he turned to his dancers and said, "Ten minutes, then we'll go through this one more time."

He spoke with no appreciable accent. He sounded like someone born in Henley-on-Thames. When she asked him about this, letting him know she'd done a little looking into a background that had told her he'd been born in Mexico City, he said he'd moved to London when he was twelve, his father a diplomat and his mother a writer of children's books. It had been important to him to assimilate into the English culture, he said. Accent was part of it as he did not wish to be marked eternally as a foreigner in this place.

He was very good-looking. Barbara could see what the attraction had been for Angelina Upman. Indeed, she could see what the attrac-tion would be for any woman. He smouldered in the way that Latin men often smouldered, helped along by a three-day growth of beard that made him look sexy instead of what it made most other men look, which was largely unkempt. His hair was dark and thick and so healthy-looking Barbara had to keep herself from touching it. She reckoned other women had the same reaction, and she also reckoned Esteban Castro knew it.

When they were alone in the room, Castro indicated the folding chairs and walked over to them. He moved as one would expect of a dancer: fluidly and with perfect posture. Like the dancers he'd dismissed, he wore a leotard that went miles to define every muscle on his legs and his arse. Unlike them, he also wore a tight white muscle-man tee-shirt that did much the same for his chest. His arms were bare. So were his feet.

He sat with his arms on his legs and his hands dangling between them. This gave Barbara a view of his package that she would have preferred not to have, so she moved her own chair to a position that kept his jewels from view. He said without preamble and without waiting to hear the reason for her call upon him, "My wife doesn't know Angelina and I were involved. I'd like to keep it that way."

"I wouldn't place money on that," Barbara told him. "Women aren't stupid, as a rule."

"She's not quite a woman" was his reply. "That was part of the problem. Have you spoken to her?"

"Not yet."

"There's no need. I'll tell you what you want to know. I'll answer your questions. But leave her out of this."

"'This'?" Barbara asked.

"Whatever this is. You know what I mean." He waited for Barbara to say something. When she gave him no assurance of any kind, he cursed and said, "Come with me."

He led the way out of the dance studio and across the lobby. He opened the other door and jerked his head in a way that told her she was to look inside. There she saw Dahlia Rourke with a group of some dozen little girls at the barre. She was attempting to position them gracefully, one arm curved above their heads. It looked hopeless to Barbara. Nice to know, she thought, that there appeared to be no real, natural grace in life. As for Dahlia, she was skeletally thin, more X-ray than human. Perhaps feeling she was being watched, she turned towards the door.

"Daughter's a potential for ballet," Castro said to her, in reference to Barbara. "She wanted a look."

Dahlia nodded. Her gaze took in Barbara but it seemed to be

without speculation. She gave a hesitant smile directed at them both and then went back to her work with the nation's future ballerinas. Castro led the way back to his own studio. He closed the door and said, "Her body functions only as a ballerina's. Nor is she interested in its functioning as anything other than a ballerina's."

"Meaning?"

"Meaning she ceased being a woman some time ago. That's largely why Angelina and I became involved."

"Are there other reasons, then?"

"Have you met her?"

"Yes."

"Then you know. She's lovely. She's passionate. She's alive. That's very appealing. Now what the hell is going on and why are you here?"

"Have you been out of the country in the last month?"

"Of course not. I'm in the middle of choreographing *Wind in the Willows*. How could I possibly leave? And let me repeat: What the hell is going on?"

"No quick trip for a weekend in the sun somewhere?"

"Like where? Spain? Portugal?"

"Italy."

"Of course not."

"What about the wife?"

"Dahlia's doing *Giselle* with the Royal Ballet. And she's got her classes here. She has no time for anything other than soaking her feet at home when she isn't working. So the answer is no and no again and I'm not saying another word until you tell me what the hell is going on, understand?" To emphasise this point, he got to his feet. He strode into the centre of the room and stood there with his arms crossed on his chest and his legs spread. Very manly pose, Barbara thought. She wondered if it was deliberate, full of the knowledge, perhaps, of how to use what he had.

She said, "Angelina Upman's daughter was snatched from a marketplace in Lucca, Italy."

Castro stared at her. His mind appeared to be coming to terms with this and with what it meant that the police had come calling upon him. He said, "And what? D'you think I did it? I don't know her daughter. I never met her daughter. Why the hell would I want to snatch her?"

"Everything has to be checked out, which means everyone whose life touches Angelina's has to be checked out. I know she dropped you without a word, just disappeared from your life. You might have taken a bit of offence at that. You might have wanted to do something to smack her round a bit—figuratively speaking. You might have wanted to play mind games with her the way she played mind games with you."

He laughed shortly. "That's going nowhere, Sergeant . . . ?" He paused.

"Havers," she said. "Detective Sergeant, actually."

"Havers," he said. "Detective Sergeant, actually. She didn't play mind games. She was here, she was gone, that was it."

"And you didn't wonder where she'd gone off to?"

"I didn't have the right to wonder. I knew that and she knew I knew it. Our rules were simple: I wasn't going to leave Dahlia for her. She wasn't going to leave Azhar for me. She'd disappeared once before for a year, but then she'd returned and she and I more or less resumed meeting. I've assumed this is the same sort of thing."

"You mean you've reckoned she'll be back."

"That's how it was in the past."

"So you knew all along about Azhar? During the entire time you were involved with her?" It was germane to nothing, but Barbara had to know, although she would have preferred it if it made no difference to her.

"I knew. We didn't lie to each other."

"And Lorenzo Mura, her other lover? What about him? Did you know about him?"

To this, Castro said nothing. He walked back to the chair on which he'd been sitting. He dropped into it and gave a sharp bark of a laugh. He shook his head. Barbara got the point. He said, "So she was . . . what? Fucking all three of us?"

"It's looking that way."

"I didn't know. But I'm not surprised."

"Why not?"

He rubbed his hands through his hair. He squeezed a handful of it as if this would drive more blood to his brain. He said, "It's this. Some women are driven by excitement. Angelina's one of them. To settle into life with one man? Where's the excitement in that?"

"She appears to be with one bloke now, though: Lorenzo Mura in Italy."

"*Appears* is the operative word, Sergeant. She *appeared* to Azhar to be with Azhar. Now she *appears* to him to be with this Italian."

Barbara thought about this in light of her knowledge of Angelina. The woman she knew was a consummate actress. She herself had been completely taken in by Angelina's air of friendliness and her spurious interest in Barbara's own life. Was it out of the question, then, that she'd managed to bamboozle everyone else around her as well? While Barbara couldn't quite get her mind round the idea of having it off with three blokes at once, she had to admit that anything was possible. She herself would worry about mistakenly shrieking the wrong name in the height of passion. On the other hand, heights of passion weren't regular occurrences in her life.

She said to Castro, "How long did your affair with Angelina last?"

"Is that important?"

"Matter of curiosity, I suppose."

He glanced at her and then away. "I don't know. A few years? Two or three? It was always off and on."

"How often did you meet when it was 'on'?"

"Generally twice a week. Sometimes three."

"Where?"

Another glance. He gave her a speculative head to toe. "What does it matter?"

"Another point of curiosity. Love to know how the other half lives, if you wouldn't mind telling me."

He looked away, his gaze settling across the room where he was reflected in the mirror. "Anywhere," he said. "In the back of cars, in a taxi, here in the studio, backstage in a West End theatre, at my place, at her place, at a particular lap dancing club."

"That must have been interesting," Barbara commented.

"She liked risk. Once we did it in the pedestrian tunnel to Greenwich. She was creative, and I liked that about her. Passion drives her. And what drives passion is excitement and secrecy. That's who she is. That's how she is."

"Seems to me that she's the sort of woman a bloke would want to hang on to, then," Barbara noted. "You know what I mean, I expect. Any time, any place, dressed, undressed, standing, sitting, kneeling, whatever. Don't blokes get off on that kind of thing?"

"Some do."

"And are you 'some'?"

"I'm Latin, Sergeant. What do you think?"

"I think it would be tough to replace her," Barbara pointed out, "once she was gone. Could have been a real heartbreaker for you."

"No one replaces Angelina," he said. "And like I told you, I expect her to be back."

"Even now?"

"With her in Italy?"

"With her living with Lorenzo Mura."

"I don't know." He looked at his watch and got to his feet, ready to resume rehearsal. "I suppose I should be glad it lasted as long as it did," he added. "Come to think of it, so should Mura."

24 APRIL

Bathsheba Ward was next on Barbara's list. Since the wily cow had lied to her about her sister—and this was looking more and more like a bloody family trait, wasn't it?—Barbara was determined to show her no pity. She was also determined to give DI Stewart and Detective Superintendent Ardery no further ammunition to fire upon her. For both of these reasons, she rose in what for her were the wee hours of the morning and headed to Hoxton. She bought a takeaway coffee on her way and used it to wash down a gratifyingly extra-large bacon butty. She was more than ready to take on the world when she arrived in Nuttall Street, where Bathsheba and her husband Hugo Ward lived in a flat on a very nicely kept estate of buildings fashioned from London brick.

No one was up and about on the estate when Barbara arrived, but that was no surprise as it was a quarter past six. She found the Ward flat with no trouble at all, and she leaned on the external bell for as long as it took until a man's voice demanded, "What in God's name do you want? Do you know what time it is?"

"New Scotland Yard," Barbara told him. "I need a word. Now."

This was greeted by silence as the man—presumably Hugo Ward—thought this one over. She gave him five seconds and then rang the bell a second time. He buzzed her inside the place without another word, and she made her way to the flat on the second floor.

Before she could knock, he had the door open. Despite the hour, he was dressed for the day in complete business regalia: three-piece suit, crisp shirt—although hideously two-toned with white collar and blue body—striped tie, and professionally polished shoes. He said, "*You're* the police?" in apparent confusion. Barbara reckoned it was her trainers, which apparently were causing him undue concern. She showed him her police identification. He admitted her into the flat.

"What's this about?" he asked, not unreasonably.

"A word with your wife," Barbara told him.

"She's asleep."

"Wake her up."

"Are you aware of the time?"

She wore a wristwatch, and she shook it next to her ear and squinted at it.

"Damn," she said. "Mickey's gone belly up." And to Hugo Ward, "You've already mentioned the time, Mr. Ward. And I don't have a hell of a lot of it to waste. So if you'll fetch your wife . . . ? Tell her it's Sergeant Havers, here to share a morning cuppa with her. She knows who I am. Tell her it's about her trip to Italy last November."

"She didn't go to Italy last November."

"Well someone did. And on her passport."

"That's not possible."

"Believe me, Mr. Ward. In my line of work, you suss out pretty fast that anything's possible."

He looked disturbed by the information. That was good. It meant he would be inclined to cooperate. His glance went from Barbara to the corridor behind him. They stood in the small square entry of the flat, where a mirror on one wall reflected a pricey-looking piece of modern art on the other. It was all lines and squiggles suggestive of nothing. But even at that, it did look as if the painter had known what he was doing, although Barbara couldn't reckon why this should be the case.

She said, "Mr. Ward . . . ? I'm short on time here. D'you want to rouse her from her beauty whatevers, or do you want me to do the honours?"

He said, "Just a moment, then," and told her to wait in the sitting room, which he called the reception room like some estate agent getting ready to sell the place. This was just off the corridor and like the entry, it was hung with a plethora of modern paintings and decorated with furniture that bore the look of Bathsheba's distinctive design style. On tables here and there were framed photographs, and Barbara sauntered over to give them the eye as Hugo Ward disappeared to fetch his wife.

She saw that the pictures were of the happy, extended Ward family: the two adult children and their spouses, a winsome grandchild, the beaming paterfamilias, the devoted second wife hanging upon him. They were in various poses on various occasions, and they all reminded Barbara of a quotation that she couldn't identify but knew that Lynley could have: Someone was protesting too much. In this case it was all about Aren't we a happy, handsome group? She gave a snort, turned away, and saw that Hugo Ward had come to the reception room's door.

"She'll see you when she's dressed and had her coffee," he said.

"I don't think so," Barbara told him. "Where is she?" She crossed the room and went into the corridor, heading towards three closed doors. "Bedroom's this way?" she said. "Since it's just us girls, she won't be showing me anything I don't own myself."

"You bloody hang on!" Ward demanded.

"Love to but you know the situation with time and tide. Is it this door?"

She opened the first that she came to as Hugo Ward blustered behind her, protesting every inch of the way. The first room was a study, beautifully appointed. She gave it a look, clocked more paintings and even more family photos, and went on to the second door, which she opened, singing out, "It's wakey-wakey time. Early bird, the worm, and you know the rest."

Bathsheba was sitting up in bed, a cup of coffee on the table next to her, and three newspapers spread out across the covers. So much for her having been asleep, Barbara thought. She eyed Hugo Ward and said, "Naughty, naughty. It's not nice to lie to the rozzers, you know. Gets right up our noses, that does."

He said, "Sorry," to Bathsheba. "She charged in, darling."

"I can see that," Bathsheba replied tartly. "Honestly, Hugo. Would it have been too difficult . . . ?" She tossed a paper to one side and reached for her dressing gown.

Barbara said to Hugo Ward, "It'll be just us girls, like I said," and closed the door in his face. She could hear him engaged in more blustering on the other side.

Bathsheba rose from the bed and worked her way into her dressing gown. She said to Barbara, "I've told you what I know, which is absolutely nothing. The fact that you've come to my home before dawn—"

"Open the curtains, Bathsheba, and have a surprise. Sun's up, birds are twittering, and the worms are dead worried."

"Very amusing. And you know what I mean. You've come at a deliberately ungodly hour to rattle me and there's nothing to rattle. This might be how the London police are used to operating, but it is *not* how I am used to operating, and believe me, I'll be talking to someone about you and your methods the moment you leave."

"Fine. I stand warned. My timbers are shivering. Now we can talk."

"I have no intention of—"

"Talking to me? Oh, I think you'll reconsider that one. You lied to me. I don't like that as a general rule. When a kid's been kidnapped, I like it even less."

"What in God's name are you talking about?"

"You're in this up to your earlobes. Hadiyyah's been missing in Italy for more than a week, and since you were in on things with your sister from the get-go—"

"*What?*" Bathsheba peered at Barbara as if trying to take a reading from her face. She shoved her hair behind her ears and strode to a dressing table, where she sat on its stool. "I have no idea what you're talking about."

"That particular kite's going nowhere this time." Barbara leaned against the bedroom door and gave Bathsheba a long and steady look. She said, "You lied to me about not having seen Angelina in donkey's years. You wrote emails to Hadiyyah pretending to be her dad, all nicely set up from University College by who the hell knows. *And you gave your sister your passport to travel to Italy last November when she left Azhar.*"

"I did nothing of the sort."

"As it happens, Angelina's given you up. On all fronts." This last was a lie. The business about the passport was a long shot. But Hugo's denial that his wife had been out of the country was helpful in the matter, so as far as Barbara was concerned, a good bluff was in order.

Bathsheba said nothing for a moment. Anyone with a true knowledge of how the police worked would have asked then and there for her solicitor, but in Barbara's experience people so seldom did. This had always been remarkable to her. In their position, she'd shut it in an instant until she had an attorney alternately massaging her temples and holding her hand. She said, "So?" to Bathsheba Ward. "Want to explain?"

"I have nothing more to say. Angelina *may* have 'given me up,' as you put it—and one wonders where you police get your colourful use of language, frankly—but as far as I know I've committed no crime and neither has she."

"Travelling on someone else's passport—"

"I have my passport. It's in a strongbox in this very flat and, shown a court order, I'll be more than delighted to share it with you."

"She would have posted it back to you as soon as she was safe. She would have taken her own with her but travelled on yours."

"If that's what you think, I daresay you have ways to uncover this. So phone up border control. Phone up customs. Phone up someone. Ring the Home Office. I couldn't care less."

"This whole bit about disliking her . . . You didn't, did you? You don't. Because if you did, why would you help her?" Barbara considered her own question in light of what she'd learned about the Upman family. There was little enough to go on, but one glaring detail explained a lot. "Unless," she said, "it was about getting her away from Azhar. A Pakistani rolling round your sister's knickers? Your parents certainly didn't like this. What about you?"

"Don't be ridiculous. If Angelina was stupid enough to involve herself with a Muslim—"

"And several other blokes at the same time, as it happens," Barbara told her. "Did she tell you that? Or did she just tell you that she'd seen the light and had to get away from the 'filthy Paki.' That's what your dad called him, by the way. What did you call him?"

But Bathsheba was looking at her oddly, Barbara saw. She was looking like a woman who'd just had a bit of a surprise sprung upon her. Barbara went back over what she'd just said to sort out what this surprise might have been, and she excavated it quickly enough in the idea of Angelina's other involvements. She said, "Esteban Castro was one of her lovers. So was a bloke called Lorenzo Mura. She's with him now. Lorenzo. That's where she was going. She told you that, didn't she? No? You didn't know it? How could you *not* know it? You told me yourself that she'd probably be with a man."

Bathsheba didn't reply. Barbara thought about this. She thought about twins and how these particular twins had grown up hating the whole idea of twinship. She considered how hating the idea of twinship could morph into hating the other twin herself. If that was the case—that Bathsheba indeed hated Angelina—then it stood to reason that she would help her only if she saw Angelina's flight as worsening her position in life and not helping it. And if Angelina had known this . . .

"She didn't tell you about Lorenzo Mura, did she?" Barbara said. "Or about Esteban Castro either. Neither of whom, by the way, is the least little bit like your Hugo out there." With a tilt of her head, she indicated the rest of the flat beyond the door.

Bathsheba stiffened. "Exactly what is that supposed to mean?"

"Come on, Bathsheba," Barbara said. "Angelina's had a string of drop-dead men from the get-go. Look Castro up on the Internet if you don't believe me. Look up Azhar and check out how he's come along in the last ten years. And now she's got Lorenzo Mura, who looks like someone Michelangelo would have sculpted. While you've got poor Hugo with that Adam's apple the size of Yorkshire and a face like—"

She surged to her feet. "That's enough!" she shouted.

"And he's getting old fast, I expect. Which means sex isn't what it used to be. Meanwhile your sister—"

"I want you out of here this instant!" Bathsheba said.

"—is getting her field plowed regularly. With a lot of skill. One man after the next and sometimes three at once—think of that, three!—and she doesn't care whether they marry her or not. Did you know that? She doesn't care." Barbara had no idea about this last point, but she did know the likelihood that Bathsheba's marriage was the only card she held that gave her the edge over her twin. She concluded with, "You didn't know any of that, though, did you? You wouldn't have lifted a hand to help her leave Azhar if you'd had a clue she was really running to another man. This one's not married, by the way. But I expect that'll change soon enough."

"Get out of here," Bathsheba said. "Bloody get *out*."

"She uses everyone, Bathsheba," Barbara told her. "Too bad you didn't know it at the time."

FATTORIA DI SANTA ZITA
TUSCANY

The film crew had been at Lorenzo Mura's home for an hour by the time Lynley arrived in the company of both Chief Inspector Lo Bianco and the public minister Fanucci. Fanucci hadn't been enthusiastic about Lynley's attendance, but when Lo Bianco pointed out to him that the reassuring presence of the liaison officer from the British police might go far to keep the parents of the missing girl calm, Fanucci acquiesced to Lynley's going along. He would, of course, remain in the background at all times, Fanucci said pointedly.

"*Certo, certo,*" Lo Bianco muttered. No one wanted to hear the opinion of the British police in this matter of the missing child, *Magistrato*.

At Fattoria di Santa Zita, they were welcomed by the *telecronista*, a sveltely dressed young woman who looked as if she'd come to television journalism via the catwalks of Milan so beautifully turned out was she. Bustling round with lights, cables, cameras, and makeup were the rest of the crew from the television news. They were unloading a van and readying an area in front of the old barn where Lorenzo Mura made his wine. There, a table of bread, cheese, biscuits, and fruit had been hospitably laid on for the crew. A table and chairs had also been set up on a terrace, wide stones overhung with wisteria coming into bloom. There had evidently been much discussion about this: the *telecronista* loving the location for its suggestion of springtime delicacy and the lighting man hating it for the complications it created in having to deal with shadows at the same time as he maintained the colour of the hanging blooms.

Fanucci strode to the location and gave it his approval. No one had asked for this, and no one apparently cared when he gave it. He said a few sharp words to a hapless young woman with a makeup case. She scurried off, returned with a third chair for the table. He sat here, apparently not intending to move from that point forward, and he indicated to her with an abrupt gesture that she was to see to his face with her powder and brushes. She did so, although it remained to be seen what she would make of his facial warts.

In the meantime, establishing shots were being taken by the cameraman: the vineyards falling off down the hillside, the donkeys grazing in a paddock beneath ancient olive trees, a few cattle down by a stream at the bottom of the hill, the many farm buildings. During this, the *telecronista* saw to her makeup in a hand mirror and applied a coat of spray to her hair. She finally said, "*Sono pronta a cominciare*," to indicate her readiness to begin. But obviously, nothing was going to happen until Fanucci gave his nod of approval.

While they were waiting for this to happen, Angelina Upman came out of the winery. Lorenzo Mura was with her, speaking quietly. Taymullah Azhar followed, keeping his distance. Lorenzo seated Angelina at the table with Fanucci, and he bent to her and continued speaking. She looked much more fragile than on the previous day, and Lynley wondered if she was managing to eat or to sleep at all. He wondered the same about Azhar, who didn't look much better than the mother of his child.

Fanucci didn't speak to either one of them. Nor did he speak to Mura. His interests apparently lay only in the filming of the report for the nightly newscast. Anything that needed to be communicated from the police to the parents could come, apparently, from Lo Bianco or from Lynley. It seemed this included sympathy for their situation.

After Fanucci examined himself in the makeup artist's mirror, they were given his approval to begin. The *telecronista* did her part first, reciting the salient details of Hadiyyah's disappearance in the rapid-fire Italian that everyone on television in the country seemed to employ. She did so with one of the olive groves as her background. It was wisely chosen, serving as a nice contrast to the rust-coloured suit she wore.

Lynley didn't try to follow her reportage, aside from listening for names. Instead, he watched the interactions among Lorenzo, Angelina, and Azhar.

Men were by nature territorial, Lynley thought, and Angelina was the territory upon which each of these men had staked a claim. It was interesting to Lynley to see how each of them demonstrated this: Lorenzo by standing behind Angelina's chair, his hands on her shoulders, and Azhar by ignoring the other man entirely and folding a handkerchief into Angelina's hands should she need it when the time arrived for them to make their appeal to the television viewers.

When the *telecronista* had completed her introduction to the piece, the scene shifted. The cameraman moved to the winery, where lights had already been set up. After a few words with the *telecronista*, he focused his lens on Fanucci.

Fanucci's was, it seemed, the fire-and-brimstone section of the report. His speech was as rapid-fire as had been the *telecronista*'s, but Lynley caught enough to know that it was filled with threats and imprecations. The malefactor *would* be found and when he was . . . They had a person of interest to whom they were speaking and he *would* reveal . . . *Anyone* who was found to know *anything* that they had not yet transmitted to the police . . . The law did not sleep . . . The police did not sleep . . . If anything *further* happened to this child . . .

Next to him, Lynley heard Lo Bianco sigh. He took a packet of chewing gum from his jacket pocket, offering it first to Lynley, who demurred. With a piece for himself, Lo Bianco walked away. Fanucci in action, it seemed, was more than he could bear to watch.

When the public minister had completed his remarks, he jerked his head to indicate that the story was now to move to Angelina

Upman and Taymullah Azhar. He rose from the table and walked to position himself behind the cameraman. There he stood like a prophet of doom.

The first movement came from Lorenzo Mura, who took himself out of the picture. There was no need to confuse the viewing public. It was enough for people to know that in front of them on their television screens were the parents of the missing girl. To throw in the complications of Angelina Upman's private life here in Italy seemed unnecessary. On the other hand, thought Lynley, seeing Lorenzo Mura on the screen might jog another kind of memory in the mind of a viewer. He walked over to Lo Bianco to suggest this to the chief inspector. Lo Bianco heard him out and didn't disagree.

Taymullah Azhar and Angelina Upman made their appeal. They did so in English—Azhar, of course, having no Italian—and it would be translated with a voice-over recording in advance of the night's broadcast. What they said was simple. It was what any parent in the same situation would have said: Please give our daughter back to us. Please don't hurt her. We love her. We will do anything to have her returned unharmed.

Lynley saw Fanucci snort at the *we will do anything*, which—although spoken in English—he evidently understood. Clearly, then, the public minister judged it ill-advised to throw an offer like that into the vast maw of an unidentified television audience. There were people out there who well might lead the parents on a merry chase when they heard such an offer: "Hand over a bundle of ransom money and watch us run you into the ground with false information about your child." Fanucci strode over to Lo Bianco's other side and said something to him tersely. Lo Bianco looked noncommittal.

Finally, it was over. At the table, Azhar said something quietly to Angelina, his hand on her wrist. Angelina pressed his handkerchief to her eyes, and he brushed her hair off her cheek. The cameraman caught this tender gesture on tape at the direction of the *telecronista*. Lorenzo Mura saw it all, scowled, and left them to each other.

He went into the winery, where Lynley assumed he would remain in something of a temper until everyone was gone. But he was wrong. Instead, Lorenzo emerged with a tray of wineglasses containing his own Chianti, along with a plate bearing slices of cake. In what Lynley thought of as a quintessentially Italian moment, he distributed wine as well as cake to everyone there.

"*Grazie*" was murmured as was "*Salute*." Wine was sipped or it was tossed back in a gulp or two. Cake was eaten. People seemed meditative, their thoughts on the child and where she might be and how she might be.

Only Azhar and Angelina neither ate nor drank, Angelina because she had been given no wine and she pushed the plate of cake aside with a shudder, and Azhar because as a Muslim he did not drink at all and the sight of the cake seemed to dishearten him.

He glanced at the others, seemed to note the wineglasses in everyone's hand, and moved his own to Angelina, saying to her, "Do you wish, Angelina . . . ?"

She glanced—was it warily? Lynley wondered—at Lorenzo who, with the tray, was crossing the farmyard to Fanucci, Lo Bianco, and himself. She said, "Yes. Yes. I think I could do with some. Thank you, Hari," and she took up the glass and drank with the others.

Lorenzo turned. His gaze went to the table where his lover and her erstwhile lover sat. He took in the instant of Angelina's drinking the wine and he cried out, "*Angelina, smettila!*" And then in English, "No! You know you must *not*."

They looked at each other across the farmyard. Angelina seemed frozen into place. Lynley sorted through what Mura had been trying to say to her: She wasn't to drink and she knew why.

No one said anything for a moment. Then Angelina finally spoke. She said, "One glass won't hurt, Renzo. It's fine." Clearly, she was willing her lover to say nothing more. Just as clearly he wasn't going to remain silent in the face of what she was apparently doing.

He said, "No! During this time especially, it is bad. You know this."

And everything changed in that instant. Utter stillness fell among them. No one moved. Into this a rooster crowed suddenly and as if in response, a burst of pigeons took to the sky from the winery's roof.

Lynley looked from Lorenzo to Angelina to Azhar. *During this time especially* did, of course, have more than one meaning: During this time especially when your child is missing, it is bad to drink, for you need to have your wits about you. During this time especially when you can neither eat nor sleep, wine will go to your head too quickly. During this time especially in the presence of these people who will be watching every move that you make, it is best to remain completely sober. There were many possibilities here. But the expression on Angelina's face said that the most wrenching of the possibilities was the one that had automatically brought the words to Lorenzo's lips. He'd said them without thinking and there could be, realistically, only one reason: During this time especially when you are carrying a child, you must not drink.

Angelina said quietly to Azhar, "You weren't meant to know, Hari. I didn't want you to know." And then desperately, "Oh God, I'm so sorry about everything."

Azhar didn't look at her. Nor did he look at Lorenzo. He didn't, in fact, look at anyone. Rather he stared straight ahead, and there was no expression whatsoever on his face. That alone told Lynley more than any words would have done. No matter how she had devastated him during their relationship, the Pakistani man was unaccountably as much in love with Angelina Upman as he had ever been.

LUCCA
TUSCANY

"Castro's a nonstarter" were Barbara Havers's words to Lynley.

His words to her were "She's pregnant, Barbara."

To which she said, "Bloody sodding hell. How's Azhar coping?"

"He's difficult to read." Lynley was careful on this topic. There was little point, he reckoned, in causing Barbara grief should her feelings for the Pakistani man be deeper than she generally pretended. "I'd say the news is a shock."

"What about Mura?"

"Obviously, he knows."

"I mean is he happy? Worried? Suspicious?"

"About what, exactly?"

She told him what she'd learned about Angelina Upman from her former lover Castro. She passed on his allusion to the fact that there might be yet another lover in Italy, beyond Lorenzo Mura. According to Castro, it was all part of the excitement she seemed to require, Barbara told him. Anyone there who might fill the bill as Angelina's little bit on the side?

He'd have to look into it, Lynley told her. Was there anything else he needed to know?

She said nothing for a few moments, which told him there *was* something more. He said her name in a way that he knew would tell her it was in her best interests to fess up immediately since he would find out eventually. She revealed to him that *The Source* had generated another story, this one about Azhar's desertion of his family in Ilford. She added, "But it's nothing I can't control," which told him volumes about what she'd been up to with the tabloid, despite her protestations on the matter.

He said, "Barbara . . ."

She said, "I know, I know. Believe me, Winnie's given me chapter and verse."

"If you persist—"

"Well, I've started something now and I've got to stop it, sir."

Lynley didn't know how she could. No one got between the sheets with *The Source* and emerged with their clothing still ironed. She should have known that. He cursed quietly.

They rang off soon after, and he considered her words about Angelina Upman. He would have to look for another lover, someone who wanted her enough to punish her if she wouldn't leave Mura for him.

He'd taken the call from Barbara on Lucca's great wall, where he'd gone to walk its perimeter and to think. He'd chosen a clockwise direction and was midway around it, at the point where a café stood offering refreshments to the scores of people who were also taking exercise up above the medieval town. He decided to stop for a coffee, and he moved towards the tables spread out beneath the leafy trees. He saw that Taymullah Azhar had evidently had the same idea. For the London professor was already at a table with a pot of tea next to him and a newspaper spread out before him.

It would probably be an English-language paper, since Lynley had already seen them on sale at a kiosk in Piazza dei Cocomeri, which adjoined one of the few uncurving streets in the town. He reckoned it was a local paper for visitors, and so it seemed to be. He gave a quick look at it as he asked Azhar if he could join him. *The Grapevine*, it was called—more a magazine than a paper—and he saw that either Azhar or the local police had managed to get a story about Hadiyyah's disappearance into it. Her picture was there, along with the simple headline *Missing*. This was good, he thought. Every avenue was being used to find her.

He wondered if Azhar knew that, in London, *The Source* was exposing the story of his family situation. He said nothing to him about it. Chances were good he was going to be told by someone eventually. Lynley didn't see the point of that someone being himself.

Azhar folded the paper and moved his chair to accommodate Lynley's bringing another to the table. Lynley ordered a coffee, sat, and gazed at the other man. He said, "The television appeal will turn up something. There'll be dozens of phone calls to the police, and most of them will be rubbish. But one of them, perhaps two or three, will give us something. Meantime, Barbara is continuing to work several angles in England. There's hope, Azhar."

Azhar nodded. Lynley reckoned that the other man knew how hope grew dimmer as each day passed. But that hope could be renewed in an instant. All it would take was a single person making a connection with something he'd seen or heard, without even knowing before the television appeal that he'd seen or heard it. That was the nature of an investigation. A memory got jogged along the way.

He told all this to Hadiyyah's father, who nodded again. Then he said to Azhar, "None of us knew she's pregnant. Now that we do know . . ." He hesitated.

Azhar had no expression on his face. He said, "Yes?"

"It's something that has to be taken on board. Along with everything else."

"And the relevance . . . ?"

Lynley looked away. The café was situated on one of the ramparts of Lucca's wall, and beyond it a group of children kicked a football on the lawn, shoving one another and laughing, slipping in the grass, shouting out. No adult was with them. They thought they were safe. Children usually did.

He said, "If, perhaps, it's not Lorenzo's child . . ."

"Whose else would it be? She left me for him. He's giving to her what I would not."

"On the surface it seems so. But because she was with Mura while she was with you, there's a chance that now she's with him, perhaps another man exists for her."

Azhar shook his head. "She would not."

Lynley considered what he knew of Angelina and what Azhar knew of the woman. People didn't change their colours rapidly, he knew. Where she had strayed once for the excitement of having a secret lover, she could stray again. But he didn't argue the point.

Azhar said, "I should have expected this."

"Expected . . . ?"

"The pregnancy. The fact that she left me. I should have understood that she would move on when I did not give her what she wanted."

"What was that?"

"First that I divorce Nafeeza. When I would not, then that Hadiyyah could at least meet her siblings. When I would not allow that, then that we should have another child. To these things I said no and no and absolutely no. I should have seen what the result would be. I drove her to all of this. What else, really, was she to do? We were happy, she and I. We had each other and we had Hadiyyah. She'd said at first that marriage was something unimportant to her. But then it changed. Or she changed. Or I did. I don't know."

"She might not have changed at all," Lynley told him. "Could it be that you never really saw her well? People are sometimes blind to others. They believe what they want to believe about them because to believe something else . . . It's far too painful."

"And you mean . . . ?"

There was no choice but to tell him, Lynley thought. He said, "Azhar, she had another lover, Esteban Castro, while she was with you. She asked me not to tell you, but we're at the point where every possible avenue needs to be travelled and her other lovers comprise one of those avenues."

He said stiffly, "Where? When?"

"As I said, when she was with you."

Lynley saw him swallow. "Because I would not—"

"No. I don't think so. I think, perhaps, she preferred things this way. Having more than one man at a time. Tell me. Was she with someone else when you first met her?"

"Yes, but she left him. For me. She left him." But for the first time, he sounded doubtful. He glanced at Lynley. "So you're saying that now if there's another man, beyond Lorenzo, and if Lorenzo knows this, has discovered this . . . But what has any of this to do with Hadiyyah? That I do not see, Inspector."

"Nor do I, at the moment. But I've found over time that people do extraordinary things when their passions are deeply involved. Love, lust, jealousy, hate, the need for revenge. People do extraordinary things."

Azhar looked into the town beneath them. He was quiet, as if in prayer. He said simply, "I just want my daughter. The rest of this . . . I no longer care."

Lynley believed the first. He wasn't sure about the second.

25 APRIL

The television appeal made the story enormous. Missing children were always news in any of the Italian provinces. Missing attractive children were significant news. But missing attractive foreign children whose disappearances brought to the doorstep of the Italian police representatives from New Scotland Yard . . . This was enough to attract the attention of journalists from far and wide. Shortly after the television appeal, they set up shop in what for them was the most logical location, as close to the *questura* as they could get since the action in the case was most likely to occur there. They blocked traffic on the way to the train station; they blocked the pavements on both sides of the street; they generally made a nuisance of themselves.

The "action in the case" was mostly defined by the police questioning of suspects. Guided by the public minister, *Prima Voce* had made its selection of prime suspect. The other newspapers were going along, and the hapless Carlo Casparia was finally where Piero Fanucci wanted someone—anyone—to be: under the journalistic microscope. *Prima Voce* was going as far as to ask the telling question: When will someone step forward as witness and name a certain drug addict in this case of the disappeared *bella bambina*?

Soon enough someone did just that. An Albanian scarf vendor in the *mercato* experienced a jog to his memory, effected by both the television appeal with its photographs of the missing child and by Fanucci's fiery sermon during that television appeal. This individual had, thus, phoned the *questura* with what he hoped was information relevant to the child's disappearance: He had seen her pass by on her way out of the *mercato*, and he was certain that he had seen Carlo Casparia rise from his kneeling *Ho fame* position and follow the girl.

Salvatore Lo Bianco was completely unconvinced that the scarf vendor had seen anything at all, but after thinking about it for a moment, he did see how this new piece of information might be useful. So he dutifully reported it to Fanucci. *Il Pubblico Ministero* declared his intention to interview Carlo Casparia personally, as Salvatore had hoped he would. By the time several officers had rounded up the young man and herded him into the *questura*, Fanucci was waiting to grill him like the martyred St. Lawrence, and representatives from seven newspapers and three television channels were gathered in the street. They already knew Casparia was inside the *questura*, which told Salvatore that someone was feeding them information. He was fairly sure it was Fanucci himself since massaging his reputation for quickly bringing criminal matters to a conclusion was dear to the *magistrato*'s heart.

Salvatore almost hated to put the drug-addled Casparia through another interrogation. But it bought him time by keeping Fanucci occupied. And *il Pubblico Ministero* was very well occupied handling this new interrogation of the addict, as things turned out. He roared, he paced, he breathed garlic into Casparia's face, he announced that the young man had been seen following this child from the *mercato* and it was time he told the police what he'd done with her.

Carlo, of course, denied everything. He looked at Fanucci with eyes so bright that he seemed to have light bulbs inside his head. They gave the instantaneous impression that Casparia was extraordinarily alert. The truth was he was high. It was anyone's guess if he even remembered what child Fanucci was talking about. He asked the *magistrato* what he would possibly want with a little girl? Fanucci pointed out that it was not what he might have wanted with her but what he actually did with her that was the question they wanted answered.

"You handed her over to someone for money. Where? Who was this person? How was this arrangement made?"

"I don't know what you're talking about" brought a slap on the back of the head from Fanucci as he paced behind Casparia's chair.

"You've stopped begging in the *mercato*. Why?" was where he went next.

"Because I can't make a move without the police pouncing on me" was Casparia's explanation, after which he put his head in his arms and said, "Let me sleep, man. I was trying to sleep when you—"

Fanucci pulled the youth upright by his filthy bronze-coloured hair and said, "*Bugiardo! Bugiardo!* You no longer go to the *mercato* because you have no need of money. You got what you needed when you passed the girl on to another. Where is she? It's in your interests to tell me now because the police will be going over every inch of those stables where you live. You didn't know that, did you? Let me tell you this, you miserable *stronzo*, when we come up with evidence that she was held there—one of her hairs, one of her fingerprints, a shred of a garment, a hair ribbon, anything—your trouble will be bigger than anything you've ever imagined in that thick head of yours."

"I didn't take her."

"Then why did you follow her?"

"I didn't. I don't know. Maybe I was just leaving the *mercato*."

"Earlier than usual? Why would you do that?"

"I don't know. I don't even remember if I left at all. Maybe I was going to take a piss."

"Maybe you were going to grab this pretty one by the arm and march her over to—"

"In your dreams, man."

Fanucci pounded the table in front of the young man. "You'll sit here till you tell me the truth," he roared.

Salvatore used this moment to slip out of the room. He could see that Fanucci would be entertained for hours. He found himself oddly grateful to poor Carlo. He himself could now get something done while Fanucci concentrated on getting "the truth" out of him.

The reality was that they'd had more than one call after the television appeal. They'd had dozens of calls and dozens of putative sightings of little Hadiyyah. Now that Fanucci was absorbed with his questioning of Carlo Casparia, the police could, in peace, sort through the information that was coming in. Something within it might be worth pursuing.

LUCCA
TUSCANY

Something indeed turned up one hour into Fanucci's interrogation of the drug addict. An officer tracked down Salvatore as he was waiting for a stained Moka to finish brewing its viscous *caffè* over the gas flame in the coffee room. There'd been a sighting of a flashy red car in the hills above Pomezzana, he reported to Salvatore. This sighting had been memorable to the caller for several reasons.

"*Perché?*" Salvatore listened to the Moka's final burbling. He reached for a marginally clean cup on the shelf above the sink, gave it a quick rinse and quick wipe, and poured the coffee. *Perfetto*, he thought. Bitter and coal-coloured. Just the way he liked it.

First, he was told, the convertible top on the car was down. The caller—this was a man who identified himself as Mario Germano, on his way to see his mamma in the village of Fornovolasco—saw the vehicle parked beneath some chestnut trees in a lay-by, and his first thought was that it was foolish to leave a car like that parked with its top down where anyone could come along and play mischief with it. So he'd given the car a second look as he drove by, and that brought them to the second reason Signor Germano remembered the car.

"*Sì?*" Salvatore sipped the coffee. He leaned against the counter and waited for more. It was soon in coming, and it made the coffee turn to bile in his mouth.

A man was leading a child away from the car and into the woods, the officer said. Signor Germano saw them and assumed that it was a father leading his child to relieve herself out of sight of the road.

"Why did he assume it was a father and child? Is he sure the child was female?" Salvatore asked.

Truth be told, Signor Germano wasn't completely sure about the sex of the child, but he thinks it was a little girl. And he assumed it was a father and child because . . . well, what else would it have been? Why would anyone assume anything else but an innocent drive in the hills on a sunny afternoon, interrupted momentarily by a child's need to squat in the bushes out of sight?

"This Signor Germano," Salvatore asked, "is he certain about the sighting?"

He was indeed because he visited his mamma on a regular schedule.

"And he takes the same route every time?"

Sì, sì, sì. The route is in the Apuan Alps, and it's the only road to get to his mamma's village.

It was too much to hope for that Signor Germano would remember in which lay-by the red car had been parked, and he did not remember. But since he'd been on his way to his mamma's village, the lay-by was, naturally, somewhere along the mountain road in advance of that place.

Salvatore nodded. This was progress indeed. It could be nothing at all, but he had a feeling this was not so. He dispatched two officers to fetch Signor Germano and to drive him into the Apuan Alps on the route to his mamma's village. If his memory was jogged as to the correct lay-by, excellent. If his memory failed him, then every lay-by would have to be checked. For the point was not the lay-by itself but the shrubbery beyond it, as well as the woods and any trail leading into the woods. Salvatore didn't want to think that the child might have been disposed of in the Alps, but every day that passed without word about a ransom and without finding her alive made that possibility ever more likely.

His order to the officers was to hold close this information about the red car in the Alps. The only people to be told would be the parents, he said. And they would be told only that a possible sighting was being looked into as there was no need to cause them further distress about a man leading a child into the woods until the police knew if this was, indeed, a relevant piece to the puzzle. Meantime, he said, he wanted an officer looking into all the car hire agencies from Pisa to Lucca. If a red convertible had been hired by someone, he wanted to know who, he wanted to know when, and he wanted to know for how long. And not a word about any of this, *chiaro*? he said. The last thing he wanted was Fanucci getting hold of the information and leaking it to the press.

PISA
TUSCANY

Salvatore decided that it was time to have a word with Michelangelo Di Massimo. He also decided that the presence of New Scotland Yard, in addition to his own presence, might go some distance towards rattling the man. Since he'd been in Lucca looking for Angelina Upman and her daughter, he was the best lead they had. While it was true that he rode a motorcycle—a powerful Ducati, according to the records that Salvatore had dipped into—there was nothing to stop him from borrowing a vehicle from another, nor was there anything to stop him from hiring one for a single day to take him first into Lucca and then into the Apuan Alps.

He rang DI Lynley and then fetched him at Porta di Borgo, one of the surviving gates of the internal, older walls that had once encircled the town. The London man had walked the short distance from the *anfiteatro*. He was waiting just outside the arch, flipping through the pages of *Prima Voce*. He slid into the passenger's seat and said in his careful Italian, "The tabloids are choosing your drug addict, it seems."

Salvatore chuckled. "They must choose someone. It is their way."

"Or, if they don't have a suspect, they go after the police, yes?" Lynley said.

Salvatore glanced in his direction and smiled. "They will do what they will do," he said.

"May I ask: Is someone leaking to the papers?"

"*Come un rubinetto che perde acqua*," Salvatore told him. "But this faucet's dripping has them well occupied. Their concentration on Carlo keeps them away from what we're doing and what we know."

"What's made you decide to talk to him now?" Lynley asked, in reference to Michelangelo Di Massimo.

Salvatore made the turn that would take them to Piazza Santa Maria del Borgo. It was crowded here, as usual, a combination of *parcheggio* for tour buses and milling tourist groups trying to orient themselves in the town as the bright sunlight fell upon their shoulders. At the piazza's north side, Porta Santa Maria gave Salvatore access to the *viale* that encircled the town. They would take this roadway to navigate quickly round the wall and glide over to the *autostrada*.

He told Lynley about the reported sighting in the Apuan Alps: a red convertible, a child, a man, their heading into the woods together. Lynley said astutely, "And this man . . . was he blond?"

Salvatore said, "This we do not know from the sighting."

"But it would seem . . ." Lynley looked doubtful. "With someone looking as Di Massimo looks, that would have been noticed certainly?"

"Who knows what will be remembered from one moment to the next, eh, *Ispettore?*" Salvatore said. "You may be right and our journey to Pisa may be for nothing, but the facts remain: He was looking for them in Lucca and he plays football for Pisa, so we have a possible connection between him and Mura. If that means something, it is time we learned what. I have a feeling about this Di Massimo."

He didn't tell the London man the rest of what he knew about Di Massimo just then. But there were reasons beyond the man's ridiculous blond hair that Salvatore knew who the Pisan was.

Michelangelo Di Massimo had an office along the river in Pisa, walking distance from Campo dei Miracoli as well as from the university. There were people who found this section of the city reminiscent of Venice, but Salvatore had never been able to see it. The only things Venice and this part of Pisa had in common were water and ancient *palazzi*. In Pisa, the first was sluggish and unclean, and the second were uninspiring. No one, he thought, would be writing poetry about Pisa's riverside anytime soon.

When they reached the building that held Di Massimo's home and office—which were one and the same—there was no answer when Salvatore rang the bell. But at the tobacconist two doors away, they discovered that the Pisan was having his regular hair appointment. They would find him, they were told, in an establishment called

Desiderio Dorato, not far from the university. It was a name that Di Massimo had obviously taken straight into his heart.

The man himself was enthroned within the place, enshrouded in a black plastic cape from shoulders to feet. His head was covered with whatever substance turned his hair from *capelli castagni* to the promised *dorati*. When they came upon him, he was deeply involved in reading a novel, a book whose traditional yellow cover announced it as a crime story.

Salvatore took it out of his hands as preamble to their discussion. "Michelangelo," he said pleasantly, "are you getting some pointers, my friend?" He felt, rather than saw, Thomas Lynley glance curiously in his direction. It was time, he decided, to tell the London man exactly who Di Massimo was.

He did it by way of introduction, emphasising Lynley's position at New Scotland Yard and revealing in a friendly fashion the London detective's purpose in coming to Italy. No doubt, he said, Michelangelo had heard of the missing child from Lucca, *non è vero*? He couldn't imagine a private investigator of Di Massimo's stature to be uninterested in a case such as this one since, above everything else that made it intriguing, the man who stood in place of the missing child's father was, like Di Massimo, a player of football.

Di Massimo plucked the book back from Salvatore's hands. He was unrattled. He said, "As you have eyes, you can see I'm in the middle of something here, Chief Inspector."

"Ah, yes, the hair," Salvatore said. "It was what made you so distinctive to the hotels and *pensioni*, Miko." He was aware of Lynley next to him adjusting to the new information. He felt a slight twinge that he hadn't told the English detective from the first about what he knew of Michelangelo Di Massimo's profession, but he didn't want the information relayed to the parents of the girl and, from them, to Lorenzo Mura. The risk was too great, and he hadn't known whether he could trust Lynley to hold his tongue.

"I don't know what you're talking about," the Pisan said.

"What I'm talking about is your presence—in my city, Miko— seeking from one hotel to the next information about a woman from London and her daughter. You even had a photo of them. Does this rattle the cage bars of your memory, my friend, or will a trip to the *questura* be necessary to do so?"

"It seems someone hired you to find them, signore," Lynley said. "And now one of them is missing, which doesn't look good. For you, that is."

"I know nothing of missing women and children," Di Massimo said. "And the fact that someone thinks I was looking for them at one time or another . . . ? It could have been anyone. You know that."

"Described such as yourself?" Salvatore asked. "Miko, how many men can be said to combine the physical attributes that blend in you so well?"

"Ask the *parrucchiere*," the Pisan advised. "Ask anyone here. They will tell you Di Massimo isn't the only man who chooses to alter the colour of his hair."

"*Vero*," Salvatore said. "But perhaps the number of these men who also wear black leather"—and here he toed the plastic cape to one side to reveal Di Massimo's trousers—"and whose whiskers sprout from his face as if in a contest to grow a full beard by this evening . . . ? I would suggest, Miko, that these two details alone set you above the others. We add to that your possession of a photo of a girl and her mother. We add to that your employment. We add to that your membership on the *squadra di calcio* and the fact that this team will have, from time to time, played matches against the team from Lucca . . ."

"*Calcio?*" Di Massimo asked. "What has *calcio* to do with anything?"

"Lorenzo Mura. Angelina Upman. The missing child. They are all connected and something has told me that you know this."

"You're fishing and your bait is off the hook," Di Massimo said.

"We shall see if that's the case, Miko, when you stand in an identity parade and the witnesses from the hotels who have identified you have a chance to see you once again. When that happens—as I assure you it will—you might then regret your reluctance to speak to us now. *Il Pubblico Ministero*, by the way, will be most interested in speaking to you once those witnesses have confirmed that the man who came into their hotels in his black leather trousers and his black leather jacket with his yellow hair and his very black eyebrows—"

"*Basta*," Di Massimo snapped. "I was asked to locate them, the girl and her mother. That is all. I search Pisa first: the hotels, the *pensioni*, even the convents that rent out rooms. Then I broaden the search."

"Why Lucca?" Lynley asked the man.

His eyes became hooded as he considered the question and, apparently, what it would reveal if he answered it.

"Why Lucca?" Salvatore repeated. "And who hired you, Michelangelo?"

"There was a bank transaction that I was told about. It came from Lucca, so I went to Lucca. You know how it works, Chief Inspector. One thing leads to another and the investigator follows trails. That's it."

"A bank transaction?" Salvatore said. "Who told you about a bank transaction? What kind of bank transaction, Miko?"

"A transfer of money. That's all I knew. The money started in Lucca. It ended in London."

"And who hired you?" Lynley asked the man. "When were you hired?"

"In January," Michelangelo said.

"By whom?"

"He's called Dwayne Doughty. He hired me to find the girl. And that, Chief Inspector, is all I know. I did a job for him. I looked for a child who was supposed to be in the company of her mother. I had a photo of them, so I did what anyone searching would do: I went to the hotels and the *pensioni*. If that's a crime, arrest me now. If it isn't, let me go back to reading my book in peace."

LUCCA
TUSCANY

Lynley rang Barbara Havers as he and Lo Bianco made the trip back to Lucca. He reached her deep into attempting to transcribe an action report for an officer whose cursive she was finding illegible. She sounded irritated and in need of nicotine. For the first time Lynley wouldn't have minded her lighting up. He knew she would need to once he imparted the information he now had about Dwayne Doughty.

There was a moment of silence when he told her: The London

private investigator had hired a Pisa private investigator to track down Angelina Upman and her daughter in Lucca. This investigator had begun his work for Doughty in January, four months earlier. To her "Bloody hell, he lied to me!" Lynley added that a bank account was involved, as was a transfer of money from Lucca to London. "Doughty has apparently known a great deal more than he's been telling you, Barbara," Lynley said.

"He's working for me," she fumed. "He's bloody goddamn working for me!"

"You'll need to have a word."

"Oh, I bloody know that," she barked. "When I get my hands on the sodding worm—"

"Just don't do it now. Don't leave the office. And if I might suggest . . . ?"

"What? Because if you think I'm handing this little matter over to someone else, you're bleeding from your ears."

"I wasn't heading there," he told her. "But you might want to take Winston with you if you're going to confront this bloke."

"I don't need protection, Inspector."

"Believe me, I know. But the cachet of authority that Winston will lend to an interview . . . ? Not to mention the implied threat of his presence . . . ? You do need that. These aren't the most cooperative of blokes, Barbara. Doughty might need convincing in the matter of talking if he's been hiding details from you."

She agreed to this, and they rang off. Lynley told Lo Bianco who Doughty was and how he had fitted into the search for Hadiyyah from the previous November. Lo Bianco whistled and shot him a look. "For an Englishman to have taken the child," he said, "this would have been an easier matter."

"Only as to language," Lynley pointed out. "Because if the Englishman doesn't live in Lucca or somewhere nearby . . . Where would he have taken her?"

At the *questura*, they quickly learned that there was an additional development. As it happened, a tourist using a local apartment in Piazza San Alessandro as a base for her trip to Tuscany had been in the *mercato* on the day of Hadiyyah's disappearance. She was an

American woman travelling with her daughter, both of them students of the Italian language, neither of them fluent, but both in town to practise as much as they could. So they read the tabloids as well as the newspapers, they watched the television and tried to understand what was being said, and they talked to the *cittadini* of the town. They'd seen the appeal on the news, and they'd looked through the thousand or more digital photos they'd taken in Tuscany to see if there was anything among them that might be of help to the police. They'd located the photos they'd taken in the *mercato* on the day that the child went missing, and they'd cooperatively delivered the memory cards from their digital cameras so that the police could examine the pictures. They'd included a message along with the memory cards: Should the police wish to question the photographers themselves, they would be that day taking in the beauties of Palazzo Pfanner.

Lo Bianco sent for someone who knew what to do with memory cards from cameras, compact discs, computers, and getting the photographs onto a monitor's screen. There turned out to be nearly two hundred that the American and her daughter had taken in the *mercato*. Lynley and the chief inspector began to go through them, studying each to see if Hadiyyah was featured in any, looking for the reappearance of anyone from one picture to the next. Especially they looked for Michelangelo Di Massimo. He would, after all, be unmistakable.

They found Lorenzo Mura doing his weekly shop at a *bancarella* featuring cheese. They found him at another featuring meat. At this one a great pig's head on the counter looked, unappetisingly, like something directly out of *Lord of the Flies*, and Mura was gazing to his left in the direction, Lo Bianco said, of Porta San Jacopo and the accordion player. They scrutinised every picture that Lo Bianco identified as being in the vicinity of that musician. Finally, they came upon two in which Hadiyyah could be seen, at the front of the crowd listening to the music and watching the man's poodle doing its dance.

The focal point of the picture was the dancing dog, not Hadiyyah, so she wasn't entirely in focus. But it was an easy matter to enlarge the picture on the screen so that the detectives could see that it was unmistakably her. To her right stood an old woman in the black of a widow, while on her left huddled three teenage girls engaged in lighting two cigarettes from the burning tobacco of a third.

Di Massimo was nowhere. But a handsome, dark-haired man stood directly behind Hadiyyah, and although his gaze, like everyone else's, was on the poodle and its master, he was reaching for something inside his jacket. Two pictures along they saw what it was. By enlarging it, they had a better image to deal with. It appeared to be a greeting card of some kind, on its front a depiction of the universal yellow smiley face. There was no photo showing exactly what he'd done with the card. There was, however, a picture of Hadiyyah bending to the accordion player's basket and putting something in it with her right hand while, in her left, she held something that could have been the card from the earlier photo.

And then . . . nothing more. There were other pictures of the accordion player, of the dancing dog, and of the crowd in attendance. But Hadiyyah was not in them. Nor was the man.

"It could be nothing," Lo Bianco said, stepping away from the monitor and going to look out of the window, which faced not only Viale Cavour but also the restless journalists gathered there.

"Do you believe that?" Lynley asked him.

Lo Bianco looked at him. "I do not," he said.

BOW
LONDON

Winston hadn't jumped on the rolling wagon of Barbara's intentions immediately. She didn't understand why until they finally reached Bow and had parked in front of Bangla Halal Grocers, where a sign offered Bangladeshi King Size Fish and two men in long white robes and tatted headgear gazed upon Barbara's old Mini with undisguised suspicion. There, Winston didn't unfold himself from the sagging seat at once, as Barbara had expected of him, considering the discomfort in which he'd had to ride all the way from Victoria. Instead, he said to her, "You got to be told something, Barb. He's checkin your story."

So caught up was she in trying to decide how she was going to make Doughty pay for his investigative crimes against her that she thought at first he meant the Bow detective. But when he went on, she understood that Winston was passing along information that had come to him via Dorothea Harriman, and this information had nothing to do with Dwayne Doughty and his questionable ethics.

"Dee says he asked her to look into where your mum was taken when she fell. She says he asked her would she do it on the sly. If no A-and-E has a record of her and no ambulance company has a record of transportin her, he's goin to use it against you. Tha's the story Dee had."

Barbara swore. "Why didn't she come to me? At least I could've rung Mrs. Flo to cook up a story."

"'Spect Dee's that worried 'bout her own job, Barb. He sees her talkin to you, he even gets word she's talked to you, we both know what he's goin to think. She's bidin her time before she gets on it—the ambulance and A-and-E business—but he's goin to be lookin for some answers soon and she's goin to have to tell him something. And when she tells him whatever she tells him, you know 's well as I do that he's goin to take steps to confirm."

Barbara thunked her head against the driver's window. How to proceed was the question. She answered it by saying, "Hang on, then," to Winston, and by making a phone call to Florence Magentry in Greenford. That good woman was going to have to lie for her, she was going to have to do so convincingly, and Barbara could see no way around it.

"Oh my dear, my dear," she said hesitantly when Barbara laid out the facts for her via mobile as Winston looked on, frowning. "I will, of course, if you think I must. A fall, an ambulance, the casualty ward . . . ? Of course, of course. But, Barbara, may I say . . . ?"

Barbara girded herself for protest. She wanted to declare that she had no choice, that she had to protect herself, that if she did not do so she would not be able to keep her mother in the secure and caring place of lodging that Mrs. Flo provided because she'd be without a job. But she said, "Yeah. Go on," and she waited for Mrs. Flo to say what she needed to say.

It was, "Sometimes, my dear, if we tempt fate this way . . . It's not a good thing, is it? What I'm trying to say is that declaring something like this—a fall, broken bones, an ambulance, casualty—"

Barbara had never taken her mother's carer to be superstitious, so she said, "You're saying that wishing makes things so? Well, I'm not wishing. I'm just saying. And if I don't 'say' something, I'm up to my neck . . . Look, a secretary from the Met will ring you, Mrs. Flo. Then a DI called Stewart'll ring you as well. You just need to tell them both that yes, Mum fell, and yes, an ambulance took her to casualty, and that's all you know since you rang me and I got onto all the rest." That would, she thought, buy her time to sort this mess out.

Up above Bedlovers, Doughty was waiting for her, as she'd phoned him and told him that—all things related to the law considered—it was in his best interests to stay put until she and he had a little confab together. She didn't mention Winston, and she noted with gratification that Doughty blanched slightly when the impressive black detective followed her into the room and blocked any escape from it. She introduced the two men. Winston meaningfully locked his eyeballs on to Doughty. Barbara then got down to business. The business was money transferred from Lucca to London. The business was hiring a Pisan called Michelangelo Di Massimo.

"You hired this bloke in January," she declared. "So let's start with how you uncovered the information about a money transfer in the first place."

"I don't reveal—"

"Do not attempt that rubbish with me. You've been playing fast and loose from the first, and if you'd like to remain a private investigator and not end up in the local nick, then you're going to talk."

Doughty was sitting behind his desk. He glanced at Winston, who stood at the door. He glanced at a metal filing cabinet, at the artificial plant covering its top surface. That, Barbara reckoned now, had to be where he had a camera that broadcast whatever went on in his office to his colleague in the other room.

"All right. Another bank account was uncovered," Doughty finally said.

"Who uncovered it? How? Who's your blagger? Because that's how you did it, isn't it, and I expect it's your 'associate' Ms. Cass who was ringing round credit card companies and banks pretending to be Angelina. Or her sister. She looked like a bird with as many talents as pores, so sweet-talking someone—"

"I'm not saying a word about Emily Cass," he said. "We use various means at our disposal to uncover information."

"Computer hacking as well, I expect. That 'computer expert' you told us about is someone who breaks and enters computer systems as easily as tumbling locks. And he or she knows someone who knows someone who knows someone else . . . Do you know how much trouble I could put you in, Mr. Doughty?"

"I'm attempting to cooperate," he said. "I learned there was a bank account here in London, an account held in the name Bathsheba Ward but in a branch nowhere near her home or her work. I found this curious and did a little . . . work on it. In . . . in time, let's say, I discovered that funds had been wired from another account, this one in Lucca. I needed someone in Italy to trace that account and to see who was at the other end of this wired money."

"Michelangelo Di Massimo was your man in Italy, then?"

"He was." Doughty pushed back from his desk. He went to the filing cabinet, made an adjustment to the artificial plant, and opened a drawer. He riffled through some files till he found what he wanted. He handed it over. It was slim enough, but it contained a copy of the report he'd written. Barbara read this quickly to see it contained the information he'd just supplied her, along with the name, the address, and the email of the private investigator in Pisa whom DI Lynley and the Italian chief inspector had interviewed that day.

Barbara closed the file and handed it back. She had a terrible feeling about what she was going to learn if she asked the next question, but she asked it anyway. "What did you do with this information?" she said.

"I gave it to Professor Azhar," he told her. "Sergeant, I've given him everything from the first."

"But he said . . ." Barbara's lips felt stiff. What had he said? Had she misinterpreted his words in some way? She tried to remember, but she was feeling turned round, down the rabbit hole, and out of her league. "Why didn't you tell me?" she asked him.

"Because I was working for him, not for you," Doughty said, not unreasonably. "And when I began working for you, what you asked me to uncover had to do with the professor's trip to Berlin and nothing else." He put the folder back and shut the drawer. He turned back to them, but he did not sit. He extended his hands in the universal gesture of look-at-me-I-have-nothing-to-hide. "Sergeant," he said and then added Winston in his remarks by saying, "Sergeants. I've told you the absolute truth at this point, and if you'd care to look through my phone records and my computer files and, yes, even my hard drive, you're more than welcome to do so. I've nothing to hide from you, and I've no interest in anything other than getting home to my wife and my dinner. Are we finished here?"

They were, Barbara said. What she didn't say, however, was that she knew how easily Doughty could have cleared his records, his hard drive, his entire life of suspicion if any of this was in the possession of a computer tech expert with inside contacts at various institutions. And there was virtually nothing she could do about it.

She and Winston left him. They descended the stairs and went into the street, where a short distance away the Roman Café was making the seductive offer of kebabs. She said to her colleague, "At least let me buy you dinner, Winnie."

He nodded and walked thoughtfully at her side. He was deep into something, and she didn't ask him what it was because she had a feeling she already knew. He confirmed this as they took a table by the window and considered the menu. He looked at it briefly and then spoke to her.

"Got to ask, Barb."

"What?"

"How well you know him."

"Doughty? 'Course he could be lying and he probably is because he's lied already and—"

"Don't mean Doughty," Winston told her. "'Spect you know that, eh?"

She did. To her sorrow and misery, she absolutely did. He was asking how well she knew Taymullah Azhar. She'd been asking herself the very same question.

BOW

LONDON

Doughty waited patiently. He knew it wouldn't be long, and it wasn't. Em Cass burst into his office not one minute after the cops' departure. He could tell how much of a lather she was in from the fact that she'd removed both her waistcoat and her tie.

"From the first," she began. "Goddamn it, Dwayne, from the—"

"It'll all be over soon," he cut in. "There's nothing to worry about. Everyone will go home happy, and you and I will fade into the sunset, ride off on our ponies, whatever."

"I think you've gone mad." She paced from one side of the office to another. She slapped one hand into the palm of the other.

"Emily," he said, "go home. Have a change of clothes and go out clubbing. Pull a new man. You'll feel much better."

"How can you even suggest . . . You're an idiot! Now it's two cops—from the Met, no less—sifting through our unwashed laundry, and you're suggesting I entertain myself with anonymous sex?"

"It'll take your mind off whatever your mind's on. Which, by the way, is an unnecessary bundle of speculations taking you nowhere. We're clean on this and we've been that way since Bryan diddled our computers and phone records."

"We're going to gaol," she said. "If you're depending on Bryan to hold out once the cops pay a call on him . . . especially that black bloke. Did you see how big he is? Did you bloody see that scar on his face? I know a scar from a knife fight when I see one and so do you. We'll be in gaol five minutes after that bloke fixes his stare on Bryan Smythe."

"They don't know any details about Bryan, and unless you decide to tell them yourself, they won't ever know any details about Bryan. Because I'm certainly not going to tell them. So it'll all be down to you."

"What're you saying? That I can't be trusted?"

Doughty looked at her meaningfully. It was his experience that no one could be trusted, but he did like to think otherwise of Emily. Still, he could tell she needed to be mollified in some way because, in her present state, one trip to the nick to spend an hour or so in the company of officers intent upon wringing the truth from her, and she might well crack.

He said carefully, "I trust you with my life, Em. I hope you trust me with yours as well. I hope you trust me enough to listen carefully to what I'm about to say."

"Which is?"

"It'll be over soon."

"What's that supposed to mean?"

"Things are in motion in Italy. The crime is about to be solved, and we'll be opening the champagne soon enough."

"Do I have to remind you that we're not in Italy? Do I have to point out that if you're depending on this Di Massimo bloke—a man you've never even bloody met, for God's sake—to carry this off without anyone being the wiser . . ." She threw up her hands. "This is more than an Italian situation, Dwayne. It became more than an Italian situation the moment the Met got involved. Which, may I remind you, was the very first instant that woman stepped into your office with the Pakistani, pretending to be an ordinary, ill-dressed heap of a female just here to support her extraordinarily intelligent, well-spoken, nice-looking, and neatly attired male friend. God, I should have known the moment I clapped eyes on them both that the very fact they were even together—"

"You did know, as I recall," he said mildly. "You told me she was a cop and you turned out to be correct. But none of that matters just now. Things are in hand. The girl will be found. And no crime was committed by you or by me. Which, I might add, is something you should hold close to your heart."

"Di Massimo gave them your name," she protested. "What's to stop him from giving them everything else?"

He shrugged. There was some truth in what she said, but he was holding on to his confidence in money being not only the root of all evil but also the oil that kept machines rolling on. He said, "*Plausible deniability*, Em. That's our watchword."

"*Plausible deniability*," she repeated. "That's two words, Dwayne."

"Merely an insignificant detail," he said.

26 APRIL

P*rima Voce* had what went for the full story, Salvatore saw. That morning's paper carried a feature on page one, complete with a photograph of Carlo Casparia—his face and bright, tangled hair covered by a jacket—being escorted between two grim-faced uniformed policemen. They would take him from the *questura* to the prison where he would be held in preventive detention during the rest of the investigation. A second photograph featured Piero Fanucci, triumphantly announcing that they at last had their confession from the malefactor, and he was now *indagato*: formally named as principal suspect. The whereabouts of the child would be forthcoming, he had told the tabloid confidently.

No journalist questioned any of this. No one asked if the unfortunate Carlo had requested or been given an *avvocato* to sit at his side and advise him of his limited legal rights. Especially nothing was asked about the confession that Fanucci had prised from the homeless man or about the means by which Fanucci had got that confession. Neither the newspapers nor the *telegiornale* brought up anything other than the coup of a case having been resolved. They all knew quite well that to do anything else would put them in danger of being accused of *diffamazione a mezzo stampa*, and it was up to *il Pubblico Ministero* himself to decide if such defamation by the press had occurred.

Lo Bianco explained all this to DI Lynley when the Englishman appeared in his office. Obviously, he was going to have to speak to the parents of the little girl as soon as possible, and he wanted to have his facts in order. He'd brought with him a copy of *Prima Voce*. He'd also brought the question about why he hadn't been rung immediately once a confession was in hand. He sounded doubtful about the entire subject of Carlo Casparia and his guilt, however. Lo Bianco wasn't surprised by this. Detective Inspector Lynley did not appear to be a fool.

Lynley indicated the tabloid when he said, "Is this information reliable, Chief Inspector? The parents might well have seen it, and they'll have questions. First and foremost will be what this bloke's said about Hadiyyah: where he took her and where she is. May I ask how"—he hesitated tellingly—"this confession came about?"

Salvatore had to be careful with what he said. Fanucci had ears and eyes in every corner of the *questura*, and any explanation he gave the Scotland Yard DI about either *il Pubblico Ministero* or the Italian laws governing both the press and criminal investigations could be misinterpreted and used against him if he didn't proceed with maximum caution. For this reason, he took Lynley from the *questura* altogether, and together they walked the distance to the Lucca train station not far away. Across the street from the station was a café. He led the other officer to its bar, ordered two *cappuccini* and two *dolci*. He waited till they were set in front of them before he faced Lynley and, leaning against the bar with a look round the café to make sure there were no other officials present, he began to talk.

Twenty hours without rest or a lawyer present, with no food and only occasional water, had been enough to convince Carlo Casparia that his interests would best be served by telling the truth, he explained to Lynley. And if there were gaps within his memory of the events surrounding the child's disappearance, that was no real problem. For after twenty hours with *il Pubblico Ministero* and other hand-picked interrogators, exhaustion and hunger crept into one's mind, stimulating one to imagine—aloud, of course—what could adequately fill the blanks in one's memory. From this combination of imagination and reality, then, a complete story of the crime's commission emerged.

That it was small part fact and large part fantasy was of no concern to *il Pubblico Ministero*. A confession was what mattered to him since only a confession mattered to the press.

"I was afraid of that," Lynley admitted. "With due respect, it *is* a decidedly odd way to proceed. In my country—"

"*Sì, sì. Lo so*," Salvatore said. "Your prosecutors do not involve themselves in an investigation. But you are in my country now, and so you will learn that often we must allow certain things to play out so that other things—unknown to the *magistrato*—can play out as well."

Salvatore waited to see if Lynley would follow what he was hinting at. Lynley observed him for a long moment as a group of tourists entered the café. They were loud and aggressive, and Salvatore winced at the hardness of their language. Two of them went to the bar and ordered in English. Americans, he thought with resignation. They always believed the entire world spoke their language.

Lynley said, "What, then, actually comprised the confession of Carlo Casparia? The parents will want to know this, and for that matter, I'd like to know it as well."

Salvatore told him how Fanucci envisioned the crime, based upon the drug addict's words, dutifully committed to paper. It was simple enough, according to *il Pubblico Ministero*: Carlo is at the *mercato* in his usual position with *Ho fame* hanging round his neck. The little girl sees this, and she gives him her banana. He sees her innocence, and in her innocence, he also sees an opportunity. He follows her as she leaves the *mercato*, heading in the direction of Viale Agostino Marti.

"But why would she be heading there?" Lynley asked.

Salvatore waved off the question. "A mere detail that does not interest Piero Fanucci, my friend."

He went on with the rest of the crime as Fanucci envisioned it: Carlo snatches the little girl somewhere along the route. He stashes her at some stables where he has slept rough since first coming to Lucca when his parents tossed him out of their Padova home. There he holds her until he can find someone to whom he can hand her off for money. This money he uses to feed his drug habit. You will note he stopped begging at the *mercato* after her disappearance, no? *Certo*, he has no need for drug money at the moment and now we know why. Mark my words well. When this monster runs out of money, he will turn to begging at the *mercato* once again.

As far as *il Pubblico Ministero* was concerned, Salvatore explained, everything was neatly in place to mark Carlo Casparia as culpable: His motive was and would always be the acquisition of money for drugs. Everyone knew that *Ho fame* indicated the vagrant's hunger for cocaine, marijuana, heroin, methamphetamine, or whatever other substance he was shoving regularly into his system. His means were as obvious as being able to rise to his feet and follow the little girl once she generously and innocently handed over her banana to assuage his supposed hunger. The *mercato* itself was his opportunity. It was, as always, crowded with both shoppers and tourists. Just as no one had noticed the child being snatched from the vicinity of the accordion player—which, of course, we now know didn't happen anyway—so also no one had noticed Casparia taking her by the arm and guiding her away.

To all of this, the Englishman remained silent, but his face was sombre. He stirred his *cappuccino*. So far, he'd not tasted it, so intently had he been listening to Salvatore's tale. Now, he drank it straight down, and he broke his *dolce* into two pieces although he ate neither. "Forgive me for not entirely understanding how you proceed when this sort of conclusion is arrived at," he said. "Has the public minister any evidence that supports this man's confession or his own picture of the crime? Does he need any evidence?"

"*Sì, sì, sì*," Salvatore told him. The *magistrato*'s instructions—coming fast on the heels of Casparia's confession—were now being followed.

"And they are?" Lynley enquired politely.

The stables where Carlo Casparia had been living rough for so long were now being sorted out by a group of scenes-of-crime officers. They would be looking for evidence of the child's being held there for whatever period was necessary before Carlo decided what to do with her.

"Where are these stables, exactly?" Lynley asked.

They were in the Parco Fluviale, Salvatore told him. He had been intending to head there when Lynley arrived at the *questura*. Would the Englishman like to accompany him to see the scene?

He would indeed, Lynley told him.

It was only a brief ride round the enormous city wall to reach the *quartiere* of Borgo Giannotti. There, from beyond its main street with its line of busy shops, one ultimately gained access to the *parco*. During this ride, Lynley asked the questions that Salvatore had been anticipating as he told the tale of Carlo Casparia's recent confession.

What about the red car? the detective enquired. What did *il Pubblico Ministero* think about it? And was it the *magistrato*'s opinion that Casparia had given Hadiyyah over to the owner of the car, who then took Hadiyyah into the hills? And if the date on which this red car, the man, and the child had been sighted was the actual day on which Hadiyyah had gone missing . . . didn't it then follow that Carlo Casparia would have had to know all along to whom he was going to deliver the child? Didn't this suggest quite a degree of planning on his part? Did Signor Fanucci envision Casparia as capable of this? Did Salvatore himself envision this?

"As to the red convertible car," Salvatore said with an approving glance at Lynley, "the *magistrato* knows nothing of this car. Even as you and I go to the *parco* to ensure his will is being carried out, one of my officers is driving into the Alps with the man who saw that car. They will attempt to identify the point at which he saw it. A search will then be conducted of the immediate area of the lay-by where the car was parked. If nothing is found, every lay-by between the village where the mother of our witness lives and the start of that road into the Alps will be searched."

"Without the magistrate's knowledge?"

"Sometimes," Salvatore said, "Piero doesn't know what's good for Piero. I must help him realise this in the best way I can."

LUCCA
TUSCANY

The stables in the Parco Fluviale stood perhaps a mile along the lane that skirted the springtime rush of the River Serchio and coursed through the southern section of the park. They comprised a derelict set of buildings, long unused for their intended purpose, and out in front of them a faded sign giving the costs of horse hiring had been the victim of ill-talented graffiti artists and hunters looking to practise their shooting on its surface.

A crime scene van was parked on a narrow gravel access road into the stable area, and Lo Bianco pulled next to the police tape that marked the site as inaccessible to the few journalists who had already received word that some kind of action was happening in the *parco*. Lo Bianco muttered when he saw them. He ignored their demands of *"Che cosa succede?"* and took Lynley into the immediate vicinity of Carlo Casparia's home away from home.

At the moment, the activity was centred on a single stable backed by a tree-studded berm. This was situated behind a line of tangled shrubbery, most of which appeared to be wild roses coming into bloom, and it comprised a line of some dozen stalls with tall doors hanging open to display the disreputable contents within. Obviously, the entire place had been used as a dosshouse for ages by any number of people, and contained within it was so much rubbish that sorting through it all for a sign of a particular little girl's presence was going to take weeks. Filthy mattresses lay everywhere. Used hypodermic needles, limp condoms, and discarded takeaway food containers were scattered on the ground. Plastic cartons, old clothing, and mildewed blankets formed mounds in corners, while carrier bags filled with rotting food sent into the air a foul miasma, which had attracted vast clouds of flies and gnats.

Within all of this detritus moved two crime scene officers. *"Come va?"* Lo Bianco called out.

One lowered his mask and answered, *"Merda!"* The other said nothing but shook his head. It seemed, thought Lynley, that they knew their occupation was going to be a useless one.

Lo Bianco said to Lynley, "Come with me, *Ispettore*. There is something more to see in this place," and he walked to the back of the stables, where a faint trail through the tall wild grass and wildflowers led up the berm and between two chestnut trees.

Here, Lynley saw, a path had been created by dog walkers, cyclists, runners, and, perhaps, families out for a *passeggiata* on long summer evenings. It was well worn, and it followed along the top of the berm in both directions, mimicking the route of the lane through the *parco* as well as the course of the river. Lo Bianco began to walk along it. In less than one hundred yards, he broke to the left, descended another berm, crossed a wooded area thick with sycamores, alders, and beeches, and came out on the edge of a playing field.

Lynley saw at once where they were. Across the field lay a patch of gravel suitable as a small car park. To the right of this two picnic tables rested beneath the trees. In front of them and across a path was the playing field, divided by more concrete paths along which saplings grew. Far to the west of all this stood a café in which, he assumed, the parents of the children who came to this place to be coached by Lorenzo Mura might wait, enjoying refreshments as they watched their budding football players undertaking another session with the man in order to improve their skills.

Lynley looked at Lo Bianco. The chief inspector, he saw, was not the fool of Piero Fanucci, no matter what the *magistrato* might think in the matter.

"I wonder," Lynley said, indicating the playing field, "if Signor Casparia might be able to 'imagine' something more, Chief Inspector?"

"What would this be?" Lo Bianco asked.

"We have, after all," Lynley said, "only Lorenzo Mura's word for it that Hadiyyah was taken from the market that day. You must have thought of that at some point."

Lo Bianco smiled slightly. "This would be one of the reasons why I have had my own suspicions about Signor Mura," he replied.

"Would you mind if I talked to him? About more, I mean, than merely explaining the nature of Carlo Casparia's 'confession.'"

"I mind not in the least," Lo Bianco said. "*Nel frattempo*, I shall be looking at the other *calciatori* on his team. One of them may drive a red convertible. This would, I think, be interesting to know."

PISA
TUSCANY

As far as he was concerned, meeting anywhere near Campo dei Miracoli was lunacy since there were dozens of other places where they could have met unnoticed in the city. But it was to Campo dei Miracoli that he'd been summoned, so he went to that site of tourism run amok. He worked his way through what seemed like five hundred people taking photographs of their mates pretending to hold up the tower, and he crossed between the Duomo and the Baptistery to the *cimitero* behind its high and forbidding walls. He went to the room he'd been instructed to find: where several of the location's *affreschi* had been moved after their restoration. No one would be there, he'd been assured. If, when the tour buses stopped and debouched their passengers at the gates to Piazza dei Miracoli, the *gitanti* were given forty minutes to scurry about and have their photographs taken before being carted off to the next site on their list, they weren't about to seek out the cemetery. With its half-demolished *affreschi* and its one decent sculpture of a woman in repose, this place would be deserted, and they would be safe from scrutiny here.

Safe from scrutiny they needed to be, he thought sardonically, considering what his employer looked like. For never had vanity led a man to such stupidity in the area of his personal appearance as it had led Michelangelo Di Massimo.

Di Massimo was already there, waiting. As promised, he was the only person in the room with the restored *affreschi*, and from a bench in the centre of the room he was studying one of them—or at least pretending to do so—with a guidebook opened on his knee and a pair of half-moon reading glasses perched on the end of his nose. The professorial air they lent him was completely at odds with the rest of him: the bleached yellow hair, the black leather jacket, the leather *pantaloni*, the stiff black boots. No one would mistake him for a professor of anything or even for a student of anything. But then, no one would mistake him for what he was, either.

There was no point to hiding his approach, so he did nothing to stifle the sharp tap of his footsteps on the marble floor. He lowered himself onto the bench next to Di Massimo, and he gazed upon the fresco to which the other man was giving his rapt attention. He saw that Di Massimo was fixed upon his namesake. Sword in hand, Michael the Archangel was either driving someone out of paradise—at least he reckoned it was paradise—or he was welcoming someone into paradise. Who really cared? For he simply couldn't work out what all the shouting was about when it came to the rescued *affreschi* in this place. They were faded and worn and in spots whatever they depicted was barely visible.

He wanted a cigarette. Either that or a woman. But the thought of women took him directly back to his wallow in the dirt with his half-mad cousin and he preferred not to think about that.

He couldn't fathom what got into him whenever he saw Domenica. She'd been pretty enough once, but that time was long past and *still* when she was in his presence, he wanted to possess her, to show her . . . something. And what did that say about him, that he still wanted the madwoman after all this time?

Next to him on the bench, Michelangelo Di Massimo stirred. He snapped his guidebook closed and deposited it into a rucksack at his feet. From this he took a folded newspaper. He said, "The British police are now involved. *Prima Voce* has the story. There's been a television appeal. You saw it?"

Of course he had not. In the evening when the *telegiornale* was broadcast, he was at his regular job at Ristorante Maestoso, unavailable to the television news. During his days, he was preoccupied with seducing the *commesse* in the fancier shops and boutiques in town in order to talk them into ringing up a pair of socks for him while they bagged a fine linen shirt instead. Thus he had no time for television or tabloids. Whatever he knew about this matter of searching for the missing child, he knew only from Di Massimo.

Di Massimo passed the copy of *Prima Voce* over to him. He scanned the story. Scotland Yard, a detective inspector in Lucca to act as liaison with the parents of the girl, more information about those parents, dismissive remarks about British policing from that idiot Fanucci, and a carefully worded statement from Chief Inspector Lo Bianco indicating cooperation between the two police forces. There was an accompanying photo of the English detective in conversation with Lo Bianco. They were in front of the *questura* in Lucca, Lo Bianco's arms crossed on his chest and his head lowered as he listened to something the Englishman was saying to him.

He passed the tabloid back to Di Massimo. He felt rather irritated with him. He hated having his time wasted, and if he'd had to come from the centre of town to Campo dei Miracoli merely to see something that he could have seen by stopping at the nearest *giornalaio* and purchasing a copy of the newspaper, he was going to be more irritated still. Thus he gestured rudely at the paper and said, *"Allora?"* in a way that indicated his impatience. To underscore this, he got up and paced the distance to the farthest wall. "This cannot be a surprise to you, Michelangelo. She's missing. She's a child. She's gone without a trace. She's British." The implication was obvious: Of course the English coppers were going to stick their fingers into this pie he and Di Massimo were baking. Had Di Massimo expected something less?

"Not the point," Di Massimo said. "Sit down. I don't want to raise my voice."

He waited till his order had been complied with before he went on. "This man and Lo Bianco . . . they came to my *calcio* practice the other day."

He felt a sudden shift in his equilibrium. "And they *talked* to you?" he asked.

Di Massimo shook his head. "They thought—I expect—that I did not see them. But this"—he tapped the side of his nose—"has a talent for knowing when the cops are present. They came, and they watched. Less than five minutes. Then they were gone."

He felt a momentary surge of relief and said, "So you do not know—"

"Aspetti." Di Massimo went on to say that the two men had come to see him on the previous day, interrupting his appointment with his *parrucchiere* in the midst of having his blond locks maintained.

"Merda!" This was the worst possible news. "How in God's name did they find you?" he demanded. "First at *calcio* and then this other? How the hell did they find you?"

"How does not matter," Di Massimo said.

"Of course it matters! If not to you, then to me. If they're on to you . . . If they've found you already . . ." He felt panic rising. "You swore to me enough time had passed. You said that no one would connect you to this matter of the girl." He thought rapidly, trying to see what other connections were possible for the police to make. For if they'd found Michelangelo Di Massimo within a week of the girl's disappearance, how much longer would it be till they found him as well? "This has to be taken care of," he said. "Now. Today. As soon as possible."

"Which is why you and I are meeting, my friend," Michelangelo told him. He looked at him levelly. "I find that it's time. We're clear on that, yes?"

He nodded once. "I know what to do."

"Be hasty about doing it, then."

FATTORIA DI SANTA ZITA
TUSCANY

Lynley wasn't entirely honest with Lo Bianco about speaking to Lorenzo Mura. He also wanted to talk to Angelina. So with the chief inspector's blessing on the matter, he drove out to the *fattoria*. It appeared to be a busy day at the place, with all evidence saying that, one way or another, life had to go on.

Workmen were crawling about the ancient farmhouse that was part of the property, some of them unloading tiles clearly meant for the roof, others of them carrying heavy boards into the structure, still others banging about inside the building with their hammers ringing in the air. At the winery, a young man was within, offering tastes of Lorenzo's Chianti to five individuals whose bicycles and discarded rucksacks indicated a spring cycling tour through the verdant district. Lorenzo stood at the fence of a paddock not far beyond the tall hedge that separated the old villa from the business end of the *fattoria*. He was speaking there to a bearded, middle-aged man, and as Lynley approached them, he saw this individual take a white envelope from the back pocket of his jeans and pass it over to Lorenzo Mura.

They exchanged a few more words before the man nodded and walked to a pickup truck that was parked in front of the wrought-iron gates giving access to the driveway up to the villa. He got in this truck and in a moment had made a quick turn around and was heading out of the place. Lynley observed him as he passed. He'd put on dark glasses and the kind of wide-brimmed straw hat that shades one's face from the sun. It was, thus, impossible to see any particulars of what he looked like aside from his beard, which was dark and thick.

Lynley approached Lorenzo. Within the paddock, he saw, five donkeys stood, a male, two females, and two foals. They were grazing beneath an enormous mulberry tree, their tails swishing to ward off flies, feasting on the fresh, sweet growth of springtime grasses. They were handsome animals, all five of them. They looked well cared for.

Without preamble, Lorenzo told him that raising donkeys for sale was another way that he supported life at Fattoria di Santa Zita. The man who had just left the property had come to purchase one of the foals. A donkey, he said, was always useful to those who lived and made their money off the land.

Lynley didn't think that the sale of one or two or twenty baby animals was going to go far in supporting everything about this particular *fattoria* that needed supporting, but instead of mentioning this, he asked about the old farmhouse and the work going on in, on, and around it.

This, Lorenzo told him, was being turned into rooms for letting to tourists who wished to experience life in the countryside by staying at one of Italy's many *agriturismi*. Eventually, he added, they would have a swimming pool, terraces for sunbathing, and a tennis court.

"Big plans, then," Lynley noted pleasantly. Big plans, of course, required big money.

Sì, there would always be plans for the *fattoria*, Lorenzo told him. And then he shifted gears entirely, saying to Lynley in English, "You must talk to her, *Ispettore*. Please, you must tell her to allow me to take her to the doctor in Lucca now."

Lynley frowned. He switched to Italian, asking Mura, "Is Angelina ill?"

"*Venga*" was Lorenzo's response, to which he added that Lynley could see for himself up at the villa. "All the day yesterday she has this sickness," he said. "She keeps nothing inside. Not soup, not bread, not tea, not milk. She tells me not to worry because this is the pregnancy. She reminds me she has not been well from the first day of it. She says to me that this will pass. She says I worry because this is *my* first child but it is not *her* first child and I must be patient because she will be well soon enough. But how can I be patient when I see she is ill, when I believe she must visit a doctor, and when *she* believes she is not ill at all?"

They were walking up the sweeping loop of the villa's formal drive as Lorenzo spoke. Lynley thought of his late wife's pregnancy. She, too, had been ill for the first part of it. He, too, had been concerned. He told Lorenzo this, but the Italian man remained unconvinced.

Angelina was on the loggia. She was lying on a chaise longue with a blanket covering her. Next to her, a mosaic-topped metal table held a transparent jug of what appeared to be blood orange juice. A drinking glass stood next to this, but nothing had been poured into it. A plate sat near to this glass, its offering of a circle of biscuits, meat, fruit, and cheese all disregarded save for one very large strawberry out of which a single bite had been taken.

Lynley could understand why the Italian man was worried. Angelina looked weak. She smiled wanly as they crossed the loggia to her. "Inspector Lynley," she murmured, as she struggled to sit upright. "You've caught me napping." She searched his face. "Has there been word of something?"

Lorenzo strode to the table and inspected its rejected offerings. He said, "*Cara, devi mangiare e bere.*" He poured orange juice into the glass and pressed it upon her.

"I did try, Renzo." She indicated the single strawberry with its marking of a minuscule bite taken. "You're worrying far too much. I'll be fine with a little bit of rest." And to Lynley, "Inspector, if there's something—"

"She must to see a doctor," Lorenzo said to Lynley. "She will not listen."

Lynley said, "May I . . . ?" and indicated a wicker chair nearby.

"Of course," she said. "Please." And to Lorenzo, "Darling, stop being foolish. I'm *not* a buttercup. And I'm also not what matters just now. So do be quiet about doctors or leave us to talk because"—she took a breath to steady what she had to say, which she directed to Lynley—"you have word of something, I expect. Please tell me."

Lynley glanced at Lorenzo, who'd flushed. He had not sat and now he walked to the rear of the loggia, where he stood behind the chaise longue with his arms crossed and his birthmark darkening noticeably.

Briefly, Lynley told Angelina of Carlo Casparia, of the "confession" extricated from the man by the public minister, and of Chief Inspector Lo Bianco's doubts regarding this confession. He related the details of the search ongoing at the stables. He mentioned a possible sighting that had taken place in the Apuan Alps. He did not speak of a red convertible or of the exact nature of the sighting: a man leading a little girl into the woods. The first was something that needed to be held back from everyone. The second would only result in the woman's terrified panic.

"The police are looking into this," he told her in reference to the Alps. "In the meantime, the tabloids . . ." He showed her the front page of *Prima Voce*. He discovered they had not seen the paper that day as neither of them had been into town to purchase a newspaper and none were delivered to the *fattoria*. "It's best, I daresay, to disregard all this. They have only limited information."

Angelina was silent for a long moment during which the hammer blows from the old farmhouse sounded faintly. She finally said, "What does Hari think?" and behind her Lorenzo let out an exasperated breath. She said to him, "Renzo, *please* . . ."

"*Sì, sì*," Mura said.

"He doesn't know any of this yet," Lynley told her, "unless he's picked up the tabloid somewhere. He was already gone from the *pensione* when I came down to breakfast."

"*Gone?*" This incredulously from Lorenzo.

"I expect he's still putting up the missing-child handbills. It's difficult for him—and for all of you, I know—just to be idle and have to wait for information."

"*Inutile*," Lorenzo said.

"Perhaps," Lynley said. "But I've found that sometimes even an act that seems useless turns out to be the single action that breaks a case."

"He won't return to London till she's found." Angelina looked out at the lawn, although there was nothing on it to hold her attention. She quietly said, "I do so regret what I did. I just wanted to be free of him, but I knew . . . I'm sorry about everything."

That desire to be free of other people, of life's complexities, of the past that often clung to one like a ragtag group of mendicant children . . . This led people into the commission of acts that paved the way to remorse. But on the pathway to regret, the corpses of other people's dreams often lay rotting. It was this that Lynley wished to talk about. But he wished to talk about it to Angelina alone, and not in the presence of her lover.

He said to Lorenzo, "I'd like a few minutes alone with Angelina, if you don't mind, Signor Mura."

Mura apparently did mind. He said, "We have no secrets from each other, Angelina and I. What you say to her can be said to me."

"I understand that," Lynley said. "But because of our previous conversation—yours and mine . . . ?" Let the man think that what he had to say to Angelina Upman involved her health and getting her to town to see a doctor, Lynley thought. Anything to have the Italian man remove himself for a few minutes of conversation that, he suspected, would only be entirely honest if Mura absented himself from it.

He did so, although with marked reluctance. He bent to Angelina first, and he kissed the top of her head. He said, "*Cara,*" quietly and then he left the loggia. He headed in the direction of the gates to the drive and the work that was going on beyond the tall hedge that marked off the old villa's immediate grounds from the rest of the *fattoria.*

Angelina turned her head to him by rolling it his way on the headrest of the chaise longue. She said, "What is it, Inspector Lynley? Is it about Hari? I know you can see . . . Renzo has no reason to be jealous of him. I give him no reason, and he *has* no reason. But the fact that Hari and I have a child . . . It's created a bond where he'd prefer there be none."

"I daresay that's normal," Lynley said. "He's uneasy, unsure of where he stands with you."

"I try to make it clear to him. He's the one. He's the . . . the endgame for me. But culturally . . . my past with other men . . . I think that's what makes it difficult."

"I have to ask this," Lynley said, moving his wicker chair closer to her. "I hope you understand. Every avenue regarding Hadiyyah's disappearance has to be explored, and this is one of them."

She looked alarmed when she said, "What is it?"

"Your other lovers."

"What other lovers?"

"Here, in Italy."

"There are no—"

"Forgive me. It's a question of the past being a form of prologue, if you understand. My concern is that if you were involved with Esteban Castro while you were also seeing Lorenzo and still living with Azhar . . . I hope you can see how that leads to the assumption that there might be others that you've been unwilling to mention in front of Lorenzo."

Her cheeks flushed with the first colour he'd seen upon them since mounting the steps to the loggia. "What's this to do with Hadiyyah, Inspector?"

"I think it has more to do with how a man might act to wound you if he discovered he wasn't your only lover. And that has everything to do with Hadiyyah."

She met his gaze for a moment so that, he assumed, he could read her face as she spoke. "There are no other lovers, Inspector Lynley. And if you want me to swear to it, I'm happy to do so. There is only Lorenzo."

He evaluated her statements: the words themselves and the way she spoke them. Her body language suggested she was telling the truth, but a woman accomplished at balancing relationships with three men at once would have to be a skilled actress to do so. That in addition to the fact that when a horse had spots, it was generally impossible to get rid of them, prompted him to say, "What would have changed you, if I may ask?"

"I don't really know," she said. "A desire not to repeat the past? A step into adulthood?" She looked down at the blanket that covered her, fingering the well-worn satin that edged it. She said, "Before, I was always searching for something that was out of my reach. Now, I think my reach and my grasp have become the same."

"What were you reaching for?"

She considered this, her delicate eyebrows drawn together. "A way to be my own person. And I kept expecting this distinct form of *me* to arrive in the hands of a man. When it didn't—for how could it possibly?—I found another man. And then another. Two before Hari. Then Hari himself, along with Esteban, and, yes, even Renzo." She looked at him. "I've hurt many people through the years, especially Hari. It's not something I'm proud of. But it's who I was."

"And now?"

"I'm making a life with Renzo. We're becoming a family. He wants to marry and I want that as well. I wasn't sure at first, but now I am."

Lynley considered this: Angelina's initial uncertainty about Mura and what that uncertainty could have meant to the man and what the man might have done to alter things. He said, "At what point did you become sure of him?"

"I don't think I understand what you mean."

"I suppose I mean: Was there a single moment when everything altered for you, when it became clear to you that what you have with Signor Mura was, perhaps, more important than seeking out other men to build—as you've said—an identity for you?"

She shook her head slowly, but when she spoke, Lynley saw that she was adept at connecting the dots among his questions. She said, "Renzo loves Hadiyyah and he loves me. And you can't sit there thinking that he might have arranged something . . . something horrible like this so that he could prove to me . . . or make me certain about him . . . And that's what you're thinking, isn't it, Inspector? *How* could you think it? How could you begin to believe that he would do something to devastate me like this?"

Because it was possible and it was his job, Lynley thought. But more than that, because it would so obviously work to engage her entirely in Mura's life if Hadiyyah should end up permanently absent.

VILLA RIVELLI
TUSCANY

Sister Domenica Giustina allowed Carina into the *giardino*. The day was hotter than normal, and the fountains in the garden were enticing to the child. Had she not embraced God's punishment for her sin of fornication, Sister Domenica Giustina might even have joined the little girl. For with her green cotton trousers rolled up to her knees, Carina was thoroughly enjoying herself. She waded in the largest of the pools, dodged laughing beneath the spray from its fountain, and splashed water in the air to form rainbows all round them. She called out to Sister Domenica Giustina, "*Venga! Fa troppo caldo oggi.*" But although the day *was* too hot, Sister Domenica Giustina knew that her suffering could not be lessened even for five minutes in the cool, pleasant water.

Forty days of punishment were necessary for what she and her cousin Roberto had done. During this period she would wear the same garments—rank though they were with the smell of him, of her, and of their mating—and she would remove them only to add thorns to the swaddling in which she wrapped her body. Nightly she would examine the wounds, for they had begun to suppurate. But this was good as the leaking pus said that her reparation was acceptable to God. God would inform her when she had done enough, and until He did so through the means of the pus's disappearance, she must continue on the path she'd chosen to illustrate the depth of her sorrow for her sins against Him.

"Suor Domenica!" the little girl cried, falling to her knees in the water so that it rose up to her waist. "*Deve venire! Possiamo pescare. Vuole pescare? Le piace pescare? Venga!*"

There were no fish in the water of this fountain, and she was being far too loud. Sister Domenica Giustina recognised this, but she could hardly bear to stifle the child's pleasure. Still, she understood it was necessary so she said, "*Carina, fai troppo rumore,*" and held a finger to her lips. She looked towards the great villa to the east of the sunken *giardino* and this look was to tell the little girl that her noise must not reach the villa's inhabitants. There were dangers everywhere.

She'd been told from the first to keep the child inside the great stone barn, and she'd disobeyed. When she'd taken him to the villa's cellar to see the little girl, he'd smiled and spoken kindly to Carina, but Sister Domenica Giustina knew him better than he knew himself and she could see round his eyes that he hadn't been pleased.

He'd made this clear to her before he left. "What stupid game are you playing at?" he'd hissed. "Keep her inside till I tell you otherwise. Can you get that into your thick skull, Domenica?" And he'd poked at her head sharply to indicate just how thick her skull was. He'd added, "God's grace, after what you've done to me, I would think . . . *Cristo*, I should leave you to rot."

She'd tried to explain. The sun and the air were good for children. Carina needed to be out of the damp, dank rooms above the barn, and had she been told to stay inside, she wouldn't have done so. No child would. Besides, there was no one about in this remote place and even if there had been someone, wasn't it time they told the world that Carina was theirs?

"*Sciocca, sciocca!*" had been his reply. He cupped her chin in his hand. His fingers increased the pressure till her whole jaw ached, and finally he threw her to one side. "She stays inside. Do you understand me? No vegetable garden, no cellar, no fish pond, no lawn. She stays inside."

Domenica said that she understood. But the day was hot and the fountains at the villa were so inviting and the child was so young. It could not hurt, Sister Domenica Giustina decided, to give her an hour to enjoy herself.

Still, she looked about nervously. She decided it would be best to stand guard from above at the edge of the *peschiera*, so she climbed the stone steps from the sunken garden to the fish pond and she made certain that she and Carina were still alone.

She walked to the spot from which the hillside fell to expose through the trees and the shrubbery the road that twisted into the hills from the valley below. Thus, she saw him. As before he raced up the road in his bright red car. She could hear, even at this distance, the roar from its engine as he changed down gears. He was going too fast, as he always did. There was a distant squeal from his tyres as he took one of the hairpin turns too sharply. He needed to slow, but he never would. He liked the speed.

Between where she stood and where he drove, the air seemed to shimmer in the heat. It made her feel indolent, and although she knew she had to get Carina out of the sunken garden, up to the rooms above the barn, and into dry clothes before his arrival, somehow she couldn't make herself move.

So it was that she saw it all when it happened. He missed a sudden hairpin turn in the road. Engine roaring and gears changing frantically, he shot through the insubstantial crash barrier. He hung there in the sky for a moment. Then the car disappeared as it dropped and dropped down the side of a cliff into whatever lay below: boulders, gnarled trees, a dried riverbed, another villa tucked away from sight. She did not know. She only saw that he was there one moment, charging into the hills, and then in the next moment he was gone.

She stood there unmoving, waiting for what would come next: perhaps the sound of impact or a fireball shooting into the sky. But nothing happened. It was as if the hand of God had struck her cousin down in an instant, his soul being called into the presence of the Almighty to account, finally, for his sin.

She returned to the sunken garden, standing above it and watching the child below. The sunlight glinted off her lovely hair, and through the spray from the fountain, she looked like someone behind a veil. Seeing her thus, joyful and open and trusting, it was difficult to believe that she, too, bore the stain of sin. But so she did and so that sin had to be dealt with.

27 APRIL

Whien Barbara walked into Detective Superintendent Isabelle Ardery's office, she knew something had gone wrong with the master plan of lies that she'd come up with to get away from the Met's offices five days earlier in order to attempt to deal with the Sayyid crisis. She reckoned that at the eleventh hour, Mrs. Flo had developed feet of ice in the matter of confirming the "fall" taken by one of the residents of her care home in Greenford. But as it turned out, that good woman had taken the decision that only an elaboration of the story of the fall would do to persuade Barbara's superior officers that everything was on the complete up-and-up regarding Barbara's absence from beneath DI John Stewart's spatulate thumb.

Stewart was in the super's office as well. He sat on one of the two chairs in front of Ardery's desk, and he turned to give Barbara a barely disguised contemptuous once-over when she joined them. The superintendent herself was standing, looking trim, fit, and well turned out as always. Beyond her shoulders, the windows offered a grey day promising more rain to confirm what that poet had said about the month of April.

Isabelle Ardery nodded as Barbara entered. She said, "Sit," and

Barbara gave idle thought to barking doglike in response. But she did as she was told. Ardery then said, "Tell her, John," and she placed both manicured hands on the windowsill, leaning against it and listening as Stewart recited what Barbara quickly saw was her likely professional epitaph.

"My flowers for your mother were undeliverable, as it happens," Stewart said. And didn't the bloody bastard look pleased about this, Barbara thought. "The hospital in question had no record of a patient with her name. I'm wondering, Sergeant . . . Has she an alias, perhaps?"

"What're you yapping on about?" Barbara asked him tiredly, although her mind started energetically darting round possibilities like a pinball scoring a multitude of points.

For the purposes of dramatic effect, Stewart had brought a notebook along, and he flipped it open in his palm. "Mrs. Florence Magentry," he announced. "An ambulance company called St. John's, she *thinks*, although it could have been St. Julian's, St. James's, St. Judith's, or any number of sanctified names beginning with J. At any rate, it was *Saint* Somebody, or so she claims despite the fact that, as it happens, there is no such creature. Next: Accident and Emergency at the local hospital and a broken hip that wasn't a broken hip at all but seemed to be so, so she was only in for an hour or a day or two or three but who really knows because the fact of the bloody matter is that she never had a sodding fall at all." He snapped the notebook closed. "Do you want to explain what the hell you're up to when no one's given you leave to—?"

"That'll do, John," Ardery said.

Taking the offensive was her only option. Barbara said to Stewart "What *is* it with you? You've got a robbery and murder case on, and you're using your time to decide whether my poor mum . . . ? You're outrageous, you are. As it happens, she was taken by a *private* ambulance to a *private* clinic because she has her own *private* insurance, and if you'd decided to sodding ask me about it instead of creeping round in the background like a third-rate housebreaker—"

"And that'll do as well," Ardery said.

But Barbara's heart was pounding. No matter what she said, Stewart was going to be able to check her story, and her only hope was to make him look worse for his compulsion to put the thumbscrews to her than she looked doing a scarper from work because she'd had to deal with that damn louse Mitch Corsico and his determination to speak to Azhar's son, Sayyid.

She said to Ardery, "He's been like this since you assigned me to him, guv. He's got me under some bloody microscope like I'm an amoeba he wants to study. *And* he's using me as a sodding typist."

"Are you actually trying to put the spotlight on me?" Stewart demanded. "You're out of order, and you damn well know it."

"You deserve the sodding spotlight on you and you've needed it on you since your wife walked out and you decided to punish every female on earth because of it. And who the hell could blame the poor woman? Life with you would make anyone prefer life on the street with a dog."

"I want her written up for this," Stewart said to Ardery. "I want it in her file and then I want a CIB1—"

"Both of you are out of order," Ardery snapped. She walked to her desk, jerked the chair out, and sank into it, looking from Stewart to Barbara to Stewart again. "I've had enough of whatever it is between the two of you. It stops here, in this office, this very minute or you're both facing disciplinary action. Now get back to work. And if I hear anything more about you"—this to Barbara—"acting in *any* way that appears remotely dodgy, you'll be facing not only disciplinary action but what follows it. Got it?"

Stewart's thin lips creased themselves into a smile. But it vanished soon enough when Ardery went on. "And you," she said to him, "are an officer in charge of a robbery and murder enquiry so *act* like an officer in charge of a robbery and murder enquiry. Which, I'd like to remind you, John, means that you assign your people in a manner that utilises their talents and does *not* appease your need for . . . for whatever the hell it is that you apparently need. Am I being clear?" She didn't wait for an answer. She picked up the phone, punched in a few numbers, and said in dismissal, "Now for God's sake get out of here and get back to work."

They did the first but paused short of the second. In the corridor, DI Stewart grabbed Barbara's arm. At his touch, she felt a surge of outrage steam through her veins and she was moments from applying her knee to a place on his body where he'd long remember the encounter. She said, "You bloody get your hand off me or I'll have you charged with—"

"You listen to me, you bleeding bovine," he whispered. "Your move in there was clever as hell. But I'm holding cards you don't even know about, and when I want to use them, I will. Understand that and act at your own peril, Sergeant Havers."

"Oh my God, you knot up my knickers," Barbara said.

She walked away, but her mind was like an arguing Greek chorus in her head. Part of it was shrieking to beware, to take heed, to walk the straight and narrow before it was too late. The other part was planning her next move and that part was quickly subdividing itself into the half dozen next moves that were possible.

Into this mental embroilment, Dorothea Harriman called Barbara's name. Barbara turned to see the departmental secretary cradling a telephone receiver in her hand. She said, "You're wanted at once down below."

Barbara cursed quietly. What now? she thought. *Down below* meant Reception. She had a visitor and was intended to go fetch him. She said, "Who the hell . . . ?" to Dorothea.

"Reception says it's someone in a costume."

"A *costume?*"

"Dressed like a cowboy?" Then Dorothea seemed to twig because Mitchell Corsico had been inside the Met offices before. Her cornflower-blue eyes got round as she said, "Detective Sergeant, it must be that bloke who was embedded—" But Barbara stopped her as fast as she could.

"I'm on it," she told Dorothea, and with a nod at the phone, "Tell them I'm on my way down, okay?"

Dorothea nodded, but Barbara had no intention of heading down to Reception to be seen in the company of Mitchell Corsico. So she ducked into the stairwell a short distance down the corridor, and she took out her mobile and punched in Corsico's number. When he answered, she was brevity itself. "Get out of here. You and I are finished."

"I've rung you eight or nine times" was his response. "No reply, no reply? Tsk, tsk, tsk, Barb. I thought a personal appearance in Victoria Street was in order."

"What's in order is for you to sod off," Barbara hissed.

"You and I need a word."

"Not going to happen."

"I think it is. So I can remain down here and ask every Tom, Dick, and Sherlock who passes by to fetch you—introducing myself to them along the way, of course—or you can come down and we can have a quick chat. What's it going to be?"

Barbara shut her eyes hard, in the hope that this would allow her to think. She had to get rid of the journalist, she couldn't be seen with him, she was a bloody fool for having used him in the first place, if anyone knew she'd been his snout in this matter of Hadiyyah and her family . . . So she had to get him clear away from the Met, and there was only one way short of killing the bugger.

She said, "Go to the post office."

"What the fuck? Are you hearing me at all, Sergeant? Do you know the damage I could do if you don't—"

"Stop being a wanker for thirty seconds. The post office is directly across the street, all right? Go over there and I'll meet you. It's either that or you and I are finished because if I'm seen with you . . . You do get the point, don't you, since you're using it to threaten me in the first place?"

"I'm not threatening you."

"And I'm your great-grandmother. Now are you going across the street or are we going to argue the finer points of blackmail: emotional, professional, monetary, or otherwise?"

"All right," he agreed. "The post office. And I hope you show, Barb. If you don't . . . Well, you won't much like what comes next."

"I'm giving you five minutes," she told him.

"That," he said, "is all I need."

Barbara rang off and considered her options. There were very few in the aftermath of her meeting with Stewart and Ardery. She rubbed her forehead and looked at her watch. Five minutes, she thought. Dorothea could surely cover her for the time it would take to get to the post office, have a word with Corsico, and get back to John Stewart's incident room.

She gave the departmental secretary the word.

"You're in the ladies'," Dorothea said cooperatively. "Female troubles, and do you need chapter and verse on what they are, Detective Inspector Stewart?"

"Ta, Dee." Barbara hurried for the lifts and made for Reception and, from there, out of the building.

Corsico was just inside the post office doors. Barbara didn't wait for him to reveal the purpose of his call upon her. Instead, she marched up to him, grabbed him by the arm, and jerked him over to a vending machine selling postage stamps.

"Right," she said. "Here I am at your beck and call, and this is happening once and once only. What do you want? This is our swan song, Mitchell, so make it good."

"I'm not here to argue." He glanced down at her hand, still gripping his arm. She released her hold on him and he took a moment to brush his fingers against the suede of his fringed jacket where she'd left an imprint.

"Great," she said. "Nice. Brilliant. So let's make this good-bye and we can part sadder but wiser with our love unfulfilled."

"Actually, that can't happen quite yet."

"And why would that be?"

"Because I want two interviews."

"I don't bloody care what you want after the Love Rat Dad story, Mitchell."

"Oh, I think you need to care. And I think you will. P'rhaps not at this precise moment, but soon."

She narrowed her eyes. "What're you on about?"

He had a rucksack with him, and from this he pulled out the digital camera she'd seen round his neck at Sayyid's comprehensive. It wasn't a palm-size suitable-for-tourist-snaps job, either. It was, instead, a professional model with a large viewing screen. He clicked it on, scrolled, and came up with what he wanted. He turned the camera so that Barbara could see what he'd photographed.

On the screen was the brouhaha that had occurred in front of

Sayyid's school. The boy and his grandfather were in a tangle, with Barbara and Nafeeza trying to separate them. Mitchell clicked from this to another photo, with Barbara hustling them all into the car. In a third, she was talking through the vehicle's open window to Nafeeza, and in the background the secondary comprehensive was clearly visible. So were the date and the time on each of the photos, comprising the very moments Barbara was putatively on her way to her mother's bedside after her tragic fall.

"What I'm thinking," Mitchell said, "is that *Met Officer Involved with Love Rat Dad* has a very nice ring to it. It's a follow-up story that opens up worlds of additional possibilities, don't you think?"

The real issue for Barbara, of course, wasn't a story in *The Source* about her "relationship" with Azhar but rather the evidence that she had both lied to her superior officers and disobeyed their orders. But Mitchell Corsico didn't know this, and Barbara was determined to keep him from finding out. She said, "So . . . what? All I see is an officer from the Met breaking up a family row. What do you see, Mitchell?"

"I see Sayyid telling me that this 'officer from the Met' is his father's extra little bit on the side. I see a score of follow-up interviews coming from every quarter, or at least the quarter relating to Chalk Farm and everyone in residence at a conversion in Eton Villas."

"You actually want to embarrass yourself like that? You don't have proof of anything, and I swear to God: You run a story like that and the next person you'll hear from is my solicitor."

"For what? Just quoting a furious young boy who hates his dad? Come along, Barb, you know the score. Facts are interesting, but innuendo is what gives a story its charm. *Involved* is the operative word in the headline. It can mean anything. The reader will decide exactly what all the comings and goings between your two abodes actually mean. You didn't mention that to me, naughty you. I hadn't a clue you actually knew these people, let alone that you live within lip-locking distance of Love Rat Dad."

Barbara thought feverishly about how to handle the reporter at this point. Temporising seemed the only possibility available to her other than caving in to his demands. If she caved in, though, she knew he had her by the throat. So stalling for time was the only direction in which she could turn.

She said, attempting to sound defeated, "Who d'you want to interview?"

"That's my girl," he said.

"I am *not*—"

"Yes, yes. Whatever," he agreed. "I want one heart-to-heart with Nafeeza. And then a follow-up with Taymullah Azhar."

Barbara knew that Nafeeza would have her tongue ripped out before she'd talk to any reporter. She also knew that Mitchell Corsico was mad as a hallucinating monkey eating plastic bananas if he thought Azhar was going to submit himself to the scrutiny of *The Source*. But the fact that there appeared to be no end to the reporter's self-delusion could, she saw, be used to her advantage for at least a day. So she said, "I'll have to speak to both of them. This will take time."

"Twenty-four hours," he told her.

"It'll take longer, Mitchell," Barbara argued. "Azhar's in Italy, and if you think Nafeeza's going to come round quickly to the idea of spilling her guts to you—"

"That's what I have to offer," he said. "Twenty-four hours. After that, it's the Met and the Love Rat Dad. Your choice, Barb."

CHALK FARM
LONDON

So she had to make a move. Barbara knew there was no point to making an attempt to convince Nafeeza that talking to *The Source* was in her best interests. Not only was it not in her best interests to say a single word to anyone representing that piece-of-rubbish-in-newspaper's-clothing, it was also Barbara's own use of the tabloid that had started them all down this road to public humiliation in the first place. To take on more of the mantle of responsibility for what *The Source* was doing to the abandoned family and would next do to the abandoned family should Nafeeza talk to them was something that Barbara wasn't about to do.

That left her with Azhar, with convincing Azhar to talk to Corsico in order to defend himself from the attack upon him as the Love Rat Dad who'd deserted wife and children. She would then have to persuade Corsico to accept this compromise of a single interview as the best she could do. She thought she could manage this manoeuvre if she explained to Azhar that her job was virtually on the line. The only question for her was whether she could live with herself after she had done so.

She hadn't spoken to Azhar since learning from Dwayne Doughty that all of the information collected by the investigator and his assistant regarding Angelina Upman's whereabouts had been handed over to him in January. If this was true, it held up to doubt everything the Pakistani professor had said and done from that point forward. And if everything he had said and done from that point forward was one variation or another on a lie, then Barbara wasn't sure what she would do about that fact or to whom she would give that information.

The only answer seemed to be food. When she arrived home, she gobbled down a double takeaway portion of haddock and chips and followed this with treacle tart and a side of Victoria sponge. She quaffed a bottle of lager as she ate and finished off her meal with a cup of instant coffee. Accompanying this, she dipped into a packet of salt-and-vinegar crisps, after which a virtuous apple assured her that her arteries would be thoroughly cleansed if she munched upon it hard and long enough.

Then, no longer could she put off the phone call to Italy without putting herself into some sort of caloric stupor. She lit a fag and punched in Azhar's number. She'd never dreaded a phone call so much in her life. She was going to have to tell him everything: from the Love Rat Dad story to the claims made by the private investigator. In neither instance did she see that she had any choice.

She wasn't prepared for where she found Azhar when she rang his mobile. He was at the hospital in Lucca. Angelina, he told her, had been taken there both at the insistence of Lorenzo Mura and the advice of Inspector Lynley. She'd been ill for two days with a variety of worrying symptoms that she believed were related to the morning sickness she'd been experiencing, but her condition had worsened and both Mura and Lynley were convinced this could be an indication of something more serious.

Barbara hated where her thoughts went immediately upon hearing this news: to how the information could best be used to appease Mitchell Corsico. A story about the mother of the kidnapped child in Italy being admitted into hospital in an emergency situation . . . possibly on the brink of losing her unborn child . . . overwrought and making herself ill because of the kidnapping of her daughter . . . desperate for the Italian police to do something—*anything*—to find her while all the time they were sitting round drinking copious amounts of vino . . . That story was a real gem, wasn't it? That exposé was certain to tug at heartstrings. Of course, it depended upon the journalist and the readers of *The Source* having hearts in the first place, but surely it was better than a front-page piece in which Azhar answered pointed questions from Corsico and ended up throwing even more mud on his own reputation. She said, trying not to sound too hopeful, "What d'you mean, 'not right with the pregnancy'?"

"Her symptoms are, according to Mr. Mura, severe and worrying," Azhar told her. "The doctors here are concerned. Dehydration, vomiting, diarrhea."

"Sounds like flu. Maybe a virus? Or that super-serious kind of morning sickness?"

"She's very weak. It was Inspector Lynley who rang me with the news. I came at once to see if there was . . . I do not know why I came."

Barbara knew why he'd taken himself to the hospital. He loved the woman and had always done so. Despite her sins against him and especially the sin of removing from him the daughter he lived for, there was something that remained strong between them. Barbara didn't understand this kind of bond between people, and she reckoned she never would.

"Have you seen her?" she asked. "Is she . . . I don't know. Is she conscious? Is she in pain? What?"

"I have not yet seen her. Lorenzo . . ." He paused, seemed to think, then changed tack. "She might be having tests just now. There are a few specialists she's seeing, I believe. This could all be related to the stress of Hadiyyah as well as to the pregnancy . . . I know very little at this point, Barbara. I hope to learn more if I remain here."

So that was why he was there, she thought. Lynley had given him the news, but Lorenzo Mura wasn't about to let Azhar near her. She herself had seen the Italian man's suspicions regarding Azhar's feelings for Angelina when they had both turned up in London trying to find Hadiyyah. He wasn't certain of her, Lorenzo Mura. But then, with her history, who would be?

Barbara wondered briefly about Angelina Upman's power over men. She wondered briefly about what Angelina Upman could drive a man to do in order to keep her as his lover.

Which brought her, of course, to the reason for her call to Azhar. There was the not insignificant matter of what she'd been told by Dwayne Doughty regarding the information that he and his cohorts had amassed during the winter, not only about the whereabouts of Angelina but also about her sister's assistance in this disappearance. According to Doughty, every single detail concerning her disappearance had been dutifully passed along to the person who'd hired him to ascertain the whereabouts of the mother and daughter: Taymullah Azhar. But Azhar had told Barbara nothing of these details over the months. So either he was lying to her by omission or Doughty was lying to her with false information.

Of the two, she knew she would believe Azhar. She felt enormous affection for him, and she didn't want to believe he might trample on that affection with any kind of betrayal.

This was no position for a police investigator to be in, and Barbara realised this. But what she needed to say to Azhar—"Doughty claims you had mountains of information in January, so what did you do with it, my friend?"—simply would not come out. Still, she needed a variation of it or she knew she couldn't live with herself. So she said, "This whole Italy thing, Azhar . . . ?"

"Yes?"

"Did you ever know or think or even guess she might be in Italy all along?"

"How could I have come up with Italy?" he replied and his reply was quick, easy, and regretful. "She could have been anywhere on the planet. Had I known where to find her, I would have moved heaven and earth to bring Hadiyyah home."

There was that, Barbara thought. There would always be that: Hadiyyah and what she meant to her father. It was inconceivable that Azhar could have discovered the child's whereabouts four months earlier and done nothing about it. He simply wasn't made that way.

But still . . . Once Doughty had raised the spectre of betrayal in Barbara's mind, it remained on the fringes of her thoughts. Despite what she knew of Azhar and despite what she earnestly believed about him, she was going to have to check up on his Berlin alibi herself. At this point, she couldn't trust Dwayne Doughty to tell her the truth about anything.

BOW
LONDON

Dwayne Doughty headed for Victoria Park. He wanted to think, and the walk itself as well as the park—should he decide to hike over to Crown Gate East—helped him to do so. To remain in the office would have meant another tête-à-tête with Emily. Her declarations of impending doom were beginning to wear on him. He had long been a believer that—significant precautions having been taken—all was going to be well at the end of the game when they scooped up the poker chips and counted the haul. But Emily didn't see things this way.

Thus, the last thing he wanted her to know was that he was actually worried. She'd been well absorbed in chasing down the assignation whereabouts of a forty-five-year-old banker and his twenty-two-year-old little bit on the side, so for the most part he'd been able to avoid her. She was very well occupied and only marginally aware of his own activities. But she'd have the goods on the banker within a day or two—photos, credit card receipts, phone information, and everything else—and just as that bloke's marriage would be kaput as a result, Dwayne's own arrangement with Emily Cass would be at that point in danger of collapsing. He needed to produce some answers for his assistant. He couldn't afford to lose her or her range of abilities, and he knew he would if he wasn't able to sort out what was going on in Italy.

This, in part, was the reason for his walk: thinking first, followed by deciding, and then acting. He began it all with the purchase of a throwaway mobile phone. If he made any dodgy calls from the office, Em would be all over him like an outbreak of smallpox.

Things should have resolved themselves by now. Nothing about this situation had ever been rocket science. He should have had the all-clear, followed by the all's well, soon to be tagged by an *arrivederci*. He had none of those and now he knew why. None of them had happened in the first place.

"I don't know" was the answer he received to his question of "What the hell is going on?" when he placed the call.

"What d'you mean you 'don't know'?" was his subsequent demand. "You're paid to know. You're paid to make things happen."

"I set everything in motion as requested. But the plan went foul somewhere and I don't know where."

"How in God's name can you not know where?"

There was a silence. Doughty listened intently. For a moment, he thought he'd lost the connection and he nearly rang off to redial the number. But then the other said, "I couldn't risk it. Not the way you wanted it done. Using the *mercato*? I'd have been remembered."

"The *mercato* came from you, not from me, you sodding fool. It didn't need to be the *mercato*. It could have been anywhere: the school, a park, on an outing, at the farm."

"None of that matters. What you do not understand is . . ." A pause and then, "No, you will *not* blame me. You wished her found, and I found her. I gave you the name. I gave you the place and its location. It was your idea to snatch her, not mine. Had you told me in advance that this was your intention, I never would have come . . . how do you say? . . . onto the train with you."

"You liked the idea of money well enough when I first found you, you bastard."

"You will think what you will think, my friend. But the fact that the police have not made progress in finding her tells me my plan was right. *Giusto*, we say."

Doughty felt a cold wind dive into his underwear when he heard *my plan*. There was supposed to be only one plan. *His* plan. Get the girl, stow her, and wait for his word to move her. That there was another plan which he'd not been told about made it nearly impossible for Doughty to speak. But he managed, "You're after the Muras' money, aren't you? That's been your scheme from the first."

"*Pazzo*" was the reply. "You listen like a jealous housewife."

"What the hell is that supposed to mean?"

"It means the cops have found me, *sciocco*. It means that had I not developed a plan different from yours, I would now be sitting in a gaol cell waiting for *il Pubblico Ministero* to decide how to deal with me. I am not in a gaol cell for the very reason you wish to berate me: I had a plan. You wished her taken. I arranged her taken. *Capisce?*"

Doughty twigged the man's meaning. "Someone *else* . . . ? Are you mad? Who took her? What did he do with her? Is it even a *he* or did you use some poor Italian grandmother in need of cash? How about an Albanian immigrant? Or an African? Or a bloody Romanian gypsy, for that matter? Did you even *know* who you were tagging to do this job? Or was it someone you picked up off the street?"

"These insults of yours . . . They get us nowhere."

"I want that kid!"

"I, too, am of the same mind, although I suspect for different reasons. I put things in motion as I told you. Something has happened, and I do not know what. She was being fetched to put an end to this matter, but the . . . the messenger sent to fetch her . . . This is what I do not know."

"What? Exactly *what* don't you know?"

"It was a . . . *come si dice?* A caution," he said. "No. A *precaution*. It seemed wise for me not to know where she was being kept, so that if the police traced me—which, as I've told you, they did—I could give them nothing of substance no matter how long they decided to question me."

"So for all you know," Doughty said, "she could be dead. This . . . this *messenger* of yours might have snatched her and killed her. She might have not been a cooperative victim of your garden kidnapping on the street, and she might well have raised a ruckus. He could have stuffed her into the boot of his car for all you know and she might have suffocated and there he was with a dead body on his hands."

"This did not happen. It would not have happened."

"How the hell do you know that?"

"My selection of . . . this messenger, let us call him . . . was carefully done. He has known from the first that complete payment for his services depends entirely on the condition of the child and on her safety at all times."

"So where is he? Where is she? What's happened?"

"This is what I'm now attempting to discover. I've telephoned, but so far I have heard not a word."

"Which means something's gone wrong. You know that, don't you?"

"*Sì. Sono d'accordo*," the other murmured. "I ask you to believe that I am attempting to discover exactly what this is. But even in this, I must proceed with caution because the police will be watching me."

"I don't care if the bloody Swiss Guards are watching you," Doughty said. "I want that kid found. I want her found today."

"I doubt that will be possible," he admitted. "Until I find the messenger sent to fetch her, I will know nothing more than you."

"Then goddamn bloody find the messenger!" Doughty roared. "Because if I have to come to Italy myself, you aren't going to be happy about it."

That said, he snapped the mobile phone in half. He was on the bridge that carried Gunmakers Lane over the Hertford Union Canal. He cursed and threw the broken pieces of the mobile into the murky water there. He watched them sink and hoped against hope that they weren't a metaphor for what was going on in his life.

28 APRIL

Salvatore Lo Bianco made the requisite offer of help to his mamma. As usual she refused. No one, she told him—also as usual—would ever wash and polish the marble cover of his father's grave during what remained of the lifetime of his devoted wife. No, no, no, *figlio mio*, this chore will take no longer than is required for my old body to hobble round the plot itself, wielding soap and water and rags and marble polish and more rags till the stone reflects this ancient, sorrowing face of mine as well as the sky with its glorious clouds above me. You may watch, however, *figlio mio*, so that you will learn how to care for this stone where my poor corpse will lie with your father's after my earthly days are done.

Salvatore told her that perhaps he would walk, instead. He would follow the path round the perimeter of this part of the cemetery. He needed to think a bit. She could call out to him if she needed help. He would not be far away.

Mamma gave a quintessential Italian mamma shrug. He could, of course, please himself in this matter. Sons so often did just that, didn't they? And then she turned and said, "*Ciao, Giuseppe, marito carissimo,*" and told the dead man how deeply she missed him, how every moment of every day brought her closer to joining him in the ground. After this, she began her work upon the grave.

Salvatore watched her and stifled a chuckle. There were certain moments in their life together, he thought, when his mamma was not his real mamma at all but rather a caricature of an Italian mamma. This was one of them. For the truth of the matter was that Teresa Lo Bianco had spent what Salvatore knew of her married life absolutely furious with his father. She'd been one of those breathtaking Italian beauties who married young and lost her looks to childbearing and a lifetime of household drudgery, and she'd never forgiven or forgotten that fact. Except, of course, when she came to the Cimitero Urbano di Lucca. Then, the instant that Salvatore parked in front of the great gates to the place, his mamma's face transformed from its habitual look of pinched irritation to an expression that mixed grief and piety so superbly that had anyone other than Salvatore seen her, she would appear as a recent widow whose loss would never be assuaged.

He smiled. He folded a piece of chewing gum into his mouth, and he began to walk. He was halfway round his first circumambulation of the quadrangle of graves decorated with saints and the Virgin and her Son when his mobile rang. He glanced at the number of whoever was placing the call.

The Englishman, he thought. He liked this man Lynley. He'd thought the Londoner would be an irritating interloper into the Italian investigation, but this hadn't proved to be the case.

His *pronto* was answered in the other detective's careful Italian. Lynley was ringing to tell him that the mother of the kidnapped girl was in hospital. "I wasn't sure if you'd know this," Lynley told him. He went on to say that when he'd seen her two days earlier at the *fattoria*, she'd been very weak and yesterday she had grown even weaker. "Signor Mura insisted she go to hospital, for a check-over at least," Lynley said. "I didn't disagree."

Lynley told him, then, of his conversations with both Lorenzo Mura and Angelina Upman. He spoke of a man who'd been at the *fattoria*, purportedly to purchase a donkey foal. A thick envelope had passed between this man and Lorenzo, and this was the payment, Lorenzo had claimed. But the British detective had begun to wonder about this exchange. What was the Mura family's financial situation? What was Lorenzo's own? And what could that mean?

Salvatore could see where Lynley was heading with this line of thought. For what Lorenzo Mura wished to do with his family's old villa, vast amounts of money would be required. His extended family were fairly wealthy—they had always been so—but he himself was not. Would they leap to assist him if the young child of his lover was endangered and a ransom demand was made? Perhaps. But no ransom demand had been made, which suggested there was no involvement on Lorenzo's part in the disappearance of Angelina's daughter.

"Yet there might be reasons other than money that he would wish for Hadiyyah's removal from her mother's life," Lynley noted.

"That would make the man a monster."

"I've seen monsters aplenty in my time and I expect you have as well," Lynley said.

"I have not entirely removed Lorenzo Mura from my thoughts," Salvatore admitted. "Perhaps it is time for us—you and I—to speak with Carlo Casparia. Piero has had him 'imagine' how this crime was committed. Perhaps he can 'imagine' more about that day in the *mercato* when the child disappeared."

He told the Englishman that he would come for him at the inner city gate where they had met before. At the moment, he was at the *cimitero comunale*, he explained, paying monthly respects to his papà's grave. "In an hour, *Ispettore*?" he said to Lynley.

"*Aspetterò*," Lynley told him. He would meet Salvatore at the gate.

And so he was waiting. Salvatore fetched Lynley at Porta di Borgo, where the detective was reading *Prima Voce* again. Carlo Casparia was all over the front page another time. His family had been located in Padova. Much was being made of their estrangement from their only son. This would keep *Prima Voce* busy for at least two days, printing stories of Carlo's fall from favour. Meantime, Salvatore thought, the police could get work done without concern that the tabloid might get too close to what they were doing.

He stopped briefly at the *questura* to fetch the laptop upon which were loaded all of the photographs taken by the American tourist and her daughter who had been in the *mercato* when the child disappeared. Then he and Lynley took themselves to the prison in which the hapless young man was being held. For once a confession was obtained from a suspect or once he was formally charged with a crime, he was whisked to prison, where he remained unless the Tribunal of Reexamination determined he could be released pending trial. Since Carlo's release depended upon having a suitable place to go—and clearly the abandoned stables in the Parco Fluviale would not qualify—his home would be the prison cell in which he currently languished. All of this Salvatore explained to Lynley as they drove to see the young man. When they arrived at the prison, however, it was to learn that Carlo was in the hospital ward. As it turned out, he wasn't taking well to the sudden absence of drugs from his system. He was taking the cure in the worst possible way, and no particular sympathy was being extended in his direction.

Thus Salvatore and Lynley found the young man in a cheerless place of narrow beds. There the patients either were restrained by one ankle to the iron footboards or were too ill to care about attempting to effect an escape by overcoming the male nurses and single doctor who were on duty.

Carlo Casparia was of this latter group, a figure huddled into the foetal position beneath a white sheet topped with a thin blue blanket. He was shivering and staring sightlessly at nothing. His lips were raw, his face was unshaven, and his ginger hair had been shorn from his head. A rank smell came from him.

"*Non so, Ispettore*," Lynley murmured uncertainly.

Salvatore agreed. He, too, didn't know what possible good this was going to do or even if Carlo would be able to hear them and respond. But it was an avenue, and it needed to be explored.

"*Ciao*, Carlo." He drew a straight-backed steel chair over to the bed as Lynley fetched another. Salvatore eased a hospital tray over and set up his laptop on it. "*Ti voglio far vedere alcune foto, amico*," he said. "*Gli dai uno sguardo?*"

In bed, Carlo was wordless. If he heard what Salvatore had said about the photos, he gave no indication. His eyes were fixed on some-thing beyond Salvatore's shoulder and, when Salvatore turned, he saw it was a clock on the wall. The poor fool was watching time pass, it seemed, counting the moments till the worst of his suffering ended.

Salvatore exchanged a glance with Lynley. The Englishman, he saw, looked as doubtful as Salvatore felt.

"*Voglio aiutarti*," Salvatore said to Carlo. "*Non credo che tu abbia rapito la bambina, amico.*" He brought the first of the tourist photographs onto the screen of his laptop. "*Prova*," he murmured. "*Prova, prova a guardarle.*"

If Carlo would only try, he himself could do the rest. Just look at the pictures, he silently told the young man. Just move your gaze to the computer screen.

He went through the entire set in vain. Then he told the addict they would try again. Did he want water? Did he need food? Would another blanket help him through this terrible time?

"*Niente*" was the first thing the young man said. Nothing would help him in the state he was in.

"*Per favore*," Salvatore murmured. "*Non sono un procuratore. Ti voglio aiutare, Carlo.*"

This was what finally got through to him: I am not a prosecutor, Carlo. I want to help you. To this, Salvatore added that nothing the young man said at this point was being taken down and nothing he said would go into a statement that he would be forced to sign while he was in extremis. They—he and this other officer from London sitting next to your bed, Carlo—were looking for the man who'd kidnapped this child and they did not think Carlo was that man. He had nothing to fear from them. Things could not get worse if he spoke to them now.

Carlo shifted his gaze. It came to Salvatore that the addict's pain made movement difficult, and he changed the position of the laptop, holding it on a level with the young man's face and slowly going through the pictures again. But Carlo said nothing as he looked at them, merely shaking his head as Salvatore paused each one in front of his gaze and asked if there was anyone he recognised as having been with the little girl.

Again and again, the addict's lips formed the word *No*. But finally his expression altered. It was a marginal change, to be true, but his eyebrows made a movement towards each other and his tongue—the colour of it nearly white—touched his scaly upper lip. Salvatore and Lynley saw this simultaneously, and both of them leaned forward to see what picture was on the screen. It was the photograph of the pig's head at the *bancarella* selling meats to the citizens of Lucca. It was the photograph in which Lorenzo Mura was making a purchase just beyond the pig's head.

"*Conosci quest' uomo?*" Salvatore asked.

Carlo shook his head. He didn't know him, he said, but he had seen him.

"*Dove?*" Salvatore asked, his hope stirring. He glanced at Lynley, and he could see that the London man was watching Carlo closely.

"*Nel parco,*" Carlo whispered. "*Con un altro uomo.*"

Salvatore asked if Carlo would recognise the other man he spoke of seeing with Lorenzo Mura in the park. He showed the addict an enlargement of the picture of the dark-haired man behind Hadiyyah in the crowd of people. But Carlo shook his head. It wasn't that man. A few more questions took them to the fact that it also wasn't Michelangelo Di Massimo with his head of bleached hair. It was someone else, but Carlo didn't know who. Just that Lorenzo and this other, unnamed man had met, and when they met, the children whom Lorenzo coached in private to improve their football skills were not present. They had been earlier, running about the field, but when this man showed up, all the children were gone.

VICTORIA
LONDON

The next time Mitchell Corsico got in touch, it was by phone. This was a case of thank-God-for-very-small-favours, though, because the tune he was singing when Barbara took the call was the same tune he'd been singing the last time she'd spoken to him. Things were ramped up at this point, though. *The Sun*, the *Mirror*, and the *Daily Mail* had begun investing some rather significant money in following the kidnapping tale by means of placing boots on the ground in Tuscany. There was competition to get new angles every day, and Mitchell Corsico wanted his own.

Tiresomely, though, he was back to *Met Officer Involved with Love Rat Dad*, Barbara discovered. He was also back to making threats. He wanted his bloody exclusive interviews with Azhar and Nafeeza, and Barbara was the means to get them for him. If she didn't manage this feat, she could expect to see her mug on the front page of *The Source*, entangled with the son and the father of Azhar in a street imbroglio.

There was no point in telling him that the angle to pursue was *Mother of Kidnapped Girl in Hospital*. *The Daily Mail* was already onto that. For its part, the *Mirror* was having fun speculating on what had put Angelina Upman into a hospital bed in the first place. They appeared to like the idea of a suicide attempt—*Distraught Mother Ends Up in Hospital*—which they were able to hint at since no one in Italy was telling their reporter a single thing.

Barbara tried to reason with Corsico. "The story's in Italy," she told him. "What the bloody hell are you still doing in London trying to follow it, Mitchell?"

"You and I both know the value of an interview," Corsico countered. "Don't pretend you think prowling round some Italian hospital is going to produce shit because we both know that's bollocks."

"Fine. Then interview someone over there. But interviewing Nafeeza or talking to Sayyid again . . . Where the bloody hell is that going to take you?"

"Give me Lynley, then," Corsico told her. "Give me his mobile's number."

"If you want to talk to the inspector, you can get your arse over there and talk to the inspector. Hang round the Lucca police station and you'll see him soon enough. Call the hotels to find him. The town's not big. How many could there be?"

"I'm not pursuing the same fucking angle every other paper's going with. We broke the story and we're planning to keep breaking it. Joining every Tom, Dick, and Giuseppe over in Tuscany gives me nothing but shit in a basket. Now, way I see it is you've got a decision to make. Three choices and I'm giving you thirty seconds to decide once I name them, okay? One: You give me the wife for an interview. Two: You give me Azhar for an interview. Three: I break the *Met Officer and Love Rat Dad* angle. Come to think, I'll give you four: You give me Lynley's mobile. Now. Do I start counting, or do you have a watch to look at to see the seconds flying by while you decide which it's going to be?"

"Look, you bloody fool," Barbara said, "I don't know how many ways to tell you the story's in Italy. Lynley's in Italy, Azhar's in Italy, Angelina is in hospital in Italy. Hadiyyah's in Italy and so's her bloody kidnapper and so're the police. Now if you want to stay here and follow the Love Rat Dad and whatever the hell you think my involvement with him is supposed to be, more power to you. You can write chapter and verse and another chapter about whatever you imagine our hot love affair is like, and you've got your scoop or whatever the hell you want to call it. *But* another rag is going to pick up the story and want to interview me for my explanation, and what I'm going to tell them—I promise you—is how I've been trying to keep *The Source* from exploiting an anguished teenager's understandable upset about his dad in order to milk a story out of him that's sixty percent fury and forty percent fantasy and perhaps they ought to look at the source—pardon the pun—of the story in *The Source* since for some reason that reporter is fixated on something having nothing to do with a little girl's disappearance in a foreign country and what does *that* tell you about the value of even buying a copy of the worthless rag, gentle readers?"

"Yeah. Right. Brilliant move, Barb. As if the unwashed public out there is the least bit interested in anything beyond gossip. You're threatening me in the wrong direction. I make my living feeding garbage to the gulls, and they're eating it up just like always."

Barbara knew there was truth in this. Tabloids appealed to the worst inclinations in human nature. They made their money off people's appetite for learning about others' sins, corruption, and greed. Because of this fact, however, she had an ace and she knew there was nothing for it but to play the card now.

"That being the case," she said to Corsico, "how about a new angle for you, then, one the other tabloids don't have?"

"They don't have *Met Officer Involved*—"

"Right. Let's give that a rest for forty-five seconds. They also don't have *Love Rat Mum Who Took Off with Her Kid in the First Place Now Up the Spout with Yet Another Bloke's Kid*. Trust me on this. They don't have that story."

There was silence at the other end. In it, Barbara could almost hear the wheels of speculation turning in Corsico's head. Because of those wheels and what they might come up with, she went on.

"You like that one, Mitchell? It's gold and it's true. Now, the bloody story's in Italy where it's been all along and I've given you something no one else has. You can use it, abuse it, or lose it, okay? As for me, I've got other things to do."

Then she rang off. Doing this was a risk. Corsico could easily call the bluff of her bravado and run with his story, whose picture on the front page of the paper would call into question how she'd got herself over to Ilford in the first place in the middle of her workday. With John Stewart scrutinising her every move, this was something so far less than desirable that Barbara knew she was in no small part mad to risk alienating Corsico by cutting him off. But she had things to do and none of them were related to dancing to the journalist's tune just now.

She'd talked to Lynley. She knew an arrest had been made, but she also knew from his description of things in Lucca that this arrest of one Carlo Casparia was based mostly on the fantasy of the public prosecutor. Lynley had explained to her how investigations proceeded in Italy—with the public prosecutor madly up to his eyeballs in the enquiry almost from the get-go—and he'd also told her that the chief inspector had ideas in conflict with the public prosecutor who headed the investigation, so "Chief Inspector Lo Bianco and I are walking rather carefully over here," he said. This, she knew, was code for "We're following our own leads in the matter." These apparently had to do with Lorenzo Mura, a red convertible, a playing field in a park, and a set of photographs taken by a tourist in the *mercato* from which Hadiyyah had disappeared. Lynley didn't say how these things related to each other, but the fact that he and the chief inspector in Italy were not satisfied with the arrest told her that there was still fertile ground to be explored both there and in London and she needed to see about exploring it.

In this, Isabelle Ardery inadvertently helped out. Since she'd instructed DI Stewart to give Barbara assignments that reflected her rank as a detective sergeant, he'd had no choice but to put her back out in the street with a suitable action assigned to her, one relating to either of the two investigations that he was supposed to be conducting. That the DI wasn't happy with this turn of events was evident in his surly manner of making the day's assignments. That he intended to dog Barbara, despite Ardery's instructions, was evident when he continued watching her like a bird of prey in search of a meal.

She had phone calls to make before she set out on her given activities, and Stewart placed himself close enough to her to hear every word of them. It was only luck that Corsico had rung her while she was making a purchase at one of the vending machines in the stairwell, Barbara realised.

She made three phone calls to set up the three interviews she'd been directed by Stewart to conduct. She made a show of taking down times and addresses, and she made more of a show of using the Internet to plot a route from one interview to the next that used her time in an efficacious manner. Then she gathered her notebook and her bag, and she headed out. Luckily Winston Nkata was still at his desk, so she stopped there, flipped open her notebook ostentatiously, and made a show of noting Winston's replies to her questions.

These were simple enough. She'd asked him to check on Azhar's Berlin alibi because she knew she couldn't risk further censure from Stewart for checking on it herself. So what had he managed to glean? she asked Winston. Was Azhar as good as his word? Had Doughty been telling her the truth when he'd pursued the Berlin story?

"'S good, Barb," Winston told her sotto voce. He made a show of pulling out a manila folder, flipping it open, and looking down upon its contents with a studious frown. Barbara glanced to see what he was using as the "evidence" under discussion. Insurance papers for his car, it appeared. "It all checks out square," he said. "He was at the hotel in Berlin the whole time. He presented two papers like Doughty told you. He was on a panel 's well."

Barbara felt the relief of having one less thing to worry about. Still she said, "D'you think someone could've been posing as Azhar?"

Winston gave her a quirky look. "Barb, the bloke's a microbiologist, yeah? How's someone goin to pretend to be that and talk the lingo with th'other blokes? First, a poser'd have to be Pakistani, eh? Second, a poser'd have to be able to talk the talk: present his paper and . . . what else d'they do? . . . answer questions 'bout it? Third, a poser'd have to wonder why the hell he was in Berlin actin the part of Azhar in the first place while Azhar was . . . what? Off in Italy kidnappin his own kid?"

Barbara chewed on her lip. She thought about what Winston had said. He was right. It was a ludicrous line of enquiry, no matter how she felt about Dwayne Doughty's half-truths. Still, she knew the wisdom of pursuing every angle, so she said, "What about someone from his lab? What about a graduate student? You know, someone wanting to oil the waters of his path to an advanced degree? How do these things work anyway, being a graduate student? I dunno. Do you?"

Winston tapped at the battle scar on his cheek. "I look like a bloke knows 'bout university, Barb?" he enquired pleasantly.

"Ah. Right," she said. "So . . ."

"Seems to me 'f you want more information, it's comin from Doughty. I say you put pressure on him. If there's more to know out there, he's the one to tell it."

Winston was right, of course. Only pressure on Dwayne Doughty was going to get her any further. Barbara flipped her notebook closed, stowed it in her bag, said, "Right. Got it. Thanks, Winnie," for John Stewart's benefit, and went on her way.

When it came to using the thumbscrews on anyone, the best way was always a visit to the local nick. So on her way to her car, Barbara rang the Bow Road station. She identified herself. She told them that in conjunction with an ongoing case in Italy that officers from Scotland Yard were dealing with, one private investigator Dwayne Doughty needed questioning. Would someone from the local station pick him up, haul him in, and hold him till she got there? Indeed, someone would, she was told. Glad to oblige, DS Havers. He'll be twiddling his thumbs, stewing in his own juices, or whatever else you wish in an interview room whenever you arrive.

Excellent, she thought. She gave a look to the locations of the interviews she needed to conduct for DI Stewart. One was south of the river; the other two were in north London. Bow Road was east. In the world of eenie, meenie, minie, and moe, there was no question in her mind where she would go first.

LUCCA

TUSCANY

By the time Salvatore and DI Lynley had returned from their questioning of Carlo Casparia in the prison hospital, the officers tracking down the cars driven by every member of Lorenzo Mura's *squadra di calcio* had finished that job. There was one red car among all the vehicles, but it was not a convertible. No matter, Salvatore told them. It was now time to trace the cars belonging to the families of every child Lorenzo coached in his private *calcio* clinic at the Parco Fluviale. Get the name of every child he coaches from Mura, get the name of every parent of every child, check their cars, then speak to each parent individually about meeting Lorenzo Mura there for a private conversation. Meantime, get a photograph of every father of every child and dig up pictures of Lorenzo's fellow team members as well.

DI Lynley remained silent during this exchange, although Salvatore could tell from the expression on the Englishman's face that he hadn't followed the rapid-fire Italian around him. So he explained how they were proceeding, and to this Lynley indicated the nature of the report he would make to the parents of the girl. Obviously, reporting anything having to do with Lorenzo Mura was out of the question. For the moment, then, it was best to tell them that information from the television appeal was continuing to be followed up on, that Carlo Casparia was attempting to be helpful, and to leave it at that.

Lynley was departing when a uniformed officer dashed down the corridor to speak to Salvatore. His face was flushed and his news was good: Regarding the red convertible seen by the driver on his way to visit his mamma in the Apuan Alps? the young man said breathlessly.

"*Sì, sì*," Salvatore responded tersely.

It had been found. Checking every lay-by on the road into the Alps prior to the turnoff for the mamma's village had gleaned them nothing, as the chief inspector would recall. But an enterprising officer had on his own time continued up that mountain road and six kilometres farther along he had found a crash barrier destroyed on a hairpin turn. The car in question had been discovered at the bottom of a gully beyond that barrier. There was no body inside. But there was a body some twenty metres away: the driver's, apparently thrown from the vehicle.

"*Andiamo,*" Salvatore said at once to Lynley. Pray God, he thought, that there was no small girl's body nearby as well.

It took nearly an hour to reach the turnoff, their route coursing along the River Serchio, first on the great alluvial plain, then into the hills, and at last into the Alps. The river was a fast-moving torrent at this time of year since snow at the highest elevation in the mountains had been melting for weeks. The result was waterfalls, sunstruck cascades, and glittering pools, all of which could be glimpsed as the police car rushed past them. The new growth of spring was thick and lush as they climbed into the mountains, and the wildflowers splashed yellow, violet, and red in swathes of colour along verges and into the trees. And the trees themselves—pines, oaks, and ilexes—grew right to the edges of villages that had no vehicular access, forming a wall of greenery that seemed to prevent the mountains themselves from descending upon and swallowing up the scattering of terracotta-roofed buildings perched precariously on the edges of cliffs that dropped hundreds of feet into more forest beneath them.

With each turn they made into a secondary or tertiary road, the way narrowed until they were at last on a route the width of the car itself. One hairpin curve followed the next. It was an ear-popping, white-knuckle ride, a by-the-grace-of-God course in which God's grace was defined by having the luck not to encounter a vehicle on its way down. Finally, they came to a police roadblock. They got out of the car, and Salvatore nodded at the uniformed officer who approached. He asked him only, "*Dov'è la macchina?*" although this was mere formality since the likely position of the red convertible was indicated some fifty metres farther along and up, by the remains of the crash barrier through which the vehicle had shot to its final resting place.

As Salvatore and Lynley approached the broken barrier, an ambulance crew came into sight, heaving a stretcher between them. On it, a body bag was strapped, its zip tightly closed, sealing the corpse from sight.

"*Fermatevi,*" Salvatore told the two attendants. He added, "*Per favore*" as an afterthought and introduced both himself and DI Lynley to them.

They did as he asked, halting their progress to the waiting ambulance. They set the stretcher on the ground, and Salvatore squatted. He steeled himself—only on television, he thought, did detectives unzip the body bags of corpses who'd lain for God only knew how many days in the hot Italian sun without preparing themselves for what they were about to see—and he lowered the zip.

Had the man been handsome in life—indeed, had he possibly been the individual behind Hadiyyah in the photographs taken by the tourists in the *mercato*—it was now impossible to tell. Those forensic specialists of the open air—the insects—had found the body as they would do, and they had worked their ways upon it. Maggots still writhed in the man's eyes, nose, and mouth; beetles had been feasting on his skin; mites and millipedes scurried into the open neck of his linen shirt. He had come to rest facedown, as well, and the settling of blood to this part of his body rendered his features purple while the gas forming within the protective covering of his skin as his tissues disintegrated had created pustules wherever he was exposed. Soon these would leak their noxious fluid, which would also seep from his orifices. Death in this manner was a horrifying sight. Nothing immured one from its impact.

Salvatore gave Lynley a look and heard the other officer whistle low as he blew out a breath and gazed on the remains. Salvatore said to the ambulance attendants, *"Carta d'identità?"* and they indicated with a simultaneous jerking of their heads that whoever was with the car below had in their possession the man's identification. Salvatore nodded and rose, thankful that he was not going to have to go through the corpse's pockets. He indicated that the body could be taken off for postmortem examination. Then, with Lynley, he approached the edge of the bluff.

Far below them was the red convertible. Two uniformed officers were with it, while two others were smoking up above them where an area of ground at the base of a boulder some eighty metres higher than the car was marked to indicate the position of the corpse. He had obviously been thrown from the vehicle as it crashed down the bluff. Wearing a seatbelt or not, he would not have survived the car's rolling *sotto sopra* as it soared from the road to its resting place. The miracle involved was that the vehicle had not burst into flames. This led to the possibility of evidence. Salvatore hoped it was evidence of life, however, and not evidence of a second individual in the convertible when it took its fatal plunge, and hence not evidence of a second body still undiscovered in the area.

Carefully, he and Lynley worked their way down to the point where the man's body had lain. He gave the officers there terse instructions: *"Cercate se ce n'è un altro."* If there was another body nearby, they were to find it.

They didn't look happy about this turn of events but when he added, *"Una bambina. Cercate subito,"* their expressions altered and they set off. If a little girl's body was somewhere nearby, it probably wasn't going to be far.

At the car, Salvatore repeated his question about the man's identification. An evidence bag was passed to him by one of the two officers at the vehicle. Inside was a black *portafoglio*. It had been tucked inside the glove box of the car, the car itself a wreck of mangled metal with one wheel missing, three others flattened, and a door ripped off. While Salvatore opened the evidence bag and removed the wallet within it, Lynley moved to look more closely at the vehicle.

The man was one Roberto Squali, Salvatore saw from his identity card. He felt a rush of excitement to see that the man was a Lucchese. This had to take them, he believed, another step closer to the missing child. Pray God she hadn't ended up here, he thought as he looked round at the wilderness. His hope lay in the fact that at least ten days separated the girl's vanishing at the *mercato* from the moment when this accident had occurred. How likely was it that she would have been in the car with this man so long after her kidnapping in Lucca?

Within Squali's wallet, Salvatore also found the man's driving licence, two credit cards, and five business cards. Three of these were from boutiques in Lucca, one was from a restaurant in the town, and the fifth was the link he had prayed to see: something that tied this man to Michelangelo Di Massimo. It was the private investigator's card and on it was his name, the number of his mobile, and the address of his questionable centre of operations in Pisa.

"Guardi qui," Salvatore said to Lynley. He handed the card to him,

waited while the other man put on his reading spectacles, and met his gaze when Lynley looked up quickly. "*Sì*," Salvatore said with a smile. "*Addesso abbiamo la prova che sono connessi.*"

"*Penso proprio di sì*," Lynley said in agreement. They had their tie between the two men. "*E la bambina?*" he continued. "*Che pensa?*"

Salvatore looked round them and then up at the mountains that surrounded them on every side. The little girl had been with this man, he thought. He was sure of that. But not at the moment when he'd gone over the cliff. He told Lynley this and the London man nodded. Salvatore returned to his inspection of the car, however, and soon enough he had what he was looking for.

It was a hair caught up in the mechanics of the seatbelt. It was long. It was dark. A test would tell them if it was Hadiyyah's. Dusting the vehicle for prints would also tell them if the child had ridden in the car. The only piece of information that the car couldn't give them was what had happened to her and where she was now.

Both men knew the hard reality of the situation with which they were faced, however: If Roberto Squali had indeed taken Hadiyyah from the *mercato* in Lucca, if he indeed had been the man seen leading a little girl into the woods somewhere along this road from which his car had toppled, where was she now? What had happened to her? For the truth was that the area in which they stood was vast, and if Squali had handed the child off to another or had killed and disposed of her somewhere to fulfill a sick fantasy, the location in which either of these things had occurred was going to prove almost impossible to find.

Salvatore considered cadaver dogs. Pray God, he thought, they would not have to use them.

VILLA RIVELLI
TUSCANY

Sister Domenica Giustina was light-headed from the fasting. She was sore from kneeling on the hard stone floor. She was thick in the brain from going without sleep, and she was still waiting for God to send her a sign about what it was He wished her to do next.

She'd failed with Carina. The child simply had not understood the crucial importance of what had lain before them both. Something within her had stirred her to fear and trepidation. And now, instead of joyful acceptance, curious playfulness, and eager cooperation with every aspect of life at the Villa Rivelli, the child kept her distance from Sister Domenica Giustina. She watched and she waited. Sometimes, she hid. This was not good.

Sister Domenica Giustina had begun to think that she had, perhaps, misinterpreted what she'd seen as she'd watched her cousin's car come roaring up the narrow mountain road. She'd known God's hand was behind the car's ripping through the crash barrier, flying into space, and disappearing. What she did not know and had to clarify was what it meant that God had placed her at that precise moment in a position to see what end had been met by her cousin Roberto. The sight of his car shooting into the void had seemed an illustration of the importance of being shriven of sins, but perhaps it meant something else entirely.

For this reason had she fasted and prayed. As a form of scourging, she tightened the swaddling that was a torment to her flesh. At the end of forty-eight hours like this, she rose with some difficulty but without the peace of knowing what she was meant to do. God's answer hadn't come from her suffering and her supplication. Perhaps, she thought, it would come from careful attention to a soft breeze that she could hear blowing through the trees of the forest that edged the immediate grounds of the villa. Perhaps God's voice would be on that breeze.

She went outside. She felt the restorative light wind on her cheeks. She paused at the top of the stone steps that led to her rooms above the barn, and she gazed upon the shuttered villa and wondered if the answers she sought might be contained within its walls. For she needed answers soon at this point. Roberto's terrible passage from the mountain road into the vacancy of space told her that.

She descended the stone steps. She began to consider an important way in which she might have misunderstood. She'd been dwelling upon Roberto's demise when, perhaps, he had not met his end at all. If that was the case, then seeking God's message in the death of her cousin would be a completely useless activity. She should, in other words, have been seeking God's message in something else.

There would be a sign of this. There had always been signs, and if she was correct in this new understanding, something was going to tell her soon. It seemed to her that the only place a sign might come to her was the same spot where she'd seen the last sign. So she went to where the low wall allowed her a view of the road that twisted up from the valley floor, and in very short order, she was given precisely what she had been praying for.

Even at this distance from the place where Roberto's car had crashed through the barrier, she could see the police cars. More important, she could see that among them *un'ambulanza* stood. As she watched, so far from them, she made out the workers carrying a stretcher up from some point below the twist of road. When they had lifted it onto the tarmac, they paused, and someone waiting for them bent over the stretcher as if to have a word with whoever rode upon it. This did not take long, after which the stretcher was loaded into the ambulance and it drove away.

Sister Domenica Giustina watched all this, her heart feeling as if it would catch in her chest. It was hard to believe what she was witnessing, but there could be no doubt in interpreting what she'd seen. Even as she had prayed and fasted within her cell, seeking to understand God's intention for her, her cousin Roberto had lain injured within the wreckage of his car. It came to Sister Domenica Giustina that both she and her cousin Roberto had been challenged. Have faith through suffering, their God had proclaimed. I will move in your life as I will.

It was *challenge*, she realised. It was all about challenge. It was about not giving up for an instant, no matter the blackness of what lay ahead.

Job had faced this. Abraham had faced this as well. In the case of that great patriarch of the Hebrews, the challenge he'd endured surpassed any other that God had ever given to man. Sacrifice your son Isaac to me, God had demanded of his servant Abraham. Take him into the mountains, build an altar of stone, and upon that altar put your sword to his throat. Let his blood flow forth. Burn his body. In this way prove your love for Me. This will not be easy, but it is what I ask. Obey your God.

Yes, yes, she understood at last. A challenge such as Abraham's could only be a challenge if it was not easy.

BOW
LONDON

She would get it all done, Barbara told herself. But first she had to talk to Doughty. After that, she'd be back on track, heading south of the river first and then doing the north London bit at the end of the day. These things always took time. No interview went like clockwork. She would be able to smooth the rough edges of her day's employment in such a way as to please anyone who decided to scrutinise it.

At the Bow Road station she identified herself and was in short order escorted to the interview room in which Dwayne Doughty was cooling his heels. He'd been there for more than an hour, she was told. His sole reaction so far had been the demand of "What the hell is going on, you sods?"

When she walked into the room, Doughty said, "*You* again?" At the narrow table, he had a plastic cup of tea with a skin of cooling milk formed on its surface. He shoved this to one side, and its contents sloshed out. "Bloody hell," he went on. "I've told you everything. What more do you want from me?"

Barbara evaluated him before she spoke. He wasn't as cool a customer as he'd been in their earlier encounters, so she reckoned this jaunt to the nick had been a very good idea. A sour smell came off him—he must have begun sweating like a glass holding a bad martini the moment uniforms had shown up in his office—and he'd loosened his necktie and unbuttoned the top of his shirt to reveal a band of oily sweat round the inside of the collar.

"What the fuck is this about?" he demanded.

She sat. She put her shoulder bag on the floor and took her time about digging out her notebook and pencil. She flipped the notebook open and then studied the detective. "Azhar's alibi checks out," she told him.

He exploded like an overblown balloon. "I bloody told you that!"

he snapped. "I looked into it myself. You paid me to do it, I did it, I made my report to you, and if that doesn't prove to you that I'm walking on the sodding right side of the bleeding law—"

"The only thing that's ever going to prove that is the full truth, Dwayne. The whole A to Z of it, if you read my meaning."

"I've given you the full truth. I've got nothing more to give. This 'interview' or whatever the hell you're up to here is bloody well over. I know my rights, and one of them isn't to sit here and have you harp on things we've already discussed. The cops asked me to come in for a few questions. I came in cooperatively. And now I'm leaving." He shoved back from the table.

"They've made an arrest in Italy," she told him.

That stopped him like a fist in the face. He said nothing, but he also didn't move.

"They're holding a bloke called Carlo Casparia," she said. "We're about twenty-four hours from tracing him to you. So what I'd suggest is that you come clean before we pack you up, put you on a plane, and deliver you to the cops in Lucca."

"You can't do that." But he sounded rather stiff when he spoke.

"Dwayne, you'd be surprised, amazed, astonished, and gobsmacked at what we can do when our little minds get going. Now the way I see things, you have a decision to make. You can tell me everything, or you can act the leaky hosepipe like you've been doing from the first, giving me information in dribs and drabs."

"I *told* you the truth," he said, but his tone had definitely altered. Barbara heard no outrage in it at this point but rather intensity, and this change was a good thing. It meant his mind was working on all cylinders and her job was to oil the gears of his brain so the entire mechanism began to operate in her direction. "I gave all the information I had to Professor Azhar," Doughty said. "I swear it. What the professor did with it, I don't know and I have no clue. He wanted the kid back, you know that. Maybe he found someone over there to snatch her for him. What *I* did—and I've already told you this—was hire a bloke in Italy once we learned a bank account in Lucca was involved. I gave him the information, the professor. I also told him the name of the bloke who did the work for me. Michelangelo Di Massimo. Now, if Professor Azhar then hired Di Massimo to take things further . . . I had nothing to do with that."

Barbara nodded, unimpressed. It was a nice performance verbally, but she watched the private detective's eyes as he spoke. They were as jittery as the rest of him was. They fairly danced in his head. And his fingers were restless, tapping in unison against his thumbs.

"So you say," she said. "But I expect this Carlo Casparia they've got over there is saying something else. See, he's not going to want to take the fall for this, not completely, because no one ever does. And what I reckon is that between him and that Michelangelo bloke, someone's not going to have your skill set when it comes to wiping hard drives, emails, and telephone records and God knows what else squeaky clean. So my guess is that in the next day or so, there's going to be a trail uncovered that leads from Casparia to Michelangelo to you, dates and times included. And *you're* going to have one bloody hell of a time trying to explain it all away. See, Dwayne, the trouble with cooking up schemes like this one to snatch Hadiyyah is that the old 'no honour among thieves'—or in this case kidnappers—always applies. You get more than one person involved, and someone's going to break, because when it comes to necks being saved, most people choose their own."

Doughty was silent. He was, of course, evaluating all this for its potential to be the truth. Barbara herself didn't know what this bloke Casparia had to do with anything, but if dropping his name and his arrest and stretching things from there was going to get her one step closer to Hadiyyah, she intended to drop it at every opportunity.

Doughty finally spoke. "All right."

"Meaning?"

He looked away from her. He was suddenly still, and only a steadying breath moved his body. "It was Professor Azhar's idea from the first."

Barbara narrowed her eyes. "What was Professor Azhar's idea?"

"To find her, to plan it all, to wait until the time was right, then to snatch her. The right time turned out to be when he was in Berlin for his conference, establishing an alibi. The kid was supposed to be snatched and held in a location until Azhar could get there and fetch her back to London."

"Bollocks," Barbara said.

Doughty's gaze flew back to her. "I'm telling you the truth!"

"Oh, are you? Aside from a few little problems having to do with getting her out of Italy and into England without a passport, what was supposed to happen when Azhar got her back to London, eh? Let me tell you: What was supposed to happen is what *actually* happened, which is why your tale is rubbish. Hadiyyah's mum showed up, demanding her back, because the first person she suspected of having snatched her daughter was the dad she'd stolen her from in the first place."

"Right, right," Doughty said. "That's how it was supposed to play out. She'd show up, he'd prove to her that he didn't have the girl, he'd return to Italy with the mother, and then—while he was in Italy—she'd be handed over to him. And he's there now, isn't he? Isn't that proof enough for what I'm trying to tell—"

"Same problem, mate. Double problem, actually. He doesn't have her, and even if he does or if he knows where she is and is putting on the performance of a lifetime for the Italian cops, my colleague over there, and everyone else, what's next on the chart for him when she's handed over? Is he supposed to bring her back to London without her mum ever knowing she's here?"

"I don't know. I didn't ask him. It didn't make any difference to me. All he wanted from me was information and that's what I gave him. End of story."

"Not quite, mate. You're doing nothing but trying to drop a load of cow manure on me. If you think that's going to come *close* to convincing me you aren't in this up to your eyeballs, then you're bloody wrong. So let's start again. And believe me, I've got hours to spare till we get to the truth."

"I've told you—"

"Hours and hours," she said pleasantly.

He seemed to think frantically of where to go next with his wild allegations, and he finally said with a snap of his fingers, "*Khushi*, then."

Barbara drew in a deep breath.

He said it again. "*Khushi*, Sergeant Havers. Would I say that if I was lying to you? Professor Azhar said this to me: 'She'll listen to someone who calls her *khushi* because she'll know the message is from me.'"

Barbara's mouth went dry. She could feel her lips sticking to the front of her teeth. *Happiness* was the definition of the word *khushi*, but it was from the word itself that the impact came. For *khushi* was Azhar's nickname for his daughter, and Barbara had heard the man say it hundreds of times in the two years that she'd known him.

She felt as if the chair she was sitting on was sinking into the floor of the room. Doughty's face got wavy in her vision. She blinked and tried to fight off dizziness.

The bloody man, she realised, was finally telling her the truth.

BOW
LONDON

Dwayne Doughty knew there was very little time at this point. He was into this mess up to his nostrils, the sweating nerve-strung personification of the best laid plans of mice and men, et cetera. Once he was back out in the street—with his hours at the Bow Road nick just an aftertaste like burnt garlic in his mouth—he made for his office. There were things to be done and he was going to have to use every one of his skills to bring about the result he needed. Failing that, he knew that the barrel-shaped and outstandingly ill-dressed Met officer was completely right: A study of Michelangelo Di Massimo's phone records and computer files was going to provide trails leading in more than one direction. Since Dwayne could hardly export the talented Bryan Smythe to deal with the Italian phone system and whatever went for the Pisan detective's technology, he—Dwayne—was going to have to set up a series of offensive manoeuvres.

In the Roman Road, he pounded up the stairs to his office. He shouted, "Emily!" as he went. Her blagging expertise was going to be required. So was the superlative hacking expertise of Bryan Smythe and every one of his well-placed contacts.

Emily's door was open. Two cardboard boxes sat outside her office in the area at the top of the stairs. They were taped and ready . . . but ready for what Dwayne didn't know until he walked into the room that housed her operation and saw exactly what she intended.

She'd removed her tailored pinstriped jacket, her waistcoat, and her tie. They all lay across the back of her chair. This chair she'd pushed against the window, the better to access the inside of her desk, her files, her supplies, and everything else that marked her employment.

She shot him a look in the midst of dumping the contents of a drawer willy-nilly into an open box. "Don't," she said.

"Don't what? What're you doing?"

"Don't ask me what I'm doing when you can see for yourself. Or don't play dumb. Or don't be a fool. How about don't put us in jeopardy? Take your pick." She reached for the Sellotape and sealed the box. She heaved it up, heaved herself likewise, and carried the box past him in the doorway. She dumped it on top of the others and returned to her office, where, at a bulletin board, she began pulling down her map of London along with bus schedules, train schedules, a map of the Underground, and—for some reason—a poster of Montacute House and three picture postcards featuring the Cliffs of Moher, Beachy Head, and the Needles on the Isle of Wight.

"This can't mean what I think it means," he said.

"I don't get paid enough to be caught up in shit like this. You do. But *I* don't."

"So you're leaving? Just like that?"

"Your powers of observation . . . ? Incredible. No wonder you've been such a howling success in your chosen line of work."

She was folding her maps and making a hash of it, paper maps always being a nightmare to put back into their original, neat form. She wasn't following the designated folds and creases. It appeared that she couldn't be bothered to do so, which told Dwayne Doughty how determined she was to be gone as soon as possible. And this told him how unnerved she was by what had happened: the cops showing up unexpectedly on their doorstep with the silver bracelets ready to be slapped on the wrists of two malefactors called Doughty and Cass.

He said, "You have a hell of a lot more nerve than this. For someone who pulls complete strangers in pubs—"

"Don't even go there," she shot at him. "If I'm not mistaken, unless things have really changed in this country, pulling strangers in pubs for anonymous sex is not going to get me hauled into the dock."

"We're not getting hauled into the dock," he told her. "I'm not. You're not. Bryan's not. Full stop."

"I'm not getting hauled to the nick, either. I'm not ringing up some solicitor to come hold my hand while the cops go through my life like it's infested with bedbugs. I'm done with this, Dwayne. I told you from the first, and you wouldn't listen because to you the bottom line is cash. Whoever pays the most is whose job we take on. Wrong side of the law? No problem, madam. We're just who you want to take the bloody fall should everything in the case go to hell. Like it has now. So I'm out of here."

"Oh, for God's sake, Em." Dwayne did his best to hide his desperation. Without Em Cass at the helm of his computer system—not to mention on the phones acting the part of whatever official was needed to glean information from sources who'd be less than cooperative faced with someone with little talent for hoodwinking them—he was sunk and he knew it. "I called in the cavalry," he told her. "I told them the truth."

She was unimpressed. "There is no bloody cavalry. I tried to tell you that right from the first, didn't I, but you wouldn't listen. Oh no. You were far too clever for that."

"Stop being dramatic. I gave them the professor. All right? Are you hearing me? I gave them the professor. Full stop. That's what you've wanted, isn't it? Well, it's been done and you and I are on our way to being in the clear."

"And they're going to *believe* you?" she scoffed. "You name a name and that's all there is to it?" She raised her head heavenward and spoke to some deity on the ceiling, saying, "Why didn't I *see* what an idiot he is? Why didn't I get out when this whole thing started?"

"Because you knew I'd never go into something without an exit strategy planned. And I have one for this. So d'you want to run off or do you want to unpack your boxes and help me set it in motion?"

LUCCA
TUSCANY

Lynley located Taymullah Azhar in the Cathedral of San Martino, which stood enormously in a large piazza along with a *palazzo* and the traditional, separate *battistero*. It was an elaborate Romanesque building not dissimilar to a wedding cake, with a façade comprising four tiers of arches, and mounted upon it was a marble depiction of the eponymous saint performing his act of kindness with garment and sword upon a mendicant at the side of his horse. Lynley wouldn't have thought to find Azhar inside this building. As a Muslim, he didn't seem like a man who'd seek a Christian church in order to pray. But when Lynley rang his mobile, Azhar's hushed voice said he was with the Holy Face inside the Duomo. Lynley wasn't certain what this meant, but he asked the Pakistani man to wait for him there.

"You have news?" Azhar asked hopefully.

"Wait for me please" was Lynley's reply.

Inside the cathedral, a tour was ongoing: A young woman with an official badge round her neck was shepherding some dozen or so people to stand at the foot of a Last Supper, the work of Tintoretto brightly lit to show angels above, apostles below, and the Lord in the midst of feeding a piece of bread to St. Peter as his companions managed to look suitably impressed with the goings on. Midway down the right aisle, a partition kept unticketed visitors away from the beauties of the sacristy, while to the left an octagonal temple was the centre of attention of ten elderly women who looked like pilgrims come specifically to the spot.

It was at this temple that Lynley found Azhar, standing respectfully back from the pilgrims but gazing upon a huge and severely stylised crucified Christ rendered in wood. The Christ had on his face an expression that looked more surprised than suffering, as if he couldn't quite come to terms with what had put him into the position in which he found himself.

"It's called the Holy Face," Azhar said to Lynley quietly as Lynley joined him next to one of the Duomo's pillars. "It's supposed to . . ." He cleared his throat. "Signora Vallera told me of it."

Lynley glanced at the other man. Here was anguish, he thought, a mental and spiritual crucifixion. He wanted to put an end to Azhar's suffering. But there was a limit to what he could tell him while so much of what they needed to know was still floating out there, waiting to be discovered.

"She said," Azhar murmured, "that the Holy Face works miracles for people, but this is something I find I cannot believe. How can a piece of wood—no matter how lovingly carved—do anything for anyone, Inspector Lynley? And yet, here I am, standing in front of it, ready to ask it for my daughter. And yet unable to ask for anything because to ask such a thing of a piece of wood . . . This means to me that hope is gone."

"I don't think that's the case," Lynley told him.

Azhar looked at him. Lynley saw how dark the skin beneath his eyes had become, acting as a stark contrast to the whites of his eyes, which were themselves sketched with red. Every day that Lynley had been in Italy, the man had looked worse than the day before. "Which part of it?" Azhar asked him. "The wood performing a miracle or the hope?"

"Both," he said. "Either."

"You've learned something," Azhar guessed. "You would not have come otherwise."

"I'd prefer to speak to you with Angelina." And when he saw the momentary terror of every parent whose child is missing shoot across Azhar's face, Lynley went on. "It's neither good nor bad," he said hastily. "It's just a development. Will you come with me?"

They set off for the hospital. It was outside the great wall of Lucca, but they went on foot as the route was not overly long and their use of the wall itself for part of the walk—sheltered by the great trees upon it—made the way both pleasant and shorter. They descended from one of the diamond-shaped *baluardi*, and from that point they made their way to Via dell'Ospedale.

When they reached the hospital, they were in time to see Lorenzo Mura and Angelina Upman together leaving the place. Angelina was in a wheelchair being pushed by an attendant. Grim-faced, Lorenzo walked at her side. He caught sight of Lynley and Azhar approaching, and he spoke to the attendant, who halted.

At least, Lynley thought, this appeared to be a piece of good news: Angelina sufficiently well to return to her home. She was very pale, but that was the extent of things.

When she saw Lynley and Azhar approaching her together, she pressed herself back in the wheelchair as if she could stop whatever news was coming. Lynley understood at once. He and Azhar arriving as one to see her . . . She would be terrified that the worst had occurred.

He said hastily, "It's information only, Ms. Upman," and he saw her swallow convulsively.

Lorenzo was the one to speak. "She wishes it. Me, I do not."

For an insane moment, Lynley thought he was referring to her daughter's death at the hands of a kidnapper. But when Lorenzo went on, his meaning became clear.

"She says she is better. This I do not believe."

Apparently, she'd checked herself out of the hospital. She had good reason, she said. The chance of infection in a hospital was greater than the benefit of being under the care of nursing staff for what amounted to morning sickness. At least, this was Angelina's belief, and she turned to her former lover for corroboration, saying, "Hari, will you explain to him how dangerous it is for me to stay here any longer?"

Azhar didn't look like a man ready to embrace a position as intermediary between the mother of his child and the father of her next child, but he was a microbiologist, after all, and he did know something about the transmission of sickness and disease. He said, "There are risks everywhere, Angelina. While there is truth in what you say—"

"*Capisci?*" she cut in, speaking to Lorenzo.

"—there is also truth in the dangers of illnesses associated with pregnancy if you don't attend to them."

"Well, I have attended to them," she said. "I'm keeping food down now—"

"*Solo minestra,*" Lorenzo muttered.

"Soup is something," Angelina told him. "And I've no other symptoms any longer."

"She does not listen to me," Lorenzo said to them.

"You don't listen to *me*. I have no symptoms. It was flu or a bad meal or a twenty-four-hour whatever. I'm fine now. I'm going home. You're the one being ridiculous about this."

Lorenzo's face darkened but that was the extent of his reaction. "*Le donne incinte,*" Lynley murmured to him. Pregnant women needed to be humoured. Things would return to normal again—at least in this matter—when Angelina was safely delivered of their child. As to the rest of their life together . . . He knew this depended on the outcome of Hadiyyah's disappearance.

"If we can speak for a moment?" he said to them. "Perhaps inside?" He indicated the doors of the hospital. There was a lobby within.

They agreed to this, and they established themselves in such a way that the light was good on all of their faces, rendering them readable to Lynley as he imparted the information. A car had been found in the Apuan Alps, he said, at the scene of an accident that had apparently occurred a few days earlier, although they wouldn't know the exact time until a forensic pathologist examined a man's body that had been near the vehicle. He hastened to add that no child's body had been at the accident site, but because the car in question matched the description of a car seen parked in a lay-by with a man and a young girl near it, the vehicle was being taken off for study. They would be looking for a child's fingerprints as well as any other evidence of her presence.

Angelina nodded numbly. She said, "*Capisco, capisco,*" and then, "I understand. You must need . . ." She didn't seem able to continue.

Lynley said, "I'm afraid we do. Her toothbrush, her hairbrush, anything to give us a DNA sample. The police will want to dust for her fingerprints, perhaps in her bedroom, so comparisons can be made."

"Of course." She looked at Azhar and then away, out of the window where Italian cypresses shielded the car park from view and a fountain bubbled on a square of gravel with benches on all four of its sides. "What do you think?" she said to Lynley. "What do they think . . . the police?"

"They'll be checking into everything about the man whose body was there."

"Do they know . . . Can they tell . . . ?"

"He had identification with him," Lynley said. And here was the important part, their reactions when he said the name. "Roberto Squali," he told them. "Is that name familiar to any of you?"

But there was nothing. Just three blank faces and an exchange of looks between Lorenzo and Angelina as they asked each other non-verbally if this was a person either of them knew. As for Azhar, he repeated the name. But it seemed more an effort to commit it to memory than an attempt to appear in the dark about who this man was.

Whatever came next, it would be from police work on the part of the Italian force, Lynley reckoned. Either that or from Barbara's uncovering something in London.

They would all have to wait.

29 APRIL

LUCCA
TUSCANY

F orse quarantotto ore." Over the telephone Dr. Cinzia Ruocco
gave Salvatore Lo Bianco the information in her usual manner
when speaking to a male: on the border between rude and
angry. She didn't like men, and who could blame her? She looked like
a young Sophia Loren, and because of this she'd suffered men's lusting
after her body for a good twenty-five of her thirty-eight years. Whenever Salvatore saw her, he lusted after her as well. He liked to think
he was good at keeping his thoughts off his face, but the medical
examiner had antennae attuned to the slightest mental image that
might pop up in the head of any male who gazed upon her bounteous
physical virtues. This was one of the reasons she preferred to do things
by phone. Again, who could blame her?

Forty-eight hours, Salvatore thought. Where had Roberto Squali
been heading, then, forty-eight hours ago when his car had flown off
the road and his life had ended? Was he drunk? he asked Cinzia
Ruocco. He was not, she replied. Not drunk and, barring toxicology
reports which would be weeks in coming, not impaired in any way.
Except, she added, in the way of all men who think ownership of a
fast sports car makes them more masculine than owning something
sensible. She wouldn't be surprised to learn this fool had possession of

a motorcycle as well. Something huge, she said, to take the place of what—she was happy to report—he *didn't* have in great size between his legs.

"*Sì, sì*," Salvatore said. He knew Cinzia lived with a man, but he had to wonder how the fellow put up with her general disdain for males of all species. He rang off and considered a map he'd posted on the wall of his office. There was so much in the Apuan Alps. It would take a century to work out where the dead man had been heading, if, indeed, where he'd been heading was relevant to the case.

Salvatore had come up with a photo of Squali in better days, which was any day prior to the day on which they'd found his body. He was a handsome man, and with the picture in his possession, it was a small matter for Salvatore to reboot the tourist photographs he'd loaded onto his laptop and to verify that it was indeed Squali standing there in the crowd behind Hadiyyah, holding the card with a yellow happy face on it. Seeing this, Salvatore considered his next options.

They had everything to do with Piero Fanucci. *Il Pubblico Ministero* was not going to be pleased when Salvatore revealed to him that he might be wrong about his prime suspect. In the past two days, Fanucci had invested a great deal into Carlo Casparia's ostensible guilt, allowing more and more details of the drug addict's "confession" to be leaked to the press. He'd even given an interview about the investigation to *Prima Voce*. This interview had ended up on the tabloid's front page as well as its website, which meant it would soon enough be translated by the British media, members of which group had started to show up in Lucca. They'd made short work of figuring out that the café down the street from the *questura* was the best spot to pick up gossip about the case, and like their Italian counterparts, they were dogged when it came to buttonholing police officials for direct questioning.

Because of this latter fact, when it came down to it, there was really no decision to make about whether to tell *il Pubblico Ministero* about the discovery of Roberto Squali, Salvatore realised. Should he not tell him, a reporter would, or—what was worse—Piero would read about it in *Prima Voce*. There would be hell for Salvatore to pay if that occurred. So there was nothing for it but to pay a call upon Fanucci.

Salvatore gave the *magistrato* every one of the details he'd so far withheld: the red convertible, the previous sighting of a man and a girl heading into the woods, the American tourist's photos of a man in possession of a card that—so it appeared—he seemed to have given to the missing girl, and now the accident site with that same man's dead body forty-eight hours in the out-of-doors.

Fanucci listened to Salvatore's recitation from the other side of his vast walnut desk, twirling a pen in his fingers and keeping his eyes fixed upon Salvatore's lips. At the conclusion of Salvatore's remarks, *il Pubblico Ministero* abruptly shoved his chair back, surged to his feet, and walked to his bookcases. Salvatore steeled himself for Fanucci's rage, possibly to include the hurling of legal volumes in his direction.

What came, however, was something else.

"*Così* . . . ," Fanucci murmured. "*Così, Topo* . . ."

Salvatore waited for more. He did not have to wait long.

"*Ora capisco com'è successo*," Fanucci said thoughtfully. He did not sound the least bit concerned about the information he'd just been given.

"*Daverro?*" Salvatore sought clarification. "*Allora, Piero* . . . ?" If Fanucci *did* indeed see how the kidnapping and everything related to it had happened, he—Salvatore—would be only too welcoming of the magistrate's conclusions.

Fanucci turned back to him with one of his inauthentic and paternal smiles, in itself a sign of worse things to come. "*Questo* . . . ," he said. "You have the link you have sought. This we must now celebrate."

"The link," Salvatore repeated.

"Between our Carlo and what he did with the girl. Now it all fits together, Topo. *Bravo. Hai fatto bene.*" Fanucci returned to his desk and sat. He continued expansively with "I well know what you will say next. 'So far,' you will say, 'there is no link to join these men Squali and Carlo Casparia, *Magistrato*.' But that is because you have not yet found it. You will, however, and it will show you that Carlo's intentions were what I have declared them to be. He did not wish this child for himself. Have I not told you that? As you can now see and as I saw the moment you told me there *was* a Carlo, he wished to sell the child to fund his drug habit. And this is exactly what he did."

"To make sure I understand, *Magistrato*," Salvatore said carefully. "You mean that you believe Carlo sold the little girl to Roberto Squali?"

"*Certo.* And Squali is the direction you are to head in: to find the point in the chain where the link exists leading you from him to Carlo."

"But Piero, what you suggest . . . A simple comparison with the tourist's photographs shows that Carlo is not likely to be involved at all."

Fanucci's eyes narrowed but his smile did not falter. "And your reason is . . . ?"

"My reason is that one of the photos shows this man Squali with a card that, in a picture that follows, appears to be in the hand of the girl. Does this not suggest that he and not Carlo followed her from the *mercato* on the day she went missing?"

"Bah!" was Fanucci's reply. "This man Squali . . . He is in the *mercato* how often, Topo? This one time? While Carlo and the girl are there weekly, *sì*? So what I'm telling you is that Carlo knew this man, Carlo knew what he wanted, Carlo saw this girl, and Carlo laid his plan, based on the girl's movements that he and not Roberto Squali had studied. So we will talk to Carlo again, my friend. And from him we will learn this Squali's intentions. Prior to this he has not mentioned the name Roberto Squali to me. But when instead I say it to him . . . ? *Aspetta, aspetta.*"

Salvatore could see how it would play out, now that Fanucci had a name to use in another interrogation of Casparia. He'd pull him out of custody and back into an interview room for another eighteen or twenty or twenty-five hours without food or drink, just enough time for Carlo to begin "imagining" how he and Roberto Squali came to be best friends, intent upon kidnapping a nine-year-old girl for reasons that would be invented on the spot.

"Piero, for God's sake," Salvatore said. "You *know* in your heart that Carlo is not involved in this. And what I'm telling you now, with these details about Roberto Squali—"

"Salvatore," *il Pubblico Ministero* said in a pleasant tone, "I know in my heart nothing of the sort. Carlo Casparia has confessed. He has signed his confession without coercion. This, I assure you, people do not do if they are innocent. And Carlo is not an innocent man."

VICTORIA
LONDON

Barbara Havers sat through the morning's meeting in the incident room with her mind in turmoil, although she managed to keep her expression attentive to DI John Stewart's endless droning. She also kept her wits about her when he required from her an oral presentation of what she'd gleaned from her three interviews on the previous day. Never mind that she'd been at the Yard past ten o'clock at night, dutifully putting her reports in order for the man's perusal. Stewart was obviously still on his mission to trip her in her tracks.

Sorry to disappoint you, mate, was Barbara's thought as she made her report. Still, it gave her little enough satisfaction to prove the DI wrong about her. For most of her was in a decided twist over what she'd heard from Dwayne Doughty when she'd spoken to him at the Bow Road nick.

Khushi had given her a very bad night. *Khushi* had insisted that she ring Taymullah Azhar in Italy and demand a few answers. What stopped her from doing this was a basic tenet about police work: You don't give away the game when you're in the middle of it, and you sure as bloody hell do not clue in a suspect that he *is* a suspect when he doesn't think he's a suspect at all.

Yet the idea of Azhar *as* a suspect felt like a hot coal lodged in her throat even now, in the midst of the morning meeting. Azhar was, after all, her friend. Azhar was, after all, a man whom Barbara thought she knew well. The idea of Azhar being in reality someone who could orchestrate the kidnap of his own daughter was unthinkable. For no matter how she looked at the matter, the same facts that she'd delivered to Dwayne Doughty remained at the core of what the private detective was alleging about Azhar: His work and his life were in London, so even if he had somehow arranged the snatching of his daughter, how the hell was he supposed to have put his mitts on her passport, eh? And even if he'd somehow managed to produce another passport for her, he would have then returned with her to London and Angelina Upman would have done exactly what she *did* do in the company of Lorenzo Mura, which was to turn up on Azhar's doorstep demanding the return of her child.

Yet . . . there was *khushi*. Barbara tried to come up with a reason why Doughty might have known this pet name that Azhar had for his daughter. She supposed Azhar might have told the man in passing, perhaps at some point referring to Hadiyyah that way. But in all the time Barbara had known him, she'd only heard him use the word when he was speaking to Hadiyyah. He never referred to her with the term. So why would he refer to her as *khushi* when speaking to Doughty? she wondered. The answer seemed to be that he wouldn't. But that answer begged the question: What was she going to do next, post Doughty's allegations?

Ringing someone seemed the only answer: ringing Lynley in order to lay before him the facts she had and to ask his advice or ringing Azhar and cleverly gleaning from him some indication that Doughty's claims were either true or false. Barbara wanted to do the first. But she knew she had to do the second. Had Azhar been in London, she could have confronted him in order to watch his face when she spoke. But he wasn't in London and Hadiyyah was still missing and she had no real choice in the matter of what to do next, did she?

She waited for an opportune moment long after the morning meeting when DI Stewart was otherwise engaged. She reached Azhar on his mobile, but the connection was bad. It turned out that he was in the Alps, he told her, and for a moment she thought he'd actually gone to Switzerland for some mad reason. When she yelped, "The *Alps*?" he clarified with, "These are the Apuan Alps. They are north of Lucca," and the connection improved as he moved into what he said was a small piazza in one of the villages tucked into those mountains.

He was searching it, he told her. He intended to search every village he came upon as he travelled higher and higher on a road that twisted into the Alps. It was from this road that a red convertible had crashed down a cliff, the driver dying when thrown from it. And inside this convertible, Barbara—

At this, the poor man's voice wavered. Barbara's hands and her feet went completely dead. She said, "What? Azhar, *what*?"

"They think Hadiyyah was with this man," he said. "They have gone to Angelina's home for her fingerprints, for DNA samples, for . . . I do not know what else."

Barbara could tell he was trying not to weep. She said, "Azhar."

"I could not just remain in Lucca and wait for news. They will compare the car—what they find in it and on it—and they will then know, but I . . . To hear she might have been with him and then to know . . ." A silence, then a barely controlled gasp. Barbara knew how humiliating it would be for him to be heard weeping by anyone. He said at last, "Forgive me. This is unseemly."

"Bloody hell," she said in a fierce whisper. "Azhar, this is your daughter we're talking about. There is *no* 'I should not' between you and me when it comes to Hadiyyah, okay?"

This appeared to make matters worse, for then he sobbed, managing only "Thank you" and nothing more.

She waited. She wished she were there, wherever he was in the Alps, because she would have taken him into her arms for what comfort she could offer in this situation. But it would have been a cold comfort indeed. When a child went missing, each day that passed was a day that lessened the possibility of that child's ever being found alive.

Azhar finally managed to give her more details as well as a name: Roberto Squali. He was at the heart of what had happened to Hadiyyah. He was the driver of the crashed car, who was dead.

"A name is a starting place," Barbara told him. "A name, Azhar, is a good starting place."

Which brought her, of course, to the pet name *khushi* and the reason for her call. But she couldn't find it in herself to mention this to Hadiyyah's father just now. He was already upset enough with this turn of events. Asking him about *khushi* or making insinuations about his putative Berlin alibi or requiring of him definitive proof that he wasn't the mastermind behind the disappearance of a most beloved child as claimed by the private investigator he'd hired . . . Barbara realised she couldn't do this to him. For the very idea that he would set off to Berlin and establish an alibi while someone he'd hired in Italy was snatching his daughter from a public market . . . It didn't make sense. Not when one put Angelina Upman into the picture. Unless, of course, the plan was to hold Hadiyyah somewhere until her mother came to believe she was dead. But what mother of a missing child *ever* gave up hope? And even if this was the plan and Azhar intended somehow to spirit his daughter back to England sans passport at some point six or eight or ten months from now, what was Hadiyyah supposed to do then? Never contact her mother again?

None of these conjectures made sense to Barbara. Azhar was innocent. He was in intolerable pain. And what she didn't need to do at the moment was to make things worse with pointed questions about Dwayne Doughty's claims and his declaration of *khushi*, as if a word in Urdu held the key to a life-and-death puzzle that seemed to enlarge with every day that passed.

LUCCA
TUSCANY

By late morning, Salvatore had the confirmation for his suspicions. The missing child's fingerprints were, indeed, in the red convertible. Forensic officers in the company of DI Lynley had gone to Fattoria di Santa Zita to obtain samples from the little girl's bedroom: fingerprints as well as DNA from her hairbrush and toothbrush. The DNA results would not come in for some time. But the fingerprints had been a matter of a few hours only, to collect them, to take them to the laboratory, and to compare them to what had been found in the car, on the sides of the leather passenger seat, on the seatbelt's buckle, and on the fascia. DNA was hardly necessary after that, but since DNA results had long since become de rigueur during trials, appropriate tests would be made.

For his own work, however, Salvatore didn't need those results. What he needed was an interview with anyone who knew Roberto Squali, and he began with the man's home address. This was in Via del Fosso, a north-south lane through the walled city. This route was, most unusually, cut down its centre by a narrow canal from which fresh ferns sprang between crevices on its edges, and Squali's residence was on the west side of this canal, through a heavy door that hid one of Lucca's fine private gardens.

Most men of Squali's age in Italy did not live alone. Rather, they lived at home with their parents, generally waited upon by their doting mammas until such a time as they married. But this did not prove true for Roberto Squali. As things turned out, Squali was from Rome and his parents still lived there. The young man himself had a residence at the home of his paternal aunt and her husband, and upon questioning them, Salvatore discovered that such had been the case since Roberto's adolescence.

The aunt and uncle—surnamed Medici (alas, no relation)—met with Salvatore in the garden, where beneath the branches of a fig tree, they sat on the edges of their chairs as if to spring away from him at the least provocation. From an earlier visit made by the police, they'd learned of their nephew's death via automobile accident; his parents in Rome had been informed; there the family were devastated; a funeral was even now being arranged.

No tears were shed in the garden for Roberto's unexpected passing. Salvatore thought this strange. Considering the length of time that Squali had lived with his aunt and uncle, it seemed to him that they would have come to consider him something of a son. But they had not, and some careful probing on his part turned up the reason.

Roberto had not been a source of pride to his family. Indeed, just the opposite was the case. At fifteen years old and enterprising well beyond his years, he'd found easy money available in running a minor prostitution ring featuring the services of immigrant women from Africa. His parents had got him out of Rome one step ahead of being arrested not only for this but also for having enjoyed the pleasures of the flesh offered—at least to hear Roberto's account of the interlude—by the twelve-year-old daughter of a family acquaintance. The parents of the violated girl agreed to a hefty financial settlement for her deflowering, and the public prosecutor had been cajoled into accepting an arrangement that guaranteed Roberto's absence from the Eternal City well into subsequent decades. Hence, an arrest and a trial associated with either matter were avoided and familial disgrace had been buried by means of the boy's removal to Lucca. There he'd remained for the past ten years.

"He is not a bad boy," Signora Medici avowed to Salvatore, less with passion than with the habit of repetition. "It is just that . . . for Roberto . . ." She glanced at her husband. It seemed a wary look.

He went on. "*Vuole una vita facile*" was how the signore put it. And to Roberto, the easy life had been defined as working as little as possible since there were pickings aplenty in their society and he'd been determined from childhood to be ready with a basket whenever something was hanging low enough on the tree. When he worked at all, it was as a waiter in one fine restaurant or another, either in Lucca or in Pisa or occasionally in Firenze. Charming as he was, he never had trouble finding employment. Keeping it, however, had always been another matter.

"We pray for him," Signora Medici murmured. "Since he is fifteen years old, all of us pray that he will perhaps grow into a man like his father or like his brother."

The fact that Roberto had a brother was a subject worth exploring, but the topic was dispatched fairly quickly. Cristoforo Squali, as things turned out, was the blue-eyed boy in the family, an *architetto* in Rome, married three years, and producing a grandchild for his proud parents eleven months after the I dos were said. With another child on the way, he was everything Roberto was not, this Cristo. He'd never put a foot wrong since the day of his birth. While Roberto . . . ? Signora Medici crossed herself. "We pray for him," she repeated. "Weekly novenas, his mother and I. But God has never heard our prayers."

Salvatore told them, then, about the location of their nephew's accident. They appeared to know little enough about his doings in Tuscany, but there was a chance that his trip into the Apuan Alps would trigger in them a memory of a conversation with him, the casual mention on his part of a friend, an associate, or an acquaintance who lived there. He did not tell them that Roberto was involved in some way in the disappearance of the English girl that had been reported in the newspapers and on the television. Telling them that would put them all on the fast track to family secrecy, considering Roberto's hushed-up brush with the law in Rome.

Salvatore didn't expect them to know much about what Roberto had been doing in the Apuan Alps. He was surprised, then, when Signora Medici and her husband looked at each other in what appeared to be consternation when he told them where their nephew's car had been found. The air among them fairly crackled with tension as the signora repeated, *"Le Alpi Apuane?"* As she spoke, her husband's face hardened on an expression that mixed loathing and fury equally.

"*Sì*," Salvatore said. If they had a *carta stradale* of Tuscany, he could show them approximately where their nephew's car had been found.

Signora Medici looked at her husband. Her glance seemed to ask him if they even *wanted* to know more at this point. They were worried about something, Salvatore concluded, perhaps trying to decide if they preferred to remain in ignorance about Roberto's activities.

Signor Medici made the decision for them both. He pushed himself to his feet and told Salvatore to come with him into the house. Salvatore followed him through an open doorway shielded from bugs by strips of plastic. This gave way into a large kitchen floored in well-scrubbed terracotta tiles. "*Aspetti qui*" told Salvatore that he was to wait, and the signore vanished through another doorway to a darkened part of the house while his wife went to the stove and from a shelf above it took a large Moka into which she began to spoon coffee. This seemed more something to do with her hands than an offer of hospitality since once she added water and put the Moka onto the flame of the *fornello*, she promptly forgot all about it.

The signore returned with a dog-eared road map of all of Tuscany. He spread it out upon a deeply dented chopping block that was a central feature of the kitchen. Salvatore studied it, trying to recall at what exact point the final turnoff appeared on the route to the accident site. With his finger he traced the route he and DI Lynley had taken. He got as far as the first turn they'd made off the main road when Signora Medici gave a whimper and her husband muttered a curse.

"*Che cosa sapete?*" Salvatore asked them. "*Dovete dirmi tutto.*" For it was obvious to him that they did know more than they wished to say about the Apuan Alps. To convince them that they indeed had to tell him whatever they knew, he saw he had no choice in the matter and told them of Roberto's possible involvement in a serious crime.

"*Ma lei, lei,*" the signora murmured to her husband. She grabbed on to his arm as if for some kind of reassurance.

"*Chi?*" Salvatore demanded. Who was this *she* to whom the signora referred?

After an agonised glance between them, Signor Medici was the one to speak. *She* was their daughter, Domenica, who resided at a cloistered convent high in the Apuan Alps.

"A nun?" Salvatore asked.

No, she was not a nun, the signore told him. She was—and here the man's lip curled with his disgust—*una pazza, un' imbecille, una*—

"No!" his wife cried. This was not true. She was *not* crazy, she was *not* an imbecile. She was, instead, just a simple girl who wanted and had been denied a life spent in the presence of God and a holy marriage to the Lord Jesus Christ. She wanted prayer. She wanted meditation. She wanted contemplation and silence, and if he did not understand that her deep love of her Catholic religion had created within their daughter a nature both massively spiritual and completely innocent—

"They would not take her," Signor Medici cut in, waving away his wife's defence of their child. "She lacked the brains. You know this as well as I do, Maria."

From all of this, Salvatore attempted to put together the pieces of a puzzle that seemed to be growing by the minute. Domenica was not a nun, then. But she lived in the convent with the other nuns? She was, perhaps, an acolyte of some sort? Perhaps a servant? A cook? A laundress? A seamstress assisting with the manufacture of vestments for the province's priests?

Signor Medici barked an unpleasant laugh. All of Salvatore's suggestions, it appeared, were far more challenging than his *figlia stupida* could have contended with. She was none of these things. Rather, she was a caretaker on the convent property, and she lived there in rooms above its hovel of a barn. She milked goats, she grew vegetables, and she fancied herself part of the community. She even called herself Sister Domenica Giustina, and she'd created out of table linens from their home here in Lucca a form of nun's habit that resembled that which the sisters themselves wore.

During the man's recitation, his wife began to weep. She looked away from her husband and clasped her hands tightly in her lap. When the man was finished, she turned back to Salvatore and said, "*Figlia unica,*" which explained something of the grief she felt and the anger harboured by her husband. Domenica was their only child. She'd held her parents' hopes for the future, which had been dashed as over the years it had become more and more obvious that the girl was not normal.

Salvatore had to ask the next question, despite their distress at having to speak of Domenica at all. Could Roberto Squali have been heading to the convent where Domenica lived? Had he and Domenica stayed in touch since she'd gone to live there?

This they did not know. Their nephew and their daughter had been close at one time as adolescents, but that time had passed as Roberto had learned the limits of what Domenica could offer anyone in companionship. This had not taken long and it was to be expected. Indeed, Domenica's life had largely been defined by abridged relationships with people who came to understand that what appeared to be a deeply spiritual nature was, in reality, an inability to exist in the world as it was.

All of this Salvatore gleaned, but none of it could eliminate the possibility of Roberto Squali's driving his convertible into the mountains in order to see his cousin. It would be a piece of luck if a visit to the convent had been his intention. No matter her simplicity, there was a very good chance that Sister Domenica Giustina could tell them something about what had happened to the English girl.

VILLA RIVELLI
TUSCANY

Domenica went to seek Carina. For the past three days the child had avoided her. During Domenica's praying and fasting, she'd heard Carina moving about in the rooms above the barn, and she'd felt the child's presence as she'd watched and waited for Sister Domenica Giustina to understand what had to be done next. Now she would be somewhere on the grounds of the Villa Rivelli. Sister Domenica Giustina felt secure in the knowledge that God would lead her to Carina without trouble.

And so it was. As if guided by the angel Gabriel, Sister Domenica Giustina made her way to the sunken *giardino* with its splashing fountains. Carina wasn't in sight, but that was of no account. For at the far end of the garden, the Grotta dei Venti stood. This *grotta* offered a chamber of stone and shell along with four marble statues from whose feet water flowed continuously into a channel from a spring far below.

This made the air within the grotto cool and inviting in the heat of the day. And here it was that Sister Domenica Giustina saw the little girl, as if waiting for her.

She was sitting on the stone floor of the place, her knees drawn up to her chin and her thin arms holding her legs in place. She was tucked into the deepest cool shadows, and as Sister Domenica Giustina entered the grotto, she saw the child shrink away.

"*Vieni, Carina,*" she said softly to the child, extending her hand. "*Vieni con me.*"

The girl looked up, her face like a haunted thing. She began to speak, but the words she used were not in Italian, so Sister Domenica Giustina understood from them only a few words. "I want my mummy," Carina said. "I want my dad. I was s'posed to see him and *where* is he and I *want* him and I don't want to be here anymore and I'mscaredandIwantmydadnownownow!"

Dad was the word Sister Domenica Giustina caught among the rush of language. She said, "*Tuo padre, Carina?*"

"IwanttogohomeandIwantmydad."

"*Padre, sì?*" Sister Domenica Giustina clarified. "*Vorresti vedere tuo padre?*"

"*Voglio andare a casa,*" the little girl said, her voice growing stronger. "*Voglio andare da mio padre, chiaro?*"

"Ah, *sì?*" Sister Domenica Giustina said. "*Capisco, ma prima devi venire qui.*"

She held out her hand once more. If the child wanted to go to her father's home, as she said, there were steps to be taken and those steps could not begin in the Grotta dei Venti.

The child looked at the hand extended to her. Her face wore an expression of doubt. Sister Domenica Giustina smiled softly to encourage her. "*Non avere paura,*" she told her, for there was indeed no reason to have fear.

Slowly, then, Carina got to her feet. She put her hand in Sister Domenica Giustina's. Together, they left the cool confines of the grotto. Together, they climbed the stairs out of the sunken garden and began to approach the great shuttered villa.

"*Ti dobbiamo preparare,*" Sister Domenica Giustina murmured to the

little girl. For she could not meet with her father unprepared. She had
to be ready: sweet and clean and pure. She explained this to the child
as she urged her forward, past the villa's wide and empty loggia, past
the sweeping steps that led up to this, round the corner of the building itself, and in the direction of the vast cellars of the place.

It was on the approach to the steps leading down to the cellars that
Carina's footsteps began to falter. She began to pull back in obvious
reluctance. She began to speak words that Sister Domenica Giustina
could not hope to understand.

"Mydadsnottherehe'snotinthecellaryousaidmydadyousaidyou
wouldtakemetomydadIwon'tgoIwon'tIwon'tit'sdarkinthereitsmells
I'mafraid!"

Sister Domenica Giustina said, *"No, no, no. Non devi . . ."* But the
child did not understand. She tried to pull away with all the strength
she had, but with surpassing strength Sister Domenica Giustina pulled
back. *"Vieni,"* she said. *"Devi venire."*

Down one step, down two, down three. An enormous effort and
she had the child within the damp, dank darkness of the cellar.

But there the little girl began to scream. And the only way to silence her was to drag her far, far inside the rooms of the cellar until
she could not be heard by the world outside the forbidding walls of
that terrible place.

LUCCA

TUSCANY

Salvatore knew that the possibility of Roberto Squali's having arranged the kidnapping of the English child on his own was remote.
Although his past clearly identified him as a player on the field of
illegal activities, there had for years been no hint of scandal or law-
breaking on his part. The logical conclusion was that although the
child had been with him, she had not come to his attention as a
kidnap victim via his own inspiration. The business card of Michelangelo Di Massimo within Squali's *portafoglio* suggested that there
was a substantial link among the private detective, Squali, and the
crime, and Salvatore was intent upon finding it.

This did not take long for the simple reason that Roberto Squali had done nothing at all to hide the link, so sure had he apparently been of the potential success of the scheme. The records of his *telefonino* revealed calls made to him by Michelangelo Di Massimo. The records of his bank account showed a significant deposit made into his account—in cash—on the very day of the girl's disappearance. This deposit far exceeded anything that Roberto Squali had put into his account at any other time. Salvatore was not a betting man, but he found himself willing to wager that an amount identical to Squali's deposit had left the account of Michelangelo Di Massimo on the very same day. Salvatore made the necessary arrangements to have those banking records sent to him via the Internet. Then he ordered the Pisan detective to be brought to the *questura*. There would be no polite visit by the police to Di Massimo's office or to the salon of his hairdresser or to any other place the man might have established himself. Salvatore wanted Di Massimo intimidated, and he knew how best to effect that reaction.

He rang DI Lynley in advance of Di Massimo's arrival. He also rang Piero Fanucci to bring him up to the minute on what he'd discovered and on which direction he was now headed with the case. On the part of Lynley, the conversation was brief: If the chief inspector didn't mind, the British detective would like to be present for the questioning of this man. On the part of Fanucci, the conversation was quite mad: They *had* their kidnapper or at least their mastermind in the person of Carlo Casparia, and Salvatore's instructions had been and still were to find the connection that existed between this Roberto Squali and *him*. If he couldn't manage that much . . . Did Fanucci need to see to it that someone else was assigned to this case, or was Topo going to come to his senses and resist the inclination to follow every wild hare that happened to hop by him?

"For the love of God, Piero" got Salvatore nowhere. So he agreed— as useless as he knew the endeavour would be—to see in what manner he could prove a conspiracy among *three* men when two of them did not even know of the existence of the third.

When Lynley arrived at the *questura*, Salvatore told him of his visit to the home of the Medici family in Via del Fosso. On a map of the province, he showed him the position of the convent as indicated by the parents of Domenica Medici, caretaker of the place. This could be something or it could be nothing, he explained to the Englishman. But the fact that Squali had been headed in the direction of this place where his cousin lived at least suggested her involvement. Once they had hammered down Di Massimo's part in what had occurred that day in the *mercato*, the convent was their next logical move.

Di Massimo's arrival caused a stir outside among the paparazzi and the reporters who were hanging about the *questura* on the scent of a new angle to the story. When he saw them, the Pisan detective covered his head—which, considering the appearance of his yellow hair, didn't seem like a bad idea—but a covered head indicated an unwillingness to be photographed, which naturally provoked the paparazzi into a frenzy of photographing him on the off chance that he was someone of interest.

Inside the *questura*, Di Massimo garnered an equal amount of attention. He wore his motorcycle leathers and wraparound sunglasses so dark that his eyes were hidden. His demands for an *avvocato* were vociferous and angry. *Per favore* was not part of what he said.

Salvatore and DI Lynley met him in an interview room. Four uniformed policemen lined along the wall to emphasise the seriousness of the situation. A tape recorder and a video camera were set up to document the proceedings. These began with polite offers of food and drink and a request for the name of Di Massimo's lawyer so that the man or woman could be sent for immediately to attend upon the needs of the suspect.

"*Indiziato?*" Di Massimo repeated at once. "*Non ho fatto niente.*"

Salvatore found it interesting that the Pisan made an immediate declaration of innocence rather than asking what crime he was suspected of having committed. Hearing this, he jerked his head at one of the uniforms and the man produced a file of photographs, which Salvatore laid in front of Di Massimo.

"Here is what we know, Miko," he explained as he opened the file and began to place the photographs on the table. "This wretched man"—and here he set before the Pisan three photos of Roberto Squali where he had been found, forty-eight hours dead in the open air of the Apuan Alps—"is the same as this man." And here he showed him two enlargements taken from the tourist photos: Roberto Squali standing behind the missing English girl and Roberto Squali having in his hand a greeting card that appeared to be later in the hand of the girl.

Di Massimo glanced at these, and as he did so, Salvatore reached over and removed his sunglasses. Di Massimo flinched and demanded them returned. An *"un attimo"* from Salvatore told him that all things—good, bad, and indifferent—would come quite soon.

"I do not know this man," Di Massimo said, folding his leather-clad arms across his chest.

"You have hardly looked at the pictures, my friend."

"I do not need to look more closely to tell you I have no idea who he might be."

Salvatore nodded thoughtfully. "Then you will wonder, Michelangelo, why he took so many phone calls from you in the weeks preceding the kidnap of this girl"—he indicated Hadiyyah—"and why he made such a large deposit of cash to his bank account once she went missing. It is a small matter, you know, for us to discover if the amount of this deposit mirrors a withdrawal from your own reserves. That is being arranged, in fact, even as we speak."

Michelangelo said nothing, but along his hairline, minuscule drops of perspiration appeared.

"I'm still waiting for the name of your *avvocato*, by the way," Salvatore added graciously. "He will want to advise you on the best manner in which to extricate yourself from the web you're caught in."

Di Massimo said nothing. Salvatore let him think. The Pisan would have no way of knowing exactly how much information the police had at this point, but the fact that he'd been brought to the *questura* was going to suggest that his trouble was deep. Since he'd already denied knowing a man to whom he'd made numerous telephone calls, his best move would be to tell the truth. Even if he'd phoned Squali a dozen times without ever having seen the man, the police still had a connection between them and this had to be explained away somehow. Salvatore's only question was how fast Di Massimo could cook up an explanation that had nothing to do with Hadiyyah's disappearance. He was betting that anyone who bleached his normally black hair the colour of *mais* was not someone who was also fast on his intellectual feet.

It turned out that his surmise was correct. Di Massimo said, *"Bene,"* on a sigh. And he began to tell his tale.

He was hired to find the child, as he had earlier admitted when the chief inspector had questioned him, no? He was hired, he found her, and he'd thought no more of the matter once he had reported her whereabouts at Fattoria di Santa Zita in the hills above Lucca. But some weeks later another, altogether different request had been made for his services. And this request was in relation to the very same child.

"What were these services?" Salvatore asked.

The orchestration of her kidnapping, he replied baldly. It was up to him to decide where this kidnapping would occur. The key to it, though, had to be the child's complete lack of fear. So he set about hiring someone to watch the family in order to find if there was anything they did that could serve the purpose of spiriting her away: something that was so much a part of their regular routine that they would never imagine anything untoward could happen to the child in the midst of it and, thus, their guard would be down. The person he hired was Roberto Squali, whom he knew as a *cameriere* at a restaurant in Pisa.

The family's weekly trips to the *mercato* in Lucca, as reported by Squali, proved to be the event he was looking for. The child's mother went off to yoga, her lover and her daughter went into the *mercato*, and there the child and the man separated so that she could watch the accordion player and his poodle. That constituted the perfect moment to snatch her, Di Massimo had concluded, but of course the snatching could not be carried out by someone as memorable in appearance as the Pisan private detective. Hence, he'd instructed Roberto Squali to carry it out.

"The child appears to have gone with Roberto willingly," Salvatore said. "She seems to have taken directions from him because she left the *mercato* on a route she'd never taken before and he followed her. There is a witness to this."

Di Massimo nodded. "Again, there was to be no fear. I gave him a word to say to her that would reassure her she had nothing to worry about."

"A word?"

"Khushi."

"What sort of word is this?"

"A word I myself was given. What it means I do not know." Di Massimo went on to say that Roberto was to tell Hadiyyah that he had come to take her to her father. He supplied Squali with a greeting card that he had been told her father had written to her. Roberto was to hand her this card and then to say this magic word *khushi*, which appeared to be some kind of *open sesame* to garner her complete co-operation. Once he had her in his company, he was to take her to a place that was safe, where she would not feel herself in any danger. There she would stay until the word came to Michelangelo that the child was to be released. With that word would also come the location of her release. He would pass this information along to Roberto Squali, who would fetch the girl, take her to the drop-off point, and leave her there for whatever was going to happen next.

Salvatore felt a wave of nausea. "What," he asked evenly, "was to happen next?"

Di Massimo didn't know. He only received bits and pieces of the plan when and as he needed to know them. And that was how it had worked from the first.

"Whose plan was this, then?" Salvatore asked.

"I've already said. A man from London."

Lynley stirred in his chair. "Are you saying that from the first, a man from London hired you to kidnap Hadiyyah?"

Di Massimo shook his head. No, no, and no. As he'd told them before, he had been hired first merely to find the child. It was only after she had been found that he was then later asked to arrange for her kidnapping. He hadn't wanted to do it—a *bambina* should never be separated from her mamma, *vero*? But when he'd been told about how this particular mamma had once abandoned this same child for a year to chase after a lover . . . This was not right, this was not good, this was not the *comportamento* of a good mamma, no? So he had agreed to snatch the child. For money, of course. Which, by the way, he had not yet received in full. So much for trusting the word of a foreigner.

"This foreigner was . . . ?" Lynley asked.

"Dwayne Doughty, as I've said from the first. The plan from start to finish was his. Why he wanted the child to be taken instead of merely reunited with her papà . . . ? This I do not know and I did not ask."

VILLA RIVELLI
TUSCANY

Sister Domenica Giustina was harvesting strawberries when she was summoned. She was using scissors to cut the fruit from the plants. She was humming an Ave that she particularly liked, and its sweet air moved her among her plants with a lightness of gait that she hadn't known in all the time she had been in this place.

Her long period of punishment was ended. She'd bathed and clothed herself anew, using upon her many wounds an ointment she herself had made. These wounds would cease their suppurating soon. Such were the loving ways of God.

When she heard her name called, she rose from the strawberries. She saw that a novice had come from the convent, the fresh breeze stirring her pure white veil. Sister Domenica Giustina recognised the young woman, although she did not know her name. A badly repaired cleft palate had left her face uneven, giving her the appearance of permanent sorrow. She was no more than twenty-three years old. That she was at this age a novice in the order of nuns spoke to how long she had lived among them.

She said, "You're wanted inside, Domenica. You're to come at once."

Sister Domenica Giustina's spirit leapt like a doe within her. She had not been inside the holy body of the convent in years, not since the day she'd learned she would not be allowed to live among the good sisters who were immured in sanctity there. She'd only been permitted a few steps inside the kitchen on the *pianoterra*. Five paces from the door to the huge pine table where she left for the nuns whatever she'd gleaned from the garden, made from the milk of the goats, or gathered from the chickens. And even then she entered only when no one else was present. That she knew this particular nun—her summoner—by her appearance was owing to having seen her arrive in the company of her parents on a summer day.

"*Mi segua*," the novice told Sister Domenica Giustina. She turned, expecting the other woman to follow.

Sister Domenica Giustina did as she had been told. She would have preferred to wash the dirt from her hands, perhaps to change her clothes. But to be asked into the convent—for surely that was the intention, no?—was a gift from which she could not turn. So she brushed off her hands, shook off her linen shift, clasped a pocketed rosary in her fingers, and followed the nun.

They went in through the great front doors, another gift to Sister Domenica Giustina and surely a sign as well. These gave onto what had once been the immense *soggiorno* of the villa, a reception room whose walls soared up to a fresco in which the magnificent god Apollo drove a chariot across an azure sky. Far beneath him, what *affreschi* had decorated the walls had long ago been whitewashed over. And whatever great silk-covered *divani* had been positioned to accommodate guests to the villa were ages gone and replaced by simple wooden pews that fanned out in front of an equally simple and rough-hewn altar. This was covered by fine, starched linen. On it stood an elaborate tabernacle of gold, accompanied by a single candle encased in red glass. The candle in red indicated that the Sacrament was present. They genuflected before it.

The air was tinctured by the unmistakable scent of incense, a heady fragrance that Sister Domenica Giustina had not smelled in many years. She was pleased when the other woman told her to wait in this place. She nodded, knelt upon the hard tiles of the floor, and crossed herself.

She found she couldn't pray. There was too much to see, too much to experience. She tried to discipline herself, but her excitement was great, and it drove her gaze first here and then there as she took in the place where she'd been left.

The chapel was dark, its windows covered by both shutters and grilles. The great doors to the loggia at the rear of the villa and behind the altar were boarded, and tapestries made by the fingers of the women within this place hung from these boards and presented scenes from the life of St. Dominic, namesake of the order of nuns who celebrated him in their needlework. Corridors led to the right and to the left from the chapel, taking one into the heart of the convent. Sister Domenica Giustina longed to wander along them, but she remained. Obedience was one of the vows. This moment was a test, and she would pass it.

"*Vieni, Domenica.*"

The voice asking her to come was barely a whisper, and for a moment Sister Domenica Giustina thought the Blessed Virgin herself had spoken. But a hand on her shoulder told her the voice was not disembodied, and she looked up to see an ancient lined face nearly hidden within the folds of a black veil.

Sister Domenica Giustina rose. The old nun nodded and, hands tucked into the sleeves of her habit, she turned and made for one of the corridors. Its opening was covered by an intricate lattice of wood, but this moved inward upon the slightest push and soon enough Sister Domenica Giustina and her companion were in a whitewashed corridor with closed heavy doors along one side and shuttered windows along the other. A few paces took them to one of the doors upon which the *vecchia* knocked softly. Someone spoke behind it. The old nun indicated that Sister Domenica Giustina was to enter, and when she had done so, the door was closed behind her.

She was in an office, simply furnished. A prie-dieu stood before a statue of the Virgin, who gazed lovingly down upon anyone wishing to pray at her feet. Across from her, St. Dominic held out his hands in blessing from a niche. Between two shuttered windows stood an uncluttered desk. At this desk sat the woman Sister Domenica Giustina had met only twice: She was Mother Superior, and she looked upon Sister Domenica Giustina with an expression of such gravity that Sister Domenica Giustina knew the moment of import had arrived.

She'd never felt such joy. She could sense it blazing out of her face because she could feel it coursing throughout her body. She had indeed been a terrible sinner, but now she had finally been forgiven. She had fully prepared her soul for God, and not only her own but the soul of another.

For years she had been penitent. She had striven to illustrate to God, through her actions, that she understood how weighty her sins had been. To pray that an unborn child—the child of her own cousin Roberto—would be taken from her body so that her parents would never learn she had carried it . . . To have that prayer granted on the very night that her parents were gone from the house . . . To have Roberto there to dispose of what had been forced so painfully from her body there in the darkness of the bathroom . . .

It had been alive, fully formed and alive, but even this matter had felt the hand of God. For a mere five months inside her had not been enough for it to live without help and that help had been denied. Or so she had come to believe because Roberto had it, Roberto had taken it, and Roberto had disposed of it. Girl or boy, she did not know. She had never known . . . until everything changed, until Roberto had made everything change.

Sister Domenica Giustina did not realise she had spoken all of this aloud until Mother Superior rose from behind her desk. She leaned upon it, her knuckles a stark white contrast to the colour of the wood, and she murmured, *"Madre di Dio, Domenica. Madre di Dio."*

So, yes and yes, the child from her body had *not* died because God worked in ways too miraculous for His humble servants ever to understand. Her cousin had returned their child into her keeping to shelter her from harm, and this is what Sister Domenica Giustina had done, up until the moment when God took the girl's father in a terrible accident among the Alps. And she—Sister Domenica Giustina—was left to try to understand what this meant. For beyond the miraculous, God also worked in incomprehensible ways and one had to struggle to understand the messages contained within His works.

"We all must prove ourselves to God," Sister Domenica Giustina concluded. "She asked me for her papà. God told me what to do. For only by doing His will—no matter how difficult—do we achieve the complete forgiveness we seek." She crossed herself. She smiled and she felt beatific, blessed by God at last to come into this place.

Mother Superior was breathing shallowly. Her fingers touched the golden ring she wore. They pressed against the crucifix upon it as if asking the martyred Lord for the strength to speak. "For the love of God, Domenica," she said. "What have you done to this child?"

30 APRIL

A heads-up is always nice, I reckon, so you're getting one."
Barbara Havers didn't need Mitchell Corsico to identify himself. At this point his tenor tones had become a permanent echo inside her skull. Had he rung her on her mobile, she could have avoided the call. As it was, he'd rung her at work, claimed to have information on "the situation DS Havers is investigating," and the bluff had proved perfectly efficacious. The call had come through, Barbara had picked it up, she'd barked, "DS Havers," and there he was.

She said, "What? *What?*"

"As my sainted mum would say, 'Don't take that tone with me,'" he returned. "She's out of hospital."

"Who? Your mum? So you should celebrate, shouldn't you? I'd tipple back one or two with you, but I've work to do."

"Don't try to be amusing, Barb. There's no story over here, and I expect you bloody well knew that. Do you have any idea what position this puts me in with my editor? *Do* you?"

He was in Italy at last. Barbara thanked her stars. "If she's *out* of hospital, I expect that confirms that she was *in* hospital," she replied. "It's not down to me that she's been released. What I gave you, I gave you in good faith."

"I'm going with the Love Rat Dad and Officer of the Met," he said. "Complete with pictures. Expect it tomorrow. I've already written it, it's attached to my breathless email on the topic of what-hot-information-I've-just-managed-to-uncover-dear-editor, and I'm about to hit send. Do you want that to happen or not?"

"What I want—" Barbara looked up as someone came to stand in front of her desk. It was Dorothea Harriman, so she said to Corsico, "Hang on," and then to Dorothea, "Something up?"

"You're wanted, Detective Sergeant Havers." She tilted her perfectly coiffed blond head in the general direction of Isabelle Ardery's office. Barbara sighed.

"Right," she said, and then to Corsico, "We'll have to have this conversation later."

"Are you completely mad?" he demanded. "Do you think I'm bluffing? The only way for you to stop this is to give me either Lynley or Azhar. You can get me access that no one else has and I swear to God, Barb, if you don't get off the bleeding fence on this one—"

"I'll speak to Inspector Lynley directly," she lied. "That satisfy you? Now, Superintendent Ardery is asking to see me and while I'd love to continue this bloody well *stim*ulating discussion with you, I've got to ring off."

"As long as you know that I'm holding off on this other story for a quarter hour, Barb. That time passes and I hit send and you look for it in tomorrow's paper."

"As always, my timbers are shivering," she said. She banged down the phone and said to Dorothea, "What's her nibs want with me? Any idea?"

"Detective Inspector Stewart is with her." She sounded regretful. This wasn't good.

Barbara thought of fortifying herself with a fag in the stairwell, but she decided that keeping Isabelle Ardery waiting when she had been summoned wasn't a particularly wise move. So she followed Dorothea to the superintendent's office, and there she found Ardery in conversation with John Stewart, who'd brought a pile of manila folders with him for some reason that probably wasn't going to be good.

Barbara joined them. She glanced from Stewart to Ardery to Stewart.

She nodded but made no other greeting. Her brain went into high gear, however. She didn't see how Stewart could have known that she'd been to see Dwayne Doughty in advance of jumping to do his bidding and conducting the interviews he'd assigned to her. And even if he *had* made that discovery, she'd got the bloody interviews done. What more did the sodding bloke want of her?

As it happened, Stewart wanted nothing of her. He'd apparently been summoned into Isabelle Ardery's office as well, and just like Barbara, he was in the dark about why the superintendent had called him in to a meeting.

Ardery didn't waste time to bring them both into the picture. She said, "John, I'm reassigning Barbara for a few days. There's a branch of the investigation in—"

"*What?*" Stewart looked like someone whose balloon had just got popped. He was staring, outraged, at Ardery as if she'd been the person wielding the pin that had popped it.

The superintendent took a moment. She let his tone act like an echo in the room. Then she said carefully, "I'd no idea your hearing was undergoing a change. As I said, I'm reassigning Barbara to another investigation."

"What bloody other investigation?" he demanded.

Ardery's spine underwent a minute adjustment. "I'm not certain you require that knowledge," she pointed out.

"You put her on my team," he countered. "And that's where she stays: on my team."

"I beg your pardon?" Ardery had been sitting behind her desk with Stewart in front of it, the manila folders still in a neat pile on his lap. She rose now and leaned her height of six feet in his direction, her well-groomed fingertips on a set of reports. "I don't think you're in a position to make those kinds of declarations," she pointed out. "Perhaps you need a moment to sort yourself? I'd take that moment, if I were you."

"Where're you putting her?" he demanded. "Every team's got enough manpower on it. If this is a power play you've decided to engage in, it's not on."

"You're out of order."

"Oh, I'm always out of order with you. D'you know what I've got here? Right here in these folders?" He lifted one and shook it at her. Barbara felt her arms go limp.

"I'm not the least interested in what you've got there unless it's the documentation for an arrest in one of the cases you've been handling."

"Oh, too right," Stewart said. "You're not the least interested in *anything* other than—" He stopped himself directly on the brink. He said, "Just forget it. All right. She's reassigned. Have her. We all know who she's going to be working with—as he's the only person who *ever* wants her on his team—and all of us know why you're only too happy to hand her to him."

Barbara drew in a sharp breath. She waited to see what the superintendent would do with this one.

Ardery said steadily, "What are you implying, John?"

"I think you know."

"And I think you'd be wise to reconsider the route you're taking. As it happens, Barbara will be working directly for me on a matter involving another police officer. And that, John, concludes what you need to know about why I require her. Are we absolutely clear on this or do we need to take our discussion to a higher level?"

Stewart stared at Ardery. She held his gaze. Her face was rigid and his was florid and Barbara knew that they were both enraged. One of them had to take a step away from the other, but she knew it wasn't going to be the superintendent. Whether it would be Stewart remained to be seen. Misogyny had been driving his behaviour for so many years, it was difficult to know if he could get it under control long enough to get himself out of the superintendent's office and back to work before she had his head on a platter.

He finally rose. "I take your meaning," he said. He turned and left the superintendent's office without a glance in Barbara's direction. She wondered what he had in those folders of his, though. She reckoned it wasn't good.

With Stewart gone, the superintendent gestured Barbara to take one of the two chairs in front of her desk. Barbara chose the one Stewart hadn't been sitting on, all the better not to besmirch her trousers with any of his essence. She waited for clarification, which was quick in coming.

"This situation in Italy has a tentacle reaching to London," she said. "I had a phone call from DI Lynley early this morning. He needs someone on the case at this end."

So it *was* Lynley, Barbara thought. Stewart, for all his odious and thinly veiled accusations, had not been very far off the mark. She blessed Lynley for his efforts to get her onto his team. He knew how deep was her concern about Hadiyyah and Azhar, he recognised the nature of her friendship with both of them, and more than anything, he understood how unwelcome it was to her ever to have to work with John Stewart. Bless him, bless him, bless him, Barbara thought. She owed him, she would repay him, she would be tireless in getting to the bottom of—

"I want to make something clear to you, Barbara," the superintendent said. "DI Lynley asked for Winston. He's the obvious choice as, let's be frank, he has a good track record of obeying orders while that's not exactly the case for you. But I'd like to give you the opportunity to prove to me directly that you can do the same. Is there anything you'd like to tell me about your time on John Stewart's team before you and I move along to what the inspector needs you to do for him?"

Here was the moment to fess up, Barbara thought. But she couldn't risk telling the superintendent that she'd gone her own way more than once in the past few days. Ardery might well pull her off the assignment she'd just put her on. So she said, "It's not anyone's secret that John Stewart and I don't get along, guv. I try. P'rhaps he tries as well. But we're chalk and cheese."

Ardery evaluated this, her gaze evenly on Barbara's. She finally said, "Right," in a slow and thoughtful drawl. Then she turned and picked up the topmost report on her desk and handed it over.

"The police in Italy have traced the kidnapping of your friend's little girl back to London."

"Dwayne Doughty, right?" Barbara said.

Ardery nodded. "They've brought in a bloke in Italy who was evidently operating on Doughty's direction. He appears to have found the child without apparent difficulty but instead of giving the word to her father, Doughty came up with a scheme to kidnap her. What's been done with her, the Italian doesn't know. He claims he was given instructions in bits and pieces: It was, he says, a case of 'Snatch her and I'll tell you what happens next.'"

"Bloody *pig*," Barbara said. "I took Azhar to meet this bloke, guv, when Hadiyyah's mum disappeared with her. He seemed to be on the up-and-up. He worked a bit on looking for her, and he finally told us there was no bloody trail and I'm-dead-sorry-I-am and that was that." Barbara didn't add anything about Azhar: the Berlin alibi, *khushi*, or anything else. Least of all did she add the claims Doughty had made when she'd seen him in the Bow Road nick since the superintendent didn't know she'd seen him in the Bow Road nick, and she didn't need to know.

Ardery said, "Yes. Well. He's involved in some way that DI Lynley needs sorted. I've been told that there was never a ransom demanded for the child, so my guess is that someone else beyond Doughty is also involved. Phone the inspector if you have more questions."

"I will," Barbara said.

Ardery handed over the report she'd received, and she eyed Barbara before giving her the word to go on her way. She said, "I want to learn at the end that you've handled every aspect of this situation in a professional manner, Barbara. Anything less than that, and you and I will be having a different sort of conversation. Am I being clear?"

As mountain spring water, Barbara thought. She said, "Yes, guv, you are. I won't disappoint you."

Ardery dismissed her. She didn't look convinced.

BOW

LONDON

Barbara decided that Doughty was not the place to begin. Presented with the facts as they'd apparently been recited by Michelangelo Di Massimo in the police station in Lucca, he would doubtless be able to produce an airtight rationale for all of them. Barbara could even imagine what it would be: I hired the bloke to find her, and he swore he tried every avenue of exploration to no avail. Are you suggesting that it's down to *me* that he found her without letting me know? That he planned her kidnapping and handed her over to God only knows who for God only knows what reason and that's down to me as well? Look, Sergeant, Di Massimo was in a far better position than I to carry this kid off into the hinterlands or wherever the hell he carried her to. I'm supposed to know enough about Italy—where, to be frank, I have never set foot—to have made a kid disappear? And why? For money? Whose money? I don't know these people. Do any of them even have money?

And on and on Doughty would go, wearing her down with logic, illogic, and everything in between. So she wouldn't begin with talking to him. Emily Cass seemed a more likely source of information.

Barbara spent some time digging up whatever might be useful in her conversation with the young woman, who turned out to be no intellectual slouch. She held an advanced degree in economics from the University of Chicago, but since attaining that degree, she'd held a string of jobs that suggested personal unsuitability for the world of business or finance: She'd been a security consultant in Afghanistan, a bodyguard to the children of a minor branch of the Saudi royal family, a personal trainer to a Hollywood actress in need of a task master to keep her body beautiful a body beautiful, and an assistant chef on a yacht whose owner was one of the biggest names in British petroleum. She was, literally, all over the map in her employment history. How she'd ended up in the employ of a private investigator was anyone's guess.

Her record was clean when it came to the law, though, and she'd sprung from a solidly middle-class family whose paterfamilias was a noted ophthalmologist and whose mother was a paediatrician. With three brothers involved in the medical field as well and another a highly successful Formula One driver, she probably wouldn't want to have her reputation sullied by any activity she might have engaged in that danced on the wrong side of the law. She was, Barbara assured herself, the better bet when it came to having a tête-à-tête with someone bearing a warrant card.

She had no intention of bearding Em Cass in the den of Dwayne Doughty's place of business. She didn't want to ring the woman either. Better not to give her time to inform the private investigator that she was going to be questioned. So she positioned herself in a window of the Roman Café and Kebab a short distance from Bedlovers, whose

upper floor housed Dwayne Doughty's office. There she waited for
Emily Cass to appear.

It took four kebabs and a jacket potato topped with cheese and chili
for this to happen. By that point, Barbara was practically a member
of the family who ran the establishment. They were looking at her a
bit askance—probably considering the nature of the eating disorder
the dishevelled woman in the window was suffering from—but they
nonetheless accepted her money in exchange for copious amounts of
food. They smiled ingratiatingly and also enquired as to her marital
status, possibly as a suitable mate for a son who hung about the place
with a suspicious dribble of drool escaping from his gaping mouth.
Barbara was grateful for the appearance of Em Cass at the end of an
extended period within the café. She was equally grateful that Emily,
who had on running clothes, set off in *her* direction and not in the
opposite, which would have made it impossible—her recent gustatory
history considered—for Barbara to catch her up.

Barbara was out of the door in a flash. She was planted on the
pavement directly in Emily's path before the young woman knew
what was happening. She was saying, "You and I need to talk" and
clamping onto her arm before Emily could either run off or dash back
to the office. Barbara hustled her across the street and into the Albert
pub—vaguely wondering why there appeared to be a pub called the
Albert in every neighbourhood of the capital—where she strong-
armed her to a table near a fruit machine with *Out of Order* hanging
prominently upon it.

"Here's what you need to know," she told her. "Michelangelo Di
Massimo has given you lot up to the Italian police. Now, this might
not be a major problem for you since, extradition being what it is, you
could be a grandmother before you found yourself standing in front
of an Italian magistrate. *But*—and I like to think of this as the nice
bit, Emily—a senior officer from the Met is over there acting as liaison for the family. One more word from him—aside from the several
words that sent me here to have this little natter with you—and you're
in trouble of the I-appear-to-need-a-solicitor variety. D'you receive
my meaning here, or do I have to spell things out more clearly?"

Emily Cass seemed to make an effort at swallowing. Barbara could hear the gulp from across the table. She idly thought about getting the woman a lager, but she reckoned she wouldn't need to go to the expense if she gave her a little time to dwell upon the significance of what she intended to say to her next.

"I expect you were more of an adjunct player in what went on. You did your bit of blagging on the phone to get information—it's what you excel in, and who can blame you for using your talents, eh?—but you did it on someone else's orders and we both know who that someone else is."

Emily had been gazing at her steadily, but she allowed her glance to go to the street and then back to Barbara. She wet her lips.

"Now my guess is that if our Dwayne has you to operate the phones and impersonate everyone from doddering old ladies to the Duchess of Cambridge, you're not the only talent he employs. He's not a fool. The bloke sets me a challenge called examine-every-one-of-my-records-here-if-you-don't-believe-me, and what that suggests to me is someone else's involvement in the whole bloody scheme, someone competent at sweeping records clean, someone who looks at that as child's play. I want that name, Emily. I suspect it's a bloke called Bryan that Doughty mentioned early on. I want his phone number, his email address, his street address, whatever. You give me that, and you and I part friends. Everyone else and I? Not so much. But there comes a point when common sense suggests one remove one's neck from the noose. We've reached that point. What's it going to be?"

That was it. Cards on the table. Barbara waited to see what would happen. The seconds ticked by. During them, a gust of wind blew a yellow carrier bag down the street and a Muslim cleric emerged from a narrow doorway with a crocodile of little boys in tow. Barbara watched them and thought how times had changed in London. No one looked innocent any longer. A simple outing took on multiple potential meanings. The world was becoming such a miserable place.

"Bryan Smythe," Emily said quietly.

Barbara turned her head back to gaze at Emily. "And he does . . . ?"

"Phone records, bank records, credit card records, emails, net searches, computer trails, all the rest. Anything having to do with computer technology."

Barbara dug out her notebook and flipped it open. She said, "Where c'n I find this stellar individual?"

Emily had to get this information from her mobile phone. She read it out—the bloke's address and phone numbers—and shoved the mobile back into her pocket. She added, "He didn't know what it was all in service of. He just did what Dwayne told him to do."

"No worries there," Barbara said. "I know Dwayne's the big fish, Emily." She pushed back from the table and dropped her notebook back into her shoulder bag. She got to her feet. "You might want to look for another line of employment. Between you and me, Doughty's private investigation business is going to have a serious setback sooner rather than later."

She left the young woman sitting in the pub. She reckoned Doughty was in his office, so that was where she took herself next. With Bryan Smythe's name in her possession, she was now holding a rather good hand of cards.

Above Bedlovers, she gave two knocks to Doughty's door, entering without being bidden to do so. She found the man in consultation with a middle-aged estate manager type. They were bent over Doughty's desk, examining photos, and in the estate manager's fingers was a handkerchief that he was in the act of crushing to bits.

Doughty looked up. "D'you mind?" he snapped. "We're conducting business."

"So'm I." Barbara took out her warrant card and showed it to the poor bloke who was being presented with the cold, hard, and no doubt slimy facts of someone's betrayal of him. "I'm going to need a word with Mr. Doughty," she said. And with a glance at the pictures—two nude young men, as it happened, cavorting together with rather too much enthusiasm in a tree-sided pond—she added, "What'd that idiot film director say? 'The heart wants what the heart wants'? I'm sorry."

Doughty gathered up the pictures and said to her, "You're a piece of work."

"For my sins," she agreed.

The estate manager had backed off from his perusal of the photos. He was taking a chequebook from his jacket pocket, but Barbara took him by the arm and urged him towards the door. "I expect Mr.

Doughty—decent bloke that he is—wants to make this one on the house." She bade him farewell, watched him go for the stairs with his head hanging low, and added her hope that the rest of his day was going to be more pleasant than his just-completed meeting in the office above Bedlovers had been.

Then she closed the door and turned to Doughty. He was red in the face, and it wasn't embarrassment making him so. He said, "How bloody dare you!"

To which she replied, "Bryan Smythe, Mr. Doughty. At least Bryan Smythe on this end. On the other end is Michelangelo Di Massimo. He doesn't have his own Bryan Smythe, as it happens. His computers won't be as squeaky clean as yours. Same goes for his telephone records, I expect. And then there's the small matter of his bank account and what it might show when we get our hands on it."

"I *told* you Di Massimo was employed to do some checking in Italy," Doughty snapped. "This is fresh off the presses for what sterling reason?"

"Because what you didn't tell me was that he was employed to snatch Hadiyyah, Dwayne."

"I didn't employ him to do that, Sergeant. I've told you that before and I'm going to continue telling you that. If you think otherwise, then it's time you took a suggestion from me."

"And that is . . . ?"

"The professor. Taymullah Azhar. It's been him from the first, but you haven't wanted to look at that, have you? So *I've* had to do your bloody job for you and believe me I'm not happy about that."

"His Berlin story—"

"Bugger Berlin. This was never about Berlin. Berlin's been a malodorous red herring from the first. Of course he was there. He was giving his paper and attending lectures and popping up all over the bloody hotel like a Pakistani jack-in-the-box. He would've had a convenient leg break in the lobby of the place if he'd needed to make certain his stay was memorable, but as it happens, he didn't need to make certain of that because all his colleagues are willing to believe every word that comes out of the blighter's mouth. As was I, as it happens. And, let's be frank here, as are you."

He went to one of his filing cabinets as he spoke. He jerked open the top drawer, and he brought out a manila folder. This he tossed on his desk, and he sat behind it. He said, "Oh, bloody sit down and let's have a rational conversation for once."

Barbara trusted the man in the same way she would have trusted a cobra sliding towards her big toe. She narrowed her eyes and observed him for anything that would allow her to read what was going on. But he looked, maddeningly, as he always looked: everything about him average save for that nose, veering in several directions before it got round to presenting his nostrils to a less-than-admiring public.

She sat. She wasn't about to let him wrest from her the reins of the conversation, however. So she said, "Bryan Smythe's going to confirm a phone sweep and he's going to confirm a computer sweep as well. Put that together with the blagging on the part of Ms. Cass and—"

"You might want to take a look at these before you cha-cha any further in that direction." Doughty opened the manila folder and handed over two documents. They were, Barbara saw, copies of plane tickets, coming from the sort of reservations made online by millions of people every day. The flight in question departed from Heathrow. It was a one-way ticket, and its destination was Lahore.

Barbara felt her heart slam against her chest and her mouth went dry. For the name of the first passenger was Taymullah Azhar. The name of the second was Hadiyyah Upman.

She found that she couldn't think for a moment. She couldn't think what it meant, she couldn't think why the tickets existed at all, and she couldn't think—because she didn't want to think—that everything she believed she knew about Azhar was about to crumble into dust.

Doughty apparently read all this on her face, for he said, "Yes. There you have it. Tied up with a ribbon and I ought to bill you hours for doing your bleeding job for you."

She said, with an attempt at bravado, "What I have here is a piece of paper, Mr. Doughty. And as you and I know, anyone can generate a piece of paper, just like anyone can buy a ticket to anyplace in anyone else's name."

"Oh, for God's sake, then have a look at the dates," he advised her.

"The date of the flight is interesting enough, but I think you'll find the date of the purchase more interesting still."

So Barbara looked at these and then she tried to decide what the two dates were telling her about her friend. The date of the flight was the fifth of July, which one could argue spoke of Azhar's hope that his daughter would be found alive and perfectly well. Or it spoke of a ticket purchase made months and months earlier, far in advance of Hadiyyah's November disappearance from London. But the date of purchase changed the playing field. It was the twenty-second of March, well in advance of Hadiyyah's kidnapping in Italy but during the time when Azhar had, ostensibly, not even known where she was. That suggested only one thing, and Barbara couldn't bear to consider the extent to which she'd been played for a fool.

She spent a moment searching for something to explain this information. She said, "Anyone could have—"

"Maybe yes, maybe no," Doughty said. "But the question is why would someone other than our friend the quiet, unassuming, and brokenhearted professor of *whatever* the hell he professes buy two one-way tickets to Pakistan?"

"Someone who wanted him to look guilty—like yourself, for example—could have made the purchase."

"You think so, eh? So ask your blokes over there in Special Branch to track this thing down because you and I both know that in these days of playing at Who's the Terrorist, anyone going to a country where people wear headscarves, towels, bedsheets, and dressing gowns in the street is going to be looked at fairly closely once you give them the word it's got to be done."

"He might have—"

"Known his kid was going to be snatched in Italy?"

"That's not what I was going to say."

"But it's what you *know*, Sergeant Havers. Now, I think you and I c'n agree it's game, set, and match we're looking at here. So are you going to continue harassing me, or are you going to do something about getting that miserable excuse of a father—if he even *is* her father—to tell the cops over there where he's stowed that poor kid?"

BOW

LONDON

Barbara sat inside her rust-dappled Mini, lit a fag, and inhaled so deeply that she could have sworn the heavenly carcinogen managed to travel all the way to her ankles. She smoked the entire thing before she would even allow herself to think. Buddy Holly helped in this. A tape deck in the car that functioned only on an off-and-on basis today was leaning towards the *on* end of things, although the very idea of Buddy's telling her that *anything* was a-getting closer was not doing much to lift her spirits.

Doughty was right. A call to Special Branch and she'd know the truth about those tickets to Lahore. It wasn't enough that Azhar was a respected professor of microbiology. That alone would never save him from scrutiny. When it came to travelling to a Muslim country, a man with a name like Taymullah Azhar was going to be looked at, even more so because he'd bought a one-way ticket to the place. In fact, he'd probably already been investigated by the blokes in SO12 because his purchase of that ticket—if indeed he was the person who had made the purchase—was going to light up the roadside flares. All she had to do was dig out her mobile, place a call to the Met, and hear the worst. *Or* hear the best, she thought. Pray God in his heaven that it was the best.

Barbara considered what she knew once she'd smoked the fag down to a dog-end the size of her little finger's nail. She flicked this into the street—apologies to the litter patrol, but her ashtray was teeming with six months of Players smoked down to various lengths and crushed therein—and she tried desperately to reason everything out. From Lynley she knew that Di Massimo was pointing every finger he had and all of his toes at Dwayne Doughty in London. Emily Cass appeared to be doing the same. Doughty had everything to lose if culpability came down to him. He knew that better than he knew anything, which was why, of course, he'd have ordered every indication that he'd been in contact with anyone in Italy wiped from the records.

Bryan Smythe could confirm this. Back him into a corner, guarantee that no visit from the Bill was going to occur if he spilled his beans onto a porcelain plate, and Bob was, let's face it, going to be your uncle. Barbara knew that she probably didn't even need to visit the bloke. These computer types? In her experience their bravado was limited to what they could accomplish behind closed doors, in a darkened room, with the glow of a computer monitor shining in their eyes. Hearing that the cops were onto him, he'd cave in an instant. He'd tell everything he knew, just as fast as his vocal cords could vibrate. Barbara just wasn't sure she wanted to know what that *everything* was.

Truth was, he was going to confirm, and she bloody well knew it. Emily Cass wouldn't have given her the bloke's name if there was any doubt in the matter. Barbara told herself that this was probably because Emily would have put him in the picture the moment Barbara and she had parted ways. And following up on that, Dwayne Doughty would have rung the bloke and given him the word. The private investigator would have concluded instantly that Emily Cass was the person who had named Smythe to Barbara, for there was no one else to do the naming. He'd deal with her later, but upon Barbara's departure from his office, Smythe would have been his very next move. Ring him and say, "There's a cop coming. She can't prove a damn thing so hold your tongue in this business and there's a bonus coming your way."

So he would hold his tongue. Or he would break and spill. Or he would run for cover. Or he would head for Scotland, Dubai, the Seychelles. Who the bloody hell knew what Smythe would do because Barbara's head was spinning, so she lit another fag.

Reality in a tablespoon? She knew what her next step was. It involved ringing Lynley with the information she had and giving him everything. But God, God, *God*, how could she ever do that? For surely there was an explanation somewhere and all she really had to do was to find it.

She could give Lynley Bryan Smythe's name. That wore the guise of progress being made. He'd tell her to haul Smythe into the nick for a proper go at him—or he would ask her why she hadn't already done so—but in any case that would buy her time. The only question was: What was she going to do with time bought? And once she admitted to herself what it was, she set her course upon doing it.

LUCCA

TUSCANY

Salvatore had no choice once Michelangelo Di Massimo named the man in London. His next encounter with Piero Fanucci wasn't going to be pleasant, but it had to be got through. Once that was taken care of, he was intent upon the Apuan Alps and that convent at which Domenica Medici was the caretaker. It was the only lead they had as to the location of the missing little English girl and, Piero Fanucci or not, Salvatore intended to follow it.

He spoke to *il Pubblico Ministero* by phone. In advance he'd done what little there was to be done to prove to Fanucci that no connection appeared to exist between Carlo Casparia and anyone else they had discovered having ties to the kidnapping case. Piero snapped that he hadn't been looking closely enough. Get back to that at once, Fanucci ordered. At this, Salvatore bridled. At this, he made a crucial error. Patiently, he said, "Piero, *capisco*. I know that you are heavily invested in the guilt of this Carlo—" At which point Fanucci morphed into *il drago* and Salvatore felt that dragon's wrath.

He listened to Piero's roaring and railing. *Il Pubblico Ministero* called into question everything from Salvatore's capabilities as a member of the police force to the various reasons—most of them having to do with Salvatore's masculinity—for the breakdown of the chief inspector's marriage. The peroration of *il drago*'s diatribe was the unsurprising information that Piero was replacing him as head of the investigation into the girl's disappearance. Someone who could follow the directions of the magistrate in charge of the investigation would be taking over, and Salvatore was to hand to this person every bit of information he had.

"Don't do this, Piero," Salvatore said. His blood had long since boiled, especially when *il Pubblico Ministero* had ventured into the area of his marriage. Indeed, Salvatore felt he had no blood left, just the burnt-copper scent of it in his body. "You have decided upon the guilt of this man based upon your fantasy. You have decided that Carlo saw an easy way to make money by following a child, grabbing her from a public market, and selling her to . . . Who, Piero? Allow me to ask you this: Is it even reasonable for you to conclude that *anyone* would go into the business of buying a child from a person like Carlo? A drug addict who is likely to tell the tale of such a sale to the first person willing to offer him the money for another purchase of whatever it is he is shooting into his body? Piero, please listen to me. I know that you are compromised in this investigation. I know that your use of *Prima Voce* to make a case for—"

That mentioning of the tabloid had done it.

"*Basta!*" Piero Fanucci roared. "*È finito, Salvatore! Capisci? È finito tutto!*"

Il Pubblico Ministero had slammed the phone down at his end. At least, Salvatore thought wryly, he would have no need of informing the *magistrato* about the convent in the Apuan Alps since Piero's poor phone would now probably be out of order. He would also have no need of telling him that more details had been amassed about one Lorenzo Mura, his fellow players on Lucca's *squadra di calcio*, and his private coaching of young *giocatori* in the Parco Fluviale.

His officers had been busy. He had photographs now of all the other city team players, which had admittedly been easy enough to come by. Less easy had been the gathering of photographs of all the parents of young boys coached by Lorenzo Mura. Getting the names of those parents had been difficult enough. Asking for them had aroused Lorenzo's suspicions and had prompted the man to demand what the parents of his football students had to do with little Hadiyyah's disappearance. Salvatore had told him the truth of the matter: Everyone whose life touched even remotely upon Hadiyyah's had to be looked at. Perhaps the parent of a child he coached was unhappy with him and felt he needed to be taught a lesson, dealt with in some way, put in his place . . . ? One never knew, Signor Mura, so every avenue had to be explored.

With pictures of those parents and the Lucchese players in hand, officers were even now on their way to the prison to show these to Carlo Casparia in the hope that what went for his memory after years of drug use might be stimulated. He had, after all, remembered a man meeting Lorenzo Mura at the place of his coaching in the Parco Fluviale. There was a slight chance that he would be able to pick this person out of the pictures with which he would be presented. And then they would have another avenue to explore.

Salvatore didn't have much time for this manoeuvre, though. He knew that Piero Fanucci would be quick about assigning this case to another. *Purtroppo*, Chief Inspector Lo Bianco would be out of his office when that individual showed up to go over the finer details of the investigation. He would be high in the Apuan Alps.

His decision to take the Englishman with him had to do with language. If by the slightest chance on earth this English girl had been taken into the Alps to that convent by Roberto Squali, then the liaison officer who spoke her own language was going to be helpful in communicating with her. If, on the other, more horrible hand, what developed from this was the news that the worst had happened and the little girl was dead, then Lynley's presence would allow him to gather information on the spot and to discuss with Salvatore in advance what details the child's parents needed to know about her death.

He fetched Lynley from their regular *luogo di incontro* by Porta di Borgo. To the Englishman's *"Che cosa succede?"* he tersely explained where they were with the collection of photos, with Lorenzo Mura, and with the need for swiftness. He spoke of this latter matter by using terms that dealt with "concerns of *il Pubblico Ministero*." What he didn't tell him was that he had been officially removed from the investigation.

He didn't seem to need to, as things turned out. The Englishman's brown eyes observed him steadily as he parted with those details he had. He even suggested politely that perhaps a siren would speed their journey . . . ? It would assist in bringing matters to a swift conclusion for you, *Ispettore*, he pointed out.

So it was with the siren blaring and the lights flashing that Salvatore and Lynley left the city. They shared little conversation as they stormed in the direction of the Alps and a convent hidden high among them.

It was called Villa Rivelli, he'd discovered. It housed a cloistered order of Dominican nuns. It was situated northwest of the point at which the unfortunate Roberto Squali had met his end, and the road that Squali had been driving upon was the single route to get to the place.

There was virtually nothing nearby, as they found when they reached the area, just a cluster of houses perhaps two kilometres in advance of the turnoff. At one time long ago these houses would have served the needs of whoever had lived within the great villa. Now they were the shuttered vacation homes of foreigners and of wealthy Italians who came to the mountains from cities like Milano and Bologna, to escape urban bustle and summer heat. It was early in the season yet, so the likelihood of anyone within the houses seeing Roberto Squali pass by several weeks ago with a child in his car was too remote to be considered. Wisdom would have dictated that Squali make his move with the child in midafternoon anyway. At that time of day, no one stirred in a place like this. People moved from *pranzo* directly to *letto* for a nap. They would have noticed nothing, even if they'd been at their houses this time of year.

When they reached the lane that led to Villa Rivelli, Salvatore nearly missed it altogether, so sheltered was it by looming oaks and Aleppo pines and so untravelled it appeared. Only a small wooden sign topped with a cross saved him from passing it by altogether. It was carved with *V Rivelli* upon it, but the letters were worn and the wood was lichenous.

The lane was narrow, cluttered with the woodland debris of a hundred winters. It had never been paved, so they lurched their way down it. They came to a great iron gate that stood open far enough to allow a car's passage. When he'd eased the car past the ornate wrought iron, he followed the driveway to the left, along a tall hedge from which birds burst, past a few decrepit outbuildings, a huge woodpile, and a *ruspa* that was more rust than steel.

The silence was complete. As the lane climbed upward, nothing broke into the stillness. So it was with some surprise that Salvatore turned into a car's-width opening perhaps a kilometre from the road below and saw, beyond the hedge, a great lawn at the other side of which stood the baroque beauty of the Villa Rivelli. Aside from the fact that it was completely abandoned in appearance, it didn't seem like a dwelling for an order of cloistered nuns. For the front of the building was fashioned with tall niches in which marble statues stood, and a single glance at them told the tale of the identities, which had more to do with Roman gods and goddesses than with saints of the Roman Catholic Church. But these were not what surprised Salvatore. It was the presence of three cars from the *carabinieri* that caused him to glance at Lynley and to worry that they might be too late.

The arrival of police at a cloistered convent was not a simple matter of knocking on the door and gaining admittance. The women within did not see visitors. Chances were better than good that if the *carabinieri* were present, it was because the *carabinieri* had been summoned. It was with this in mind that Salvatore and Lynley approached two armed officers who were gazing at them expressionlessly through very dark glasses.

It was, Salvatore discovered, much as he'd thought. A telephone call from the convent had brought them to this remote villa. Captain Mirenda had been admitted, and she was presumably speaking to whoever had made the call. As for the rest of them . . . ? They were having a look round the grounds. It was a beautiful spot on a beautiful day, eh? Such a pity that the ladies who lived here never got to enjoy what it had to offer. *Giardini, fontane, stagni, un bosco* . . . The officer shook his head at the waste of such pleasures.

"*Dov'è l'ingresso?*" Salvatore asked him. For it didn't seem conceivable that access to the convent was gained by merely knocking upon the two great front doors. In this, he was right. The superior officer of the two *carabinieri* had gone round the side of the building. Salvatore and Lynley did the same. They found yet another officer stationed outside of a plain door set down a few steps. To him, they showed their identification.

The police were notoriously territorial in this part of the world. Because there were so many divisions of them, turf wars were common when it came to an investigation. Often the first branch of *polizia* on the scene was the branch that wrested control of an investigation, and this was particularly the case when it came to the *polizia di stato* and the *carabinieri*. But things were much different on this day, Salvatore found. After examining their identification and gazing at them both as if their faces held secret information for him, the officer stepped away from the door. When it came to entering the convent, they could suit themselves.

They went in through a vast kitchen, which was completely deserted. They climbed a stone stairway, their footsteps echoing between the plastered walls. The stairway took them into a corridor, which was also deserted. This they followed and finally arrived in a chapel, where a candle lit for the Sacrament was the first indication of life in the building since someone from within would have had to light it unless Captain Mirenda had done the honours.

Four separate corridors led from the chapel, each of them at a corner of the room and one of which they'd just travelled. Salvatore was trying to decide which of the remaining three might lead them to a human presence, when he heard the sound of women's voices, just a quiet murmur in what otherwise would have been a place of silence and contemplation. Footsteps accompanied these voices. Someone said, "*Certo, certo. Non si preoccupi. Ha fatto bene.*"

Two women emerged from behind a wooden lattice that served to cover the doorway of the corridor nearest the chapel's altar. One of them wore the habit of a Dominican nun. The other wore the uniform of a *carabinieri* captain. The nun halted abruptly, the first of them to catch sight of the two men—both in the clothing of civilians—standing in the convent chapel. She looked behind her for a moment, as if to retreat to safety behind the lattice, and Captain Mirenda spoke sharply.

"*Chi sono?*" This was, she told them, a cloistered convent. How had they gained entrance?

Salvatore identified himself and explained who Lynley was. They were there, he said, on the matter of the English girl who had vanished from Lucca, and he felt confident that Captain Mirenda was aware of that case.

She was, of course. How could she be otherwise since, unlike the nun who'd stepped into the shadows, she did not live in a protected world. But it seemed that she had either been summoned to the convent on another matter entirely, or she had not connected the reason she'd been summoned to anything that had gone before this moment, especially in a *mercato* in Lucca.

The nun murmured something. In the shadows, her face was hidden.

Salvatore explained that he and his companion were going to have to speak to the Mother Superior. He went on to say that he knew it was irregular for any of the nuns to meet with an outsider—particularly if that outsider was male—but there was an urgent need since a direct relationship existed between a young woman of the name of Domenica Medici and a man who had taken the little girl from Lucca.

Captain Mirenda glanced at the other woman. She said, *"Che cosa vorrebbe fare?"*

Salvatore wanted to tell her that it was not a matter of what the nun wished to do at this point. This was a police matter, and the traditions of the cloister were going to have to be set aside. Where, he enquired, was Domenica Medici? Her parents had indicated she lived in this place. Roberto Squali had died on his way here. Evidence in his car proved the child had been a passenger at some point.

Captain Mirenda told them to wait in the chapel. Salvatore didn't like this, but he decided a compromise was in order. The *carabinieri* had sent a woman for obvious reasons, and if it was down to her to open doors in this place, he could live with that.

She took the arm of the nun, and together they disappeared behind the lattice from which they'd emerged. In a few minutes, though, the captain was back. With her was a different nun altogether, and she didn't shrink from their presence as had the other. This was Mother Superior, Captain Mirenda told them. It was she who had summoned the *carabinieri* to Villa Rivelli.

"Your wish is to see Domenica Medici?" Mother Superior was tall and stately, appearing ageless in her black-and-white habit. She wore the rimless spectacles that Salvatore remembered on the nuns of his youth. Then those glasses had seemed quirky, an antique fashion long out of vogue. Now they seemed trendy, striking an odd note of modernity out of keeping with the rest of Mother Superior's attire. Behind the glasses, she fixed upon him a gaze that he remembered only too well from the classroom. It demanded truth, and it suggested that anything less would be quickly uncovered.

He recounted what he'd learned from the parents of Domenica Medici: that she lived on the grounds of Villa Rivelli and that she served as a caretaker. He added to this what he'd already told Captain Mirenda. This was a matter of some importance, he concluded. A child's disappearance was involved.

It was Captain Mirenda who spoke. "Domenica Medici is here on the grounds," she said. "And there is no child within the convent walls."

"You have made a search?" Salvatore said.

"I have not needed to," Captain Mirenda said.

For a moment, Salvatore thought she meant that the word of Mother Superior was good enough, and he could tell that Lynley thought the same, for the other man stirred next to him and said quietly, "*Strano*," in a low voice.

Strange indeed, Salvatore thought. But Mother Superior clarified. There *was* a child, she said. From within the convent, she herself had both seen and heard her. She had assumed the girl was a relative come to stay for a time with Domenica. The reason for this was that she'd been delivered to the place by Domenica's cousin. She played on the grounds of the villa and helped Domenica with her work. That she might not have been a member of Domenica's family had not occurred to anyone in the convent.

"They have no contact here with the outside world," Captain Mirenda said. "They did not know that a child has gone missing from Lucca."

Salvatore very nearly didn't want to ask why the *carabinieri* had been sent for, then. This was of no import, however, since DI Lynley did the asking himself.

Because of the screaming, Mother Superior told them quietly. And because of the tale Domenica had told when she'd been sent for by the nun and questioned about it.

"*Lei crede che la bambina sia sua,*" Captain Mirenda interjected abruptly.

Her *own* child? Salvatore thought. "*Perché?*" he asked.

"*È pazza*" was the captain's answer.

Salvatore knew from speaking to Domenica's parents that the girl was, perhaps, not right in the head. But for her to believe that the child brought here by her cousin was her own daughter took things in a direction so strange that it suggested the girl was, indeed, more mad than she was slow.

Mother Superior's quiet voice filled in the rest of the details and comprised the information she'd gathered preceding her phone call. This man who had brought the child to the villa had once made Domenica pregnant. She'd been seventeen at the time. She was now twenty-six. To the poor girl, the age of the child seemed right. But it was, of course, no child of hers.

"*Perché?*" Salvatore asked the nun.

Again, the captain answered for her. "She prayed for God to take that child from her body so that her parents would never know she was pregnant."

"*È successo così?*" Lynley asked.

"*Sì,*" Captain Mirenda confirmed. That was indeed what had occurred. Or at least that was the tale Domenica had told Mother Superior when she'd been summoned into the convent upon the terrible screaming of the little girl. Captain Mirenda herself was on her way to question Domenica Medici about this. She would have no objection to the other policemen attending her.

Mother Superior spoke one last time before they left her. She murmured, "I did not know. She said it was her duty to prepare the little girl for God."

VILLA RIVELLI
TUSCANY

Lynley had followed the conversation perfectly well, but he very nearly wished he hadn't been able to do so. To have managed to track Hadiyyah to this place—for who else could it be but Hadiyyah brought into the Alps?—and to find themselves just hours too late . . . He couldn't imagine how he was going to tell the girl's parents. He also couldn't imagine how he was going to relay the information to Barbara Havers.

He walked slowly in the wake of the *carabinieri* officer and Lo Bianco. Captain Mirenda had been told where Domenica Medici was to be found. A short distance from the villa and sheltered from it by a hedge of camellias in bloom, a stone barn stood. Within this barn a woman dressed in garb similar to the Mother Superior's sat on a low stool milking a goat, her cheek resting on the animal's flank and her eyes closed.

Lynley would have thought she was a nun herself, save for the subtle differences in her clothing from the habit worn by the Mother Superior. The essentials of it were the same: a white robe, a simple black veil. Most people, seeing her, would assume she was a member of the cloistered community.

She was so involved in what she was doing that she wasn't aware anyone had entered the barn. It was only when Captain Mirenda said her name that her eyes opened. She wasn't startled by the presence of outsiders. Less was she startled by the fact that one of them wore the uniform of the *carabinieri*.

"*Ciao, Domenica,*" Captain Mirenda said.

Domenica smiled. She rose from her stool. A gentle slap on the flank of the goat sent it on its way, and it moved to join three others who were gathered at the far end of the barn, near a door the top half of which was open, revealing a fenced paddock beyond it. She brushed her hands down the front of the garment that went for her false nun's habit. In a gesture reminiscent of cloistered nuns Lynley had seen depicted on television and in films, she buried her hands in the sleeves of this garment, and she stood in an attitude that mixed humility with anticipation.

Lo Bianco was the one to speak although Captain Mirenda shot him a look that indicated he was out of place to be doing so. The *carabinieri* had, after all, been the agency of police first on the scene. Courtesy demanded that Lo Bianco allow the other officer to get down to business while he and Lynley observed.

He said to the young woman, "We have come for the child that your cousin Roberto Squali gave into your keeping, Domenica. What have you done with her?"

At the question Domenica's face took on a look of such placidity that for a moment Lynley doubted they'd found the right person. "I have done God's will," she murmured.

Lynley felt the grip of despair. His gaze took in the barn. His thoughts shot from one place to another where the mad young woman could have hidden the body of a nine-year-old girl: somewhere in the woods, somewhere on the grounds, a shadowy corner of the villa itself. They would need to bring in a team to find her unless the woman could be made to speak.

"What will of God have you done?" Captain Mirenda said.

"God has forgiven me," Domenica replied. "My sin was the prayer and the relief in having the prayer granted by Him. Ever since, I have walked the path of penitence to receive His absolution. I have done His will. My soul now magnifies the Lord. My spirit rejoices in God my Saviour." Again her head bowed, as if she'd said all she was going to say on the subject.

"Your cousin Roberto Squali would have told you to keep the child safe," Lo Bianco said. "He would not have told you to harm the child. You were to keep her until he came for her. Do you know your cousin Roberto is dead?"

She frowned. For a moment she said nothing, and Lynley thought that the news alone might loosen her tongue as to the whereabouts of Hadiyyah. But then she said, surprisingly, that it was the will of God that she should have witnessed what happened to Roberto. She, too, had thought her cousin was dead because God had clearly taken his car from the road and sent it soaring into the air. But the *ambulanza* had come for him and she'd understood from this that patience was required when one sought to understand the greater meanings behind God's hand in one's life.

"*Pazza*," Captain Mirenda said tersely. Her voice was low, and if Domenica heard this declaration, she said nothing in reply to it. Slings and arrows couldn't hurt her now. Obviously, she'd moved to an unearthly realm in which the Almighty had blessed her.

"You witnessed this accident to your cousin?" Lo Bianco said.

That, too, was God's will, Domenica told him.

"And then you wondered what next to do with the child you were supposed to be keeping for him, *vero*?" Lo Bianco clarified.

All that was required was to do God's will.

Captain Mirenda's expression said that she wished God's will to be that she herself should throttle the young woman. Lo Bianco's looked only marginally different. Lynley said to Domenica, "What was God's will?"

"Abraham," she told him. "Deliver your beloved son to God."

"But Isaac did not die," Lo Bianco said.

"God sent an angel to stop the sword from falling," Domenica said. "One only has to wait for God. God will always speak if the soul is pure. This, too, I prayed to know: how to purify and ready the soul for God so that the state of grace we all seek to be in at the moment of death could be acquired."

The moment of death was enough to spur Lo Bianco to action. He went to the young woman, grasped her arm, and said, "God's will is *this*," in a voice that boomed in the stone walls of the place. "You will take us to this child at once, wherever she is. God would not have sent us into the Alps to find her if God did not intend her to be found. You understand this, *sì*? You understand how God works? We must have that child. God has sent us for her."

Lynley thought the young woman might protest, but she did not. She also did not appear cowed by the demand or its ferocity. Instead, she said, "*Certo*," and seemed happy to comply. She headed for the great doors of the barn.

Once outside she went to a stairway that climbed to a door on the barn's south side. The others followed her up these stairs and into a dimly lit kitchen, where the sight of fresh, bright vegetables in an ancient stone sink and the fragrance of newly baked bread acted as a mocking contrast to what they understood they were about to find in this place.

She approached a door on the far side of the room, and from her pocket she withdrew a key. Lynley girded himself for whatever was behind the door, and when she said, "The waters of God washed away her sins, and her purity made her ready for Him," he saw Captain Mirenda cross herself and he heard Lo Bianco give a quiet curse.

Domenica didn't cross the threshold of the room beyond the door. Instead, she welcomed them to do so. They hesitated, and Domenica smiled. "*Andate*," she urged them, as if eager for them to see what God's handmaiden had done in the name of Abraham.

"*Dio mio*" was Lo Bianco's murmur as he passed the young woman and entered the room.

Lynley followed him, but Captain Mirenda did not. She would, he knew, want to prevent Domenica Medici from fleeing the scene. But Domenica made no move to do so. Instead, as the two men entered a small chamber furnished with only a narrow bed, a small chest of drawers, and a prie-dieu, she said, "*Vuole suo padre,*" and the little girl cowering in the corner of the room repeated this declaration in English.

"I want my dad," Hadiyyah said to them. She began to cry in great heaving sobs. "Please can you take me to my dad?"

VILLA RIVELLI
TUSCANY

Salvatore allowed DI Lynley to carry the little girl from the place. She was gowned in white from head to toe, like a child dressed for a Christmas pageant, and she clung to him, burying her face in his neck.

The Englishman had crossed the room to her in three steps. He'd said, "Hadiyyah, I'm Thomas Lynley. Barbara has sent me to find you," and she'd held out her arms like a much younger child, trust established at once by his use of English and by the mention of this name. Salvatore did not know who this person was, this Barbara. But if it served to comfort the child in some way to hear her name spoken, he was more than happy to have Lynley invoke it.

"Where is he? Where's my dad?" the child wailed.

Lynley picked her up, and she clung to him, thin legs round his waist, thin arms round his shoulders. "Barbara's in London waiting for you," he told the child. "Your father's in Lucca. Shall I take you to him? Would you like that?"

"But that's what *he* said . . ." And she cried anew, somehow not comforted by the idea of being taken to her father but rather terrified anew in some way.

Lynley carried her outside and down the stone steps. At their bottom a rustic table and four chairs stood in a square of bright sunlight. He set the girl on one of these chairs and drew a second chair close to her. Gently, he smoothed her chestnut hair, saying, "What did he say to you, Hadiyyah? Who?"

"The man said he'd take me to my dad," she told him. "I want my dad. I want Mummy. She put me in water. I didn't want it and I tried to stop her but I couldn't and then she locked me up and . . ." She wept and wept. "I wasn't scared at first 'cause he said my dad . . . But she made me go into the cellar . . ."

The story came in fits and starts and from it Salvatore picked up snatches and the rest was translated by Lynley as the little girl spoke, telling the tale of what in her confused mind Domenica Medici had determined to be the will of God. A visit to the cellar clarified matters further, for deep within the labyrinthine shadowy place was an ancient marble bathing pool in which disturbingly green and cloudy water had waited for the immersion of a frightened child, baptising her and washing away whatever "sins" stained her soul and made her less pleasing to the sight of God. Once she'd been thus baptised, locking her away was the only manner in which her keeper Domenica could assure her continued purity while she herself awaited the next sign from God to tell her what to do with the child.

When Salvatore saw the place to which Domenica Medici had dragged the little English girl, he understood the screaming that had brought the *carabinieri* to the convent. For the vast and vaulted cellar of the Villa Rivelli would be a place of nightmares for any child, with one crypt-like chamber giving onto another, with looming dusty disused wine barrels the size of military tanks in rows, with ancient olive presses looking like instruments of torture . . . It was no wonder that Hadiyyah had screamed in terror. There was more than a good chance that she would wake up screaming from her dreams for a very long time to come.

It was time to get her out of this place and back to her parents. He said to Lynley, "*Dobbiamo portarla a Lucca all'ospedale,*" for Hadiyyah would have to be examined by a doctor and spoken to by a specialist in childhood trauma if one could be found whose English was adequate.

"*Sì, sì,*" Lynley agreed. He suggested that they phone the parents and have them meet them there.

Salvatore nodded. He would make that call once he spoke to Captain Mirenda. The *carabinieri* would, for the present, take charge of Domenica Medici. He doubted they would get much more from the young woman than they'd got already, but she had to be dealt with. She didn't seem to be an accomplice so much as an instrument of her cousin Roberto Squali. But buried within the confusion of her mind could be something that would tell them more about the commission of the crime. She, too, would need to be examined by a doctor. This doctor, however, would be one of the mind so that an assessment could be made of her.

"*Andiamo*," Salvatore said to Lynley. Once these things were accomplished, their work here was finished and whatever details Hadiyyah herself might be able to provide about her kidnapping, those could wait until she'd been seen to at the hospital and until she was reunited with her parents.

VICTORIA
LONDON

It wasn't as difficult as it had used to be, getting an officer from Special Branch to talk. Time was when the blokes from SO12 were a deeply secretive lot, not only closemouthed but also nervy. They had trusted no one, and who could blame them? In the days of the IRA and bombs on buses, in cars, and in rubbish bins, pretty much everyone looked Irish to them, so it didn't matter if a questioner happened to be from another branch of the Met. The SO12 blokes were tight-lipped and all the et ceteras. Prying information out of them generally took a court order.

They were still careful, but sharing information was sometimes necessary in these days of fiery clerics in English mosques exhorting their listeners to *jihad*, British-born young men schooled in the beauties of martyrdom, and professionals from unexpected fields like medicine deciding to alter the course of their lives by wiring their cars with explosives and planting them where they would do the most harm. No one could afford unsafe convictions in any of these matters, so if one agency within the Met needed information from another agency within the Met, it wasn't impossible to find someone who could impart a few details if a name was given.

Barbara got inside to talk to Chief Inspector Harry Streener by using the magic words *Pakistani national living in London* and *a developing situation in Italy*. The bloke had the accent of someone who should have been whistling commands to his sheepdog in the hills of Yorkshire and the pasty cue-ball complexion of a poor sod who hadn't seen the sun for the past ten years. His fingers were yellow from nicotine and his teeth weren't much better, and when she saw him, Barbara made a mental note that giving up smoking wasn't an entirely bad idea. But she set this aside for future consideration and gave him the name she was loath to give him.

"Taymullah Azhar?" Streener repeated. They were in his office, where an iPod in a docking station was playing something that sounded like hurricane-force winds in a bamboo grove. Streener saw her glance in its direction. "White noise," he said. "Helps me to think."

"Got it," she said with a wise nod. It would have driven her to the nearest Underground station for shelter, but everyone's boat floated on different water.

Streener tapped at his computer's keyboard. After a moment, he read the screen. Barbara itched to get out of her seat, crawl over his desk, and have at the information, but she forced herself to wait patiently for whatever it was that Streener decided to impart. She'd already sketched in the facts for him: Azhar's employment at University College London, his entanglement with Angelina Upman, their production of a child together, Angelina's flight with Hadiyyah to destinations unknown, and Hadiyyah's disappearance via kidnapping. Streener had listened to all this with a face so impassive that Barbara wondered if he was actually hearing her. At the end of her recitation, she'd said, "Superintendent Ardery's put me onto the London end of things while DI Lynley's working the Italian end. I thought it best to check with you lot and see if you've been having a look at the bloke."

"And your thought as to why SO12 would be onto this . . . What was the name again?" Streener said.

Barbara spelled it out for him. "Just seemed like an *i* that needed to be dotted," she told him. After a moment, she added, "Pakistan? You know what I mean. I don't have to be PC with you, do I?"

Streener guffawed. The last thing cops needed to be was politically correct with each other. He typed a bit. Then he read. His lips formed a whistle that he didn't make. He nodded and said, "Yeah. He's here. Ticket to Lahore triggered the usual alarms. One-*way* ticket upped the noise."

Barbara felt her gut clench. "C'n you tell me . . . Were you looking at him before the one-way ticket?"

Streener glanced at her sharply. She'd tried to keep her voice intrigued by this development but not involved other than as a professional doing a job. He seemed to evaluate her question and what it might imply. He finally looked back at his screen, scrolled a bit, and said slowly, "Yes, it appears that we were."

"C'n you tell me why?"

"It's the job," he said.

"I know it's your job, but—"

"Not mine. His. Professor of microbiology? He has his own lab? You can fill in the blanks there, can't you?"

She could indeed. As a professor of microbiology, as a professional with his own lab . . . God only knew what tasty weapon of mass destruction he could be cooking up. As she herself had said, the magic words were *Pakistani national living in London. Pakistani* meant *Muslim. Muslim* meant *suspicious.* Put one and one together among this lot in SO12, and you came up with three every time. It wasn't fair but there you had it.

She couldn't really blame them. To them, Taymullah Azhar was just a name just as, to them, terrorists were hiding in every garden shed. The job of SO12 was to make sure those blokes didn't emerge from those sheds with bombs inside their shorts or, in the case of Azhar, with a Thermos filled with God only knew what, sufficient to contaminate the water supply of London.

She said, "Have you blokes been following the kidnap situation, then?"

Streener looked some more, then nodded slowly. "Italy," he said. "He landed in Pisa."

"Any indication that Azhar's contacted an Italian there? Michelangelo Di Massimo would be the name."

Streener shook his head, his eyes on the computer's screen. "Doesn't seem to be, but this goes back forever. Let me try . . ." He typed. He was fast, using only two fingers but getting the job done. There was nothing on a Michelangelo Di Massimo, he reported. There was nothing, in fact, in Italy at all aside from his landing in Pisa and the name and location of his B & B.

Thank God was Barbara's thought when she heard this. Whatever the tickets to Pakistan meant, in this one matter Azhar was clean.

She'd taken notes throughout, and now she flipped her notebook closed. She made her thanks to Streener and got herself out of his office and into the nearest stairwell, where she lit a fag and took five deep drags. A door opened some floors below her and voices floated upward as someone began climbing. Hastily, she crushed the fag out, put the dog end in her bag, and ducked back into the corridor, where she was making for the lifts when her mobile rang.

"Page five, Barb," Mitchell Corsico said.

"Page five what?"

"That's where you'll find yourself and the Love Rat Dad. I tried for page one, but while Rod Aronson—that's my editor, by the way— liked this new twist of the Love Rat Dad having it off with an officer from the Met, he wasn't exactly impassioned by it since there's nothing fresh on the kid's disappearance that I c'n give him from over here. So he's putting it inside. Page five. You got lucky this time."

"Mitchell, why the hell are you doing this?"

"We had an agreement. Quarter of an hour. That was . . . how many hours ago exactly?"

"It might interest you that I'm working, Mitchell. It might interest you to know that I'm about to break this case wide open. It might be a grand idea for you to stay on my good side because when the story's ready for—"

"You should have told me, Barb."

"I don't report to you, in case you haven't noticed. I report to my guv."

"You should have given me something. That's how this game is played. And *you* know *that*. If you didn't want to play, you shouldn't have climbed into my sandbox. D'you understand?"

"I'm *going* to give you . . ." The lift arrived. It was filled to capacity. She couldn't continue the conversation. She said, "We c'n sort this out. Just tell me that there're no dates involved, and we're back in business."

"On the pictures, you mean? Are the dates removed from the pictures?"

"That's what I mean."

"And can I guess why that's important to you?"

"Oh, I expect you can work that one out. Are you going to answer me?"

There was a moment. She was in the lift and the doors were closing and she was in terror that either he wouldn't reply or they'd be cut off.

But he finally said, "No dates, Barb. I gave you that much. We'll call it a sign of good faith."

"Right," she said as she rang off. They would definitely call it something.

LUCCA
TUSCANY

Hadiyyah wanted Lynley to sit in the back seat of the police car with her, and he was happy to oblige. Lo Bianco phoned ahead to the hospital in Lucca, and he then notified Angelina Upman and Taymullah Azhar that Hadiyyah had been found at a Dominican convent in the Apuan Alps, that she was alive and well, and that she would be at the hospital within ninety minutes for a general exam. If they would be so good as to meet DI Lynley and himself at this location . . . ?

"*Niente, niente*," he murmured into the mobile, an apparent brushing off of copious expressions of gratitude from the other end. "*È il mio lavoro, Signora.*"

In the back seat, Lynley kept Hadiyyah tucked next to him, which seemed to be her preference. Considering the length of time that she'd been held at Villa Rivelli, she did not appear to be the worse for the experience, at least superficially. Sister Domenica Giustina, as Hadiyyah called Domenica Medici, had taken good care of her. Up until the last few days, the child had apparently had the run of the villa's grounds. It was only in the end that she had become frightened, Hadiyyah said. It was only when Sister Domenica Giustina took her into the cellar to that mouldy, smelly, creepy chamber with the slippery and slimy marble pool in the floor that she had known the slightest bit of terror.

"You're a very brave girl," Lynley said to her. "Most girls your age—most boys as well—would have been frightened from the very start. Why weren't you, Hadiyyah? Can you tell me? Do you remember how all of this began? What can you tell me?"

She looked up at him. He was struck by how pretty a child she was, everything attractive in both of her parents blending together to form her innocent beauty. Her delicate eyebrows knotted as she heard his questions, though. Her eyes filled with tears, possibly at the realisation that she might well have done something wrong. Every child knew the rules, after all: Don't go anywhere with a stranger, no matter what that stranger says to you. And both he and Hadiyyah knew that that was what she had done. He said quietly, "There's no right or wrong here, by the way. There's just what happened. You know I'm a policeman, of course, and I hope you know that Barbara and I are very good friends, yes?"

She nodded solemnly.

"Brilliant. My job is to find out what happened. That's it. Nothing else. Can you help me, Hadiyyah?"

She looked down at her lap, "He said my dad was waiting for me. I was in the market with Lorenzo and I was watching the accordion man near the *porta* and he said 'Hadiyyah, this is from your father. He is waiting to see you beyond the city wall.'"

"'This is from your father'?" Lynley repeated. "Did he speak English or Italian to you?"

"English."

"And what was from your father?"

"A card."

"Like . . . a greeting card, perhaps?" Lynley thought of the pictures they had from the tourists in the *mercato*, Roberto Squali with a card in his hand, then Hadiyyah with something similar in hers. "What did the card say?"

"It said to go with the man. It said not to be afraid. It said he would bring me to him, to my dad."

"And was it signed?"

"It said 'Dad.'"

"Was it in your father's handwriting, Hadiyyah? D'you think you would recognise his handwriting?"

Slowly she sucked in on her lip. She looked up at him, and her great dark eyes began to spill tears onto her cheeks. In this, Lynley had his answer. She was nine years old. How often had she even *seen* her father's handwriting and why would she ever be expected to remember what it looked like? He put his arm round her and pulled her closer to him. "You didn't do anything wrong," he said again, this time pressing his lips to her hair. "I expect you've missed your father badly. I expect you'd very much like to see him."

She nodded, tears still dribbling down her face.

"Right. Well. He's here in Italy. He's waiting for you. He's been trying to find you since you went missing."

"*Khushi*," she said against his shoulder.

Lynley frowned. He repeated the word. He asked her what it meant and she told him *happiness*. It was what her father always called her.

"He said *khushi*," she told him with trembling lips. "He called me *khushi*."

"The man with the card?"

"Dad said he'd come at Christmas hols, see, but then he didn't." She began to weep harder. "He kept saying 'soon, *khushi*, soon' in his emails. I thought he came as a big surprise for me and was waiting for me and the man said we had to drive to him so I got in the car. We drove and drove and drove and he took me to Sister Domenica Giustina and Dad wasn't *there*." She sobbed and Lynley comforted her as best he could, no expert in the ways of little girls. "Bad, bad, bad," she wept. "I did bad. I made trouble for everyone. I'm *bad*."

"Not in the least," Lynley said. "Look at how brave you've been from the start. You weren't frightened and that's a very good thing."

"He said Dad was on his way," she wailed. "He said to wait and Dad would come."

"I see how it happened," Lynley told her. He stroked her hair. "You did brilliantly, Hadiyyah, from beginning to end and you're not to blame. You'll remember that, won't you? You are not to blame." For at that point, Lynley thought, what else was the child to do but wait for her father? She had no idea where Squali had taken her. There was no nearby house to which she could have run. Inside the cloister, the nuns might have seen her but they assumed she was a relative of their caretaker. Nothing appeared out of the ordinary to them, for the child played on the villa's grounds. If she acted like anything at all, what she didn't act like was a kidnap victim.

He fished his handkerchief out of his pocket and pressed it into Hadiyyah's small hands. He met the gaze of Lo Bianco in the rearview mirror. He could see what the chief inspector was thinking: They needed to get their hands on that card Squali had given the child, and they needed to find the connection between him and anyone who knew Hadiyyah's nickname was *khushi*.

When they arrived at the hospital in Lucca, Angelina Upman rushed at the car. She flung open the rear door and grabbed her daughter, crying her name. She looked terrible, everything from her difficult pregnancy to her anxiety about her child having taken a grievous toll upon her. But at the moment, the only thing of import was Hadiyyah. Angelina cried, "Oh my God! Thank you, thank you!" and she ran frantic hands over Hadiyyah from head to toe, a desperate search for any possible injuries.

For her part, Hadiyyah only said, "Mummy," and "I want to go *home*," and then she saw her father.

Azhar was approaching from the hospital doors with Lorenzo Mura following him. Hadiyyah cried out, "Dad! Dad!" and the Pakistani man broke into a sprint. When he reached Angelina and his daughter, he swept both of them into his arms. They formed a tight unit of three, and Azhar bent to kiss Hadiyyah's head. He pressed his lips to Angelina's as well. "The best of all conclusions," he said. And to Lynley and Lo Bianco as they got out of the car, "Thank you, thank you."

Lo Bianco murmured again that this was his job: to reach a successful conclusion to a bad situation. For his part, Lynley made no reply. He was, instead, watching Lorenzo Mura and trying to determine what it meant that his expression was black and his eyes mirrored fury.

LUCCA

TUSCANY

Lynley was not long in the dark on this matter. While Angelina accompanied her daughter to be examined by one of the doctors in casualty, Lynley and Lo Bianco remained with Lorenzo and Azhar. They found a sheltered corner of the waiting room, where they could speak in private, and here the two police officers explained not only what had happened in the *mercato* on the day that Hadiyyah had disappeared but also where she had been taken and by whom and for what reason.

"He has done this!" was Lorenzo's reaction the moment that the police had reached the conclusion of the story. In case they didn't know to whom he was referring, Lorenzo went on, indicating Azhar with a jerk of his head in the Pakistani man's direction. "Can you not see he has done this?"

Azhar's dark eyebrows drew together. "What do you mean?"

"*You* have done this to her. To Angelina. To Hadiyyah. To *me*. You found her and you want her suffering—"

"*Signore, Signore,*" Lo Bianco said. His voice was calm and conciliatory. "*Non c'è la prova di tutto ciò. Non deve—*"

"*Non sa niente!*" Lorenzo hissed. And what followed was Italian so rapid-fire that Lynley could follow none of it. What he did understand was Lo Bianco's statement about proof: There was nothing to indicate that Azhar had been involved in this matter. He also understood that there might be, that the London connection between Michelangelo Di Massimo and the private investigator Dwayne Doughty did not look good. But this was a matter about which Lorenzo Mura knew nothing. At the moment he was operating on nerves alone, and God knew his had been strung out for weeks.

Azhar was silent, his face immobile. He watched the heated conversation between Lo Bianco and Mura, and he did not ask for a translation. In part, Lynley could tell, no translation was necessary. The murderous looks Lorenzo was shooting the Pakistani man were enough indication that something accusatory was being said.

Angelina approached them at this point, Hadiyyah's hand in hers.

Lynley could tell she took in the situation with a single glance, because she stopped and bent to her daughter. She smoothed her hair, took her to a nearby chair that was well within her sight, parked her there with a kiss on the top of her head, and came to join the men.

"How is Hadiyyah?" Azhar asked at once.

"Oh, he asks this now," Lorenzo scoffed. "*Vaffanculo! Mostro! Vaffanculo!*"

Angelina blanched, which was something to see as she had virtually no colour in her face to begin with. She said, "What's going on?"

"How is Hadiyyah?" Azhar repeated. "Angelina . . ."

She turned to him. Her face was soft. "She's well. There was no . . . She's unhurt, Hari."

"May I . . ." He nodded at his daughter, who watched them with her great dark eyes so solemn and confused.

"Of *course* you may," Angelina said. "She's your daughter."

Azhar nodded, even managing a small and formal bow. He strode across to Hadiyyah and she jumped from her chair. He swung her up and into his arms, and the child buried her face in his neck. Angelina watched this, as did everyone.

"*Serpente*," Lorenzo hissed at Angelina, indicating Azhar with a scornful jerk of his head in the Pakistani's direction. "*L'uomo è un serpente, cara.*"

She turned to him. She examined him in a way that suggested she was only seeing Lorenzo Mura for the very first time. She said, "Renzo, my God. What are you saying?"

"*L'ha fatto*," he said. "*L'ha fatto. L'ha fatto.*"

"He did what?" she asked.

"*Tutto, tutto!*"

"He did *nothing*. He did nothing at all. He's been here to help find her; he's made himself available to the police, to us; he's suffered every bit as much as I have suffered and you can*not*, Lorenzo, no matter how you feel and what you want, accuse him of anything but loving Hadiyyah. *Chiaro*, Lorenzo? Do you understand?"

The Italian's face had flooded with colour. One hand knotted into a fist. "*Non è finito*" was what he said.

VICTORIA
LONDON

Barbara was in the midst of planning out her next confrontation with Dwayne Doughty when the call from Lynley came. She was at her desk, she was reorganising her notes, and she was ignoring the baleful glares from John Stewart that the DI was firing at her from across the room. He'd not stopped his ceaseless observation of her despite being warned off by their guv. He seemed to be turning his mania for ruining her into a form of religion.

"We have her, Barbara" was how Lynley began. "We've found her. She's fine. You can set your mind at rest."

Barbara was unprepared for the explosion of emotion inside of her. She said past something that occluded her throat, "You have Hadiyyah?"

They indeed had Hadiyyah, Lynley told her. He spoke of a place called Villa Rivelli, of a young woman who thought herself a Dominican nun, of the same young woman's delusions about having the care of Hadiyyah placed into her hands, and of an aborted "baptism" of Hadiyyah that had frightened the child enough to raise the alarm and gain the notice of the Mother Superior inside the cloistered convent. When he was finished, all Barbara could say was "Bloody hell, bloody hell. Thank you, thank you, sir."

"Thanks go to Chief Inspector Lo Bianco."

"How's . . ." Barbara thought how to phrase it.

Lynley kindly intercepted her question. "Azhar's fine. Angelina is a little worse for wear. But she and Azhar have made their peace, evidently, so all's well that ends well, I daresay."

"Peace?" Barbara asked.

Lynley explained the scene at Lucca's hospital, where Hadiyyah was taken after her rescue from the convent. Post a number of accusations from Lorenzo Mura on the matter of Azhar's putative involvement in Hadiyyah's disappearance, Angelina and her former lover were able to reach a rapprochement with each other. For her part, Angelina had admitted to doing Azhar a grave injustice in leading him to believe she'd returned to him while all the time planning the disappearance of his daughter. For his part, Azhar asked forgiveness for having been unwilling from the first to give Angelina what she had so wanted: marriage or a sibling for their daughter. He'd said that he was wrong in this. He said he understood that it was too late for them now—for Angelina and himself—but he hoped that she could forgive him as he fully, wholeheartedly, and freely forgave her.

"Did Mura hear all this?" Barbara asked.

"He'd already departed in something of a temper. But I have a feeling things aren't finished there. He indicated as much before exiting stage left. He's convinced that Azhar's at the bottom of everything that's gone on. I must tell you that chances are you'll be hearing from Chief Inspector Lo Bianco or whoever's replaced him."

"Was he pulled from the case?"

"He was, so he tells me. And Hadiyyah explained that . . ." He stopped for a moment. He spoke to someone in Italian. Barbara caught *pagherò in contanti* and a woman's voice in the background saying "*Grazie, Dottore.*" He continued, "Hadiyyah told me that she went with a man who told her he was taking her to her father. She said he had a card— a greeting card, I think—with a message purporting to be from Azhar telling her to go with the man as he'd bring her to her father."

Barbara felt a frisson at this. "Have you seen the card?"

"As yet, no. But the *carabinieri* have Domenica Medici in hand, which means they have the entire convent in hand. If there's a card at Villa Rivelli and Hadiyyah kept it, it'll turn up soon enough."

"It could be elsewhere," Barbara said. "And anyone could have written that message, sir."

"My first thought as well, as she apparently wouldn't recognise his writing. But then she told me something curious, Barbara. The man who took her from the market called her *khushi*. Have you ever heard Azhar use that term? She said it's his nickname for her."

Barbara's stomach turned to liquid. She casually repeated, "*Khushi*, sir?" to buy a few moments in which her thoughts jumped feverishly from one point to another, like fleas indicating directions on a map.

"She said that's why she went with him. Not only because of the card holding out the promise of her father, but also because he called her *khushi*, which meant to her that Squali had to be telling the truth, for how else would he have known the term?"

Doughty, of course, Barbara thought. That king of rats. He would have passed the nickname on. But there were several reasons he may have done so, and offering any of them to Lynley was to take a route that led nowhere remotely helpful. So she said, "Azhar might've called her that round me, but I bloody well don't remember, sir. On the other hand, if it *is* a nickname, I reckon Angelina knew it, too."

"I take it you're suggesting a path from Angelina to Lorenzo Mura?"

"It makes sense in a way, doesn't it? From what you've said, sounds to me like Mura's got a very wide streak of jealousy running up his spine. Also sounds to me like he hates Azhar and it doesn't take too much of a jump to get from there to him wanting to cut the tie between Azhar and Angelina permanently in some way. Plus . . ." And here Barbara put into words what didn't bear thinking of, "What if he's also jealous of Angelina's bond with Hadiyyah? What if he wants Angelina only for himself? P'rhaps the plan was to set Azhar up with a kidnap charge and to . . ." At the end, she couldn't put it into words.

Lynley did it for her. "Are you suggesting his intention would have been to eliminate Hadiyyah?"

"We've seen nearly everything in our line of work, sir."

He was silent. He would, of course, know this was true.

"What about Doughty?" Lynley asked. "What have you turned up on him?"

Barbara didn't want to go within fifty yards of what she'd learned about Doughty, leading as it did to his claims about Azhar. What she wanted was a chance to talk to Azhar, to ask him questions and to study his face as he gave his answers. But her brief had been to dig into Doughty's part in Hadiyyah's disappearance, so she had to give Lynley something and she quickly made her choice. "I've come up with a bloke called Bryan Smythe," she said. "He does computer work for Doughty, the kind requiring a special touch of the hacking variety."

"And?"

"Haven't put the thumbscrews to him yet. That's on for tomorrow. But what I hope to learn is that Doughty employed him to wipe clean all traces of communication between himself and one Michelangelo Di Massimo. Which'll more or less confirm that Doughty's involved."

Lynley said nothing. Barbara waited in a welter of anxiety for him to take the next step, which logically demanded that Barbara check for a connection between Doughty and Azhar. He said finally, "As to that . . ."

She cut in hastily with what she hoped sounded like a conclusion. "Someone would have hired him, of course. Way I see it, it could go two directions. Either someone here hired him to execute a plan to snatch Hadiyyah—"

"And that would be?"

"Anyone who hated Azhar, I expect. Angelina's relatives top that list. They knew Hadiyyah was missing from London 'cause I went to see them when she first disappeared. Azhar went as well. They hate him, sir. To do something to hurt him? Nothing they might pay for that pleasure would be too much, believe me."

"And the other direction?"

"Your end. Someone in Italy setting everything up, including creating a line to a private detective in London for purposes of making someone in London look suspicious. Who does that suggest to you?"

"We know Lorenzo Mura is probably acquainted with Di Massimo. They both play football for their cities' teams." He was quiet for a moment, then she heard him sigh. "I'll pass all this on to Lo Bianco," he finally said. "He can hand it over to his replacement."

"D'you still want me to—"

"Complete your work on the Doughty end of things, Barbara. If you come up with something, we'll send it to Italy when I get back. Everything's in the hands of the Italians now. As liaison officer, my work is finished."

Barbara let out her breath, which she'd been holding as she'd waited for his reaction to the tale she'd spun. She said, "When d'you come back home, sir?"

"I've a flight out in the morning. I'll see you tomorrow."

They rang off then, and Barbara was left at her desk with the malignant stare of DI Stewart upon her. Across the room as he was, he hadn't been able to hear any part of her conversation with Lynley, but he had on his face the expression of a man who had no intention of letting any sleeping dog alone if there was a chance he could kick it soundly in the ribs.

She returned his stare until he shifted in his chair and went back to wasting his time in a putative examination of paperwork on his desk. Barbara sorted through her feelings about what she had just done and not done in her phone call with Lynley.

She was fast approaching a professional line. Should she cross it, that move would forever define her. She asked herself what was owed to the people she loved, and the only answer she could come up with was absolute loyalty at all costs. The difficulty was in choosing those people. The additional difficulty was attempting to understand the exact nature of the love she felt for them.

1 MAY

Inside the kitchen of Torre Lo Bianco, Salvatore fondly watched the interaction of his two children with their *nonna*. The previous night had been one of those designated for the children to spend with their father and, as it happened because of his current abode, with their *nonna*. Salvatore's mother was taking full advantage of the presence of her *nipoti*.

She'd given them a breakfast heavily reliant upon *dolci*, which naturally would have met with Birgit's outraged protests. She'd made a vague bow to nutrition with *cereale e latte*—thanks be to God she'd at least chosen bran flakes, Salvatore thought—but after that she'd brought out the cakes and the *biscotti*. The children had devoured far more than was good for them and were showing the effects of so much sugar. For her part their *nonna* was plying them with questions.

Were they attending Mass every Sunday? she wanted to know. Had they gone to services on Holy Thursday? Were they on their knees for three hours on Good Friday? When was the last time they'd received the Blessed Sacrament?

To every question, Bianca answered with lowered eyes. To every question, Marco answered with an expression so solemn that Salvatore wondered where he had learned to master it. On the way to school he informed them that lying to their *nonna* should be Topic Number One when next they went to confession.

Before he left them at Scuola Dante Alighieri, he told Bianca that her little friend Hadiyyah Upman had been found. He hastened to assure her that the child was well, but he also spent some moments making absolutely certain that Bianca understood—"*anche tu, Marco,*" he added—that she was never, ever upon her immortal soul to believe *anyone* who might tell her to accompany him for any reason. If that person was not her *nonna*, her mamma, or her papà, then she should scream for help and not stop screaming until help got to her. *Chiaro?*

Hadiyyah Upman's love for her father had been her downfall. She missed him terribly, and no false emails from her aunt purporting to be from her father had assuaged her feelings. All someone had to do to gain her trust was to promise the little girl that she'd be taken to the man. Praise God that she'd only ended up in the care of mad Domenica Medici. There were far worse fates that could have befallen her.

Once Hadiyyah and her parents had been reunited at the hospital, Salvatore and the London detective had gone their separate ways. Lynley's job as liaison was complete, and he did not wish to intrude further into the Italian investigation. "I'll pass along to you the information that my colleague in London gathers," he said. He himself would be returning to London. "*Buona fortuna, amico mio,*" he'd concluded. "*Tutto è finito bene.*"

Salvatore tried to be philosophical about this. Things had indeed finished well for DI Lynley. They had finished far from well for himself.

He brought *il Pubblico Ministero* into the picture as soon as he and Lynley had parted. Fanucci, he reasoned, would want to know that the child had been found alive and well. He also assumed that Fanucci would want to know what Hadiyyah herself had reported: about the card ostensibly in her father's handwriting, about Roberto Squali's use of her nickname, and most of all about what these two facts suggested about culpability for her disappearance. She had, after all, not said one word about Carlo Casparia.

What he hadn't reckoned on was Fanucci's reaction to what he perceived as Chief Inspector Lo Bianco's defiance. He'd been removed from the case, hadn't he? He'd been told the investigation was being handed over to another officer, *nevvero*? So what had he been doing voyaging off into the Apuan Alps when he should have been sitting in his office, awaiting the arrival of Nicodemo Triglia, who was taking the case off his hands?

Salvatore said, "Piero, with the safety of a child in jeopardy, surely you did not expect me to sit upon information I had as to her possible whereabouts? This was something that had to be dealt with without delay."

Fanucci allowed that Topo had returned the child to her parents unharmed, but that was as far as he would go in the area of congratulations. He said, "Be that as it may, everything now goes into the hands of Nicodemo, and your job is to give to him whatever it is that you have gathered."

"Allow me to ask you to reconsider," Salvatore said. "Piero, we parted badly in our last conversation. For my part, I am filled with apology. I would only wish—"

"Do not ask, Topo."

"—to be allowed to finish with the final details. There are curious matters concerning a greeting card, also matters concerning the use of a special name for the child . . . The lover of the girl's mother insists that this man—the girl's father—must be considered before he leaves the country. Let me tell you, Piero, it is not so much that I believe the lover but that I believe something more is going on here."

But this Fanucci did not want to hear. He said, "*Basta, Topo*. You must understand. I cannot allow defiance in an investigation. Now, it must please you to wait for Nicodemo's arrival."

Salvatore knew Nicodemo Triglia, a man who had never missed his afternoon *pisolino* in his entire career. He carried a gut upon him the size of an Umbrian wild boar, and he'd never encountered a bar that he passed by without stopping in for a *birra* and the thirty minutes that were required for him to savour it.

Salvatore was brooding upon this at the *questura* while he waited for the old stained Moka in the little kitchen to finish its coffee business for him on the two-burner stove. When it had done so, he poured himself a cup of the viscous liquid, dropped in a sugar cube, and watched it melt. He carried it to the room's small window and looked out at a view that was limited to the *parcheggio* for the police vehicles. He was staring at them without really seeing them when one of his officers interrupted.

"We have an identification," a woman's voice said.

So deep into his thoughts was Salvatore that, when he turned, he did not remember the officer's name. Just a crude joke that had been in the men's toilet about the shape of her breasts. He'd laughed at the time, but now he felt shame. She was earnest about her work, as she had to be. It was not easy for her in this line of employment that had for so long been dominated by men.

"What identification?" he asked her. He saw that she was carrying a photo and he tried to remember why any of his officers were showing photographs to anyone.

She said, "Casparia, sir. He's seen this man."

"Where?"

She looked at him oddly. She said in some surprise, "*Non si ricorda?*" but hastily went on lest her question sound disrespectful. She looked about twenty years old, Salvatore thought, and she probably thought the antiquity of his forty-two had begun to affect his memory. She said, "Giorgio and I . . . ?"

At which point he remembered. Officers had taken photographs to the prison for Carlo Casparia's perusal. These comprised pictures of the soccer players on Lucca's team as well as the fathers of the boys Lorenzo Mura coached. And Carlo Casparia had recognised someone? This was an extraordinary turn of events.

He held out his hand for the picture. "Who is this?" he asked. Ottavia was her name, he thought. Ottavia Schwartz because her father was German, she'd been born in Trieste, and suddenly his head was filled with utterly useless information. He looked at the picture. The man looked roughly the same age as Lorenzo Mura, and with one glance Salvatore could see why the drug addict had remembered this individual. He had ears like conch shells. They stood out of his head in misshapen glory, and they transmitted light as if torches were being held behind them. This man in the company of anyone would be unforgettable. It could be, he thought, that they had just experienced a piece of luck. He repeated his question as Ottavia wet her forefinger on her tongue and flipped open a small notebook.

She said, "Daniele Bruno. He is a midfielder on the city team."

"What do we know about him?"

"Nothing yet." And when his head rose abruptly, she went on in haste. "Giorgio's on it. He's compiling enough information for you to—"

She looked startled as Salvatore stepped forward and closed the door of the tiny kitchen. She looked more startled when he spoke to her urgently in a low voice.

"Listen to me, Ottavia, you and Giorgio . . . You give this information to no one else but myself. *Capisce?*"

"*Sì, ma . . .*"

"That is all you need to know. Whatever you have, you hand over to me."

For he knew where things would head should Nicodemo Triglia be given Ottavia's information. It was already written in the stars and he had seen this on Piero Fanucci's unfortunate features. The Big Plan was how he thought of it, and it comprised how Piero was going to save face. There was only one way for him to do it at this point since nothing that had happened to Hadiyyah Upman related in any way to Piero's main suspect in her kidnapping. So Piero could only save face by burying information now and by biding his time until the moment that the tabloids had found other stories to pursue once the excitement of the child's return to her parents had subsided. Then Carlo would be released very quietly to his life, and everyone else's life—particularly Piero's—could simply go on.

Ottavia Schwartz frowned but asked if the chief inspector wished her to put her notes into a report for him. He told her no. Just hand them over as they are, he said, and let this conversation between us slip from your mind.

LUCCA
TUSCANY

Lynley did not see Taymullah Azhar again until breakfast. The Pakistani man had gone to Fattoria di Santa Zita to be with his daughter once Hadiyyah was released from the examination she'd undergone at the hospital. As liaison officer, Lynley had no need to accompany them. But his mind was uneasy in the aftermath of Hadiyyah's rescue and Lorenzo Mura's accusations. On the one hand, his own work was finished. On the other hand, he had questions, and it seemed reasonable to ask them of Azhar when they stood at Signora Vallera's breakfast buffet table, spooning cereal into their bowls.

He began with "All's well, I hope?"

Azhar said, "There is no sufficient way that I can thank you, Inspector Lynley. I know that your presence is Barbara's doing as well as your own, and there is no way I can thank her either." And then in answer to his question, "Hadiyyah is well. Angelina is less so."

"One hopes her condition will now improve."

Azhar moved towards his table and politely asked Lynley to join him. He poured coffee for them both from a white crockery jug.

"Hadiyyah told us about a card," Lynley said as he sat. "This was a greeting card that the man Squali handed to her in the marketplace before she left with him. She said it contained a message from you, telling her to go with him as you were waiting for her."

"She told me this as well," Azhar said. "But I know nothing about such a card, Inspector Lynley. If there is one somewhere—"

"I believe there is." Lynley told the other man of the tourist photographs, of the particular pictures of the happy face card in the hand of Roberto Squali, and then of the photo of Hadiyyah holding what looked like the very same card.

"Have you seen this card, Inspector?" Azhar then asked. "Was it with Hadiyyah's belongings where she was found?"

This was something Lynley didn't know. If there had been a card, though, it would now be in the hands of the *carabinieri* who'd arrived at the convent first and who had taken Domenica Medici away. These policemen would have searched the premises for anything connected to the child who'd been held in the place.

"Who else knew about Hadiyyah's disappearance?" Lynley asked him. "I'm talking about her disappearance from London last November. Who else knew, aside from Barbara and myself?"

Azhar named the individuals he'd told over the initial weeks: colleagues at University College London, friends in the field of microbiology, Angelina's parents and her sister Bathsheba, and his own family much later, of course, once Angelina and Lorenzo had arrived in London insisting that Hadiyyah had been snatched from the Lucca marketplace by him.

"Dwayne Doughty knew about her disappearance as well, did he not?" Lynley watched Azhar's face closely as he said the London investigator's name. "We've been told by Michelangelo Di Massimo, an investigator in Pisa, that Doughty hired him to find Hadiyyah."

"Mr. Doughty . . . ?" Azhar said. "But I hired this man to try to find Hadiyyah straightaway when she went missing, and he told me there was no trace of her, that Angelina had left no trail from London to . . . to anywhere. And now you are saying that . . . what? That he discovered that Angelina had gone to Pisa? Last winter he knew this? While telling me that there was no trail?"

"When he told you there was no trace of her, what did you do?"

"What could I do? There is no father of record on Hadiyyah's birth certificate," he said. "No DNA test has ever been done. Angelina could have claimed anyone was my daughter's father, and without a court order she still could do so in the absence of such tests. So you see, to everyone who might have helped me, I had no real, legal rights. Only the rights Angelina chose to give me. And those rights she had withdrawn when she left with Hadiyyah in the first place."

"If that's the case," Lynley said quietly, reaching for a banana, which he peeled upon his plate, "then kidnapping Hadiyyah might well have been your only option if you were able to find her."

Azhar assessed him steadily, with no indication of protest or outrage. "And had I done such a thing and then taken her back with me to London? Do you know what that would have gained me, Inspector Lynley?" Azhar waited for no reply, going on to say, "Let me tell you what it would have gained me: Angelina's enmity forever. Believe me, I would not have been that stupid no matter how much I wanted—and still want—my daughter home with me."

"Yet someone took her from the marketplace, Azhar. Someone promised her you. Someone wrote a card for her to read. Someone called her *khushi*. The man who took her left a trail behind him, one that led to Michelangelo Di Massimo. And Di Massimo gave us the name of Dwayne Doughty in London."

"Mr. Doughty told me there was no trail," Azhar repeated. "That this was not true . . . that he might have known all along this was not true . . ." His hands shook slightly as he poured more coffee. It was the first indication that something moved within him. "In this . . . I would like to do something to this man, Inspector. But because of what he did or intended to do or tried to do, Angelina and I have finally made peace. This terrible fear that we would lose Hadiyyah . . . It brought about something good in the end."

Lynley wondered how a child's kidnapping could truly result in something good, but he inclined his head for Azhar to continue.

"We have come to agree that Hadiyyah needs both of her parents," he said, "and that both of her parents should be in her life."

"How will this be effected with you in London and Angelina in Lucca?" Lynley asked. "Forgive me for saying it, but her situation at Fattoria di Santa Zita seems fixed at this point."

"It is. Angelina and Lorenzo will marry soon, after the birth of their child. But Angelina agrees that Hadiyyah will spend all her holidays with me in London."

"Will that be enough for you?"

"It will never be enough," he admitted. "But at least I can find peace in the arrangement. She'll come to me the first of July."

SOUTH HACKNEY
LONDON

Barbara found Bryan Smythe's place of business in the same location where she found his house. This was not far from Victoria Park, in a terrace that looked ready for the wrecking ball. The houses were built of the ubiquitous London brick, outstandingly unwashed in this case. Where homes weren't looking in danger of imminent collapse, they were streaked with one hundred years of grime and guano, and the wood of windows and doors was split and rotting. However, Barbara discovered soon enough that all of this was clever camouflage. For

Bryan Smythe, as it happened, owned six of the dwellings in a row and although the curtains that hung in their windows looked like the ill wishes of an envious sibling, once inside the door everything altered.

He was prepared for her visit, of course. Emily Cass had alerted him. His first words to Barbara were "You're the Met, I presume," and although he took in her appearance from head to toe, his facial expression didn't alter when he read her tee-shirt's message of *No Toads Need to Pucker Up*. Barbara clocked this. He was going to be good at dissimulation, she decided. He added, "DS Barbara Havers. That's right, isn't it?"

She said, "Last time I looked," and elbowed her way into his house.

The place opened up like a gallery in both directions, with various large canvases of modern art on the walls and bits of metal sculpture depicting God only knew what writhing on tables, with sparse leather furniture and tasteful rugs beneath which a hardwood floor gleamed. The man himself was nothing to look at and less to talk about: ordinary except for his dandruff, which was extraordinary and copious. One could have cross-country skied on his shoulders. He was as pale as someone who rubbed elbows regularly with the walking dead, and he appeared malnourished. Too busy hacking into people's lives to eat, Barbara reckoned.

"Nice digs," she told him as she looked round the place. "Business must be booming."

"There are good times and bad," he replied. "I offer independent technological expertise to various companies and occasionally to individuals in need. I deal in making sure their systems are secure."

Barbara rolled her eyes. "Please. I'm not here to waste your time or mine. If you know my name, you know what's up. So let's get to the point: I'm more interested in Doughty than I am in you, Bryan. C'n I call you Bryan? I hope so." She sauntered into the gallery space and stood before a canvas painted red with a single blue stripe at the bottom. It looked like a proposal for a new EU road sign. She decided her preference was to remain in ignorance when it came to the subject of modern art. She turned back to Smythe. "Obviously, I c'n bring you down, but at present, I'm not ready to play that card."

"You can try what you want," Smythe told her blithely. He'd shut the door behind her and he'd shot the bolt home. She reckoned this had more to do with the value of the art on the walls than her presence, though. He went on to say, "Let's look at the facts. You shut me down, I'm back up in twenty-four hours."

"I expect that's true," she admitted. "But your regular customers might not like reading the news—or hearing about it on the telly—that their 'technological security expert' has had his gear carted off to the techies at New Scotland Yard for a lengthy scrutiny that doesn't bode well. I can make that happen. You can, as you say, set yourself up with a whole new system before our forensic tech blokes can unpack your belongings in some cobwebbed basement in Victoria Street. But I expect the serious hit your business will take as a result of the publicity might require a rather long recovery period."

He eyed her. She eyed his art. She picked up a sculpture that sat on a table of solid glass and she tried to make out what the thing was. Bird? Plane? Prehistoric monster? She looked from it to him and said, "Should I know what this bloody thing is?"

"You should know enough to be careful with it."

She made a feint at dropping it. He took a quick step forward. She winked at him. "Us rozzers, Bryan? Believe me, we are thick as shoe soles when it comes to art. We are bulls in the bloody you-know-what, especially the blokes who come to cart off one's belongings for inspection."

"My art has nothing to do with—"

"The job? This technological expertising you do? I expect that might be the case, but the blokes who show up with court orders in their grubby hands . . . ?" She placed the sculpture carefully on the table. "They don't know that, do they?"

"What sort of court order do you actually expect—"

"Emily Cass gave you up. You know that, Bryan. Pushed into a corner, she did not exactly come out swinging. You're into bank records, phone records, mobile records, travel records, credit card records, and God only knows what other records. Do you really believe the local magistrate isn't going to want to know what's going on when you sit down at your keyboard and get in touch with your embedded mates? Where is that keyboard, by the way? Does a magic button somewhere do the business and a wall swings aside to reveal basement stairs?"

"You've seen too many films."

"For my sins," she admitted. "So what's it to be?"

He thought about this. He wouldn't know that she'd already determined to talk to Azhar before she reported to Lynley or to anyone else about *any* of her findings. He wouldn't know that she'd decided she had to see her Pakistani neighbour in person in order to look him squarely in the face. He wouldn't know that she could not for a moment believe that Azhar would endanger his daughter, frighten his daughter, or do anything else to his daughter in aid of either keeping her or getting her away from her mother. But those tickets to Pakistan suggested the worst and until she spoke to him and read whatever she could read from his expression or in his eyes, Barbara's level of desperation was such that even staying calm in the presence of this bloke Smythe was taking every resource she had.

He finally said, "Come with me. At least I can enlighten you on one thing."

He crossed the gallery space and slid open two silent pocket doors. Beyond them, a room similar in size to the gallery looked through a bank of pricey double-glazed windows out into a garden. This was brilliant with spring flowers and defined on its boundaries by ornamental cherry trees in bloom. A perfect lawn held a white gazebo. A rectangular pond supporting lily pads lay in front of this, a fountain at its centre.

The room into which he walked was his working space, as far from the cinematic version of a computer whiz's lair as could be imagined. In films, the hacker holed up in a basement where the only light came from the monitors of the multitude of computers that encircled him. In Bryan Smythe's reality there was a laptop on a fine stainless steel desk that faced his garden. Next to the laptop, three memory sticks sat in a holder. Another holder held sharpened pencils; another held pens. Next to the laptop were a pristine legal pad, one expensive designer fountain pen, and a printer.

Aside from that, the room morphed into a high-end kitchen at one end and a higher-end entertainment centre at the other. Speakers in the ceiling spoke of surround sound. Everything spoke of big money.

Barbara whistled soundlessly. She said, "Nice garden," and went to look out of the window while her mind whirled into action and she tried to decide how best to wring the information from him. "Thinking of the Chelsea Flower Show, are we?"

"I like to have something pleasant to look at," he said, and the slight emphasis he put upon the adjective indicated that Barbara wasn't a sight for eyes even mildly sore. "While I work, that is," he added. "Hence the positioning of the desk."

"Always a good idea," she acknowledged. "I expect you'd like to keep things that way."

"Meaning?"

"Meaning it's decision time for you, and let me be plain in case I haven't been so far. Doughty is the fish we're after. We're looking at him for a kidnapping charge, something he orchestrated to occur in Lucca, Italy. It involves a nine-year-old English girl who was snatched by her mum last November and carted off to eat copious mounds of pasta, if you get my meaning. He was hired to locate her but he did more than that. He located her, claimed he hadn't done, and then arranged to have her snatched. And then, he had you wipe every record clean. These would be all the records having anything to do with the nine-year-old girl, the original snatching, et cetera, et cetera. Are we on the same page so far?"

His mouth made a disparaging moue. She took this for acknowledgement and charged on.

"You confirm this, and our relationship—that would be yours and mine, and believe me I've been chuffed by it beyond my wildest dreams—is over. You refuse to confirm . . . ?" She waggled her hand. "The local rozzers, the local magistrate, and the Met'll be wild to make your acquaintance."

"So are you saying," he said, "that if I confirm your imaginative theories about this nine-year-old—and I'm not confirming anything, by the way—my name does *not* get handed over to the Met at once? Or to the local police? Or to anyone?"

"Bryan, you are one clever lad. That is *exactly* what I'm saying. So what's it going to be? Admittedly, Doughty isn't going to want your services after this, but you can't blame him for that, eh? Small price to pay for your continuing ability to do business at all, you ask me."

He shook his head. He walked over to gaze at his garden. He finally turned back to her and said, "What the bloody hell kind of cop are you?"

She was taken aback by the force of loathing behind his words, but she managed to keep her face a perfect blank as she said, "Meaning?"

"You think I don't see where this is heading?"

"Where?"

"Today what you want is confirmation and tomorrow it's cash. Not wired to some account on the Isle of Man or tucked away in Guernsey or God knows where but handed over in an envelope in tens and twenties and fifties and next week more and next month more and always this 'D'you really want the Met to know about you, mate?' You're dirtier than I am, you miserable cow. And if you think I'm going to—"

"Rein in the ponies," Barbara said to the man, although her heart was pounding in her temples. "I told you I want Doughty, and Doughty's who I want."

"And your word on that is good, is it?" Bryan laughed, a high whinny that spoke of how desperate *he* was feeling. It came to Barbara that they were like two Wild West ne'er-do-wells out in the street in front of the saloon, both of them having drawn their rusty pistols at the exact same moment, both of them trying to work out how to walk away from the confrontation instead of ending up in the dust with a bullet in the chest.

She said, "Looks to me like we've got each other by the you-know-whats, Bryan. But between us, I think I've got the better grip. I'm telling you for the last time that I want Doughty and only Doughty and that's an end to this. Either you go for that or you decide you'd rather risk it by escorting me to the door and seeing what I'll do next."

His jaw moved, teeth biting down on something unpalatable. She understood. Her teeth were doing much the same thing.

He said, "You have your confirmation. I wiped Doughty's records. Everything having to do with a bloke called Michelangelo Di Massimo. Everything having to do with a bloke called Taymullah Azhar. Emails, bank statements, phone calls, mobile calls, wire transfers of money, websites looked at, anything discovered via search engines having to do with Lucca, Pisa, or anywhere else in Italy. Whatever you can think of, it was dealt with. As deeply as I and a few . . . a few colleagues here and there could go. All right?"

"One more thing."

"Christ, what else?"

"When?"

"When what?"

"When did all these records begin?"

"What does it matter? I went back in time and got it all."

"Right. Brilliant. Got that in a trap. What I'm asking is the date all these records having to do with Italy got wiped."

"What's that got to do with—"

"Believe me. It does."

Astoundingly, then, Bryan went to something worthy of Dickens to sort this one out. He opened the desk and brought out—of all things—a pocket diary. He began to leaf through it, back into time. He found nothing. He rooted in his desk and brought out another. As he did so, Barbara felt her stomach tighten into a ball.

"Last December," he said. "The fifth. That's when it all began."

God, Barbara thought. In advance of Hadiyyah's kidnapping in Lucca. In advance of everything. She said, " 'It'? What's 'it' supposed to be?"

A small smile, containing just enough triumph to tell Barbara she'd won the battle but lost the war. "I expect you can work that one out," he said. To this he added, "If you're planning your next stop to be in Bow, then you'd be wise to plan on something else as well."

"And that would be?" she asked, although her lips were barely working at this point.

"A fail-safe position, a backup plan, whatever you want to call it," he told her. "Dwayne's not stupid and he's going to have one."

"And you know this because . . ."

"Because he always does."

BOW

LONDON

Dwayne Doughty was not surprised to see her. Barbara was herself not surprised to discover that this was the case. The Doughty-Cass-Smythe operation had been up and running for quite some time. They might give each other up like third-rate burglars hoping to strike a deal with the cops, but they would also let each other know that they had done so. She readied herself to do battle with the man. She readied herself to see what the private investigator's fail-safe position was going to be.

He said to her, "Very good time from South Hackney," just in case she needed the full score on exactly whose loyalties were going to lie where. He looked at his watch. "Quarter of an hour. Did you hit all the lights green or did you use a siren?"

"I think this is about the jig being up," Barbara told him. "And as there's no music, we're not talking about dancing."

"Your way with metaphors continues to astound," Doughty said. "But one of the reasons Bryan Smythe has at one time or another been in my employ has to do with his talent at wiping away any sign that he's actually been in my employ."

"Does this mean you're assuming the Met doesn't employ blokes whose talents match the redoubtable Bryan's?" Barbara asked him. "Does it mean you've somehow jumped to the conclusion that the Met has no way to contact the cops in Italy who will come up with equally talented blokes who c'n deal with Michelangelo Di Massimo's records? You seem to believe that no stone has been left unturned by Bryan's magical power to erase your past manoeuvres, mate, but here's what I've learned from years of dealing with villains of every make and variety: No one thinks of everything and the thing about stones and turning them over . . . ? There's always a pebble nearby that goes unnoticed."

He gave a little salute. "Once more with the metaphor. You do amaze." He leaned back in his chair. It was the sort that gave way when pressure was put upon its back, and Barbara sent a fleeting prayer heavenward that he'd lean too far, fall over, and bash himself senseless on the floor. No such luck. But what he did was roll the chair over to a filing cabinet and slide open its bottom drawer. From this he took a memory stick. He said, "You can go that route with the cops in Italy, the tech experts at the Met, and the tech experts in Italy. But it isn't something that I'd advise. To attempt your own skill at metaphor: That's a road I wouldn't drive a donkey cart on."

When Barbara saw the memory stick, she reckoned they were at the fail-safe that Bryan Smythe had mentioned. There was nothing for it but to see what Doughty had on it, and she knew that all she had to do was wait for the revelation.

He gestured affably for her to sit. He offered coffee, tea, a chocolate digestive in an irritatingly specious display of manners. Her response to this was "Get to the bloody point," and she remained standing.

"As you will," he said, and he plugged the memory stick into his computer.

He was well prepared. It took him a two-breath moment to find what he wanted. He tapped three or four keys, turned the monitor in her direction, and said, "Enjoy the show."

It was a film in which the stars were Dwayne himself and Taymullah Azhar. Its setting was here in Doughty's office. Its dialogue comprised Doughty revealing every bit of information on Hadiyyah's whereabouts in Italy as discovered by Michelangelo Di Massimo. Fattoria di Santa Zita came first, in the hills above a town called Lucca, in the home of one Lorenzo Mura, whose apparent idiocy in the arena of wiring money from Lucca to London so that Angelina would be able to finance her escape from Azhar had left a trail not of breadcrumbs but of veritable pieces of foccacia. A secondary bank account this was, as Dwayne explained to Azhar, in the name not of Angelina but of her sister Bathsheba, on whose passport Angelina departed the country on the fifteenth of November.

Barbara heard her heart pounding in her ears. But she said casually, "And your point is what, Dwayne? Way I recall things, we know all this. So you want me to know you told Azhar when I wasn't present? Am I supposed to be impressed?"

Doughty paused the film, freezing it on a single image.

"You don't look thick," he said, "but I'm getting the impression that your eyesight is failing. Look at the date of the film."

And there it was. The seventeenth of December. Barbara said nothing, although what she felt was alarm. It shot through her arms and down into her fingers. She tried to keep her face impassive although she knew if she tried to raise her arms, she'd display the degree to which her hands were shaking.

Doughty flipped back through a diary on his desk, a large one that displayed every hour of the workday and every individual he'd seen. "You're a busy bird, I reckon, with a social calendar that would slay an It girl, so let me help you. Our final meeting—this would be you, the professor, and yours truly here—took place on November thirtieth. If you need the math on it, this meeting you've just watched between that lofty bloke and me happened seventeen days later. To be additionally helpful—since that's the kind of individual I am—let me jog your memory about one minor detail of that final meeting the three of us had. I handed the professor my card. I invited him to get in touch if there was *any* other way I could be helpful to him. For his part? The professor got the message."

"Bollocks," Barbara said. "What message?"

"I had a feeling about our professor, Sergeant. Desperate times, measures, and you know the rest. I thought I could be of further assistance to him. If he was interested, that is. It turned out he was." Dwayne leaned into the keyboard and made a few adjustments with the mouse as well. "Here's how he expressed himself . . . and his interest, as it happened, two days later."

The setting and the characters were the same. The dialogue, though, was entirely different. In the world of critical exegesis of cinema, it would have been breathlessly described as "electrifying dialogue." In the world of reality, it was damning evidence. Barbara watched in gut-wrenching silence as Taymullah Azhar broached the subject of kidnapping his own daughter. Could it be done? Could this previously mentioned Michelangelo Di Massimo somehow arrange it? Could the Italian get to know the movements of Lorenzo Mura, Angelina, and Hadiyyah well? If he could, was there a way to take Hadiyyah from her mother with a promise that she would be returned to her father?

And on and on went the discussion between Azhar and Dwayne

Doughty. On the film, Doughty listened sympathetically: fingers steepled at his chin, nodding when nodding was called for. The bloke was the very image of caution as, no doubt, in his head the till was ringing up how much money he was going to make if he got involved in an international kidnapping scheme.

Doughty said on film in what bordered on religious tones, "I can only put you in touch with Mr. Di Massimo, Professor Azhar. What you and he decide between you . . . ? Obviously, my work for you is finished and I would be no part of anything from this point forward."

Oh, too bloody right, Barbara scoffed. When the film was over, she said, "This is a load of bollocks."

Dwayne wasn't affected by this. He said pleasantly, "Alas. It is what it is. My point is this: You take me down, I take him down, Barbara. May I call you Barbara? I have a feeling we're growing closer here."

She had a feeling violence was in the offing and it would be demonstrated by her jumping over the bloke's desk and throttling him. She said, "The whole kidnap idea is rubbish on toast. Once Hadiyyah was found by this Di Massimo bloke, all Azhar had to do was show up on Angelina's doorstep unexpectedly and demand his rights as her father. With Hadiyyah thrilled to bits to see him, with Azhar standing on her front porch or whatever the hell they have over there, what was Angelina Upman going to do then? Run from one *fattoria*—whatever that is—to another for the rest of her life?"

"That would have been sensible," Doughty admitted graciously. "But haven't you noticed—and I would think you have, in your line of work—that when passions become inflamed, good sense tends to fly right out the window?"

"Kidnapping Hadiyyah would have gained Azhar nothing."

"In the normal garden kidnapping, how true. But let's suppose—you and I, Barbara—that this wasn't a garden kidnapping at all. Let's suppose the professor's brainchild was to have Hadiyyah kidnapped because he knew very well that the first thing her mummy would do in that case was exactly what her mummy did: come to London with the boyfriend in tow, hot in her demands to have her child back." Doughty raised his hands to his mouth in mock horror. "But when she gets to London, it is only to find that the professor has not the slightest idea that the child is missing. My God, she's been *kidnapped*? the professor says. Search my house, search my office, search my lab, search my life, search where you like because I did not do this . . . and all the rest. While all along the plan is in motion for Michelangelo Di Massimo to snatch the kid, to stow her some place very safe and very out of sight, and then—when the time is right—to release her in an equally very safe location where she can be 'found' by someone who has seen the news of her scurrilous kidnapping. Meantime, her dad is off to Italy to assist in the search, demonstrating his anguish by putting handbills up in every village and town, establishing himself as bereft beyond measure, having previously established an ironclad alibi for the time of her disappearance through means of a conference he was long scheduled to attend in Berlin. When the child is found, the re-union is emotional, blessed, sanctified, and all the rest. And Azhar has access to his daughter once again, this access blessed by Angelina."

"Ridiculous," Barbara said. "Why go to all this trouble, Dwayne? If you'd found Hadiyyah, why would Azhar want her kidnapped? Why would he terrify her or put her at risk or do *anything* at all besides show up one day and demand access to her as her father? He knows where she is. He knows from whatever he's found out about Mura that she's not going anywhere."

"You've made that point already," Doughty admitted. "But there's one small thing you're forgetting here."

"Which is what, exactly?"

"The larger picture."

"Which is what, exactly?"

"Pakistan."

"What? Is your claim actually going to be that Azhar's plan—"

"I'm claiming nothing here. I'm merely asking you to follow the dance steps because you know the music. You aren't stupid, despite what you might feel towards our brooding professor. He had her snatched, and when the time was right, he was going to take her to Pakistan and disappear."

"He's a bloody professor of—"

"And bloody professors don't commit crimes? Is that what you want to tell me? Dear sergeant, you and I both know that crimes are not the especial province of the unwashed masses. And you and I both know that if this particular professor took his daughter to Pakistan, the door of possibility of Mummy's getting her back would be slammed for years, locked with a key, and Angelina would be left banging on it till her fists were bloody. Trying to get a kid from the kid's father in Pakistan? The kid's Pakistani father? The kid's Muslim father? Exactly how many rights do you think a mere Englishwoman would have, *if* she was even able to find him in the first place?"

Barbara felt the persuasive truth of all this, but accepting that truth . . . ? She knew there was another explanation. She also knew that to sit in the office and to argue the cause of that explanation to Doughty was a useless endeavour. Only a conversation with Azhar was going to shed light on everything. Doughty was as dirty as the inside of a Hoover. That was the truth that she had to cling to.

It was as if he'd read her mind, though, when Doughty next spoke. "The professor is dirty, Sergeant Havers," he said. He pushed away from his desk and returned the memory stick to his filing cabinet, which he then locked. He turned back to Barbara and held out his wrists in mock surrender. "Now . . . You can cart me off to the nick, and I can go through this all again for whoever's interested in listening. Or you can start building a case where it's meant to be built: right in the professor's front garden."

VICTORIA
LONDON

Lynley arrived in London by early afternoon, weathering a crowded flight from Pisa in which he'd suffered his six-foot-two-inch frame being jackknifed into the middle seat with a rosary-saying nun on one side of him and an overweight businessman with a very large newspaper on the other. Prior to leaving the vicinity of Lucca, he'd had a final word with Angelina Upman. She confirmed every detail of Azhar's story on the subject of their parting on the previous night. Forgiveness was the theme of what had passed between them, as were future arrangements for Hadiyyah so that she could continue to be part of the London life of the father she adored. Only Lorenzo Mura was opposed to these plans. He didn't like Azhar, he didn't trust Azhar, and Angelina was a fool to consider allowing Azhar access to her daughter.

"Darling, she's Hari's daughter as well" did not soothe Mura. He stormed from the room breathing the fire of angry Italian into the air. Angelina sighed. "It's not going to be easy," she told Lynley, "but I want to do what's right for us all."

In her presence, Lynley had given thought to the toll this entire affair had taken upon Angelina. He reckoned she was normally a beautiful woman, but the circumstances she'd been caught in had temporarily robbed her of her looks, leaving her gaunt, lank-haired, and hollow-eyed. She needed to recover and she needed to do so as quickly as possible to safeguard the life she carried within her. He wanted to tell her this, but she would know it already. So he said to her, merely, "Be well," and he departed.

In London, he went directly to the Yard. There, he met with Isabelle Ardery to make his report to her. It was a good result, culminating in the safe return of Hadiyyah Upman to her mother. The affair was in the hands of the Italian police now, and on the Lucca end of things, there was nothing more to be done as the public minister would determine what to do with the evidence uncovered by Chief Inspector Salvatore Lo Bianco and whoever followed him as head of the case.

"The investigation was taken away from him yesterday," Lynley explained. "He and the public minister didn't see eye to eye on things, as it happened."

Isabelle picked up a phone, saying to him, "Let's have Barbara's report, then," and she summoned Barbara to join them.

Lynley sighed and shook his head inwardly when he saw the sergeant's appearance. Her hair was still a chopped-up mess, and she'd returned to a manner of dress certain to set Isabelle's teeth on edge. At least on this day, she'd eschewed a slogan-embossed tee-shirt in favour of a jersey. Its zigzag horizontal pattern of neon colours, however, did nothing to enhance her charms. Her trousers—baggy at the seat and the knees—looked like something her grandmother had discarded.

He glanced at Isabelle. She looked at Havers, looked at him, and admirably controlled herself. She said, "Sergeant," and indicated a seat.

Barbara shot Lynley a look that he couldn't read, although she seemed to think she was being called onto the carpet for something. He couldn't blame her for that. Rarely was she summoned into a superior's office for any other thing. He said, "I've just brought the guv up-to-date on Italy," and Isabelle said, "As to the London end of things, Sergeant . . . ?"

Havers looked relieved. She said by way of introduction, "Way I see it, guv, things're going to come down to one slimy bloke's word against another slimy bloke's word." She balanced the ankle of a red-trainer-shod foot on her knee and displayed a length of white sock printed with cupcakes. Lynley heard Isabelle's sigh. Havers went on. Doughty, she told them, did not deny employing one Pisan called Michelangelo Di Massimo in an attempt to trace Hadiyyah and her mother. He claimed he had done so on behalf of Azhar, and that was the extent of what he'd done. He said that *whatever* money flowed from a London bank to an Italian bank—into the account of Di Massimo—was merely in payment for this service. But it proved to be a service that had gained him nothing, according to Doughty. Di Massimo had declared that the trail went dead early on. Havers said, "I reckon we have to decide which one of these blokes is the real liar. Since Di Massimo's got the Italian cops on his back, could be we should just wait and see what comes of that."

Isabelle hadn't won her position as detective superintendent by failing to see where the net of an investigation had one or two gaping holes. She said, "At what point did Taymullah Azhar learn the name of this Italian private investigator, Sergeant?"

To which Havers's reply was, "Never, guv, as far as I know. At least not before the inspector here sussed things out with the Italian coppers. And that's really the crux of the matter, isn't it?" Before Isabelle could answer, Havers continued with "SO12's been onto Azhar, by the way. He's clean."

"SO12?" Lynley and Isabelle said simultaneously. Isabelle continued. "What have SO12 to do with things, Sergeant?"

Havers explained that she'd been intent on exploring every single avenue and—"Let's admit it, guv, since you just brought him up, one of those avenues was Azhar"—she'd had a talk with Chief Inspector Harry Streener to see if his team had been looking into Azhar for any reason. Azhar had been in Berlin at the time of the kidnapping, and that didn't look good, so she had figured if there was anything questionable going on, SO12 would have found it. "Azhar's a microbiologist, guv. Azhar's Muslim. Azhar's Pakistani. To the SO12 blokes . . . You know how they are. I reckoned if there was anything to be turned up about him, they would have done the spadework."

But there had been nothing, Havers said. Her conclusion was the same as DI Lynley's. This entire mess was better left in the hands of the Italian police.

"Get me your final written report then, Barbara," Isabelle said. "You as well, Thomas." And she signalled an end to their meeting by gesturing towards the door.

Before Lynley could follow Barbara through it, though, Isabelle said his name once again. He turned and she lifted a finger that told him to stay where he was. A nod instructed him to shut the door.

He returned to the seat he'd taken. He watched the detective superintendent. He'd come to know how expert she was at hiding things—particularly the workings of her mind and her heart—so he waited to hear what she wished to say, knowing how unlikely was the possibility that he could guess it in advance.

She pulled open the bottom drawer of her desk. He took a sharp breath. Isabelle was a drinker, and she knew he knew this. She believed she had the problem under control. He did not. She was aware of his belief, but she was also aware of the tacit understanding between them: He would not betray her as long as she kept her drinking away from Victoria Street and away from the job should the job take her elsewhere. He could see the slight tremor in her hands, however, and he said her name.

She shot him a look. "I'm not entirely stupid, Tommy. I have things under control" was her expected remark. Instead of a bottle, she brought out of the drawer a folded tabloid, which she opened, smoothed, and began to flip through.

He could see it was *The Source*, the most scurrilous of the London rags. He felt wary when he considered the implications behind Isabelle's having stowed it in her desk as well as her dismissal of Barbara Havers and her indication that she wished to speak to him alone. These were unfortunate signs. They transformed themselves into ill realities when she found what she was looking for and turned the paper towards him so that he could see for himself what was causing her concern.

He reached in his jacket for his reading glasses, although the truth was that he didn't need them, at least for the headline of the story: *Love Rat Dad's Ties to the Met* spread across the top of pages four and five. Accompanying this was a photograph of Taymullah Azhar inset onto another, larger photograph of some sort of brouhaha in a London street. This involved a shouting teenage boy in a school uniform, an enraged man who appeared to be in his late sixties, a frightened-looking woman in a *shalwar kameez* and headscarf, and Barbara Havers. Havers was in the act of attempting to get the old man to release his hold on the boy; the headscarf woman was in the act of attempting to get the boy away from the man. The man himself was in the act of trying to stuff the boy into a car, its back door open and waiting for him.

Lynley scanned the story, which was typical of *The Source*. It bore a by-line that he knew only too well: *Mitchell Corsico*. It contained the breathless sort of writing that was *The Source*'s stock-in-trade. This was of the hot-breaking-news variety in which the named reporter had uncovered a close connection between a detective sergeant from the Met and the Love Rat Dad whose daughter had recently been kidnapped in Italy. This female officer from the Met would be, gentle readers, a presence in the life of the Love Rat Dad in addition to the deserted wife in Ilford *and* the lover who had borne the man's child. They live cheek by jowl, as it happens, in a north London neighbourhood where they keep separate residences on the very same property under the watchful eye of neighbours only too happy to express their opinions on the topic of the mild-mannered university professor and what was turning out to be a veritable stable of women willing to partner him.

The article followed the same pattern as so many stories featured in the daily tabloids. Their meat and potatoes had for generations consisted of destroying reputations. They built someone up one week as a hero or a sympathetic victim or a luck-struck winner of a national lottery or a grand success in the arts or an admirable self-made man . . . only to tear him down the next week when every slighted friend or colleague he had in his life crawled out of their personal rubbish tip to report "new facts" about him. Just to bring him down a few pegs, of course.

Lynley looked up when he completed his reading of the article. He wasn't quite sure where to go with any remark he might make because he wasn't quite sure what Isabelle knew about Barbara and Taymullah Azhar. Nor, he had to admit, was he.

She said, "What am I to make of this, Tommy?"

He took off his glasses and returned them to his jacket pocket. "It looks to me like an officer of the police coming to the aid of an adolescent boy being struck about the head by an older man."

"Oh, I can see that. I can even tell myself that all this photo depicts is a moment in which DS Barbara Havers happened upon a conflict in the street and stepped in to sort it like the Good Samaritan we know her to be. I could do all that happily, but what prevents me is the fact that this adolescent boy is the son of Taymullah Azhar. Not to mention the fact that the older man is the father of Taymullah Azhar. I'm not to make a coincidence of that, am I, Tommy?"

"The picture could have a thousand and one interpretations, Isabelle, as can the article. Anyone reading it and looking at the picture can see that much."

"Naturally. And one of those interpretations is that Barbara Havers may very well have a vested interest—a deeply personal and not an objective professional interest—in matters that should not concern someone involved in an investigation."

"You can't possibly think that Barbara—"

"I don't know what the hell to think about Barbara," Isabelle cut in sharply. "But I do know what I see with my eyes and I do know what I hear with my ears, and—"

"'Hear'? From whom? What? About Barbara?" Lynley studied her for a moment before he went on. She watched him do so and she met his gaze steadily. He finally looked away from her and at the paper still spread on her desk.

Lynley knew she wasn't a tabloid reader. He didn't flatter himself in thinking he knew everything about her from the months they'd spent naked in each other's beds, but he did know that much. She didn't read tabloids. So how had this one fallen into her hands? He said, "Where did you get this?" with a gesture at the paper.

"That's hardly as important as the 'news' it contains."

Lynley glanced over his shoulder at the closed door and what lay beyond it. And then, quite simply, he knew. "John Stewart," he said. "And now he's waiting to see what you intend to do about her. While all along what you should be intending to do is something about John."

"I plan to deal with John in due time, Tommy. Just now we're dealing with the issue of Barbara."

"There is no issue of Barbara. She may know Azhar, but as to there being the slightest indication of a romantic involvement, a physical involvement, *any* involvement between them other than simple friendship . . . It's just not on, Isabelle."

She considered this for a very long moment. Outside her office, the sounds of a typical day's activities were ongoing. Someone called out for "a copy of that article on peat preservation Philip was going on about," and a trolley rattled by. Inside her office, they engaged in a stare-down which Isabelle finally broke by speaking.

"Tommy, we all have blind spots," she said.

"Barbara doesn't," he returned as firmly as he could. "Not in this matter."

She looked infinitely sad when she dismissed him with the reply, "I'm not talking about Barbara, Inspector."

VICTORIA
LONDON

He wasn't as certain about Barbara Havers as his words had been. He wasn't, in fact, certain about anything. For this reason, he read the activity reports Barbara had turned in during the time she'd worked on John Stewart's team, and from there he went to spend ten minutes with Harry Streener in SO12. The fact that now two CID officers were interested in SO12's concerns about one Taymullah Azhar gave Streener pause, but Lynley soothed him with a claim that loose ends were being tied up upon the request of Detective Superintendent Ardery and he was the bloke given the job of tying.

Thus Lynley discovered the airline tickets to Pakistan in very short order. Thus Lynley also discovered to his dismay that Barbara was withholding information. He didn't particularly want to think what all of this meant: about Taymullah Azhar and the kidnapping of his daughter as well as about DS Barbara Havers. But he knew he had to speak to Barbara at once. For the reality she needed to face was simple: If he had learned she was withholding information about Taymullah Azhar, it stood to reason that John Stewart would unearth this fact sooner or later and turn it over to Isabelle. At that point Isabelle's hands would be tied and so would his own be. He couldn't let that happen.

He found Barbara at work at her desk, every inch of her announcing that she was nothing less than a nose-to-the-grindstone officer intent upon doing her duty. He said to her quietly, "I need a word, Barbara," and he could see from her immediate expression of alarm that he'd perfectly telegraphed to her the seriousness of the situation.

He left her and went to the lifts. When she joined him there, he pushed for the fourth floor. He led her to Peeler's. Some tables were occupied with the last of the lunchtime crowd, but most were empty. He selected one far away from the remaining hubbub of the place, and by the time they had reached the table, sat, and ordered coffees, he could tell that the sergeant was as rattled as he wanted her to be.

He said, "John Stewart's given Isabelle a copy of *The Source*. There's a story in it written by Mitch Corsico—"

"I went to the school, sir," Barbara told him hastily. "Sayyid's comprehensive. I'd had word from Corsico that he was intent on interviewing the kid, and I knew Sayyid would spew all sorts of rubbish about Azhar. It wasn't only about Azhar that I went to the school, though. I knew whatever *The Source* might print would hurt everyone: his mum, his dad, Sayyid himself. I thought—I *believed*—I had to—"

"That's not what I want to talk to you about, Barbara," Lynley told her. "John has his reasons for handing over the tabloid, and I expect we'll discover what they are sooner rather than later. The point is that you're in this too far, that fact is playing itself out in the paper, and that makes your work suspect."

Havers said nothing as their coffee was delivered to the table. When cups and saucers had been laid before them and the coffee poured, she did her business with the milk and sugar and set the spoon aside but didn't drink. She said, "I hate that bloke."

"You've reason," Lynley told her. "I wouldn't waste the breath to argue otherwise. But you've fallen into John's hands with the way this business of Hadiyyah's kidnapping has played out. So if you've given him any other evidence of your lack of objectivity in the investigation, then I think it's to your benefit to tell me now before he discovers it and reports it to Isabelle."

He waited then. It was, he knew, a do-or-die moment for Havers, one that was going to define what the nature of their partnership was and what, if anything, he could do to help her out of the mess into which she seemed to have got herself. It was obvious to him that DI John Stewart had loosed the dogs of an informal investigation upon her. She had to see that, and she also had to see that only a complete display of the cards she was holding would allow him to develop a strategy on her behalf.

Come on, Barbara, was what he thought. Move yourself in the right direction.

At first, he thought she was going to do just that. She said, "Sir, I lied about my mum." And she told him of a tale she'd spun for Isabelle in order to buy herself time from work. It was about her mother's having taken a fall. She gave him an account of everything fictitious that had followed the ostensible fall: from the ambulance service to the private hospital and all points in between. She also told him of the use she had made of her time while she was supposed to be engaged in activities assigned to her by DI Stewart. She gave an account of her dealings with Doughty and of her confrontations with that man's associates. On the surface, it appeared that she was telling him everything. But she said nothing about airline tickets to Pakistan, and Lynley knew this damned her.

That knowledge felt like a crack in his chest. He hadn't actually understood until that moment how important his partnership with Barbara was to him. She was at most times a maddening woman whose personal habits set his teeth on edge. But she had always been a decent cop with a very good mind, and God knew he enjoyed her fractious company. And it had to be said: She had also saved his life on a night when he hadn't cared in the least if that life was going to be taken from him by a serial killer.

It wasn't so much that he believed he owed Barbara Havers something, though. It was that he cared deeply for the bloody woman. She was more than a partner. She was a friend. As such, she was like the other people in his small circle of trusted intimates: She was part of the fabric of his life, and he wanted to keep that fabric as whole as he could make it considering the rent that he'd had to repair when Helen had been torn from him.

She talked on and on. Her monologue had the appearance of the unburdening of one soul to another. He waited and hoped she would be totally frank with him. When she wasn't, he had no further choice.

He said at the end of her remarks, "Pakistan, Barbara. You've left that out."

She took a slurp of her coffee. Then she took three more gulps in rapid succession and looked round Peeler's for a top-up. She said casually, "Pakistan, sir?"

He said, "Airline tickets. One in the name of Taymullah Azhar. The other in the name of Hadiyyah Upman. Purchased in March for a flight in July. You've not mentioned that, but SO12 was happy to."

Her gaze met his. He tried to read her face, but he couldn't tell if what he was looking at was defiance or chagrin. She said, "You bloody checked my work. I can't believe that."

"SO12 raised questions. In my mind and, more important, in Isabelle's."

"'Isabelle,'" she repeated. "Not 'the guv' and not 'the superintendent.' I reckon I know what *that* means, don't I?" Her words were bitter.

"I reckon you don't," Lynley told her evenly. "SO12 was my own initiative."

They were eyeball to eyeball for a moment. "Sorry, sir," she said at last, looking away from him.

"Accepted," he replied. "As to the airline tickets . . . ? You must see how it's going to look when it comes out that you withheld this information. If I discovered it with a simple call upon Harry Streener, then it stands to reason that DI Stewart's going to uncover the very same thing."

"I c'n handle Stewart."

"That's where you go wrong. You want to 'handle' him and you think you can 'handle' him because I daresay you believe the truth will out and the truth will set you free and whatever other aphorisms you'd like to apply to this situation."

"The 'truth' is he hates me and everyone knows it, including, pardon me, *Isabelle*, sir. And if we want to look at how she positioned me into working for the bloke so that—as you and I both bloody well know—I'd eventually be kicked back down to uniform when I stepped out of order, then what *I* 'daresay' is we're going to see a master plan at work."

Lynley had not worked as a homicide detective for years to be unaware that Havers was attempting to wrest control of their conversation in order to divert it away from the more crucial matter onto something she could bear to speak about. So he said, "Pakistan, Barbara. Airline tickets. Let's get back to that, shall we? Anything else takes us into the realm of speculation and wastes our time."

She ran a hand through her chopped-up hair. She said, "I don't *know* what it means, all right?"

"Which part? The fact that he's holding tickets to Pakistan, the fact that he purchased them in March when he ostensibly didn't know where his daughter was, or the fact that you've withheld this detail? Which part is the part whose meaning you don't know, Barbara?"

"You're cheesed off," she said. "You've a right to be."

"Don't let's go there. Just answer me."

"I don't know what it means that he bought those tickets."

"He told me she's coming to him in July, Barbara. Spending her holidays with him is the agreement he reached with Angelina once Hadiyyah was safely returned from the convent in the Alps. That first holiday commences in July."

"I still don't know what it means," she insisted. "I want to talk to him. Until he gets back to London, I won't know what his intentions are. Until he can explain himself to me—"

"You're intent on believing whatever he says?" Lynley asked her. "Barbara, you've got to see how mad that is. What you should be doing is what you should have been doing all along: following the money, the money going from Azhar to anyone else."

"He would have paid Doughty for his services in looking for Hadiyyah," she said. "What's that supposed to prove? The man's daughter disappeared with her mum, Inspector. The cops here were doing nothing about it. He had no rights and—"

"The dates of the transfers out of his account are going to tell us volumes," Lynley said. "You know that very well."

"*Anything* can be argued about dates. Azhar paid Doughty when he'd gathered enough money to pay him. It was more expensive than he'd thought it would be, so he made more than one payment. He had to do it . . . over a period of months, say. And what he paid him *for* was to hire someone over in Italy to find his daughter. Everything else was on Doughty's head."

"For the love of God, Barbara—"

"Doughty saw a way to make more money out of this. Hold her long enough to make everyone desperate, make a demand for ransom a few weeks from now, and Bob's the rest of it."

Lynley sat back in his chair. He stared at her, his breath taken with her self-delusion. He said, "You can't possibly believe that. There *was* no demand for money, and Azhar's damned by those airline tickets."

"He bought them to reassure himself that she would be found. It was like hedging his bets."

"For Christ's sake, she hadn't even been kidnapped from the *mercato* in Lucca when he bought them."

"There's an explanation. I'm going to find it."

"I can't let you decide—"

She grabbed his arm fiercely. "I need to talk to Azhar. Give me time to talk to Azhar."

"You're walking on the wrong side in this. The consequences are going to come down on your head like the wrath of God. How can you expect me—"

"Just let me talk to him, sir. There's going to be an explanation. He'll be back soon. A day. Two or three at the most. He has students at work in his lab at University College. He has courses to teach. He's not going to hang round Italy waiting for July to roll round. He *can't* do that. Just give me a chance to talk to him. If there's no explanation he can offer for those tickets and when he bought them and all the rest, I'll tell the guv about them and I'll give her my conclusions. I swear to God I'll do that. If you'll give me the time."

Lynley gazed at the raw appeal on her face. He knew what he was meant to do: report the entire twisted mess at once and let the inevitable gear itself up to happen. But years of partnership lay between him and what he was meant to do. So he sighed deeply and said, "Very well, Barbara."

She breathed, "Thank you, Inspector."

"I don't want to regret this," he told her. "So once you've spoken to Azhar, you're to speak to me straightaway. Are we clear on this?"

"We're absolutely clear."

He nodded, got to his feet, and left her nursing the rest of her coffee.

There was absolutely nothing he liked about the situation. Everything was screaming Taymullah Azhar's involvement. Since Barbara had withheld the information about those tickets to Pakistan, it stood to reason that there were other damning details she was withholding as well. He now knew she was in love with Azhar. She would never admit the fact to herself, but her relationship with the Pakistani professor went far beyond her friendship with his daughter, and it had been heading in that direction from the first. Could he rationally expect her to turn against the Pakistani man if his involvement turned out to be more than a father's desperate search for his child? Would he himself have turned against Helen had he discovered something questionable that she had done? More to the point, would he turn against Havers now?

He cursed at the web this entire investigation had become. Barbara needed to march into Isabelle's office, reveal everything, and throw herself upon the superintendent's mercy. She had to take the bitter medicine Isabelle would then dole out to her. But he knew that Havers would never do it.

His mobile rang. For a moment he allowed himself to think that Barbara had seen sense. She'd thought rationally as she'd finished her coffee, and here she was to announce that she'd reconsidered.

But a glance at his phone told him it wasn't Barbara phoning at all. It was Daidre Trahair.

"This is a pleasant surprise," he told her in answering the mobile's ring.

"Where are you?"

"Ringing for the lift as it happens."

"Does that mean a lift in Italy or somewhere else?"

"It means London."

"Ah. Lovely. You're back."

"Only just now. I flew in from Pisa late this morning and came directly to the Met."

"How is it that you coppers put things, then? Did you have a 'good result'?"

"We did." The lift doors opened, but he waved it off, not wanting to chance losing the signal. He gave Daidre a few details about Hadiyyah's safe return to the arms of her parents. He didn't tell her about SO12, Pakistan, or Barbara's perilous situation.

She said, "You must be enormously relieved to have it turn out so well. She's safe, she's healthy, her parents are . . . what?"

"Certainly not reconciled to each other, but in acceptance of the reality that they must share her. Admittedly, it's not the best situation for a nine-year-old, shuttling between parents in two different countries, but it's how things must be."

"This is how it is for so many children, isn't it, Tommy? I mean, going between two parents."

"You're right, of course. More and more, it's the way of the world."

"You sound . . . not quite as relieved as I'd think you'd be."

He smiled at this. She had read him astutely, and he found, unexpectedly, that he liked that fact. He said, "I suppose that I'm not. Or perhaps I'm merely tired."

"Too tired for a glass of wine?"

His eyes widened. "Where are you? Are you not phoning from Bristol?"

"I'm not."

"Dare I hope . . . ?"

She laughed. "You sound like Mr. Darcy."

"I thought women liked that. Along with those tight trousers."

She laughed again. "As it happens, they do."

"And . . . ?"

"I'm in London. On business, of course—"

"Of the Kickarse Electra kind?"

"Alas, no. This is business of the veterinarian kind."

"Might I ask what a large animal veterinarian is doing in London? Have we a camel at the zoo in need of your expert ministrations?"

"That brings us back to the glass of wine. If you've time this evening, I'll explain it to you. Have you the time?"

"Name the place and I'm there."

She did so.

BELSIZE PARK
LONDON

The wine bar she suggested was in Regent's Park Road, north of both Regent's Park and Primrose Hill. It was situated rather unceremoniously between a newsagent's and a kitchen shop, but its exterior position was deceptive. Inside, all was candlelight, velvet-draped windows, and linen-covered tables for two.

As the hour was still early and the place largely unoccupied, he saw

Daidre at once. She was seated at a table tucked into a corner, where a painting on the wall either featured a modern look-alike to William Morris's wife—God, what was her name? he wondered—or there was a Pre-Raphaelite extant that he wasn't aware of. A light shone brightly upon the piece, giving Daidre sufficient illumination to inspect a set of papers she'd spread on the table. She was also speaking to someone on her mobile.

He paused before crossing the wine bar to join her, aware of experiencing a decided rush of pleasure at seeing Daidre again. He took a rare opportunity to study her without her knowledge, noting that she was wearing new spectacles—rimless and virtually unnoticeable—and that she was dressed for business in a tailored suit. The scarf she wore bore a mixture of colours that matched her sandy hair and, it was likely, her eyes as well, and it came to him that he and she could actually pass for brother and sister, so similar was their colouring.

As he approached, he saw other details. She was wearing a simple pendant necklace: its decoration a gold depiction of the wheelhouse of one of the Cornish mines from the area of her birth. She had gold studs in her ears as well, but they and the necklace comprised her only jewellery. Her hair was slightly longer now, reaching below her shoulders, and she was wearing it back from her face and fastened somehow on the back of her head. She was a handsome woman, but not a beautiful one. In a world of thin, young, airbrushed things on the covers of fashion magazines, she would not have garnered a second look.

She'd already ordered a glass of wine, but it seemed untouched. Instead, she was jotting notes on the margin of her paperwork, and as he reached the table, he heard her say into her mobile, "I'll send it on to you then, shall I? . . . Hmm, yes. Well, I'll wait for your word. And thank you, Mark. It's very good of you."

She glanced up then. She smiled at Lynley and held up a just-a-moment finger. She listened again to whatever was being said to her by whoever was on the other end of the mobile, and then, "Indeed. I depend on you," and she rang off.

She stood to greet him, saying, "You've made it. It's lovely to see you, Thomas. Thank you for coming."

They engaged in air kisses: one cheek, then the other, with nothing touching anyone's flesh. He asked himself idly where the maddening social nicety had come from.

He sat and tried not to notice what he noticed: that she quickly put all the paperwork into a large leather bag by the side of her chair, that a faint blush had risen to her cheeks, and that she was wearing something on her lips that made them look soft and glossy. Then it came to him suddenly that he was taking in aspects of Daidre Trahair that he hadn't taken in, in the presence of a woman, since Helen's death. Not even with Isabelle had he noted so much. It discomfited him, asking him to identify what it meant.

He wanted, of course, to ask who Mark was. But instead, he nodded at the large bag on the floor and said, "Work?" as he drew out a chair to sit.

She said, "Of a sort," as she sat again herself. "You're looking well, Thomas. Italy must suit you."

"I daresay Italy suits most people," he told her. "And Tuscany in particular suits everyone, I expect."

"I'd like to see Tuscany someday," she said. "I've not been." And in less than a second and most typical of Daidre, "Sorry. That sounds as if I'm begging an invitation."

"Perhaps coming from someone else," he said. "Coming from you, no."

"Why not from me?"

"Because I've got the impression that subterfuge isn't part of your bag of tricks."

"Well . . . yes. Admittedly, I have no bag of tricks."

"Exactly," he said.

"I ought, I suppose. But I've never quite had the time to develop tricks. Or to sew the bag for them. Or whatever. Are you having wine, Thomas? I'm drinking the house plonk. When it comes to wine, I'm hopeless. I doubt I could tell the difference between something from Burgundy and something made here in the cellar." She twirled her wineglass by the stem and frowned. "I appear to be making the most disparaging remarks about myself. I must be nervous."

"About?"

"As I was in complete order a moment ago, I must be feeling nervous with you here."

"Ah," he said. "Another glass of wine, perhaps?"

"Or two. Honestly, Thomas, I don't know what's wrong with me."

A waitress came to them, a girl who had the look of a student and the accent of a recent arrival from the Eastern Bloc. He ordered wine for himself—the same plonk that Daidre was drinking—and when the girl took herself off to fetch it, he said, "Whether you're nervous or not, I'm quite glad you rang me. Not only is it a fine thing to see you again, but frankly, I was in need of a drink."

"Work?" she asked.

"Barbara Havers. I had an encounter with her that disturbed me rather more than I like to be disturbed by Barbara—and believe me she's been disturbing me in one way or another for years—and getting thoroughly soused seems like a reasonable reaction to the entire mess she's in. Either that or being diverted by your presence."

Daidre took up her own wine but waited till he had been served his. They clinked glasses and drank to each other's health, whereupon she said, "What sort of mess? It's not my business, of course, but I'm available to listen should you have a mind to talk about it."

"She's gone her own maddening way in an investigation and not for the first time."

"This is a problem?"

"She's skirting far too close to ignoring her ethical responsibility as a police officer. It's a complicated matter. Enough said on the subject. For the moment, I'd like to forget all about it. So tell me, then. What are you doing in London?"

"Interviewing for a job," she said. "Regent's Park. London Zoo."

He found himself brightening, sitting up straighter all at once. Regent's Park, the zoo . . . He had a thousand questions about what it all meant that Daidre Trahair was thinking of making a change from Bristol, but all he could manage was, stupidly, "As veterinarian?"

She smiled. "It is, more or less, what I do."

He shook his head sharply. "Sorry. Stupid of me."

She laughed. "Not at all. They might have wanted me to teach the gorillas to play chess or to train the parrots. One never knows." She took more wine and gazed at him with something that looked to him like fondness. "I was contacted by a head hunter, someone employed by the zoo. I didn't seek the position out, and I'm not altogether sure I'm interested in it."

"Because . . . ?"

"I'm quite happy in Bristol. And, of course, Bristol is that much closer to Cornwall and I do love my cottage there."

"Ah, yes, the cottage," Lynley said. It was where they had first met, himself an intruder who'd broken a window to get to a phone, herself the owner of the place who'd arrived for a getaway only to find an unknown man tramping mud on her floors.

"And then, there's my commitment to Boadicea's Broads as well as my regular darts tournaments."

Lynley lifted an eyebrow at this.

She laughed and said, "I'm quite serious, Thomas. I take my discretionary time to heart. Besides, the Broads rather depend on me—"

"A good jammer being difficult to find."

"You're teasing, of course. And I do know that I could join the Electric Magic. But then I'd be skating on occasion against my former teammates, and I don't know how I feel about that."

"These are serious matters," he said. "I suppose it must come down to the job itself, then. As well as the benefits attached to taking it, should it be offered."

They gazed at each other for a moment in which he saw the colour rise appealingly to her cheeks. He liked the look of her when she blushed. He said, "Have you listed them?"

"What?"

"The benefits. Or is it early days for that? I assume they're interviewing other large animal vets as well. It's an important position, isn't it?"

"Yes and no."

"Meaning?"

"Meaning they've done the interviews. All of the interviews. The initial ones, the secondary ones. The paper screening and checking of documents and references and all of that."

"So this is something that's been going on for a while," he said.

"Since early March. That's when I was first contacted."

He frowned. He observed the ruby colour of his wine. He asked himself how he felt about this: that since early March she'd been part of a process that might bring her to London but she'd not told him. He said, "Since early March? You haven't mentioned it. How am I to take that?"

Her lips parted.

He said, "Never mind. Terrible question. My ego was speaking for me. So where are you in the process, then? Tertiary interviews? Who knew so much was involved in vetting a vet, if you'll pardon the pun. *Is* it a pun? I don't quite know. You're leaving me at sixes and sevens, Daidre."

She smiled. "It's made difficult by—"

"What is?"

"My decision. They've offered me the job, Thomas."

"Have they indeed? That's wonderful! Isn't it?"

"It's complicated."

"Of course. Moving house is always complicated, and you've already listed your other concerns."

"Yes. Well." She took up her wine and drank. Looking for courage? he wondered. She said, "That's not exactly what I mean by complicated."

"Then what?"

"You, of course. But you know that already, I expect. You're a complication. You. Here. London."

His heart had begun to beat more heavily. He tried for lightness in his response. "It's a disappointment for me, of course. If you take the job, I won't have the opportunity of enjoying the personal tour of the zoo in Bristol that you once promised me. But I assure you we'll be able to soldier on under the burden of my disappointment. Rest your mind on that score."

"You know what I mean," she said.

"Yes. Of course. I suppose I do."

She looked away from him, across the wine bar to where a couple had just been seated. They reached spontaneously for each other's hand, twined fingers, and gazed into each other's eyes across the candlelight. They looked to be somewhere in their twenties. They looked to be somewhere in the first stages of love.

She said, "You see, I don't want to see you, Thomas."

He felt himself blanch, her words unexpectedly like a blow to him.

She moved her gaze from the young couple to him, apparently saw something on his face, and said quickly, "No, no. I've said that badly. What I mean is that I don't want to *want* to see you. There's too much danger in that for me. There's . . ." Again she diverted her gaze from him, but this time she put it on the candle's flame. It guttered as someone new entered the wine bar. Voices called out a greeting to the young lovers at the table. Someone said, "Don't trust that bastard, Jennie," and someone else laughed.

Daidre said, "There're too many possibilities for pain here. And I promised myself some time ago . . . It's that I've had enough of pain. And I *hate* saying that to you, of all people, because what you've endured and what you've somehow come out whole from *having* endured makes anything I've gone through in my little life a very paltry thing and believe me, I know it."

It was her honesty that he admired, Lynley realised as she spoke. It was her honesty that he knew he could grow to love. Understanding this, he was in that moment as afraid as she was, and he wanted to tell her this. But instead he said, "Dear Daidre—"

"God, that sounds like the beginning of the end," she declared. "Or something very like."

He laughed, then. "Not at all," he said. He considered their predicament from several different angles as he took up his wineglass and drank. He said, "What if you and I screw up our courage and approach the precipice?"

"What precipice would that be exactly?"

"The one in which we admit that we care for each other. I care for you. You care for me. Perhaps we'd both rather not since, let's face it, caring for anyone is a messy business. But it's happened and if we get it into the air between us, we can decide what, if anything, we'd like to do about it."

"We know the truth of things, Thomas," she said firmly and, he thought, a little fiercely. "I don't belong in your world. And no one knows that better than you."

"But that's what's at the bottom of the precipice, Daidre. And just now . . . Well, isn't the truth that we don't even know if we want to jump?"

"Anything can lead to jumping," she said. "Oh God. Oh *God*. I don't want that."

He could *feel* her fears. They were as real a presence at the table as was Daidre herself. Their cause was far different from the fears he himself felt, but they were nonetheless as strong as his own. Loss wears so many guises, he thought. He wanted to tell her this, but he did not. The time wasn't right for it.

He said, "I'm actually willing to approach the precipice on my own, Daidre. I'm willing to say that I care for you, that I would welcome your presence in London for what it might mean in my life to have you closer than an extremely lengthy drive down the M4 to Bristol. Whether you wish to approach the precipice any closer just now . . . ? That's up to you, but it's not required."

She shook her head and her eyes were bright and he wasn't at all certain what this meant. She clarified with a nearly voiceless "You're a very good man."

"Not at all, really. My point is that we can be whatever we wish to be in each other's life. What that is . . . ? We don't need to define it here. Now, have you had your dinner? Would you like to have dinner with me? Not here, actually, because I have a few doubts about the quality of their food. But perhaps somewhere nearby?"

She said, "There's a restaurant at my hotel." And then she looked horrified and hastily added, "Thomas, you aren't intended to think I meant . . . because I didn't mean . . ."

"Of course you didn't," he said. "And that's precisely why it's so easy for me to say that I care for you."

5 MAY

Barbara Havers was sitting up in bed reading when Taymullah Azhar knocked on her door. His knock was so soft and her interest in her book so intense that she very nearly didn't hear him. After all, Tempest Fitzpatrick and Preston Merck were in mutual torment over Preston's mysterious past and his agonising inability to act upon his acutely passionate love for Tempest—although Barbara thought they would be better off in torment over his rather strange and unheroic surname—and she was paragraphs away from discovering how they were going to resolve this troubling issue. Had Azhar not also tentatively called out, "Barbara? Are you awake? Are you there?" she might have missed his visit to her bungalow altogether. As it was, though, when she heard his voice, she cried out, "Azhar? Hang on," and she leapt out of bed.

She looked round frantically for something to put on as a cover-up. She was wearing one of her sleeping tee-shirts, this one with a faded caricature of Keith Richards on it along with the words *Forget His Money . . . I Want His Constitution* written below it. She reached for her tattered chenille dressing gown but noticed as she tied its belt that she'd not laundered it since spilling tinned beef goulash down the front of it six weeks earlier. She threw it off and grabbed her mac from the wardrobe. It would have to do.

She drew the bedcovers over the disarray of sheets, pillows, and Tempest and Preston's amorous difficulties. She hurried to the door.

She'd waited four days to talk to Azhar. Every evening, she'd arrived home from work and had immediately checked for his return from Italy. Every morning, she'd had to report to DI Lynley that he'd not yet come back to London. Every day, she'd had to repeat that she wanted to speak to Azhar face-to-face about everything that she'd uncovered concerning the kidnapping of his youngest child. And in response, Lynley's reply had been unvarying: I want a report from you, Barbara, and I do not want to discover at some later date that Azhar's been back since the evening of the first of May. She'd said passionately, I'm not lying to you. I *wouldn't* lie to you. A raised aristocratic eyebrow told her exactly how seriously he took that claim.

When she swung the door open, it was to see Azhar standing hesitantly in the shadows. She flipped on the light above the front step, but it wasn't helpful in the illumination department as it flashed brightly once like a bolt of lightning and then went dead. She said, "Oh, bloody hell," and then, "Come in. How are you? How's Hadiyyah? Are you only just back?"

She stepped away from the door, and he came into the light from the bungalow. He looked good, she thought. The relief he was feeling had to be enormous. She didn't ask herself what the relief's source was: having his daughter safe, having escaped Italy without anyone's suspicions falling on him, or having a plan in place to spirit Hadiyyah to another country when the time was right. These things she shoved to the back of her mind. Not yet, she told herself.

He was carrying a plastic carrier bag, which he handed to her, saying, "I have brought you something from Italy. A very small way to say thank you for everything, Barbara. I am and have been so grateful to you."

She took the bag from him and closed the door as he entered. He'd brought her olive oil and balsamic vinegar. She'd not the slightest clue what to do with the former—perhaps a Mediterranean fry-up? she thought—but she reckoned the latter would be smashing on chips. She said, "Ta, Azhar. Sit, sit," and she went to the kitchen area and put on the kettle.

He was looking at her bed, at the light on next to it, at the cup of Ovaltine next to the light. He said, "You were in bed. Indeed, I thought you might be because of the hour, but I wanted to . . . Yet I probably should not have—"

"You *should* have," she told him. "And I wasn't asleep. I was reading." She hoped he didn't ask *what* she was reading because she'd have to lie and tell him Proust. Or perhaps *The Gulag Archipelago*. That would go down a real treat.

She brought out the PG Tips, a bowl of sugar—from which she removed the clotted evidence of a wet spoon having been dipped into it with rather too much regularity—and a jug of milk. She took mugs from a shelf and bustled round like the owner of a third-rate B & B accommodating a late-night arrival. Jaffa Cakes on a plate, two paper napkins, two spoons, then a "whoops" and a replacement for one of them when she saw it was dirty . . . Back and forth from the kitchen to the table she went until there was nothing left but to pour the water over the tea bags and sit and talk to this man whom she knew and did not know all at once.

He watched her solemnly. He knew something was up. He said nothing at first.

Then his initial statement: "Inspector Lynley will have told you the details."

"Most of them, yeah," Barbara said. "I would have rung you to get the rest of them, but I reckoned you had a lot to cope with. With Hadiyyah, with Angelina and Lorenzo. With the coppers as well, I expect." She watched his face as she said this last, but he was busying himself with the tea, much dunking of the tea bag and then a questioning look as to where he was supposed to put it. She fetched an ashtray for the bag. She fetched her fags as well. She offered him one but he demurred and she found she didn't feel much like a smoke either.

He said, "There was much to discuss. The nightmare has, I believe, finally ended."

"Which means what exactly?"

He stirred his tea. He'd used sugar but no milk. Barbara saw to hers and waited for his answer. She found that nerves were making her suddenly ravenous. She grabbed up a Jaffa Cake and shoved it into her mouth.

"Not that Hadiyyah is restored to me," he said, "but that she will come to me and I may go to her—to Lucca—as often as I like. I need only ring Angelina first. I believe it took this . . . this loss of Hadiyyah to allow Angelina to see that to either parent, the loss of a child cannot be contemplated, let alone endured. I think she did not realise this, Barbara."

"Bollocks. She has to have known that."

"I think not. She wanted Hadiyyah with her. She wanted Lorenzo and the life she now is making with him. She knew no other way to achieve this. She is not, at heart, an evil woman."

"She's capable of evil," Barbara noted.

"Perhaps we all are," Azhar said quietly.

It was as good an entrée as she was going to get. She said, "Where do things stand between you now, Azhar? Between you and Angelina?"

"We have an uneasy peace. I hope that trust might develop between us in time. There has been little enough of that in the past."

"Trust," she noted. "Always important in relationships, isn't it?"

He didn't reply. He was looking at his tea. She said his name questioningly. He looked up then, and when their gazes met, she tried to read his dark eyes for something—anything—that would tell her he hadn't used her in the worst possible way, putting everything she was and everything she had in jeopardy. She saw nothing. His eyes looked peculiarly flat, and she tried to tell herself their lack of depth was owing to the overhead light.

She forged ahead. "Dwayne Doughty was someone you shouldn't have trusted, Azhar. I'm partly responsible, I reckon, because I took you to him. I checked him out, and he seemed completely on the up-and-up. He probably *is* in a lot of ways, long as what he's asked to do is perfectly in order and on the up-and-up as well. When it isn't, though . . . ? When something tempts him . . . ? He protects himself. I expect you didn't know that, did you?"

Still he said nothing. But he reached for her packet of Players and he lit one and she could see that his hand wasn't steady. So could he. He glanced at her as he shook the match out. He waited. Good move on his part, she thought.

She said, "Doughty's office is wired. Both for film and for sound. In his line of work, it's not a bad idea when you think of it. And I *should* have thought of it. Or perhaps you should have." She lit a cigarette herself. She saw that her own hands were none too steady. "So every meeting you and I had with him is documented, backed up, signed, sealed, and whatever. So is every meeting you had with him alone. 'Course, I don't know how many there were—those you-and-him meetings—'cause he only showed me two. But then, two was all it took, Azhar."

The Pakistani man had gone as pale as someone with pecan-coloured skin could go. He said in a nearly inaudible voice, "I did not know how . . ." But he did not continue.

She said, "How what, Azhar? How to tell me? How to get Hadiy-yah back? Or how bloody wretched I was going to feel when I saw the film of you making the suggestion that you and our Dwayne find a way that she could be snatched? How *what*? You'd best tell me because the water you're in is hot and promising to get a hell of a lot hotter now you're back in London."

"I did not know what else to do, Barbara."

"About what? Hadiyyah? Angelina? Life? What?"

"That day I rang you in December," he said. "You were in Oxford Street. You remember this. I rang to tell you that Mr. Doughty had found no trace." He waited for her nod before continuing. "I lied to you. He told me that day that he had traced her to Italy on Bathsheba's passport. Hadiyyah's passport was the same, of course. He found that they had landed in Pisa, but there the trail ended."

"Why didn't you tell me? Why did you lie?"

"He said that we—he and I—could hire an Italian detective if I wished. It would be costly, he said, for an Italian to conduct a search such as we needed, but if I wished him to carry on . . . ? This, of course, I wished. So he hired a Pisan, and the Pisan eventually found them. Mr. Doughty reported it all to me as the Pisan discovered it: Lucca, the farm in the hills, Lorenzo Mura, Angelina's presence at his farm, Hadiyyah's presence, the name of her school. All of it. Every-thing. I could tell this man was very thorough. I asked myself what was possible with so thorough a man. Could he, I wondered, discover more? What their days were like? What their lives were like? This I asked Mr. Doughty, and he made the arrangements for the Pisan detective to do more research. This the man did. He made a report of their daily movements. The markets they went to, the shops they frequented, their lives on the farm, the *mercato* near Porta Elisa, Angelina's yoga class, Hadiyyah's watching and listening to the accordion player. All of this the Pisan detective sorted out. He was very good."

"When?" Barbara's throat felt sore and dry, and she gulped down tea to relieve the tightness in it. "When did you know everything? Everything you just told me."

"All of the details? In February. By the end of the month."

"And you didn't tell me." Instead, he had let her agonise about his state of mind, about his daughter, about what to do and how to make things different for him, her friend. "What kind of friendship—"

"No!" He crushed out his cigarette so abruptly that he upended the ashtray and the sodden tea bags within it. Neither of them moved to alter the mess that dripped onto the table like the remains of a doused fire. "You must *not* think this. You must *not* think I valued you any less because I kept silent about this. I believed that at the end of the knowledge I had acquired about Angelina and where she'd taken my daughter was losing her completely. You must understand this. I have no rights. Not without tests, which Angelina would have denied me. And not without a case brought to court and where would that court case be held? Here? In Italy? And Angelina would fight like a tiger if it came to a court case and through all this would Hadiyyah be dragged and how could I do that to my own daughter?"

"So you did . . . what, Azhar? What the bloody hell did you do?"

"If there is a film and you have seen it, then you know what I have done."

"You planned her kidnapping. You planned it to take place when you were in Berlin with a cast-iron alibi. You knew Angelina would turn up here. And then what, for God's sake? You would go to Italy and play the part of the distraught father in search of his daughter till she turned up unharmed in some village God knows where after having been traumatised—" To her horror, her voice broke and she felt the swelling behind her eyes that signalled tears were on their way.

"I could see no other way," he said. "You must understand this,

Barbara. It seemed to me the lesser evil. And this man in Italy . . . he had his instructions. Tell Hadiyyah he was going to bring her to me, call her *khushi* so she will know it's the truth, take her to a very safe place where she will *not* be frightened, and when word is sent to you, take her to a town or a village that will be named—because I myself will have gone to Italy and will have found that village and will know it is safe—and release her close to the police station there because I will have found the police station in advance. Thus she will be returned by those police to her mother at once, but I will be there as well. And having gone through this trial, having seen me there suffering as she herself will suffer, Angelina will no longer deny Hadiyyah her father because Hadiyyah will see me there in Italy and she will want her father back in her life."

Barbara shook her head. "No. That's not it. You could have accomplished the same bloody thing by turning up on the doorstep of that farmhouse or whatever the hell it is and saying, 'Yoo-hoo, surprise, I'm here to collect the daughter you snatched.' If you knew the school, you could have gone to the school. You could have shown up in the market yourself. You could have done a dozen different things, but instead—"

"You do not see. Angelina had to *feel*. And none of those things would have allowed her to feel. She had to see what she had done to me. She had to feel in equal measure. It was the only way. You must know this, Barbara, as you know Angelina."

"You've bollocksed everything up. *You* must know that."

"What I did not know was that this Italian detective would hire someone else to carry the plan off. I still do not know why he did that. But so he did, and that person was killed as he went to fetch Hadiyyah from the Alps. And then none of us knew where he had taken her. And then I saw how badly I had gone wrong with this plan. But what was I to do at that point? What would you have done? Had I told the truth . . . Have you any idea what Angelina would have done then, had she learned that Hadiyyah's father had arranged for her kidnapping? You cannot think she would have dealt with me in a way that indicated a sudden understanding of how much I wanted and was desperate for my daughter's return."

"There are trails, Azhar," Barbara said. Other than numb to her soul, she wasn't sure what else she felt and, worse, she found herself wondering if she would ever feel anything again other than numb to her soul. "There are trails between you and Doughty. And who paid Di Massimo? You? And what about the other bloke? Who the bloody hell paid him? You can't be thinking that all of this mess was handled without a trace of your involvement, and once the Italians sort this out—which they will, let me tell you—then how exactly are you going to commune with Hadiyyah from inside a bloody Italian prison? And how the hell is Angelina going to feel when she learns you were behind the whole thing? And what sodding court in the world is going to allow you shared custody or even visitation or *whatever* else when it's proved you were behind her kidnapping?"

"Mr. Doughty told me of a man," he said. "He spoke of his skills with computers and the trails they leave."

"Of course he bloody well told you because what Bryan Smythe really did—and you c'n bet your life on this—was wipe out any connection between Doughty and Di Massimo, not between you and anyone. And as to the rest . . . ? As to your connection with any of these blokes . . . ? What the hell did you think? That once Hadiyyah was restored to her mum, the Italian cops were going to let everyone kiss and make up and there would be no further investigation? You can't have been that bloody mad, Azhar. Don't ask me to believe that you were because—"

And then she knew. She stopped herself. All of the facts spread out in front of her like a map of the world and she recognised every country depicted. She breathed, "Oh my God. Pakistan. That was it all along."

He said nothing. He watched her. She wondered if she'd ever really known him. A chasm seemed to exist between who she'd thought he was and who he was turning out to be, and in that moment what she truly wanted was to fling herself into the void created, so stupid had she been, such a dupe, such a fool.

"Doughty was right," she said. "He found those tickets, Azhar. I expect he didn't tell you that. SO12 found them as well, in case you're interested. One-way to Pakistan and yourself a Muslim? That sort of purchase is like lighting firecrackers on a carriage in the Underground at half past five in the afternoon. It gets you noticed. It gets you investigated. Didn't you think of that?"

Still, he said nothing although she saw his jaw shift. He fixed his gaze on hers, but other than his jaw, he didn't move a muscle.

She said, "You're taking her there. You bought the tickets in March because by then all the kidnapping plans were in place, weren't they? You knew when and you knew how and you knew what Angelina would think and would do and by God she did it. She came to London, you returned with her to Italy, and everything played out according to plan except that one unfortunate car wreck and a dead man, but at the end of the day, you got her back and all was well. And you had— you *have*—no bloody intention of sharing Hadiyyah with Angelina at all. You're going to take her to Pakistan and you're bloody well going to disappear with her because that's the only hope you have of getting Hadiyyah permanently. And once you knew that Angelina had taken up with another man, you *wanted* her permanently. You've family in Pakistan. Don't tell me you don't. And as far as getting employment there . . . ? For a man like you . . . ? A man with your education and background . . . ?"

Nothing from him. Not a change in expression, not a shifting in his chair, not a shuffling of his feet beneath the table. She thought she saw a pulse in the vein on his temple, but she also thought she saw it only because she wanted to see something in place of the nothing that she was seeing as she spoke.

"Tell me, Azhar. You goddamn bloody hell tell me what those tickets to Pakistan mean. Because Inspector Lynley knows about them, and he also knows the arrangement you and Angelina have: that Hadiyyah will come to you for her holidays and the first one begins in July."

He shifted his gaze at last. It moved to the tiny fireplace across the room. He said, "Yes."

"Yes to what?"

"That was what I was going to do."

"And you still intend to do it, don't you? You've got the tickets, and when she comes to you, she'll have her passport because she'll be coming from Italy. After a few days here to reassure her and everyone else that peace reigns between you and Angelina, off you'll go. And there's no way in hell that Angelina will be able to get her back. Not for years. Not for bloody decades."

He looked at her then. His eyes were startled. He said, "No, no. You are not listening to me. I said that Pakistan *was* what I intended. It is not what I now intend. There is no need. We will share her, and both of us—Angelina and I—will make this work."

Barbara stared at him. Finally, she felt something. It was incredulity and it was sweeping into her with the force of a polluted effluent pouring into a river. She couldn't speak. She didn't know the words.

He said, "Barbara, what else was I to do? You see this. I know you must see this. She is all I have. My family here is lost to me. You have seen this yourself. I could not lose her when I have lost so much already."

"I can't let you disappear with Hadiyyah into Pakistan. I won't do that."

"I will not. I will *not*. I thought I would. I intended to do it. But now, I will not, and I swear this to you."

"And I'm supposed to believe you? After everything that's passed? Do you think that's reasonable?"

"I beg you," he said. "I give you my word. When I bought those tickets . . . You must understand how I saw Angelina at that time. She had betrayed me. She had disappeared with my child. I'd had no way of knowing where they had gone or if I would ever be able to find them. I'd had no way of knowing if I would ever see Hadiyyah again. I swore to myself in November that if I could find her, I would make a way never to lose her again. Pakistan was that way. But it is not the way now. We have made our peace. It is not perfect, but it cannot be perfect. We will share Hadiyyah and I will see her on her holidays and whenever else I like. Should she wish to return here when she is of age, she will do so. I will be her father and she my daughter and this is how it will be."

"But not if the Italian coppers track you down," Barbara told him. "Don't you see that?"

His fingers closed over the packet of Players on the table between them, but he did not take another one. He said, "They must not track me down. They must not make any further connections."

"Di Massimo's not planning to take the fall for this alone. He's given them Doughty. And when it comes down to it, Doughty's going to give them you."

"Then we must stop him," Azhar said simply.

For a crazy moment, Barbara thought he was suggesting murder. For a crazier moment, she considered the likelihood of his having meddled with the car that had sent Roberto Squali to his death. At that point, anything was beginning to seem possible when it came to Azhar. But then he spoke.

"Barbara, I beg you from the fullness of my heart to help me. I may have committed an act of evil. But this act in the end brought about vast good, not only for me but also for my daughter. You must see that. This man Bryan Smythe . . . If he has removed all traces of connection between Mr. Doughty and the Italian detective Di Massimo, can he not do the same for me?"

"It doesn't matter," Barbara said.

"I do not see why."

"Because Doughty has those films. Every meeting. Every plan. Every request you made. I expect he denied them all when you were in his office. I expect he phoned you later—from a call box or a throwaway mobile—and said he'd thought things over and p'rhaps there *was* a way he could help. What I'm saying is you can rest assured there's nothing on those films that makes him look bad and everything on them that puts you in an Italian gaol for ten years and counting."

He was quiet for a moment as he considered this. He finally said quietly, "Then we must get those films."

Barbara did not miss his use of the plural pronoun.

6 MAY

B arbara rang the Yard in advance of what she presumed was Superintendent Ardery's normal arrival time. She left a carefully crafted message. She was on her way to Bow for a final word with Dwayne Doughty, she told Dorothea Harriman. There were a few more details that needed to be hammered down, sewed up, or whatever, with regard to the private investigator's place in the kidnapping of Hadiyyah Upman, and once she'd accomplished this, she'd be able to write the report that the superintendent was anticipating. Harriman asked if Detective Sergeant Havers wished her to fetch the guv so that she could give her the message personally. "She's only just arrived," the departmental secretary revealed. "Gone off to the ladies'. I c'n fetch her in a tick, if you'd like to speak with her yourself, Detective Sergeant."

Speaking with Isabelle Ardery was not high on the list of things Barbara wanted to do. She replied with an airy, "No need for that, Dee," but added that she'd be grateful if Dorothea would let DI Lynley know what she was up to when he showed his face in Victoria Street. Barbara knew quite well that she was on uneven ground with Lynley as it was. She also knew she'd go under entirely if she didn't keep him in the loop of what she was up to. More or less.

The detective inspector was already there as well, Dee Harriman told her. So she'd give him the word as soon as they rang off. The poor man had been cornered by DI Stewart for some sort of ear bending when last she'd seen him. She'd pop round and rescue him by means of passing along the detective sergeant's message. "Any message from you for Detective Inspector Stewart?" Harriman asked impishly.

"Very amusing, Dee," Barbara told her. And she thought how far, far better a thing it was that Lynley and not herself be on the receiving end of one of Stewart's diatribes.

She fetched Azhar from the ground-floor flat at the front of the big house in Eton Villas as soon as her phone call was completed. They set off, but not for Bow. Their destination was South Hackney and Bryan Smythe.

They'd been up till after two in the morning developing a strategy for dealing with Bryan Smythe. They had a separate strategy for dealing with Dwayne Doughty. But one would not function without the other.

During all of their discussing and planning, Barbara had tried to keep her mind on both Azhar and Hadiyyah and away from where she was placing herself in dealing with this situation. Azhar had been desperate, she told herself. Azhar had a right to his child. To this she added that little Hadiyyah deserved a loving father in her life. All of these facts she'd repeated to herself like a mantra. She massaged her brain with them. It was the only thing she could bear to think of.

What she hadn't dared consider was how far she was sliding off the rails in this personal spate of employment in which she was engaged. There would be time for that later. Now, however, there was only coming up with a way to mitigate the jeopardy into which Azhar had placed himself in the cause of finding the daughter he loved.

When he opened the door to her persistent knocking, Bryan Smythe did not seem wildly chuffed to see Barbara standing on his doorstep with an unidentified dark-skinned man at her side. She couldn't blame him for this. In his line of work, he probably didn't much like unexpected visitors. He probably also didn't much like attention being drawn to his house. She was betting on this latter assumption as the best means of gaining entrance to his lair should he not be ready to roll out the red carpet for them.

She said, "You were right, Bryan. Honours to you. Doughty had everything backed up on film."

He said, "What're you doing here? I told you what you wanted to know, and I said he'd have a fail-safe position. He had one, so the story ends there." He glanced right and left as if with the concern that his neighbours—such as they were in this street—were behind the dismal, sagging curtains at their filthy windows taking snapshots of his tête-à-tête with a rozzer. A car turned at the corner and began rolling in their direction, its driver cruising slowly as if hunting for the proper address. Bryan gave a curse and jerked his head towards the inside of his house.

Barbara inclined her head to Azhar. She gave mental thanks that Smythe's sense of caution tended to make him both jumpy and suspicious. They needed Bryan Smythe in their corner. If they couldn't manoeuvre him there in the coming minutes, the game was over.

"You'll get no aggro from me on that front," Barbara told him as she passed over the threshold. "That's not why we're here." She introduced him to Azhar. She watched as Bryan took in the other man and made whatever mental adjustments were necessary to align the reality of the Pakistani he was looking at to whatever mental image he'd had of him. "So be hospitable, eh? Make us a cuppa, toast us a teacake, and we'll tell you what we need."

"*Need?*" Bryan said incredulously. He shut the door smartly and locked it for good measure. "As I see it, you're not in the position to be *needing* anything. At least nothing more than I've already given you."

Barbara nodded thoughtfully. "I c'n see why you reckon that. But I think you're forgetting a salient point."

"What would that be?"

"That I'm the only one of you lot who's clean. You watch every one of Dwayne's films—'cause I bet he's got dozens, if not hundreds—and you look through every record you c'n find on me out there in cyberland, and there's nothing that connects me to this Italian business because I *wasn't* connected to this Italian business. Whereas the lot of you . . . ? You're all hanging from the precipice by broken fingernails, Bryan."

"Including your friend here." He jerked his head at Azhar.

"No one's saying otherwise, mate. Now, how about that cuppa? I like mine with the works. Azhar goes with sugar. Do you lead the way or do I?"

He had little choice but to see what she was up to, so he went through to the other half of his house. There, the enormous flat screen television had been muted but was showing a chat show in which five badly dressed women appeared to be measuring the size of their bums against a life-size poster featuring the bony arse of a catwalk model. Bryan had apparently been enthralled with this when they'd knocked on his door, for on a coffee table in front of a fine leather sofa with a superb view of the telly, breakfast for one was still laid out. Eggs, bacon, sausage, tomato, the works. Barbara's stomach rumbled. She nearly regretted her single Pop-Tart and cup of coffee.

Bryan took himself to the kitchen end of the huge room, where he filled a stainless steel electric kettle. It was sleek and modern like the kitchen itself, and it matched the handles on the cabinets as well as the lighting fixtures. From an impressive fridge—also of pristine stainless steel—he brought out milk and sloshed some into a jug. Barbara told him they'd wait in the garden.

"Gorgeous day," she said. "Out in nature. Fresh air and all the et ceteras. Don't see gardens like this in our neighbourhood, do we, Azhar?" She led him out.

Midway between the pool with its lily pads and its sparkling fountain, there was a seating area fashioned from bluestone benches. Behind it grew a plethora of brilliant flowers artfully planted to look unarranged. Here, Barbara sat and gestured for Azhar to do the same. In the garden, Barbara reckoned, Bryan wouldn't have a system to record whatever was said between them. For he did his business in the house itself, and she didn't think it likely that he invited anyone who employed him to enjoy the fruits of his labours beyond the windows. Indeed, she thought it was probable that those who employed him never came to his house anyway. But better safe than sorry was how she looked at it.

She sat with Azhar next to her. When Bryan joined them with tea on a tray—the thoughtful bloke had actually provided the teacakes as requested, she saw—he sat opposite them. The tray he placed on the stone bench next to him. Barbara reckoned his hospitality didn't extend to being mother, so she did the honours and she also scored a teacake for herself. It was tasty and the butter was real. There was nothing second-rate about the bloke.

Except perhaps his manners since he said, "You have your tea. Now what do you want? I've work to do."

"Didn't look that way from the telly."

"I don't care what it looked like. What do you want?"

"To employ you."

"You can't afford me."

"Let's say Azhar and I are pooling our resources, Bryan. Let's also say that, all things considered, we reckon you'll give us something of a cut-rate price."

"What things?"

"What 'what things'?"

"You said 'all things considered.'"

"Ah." She chowed down on more of the teacake. It had very nice currants in it, not at all dried out. Lovely, she thought. The thing had to have come from a bakery. No way did one score such a delicacy from the local Tesco. "In that, we go back to your line of work," she said, "and what happens to it if I give the word to the blokes in Victoria Street who look into Internet crimes. We've been through this before, mate, so let's not beat the horse while it's lying in the dust. You've wiped all the records to make Doughty clean, and now you're going to do something similar for Azhar. It'll be trickier, but I reckon you're the bloke to do it. We've got air tickets to Pakistan that need to be altered in the records at the Met. No worries that there's terrorism involved. There isn't. Just a detail on the tickets that needs changing in a file on someone who's been investigated and vetted and is in the clear. That's Azhar, by the way. He look like a terrorist to you?"

"Who bloody knows what a terrorist looks like these days?" Bryan said. "They're jumping out of rubbish bins. And it's impossible to do what you ask. Hacking into that system . . . ? D'you know how long that would take? D'you have any idea how many backups exist? I'm not talking about backups just at the Met, either. I'm talking about backups at the airline, on their main databases, on their alternative databases. I'm talking about backups on tape that you can alter only if you have the tape itself. Plus, there're computer applications that've been written by hundreds of people over dozens of years and—"

"If we needed all that," she cut in, "I c'n see it'd be something of a headache for you. But as it happens, we want the airline ticket altered, like I said, and it only needs to be altered in the Met's system. The date of purchase needs to be changed, and it needs to be round-trip instead of one-way. That's it. There's one in Azhar's name and one in the name of Hadiyyah Upman."

"And if I can't get into the Met's system . . . Which department are we talking about? Who's got the records?"

"SO12."

"Completely impossible. Laughable even to suggest it."

"Not for you, and you and I know it. But to give you a little practice in advance—a bit of a way to exercise your typing skills, let's say—we also need you to take care of a few bank records. Not a big deal for a bloke with your talents, and it's an alteration again, not an erasure. Azhar here needs to have paid Doughty less: just enough to cover his services up to the point where the trail Angelina Upman left—such as it was—went dead as a corpse. That's it, Bryan. Airline tickets and payments to Doughty and we're out of your life, more or less."

"Meaning?"

"Meaning I want you to hand over your fail-safe position. Just for an hour or two and you'll have it back, but I'm going to need to take it with me. Today."

"I don't know what you're talking about."

Barbara hooted. She said to Azhar, "You're not to mind that he thinks we're idiots. Computer nerds and their attitude problems? Hand in glove, if you know what I mean." And then to Smythe, "Bryan, the one thing you're not is stupid. You've backed up all of the information you removed from Doughty's records. Wherever you have it—and I expect it's right here in the house in a very nice safe with a very secure combination on it—I want it. Like I said, I need it for an hour or two and then you'll have it back. And stop denying that you have it because you're the sort of bloke who knows how to put the full stops where they belong."

He said nothing at first. His expression was hard, his eyes flinty.

He looked from Barbara to Azhar to Barbara and he said to her, "How many more of you are there?"

Azhar stirred next to her, but Barbara put her hand on his arm. She said, "Bryan, we're not here to discuss—"

"No. I want to know. How many more dirty cops're going to crawl out of the woodwork if I cooperate with you? And don't please tell me you're the only one. Your sort doesn't exist alone."

Barbara felt Azhar glance in her direction. For her part, she was surprised at how Smythe's words stung. It wasn't the first time he'd accused her of being dirty, but the fact was that this time, he was speaking the truth. That she was dirtying herself in the cause of a larger good, however, was not something she wished to debate with the man. So she said to him, "This is a one-time operation. It's about Azhar, it's about his daughter, and after that, it's about us being gone from your life."

"I'm expected to believe that?"

"I don't see that you have a choice." She waited as he thought things over. Birds were chirping pleasantly from the ornamental cherry trees in the garden, and within the pool a goldfish surfaced in the hope of feeding time's approach. She said, "My grip's better than yours is, mate. Face up to it and we're out of here and you c'n go back to your breakfast and those ladies' arses."

"Grip," he repeated.

"On the whatsies. We're all hanging on to each other's, let's face it. But just now I've got the better hold. You know it. I know it. Let's have your fail-safe data so Azhar and I c'n get on with things."

"You're heading for Doughty next," he said.

"Bob's definitely your uncle, mate."

BOW

LONDON

"This is too much, Barbara" were Azhar's first words. He'd said nothing at all during their encounter with Bryan Smythe, but once they were in Barbara's car and heading over to Doughty's office, he pressed fingers to his forehead as if trying to contain the pain in his head. "I am so sorry," he said. "And now this. I cannot—"

"Hang on." She lit a fag and handed him the packet. "We're in it now, so it's not the time to lose your nerve."

"This is not a matter of nerve." He took a cigarette and lit it, but after one drag on it, he threw it out of the window in disgust. "This is a matter of what you are doing because of me. Because of my decisions. And I . . . Silent like a miserable statue in that man's garden. I despise myself."

"Let's stick with the facts as we know them. Angelina took Hadiyyah. You wanted her back. The wrong involved here started with her."

"Do you think that matters? Do you think that *will* matter should the details of this morning excursion of ours come to light?"

"Details won't come to light. Everyone's at risk. That's our guarantee."

"I should not have . . . I cannot . . . I must stand like a man and tell the truth and—"

"And what? Go to gaol? Spend some time in a prison learning how to say 'Touch me there and I'll cut off your hand' in Italian?"

"They would have to extradite me first and then—"

"Oh, too right, mate. And while you're waiting to be extradited, Angelina is going to be doing what? Sending Hadiyyah for pleasant, extended visits with the man who arranged her kidnapping and—oh, by the way—also bought one-way tickets to Pakistan for himself and her?"

He was silent, and she glanced at him. His face was anguished. "All of this is down to me," he said. "No matter how Angelina has behaved in the past, the first sin was mine. I wanted her."

At first, Barbara thought he was talking about the daughter he and Angelina had created. But when he went on, she saw that was not what he meant at all.

"How wrong could it be, I asked myself, to want a lovely young woman in my bed? Just once. Or twice. Three times, perhaps. Because, after all, Nafeeza is heavy with child and wishes to be left in peace until she delivers and as a man, I have my needs and there she is, so lovely, so fragile, so . . . so English."

"You're human," Barbara said, although the words did not come easily to her.

"I saw her at that table at University College, and I thought, What a particularly lovely English girl she is. But I also thought what Middle Eastern men—men like me—are schooled to think of particularly lovely English girls, of all English girls: They are not like our women, their clothing alone illustrates how easy they are with their chastity, and these things that rob them of their virtue mean very little to them. So I sat with her. I asked her if I could join her at her table, and as I did so, I knew exactly what I wanted from her. What I did not think was that the wanting would increase, the 'must have' would dominate, and I would bring ruin upon my world. And now I am set upon the same course, but the world to be ruined is going to be yours. How, then, do I live with that?"

"You live with that by knowing that this is *my* decision," she told him. "We have another half hour to live through, and then we're through it, all right? We have Bryan where we want him and all that's left is putting Doughty into line behind him. But that's only going to happen if you *believe* it's possible because if you don't—if you go into that office broadcasting on your face that the only end reachable is the one with you sitting in the dock in a Lucca court-room—we're finished, Azhar. We, not you. We. And I'd like to hold on to my job."

She pulled to the kerb and let the Mini idle. They were round the corner from Doughty's office, parked near a primary school where the happy noise of children running about a schoolyard came to them through the open windows of the car. They listened to this in silence for a moment. Barbara shut off the Mini's ignition and said, "Are we on the same page, Azhar?"

At first he did not answer. Like her, he listened to the children. Like her, he was also probably thinking of his own child, perhaps of all his children. He raised his head and closed his eyes briefly. He finally said firmly, "Yes. Yes. All right," and together they climbed out of the car.

Doughty wasn't in his office. They found him, however, in the office next door, where Em Cass was set up. She'd obviously just arrived at work since she was wearing running clothes, trainers, and a sweatband round her head, and at first it looked from his position as if Doughty was taking in the fragrance of her armpits since he was sitting at her table of computers and she was bent forward across him to use the mouse. She was saying, "No. The hotel records indicate—" But she straightened, ceasing her words abruptly, when Barbara pushed open the door. Doughty turned and said, "What the hell . . . You're out of order walking in unannounced."

Barbara said, "I think that's a social nicety we can all wave farewell to at this point, Dwayne."

"You can go wait in my office," he said. "And you can thank your stars I don't toss you and the professor back down the stairs you just tramped up."

"We will all speak together," Azhar said. "Either in your office or in this office but in either case now."

Doughty rose from his chair. "Where'd *your* manners take themselves off to? I don't take orders from people who aren't employing me."

"Got that in a biscuit box, Dwayne." Barbara brought out of her pocket Bryan Smythe's memory sticks and dangled them from her fingertips. "But I expect you take orders from someone who's hanging on to these trying to decide which department at the Met is going to be happiest to see them. They're on loan, by the way. Bryan handed them over."

There was a moment of tight, evaluative silence among them. From below in the street, the sound of Bedlovers' protective grille being raised came to them like the noise of a castle's portcullis. Someone coughed, hacked, and spit with the force of a minor explosion. Em Cass grimaced at the sound. Obviously, a woman who disapproved of life's indelicacies, Barbara thought. That was a very good thing, she reckoned, since they were well in the midst of one of them.

"Are we going to talk or are we going to stand here staring at each other?" Barbara asked.

Doughty said, "I know a bluff when I'm looking at one."

"Not in this case, mate. You c'n ring Bryan if you like. Like I said, these're on loan from him. He feels a bit like you do when it comes to the Bill. *Anything* to clear one's house of the coppers."

"She's telling the truth," Em Cass said. "Christ, Dwayne. I don't know why I ever listen to you and your plans and your I've-got-everything-under-control. I should have done a runner when I was packed."

Barbara liked even more the fact that, along with her delicacies, Emily Cass also appeared to be someone who preferred that her line of employment not lead her in the direction of arrest. This of course begged the question: What was she doing working as a blagger for Dwayne Doughty in the first place? But economic times were tough. Perhaps it had been that or becoming a barista.

She said, "Let's decamp to your office, Dwayne. Without the filming this time, 'f you don't mind. You come, too, Emily. It's roomier, there're chairs, and someone might go weak at the knees." She made a sweeping gesture to the doorway. She was gratified to see Emily the first person through it. Doughty followed her, giving Barbara a withering glance and ignoring Azhar altogether.

Inside his own office, Doughty removed the hidden camera, placed it in a drawer, and positioned himself behind his desk. Barbara wanted to guffaw at this final I'm-in-charge move. She sat, Emily went to the window and leaned against its sill, and Azhar took the other chair. Doughty said, "It wouldn't take all those memory sticks, in case you're actually thinking Bryan isn't having you for a fool."

"When I said everything, I meant everything," Barbara replied. "I've got his entire system here, Dwayne. Not just you but everyone else. My fail-safe position, if you'd like to call it that. Sometimes people need a little urging when it comes to cooperating, I find. Now what I wonder is how much urging you're going to need."

"To do what, exactly?"

"To hand over *your* fail-safe position—"

"In your bloody dreams."

"—and to assure us you've seen the light of salvation and it's called Di Massimo."

"What the bloody hell are you talking about?"

Emily Cass stirred. "I expect it's a good idea to hear her out."

"Oh, you *expect* that, do you? Did you *expect* that when you gave her Smythe? Which, by the way, is the only way she could have dug him out of whatever molehill he happens to operate from and don't think I haven't worked that one out."

"Let's not start pointing fingers," Barbara said. "It wastes my time and I've wasted enough of it already dealing with you lot. Now we can get down to business or, like I said, I can—"

"Sod you," Dwayne told her. "Sod the professor."

Barbara looked at Emily. "He always this stupid?"

"He's a man," Emily said in reply. "Go on. Pretend he's not here."

"I want him on board."

"He is. He won't tell you that, but he is."

Barbara turned to Azhar. "How did Di Massimo come into this mess?"

"Mr. Doughty found him," he said, telling her what she already knew and what had been established between them on their long night of planning. "He said that we needed a detective in Italy who spoke English, and Mr. Di Massimo was that detective."

"How often did you speak to him?"

"To Mr. Di Massimo? Never."

"How often did you contact him by email?"

"Never."

"How did he get paid?"

"Through Mr. Doughty. I paid him and he transferred the money to Italy."

"Keeping some for himself, you reckon?"

"Are you bloody accusing—"

"Relax, mate," Barbara told Doughty. "You employed a subcontractor. You took your cut. It's the way of the world." She held up the memory sticks another time and she said to Azhar, "What d'you reckon these're going to show, then?"

"The movement of money, among other things. From my bank account to Mr. Doughty's to Mr. Di Massimo's. Internet activities: emails and searches. Telephone records. Mobile records. Credit card records."

"So what you're saying," she said to Azhar, "is that over there in Italy, at this very moment while Michelangelo Di Massimo is being the canary on matters having to do with the snatching of Hadiyyah, what I've got here in my grubby hands is proof that the bloke is telling the truth."

Azhar nodded. "It does appear that way, Barbara."

She turned to Doughty. "The point being that the interests of everyone—that would include you, Dwayne—would best be served if we took a solid look at where we ought to be applying our talents, such as they are."

He opened his mouth, but she cut him off before he could speak.

"And," she said, "I'd suggest you think that one over before you reply. We've got Di Massimo, but we've also got a dead bloke called Squali and all the information he may have left behind, which I reckon is plentiful. Now, do we climb into the boat and plug its holes and float it together, mate, or do we let it sink on its bloody own?"

Doughty examined her before he shoved his chair back and opened the drawer in which he kept his own fail-safe memory stick.

"You and your sodding metaphors," he replied.

VICTORIA
LONDON

Lynley wasn't sure what his preoccupation actually meant. He'd come into the Yard early upon Isabelle's request, he'd been buttonholed by John Stewart for an extended and unpleasant conversation about Barbara Havers's tendency towards insubordination, he'd finally managed to wrest himself away from the other DI, and now as he waited in Isabelle's office, he realised that he hadn't taken in whatever it was that Stewart had been implying about Barbara's performance while on his team.

The reason was Daidre Trahair. They'd had a fine dinner together at her hotel, conversation flowing easily between them until the moment that he'd finally got up the nerve to ask her who Mark was—"That bloke you were speaking to on your mobile when I came into the wine bar?" he said to her when she looked utterly puzzled by the question—and he'd been unaccountably relieved to learn that Mark was her solicitor in Bristol. He would be looking over the contract that London Zoo had offered Daidre because, as she put it, "I'm hopeless when it comes to the 'party of the first part' and 'pursuant to

Clause One,' and that sort of thing, Thomas. Why do you ask about Mark?"

That was certainly the question, he admitted. Why did he ask? He hadn't been this preoccupied by a woman since before his marriage to Helen. And what was puzzling to him was that Daidre Trahair was absolutely nothing like Helen. He couldn't quite work out what it meant: that the first woman to interest him seriously was someone completely different from his dead wife. So he had to ask himself if he was truly interested in Daidre or merely interested in making Daidre interested in him.

He'd said to her, "The answer to that question. It's something I'm working on. Not very adeptly, I'm afraid."

"Ah," she said.

"Ah, indeed. Like you, I'm a bit at sixes and sevens."

"I'm not entirely sure I want to know what you mean."

"Believe me, I understand," he'd said.

At the end of their meal, she walked with him through the lobby of the hotel to the front door of the place. It was a large hotel, part of an American chain, the kind of place where businessmen and -women stayed and their comings and goings went largely ignored by the staff. This meant all sorts of things, among which was the fact that when someone went to someone else's room, no one took note of that unless observation of the CCTV films became necessary later. He found himself acutely aware of this. He felt a sudden need to get out of the place unscathed. And what did *that* mean? he asked himself. What was bloody wrong with him?

She walked out onto the pavement in his company. There, the night was inordinately pleasant. She said, "Thank you for a lovely evening."

He said, "Will you tell me when you've decided about the job?"

"Of course I will."

Then they looked at each other, and when he kissed her, it seemed like a natural thing to do. He fingered a piece of her sandy hair that had come loose from the slide at the back of her head, and she reached up and caught his fingers and squeezed them lightly. She said, "You're a lovely man, Thomas. I would be every way the fool if I didn't see that."

He moved his hand to her cheek—he could feel her blush, although in the dim light he couldn't see it—and he bent to kiss her. He held her briefly and breathed in the scent of her and acknowledged that her scent was not the citrus of Helen that he'd so loved and realised that this was not a bad thing. He said, "Ring me, please."

"As you recall, I did. And will do again."

"I'm glad of that, Daidre," he told her and then he left.

There was no question of his going to her room. He didn't want to. And what, he wondered, did *that* mean, Thomas?

"Are you listening to me, Tommy?" Isabelle asked. "Because if you are, I'd expect at some point you'd grunt or nod or look reflective or, for God's sake, something."

"Sorry," he said. "Late night and not enough coffee this morning."

"Shall I have Dee bring you a cup?"

He shook his head. "John bent my ear when I got here," he told her. "Taking that decision to put Barbara on his team, Isabelle—"

"It was a brief enough period. It hardly killed her."

"Still, his antipathy for her—"

"I hope you're not about to tell me how to run the department. I doubt you did that with Superintendent Webberly."

"I did, as it happens."

"Then the man was a saint."

Before he could reply, Barbara Havers joined them. She came in in a rush. She was the personification of all business, aside from her clothing, which was, as usual, a bow to the fashion of an era that had never existed. She'd at least eschewed the cupcake socks. She'd replaced them, however, with Fred and Wilma Flintstone. They more or less made a piece with her tee-shirt: She was wearing the bones of the Natural History Museum's T-rex across her chest.

She said, "Here's how it looks," after she acknowledged the tardiness of her arrival with "Sorry. Traffic. Had to buy petrol as well." She went on with, "Everything points to Di Massimo trying to finger Doughty for what he himself cooked up. He knows there'll be records of communications between him and Doughty—and there are—and he reckons that as there was no ransom request, we're going to fall into line with whatever he claims. But the link from him to Squali is what's going to bring him down. He's telling partial truth and partial lie, and his idea is that if he muddies the waters enough, no one is going to sort it all out."

"Meaning what, Barbara?" Isabelle said.

Lynley said nothing. He merely noted that the sergeant's colour was high and he wondered if this was due to the rush she was in or the tale she was telling.

"Meaning Doughty hired Di Massimo to start at the airport in Pisa, which was as far as he—Doughty, that is—was able to get in working out where Angelina Upman had taken Hadiyyah. He didn't give Azhar the information because he didn't know where it would lead. Di Massimo's brief was to find Angelina and report back. He was told to do whatever it took to find her because—according to Doughty's tale—whatever it took was ultimately going to be funded by her dad. Only once Di Massimo knew where she was, it was a short journey from there to who's-got-more-dosh and the answer to that was the extended Mura family. So he hired Squali to snatch her but what he told Doughty was that he couldn't find her at all. Records show all communication between him and Doughty ended at the point he made his report."

"Which was when?"

"December fifth."

"What records are we talking about, Barbara?" Lynley asked quietly.

Another slight rush of colour to her cheeks. He reckoned that she hadn't expected him to be sitting in Isabelle's office as a party to this meeting. She had a few decisions to make as a result of his presence. He could only pray she made the right ones.

"Doughty's," she said. "He opened them to me, sir. He's printing up the whole lot of them and he'll be shipping them over to the bloke in Italy who's dealing with that end of things once we give him the name. 'Course he'll want someone to translate, but they'll have someone for that." She licked her lips, and he saw her swallow. She turned back to Isabelle and went on. "What I can't work out is the ransom request."

"There wasn't one as I understand it," Isabelle said.

"That's the screw in the works," Barbara acknowledged. "What

I reckon is that once Di Massimo worked out how much money the Mura family has, he planned one of those typical Italian kidnappings. Think of it: Here's a country with a big tradition of holding people for months to get what they want. Sometimes the demand comes quickly; sometimes they like to wait till the family is ready to blow itself to bits with worry. Look at the poor Getty kid all those years ago."

"I doubt the Muras have pockets quite so deep as the Gettys," Lynley said evenly, watching Barbara. Her upper lip looked damp.

"True. But what I reckon is everything depended on what Di Massimo wanted. Was it money, land, cooperation, stock options, political influence . . . who the bloody hell knows? I mean, how much do we know about the Muras, sir? What does Di Massimo know that we don't?"

"You're doing a great deal of 'reckoning,'" Lynley said. His tone was dry and he felt, rather than saw, Isabelle glance his way.

"I was thinking the same," she said to Havers.

"Well, right. Yes. Of course. But isn't our part of the investigation to turn over what we have to this bloke in Italy . . . What's his name, sir?"

"Salvatore Lo Bianco. But he's been replaced. I've no idea who has the case now."

"Right. Well. I expect we can sort that out with a phone call. Point is that it's an Italian situation and it seems to me our part is finished."

Of course, their part wasn't finished at all, and Lynley waited for Havers to bring up all those things that she was leaving out of what was going for her report to the superintendent. The list of those things was topped by one-way tickets to Pakistan. The fact that she was saying nothing about them was so damning that Lynley felt its pressure upon his chest like a pallet of bricks.

Havers said, "Far as I can tell and far as the records're going to show, no crime was committed on British soil, guv. Everything's up to the Italians now."

Isabelle nodded. She said, "Include that in your written report, Sergeant. I don't want another day to pass without my seeing it on my desk."

Havers remained where she was, obviously waiting for more. When nothing else appeared to be forthcoming, she said, "That's it?"

"For now. Thank you."

It was more than clear that Isabelle was dismissing her. It was additionally clear that she wasn't dismissing Lynley. Havers caught this and Lynley saw her do so. She cast a look in his direction before she took herself out of the superintendent's office.

When the door closed behind her, Isabelle stood. She went to her window and gazed at the sunny day outside, at what she could see of rooftops and fresh green treetops and in the distance St. James's Park. Lynley waited. He knew more was coming from her or she would have dismissed him along with Barbara.

She went to a filing cabinet and brought out a manila folder. She returned to her desk. She handed it to him wordlessly, and he knew that whatever was within it was something he wasn't going to want to see. He could tell that much from her expression, which seemed caught in the undecided no-man's-land between hardness and compassion. The hardness came from the set of her jaw. The compassion came from her eyes.

She sat again. He put on his reading glasses and opened the folder. It contained a series of documents. They were official activities reports, but the activities they documented were unofficial in the extreme. Every out-of-line and off-the-record move Barbara Havers had made since the earlier time of being put to work as a member of John Stewart's team was contained in the report of activities. Stewart had continued this surveillance of her after Isabelle had reassigned her. He had assigned two detective constables to shadow Havers, to check on her work or the lack thereof, to confirm the reasons for her every absence from the Yard. He'd verified details about her mother's life in Greenford at the home of Florence Magentry. He'd identified every person with whom she met: Mitchell Corsico, the family of Taymullah Azhar, Dwayne Doughty, Emily Cass, Bryan Smythe. The only thing missing was SO12. There was no mention of the airline tickets to Pakistan. Lynley wasn't sure why this was the case except that as it had to do with Barbara's actions inside the Met's actual buildings, perhaps there had been no need to shadow her. Or, he thought, perhaps John Stewart was holding back on this as the pièce de résistance on the off chance that Isabelle decided to do nothing about what his unauthorised investigation had revealed.

Lynley handed the report back when he'd finished it. He said the only thing he could. "You and I both know you're going to have to do something about him, Isabelle. That he'd be using the Met's manpower to conduct his own investigation . . . It's outrageous and we both know that. Did any of this"—with what he hoped was a dismissive gesture at Stewart's paperwork—"get in the way of Barbara's completion of whatever John assigned her to do? If not, then what does it matter that she did this as well?"

Her gaze upon him was perfectly even and quintessentially Isabelle. She looked at him unspeaking for a good thirty seconds in which she kept her gaze on him before she said quietly, "Tommy."

He had to break the look. He didn't want to hear what she had to say and he certainly didn't want to know what she might ask of him.

She said, "You know that Barbara's completion of John's assignments isn't the point. Nor is the when and how of her completing them. You know that what occurred just now among the three of us says it all. I *know* you know that. In what we do, there's no place for a sin of omission, no matter who's involved."

"What are you going to do?"

"I'm going to do what needs to be done."

He wanted to plead, which told him how far he himself had waded into the river into which Barbara Havers had dived headlong. But he did not do so. Instead he said, "Will you give me a few days to deal with this? To try to sort things out?"

"Do you actually suppose there's something to sort at this point? More important, do you really think there's something exculpatory that will come out of the sorting?"

"There probably isn't, but I'm asking all the same."

She picked up the folder and tapped the papers within it neatly so that they were aligned. She handed it to him and said, "Very well. This is your copy. I've another. Do what you must."

SOUTH HACKNEY
LONDON

He was caught between anger and sorrow, in the land of others' expectations of him. He asked himself what sort of person he seemed to be to other people and in particular to his longtime partner Barbara Havers. She clearly expected him to hold his tongue, to take her part, to be the breathing personification of like-a-bridge-over-troubled-water in her life, no matter what she did or how far out of order she took herself. This expectation on her part angered him: not only that she would have it but that he would have—through his own past actions—somehow schooled her into having it. And what, he wondered, did that say about him as an officer of the Met?

More, what did the information contained within John Stewart's report say about Barbara, and what was he to do with what it said? He needed to think about this and to consider it from every angle, and he couldn't do so standing in the corridor at the door to Isabelle's office, so he took himself down to the underground car park—avoiding conversation with everyone on his way—and he climbed into the Healey Elliott. There, he opened the manila folder and read every word of the damning information inside and tried like the devil to think what it meant beyond what DI Stewart wanted it to show, which was Barbara's normal means of doing business, with her the living embodiment of going her own way whenever the inclination came upon her.

From the first Barbara had been on the wrong end of things when it came to Hadiyyah's disappearance in Italy. Like his personal snout inside the Met, she'd given the story to Mitchell Corsico and *The Source*. She'd done so in order to force Isabelle's hand because she herself wanted to be in Italy, and he had to ask himself what this said about Barbara. Was it an indication of her love for Hadiyyah? Her love for Azhar? Or, more difficult to face, was it an indication of her own involvement in the child's kidnapping for some reason that, as yet, he did not clearly see? And what in God's name did it mean that in Isabelle's presence she said nothing about those tickets to Pakistan? She was protecting Azhar, of course, and there could be only one reason for this, a reason that went far beyond whether Barbara loved the man or not: She was doing it because he *needed* protecting in this matter of his daughter's kidnapping, obviously. But wasn't the truth that he himself—Detective Inspector Thomas Lynley—had also said not a word to Isabelle about those tickets to Pakistan? So if Barbara was protecting Azhar for whatever reason, wasn't the truth that he was protecting Barbara?

He forced his mind away from the whys and wherefores, and he directed it to the immediate problem: Stewart's report and the evidence it contained. Among the other information that Barbara had omitted in Isabelle's office was her visit to South Hackney, to someone that Stewart's man had identified as Bryan Smythe. An address was included, the time and length of her call upon him, and her call upon Dwayne Doughty in Bow immediately upon the conclusion of her dealings with Smythe. It seemed, then, that Smythe was the logical place to begin. But Lynley had to admit to himself that the thought of beginning what could well end with Barbara's sacking from the Met produced in him such a heaviness of spirit that it invaded his body as well, making the very effort of pushing his key into the Healey Elliott's ignition a matter of will that he did not know if he possessed. How had they come to this moment? he wondered. Barbara, he thought, what in God's holy name have you done?

He couldn't bear to consider the answer to that question, so he started the car and he left the Yard and he took himself to South Hackney with as little thinking as possible involved, listening instead to Radio 4 and an amusing wordplay programme in which various celebrities matched wits with each other. It was a poor substitute for what he really wanted—which was total liberation from thought itself—but it did the trick for now.

He found the street in which Bryan Smythe lived without any trouble. It wasn't a thoroughfare the salubrious nature of which encouraged him to park his car. Indeed, it was insalubrious in the extreme, but there was nothing for it but to guide the Healey Elliott to the kerb and to hope for the best.

What he concluded from Barbara's actions on the day that she had called upon Smythe was that, whoever the bloke was, he was also involved in this business of Hadiyyah, Azhar, and Italy. He could see no other reason that Barbara would come to call upon the man and then go from him directly to Dwayne Doughty. So his expectation of Smythe was that the man would stonewall, and he was going to have to come up with a way to break through whatever barriers Smythe put up once he opened the front door upon Lynley's knock upon it.

Smythe was nondescript, completely ordinary save for his dandruff, which was mightily impressive. Lynley had not seen such dandruff since he'd been at Eton and Snow-on-the-Mountain Treadaway had been his history master.

He took out his warrant card and introduced himself. Smythe looked from the police ID to Lynley to the police ID to Lynley again. He said nothing, but his jaw hardened. He looked beyond Lynley to the street. Lynley told him he'd like a word. Smythe said he was busy, but he sounded . . . Was that anger in his tone?

Lynley said, "This won't take long, Mr. Smythe. If I might come in . . . ?"

"No, you may not" would have been the wise answer, followed by Smythe's closing the door, striding to the phone, and ringing his solicitor. Even "What's this about, then?" might have been the reasonable response of an innocent person. As would any indication that something untoward might have happened in the neighbourhood and here was an officer of the Met to ask him questions about it. But none of that was forthcoming from Smythe because no one guilty of something ever thought of the list of replies that an innocent person might make when faced unexpectedly with a policeman on his doorstep.

Smythe stepped back from the door and indicated with an impatient jerk of his head that Lynley could enter. Inside, Lynley saw, was an impressive collection of Rothko-esque paintings along with various other objets d'art. Not exactly what one expected to find in a South Hackney sitting room. Parts of the borough were on a galloping course towards gentrification, but Smythe's home was extreme. As was the fact that he appeared to own an entire row of the terrace in which his house stood and had bashed his way from one house to the next in order to fashion a showplace of all of them.

He had money by the lorryful. But from what? Lynley doubted its source was on the up-and-up. He said to Smythe, "Your name has come up, Mr. Smythe, in an investigation into the kidnapping of a child in Italy."

Smythe said at once and nearly by rote, "I know nothing about a kidnapping of any child in Italy." His Adam's apple, however, jumped in a rather revealing fashion.

"You don't read the newspapers?"

"From time to time. Not recently, as I've been rather busy."

"Doing?"

"What I do."

"Which is?"

"Confidential."

"Related to someone called Dwayne Doughty?"

Smythe said nothing, but he looked round as if with the wish that he could do something to move Lynley's attention off him and onto one of his art pieces. He was, at that precise instant, probably bitterly regretting admitting Lynley into his house. He'd done it to look less guilty as if with the belief that a show of reluctant cooperation on his part would mean something other than having very little sense.

Lynley said, "Mr. Doughty is connected to this Italian kidnapping. You're connected to Mr. Doughty. Since your work is"—with a gesture to acknowledge the room itself and its art collection—"quite obviously profitable, it leads me in the direction of believing that it also violates any number of laws."

Unaccountably, then, and contrary to Lynley's expectations of him, Smythe muttered, "Jesus *Bloody* Christ."

Lynley raised an eyebrow expectantly. Calling upon the Saviour wasn't the reaction he'd thought he might get. Nor was what came next from the man.

"I don't know who you are, but let's get this straight. I don't bribe cops, no matter what you think."

"How very good to know," Lynley replied, "as I'm not here to be bribed. But I expect you see how the suggestion on your part doesn't actually clarify your connection to Mr. Doughty, although it does leap in the direction of admitting you're operating something here that's illegal."

Smythe seemed to be evaluating this for some reason. The reason became marginally clear when he said, "Did she give you my name?"

"She?"

"We both know who I mean. You're from the Met. You're a cop. So is she. And I'm not stupid."

Not entirely, Lynley thought. He had to be speaking about Havers, so another connection was made. He said, "Mr. Smythe, what I know is that an officer of the Met came to see you and, after her call upon you, went directly to the office of a private investigator called Dwayne Doughty who was—earlier in the year—engaged in a search for a British child kidnapped in Italy. This same Mr. Doughty has been named by a man under arrest in Italy for his own involvement in the kidnapping. Now, the Smythe-to-Doughty business asks for conclusions to be drawn, and that's my job. It also asks whether there might be Smythe-to-Doughty-to-bloke-under-arrest-in-Italy conclusions to be drawn as well, which is also my job. I can happily draw those conclusions or you can clarify. Frankly, I don't know what we have here unless you tell me." And when Smythe's expression bordered on the complacent at the end of these remarks, Lynley added, "So I suggest you enlighten me lest the report I give to my guv indicates that a more thorough investigation of you is necessary."

"I've told you. I work for Doughty occasionally. The work's confidential."

"A broad idea would be fine."

"I compile information on cases he's working on. I pass the information to him."

"What's the nature of the information?"

"Confidential. He's an investigator. He investigates. He investigates people. I follow trails that they leave and I . . . Let's say I map those trails, all right?"

Trails suggested only one thing in this day and age. "Using the Web?" Lynley said.

Smythe said, "Confidential, I'm afraid."

Lynley smiled thinly. "You're a bit like a priest, then."

"Not a bad analogy."

"And for Barbara Havers? Are you her priest as well?"

He looked confused. Clearly, he had not expected the river to course in this direction. "What about her? Obviously, she's the cop who came to see me and she went from me to Doughty. You already know that. And as to what I told her or what sent her there . . . If I don't keep my work confidential, Inspector . . . What did you say your name was?"

"Thomas Lynley."

"Inspector Lynley. If I don't keep my work confidential, I'm out of business. I'm sure you get that, eh? It's a bit like your own work when you think about it."

"As it happens, I'm not interested in what you told her, Mr. Smythe. At least not at present. I'm interested in why she showed up on your doorstep."

"Because of Doughty."

"He sent her to you?"

"Hardly."

"She came on her own, then. For information, I daresay, since—if you work for Doughty—supplying information is your business. We seem to have come full circle in our conversation and what's left is for me to repeat the obvious: Gathering information appears to be paying you quite well. From that and the look of your home, I expect what you're doing can lead you to trouble."

"You've said this."

"As I noted. But your world, Mr. Smythe"—he glanced round the large room—"is about to undergo a seismic shift. Unlike Barbara Havers, I'm not here on my own behest. I've been sent, and I expect you can put the pieces together and come up with the reason why. You're on the Met's radar. You're not going to be happy to be there. To use an analogy that I'm certain you'll understand, you're living in a house of cards and the wind has now begun to blow."

"You're investigating her, aren't you?" he said, with dawning understanding. "Not me, not Doughty, but her."

Lynley didn't reply.

"So if I tell you—"

Lynley interrupted him. "I'm not here to make deals."

"So why should I bloody—"

"You can do as you like."

"What the *hell* do you want?"

"The simple truth."

"The truth's not simple."

Lynley smiled. "As Oscar himself once said. But let me make it simple. At your own admission you look for trails and create 'maps' of them for Dwayne Doughty and, I expect, for others. As this pays you extraordinarily well by the look of your home, I'm going to assume you also 'uncreate' maps by removing those trails, an activity for which you charge rather more. Since Barbara Havers was here, I suspect—due to some glaring omissions in her reports to me—that she's employing you to engage in uncreating and removing. What I need from you is confirmation of this fact. A simple nod of your head."

"Or?"

" 'Or'?"

"There's always an *or*," he said angrily. "Spit it out for God's sake."

"I've mentioned the wind. I think that's sufficient."

"What the *hell* do you want?"

"I've said—"

"No! *No!* There's always something bloody more with you lot. First it was her and I cooperated. Then it was her and him and I *still* cooperated. Now it's you and where the hell is it going to end?"

" 'Him'?"

"The bloody Paki, all right? She came alone first. Then she brought him. Now you're here and for all I know, the bloody Prime Minister is going to show up next."

"She was here with Azhar." That wasn't in the report and how, Lynley wondered, had John Stewart missed that?

"Of course she was bloody here with Azhar."

"When?"

"This morning. When d'you think?"

"What did she want?"

"My backup system. Every record, all my work. You name it, she wanted it."

"That's all?"

He looked away. He walked to one of his paintings—this one largely red with a blue stripe at the bottom that bled almost imperceptibly into a purple haze. Smythe gazed on it as if evaluating what would become of it once the appropriate Met officers started swarming round the place. "As I said," he explained to the painting rather than to Lynley, "she wanted to hire me as well. One job only."

"Its nature?"

"Complicated. I've not even done it yet. I've not even begun."

"So its revelation should present no . . . no moral or ethical dilemma for you."

Still, Smythe kept his gaze on the painting. Lynley wondered what he saw there, what anyone saw when they tried to interpret someone else's intentions. Smythe finally said with a sigh, "It involves altering bank records and phone records. It involves a date change."

"What sort of date change?"

"On an airline ticket. On two airline tickets."

"Not their elimination?"

"No. Just the date. That and making them round-trip."

Which would, Lynley thought, explain why Barbara had said nothing to Isabelle about those tickets to Pakistan that SO12 had uncovered. Altering them would remove suspicion from Azhar entirely, especially if the change involved the date of purchase. So he said, "Purchase date or flight date?" and he waited for what, at heart, he knew Smythe would say.

"Purchase," he said.

"Are we talking about the airline's records, Mr. Smythe, or something else?"

"We're talking about SO12," he said.

SOUTH HACKNEY
LONDON

He'd given up smoking long before he and Helen had married. But as Lynley stood with the key to the Healey Elliott in his hand, he longed for a cigarette. Mostly, it was for something to do other than what needed doing. But he had no cigarettes, so he got into the car, rolled down the window, and gazed sightlessly at the London street.

He understood why Barbara's call upon Smythe with Taymullah Azhar in tow had not been part of John Stewart's report. It had only occurred that morning, itself the reason she'd arrived late at the Yard. But he had no doubt that it would be included as an addendum that Stewart would hand over to Isabelle at the appropriate moment. The only question was when and what, if anything, he himself was going to do about it. Obviously, there was no stopping Stewart. There was only preparing Isabelle in advance.

In this, he saw that he had two options. He could either manufacture a reason that Barbara had paid a call on Bryan Smythe. Or he could report to Isabelle what he'd discovered and let matters develop from there. He'd asked the guv for time to sort all of this out but what, really, was there to sort at this point? The only saving grace that he could see was that his own call upon Smythe had obviated any tinkering the hacker might have been about to do inside the records of SO12, if he could, indeed, even get inside them in the first place. At least that blot on the copybook of Barbara's career would not be present. As to everything else . . . The truth was that he didn't know how far she was steeped in the sin of this mess and there was only one way to find out and he didn't want to do it.

He'd never been a coward when it came to confrontations, so he had to ask himself why he was feeling such cowardice now. The answer seemed to be in his longtime partnership with Barbara. The truth was that she'd apparently gone bad, but his years working with her told him that, in spite of everything, her heart was good. And what in God's name was he supposed to do about that? he asked himself.

LUCCA
TUSCANY

Salvatore's removal from the kidnapping investigation put him in the position of ship-without-harbour. This left him daily slinking by the morning meeting of Nicodemo and his team, a displaced policeman trying to catch a word here and there that would allow him to know where the investigation stood. No matter that the child had been returned to her parents unharmed. There were things going on here that needed understanding. Unfortunately, Nicodemo Triglia was not the person to sort through them.

Salvatore caught the eye of Ottavia Schwartz on his fifth morning venture by the meeting. He went on his way but was gratified when a minute later, she came to find him. He was, ashamedly, even more gratified when the young woman murmured, "*Merda*. It goes nowhere," but he was professional enough to give Nicodemo a minor show of support by murmuring back, "Give him time, Ottavia."

She gave a sputter that communicated *as you like* and said, "*Daniele Bruno, Ispettore.*"

"The man with Lorenzo in the Parco Fluviale."

"*Sì*. A family with very big money."

"The Brunos? But not an old family, *non è vero*?" By this he meant, not old money handed down through the centuries.

"Twentieth century. It all comes from the great-grandfather's business. There're five great-grandsons and they all work for the family company. Daniele's director of sales."

"The product?"

"Medical equipment. They sell a lot of it if looks say anything."

"Meaning?"

"Meaning they live on a compound outside Camaiore. Much property and all the houses together behind a great stone wall. Everyone's married with children. Daniele has three. His wife's an *assistente di volo* on the Pisa–London route."

Salvatore felt a little rush of excitement at this connection to London. It was something. Perhaps it was insignificant, but it *was* something. He told Ottavia to look into the wife. Keeping it all very quiet, he said. "*Puoi farlo, Ottavia?*"

"*Certo*," She sounded a little offended. Of course she could do this. Keeping things quiet was her middle name.

Shortly after they parted, Salvatore took a call from DI Lynley. The London man claimed that, as he did not know how to reach the new chief investigator, perhaps Salvatore could pass along some information they'd uncovered in London . . . ? Between the lines, Salvatore read the truth of the matter, which was that DI Lynley was kindly keeping him informed. He played along, assuring the other detective that he would indeed tell Nicodemo whatever Lynley wished him to know.

"*Non è tanto,*" Lynley said. The private investigator in London named by Di Massimo claimed that he had hired the Italian to look for the girl in Pisa but that Di Massimo had reported to him that the trail went dead at the airport. He was, in fact, sending a report to Salvatore in proof of this. "He claims," Lynley said, "that once the trail went dead at the airport, everything from that point on had to have come from Di Massimo on his own initiative as he—Doughty— knows nothing of it, and there's no evidence pointing otherwise."

"How can there be no evidence?"

"There's a computer technology wizard involved here in London, Salvatore. Chances are very good that he's wiped all superficial traces of a connection between them. They'll be somewhere deep on God only knows what kind of backup system there is, and we can certainly find them in time, but I think it's going to come down to whatever can be unearthed at your end if you want to settle this quickly. And whatever you unearth, Salvatore . . . ? It's going to have to be solid evidence."

"*Chiaro,*" Salvatore said. "*Grazie, Ispettore.* But it is out of my hands now, as you know."

"But not, I suspect, out of your mind or out of your heart."

"*È vero,*" Salvatore said.

"So I'll keep you informed. And you may pass information on to Nicodemo as you will."

Salvatore smiled. The London officer was a very good man. He told Lynley of the wife of one Daniele Bruno: a flight attendant on the Pisa–Gatwick route.

"Any connection to London needs to be explored as well," Lynley concluded. "Give me her name and I'll see what I can do from this end."

Salvatore did so. They rang off with promises to keep each other informed. And less than five minutes later he had his first piece of new information.

LUCCA
TUSCANY

It came from Captain Mirenda of the *carabinieri*. It came by special messenger. It was a copy of the original, which she was keeping, but it included a note from the captain in which she explained that a thorough search of the rooms above the barn at Villa Rivelli had turned it up. All of this information was contained on the cover page of three pages that were clipped together. Salvatore removed this top one and looked to see what he had been sent.

The second page comprised the front and back of a greeting card, unfolded so as to show it in its entirety on one sheet of paper. It was a smiley-face sun with no message printed. Salvatore glanced at it, removed it, and looked at the third page.

This was the message contained within the card. It was handwritten. It was in English. Salvatore could not translate the message completely, but he recognised key words.

He rang Lynley back at once. He knew he could have—should have—gone to speak with Nicodemo Triglia instead, not only because he was holding something that could indeed be vital to the case he was now assigned but also because, unlike himself, Nicodemo spoke English. But he told himself it was a case of quid pro quo, and when Lynley answered, he read him the message.

> *Do not be afraid to go with the man who gives you this card, Hadiyyah. He will bring you to me.*
>
> *Dad.*

Lynley said, "God," and then he translated the message into Italian. He said, "What remains is the handwriting. Is the message in cursive, Salvatore?"

It was, and thus they needed to see a sample of the Pakistani man's handwriting. Could Ispettore Lynley get a sample? Could he fax it to Italy? Could he—

"*Certo*," Lynley said. "But I expect there's a source more immediate, Salvatore." Taymullah Azhar would have filled out paperwork at the *pensione* where he had stayed in Lucca. This was Italian law, no? Signora Vallera would have that paperwork. There would not be a lot of writing upon it, but perhaps there would be enough . . . ?

Salvatore said that he would see to it at once. And in the meantime, he would send to Lynley a copy of the card and its contents, exactly as it had been sent to him.

"And the original?" Lynley said.

"It remains with Captain Mirenda."

"For God's sake, tell her to keep it safe," Lynley said.

Salvatore went on foot to Pensione Giardino. It was a half-mad way of making a bargain with Fate. If he went by car, there would be nothing at the *pensione* in the handwriting of Hadiyyah Upman's father. If he went on foot—walking briskly—there would be something he could use to identify the writer of the card as Taymullah Azhar.

The *anfiteatro* was filled with sunlight and activity when Salvatore arrived. A large group of tourists encircled a tour guide at the centre of the place, people were charging into and out of the shops in search of souvenirs, and most of the tables at the cafés were occupied. Tourist season was hard upon Lucca now, and in the coming weeks the town would become more and more crowded as guides with their duckling charges in tow began to explore the many churches and *piazze*.

The greatly pregnant owner of Pensione Giardino was washing windows, a small child in a pushchair next to her. She was putting a great deal of energy into the activity, and a fine sheen of perspiration glistened upon her smooth olive skin.

Salvatore introduced himself politely and asked her name. She was Signora Cristina Grazia Vallera and, *Sì, Ispettore*, she remembered the two Englishmen who stayed at the *pensione*. They were a policeman and the anguished father of the little girl who'd been kidnapped here in Lucca. By the grace of God, it had all ended well, no? The child had been found safe and healthy, and the newspapers were full of the happy conclusion to what could have been a most tragic tale.

"*Sì, sì*," Salvatore murmured. He explained that he was there to check upon a few final details and he would like to inspect any documents in the signora's possession that the kidnapped girl's papà had filled out. If there was anything else he had written upon in addition to those documents, that would be helpful as well.

Signora Vallera dried her hands on a blue towel tucked into the apron she was wearing. She nodded and indicated the *pensione*'s front door. She guided the pushchair into the dim, cool entry of the place and invited Salvatore to sit in the breakfast room while she searched for something that might answer his need. She kindly offered him a *caffè* while he waited. He demurred politely and said he would prefer to entertain her *bambino* while she assisted him.

"*Il suo nome?*" he enquired politely as he dangled his car keys in front of the toddler.

"Graziella," she said.

"*Bambina*," he corrected himself.

Graziella was not overly enthusiastic about Salvatore's car keys. Give her a few years, he thought, and she'd be delighted to have them dangled in front of her eyes. As it was, she watched them curiously. But she just as curiously watched Salvatore's lips as he made a series of bird noises that she doubtless found strange emanating from a human being.

In short order, Signora Vallera returned. She had with her a registration book in which her guests filled out their names, their street addresses, and—should they wish—their email addresses as well. She also had with her a comment card with which each of her rooms was supplied in order that she might better meet the needs of her guests in the future.

Salvatore thanked her and took these things to a breakfast table beneath one of the front windows that the signora had been washing. He sat and unfolded from his pocket the copy of the card that Captain Mirenda had sent to him. He began with the reception book and he went on to the comment card on which Taymullah Azhar had thanked Signora Vallera for her great kindness to him during his stay, adding that he would have changed nothing about the establishment other than the reason that had necessitated his stay within its walls.

It was the comment card that Salvatore found most useful. He set it next to the copy of the card from Captain Mirenda. He took a deep breath and began his perusal of first one, then the other. He was not an expert, but he did not need to be one. The handwriting on each was identical.

8 MAY

B arbara Havers stormed home after her seventh frantic phone
call to Taymullah Azhar produced nothing more than the previous six, his recorded voice asking her to leave a message. This
one time, though, she left nothing. "Azhar, ring me at once" had got
her nowhere. That being the case, she knew he wasn't planning to
answer or he was already on his way to Italy.

When word had come from Lucca, that word had gone to Lynley's
mobile. Barbara had seen him take the call, and she had clocked the
quick alteration in his face. She had also seen him glance at her before
he left the room.

She followed. She saw Lynley do what she expected he would do:
He made his way to Isabelle Ardery's office.

None of this was good. And nothing that had preceded it was good,
either.

For two days, Bryan Smythe had reported that all his attempts to
hack into SO12's records had been unsuccessful. He'd declared that
he'd gone at the problem every which way to Sunday, but with regard
to SO12, the Met was impenetrable. Certainly, he could get into
personnel records and the PNC wasn't exactly a problem requiring
an IQ above the level of Einstein's. But when it came to documents

under the protection of the anti-terrorist squad . . . Forget about it, Sergeant. It's impossible. This is national security we're talking about. These blokes work hand in glove with MI5, and they aren't about to leave gaps in their system.

Barbara didn't believe him. There was something in his voice that told her something else was up.

He went on to declare briskly that *as* he'd done everything he could and *as* he couldn't help her and *as* he'd shown good faith in at least making every possible attempt at fulfilling her wishes, he wanted all his backup information that she was carrying round with her returned to him.

It was the briskness that gave him away. But "It doesn't work that way, Bryan" didn't get her far.

"You're in this deep and so am I and what I suggest is that we protect each other" was his immediate reply.

That was all he would say. But the fact that he would say it when *she* was the person holding the information that would land *him* in gaol suggested that he was holding information about her as well, and it wasn't of the nature that Doughty's was: just filmed documentation of her innocent visits to the man.

She said sharply, "What's going on, Bryan?"

He said, "Give me the memory sticks and I'm happy to share on that subject."

"Are you actually trying to blackmail me?"

"Go to bed with thieves and don't complain when they steal your jimjams," he replied evenly. "In a word—or three—things have changed."

"Then I'll ask again: What's going on?"

"And I'll say the same: Return my backup system."

"You can't be claiming you have only one system, Bryan. Bloke like you? You wouldn't make a mistake like that."

"That's hardly the point."

"Then what *is* the point?"

"The point is the mistakes *you've* made, not those that you'd like to assign to me. Full stop."

That was his final word. What was left to her was to decide if he was bluffing on the subject of her alleged mistakes. In his position, she would have bluffed her way to hell and back. But in his position, she also would have reckoned that the information on his memory sticks could be copied endlessly so what was the advantage to him in demanding their return?

And what did it matter since he had to know that she couldn't return his backup. Do that, and her leverage over him was gone. She said, "I'm holding on to what I've got till you manage our little SO12 problem. I don't believe that you can't do it, and I don't believe you're friendless in the area of hacking, either. You can't do it, you know someone who can. So get on the blower—or however else you contact your techno mates—and find a bigger genius than yourself."

"You aren't hearing me very well," he told her. "I do that, and I'm finished. But here's what you ought to look at more closely: So are you. Am I being clear? I change those tickets, you're finished, Sergeant. You hang on to my backup files, you're finished as well. You're as good as finished anyway and so am I, but the only thing that proves it is the backup system, which—in your possession, *mate*—also proves you're finished. Because it proves what I've already told them and how much clearer am I going to have to be with you, eh? I'm doing what I do for a living which, let's face it, is illegal as hell. But what *you're* doing is *not* what you're supposed to be doing for a living and the bloody gaff is bloody blown so if you have any bloody sense, you're going to give me the memory sticks and you're going to make sure that no one else has a copy of what's on them."

Hearing this, she'd thought back frantically. When it came to Doughty and his merry crew, she'd been more than careful with what she'd reported to Lynley while he'd been acting as liaison officer. And when it came to Smythe, Lynley knew nothing at all. She'd covered her tracks by making absolutely sure she saw to the work assigned to her by John Stewart, and even if the ground was shaky when it came to everything she'd declared about her mum, it wasn't as if that ground was going to crumble beneath her. No, she had to move forward and stick to the plan and get Azhar cleared of this mess.

"Find the genius we need or do it yourself, Bryan" was her parting remark to the man in South Hackney. She wasn't about to let Azhar go down for kidnapping.

That final thought was fixed inside her head as she careened home. She sent a message of thanks heavenward when she saw that Azhar's car was in the driveway next to the house. She sent a second message heavenward when she blasted out of her own car—parked behind his to block him although she wouldn't admit that to herself—when she went through the gate and saw that the French windows of the ground-floor flat were open to the pleasant day.

She hurried over to the flat. At the doors, she called out his name. He came from the bedroom as if materialising out of shadow. One look at his face and she knew he'd been told. Lynley had promised her he would make no attempt to reach Azhar, but he'd also informed her that the Italians would probably contact him. Or perhaps Lorenzo Mura would. But in any case, it was likely that he already knew.

"Inspector Lo Bianco only phoned me as a courtesy" was how Lynley had put it.

"Did he say anything about Hadiyyah?" Barbara had asked.

"Only that she remains with Mura for now."

"For God's sake, how did it happen?" she demanded. "This isn't the sodding nineteenth century. Women don't just die of morning sickness."

"Everyone's in agreement on that."

"Which means?"

"There'll be an autopsy."

Now, confronted with Taymullah Azhar, Barbara said, "Bloody hell, Azhar. What happened to her?"

He came to her and without a thought she took him into her arms. He was wooden. He said, "She would not listen. Lorenzo wanted her to remain in hospital, but she would not agree to that. She thought she knew best when she didn't know at all."

"How is Hadiyyah? Have you spoken to Hadiyyah?" She released him and gazed into his face. "Who phoned you with the news? Lorenzo?"

He shook his head. "Her father."

"Oh my God." Barbara could only imagine how the conversation with Angelina's father might have gone. Probably along the lines of "She's *dead*, you bloody bastard, and since it's down to you that she ever took herself to Italy in the first place, I hope you choke on the sodding champagne you're going to want to swill."

"But what *happened* to her?" Barbara led Azhar to the sitting room, where she urged him onto the sofa and sat at his side. He seemed a combination of still stunned from the news and trying to come to terms with it. She put her hand on his arm, raised it to his shoulder.

"Kidney failure," he said.

"How the hell is that possible? Why the hell wouldn't the doctors have known? There would have been signs, wouldn't there? There would have to be signs."

"I do not know. Her pregnancy was difficult, evidently. It had been so when she carried Hadiyyah as well. When things worsened for her, she thought she'd eaten something bad. But then she recovered—or she *said* she'd recovered—but I think perhaps . . . This was due to Hadiyyah."

"Her illness?"

"Her wanting to leave hospital. Her insisting upon that. How could she stay there when Hadiyyah was missing and when Hadiyyah—and not Angelina—was what was more important? So by the time she had Hadiyyah back unharmed and by the time she became ill once again, it was too late. She was more ill than anyone suspected." He looked at her. His eyes seemed hollow. "This is all I know, Barbara."

"Have you spoken to Hadiyyah?"

"I rang at once. He would not allow it."

"Who? You mean Lorenzo? That's bloody insane. What right has he to keep you from . . ." Her voice drifted off, and her throat grew so tight as the logical question rose to her lips unbidden. "Azhar, what's to happen to Hadiyyah? What's going on?"

"Angelina's parents are going to Italy. Bathsheba as well. They're on their way now, I expect."

"And you?"

"I was packing when I heard your voice."

LUCCA

TUSCANY

Nicodemo Triglia wasn't concerned about the sudden death of Angelina Upman other than as the misfortune it was. His brief was the kidnapping of the woman's daughter, and Nicodemo was a man who stuck to his brief like a fly in a pool of honey. Unless he was told there was a connection between two events, he assumed there was none. Salvatore knew this about the man. Nicodemo's tunnel vision was legendary, which made him useful to *il Pubblico Ministero* and maddening for anyone else who had to work with him. But in this instance, that tunnel vision was going to be of benefit to Salvatore.

For safety's sake, he was meeting with Cinzia Ruocco in a neutral environment. Piazza San Michele was littered with cafés facing the white Chiesa di San Michele in Foro, and on this particular day its vicinity was enhanced by a clothing and dry goods market that had been set up on the church's south side. So the piazza was crowded both with visitors to Lucca and with Lucchese searching for bargains among the cheap clothes. His meeting with Cinzia would thus be unnoticed, which was important to Salvatore.

He had been informed of the sudden death of Angelina Upman by Lorenzo Mura in the late evening of the previous day. The man had turned up at Torre Lo Bianco—it was hardly a secret where Salvatore lived—and had charged up the stairs to the very top of the tower when Salvatore's mamma had pointed the way. Salvatore was enjoying his regular evening's *caffè corretto* when pounding footsteps on the stairs to his aerie caused him to turn from his view of the city.

Mura was a man deranged. At first, Salvatore had no idea what he was talking about. When he cried out, "She's dead! Do something! He killed her!" and raised his hands to beat upon his temples as he wept, Salvatore had only stared at him in incomprehension. His first horrified thought was of the child.

He said, "What? How?"

Lorenzo crossed the tower to him and grabbed his arm in a grip that crushed his sinews right to the bone. "He did it to her. He would stop at nothing to have the child back. Do you not see? I know he has done this."

At that, Salvatore knew what he should have known the moment Lorenzo had come into his view. He was speaking of Angelina. Somehow Angelina Upman had died, and Mura's grief was unmanning him.

But how was it even possible that the woman had died? he asked himself. To Lorenzo, he said, "*Si sieda, signore*," and he led him to one of the wooden benches that sided the large square planter in the centre of the roof. "*Mi dica*," he murmured, and he waited for Lorenzo to calm himself enough to tell him what had happened.

She had become weak, Mura told him. She had become lethargic. She could not eat. She would not move from the loggia. She kept declaring she would soon enough be well. She kept promising that she needed only to regain her strength after the terrible ordeal when Hadiyyah had been missing. And then she could not be awakened from an afternoon *pisolino*. An ambulance was called. She died the next morning.

"He did this to her," Lorenzo cried. "*Do* something, for the love of God."

"But, Signor Mura," Salvatore had said, "how could anyone be involved in this, let alone the professor? He is in London. He has been there for days. Tell me what the doctors are saying."

"What does it matter what they say? He fed her something, he gave her something, he poisoned her, he poisoned our water, it all took time so that she would die after his departure to London."

"But, Signor Mura—"

"No!" Mura shouted. "*Mi senta! Mi senta!* He pretends to reach peace with Angelina. This is easy for him because already he has killed her and what he's given her resides within her, waiting . . . just waiting . . . And when he's gone, she dies and this is what happened, and you must do something."

So Salvatore promised he would explore what had happened. Cinzia Ruocco was his first step. A sudden death such as this . . . There would be an autopsy. Angelina Upman had been under the care of a doctor, *sì*, but this care had been for her pregnancy and that doctor certainly would sign no certificate declaring that one of his patients had died of pregnancy. So he would meet with and speak to Cinzia Ruocco, the medical examiner.

Now, Salvatore stood when he saw Cinzia approaching through the crowded piazza. God, he thought in his usual response to the sight of her, such a beautiful woman to be carving up bodies, such a heart beating within her magnificent chest. She was the kind of woman willing to mar her own beauty and then to display the result of that marring for all to see, as she did now. She wore a sleeveless dress so the scars from the acid she'd poured down her arm were fully displayed. These had spared her from the marriage that her father had insisted she make in Naples. She never spoke of this, but Salvatore had looked into her past and her family's connection to the Camorra. It had been a simple matter to learn that Cinzia Ruocco allowed no person other than herself to dictate her fate.

Salvatore raised a hand so that she would see him. She nodded briskly and strode to join him, oblivious to those whose stares went from the perfection of her face and her figure to the terrible disfigurement of her arm. She'd spared her hand when she'd used the acid. She had been desperate when she'd done it, but she'd never been a fool.

"*Grazie per avermi incontrato,*" Salvatore told her. She was busy and to take time from her schedule to meet him here in the piazza was an act of friendship he would remember.

She sat and took his offered cigarette. He lit it for her, lit one for himself, and raised his chin at a waiter lingering by the door that led into the café's interior with its display of baked goods. When the waiter advanced upon them, Cinzia glanced at her watch and ordered a *cappuccino.* Salvatore requested another *caffè macchiato.* He shook his head at the offer of *un dolce.* Cinzia did the same.

She leaned back in her chair and gazed at the piazza. Across from them beneath a loggia, a guitarist, a violinist, and an accordionist were setting up shop for the day. Next to them, a *venditore dei fiori* did likewise, filling buckets with bouquets.

"Lorenzo Mura came to see me last evening," Salvatore told her. "*Che cos'è successo?*"

Cinzia drew in on her cigarette. Like a woman of fifty years in the past, she made cigarette smoking look glamorous. She needed to give it up, as did he. They would both die of it if they were not careful. She said, "Ah. Signora Upman, no? Her kidneys failed, Salvatore.

They were failing all along, but because of the pregnancy . . ." She flicked ash expertly from the cigarette. "Doctors don't know it all. We put our faith in them when often we should listen to what our bodies are telling us instead. Her doctor heard from her some symptoms: vomiting, diarrhea, dehydration. A bit of spoiled food, he decided, along with the morning sickness, was at the root of the problem. She was in a delicate state anyway—susceptible to illness, eh?—so perhaps a bug of some sort had easy access to her system. Give her much fluid, take a family history from her, do a few tests, and in the meantime, just for safety's sake, treat her with a course of antibiotics." Again she drew in on her cigarette. Again she tapped it on an ashtray at the table's centre, and she added, "I suspect he killed her."

"Signor Mura?"

She eyed him. "I speak of the doctor, Salvatore."

He said nothing for a moment as their coffees were placed on their table. The waiter took a quick opportunity to gaze admiringly at Cinzia's cleavage, and he winked at Salvatore. Salvatore frowned. The waiter departed hastily.

Salvatore said, "How?"

"I suspect his treatment did the job. Consider, Salvatore: A pregnant woman goes to hospital. She presents her symptoms to the doctor. She can keep nothing in her system. She is weak, dehydrated. There is blood in her stool and this suggests something more is involved than morning sickness, but no one living with her is ill—an important point, my friend—and no one elsewhere has presented the same symptoms. So an assumption is made and a course of treatment that grows from that assumption is prescribed. In the ordinary way of things, this course of treatment would not kill her. It might not cure her, but it would not kill her. Her condition improves, and she goes home. Yet the sickness returns in double force, in triple force. And then she dies."

"Poison?" Salvatore said.

"*Forse,*" she replied, but she looked thoughtful. "I suspect, though, it is not the kind of poison we think of when the word itself is said. You see, we consider poison as something introduced: into food, into water, into the air we breathe, into a substance we use in the ordinary course of events in our lives. We do not think of poison as something produced within us because of an error on the part of our doctors, these fallible people in whom we place our trust."

"You're saying that something the *doctors* did triggered a poison inside her body?"

Cinzia nodded. "That is what I'm saying."

"This is possible, Cinzia?"

"It is indeed."

"Can it be proven? Can it be established for Signor Mura that no one is at fault in this matter? What I mean is that no one poisoned her. Can this be established?"

She glanced at him as she stubbed out her cigarette. "Ah, Salvatore," she said. "You misunderstand me. That no one is involved in her death? That this was merely a terrible mistake on the part of her doctors? My friend, that is not what I'm saying at all."

11 MAY

S he was not Catholic but the Mura family had extraordinary influence, so she was given a Catholic funeral and an impressive burial at Cimitero Urbano di Lucca. Salvatore went to the funeral out of respect for the Muras in general and to show Lorenzo in particular that he was indeed looking into the untimely death of the woman he loved and the child she carried. He went to the burial for another reason entirely: to observe the behaviour of every person there. At a great distance from the gravesite, Ottavia Schwartz observed as well. She was tasked with surreptitiously taking photos of everyone present.

There were three camps of people: the Muras and their friends and associates, the Upmans, and Taymullah Azhar. The Mura contingent was vast, in keeping with the extraordinary size of their family and the length of time they'd held influence in Lucca. The Upmans were a party of four consisting of Angelina's parents, her sister—an astonishing identical twin of the dead woman—and this sister's spouse. Taymullah Azhar was a party of two: himself and his daughter. This poor child's confusion was total, her understanding of what had happened to her mother imperfect. She clung to her father's waist at the gravesite. Her face was a study in incomprehension. As far as she had known, her mummy had had an upset tummy when she'd lain on a chaise longue on the loggia. She'd drifted into sleep and had not awakened. Then she was dead.

Salvatore thought of his own Bianca, nearly the same age as Hadiyyah. He prayed as he looked upon this little girl: God forbid that anything should happen to Birgit. How does a nine-year-old child recover from such a loss? he asked himself. And this poor child . . . kidnapped from the *mercato*, then taken to reside at Villa Rivelli with the half-mad Domenica Medici, and now this . . .

But that chain of thought led him ineluctably to the Pakistani professor. Salvatore observed Taymullah Azhar's solemn face. He considered the way in which everything had come about to result in this moment of his daughter clinging to his waist. She was returned into his sole care, her remaining parent. There would be no sharing of her required, no to-ing and fro-ing from London for visits that would end all too soon. Was this present situation the terrible synchronicity of random and apparently unrelated events, or was this what it appeared to be: a convenient conclusion to the dispute over possession of a child?

Lorenzo Mura clearly thought the latter, and he had to be restrained from a graveside confrontation with Azhar. His sister and her husband held him back. "*Stronzo!*" he cried. "You wanted her dead and now you have it! For God's sake, someone do something about him!"

It was an unseemly graveside display, but one not out of keeping with Mura's nature. He was passionate in the first place. And now as a man who has suddenly lost the woman he loves and the child she carries . . . their future planned out together and then gone in an instant . . . ? The English present at the funeral and gravesite would always practise their stiff upper lips faced with a tragedy such as this. But an Italian? No. A release of grief, a reaction to grief . . . These things were natural. Reticence in the face of these things was what was inhuman. Salvatore only wished that the child of Angelina Upman did not have to witness it or hear what Lorenzo was shouting across the grave at her father.

Mura's family seemed to feel likewise. His sister urged Lorenzo from the grave and their mamma drew him to her sumptuous bosom. He was soon encircled by his relations and they moved as one unified body away from the grave and towards the cemetery's grand entrance where their cars had been left.

The Upman family approached Taymullah Azhar. Salvatore's English was too limited for him to understand all that they said, but he could read their expressions well enough. They hated this man, and they cared little for the child he had produced with the dead woman. They looked upon her as if she was only a curiosity to them. They looked upon him with loathing. At least Angelina's parents did so. Her sister extended a hand to the child, but Azhar moved Hadiyyah out of her reach.

"This is how it finishes," the father of Angelina said to the Pakistani man. "She died as she lived. As will you. And soon, I hope."

His wife, the mother, looked at the child. She opened her lips to speak, but before she could do so, the husband had her by the arm and was marching her in the same direction the Muras had taken. The twin sister said, "I'm sorry how it's ended. You should have given her the only thing she wanted. I expect you know that now," and she walked off as well.

Soon enough Salvatore alone remained at the gravesite with Taymullah Azhar and his daughter. He wished that little Hadiyyah did not have to hear what he was going to say. Certainly she had already heard enough for one day, and she didn't need to know the various ways in which her father was under suspicion.

"There are some things you need to know, Salvatore" was how Cinzia Ruocco had put it to him as they sat in Piazza San Michele. "In this woman's gut was something very strange. No one yet wishes to talk about it, but we call it a biofilm."

"What is this, then? Is it something that harms?"

"An aggregate of bacteria," she said, and she used her hand in a cupping motion as if to demonstrate. "A collection of it that was most unexpected. It was . . . Salvatore, it was highly evolved. It should not have been there in her gut. And I must tell you this, my friend. It is nowhere else. And it should be."

He was confused. It should not have been there in her gut. It was not elsewhere, yet it should have been. What kind of medical riddle was this? He said, "She did not die of kidney failure, then?"

"*Sì, sì*, she did. But it was triggered."

"By this . . . what did you call it?"

"A biofilm. But no, the biofilm—this thing in her gut—it *began* the process. But a toxin killed her."

"She was poisoned, then."

"She was poisoned, *sì*. Just not in the way her doctors would immediately recognise because, you see, she had already been ill. It was very clever. Someone was either very lucky to kill her in this way, or someone had thought of everything. Because, you see, in the normal course of events, it would be assumed that her death was natural, especially since she had been so ill from the pregnancy. But nothing about this death was natural. It was a chain reaction, as inevitable as knocking dominoes over."

Which left Salvatore with the job he had to do now. He approached Taymullah Azhar to do it.

CHALK FARM
LONDON

Barbara kept watch. Once she arrived home at the end of her workday, she went immediately to Azhar's flat. His intention had been to return to London directly after Angelina's funeral, bringing Hadiyyah with him, all the better to return the little girl to the environment she'd known for all of her life save for the past few months. But he had not yet arrived.

She wasn't concerned at first. The funeral had been scheduled for the morning, but there would have been a reception of some sort afterwards, wouldn't there? People would want an opportunity to express further condolences and to do what they could to suggest to the bereaved that life would go on. After that, Hadiyyah's things would need to be packed, if they weren't already, and the drive to Pisa would have to be made. Then there was the wait at the airport and the flight itself, and of course she shouldn't have expected them before evening at the earliest.

But evening came and went and darkness fell, and still Azhar and

Hadiyyah did not return. Again and again, Barbara left her bungalow to pace to the front of the building, thinking that they had returned without letting her know for some reason. Finally, at half past nine, she rang Azhar's mobile.

"How did it go?" she asked him. "Where are you?"

"Still in Lucca," he said. He sounded exhausted as he added, "Hadiyyah is asleep."

"Ah. I did wonder . . . I expect it was too much for her, wasn't it?" Barbara said. "Everything that's happened and then the funeral and on top of that a flight to London? I didn't think of that. I won't keep you, then. You must be all done in as well. When you get back to town, we c'n—"

"He took my passport, Barbara."

A fist gripped her heart. "Who? Azhar, what's happened?"

"Chief Inspector Lo Bianco. It was after the . . . her burial."

"He was there?" Barbara knew only too well what it meant when the coppers went to the funeral of someone with whom they were not personally involved.

"Yes. At the church and then at the cemetery. This is where . . . Barbara, Hadiyyah was with me. She did not hear him as he took me aside, but she will wonder why we do not leave in the morning. What am I to tell her?"

"Why does he want your passport? Never mind. What a bloody stupid question. Let me think." But she found it was nearly impossible to do so because every thought led her to one place only and that was a place in which Dwayne Doughty had cut a deal with someone to save his own neck and had provided the necessary information pointing to Azhar's involvement in his daughter's kidnapping. Or perhaps Di Massimo had done so, although, according to Azhar, he'd never spoken to the man. Or perhaps it was Smythe, with a backup to his backup sent by express to the Italian police. Or . . . God only knew because the real point was that without his passport, Azhar was stuck in Lucca at the mercy of the coppers. "They've not questioned you, have they?" she asked him. "Azhar, if they want to ask you questions, you must find a solicitor at once. D'you understand? Don't say a sodding word to those people without a solicitor sitting next to you."

"They have not even asked to question me. But, Barbara, I fear that perhaps Mr. Doughty . . . or one of his associates . . . Someone must have told the inspector something to make him begin to think that I . . ." He was silent for a moment and then, quietly, "Oh God, I should have let it all go."

"Let what go? Let your own daughter go? How the bloody hell were you supposed to do that, eh? Angelina *took* her. She disappeared. You did what you had to do to find her."

"It fell apart, Barbara. This is what I fear."

She couldn't tell him his fears were unreasonable. Yet unless the Italians had sent someone from Italy to talk to Doughty or unless Smythe somehow had contacted them, the only person who could have told them anything would have been Di Massimo. And according to Azhar, he'd engaged in no communication with the Italian detective at all, all of that being done by Doughty with every trail removed by Bryan Smythe. So it was likely that the Italian cops had something more, something different beyond information they would have gleaned from an interrogation of Di Massimo. She had to find out what that was. Until she discovered it, they could plan no further.

She said to Azhar, "You listen to me. First thing tomorrow, you ring the embassy. Then you ring for a solicitor."

"But if he asks me to come to the *questura* . . . and what of Hadiyyah? Barbara, what of Hadiyyah? I am not innocent in this matter. Had I not arranged to have her taken—"

"Just stay where you are and wait till you hear from me."

"What will you do? From London, Barbara, what *can* you do?"

"I c'n get the information we need. Without that, we're wandering in the dark."

"If you could have seen how they looked upon us," he murmured. "Not only upon me but upon Hadiyyah."

"Who? The coppers?"

"The Upmans. That I am worse than nothing to these people is something I can bear. It is as it has always been. But Hadiyyah . . . They looked at her as if she carried a disease, some deformity of body . . . She is a child. She is innocent. And these people—"

"Set them aside, Azhar," Barbara cut in. "Don't think about them. Promise me that. I'll be in touch."

They rang off. Barbara spent the rest of the evening and far into the night sitting at the table in her tiny kitchen, smoking one fag after another, and trying to work out what she could do that did not involve anyone other than herself. She knew this was a pointless activity, but she engaged in it anyway till she had to admit there was only one action she could take next.

12 MAY

The fact that Isabelle Ardery had made no move to deal with Barbara Havers suggested to Lynley that she was either giving him the time he had asked for to try to sort out what Barbara had been up to or she was herself building a case against Barbara that would give her the result she'd been looking for since first encountering the sergeant as a difficult member of her team. Isabelle was someone who wanted things to run smoothly, and it couldn't be argued that Barbara lent to the machinery of a police investigation the constant oil of her cooperation.

Isabelle had, of course, asked for a report from him. He told her of his conversation with Bryan Smythe, but he made no mention of either the airline tickets to Lahore or what Barbara Havers had asked Smythe to do. He left out the information that she had gone to see Smythe in the company of Azhar as well. This proved to be a misstep on his part.

Isabelle slid the report across her desk to him. He put on his glasses, opened it, and read.

John Stewart had been on top of the call upon Bryan Smythe made by Havers and Azhar. He'd merely not had a chance to hand it over to Isabelle when Lynley and she had met earlier with the sergeant. When

Lynley asked the superintendent why she had not yet turned Barbara over to CIB, her steady reply of "I'm waiting to see how far this reaches" told him that his own actions would be scrutinised as well.

"Isabelle, I admit that I'm trying to find excuses for her" was what he told the superintendent.

"Looking for reasons is understandable, Tommy. Looking for excuses is not. I expect you see the difference between the two."

He returned Stewart's report to her, saying, "And as for John . . . his reasons? His excuses? What are you planning to do about him?"

"John's well in hand. You're not to concern yourself with John."

He could hardly believe what she was saying since it had to mean she'd actually *set* DI Stewart to the task of watching Havers closely and noting her movements. If that was the case, Isabelle was giving Barbara rope. She also was telling him not to wrest that rope from Barbara's grasp only to wrap it round his own neck.

All that was wanted to finish Barbara off was Lynley's own report on the full contents of the conversation he'd had with Bryan Smythe. For although Stewart knew where Barbara had gone and when she'd gone there and with whom, what he had not known from the first was what she was up to. Only Lynley himself—and Barbara—knew that.

Early in the morning, he went into the garden behind his house. His place was laid for breakfast, his newspapers were on the dining room table precisely angled from his fork, and the scent of bread toasting under Charlie Denton's watchful eye was emanating from the kitchen. But he walked to the window, looked out on the bright spring day, and saw how beautifully the roses were blooming. He went outside to look them over, aware that in the time since Helen's death, he'd not once ventured out into the garden she'd loved. Nor, he realised, had anyone else.

Among the rose bushes he found a pail. Within it pruned branches from the plants leaned. Hooked over the pail's side was a small pair of secateurs, rusty now from being exposed to the weather for more than a year. The bushes themselves told the tale of why the pail, its contents, and the secateurs had been left out here for so long. Helen had been in the midst of pruning them when she'd been murdered.

Lynley thought of how he'd watched her once from the window of his library above stairs. He'd gone to join her in the garden and even now her words came to him, spoken in her typical self-deprecating, droll fashion. *Tommy darling, I do think this might be the* only *useful activity I could possibly become adept at. There's something so satisfying about grubbing round in the dirt. I think it takes one back to one's roots.* And then she thought about what she'd said and laughed. *What a terrible pun. It was completely unintentional.*

He'd offered to help her, but she wouldn't let him. *Don't please rob me of my one opportunity to excel at something.*

He smiled now at the thought of her. Then he was struck by how the thought of Helen had for the first time not been accompanied by searing pain.

A door opened behind him. He turned to see Denton opening it for Barbara Havers. Seeing her, Lynley glanced at his watch. It was seven twenty-eight in the morning. What on earth was she doing in Belgravia? he wondered.

She crossed the lawn to him. She looked horrible. Not only was she more thrown together than usual, but she also seemed to have spent an entire night without sleep. She said to him, "They have Azhar."

He blinked. "Who?"

"The cops in Lucca. They've taken his passport. He's being detained. He doesn't know why."

"Is he being questioned about something?"

"Not yet. He just can't leave Italy. He doesn't know what's going on. *I* don't know what's going on. So how do I help him? I didn't know what else to do. I don't speak Italian. I don't know their game. I don't know what's happened." She took three paces along the flowerbeds before she swung round and said abruptly, "C'n you ring them, sir? C'n you find out what's happening?"

"If they're detaining him, it's obviously because they've got questions about—"

"Look. Right. Whatever. I know. For what it's worth, I've told him to ring the embassy. And to get a solicitor, just in case. I've *told* him that. But there must be something more I c'n do. And you *know* these blokes and you c'n speak Italian and you c'n at least . . ." She punched a fist into her palm. "Please, sir. Please. It's why I've come from Chalk Farm. It's why I couldn't wait till you got to work. Please."

He said, "Come with me," and took her to the house. Inside the dining room, he saw that Denton was already laying another place for breakfast. Lynley thanked him, poured two cups of coffee, and told Barbara to serve herself some eggs and bacon from the sideboard.

"Already eaten," she said.

"What?" he asked.

"Chocolate Pop-Tart and a fag." She cocked her head at the sideboard and added, "Anything nutritious'll probably put my system into shock."

"Humour me," he told her. "I don't wish to eat alone."

"Sir, please . . . I need you to . . ."

"I'm completely aware of that, Barbara," he said steadily.

Reluctantly, she spooned herself some scrambled eggs. She added to this two rashers of bacon. She got into the spirit of things with four mushrooms and a piece of toast. He followed her lead and then joined her at the table.

She said with a nod to his newspapers, "How d'you read three bloody broadsheets every morning, for God's sake?"

"I take the news from *The Times* and the editorials from *The Guardian* and *The Independent*."

"Seeking balance in life?"

"I find it's wise to do so. The overuse of adverbs in journalism these days is becoming something of a distraction, though. I don't like to be told what to think, even surreptitiously."

They locked eyes at this. She broke away first, scooping up some of her scrambled eggs and piling them up on a portion torn from her toast. She chewed quite a bit. Swallowing, however, did not appear easy for her.

Lynley said, "Before I make the call to Inspector Lo Bianco, Barbara . . . ?" He waited for her gaze to meet his. "Is there anything you want to tell me? Anything I need to know?"

She shook her head.

"You're certain?" he said.

"Far 's I know," she told him.

So be it, he thought.

BELGRAVIA
LONDON

For the first time in her life, Barbara Havers cursed the fact that she had no language other than English. While it was true that she'd had moments of desire to learn a foreign tongue—most of them having to do with understanding what the cook at her local curry house was really yelling about the lamb *rogan josh* before he slopped it into a takeaway container—for the great majority of her life she'd had no need of one. She had a passport, but she'd never used it to go anywhere a foreign tongue was spoken. She'd never used it at all, in fact. She only had it on the off chance that a heretofore unknown Prince Charming might show up unexpectedly in her life and wish to take her on a luxury Mediterranean holiday in the sun.

But now, watching Lynley as he spoke to Chief Inspector Lo Bianco in Lucca, she tried to pick up anything she could. She listened hard for words she might recognise. She tried to read his face. From the words, she only picked up names: Azhar, Lorenzo Mura, Santa Zita—whoever the hell that was—and Fanucci. She thought she also heard Michelangelo Di Massimo mentioned as well as *information*, *hospital*, and *factory*, for some reason. Most of what she learned came from Lynley's face, which grew graver as the conversation continued.

He finally said, "*Chiaro, Salvatore. Grazie mille. Ciao,*" which told her the conversation was ending.

Barbara felt only dread when he rang off, but the dread didn't stop her. "What?" she asked. "*What?*"

"It appears to be *E. coli*," he said.

Food contamination? she thought. *Food?* She said, "How the bloody hell did she die of food poisoning in this day and age? How does *anyone* die of food poisoning now?"

"Evidently, it was an enormously virulent strain, and the doctors didn't recognise what it was because she reported being ill earlier due to her pregnancy. That's what they initially thought they were still dealing with: a more serious version of morning sickness. Once they believed they had that sorted, they did other tests and those were all negative."

"What sort of tests?"

"Cancers, colitis, other diseases. Colon and bowel. There was nothing, so they assumed she'd picked up a bug of some sort, as people do. They gave her a course of antibiotics as a precaution. And that's what killed her."

"*Antibiotics* killed her? But you said *E. coli* . . . ?"

"It was both. Evidently with *E. coli*—at least with this strain of it, as far as I can tell from what Salvatore said—antibiotics cause a toxin to be produced. Shiga, it's called. It finishes off the kidneys. By the time the doctors realised from Angelina's symptoms that her kidneys were going, it was too late to save her."

"Bloody hell." Barbara took this all in, and what seeped slowly into her consciousness was the fact that her body was relaxing for the first time in twelve hours and her mind was chanting, Thank God, thank God, thank God, thank God. Food poisoning ultimately leading to death, as unfortunate as it was, did not mean . . . what she did not want it to mean.

She said, "It's over, then."

Lynley gazed at her long before he said, "Unfortunately, it isn't."

"Why not?"

"No one else is ill."

"But that's good, isn't it? They dodged the—"

"No one, Barbara. Anywhere. Not at Fattoria di Santa Zita—that's the land Lorenzo Mura owns—not in any surrounding village, and not anywhere in Lucca. No one, as I said. Anywhere. Not in Tuscany. Nor in the rest of Italy. Which is one of the reasons the doctors didn't recognise what they were dealing with immediately."

"Should I be following this?"

"When *E. coli*'s involved, it's generally referred to as a breakout. Do you see what I mean?"

"I see that this was an isolated case. But like I said, that's good, isn't it? That means . . ." And then she indeed saw what it meant, as clearly as

she saw Lynley regarding her. Her mouth went dry. She said, "But they'd
be checking *everywhere* for the source, right? They'd have to do that to
prevent anyone else from getting infected. They'd be looking at everything Angelina ate and . . . Are there animals at this *fattoria* place?"

"Donkeys and cows, yes."

"Could the *E. coli* have come from them? I mean, don't animals
pass this stuff on in some way? Aren't we talking about . . . you
know . . ."

"Evidently cattle are a reservoir for the bacteria, and it passes
through their system. Yes. But I don't believe there will be evidence
of *E. coli* at Fattoria di Santa Zita, Barbara. Neither does Salvatore."

"Why not?"

"Because no one else who ate there is ill. Hadiyyah, Lorenzo, even
Azhar in the immediate days after Hadiyyah was found."

"So maybe it's . . . Does it incubate or something?"

"I'm vague on the details, but the point is someone there would
have fallen ill by now."

"Okay. Let's say she went for a walk. Let's say she got too near to
a cow. Or let's say she . . . P'rhaps she got it somewhere else. In town.
At the marketplace. Visiting a friend. Picking something up off the
road." But even Barbara could hear the desperation in her voice, so
she knew Lynley would clock it, as well.

"We go back to no one else being ill, Barbara. We go back to the
strain itself."

"What about the strain?"

"According to Salvatore"—with a nod at his mobile phone lying
by his plate—"they've never seen anything like it. It's to do with the
virulence. A strain this virulent can take out an entire population
before they identify its source. But that population falls ill quickly, in
a matter of days. The health authorities become involved, and they
begin looking at anyone else who might have seen a doctor or ended
up in casualty with similar symptoms. But as I said, no one else has
been ill. Not before Angelina. Not after Angelina."

"I still don't see how that's such a bad thing. I don't see why
Azhar's been detained unless . . ." Again that steady gaze upon her.
She read the grim nature of it, but she read something else, and she

wanted more than anything in her life not to be able to understand that look. She said lightly, "Oh, I see. They're keeping Azhar in Lucca because they don't want him to pass it on to someone else, I expect. If he's got it in him—like dormant or something—and he brings it back to London . . . I mean, he could be a modern-day Typhoid Mary, eh?"

The look on Lynley's face was unchanging. He said, "It doesn't work that way. It's not a virus. It's a bacteria. It's—if you will—a microbe. A quite dangerous microbe. You do see where this is leading, don't you?"

She felt her face going numb. "No. I . . . I don't, actually." All the time, however, her brain was pounding inside her skull, a chant of Oh my God, Oh my God.

Lynley said, "If no source can be found at the *fattoria* itself or in the food supply that Angelina had access to both there and in Lucca and anywhere else she might have gone and if she remains the sole person infected, then where this all leads is to someone putting his hands on a virulent strain of the bacteria and putting it into Angelina's system. Through her food is the most obvious means."

"But why would someone . . . ?"

"Because someone wanted her dangerously ill. Someone wanted her dead. You and I both know that's where all this is leading, Barbara. That's why Azhar has been asked to turn in his passport."

"You can't possibly think that Azhar . . . How the bloody hell was he supposed to do it?"

"I think we also both know the answer to that."

She pushed away from the table although she wasn't sure where she was intending to go. She said, "He has to be told. He's under suspicion. He has to be told."

"I expect he knows already."

"Then I've got to . . . We've got to . . ." She brought her knuckles to her mouth. She considered everything: from the moment Angelina Upman had taken her daughter from London the previous November to where they were now with Angelina dead. She refused to believe what was lying in front of her like a dead dog on the path she was hiking. She said, "No."

"I'm sorry."

"I have to—"

"Listen to me, Barbara. What you have to do now is to take yourself out of this at once. If you don't do that, I can't help you. Frankly, I don't think I can help you as it is although I'm trying."

"What's that s'posed to mean?"

Lynley leaned forward. "You can't think Isabelle is unaware of what's been going on, of what you've been up to, of whom you've seen, of where you've been. She knows it all, Barbara. And if you don't begin walking the straight and narrow this very moment—here, now, and right in this room—the jeopardy you'll be facing could cost you everything. Am I being clear? Do you understand?"

"Azhar didn't kill her. He had no reason because they'd made peace and they were going to share Hadiyyah and . . ." It was Lynley's face that cut off her words. Even beyond what she herself knew about Azhar and about what he'd done to bring about his daughter's kidnapping and to position himself to be there in Italy when she was "found," it was the compassionate sympathy in Lynley's face that did her in. All she could say was "Really. He couldn't."

"If that's the case," Lynley replied, "Salvatore Lo Bianco will sort it all out."

"And in the meantime . . . What the bloody hell do you suggest I do?"

"I've made the suggestion: get back to work."

"That's what you would do?"

"Yes," he said steadily. "In your position, that's what I would do."

She knew he was lying when he said it, though. For the one thing Thomas Lynley would never do was desert a friend.

LUCCA
TUSCANY

Salvatore Lo Bianco received the request for a meeting not from *il Pubblico Ministero* himself but from Piero Fanucci's secretary. She rang his mobile and brusquely instructed him to go to the Orto Botanico, where he would find the *magistrato* waiting for him. "He wishes to have a private word with you, *Ispettore*," was how she put it. "Now?" was how Salvatore responded. "*Sì, adesso*," she replied. Signor Fanucci had arrived at work that morning in something of a state, and a few phone calls both made and received by him had heightened that state. It was her suggestion that Ispettore Lo Bianco leave at once for the botanical gardens.

Salvatore swore but he cooperated. The fact that phone calls had been made by Fanucci and received by him suggested he was on the trail of something. The fact that he had followed these phone calls with a demand for Salvatore's presence suggested he was on the trail of what Salvatore himself was up to.

The botanical gardens were inside the wall of the old city, on its southeast edge. In the month of May, they were flourishing, and where flowers had been planted, they were gloriously abloom. Very few people were within the garden's walls, however. At this hour, the Lucchese were themselves at work, while tourists generally stuck to visiting the churches and *palazzi*.

Salvatore found Fanucci admiring a mass of wisteria, which over-hung an ancient stone trough that was filled with water lilies. He turned from the sight of branches dipping low with clusters of purple flowers as Salvatore approached him on the gravel path.

Piero was smoking a thick cigar, newly lit. He regarded Salvatore with an expression that managed to mix personal sorrow with pro-fessional anger. The anger, Salvatore thought, was real. The sorrow, he reckoned, was not.

"Talk to me, Topo" comprised Fanucci's opening remarks. He flicked some ash from his cigar onto the path. He ground it into the *sassolini* with his foot. "You and the lovely Cinzia Ruocco have been meeting, *no*? You have an earnest talk with her in Piazza San Michele, and why do I suspect the two of you discuss matters from which you were told to step away? What has this to do with, Salvatore?"

Salvatore said, "Of what importance is Cinzia's speaking with me? If I wish to meet a friend for a *caffè*—"

Fanucci held up a minatory finger. "*Stai attento*," he snapped.

Salvatore did not appreciate the threat implied in being spoken to in such a way. He'd had quite enough of Fanucci. He felt his temper rise. He sought to control it. He said, "I see the unfortunate death of this woman Angelina Upman as suspicious. My job is to look at things when they seem suspicious. To me, there is a connection here."

"Between what, may I ask?"

"I think you know."

"Between the kidnapping of this woman's child and her own death? Bah. *Che sciocchezza!*"

"If that is the case, then the only fool will be me. So what difference does it make that I speak to Cinzia about how this unfortunate woman died? I would think it pleases you anyway, to have her dead."

Fanucci's face reddened. His lips moved round the cigar and Salvatore could see his teeth clamp down. He, too, was trying to hold on to his temper. It was, he knew, only a matter of moments before one of them let loose.

"What is that supposed to mean, my friend?" Fanucci asked.

"It means that now this story of her death takes over the headlines. *Poor Mamma of Kidnap Girl Dead in Her Sleep.* And this turn of events directs the spotlight away from the kidnapping and away from Carlo Casparia at long last. It means that now you can release poor Carlo back into his life, which—as we both know, Piero—you were going to have to do quite soon anyway."

Fanucci's eyes narrowed. "I know nothing of the sort."

"Please, do not think me a stupid man. You and I have been acquainted far too long for that. You know you have been wrong about Carlo. And since you cannot bear to be wrong, you have refused to release him. For then you would have to face scrutiny and commentary in the press, and this is something you cannot abide."

"You dare to insult me this way, Salvatore?"

"The truth is not an insult. It is merely the truth. And to this truth, I would have to add with due respect that, in your position, an inability to face one's errors is a very dangerous quality to possess."

"As is jealousy," Fanucci snapped. "Professional or personal, it robs a man not only of his dignity but also of his ability to do his job. In all of your thinking and *respecting*, Salvatore, have you ever once considered this?"

"Piero, Piero. Do you see how you try to alter our conversation?

You wish to make it about me when it should be about you. You have wasted time and resources trying to mould what few facts you had into a case you could build against Carlo. Then when I would not accompany you down this ridiculous path you were determined to walk, you brought in Nicodemo, who would."

"And this is how you see things?"

"Is there another way?"

"*Certo.* For your jealousy blinds you to the facts in front of you. It has done so from the moment this little English girl disappeared from the *mercato.* This has always been your weakness, Topo. This jealousy of yours infects all that you do."

"You propose that I am jealous of what?"

"You are a man broken by his divorce, living back at home with his mamma, no other woman willing to abide you. And we must ask what it must do to your manhood to see someone else—someone like me, so ill formed, so repulsive to look upon—*still* with women eager to be bedded. Bedded by me, a veritable toad. And on top of that, to have this same toad order your replacement in an investigation because your work was not what it should have been . . . ? How does that feel? How do your colleagues look upon you? What do they think of you as they follow Nicodemo's orders instead of yours, eh? Little Topo, have you wondered why you cannot step away from this case as you've been ordered? Have you asked yourself what you try to prove with all of these actions behind my back?"

Salvatore understood now why *il Pubblico Ministero* had wanted this meeting to occur away from his office. Fanucci had a larger plan in mind than merely goading and humiliating Salvatore, and Salvatore could only assume it had to do with saving face in the one way he could.

He said, "Ah. You are afraid, Piero. Despite what you say, you do see there may indeed be a connection between these events. The child is kidnapped. Then her mother dies. If there's a connection between these two occurrences, it cannot possibly be a connection having to do with Carlo Casparia, Michelangelo Di Massimo, and Roberto Squali, can it? For Casparia's in custody, Squali's dead, and that leaves Michelangelo Di Massimo somehow putting his hands on a dangerous bacteria and *also* somehow getting Angelina Upman to ingest it without her knowledge. And how, possibly, could that have happened? So if there is a connection, it follows that someone else—"

"I have said it. There is no connection," Fanucci said. "They are both unfortunate events but they are unrelated."

"As you wish," Salvatore said. "To believe otherwise . . . This would be a problem for you, *sì*? But at least the unfortunate Carlo is no longer a problem, Piero, for if you wish it, you can release the information of this death from *E. coli* to *Prima Voce* in your usual manner, as a leak. Then the paper will fan the flames of public panic to find the source of this deadly contamination. And while that is happening, you can ease Carlo out of the prison and by the time the papers have wind of it"—he snapped his fingers—"it has become old news. And hardly worthy of a story on the first page of the paper, eh? Death trumps kidnapping, after all, even if the corpse is not that of the kidnapped individual. You should be thanking me for making this possible, Piero, not quarrelling with me because I spoke to Cinzia Ruocco about how that poor woman actually died."

"You are being ordered, here and now, Topo, to stand down from this matter. You are being told to hand over to Nicodemo Triglia every bit of information you possess on anything related to the kidnapping of the English girl *and* the death of her mother."

"So you, too, believe they are related, despite your earlier words, eh? And what do you intend to do about that? Bury the evidence of murder so that you can pursue . . . Who is it you intend to pursue in the kidnapping now? It must be the hapless Di Massimo. He will be made guilty of the kidnapping while the death of the mother will merely be an unfortunate coincidence, a senseless tragedy following her daughter's safe return. That is how it must be played so that you are not made to appear in the papers what you actually are. Blind, stubborn, lacking in all objectivity, and a fool."

That did the job. Fanucci erupted. *Il drago* could no longer contain himself. He advanced on Salvatore and, when the blow came, it was with some surprise that Salvatore realised how strong the *magistrato* actually was. He delivered the uppercut with brutal accuracy. Salvatore's head flew back, his teeth driven into his tongue, and then the second punch hit him. This was a blow to his guts, which readied him for the third punch. This one put him onto the ground. He half expected Fanucci to fall upon him then, so that they would roll in the gravel like two schoolboys. But as it turned out, that might have damaged *il Pubblico Ministero*'s bespoke suit. So instead, Piero delivered an agonising kick to Salvatore's kidneys.

"You." Piero grunted with each subsequent kick. "Speak. To. Me. In. This. Way."

Salvatore could do nothing but protect his head as Piero Fanucci went for the rest of his body. He managed to say, *"Basta, Piero!"*

But it was not enough for Fanucci until Salvatore lay motionless on the ground. And by then Salvatore could only dimly hear the magistrate's final words to him. "We shall see which of us is the greater fool, Topo."

Which was, Salvatore decided as Fanucci walked off, Piero's way of giving him permission to investigate the death of Angelina Upman to his heart's content.

Bene, he thought. It very nearly made the beating worthwhile.

LUCCA

TUSCANY

He could barely get his key in the lock. Luckily his mamma heard the scraping of metal against metal. She came to the door, demanding to know who was there, and when she heard his weak voice, she threw the door open. He tumbled directly into her arms.

She screamed. Then she wept. Then she cursed the monster who had laid his brutal hands upon her only son. Then she wept some more. Finally, she helped him into a chair only three feet from the doorway. He was to sit, sit, sit, she told him. She was going to phone for *un' ambulanza*. And then she was going to phone the police.

"I am the police," he reminded her feebly. He added, *"Non ho bi-sogno di un'ambulanza. Non la chiamare, Mamma."*

What? she demanded. He didn't need an ambulance? He couldn't walk, he could barely talk, his jaw looked broken, his eyes were blacked, his mouth was bleeding, his lips were cut, his nose could be broken, and inside his body God alone knew what damage had been done. She wept anew. "Who did this to you?" she demanded. "Where did this happen?"

He was too embarrassed to tell his mamma that *il Pubblico Ministero*—a man more than twenty years his senior—had beaten him so. He said, "*Non è importante, Mamma. Ma puoi aiutarmi?*"

She took a step back from him. *What* was he asking? she demanded, a hand at her breast. Did he think his own mamma might not help him? Would she not give her life for him? He was her blood. All of her children and their children were her reason for living in the first place.

So she bustled round and began to see to his injuries. She was accomplished at this, a woman who was mother to three and *nonna* to ten. She'd bound more wounds than she could remember. He was to put himself into her hands.

She did it well. She still wept as she worked, but she was tenderness itself. When she had finished her ministrations, she helped him carefully to a *divano*. He was to lie there, she told him, and he was to rest. She would call his two sisters. They would want to know what had happened. They would want to visit. And she herself would make his favourite *farro* soup. He would sleep while she worked upon this, and—

"*No, grazie, Mamma,*" Salvatore told her. He would rest a quarter of an hour and then he would return to work.

"*Dio mio!*" was her response to this idea. They went back and forth on the subject of his continuing his day as if nothing untoward had occurred. She would not hear of it, she would bar the door, she would cut off her hair and pour ashes on her head if he so much as put one toe outside of Torre Lo Bianco, *chiaro*?

He smiled weakly at her drama. Half an hour, he compromised. He would rest that long and that was all.

She threw her hands up. At least he would take a fortifying glass of wine, no? An ounce or two of *limoncello*?

He would take the *limoncello*, he told her. He knew that she was going to be relentless till he agreed with at least one of her suggestions.

At the half-hour mark, he eased himself off the *divano*. A wave of dizziness passed over him, followed by a surge of nausea, and he wondered if he'd been concussed. He made his way to a mirror near the entry to the tower and had a look at his reflection to assess the damage.

He thought wryly that at least the scars on his face from adolescent acne were now unremarkable since his features were at present so much more interesting than the remains of what those eruptions on his face had done to his skin. His eyes were swollen, his lips looked lumpy as if injected with a foreign substance, his nose was indeed possibly broken—its position seeming somewhat different from what he remembered—and already the bruising from Piero's fists was starting to appear. He felt additionally bruised on every part of his body, as well. Cracked ribs were likely. Even his wrists hurt.

Salvatore had not known that Piero Fanucci was such a fighter. But on consideration, he had to admit that it made sense. Ugly beyond all possibility of self-reconciliation to this fact, possessing that unsettling adventitious finger upon his hand, springing from poverty and familial ignorance, exposed to the derision of others . . . Who could doubt that, given the alternative between life as a victim and life as an aggressor, Piero Fanucci had made the better choice? Reluctantly, Salvatore rather admired the man.

But he would have to do something about his own appearance lest he frighten women and children in the street. And there was the small matter of his clothing as well, which was filthy and, in some places, torn. So before he went anywhere, he was going to have to make himself presentable. This meant he was going to have to climb three flights of the tower steps to his bedroom.

He managed it, just. It took a quarter of an hour, and he did it mostly by dragging himself up via the handrail while below him his mamma clucked and chattered and called the Blessed Virgin to bring him to his senses before he killed himself. He staggered into his boyhood bedroom and did his best to remove his clothing without crying out in pain. It was the effort of another quarter hour that allowed him to succeed in fighting his way into a change of clothing.

In the bathroom he found the *aspirina*, and he downed four of them with big gulps of water from the tap. He washed his face, told himself he was feeling better already, and made his way back down the stairs. His mother waved both of her arms in a gesture declaring that, Pilate-like, she was not about to take responsibility for whatever lunacy he chose to commit himself to next. She decamped into the kitchen and started to bang round with her pots and pans. She would, he knew, make the *farro* soup. If she couldn't stop him, at least she could nourish him on his return.

Before he left the *torre*, Salvatore placed the phone calls that would bring him up to the minute on the subject of the source of the *E. coli* that had resulted in Angelina Upman's death. What he discovered was that the health authorities were playing a careful waiting game. Word had not gone out far and wide as to the cause of death because it had so far been an isolated incident. Steps had been taken at Fattoria di Santa Zita to locate a source of the bacteria there. All results of all tests were negative. So the health officials had moved on.

Every place Angelina had been in the weeks before her death was being considered, he was told. But still the curiosity of only a single person being affected by the bacteria had not yet been resolved. This was unheard of. It brought into question Cinzia Ruocco's findings and the findings of the laboratory that had done the tests on the samples Cinzia had sent. Cross-contamination of some sort was now being considered. Cinzia's own workplace was being evaluated. Nothing, frankly, about the death of the Englishwoman was making sense.

Salvatore noted all of this and from it he could draw only one conclusion. Her death from the bacteria made no sense to the health officials because they were looking at it the wrong way round. They were still seeing it as an accidental ingestion when it was nothing of the kind.

When it came to murder, the starting point was generally motive. In this case, though, it was also—and more important, perhaps—access to means. But Salvatore chose to look at motive first. It was a glaring one that could not be denied. It pointed directly at Taymullah Azhar.

When the question was, Who benefited from Angelina Upman's untimely death?, the answer was the father of her child. When the question was, Who most probably would wish her dead?, the answer again was the father of her child. Her death gained him the return of Hadiyyah into his care permanently. Her death also garnered the vengeance he might have been seeking for having put him through the ordeal of losing her in the first place, not to mention the humiliation of his woman having had an affair while still living with him. No one else had a reason to murder her unless, possibly, there was someone in her life the police had yet to learn about. Another man, perhaps? A thwarted lover? A jealous friend? Salvatore supposed any of these were possible. But not likely, he thought. Sometimes the reason for the dog not barking at night was the most obvious reason of all.

Doing his homework on Taymullah Azhar was a simple enough thing. It required only access to the Internet, followed by a phone call to London. Taymullah Azhar was doing nothing to hide who he was, anyway. And the list of who he was was a point of significant interest: a professor of microbiology with a laboratory at University College London and an impressive list of academic papers to his name, the topics of which were indecipherable to Salvatore. But they were not as important as that one detail, microbiology. It was time to have a talk with the good professor, he decided. But to do that he would need the assistance of a discreet translator, his own English being far too limited to do justice to an interrogation.

He decided to have his conversation with Taymullah Azhar at the *pensione* where the man was staying. In advance of going there, he phoned the *questura*. He spoke to Ottavia Schwartz. Could the resourceful Ottavia arrange a translator to meet him inside the *anfiteatro*? he enquired. Not a police translator, mind you, but perhaps one of the many tour guides in the town . . . ?

"*Sì, sì,*" she told him. This would not be a problem, *Ispettore*. "*Ma perché non un traduttore dalla questura?*" she asked, and truthfully, it wasn't an unreasonable question since they had a multilingual translator on staff who worked among all the police agencies in Lucca. But to involve that person would also involve word filtering over to Piero, and Salvatore had had enough of the *magistrato* for one day.

He told Ottavia it was more of the same that had gone before. Better for no one to know what he was up to until he had all his soldiers lined up for the attack.

This arrangement made, he went for his car and drove carefully to the *anfiteatro*. As with the narrow streets on which he travelled, one of the arched entries to the amphitheatre was wide enough for a small car, so he drove straight in and parked in front of the ample display of succulents arranged in tiers beneath Pensione Giardino's windows. There he waited. He phoned London in the meantime and made a single request of Inspector Lynley. Lynley agreed to be of assistance in this matter. And yes, he said, he believed he could manage it without anyone at University College becoming wise to the matter.

Salvatore went across the piazza for a quick espresso, taken at the inside bar and mindful of the curious looks his appearance was garnering from the barista. He took his time about downing the *caffè*, and when he'd finished, he headed back to his car to see that the translator was waiting for him there.

He took a sharp breath that hurt his chest. He wondered if Ottavia's selection of translator was deliberate or merely a chance assignment given by whatever independent organisation the young police officer had phoned. For leaning against the police car across the piazza and gazing round through enormous sunglasses for the policeman she was to meet was Salvatore's own former wife.

He'd had no idea Birgit had taken up doing translating on the side, away from her work at the university in Pisa. It seemed out of character in her although, as a Swede, Birgit spoke six languages equally well. She would be in demand if she wished to make extra money as she no doubt did. On a policeman's salary, Salvatore had little enough to give her in the way of child support.

She leaned against the side of his car, smoking a cigarette, as blond and shapely and attractive as ever. Salvatore girded himself to greet her. When he got to the car, she peered at him. She pursed her lips, then shook her head. "*Non voglio che i tuoi figli ti vedano così,*" she said abruptly. Typical of her. Not a question about what had happened to her poor former husband but rather a declaration about the children not seeing him in such a state. He couldn't actually blame her, however. He didn't want the children to see him looking like this either.

He told her he was surprised that she had taken up translating. She shrugged, a quintessential Italian movement that she'd learned from her years living in Tuscany. He had never seen it from another Swede. "Money," she told him. "There's never enough."

He looked at her sharply to see if this was a dig. She wasn't giving him one of her sardonic glances, though. He contented himself with understanding that she was merely stating a fact. He said, "You will explain to Bianca and Marco why their papà cannot see them for a day or two, Birgit?"

"I'm not heartless, Salvatore," she told him. "You only think I am."

This was not true. He only thought that they had been from the first badly matched, and this was what he told her.

She dropped her cigarette, crushing it with the toe of one of the stilettos that made her six inches taller than he. She said, "No one sustains lust. You thought otherwise. You were wrong."

"No, no. At the end I still lusted—"

"I'm not speaking of you, Salvatore." She nodded at the *pensione*. "Our English speaker is here?" she said.

He was still trying to wrest the sword from his throat. He nodded and followed her to the door.

Signora Vallera greeted them. *Sì*, Taymullah Azhar was still within the *pensione*, she told Salvatore, casting a curious glance at Birgit and taking in her great Swedish height, her tailored suit, her silk scarf, her sunlight hair, her silver earrings. The professor and his daughter had been making a plan to purchase flowers and ride bicycles to the *cimitero comunale*, but they had not yet left, she told them. They were in the breakfast room, studying the *pianta stradale* to plan a route. Should she fetch . . . ?

He shook his head. She pointed out the way, and he headed there with Birgit following. The *pensione* was small, so all that was needed was the sound of a conversation and in particular the sound of Hadiyyah Upman's sweet voice. He wondered if, at nine years old, she was completely aware of what the loss of her mother meant to her now and was going to mean to her in the future.

Taymullah Azhar saw them at once, and he put a protective hand on Hadiyyah's shoulder. His dark eyes moved as his gaze took in Birgit first and Salvatore second. He frowned at the state of Salvatore's appearance. "*Un incidente*," Salvatore told him.

"An accident," Birgit translated. Her face looked as if she wanted to add "with someone's fists," but she didn't do so. She told him that Ispettore Lo Bianco had some questions he wished to ask. She explained her purpose needlessly, but Salvatore didn't stop her from doing so: Ispettore Lo Bianco, she said, had only limited English. Taymullah Azhar nodded although, of course, he knew this already.

He said to Hadiyyah, "*Khushi*, I will need to talk to these people for a few minutes. If you wait for me . . . Perhaps Signora Vallera will allow you to remain in the kitchen to play with little Graziella . . . ?"

Hadiyyah looked from his face to the face of Salvatore. She said, "Babies don't play much, Dad."

"Nonetheless," he said, and she nodded solemnly and scooted out of the room. She called out something in Italian, but Salvatore didn't catch it. He and Birgit moved to the table on which the street plan of the city was spread out. Azhar folded the map neatly as Signora Vallera came to the door of the breakfast room. She asked if they wanted *caffè* and they accepted. As they waited for her to bring it to them, Salvatore enquired politely about Hadiyyah's well-being as well as Azhar's.

He watched the Pakistani man carefully, the answers of little import to him. What he thought about was what he had learned about the London professor in the hours since Cinzia Ruocco had revealed what her findings were and what her thoughts were as they related to the findings. What Salvatore knew about Taymullah Azhar at that point was that he was a microbiologist of some considerable reputation. What he didn't know was whether one of the microbes he studied was *E. coli*. Nor did he know how that particular bacteria might be transported. Nor did he know how, having transported it, one managed to get a single individual to ingest it without her knowledge.

He said through Birgit, "*Dottore*, can you tell me about your relationship with Hadiyyah's mamma? She left you for Signor Mura. She returned to you at some point into her relationship with Signor Mura, *sì*?, to soothe you into believing she'd come back. She disappeared then with Hadiyyah. You were left not knowing what had become of them, *vero*?"

Unlike so many people who rely on a translation of the speaker's words, Azhar didn't look at Birgit as she repeated Salvatore's statements in English. Nor would he do so for the rest of the interview. Salvatore wondered at this unnatural form of discipline in the man.

"It was not a good relationship," Azhar said. "How could it have been otherwise? As you have said, she took Hadiyyah from me."

"She had other men from time to time, *vero*? While you and she were together?"

"I understand this now to be the case."

"You did not know this previously?"

"While she lived with me in London? I did not know. Not until she left me for Lorenzo Mura. And even then I did not know about him. Just that it was likely there was someone, somewhere. When she returned to me, I thought she had . . . returned to me. When she left with Hadiyyah, my thought was that she had gone back to whoever it was she had left me for. To him or to someone else."

"Do you mean that the first time she left you, she might have left you for someone other than Signor Mura?"

"That is what I mean," Azhar affirmed. "We did not discuss it. When we saw each other again once Hadiyyah had been taken, there was no point to that sort of discussion."

"And once you reached Italy?"

Azhar drew his eyebrows together as if to say, What about it? He didn't answer at first as Signora Vallera came into the room with the *caffè* and a plate of *biscotti*. They were shaped like balls and covered with powdered sugar. Salvatore took one and let it melt in his mouth. Signora Vallera poured *caffè* from a tall crockery jug.

When she'd departed, Azhar said, "*Non capisco, Ispettore*," and waited for elucidation.

Salvatore said, "I wonder if you carried with you the understandable anger at this woman for her sins against you."

"We all commit sins against each other," Azhar said. "I have no immunity from this. But I think she and I had forgiven each other. Hadiyyah was—she is—more important than the grievances Angelina and I had."

"So you did hold grievances." And when Azhar nodded, "Yet in your time here, those did not rise between you? You did not accuse? There were no recriminations?"

Birgit stumbled a bit with the word *recriminations*. But after a pause to consult a pocket dictionary, she carried on. Azhar said that there had been no recriminations once Angelina understood that he had had nothing to do with their daughter's disappearance, although it had taken him much to convince her of this, including a call upon his estranged wife and their children as well as proof of his own presence in Berlin at the time of Hadiyyah's disappearance.

"Ah, yes, Berlin," Salvatore said. "A conference, *vero*?"

Azhar nodded. A conference of microbiologists, he said.

"Many of them?"

Perhaps three hundred, Azhar told him.

"Tell me, what does a microbiologist do? Forgive my ignorance. We policemen . . . ?" Salvatore smiled regretfully. "Our lives, they are very narrow, you see." He put a packet of sugar into his *caffè*. He took another *biscotto* and let it melt on his tongue like the other.

Azhar explained, although he didn't look convinced by Salvatore's declaration of ignorance. He spoke about the classes he taught, the graduate and postgraduate students he worked with, the studies carried out in his laboratory, and the papers he wrote as a result of those studies. He spoke of conferences and colleagues as well.

"Dangerous things, these microbes, I would think," Salvatore said.

Azhar explained that microbes came in all shapes and sizes and levels of danger. Some, he said, were completely benign.

"But one does not interest oneself with those that are benign?" Salvatore said.

"I do not."

"Yet to protect yourself from the danger of exposure to them? This must be crucial, eh?"

"When one works with dangerous microbes, there are many safeguards," Azhar informed him. "And laboratories are differently designated according to what's studied within them. Those that have higher biohazard levels have more safeguards built into them."

"*Sì, sì, capisco.* But let me ask: What, really, is the point of studying such dangerous little things as these microbes?"

"To understand how they mutate," Azhar said, "to develop a treatment should one be infected by them, to increase the response time when one is trying to locate the source. There are many reasons to study these microbes."

"Just as there are many types of microbes, eh?"

"Many types of microbes," he agreed. "As vast as the universe and mutating all the time."

Salvatore nodded thoughtfully. He poured more *caffè* into his cup from the crockery jug and held it up to both Birgit and Azhar. Birgit nodded; Azhar shook his head. He tapped his fingers against the table-top and looked beyond Salvatore towards the door of the room. Hadiyyah's high, excited chattering came to them. She was speaking Italian. Children, he thought, were so quick to pick up languages.

"And in your laboratory, *Dottore*? What is being studied there? And is this laboratory a . . . what did you call it? A biohazard laboratory?"

"We study the evolutionary genetics of infectious diseases," he said.

"*Molto complesso*," Salvatore murmured.

This required no translation. "It is complex indeed," Azhar said.

"Do you favour one microbe over another in this biohazard laboratory of yours, *Dottore*?"

"*Streptococcus*," he said.

"And what do you do with this *Streptococcus*?"

Azhar seemed thoughtful at this. He frowned and once again his eyebrows drew together. He explained his hesitation by saying, "For-give me. It is difficult to—forgive me—to simplify what we do for a layman's understanding."

"*Certo*," Salvatore acknowledged. "*Ma provi, Dottore.*"

Azhar did so after another moment of thinking. He said, "Perhaps to make it simple, it's best to say that we engage in a process that al-lows us to answer questions about the microbe."

"Questions?"

"About its pathogenesis, emergence, evolution, virulence, transmission . . ." Azhar paused to give Birgit time to work upon the more complicated words in Italian.

"And the reason for all this?" Salvatore asked. "I mean, the reason for all this in *your* laboratory?"

"The studying of mutations and how they affect virulence," he said.

"In other words, how the mutation makes the microbe more deadly?"

"This is correct."

"How the mutation makes the microbe more likely to kill?"

"This is also correct."

Salvatore nodded thoughtfully. He observed Azhar at greater length than was called for by their conversation about his work. This obviously told the Pakistani man that something was up and, considering that he had been asked to turn his passport over to the police, what was up was obviously the death of his daughter's mother and its possible connection to his own work.

Azhar said with apparent great care, "You are asking me these questions for a reason, Inspector. May I know what it is?"

Instead of replying in answer, Salvatore asked, "What happens to these microbes of yours if they are transported, *Dottore*? What I mean is, what happens to them if someone transports them from one place to another?"

"It depends on how they're transported," Azhar said. "But I don't understand why you ask me this, Inspector Lo Bianco."

"So they can indeed be transported?"

"They can. But again, Inspector, you ask me these questions because—"

"The kidneys of an otherwise healthy woman fail," Salvatore cut in. "Obviously, there must be a reason for this."

Azhar said nothing at all in reply. He was still as a statue, as if any movement he made would tell a tale he did not wish to be told.

"So you see, we ask you to remain in Italy for a bit of time," Salvatore went on. "You would wish, perhaps, to have an English-speaking attorney at this point? You would wish, perhaps, to see to it that little Hadiyyah has someone to care for her in the event—"

"I will care for Hadiyyah," Azhar said abruptly. But he sat so stiffly in his chair that Salvatore could imagine every muscle in his body tensing as all the implications behind Salvatore's questions, his own frank responses, and the advice about an *avvocato* fell upon him.

"What I would suggest, *Dottore*," Salvatore said carefully, "is your preparation for all possible outcomes to this conversation you and I are having."

Azhar rose then. He said quietly, "I must go to my daughter now, Inspector Lo Bianco. I have promised her that we will take flowers to her mother's grave. I will keep that promise."

"As a father should," Salvatore said.

CHELSEA
LONDON

The glorious May weather made Lynley long for a convertible as he coursed along the river. There were other routes to get to Chelsea from New Scotland Yard, but none of them provided what first Millbank and then Grosvenor Road provided on this day: trees bursting forth with brilliant green leaves still untouched by the city's dust, dirt, and pollution; the sight of runners taking exercise on the wide pavement that followed the course of the Thames; barges in the water and pleasure craft heading towards Tower Bridge or Hampton Court. Gardens were brilliant with grass renewed and with shrubbery bearing its new spring growth. It was a fine day to be alive, he thought. He breathed in life deeply and felt momentarily at peace with his world.

That had not been the case a few minutes earlier when he'd reported to Superintendent Ardery the phone call he'd received from Salvatore Lo Bianco. Her immediate response was "Christ. This becomes worse and worse, Tommy," and she'd left her desk and begun to pace her office. On her second circuit of the room, she'd closed the door upon anyone who might wander by.

The fact that she was in mental disarray was unlike her. Lynley said nothing but merely waited for what was coming next. It was "I need some air and so do you," to which his admonitory "Isabelle" was met with her sharp "I said *air*, for God's sake. Do me the courtesy of taking me at my word until you find me passed out on this floor with a vodka bottle in my hand."

He winced at how well she knew him. He said, "Right. Sorry," and she accepted this with a sharp nod. Then she strode to the door that she'd just closed, and she threw it open. She said to Dorothea Harriman—always lingering nearby to be of assistance or to glean gossip—"I have my mobile," and she headed in the general direction of the lifts.

The two of them went outside, where Isabelle stood for a moment in the vicinity of the Met's revolving sign. She said, "At moments like this, I wish I still smoked."

He said, "If you tell me what's happened, I'll let you know if I feel the same."

"Over there." She inclined her head towards the junction of Broadway and Victoria Street. A park lay there, its grass shaded by great London plane trees. At a far corner stood a memorial to the suffragette movement, but she didn't move towards this immense scroll but rather to one of the trees. She leaned against it.

"So how do you propose to do this without alerting Professor Azhar?" Isabelle asked him. "Obviously, you can't go yourself. And sending Barbara would be tantamount to shooting yourself in a crucial bodily organ. You do know that, Tommy. At least and by God, I hope you know that."

The passion with which she said her last bit told Lynley she'd either been withholding information the last time they'd spoken or she'd received yet another damning report from DI Stewart. It turned out to be the latter.

She said, "She's been to see both the private investigator—"

"Doughty," he said.

"Doughty," she agreed. "And this Bryan Smythe."

"But we knew that, Isabelle."

"In the company of Taymullah Azhar, Tommy," Isabelle added. "Why wasn't this part of her report?"

He cursed inwardly. This was something new, something more, another brick in the wall, nail in the coffin, whatever on earth one wanted to call it. He said, although he knew the answers as well as he knew his own name, "When did she see him? When did they go? And how did you—"

"That's where she was the morning she claimed whatever she claimed—Was it a stop for petrol? Traffic? God, I can't even remember now—about why she was late to our meeting."

"John Stewart again, then? Christ, Isabelle, how much longer are you going to put up with his machinations? Or did you order him, at this point, to start tailing Barbara?"

"Don't let's make this about something other than what it is. And what it is is beginning to look like a cover-up, which as you bloody well know is far more serious than creating a story about her miserable mother falling over a stool or *whatever* the hell it was supposed to be in her care home."

"I'm the first to admit she was out of order doing that."

"Oh, let me call on the saints and angels in praise," Isabelle said. "And now what we have is a set of behaviours on the part of Sergeant Havers that strongly suggest she's stitching up evidence."

"We have no UK crime," he reminded her.

"Don't take me for a fool. She's over the side, Tommy. You and I both know it. I may have started out investigating arson in my career, but one thing I learned from examining fire scenes is that if my nose is picking up the scent of smoke, there's bloody well been a fire."

He waited for her to tell him the rest, which constituted those airline tickets to Pakistan. Still she did not. He concluded once again that, for whatever little good it did Havers, Isabelle continued not to know about the tickets. Had she known, she would have told him at this point. There was no reason to hold back that information.

She said to him, "Did you know she'd been to see Smythe and Doughty in the company of Azhar?"

He looked at her steadily as he formulated his reply: which way to go and what it would mean if he went there. He had hoped she wouldn't ask the question, but as she said, she wasn't a fool.

"Yes," he told her.

She looked heavenward, crossing her arms beneath her breasts. "You're protecting her by stitching up evidence yourself, I take it?"

"I am not," he said.

"So what am I to think . . . ?"

"That I don't know everything yet, Isabelle. And until I know it, I saw no reason to worry you."

"You mean to protect her, don't you? No matter the cost. God in heaven, what's wrong with you, Tommy? This is your bloody career we're talking about." And when he didn't answer, she said, "Never mind. It *isn't*, is it? What was I thinking? The earldom awaits. Is that what they call it, by the way, an earldom? And the family pile in Cornwall is always there ready for you to decamp to if you want to throw all of this over. You don't need to do this kind of work. It's all a lark for you. It's a walk in the park. It's a bloody joke. It's—"

"Isabelle, *Isabelle*." He took a step towards her.

She held up her hand. "Don't."

"Then what?" he asked her.

"Can you not for one moment *see* where this is heading, for all of us? Can you not look beyond Barbara Havers for a bloody instant and realise the position she's putting us in? Not only herself, but us as well."

He had to see it because, like her, he was not a fool. But he also had to admit to himself that before this moment he hadn't thought about the impact Barbara's behaviour would have upon Isabelle herself should all of what she had done come out into the open. Hearing Isabelle's voice tinged as it was with despair, he felt as if the clouds were parting and where the sun was shining was not, at this moment, upon Barbara. For Isabelle Ardery was in charge of all the officers, and the responsibility for what the members of her squad did and did not do ultimately rested upon her shoulders.

Cleaning house was what it was generally called in the aftermath of corruption's coming to light. The rubbish got tossed to appease the public, and Isabelle Ardery stood in very good stead to be part of that rubbish.

He said to her, "This situation . . . It's not going to come to that, Isabelle."

"Oh, you know that, do you?"

"Look at me," he said. And when she finally did so and when he read the fear in her eyes, he said, "I do. I won't allow you to be damaged. I swear it."

"You don't have that power. No one does."

Now as Lynley guided the Healey Elliott into Cheyne Walk, he tried to put his promise to Isabelle from his mind. There were bigger issues even than Barbara's involvement with Taymullah Azhar, Dwayne Doughty, and Bryan Smythe, and those needed to be dealt with as soon as possible. Still, his heart was heavy as he parked the car near the top of Lawrence Street. He walked the distance back to Lordship Place and went in through the gate that led to a garden he knew as well as he knew his own.

They were in the last stages of an alfresco lunch beneath a cherry tree in magnificent bloom in the centre of the lawn: his oldest friend, that friend's wife, and her father. They were watching an enormous grey cat slinking along an herbaceous border thick with lunaria, bellis, and campanula. They were apparently hot into a discussion on the subject of Alaska—said cat—and whether his best mousing days were over.

When they heard the squeak of the garden gate, they turned. Simon St. James said, "Ah, Tommy. Hullo."

Deborah said, "You're just in time to settle an argument. How are you on the subject of cats?"

"Nine lives or otherwise?"

"Otherwise."

"Not an expert, I'm afraid."

"Damn."

Deborah's father, Joseph Cotter, rose to his feet and said, "Afternoon, m'lord. A coffee?"

Lynley waved Cotter back to his seat. He fetched another chair from the terrace at the top of the steps that led to the house's basement kitchen. He joined them at the table and took a look at the remains of their meal. Salad, a dish with green beans and almonds, lamb bones littering their plates, the tail end of a loaf of crusty bread, a bottle of red wine. Cotter had been cooking, obviously. Deborah's talents were artistic, but her artistry was decidedly minimal in the kitchen. As for St. James . . . If he managed marmite on toast, it was cause for massive celebration.

"How old is Alaska?" he enquired, preparatory to giving his opinion.

"Lord, I don't know," Deborah said. "I think we got him . . . Was I ten years old, Simon?"

"He can't possibly be seventeen," Lynley said. "How many lives can he have?"

"I think he's been through eight of them at least," St. James told him. He said to his wife, "Perhaps fifteen."

"Me or the cat?"

"The cat, my love."

"Then I proclaim his mousing days . . . still ongoing," Lynley said. He made a hasty benediction over the animal, who was at that moment attacking a fallen leaf with an enthusiasm that suggested he thought it was dinner.

"There you have it," Deborah said to her husband. "Tommy knows best."

"Having vast experience with felines?" St. James asked.

"Having vast experience of knowing with whom I ought to agree when paying a social call," Lynley said. "I had a feeling that Deborah was on the side of mousing. She's always been an advocate for your animals. Where's the dog?"

"Being punished, if one can actually punish a dachshund," Deborah told him. "She was being far too insistent about having her share of lamb, and she's been put back into the kitchen."

"Poor Peach."

"You only say that because you weren't present to witness her machinations," St. James told him.

"We call it 'love eyes,'" Deborah added. "She casts them upon one and it's impossible to deny her."

Lynley chuckled. He leaned back in his chair and took a final moment to enjoy their company, the day, the simple pleasure of gathering in the garden for lunch. Then he said, "It's business I've come on, actually," and as Joseph Cotter then rose as if to make himself scarce, Lynley told him to stay if he wished as there was no secret involved in his mission in Chelsea.

But Cotter said it was time for him to do the washing up. He took a tray from its resting place on the lawn and loaded it efficiently. Deborah helped him, and in a moment she and her father left the two men alone.

"What sort of business?" St. James asked him.

"Scientific, actually." Lynley brought him into the picture regarding the death of Angelina Upman in Italy. He related the details from the phone call Salvatore Lo Bianco had made to him. St. James listened in his usual fashion, his angular face reflective.

At Lynley's conclusion, he was silent for a moment before he said,

"Could there have been a laboratory error? Having an isolated case of so virulent a strain of bacteria . . . To me, it doesn't suggest murder as much as it suggests human error in examining what came from the dead woman's gut. The point at which bacterial involvement is suspected . . . ? That should have happened while she was alive. It's going to be difficult for Lo Bianco to prove anything, isn't it? For example, how the *E. coli* entered her system at all."

"I suppose that's why he wants to begin with the lab. Will you do it for me?"

"Pay a call at University College? Of course."

"Azhar claims his lab's studying *Streptococcus*. Lo Bianco's looking for anything else they might be studying. As for transport . . ." Lynley shifted in his chair. Movement in the corner of his eye caught his attention. Alaska had dived into the herbaceous border and a furious battle appeared to be going on among a patch of violas. He said, "*Could* he have transported a bacteria safely from London to Lucca, Simon?"

St. James nodded. "It merely needs to be put on a medium that allows it to survive, a broth and a solidifier. Onto the solid, one would streak the bacteria. Placed onto a petri dish, it not only would survive but grow."

"How much would be needed to kill someone?"

"That depends, doesn't it?" St. James said. "Toxicity is the key."

"I have the impression from Salvatore that the *E. coli* we're seeking is particularly toxic."

"I'll have to be careful, then," Simon said. He folded his linen table napkin and pushed himself to his feet. He was disabled, so rising was always a rather awkward business for St. James, but Lynley knew better than to offer his assistance.

VICTORIA
LONDON

When Barbara saw who was ringing her mobile, she ducked into the stairwell to take the call. There were voices echoing up the stairs from somewhere far below, but they disappeared as whoever was climbing left the stairwell for one of the lower floors. She said to Azhar, "How are you? Where are you? What's happening over there?" and although she tried to keep from her voice the desperate urgency that she was feeling, she could tell from his hesitation prior to responding that he heard it and wondered about it.

"I have a solicitor," he told her. "He is called Aldo Greco. I wanted to give you his phone number, Barbara."

She had a pencil but no paper, and she searched the floor frantically for something to write on before she had to give in and use the faded yellow wall. She took the number down for later programming into her mobile. She said, "Good. That's an important step."

"He speaks English very well," Azhar said. "I'm told that it is lucky indeed that I found myself in need of a solicitor while being detained in this part of Italy. I'm told had this . . . this situation occurred in one of the small towns deeply south of Naples, it would be more difficult as a solicitor would have had to be willing to come from a larger city. I do not know why this is the case. It is merely what they told me."

Barbara knew he was only making conversation. Her heart cracked a little at the thought that he would have to do this with her, his friend. She said, "What's the embassy going to do? Have you spoken to any-one there?"

He said that he had, that it was the embassy who had given him a list of solicitors in Tuscany. But aside from that list, they could do little else for him beyond phoning his relatives, which he hardly wanted them to do. "They say that when a British national gets into difficulties on foreign soil, it's up to that British national to get him-self out of those difficulties."

"Nice of them, informing you of that," Barbara noted sardonically. "I always did wonder what our bloody taxes are going for."

"Of course they have other concerns," he said. "And as they do not know me and only have my word that there is no reason for the police to wish to question me . . . I suppose I can understand."

Barbara found she could see him even without his presence. He'd be wearing one of the crisp white shirts he usually wore, she reckoned, along with trousers that were dark and simple. Cut well to fit him, the clothing would inadvertently reveal his slender frame. He'd always looked so delicate, she thought, so insubstantial when compared to other men. His appearance along with how well she knew him—and she knew him well, she told herself—spoke of his essential goodness. Which was, at the end of the day, why she gave him the information he needed in order to prepare himself for what was coming. This wasn't about her loyalty to anyone, she told herself. This was about basic fairness.

She said, "Her kidney failure was caused by a toxin, Azhar. Shiga toxin it's called."

There was silence for a moment. Then he said, "What?" as if he hadn't heard her clearly or, hearing her, couldn't quite believe what she was telling him.

"DI Lynley rang the Italian bloke for me. He got the information."

"From Chief Inspector Lo Bianco?"

"That's the name. This bloke Lo Bianco said that Shiga toxin caused her kidneys to fail."

"How is this possible? The strain of *E. coli* that results in Shiga toxin—"

"She picked it up somewhere, the *E. coli*. Apparently a bloody nasty strain of it. The doctors didn't know what they were dealing with because of her earlier problems with the pregnancy, so they did a few basic tests and when the tests were negative or whatever they gave her a course of antibiotics—"

"Oh my God," he murmured.

Barbara said nothing, and after a moment, he seemed to begin thinking aloud because he went on in a meditative tone with, "This is why he asked me about . . ." And then his voice altered to insistence as he said, "It has to be a mistake, Barbara. For one person alone to die from this? No. Virtually impossible. This is a bacteria, *E. coli*. It infects a food supply. Someone else would fall ill. Many people would fall ill because they would eat from the same food supply as Angelina. Do you see what I mean? This cannot have happened. There has to be a laboratory error."

"As to laboratories, Azhar . . . You see where they're heading, don't you? The Italian coppers? With the whole idea of laboratories?"

He was silent then. The pieces were clicking into place. Or at least that was what Barbara had to believe. He wasn't speculating in this silence, he wasn't wondering, and he wasn't planning his next move. He was merely concluding, completing for himself the chain of events that began with Angelina's disappearance from London with their daughter in tow and ended with her death in Lucca.

He finally said quietly, "*Streptococcus*, Barbara."

"What?"

"This is what we study in my laboratory at University College: *Streptococcus*. Some laboratories study more than one bacteria. We do not. We study more than one strain of it, of course. But only strains of *Streptococcus*. Of personal interest to me is the *Strep* that causes meningitis in newborn infants."

"Azhar. You don't have to tell me this."

"The mother, you see," he said insistently as if she hadn't spoken, "passes it to the infant as the baby travels through the birth canal. From this develops—"

"I believe you, Azhar."

"—the infant's meningitis. We're seeking a way to prevent this."

"I understand."

"And there are other forms as well, other forms of *Strep* that we study in the lab since the graduate students are working on dissertations and the postgraduates are working on papers to be published. But the one I study . . . It is as I said. And of course Angelina was pregnant so they will ask about this, won't they? How coincidental is it that I would study a bacteria found in pregnant women? And they will wonder as you are wondering because, after all, I arranged the kidnapping of my own child—"

"Azhar, *Azhar*."

"I did not harm Angelina," he said. "You cannot think I harmed her."

She hadn't been thinking that. She couldn't even bring herself close to thinking that. But the truth was that in this entire Italian situation, there was more than one kind of harm, and Azhar knew this as well as Barbara herself. She said, "The kidnapping. Those tickets to Pakistan. You have to see how it's going to look in conjunction with her death if word gets out."

"Only you and I know about these things, Barbara." His voice was wary.

"What about Doughty and Smythe?"

"They work for us," he said. "We do not work for them. They've been instructed . . . You must believe me because if you of all people do not believe . . . I did not harm her. Yes, the kidnapping was a terrible thing to arrange, but how else could she ever be made to experience what it feels like when your child is there one day and gone the next and you have no idea . . . ?"

"Pakistan, Azhar. One-way tickets. Lynley knows about them. And he's doing his homework."

"You are not thinking," he cried. "Why would I purchase tickets for July but arrange Angelina's death in May? Why would I do that when I would have no need of tickets to Pakistan with Angelina dead?"

Because, Barbara thought, those tickets absolve you of suspicion and I did not see that until this moment because I *couldn't* see it until I learned how Angelina Upman died. She said none of this, but her silence seemed to tell Azhar that something more was required of him, if not now then the next time Inspector Lo Bianco wanted to question him.

He said, "If you think I harmed her, you must ask yourself where I got this bacteria. Of course, someone somewhere in England studies it and perhaps in London but I do not know who. And yes, of course, this is an easy enough thing for me to find out. So I could have found out. But so could anyone else."

"I see that, Azhar. But you have to ask how likely it is . . ." And here she paused because she had to consider what she owed: not only to Lynley, to Azhar, to Hadiyyah, but also to herself. She said, "The thing is . . . you lied to me once and—"

"I do not lie now! And when I did lie . . . How could I tell you what I had planned? Would you have allowed me to go forward and kidnap her? No, you would not. An officer of the police? How could I have expected this of you? It was something that had to be done on my own."

As murder is generally done, she thought.

A silence endured between them, broken finally by Azhar. "Is there nothing you are willing to do to help me now?" he asked.

"I haven't said that."

"But it's what you think, isn't it? 'I must distance myself from this man because if I do not, it could cost me everything.'"

Which was, Barbara thought wryly, not that far off from what DI Lynley had told her. Everything was on the line for her unless she could think of a way to get herself one step ahead of the Italian police.

THE WEST END
LONDON

Mitchell Corsico was the way, she decided. Once she programmed the phone number of Azhar's solicitor into her mobile and rubbed it off the stairwell's wall, she rang the reporter and said, "We need to meet. Angelina Upman's dead. Why'd you blokes not pick up on the story?"

His fire wasn't lit. "Who says we didn't pick up on the story?"

"I sure as hell didn't see it."

"Are you saying I'm responsible for what you see or don't see in the paper?"

"Are you saying it was in the paper but it didn't make front-page news? You are seriously out of the loop, son. We better meet, pronto."

He still didn't bite, the wily bastard. "Tell me why this is front-page news, and *I'll* tell *you* if we need to meet, Barb."

She refused to be irritated by the bloke's arrogance. She said, "*Did* it even make *The Source*, Mitchell? A British girl is kidnapped from a crowd of people, then she's found stowed in a convent in the Italian Alps under the care of a mental case who thinks she's a nun, then her mother dies unexpectedly. What part of this isn't the kind of story that's meat and potatoes to you lot?"

"Hey, she made page twelve. If she'd done us a favour and offed herself, she'd've made page one, but what can I tell you? She didn't, so she got buried inside." He guffawed and added, "Pardon the pun."

"And what if she actually did you blokes a real page-one favour and died in a way that the powers in Italy want hushed up?"

"What, are you saying the Prime Minister killed her? What about the Pope?" Another irritating guffaw from the bloke. "She died in hospital, Barb. We got all the facts. She slipped into a coma and she never came out of it. Her kidneys were done for. So what're you suggesting: that someone tiptoed into her hospital room and put kidney poison in her drip bag?"

"I'm suggesting you and I need to talk and I'm not prepared to talk till I see your face."

She allowed him to dwell on this while she herself feverishly considered which of the many ways possible would be best to spin the story in order to hook *The Source*. Politically the rag had become so nationalist over the years, it was practically Nazi in its leaning. She decided flag waving was the way to go. Brits versus the Pasta Eaters. But not yet. Not till she had him hooked.

He finally said, "All right. But this had better be very good, Barb."

She said, "It is," and just to be pleasant, she allowed him to name the place of their meeting.

He chose Leicester Square, the half-price ticket booth. The *real* half-price ticket booth, he told her, not some wannabe. There was a fancy notice board next to the real one where tickets on offer for the dramas, comedies, and musicals were announced. He'd meet her there.

She kept her voice airy. "I'll wear a rose in my lapel."

"Oh, I expect I'll know you by the sweat of your desperation," he said.

They set up a time, and she got there early. Leicester Square was, as usual, a terrorist's wet dream, with the crowds only getting worse as summer came on. Now there were masses of tourists gathered at open-air restaurants, in front of buskers, buying tickets for the cinema, and attempting to negotiate terms for theatrical productions in need of an audience. By mid-July the masses would have morphed into hordes, and moving through them would be nigh impossible.

She planted herself in front of the notice board and made a show of studying its offerings. Musicals, musicals, musicals, musicals. Plus Hollywood celebrities trying to be stage actors. Shakespeare was spinning in his grave, she reckoned.

She was seven and a half minutes into listening to various debates all round her—what to see, how much to spend, whether *Les Miz* could possibly run for yet another century or maybe two—when the scent of aftershave worked on her like smelling salts. Mitchell Corsico was at her side.

She said, "What the bloody hell are you wearing? Essence of horse? Christ, Mitchell." She waved a hand in front of her face. "Isn't the get-up enough for you?" How long, she wondered, could one man possibly keep wearing clothes that suggested a bloke on a quest to find Tonto?

He said, "You wanted this meeting, right? So it needs to be important or I'm not a happy horseman."

"How does an Italian cover-up sound?"

He glanced round. The jostling of people trying to see the notice board was something of a trial, so he moved towards the edge of the square in the direction of Gerrard Street and its one-hundred-yard claim of being London's Chinatown. Barbara followed. He planted himself squarely in front of her, then, and said, "What're you talking about? You better not be playing me."

"The Italians have the cause of death. They're not saying officially what it is. They don't want the papers getting a whiff of it because they don't want to start a panic. Either among the people or in the economy. Is that enough for you?"

His gaze shifted from her to a balloon seller to her again. "Could be," he said. "What's the cause?"

"A strain of *E. coli*. A super strain. A deadly strain. The worst there is."

His eyes narrowed. "How d'you know this?"

"I know it because I know it, Mitchell. I was there when the call came through from the rozzers."

"'Came through'? Where?"

"DI Lynley. He got the word from the chief investigator in Lucca."

Mitchell's eyebrows locked. He was, she knew, evaluating her words. He wasn't a fool. Content was one thing. Meaning was another. The fact that she would bring Lynley into anything at all was raising his warning hairs.

He said, "Why would you be telling me? That's what I'm wondering."

"It's obvious, isn't it?"

"Not to me."

"Bloody hell, Mitchell. You know *E. coli* comes from food, don't you? *Contaminated* food."

"So she ate something bad."

"We're not talking about a single vinegar crisp, mate. We're talking about a *supply* of food. Who knows what? Spinach, broccoli, minced beef, tinned tomatoes, lettuce. For all I know it got baked into her lasagna. But the point is, if the word gets out, that whole industry in Italy takes a hit to the solar plexus. A whole section of their economy—"

"You can't be suggesting there's a lasagna industry."

"You know what I mean."

"So maybe she had a burger somewhere and a worker went to the loo and didn't wash his hands before stacking on the tomatoes?" He shifted his weight from one cowboy-booted foot to the other and pushed his Stetson farther back on his head. He was garnering one or two curious glances from people who looked to be seeking whatever violin case or other receptacle in which they were supposed to deposit appreciative ten-pence pieces for his costuming, but there weren't many of those since, in Leicester Square, far more interesting sights existed than the one presented by a London man in a cowboy get-up. "And anyway, the fact that only one person died . . . That pretty much supports the idea, doesn't it? One person, one burger, one bad tomato."

"With this bloke, whoever he was, and assuming they even serve burgers in Lucca, Italy—"

"Christ. You know what I mean. The burger's an example. Say it was a salad. What about that salad with tomatoes and that Italian cheese and whatever that green crap is they put on it? That leafy bit."

"I look like I would know that, Mitchell? Come on, I'm giving you a significant heads-up on a story that's going to break in Italy at any moment, only *you* now have the edge because, believe me, the cops and the health blokes over there aren't about to release it and cause a stampede away from Italian products."

"So you say." But he wasn't a fool. "Why're you into this anyway, Barb? This got to do with . . . ? Where's our Love Rat Dad these days?"

There was no way she wanted him anywhere near Azhar. She said,

"Haven't spoken to him. He went to Lucca for the funeral. I expect he's back now. Or still there with the kid, getting her packed. Who the bloody hell knows? Listen, you can do what you want with this story, mate. I think it's gold. You think it's lead? Fine, don't run it. There're other papers who'd be happy to—"

"I didn't say that, did I? I just don't want this to be another bomb like the other."

"What d'you mean, 'bomb'?"

"Well, let's face it, Barb, the kid was found."

Barbara stared at the man. She wanted so badly to punch his Adam's apple that her fingernails clawed at the skin of her palms. She said slowly as her blood pounded so hard in her head that she thought she would soon see stars, "Too right, Mitch. That was a blow for your lot. So much better to have had a corpse. Mutilated, too. That would move those copies right off the newsstand."

"I'm only saying . . . Look, this is an ugly business. You know that. Fact is, you and I wouldn't be talking in the first place if you thought it was anything else."

"If we're talking ugly, Italian cops and Italian politicos in bed with each other is bloody ugly. That's your story, at the cost of an English-woman's life with more lives in jeopardy. You can take it or leave it to another rag. Decision is yours."

She turned and began to stride towards Charing Cross Road. She would walk the distance back to New Scotland Yard. She needed the time to cool off, she reckoned.

WAPPING
LONDON

Dwayne Doughty had lots of ideas on the subject of how Emily Cass afforded her flat in Wapping High Street but he decided not to pursue them. He could tell, however, that Bryan Smythe was mentally listing the potential sources of income allowing her to occupy a second-floor conversion in a Grade II–listed warehouse overlooking the Thames. She couldn't possibly own it, Smythe was thinking. Therefore she had it on let. But the cost would be enormous. She couldn't pay it on her own. There was a man involved then, depend upon it. She was—*gasp!*—a kept woman. Or someone's live-in lover, more likely. In exchange for sexual favours accomplished in the astounding athletic positions of which a woman in her physical condition was capable, she domiciled herself within brick walls, exposed beams and pipes, and mod cons of stainless steel. It was a subject worthy of some considerable teeth gnashing. Doughty reckoned Smythe's poor molars would be worn to the nubs by the end of their confab.

They were meeting in Wapping at Emily's suggestion. With what they were up to, she had insisted, they could no longer risk any location where the cops had shown their faces and might do so again or any *other* location in a public place. That left her flat. Hence their presence in a conversation grouping of low-slung leather furniture surrounding an even lower glass-topped coffee table, all of it overlooking the river. She'd placed a stainless steel coffee service on this, along with cups and a plate of bakery items supplied by Bryan. He—Dwayne—was enjoying an apricot-filled croissant and meditating on how to score an apple tart next, knowing that Emily wasn't about to touch any of it.

Dwayne was also aware of the fact that Emily's insistence upon meeting elsewhere had to do with the disintegrating nature of the little trinity of malefactors that they comprised. She wouldn't trust him not to document their every word in some fashion in his office, and she wouldn't trust Bryan Smythe not to do the same in his palace in South Hackney. Here in Wapping she had some semblance of control. Dwayne had decided to give her that.

Their purpose in meeting was to make certain they were all on the same page, in the same loop, and dancing the same dance when it came to what they had begun referring to as the Italian Job. Much of what was being done was being done by Bryan, so he had the floor. Despite being miles away from anyone who would have been remotely interested in what they had to say to one another, the three of them hunched round the coffee table, speaking in murmurs and looking at what documents Bryan had generated in order to spot any weaknesses in them.

What Bryan Smythe had created, with the participation of hackers and insiders whom he knew by the dozens, was the necessary trail, which illustrated the veracity in the claims Doughty had made and was continuing to make about one Michelangelo Di Massimo. Thus, for their delectation, he was presenting to them the invoices that showed all the payments that had been made to Di Massimo for his ostensibly brief search for Angelina Upman and her daughter in Pisa, Italy. Additionally, however, they were examining the documents that would allegedly prove that—having reported his failure to find the missing people while all the time knowing where they were—Di Massimo had begun moving sums of money from his own account to Roberto Squali's account in supposed payment for Squali's planning and kidnapping of the child. Thus actual bank transactions from London to Pisa proved that Doughty had been paying small amounts for Di Massimo's expenses—petrol, mileage, meals, et cetera—and for his hourly billing, while Smythe-created bank transactions from Pisa to Lucca looked as if Di Massimo had been paying large amounts to Squali for something questionable about which, alas and despite anything Di Massimo might be saying, Doughty knew nothing at all. Bryan had gone so far as to create the receipts as well.

The reliability of this information, of course, depended upon the Italian coppers not delving into too many layers of the British banking system or any British system, for that matter. For of course there were backups, counter-backups, and massive storage systems in hundreds of locations. But Doughty et al. were depending upon the general incompetence and known corruptibility of all Mediterranean countries when it came to complicated legal, political, and technological issues. This, they reckoned, would allow the team of Cass-Smythe-Doughty to carry the day.

The Di Massimo Problem of the Italian Job massaged into a form that the Italian police were likely to swallow, what remained was the DS Barbara Havers Problem. The infuriating woman still had in her possession the backups that could sink all of them, and because of this, she had to be dealt with. This was more difficult but not impossible: Sums matching what Di Massimo had transferred to Squali were shown to have been earlier wired from the account of one Barbara Havers to the account of Michelangelo Di Massimo. And sums matching *this* amount were shown to have been wired from the account of Taymullah Azhar to the account of Barbara Havers in advance of that movement. Thus, Barbara Havers would soon discover that she was now complicit in the kidnapping of Hadiyyah Upman.

Wasn't techno-wizardry incredible, mate?

13 MAY

Bah! was Salvatore's reaction when the packet of information from London arrived on his desk. It was—*merda!*—entirely in English. But Salvatore recognised the name repeated on nearly every sheet: Michelangelo Di Massimo.

Salvatore knew he was meant to turn this material over to Nicodemo Triglia. Nicodemo was, after all, in charge of all matters relating to the kidnapping enquiry. As it was, though, he decided to hold on to it until he better understood its contents. For this, he needed an English speaker who had nothing to gain from reporting Salvatore Lo Bianco's activities to *il Pubblico Ministero* for personal gain. That left out everyone associated with the police. Remaining, once again, was Birgit.

His ex-wife would not allow him at her house, she told him briskly when he phoned. He couldn't blame her. Just as she had no wish for Bianca and Marco to see his beaten face, so also did he not wish it. They agreed to meet across the street from Scuola Dante Alighieri. There, a children's park contained benches for their parents as well as swings, slides, roundabouts, and such, and Birgit would wait for him on one of those benches. He was to make certain that their children were fully enclosed in the embrace of the *scuola* before he arrived, *chiaro?*

Chiaro, he assured her.

He found her on the bench farthest from the school, shaded by a large sycamore tree. Nearby, two women with toddlers in pushchairs sat on opposite ends of a bench in the pleasant sunlight, smoking and speaking on their mobile phones. Their children dozed in the warm morning air.

Salvatore walked to join his ex-wife. He eased himself onto the bench. He'd wrapped his chest tightly with elastic bandages, and while they did something for the pain in his ribs, they constricted his movement and made his breathing shallow.

"How is it?" she asked. "You look even worse." She shook a cigarette from a pack and offered him one. He thought the taste would be nice and the nicotine nicer. But he didn't believe his lungs could handle the experience.

"It's the bruising," he replied. "It has to go purple first, then yellow. I'm fine."

She tutted. "You should have reported him, Salvatore."

"To whom? To himself?"

She lit her cigarette. "Then you should beat him senseless when you have the chance. What's Marco to think if his own father won't defend himself when he is set upon?"

There was no good answer to this question, and after their years of marriage, Salvatore liked to think he was wise enough not to engage Birgit in these sorts of vague philosophical debates. So from a manila envelope he took the report and he handed it to her. He understood the bank statements, the receipts, and the telephone records, of course, he informed Birgit. It was the larger reports he needed her help in translating.

"You need to work on your English," she told him with a scowl. "How you've got this far without more than one language . . . And don't tell me that at least you have French, Salvatore. I remember rescuing you from trying to speak to the waiters in Nice." She began to read.

For some minutes she did this in silence. He watched one of the toddlers struggling to get out of his pushchair as the poor child's mother continued her chat on her mobile phone. The other woman had ended *her* conversation, but she'd promptly begun texting and her child went ignored. Salvatore sighed and silently cursed modern life.

Birgit flicked ash from her cigarette, flipped the page, continued reading, made a few *hmphs*, gave a few nods, and looked up at him. "This is all from a man called Dwayne Doughty," she said, inclining her head at the document, "sent to you as directed by an officer of New Scotland Yard. This Doughty gives you an account of hiring Michelangelo Di Massimo to assist in the finding of a London woman who disappeared with her daughter. He tracked them himself to Pisa airport by means of their ticket purchases and through information provided by the border agents in England. He asked Michelangelo Di Massimo to take it from there and Michelangelo made the attempt. He describes the various methods this Michelangelo used and, as proof of this, he sends you also copies of his bills for services and costs incurred. He says that having checked with trains, with taxis, with private car companies, and with the buses—both touring buses and city buses—Signor Di Massimo claimed to have found no trace of the woman beyond the airport. All of the car hire agencies, too, showed no trace of her having picked up a hire car, either at the airport or in Pisa. What's known is that she landed at Galileo with her daughter and then disappeared. According to Signor Doughty, his conclusion— Michelangelo Di Massimo's—was that the woman and girl had been fetched by a private party and taken somewhere. This is what he told the London detective in his reports and the London detective tells *you* that he relayed this information to the child's father, along with Signor Di Massimo's name and details. He says it is his belief that all arrangements from that point were made between these two men privately as he had nothing more to do with the matter."

Salvatore speculated upon the information. That it contradicted what Di Massimo was telling the police came as no surprise to him. In a situation like this, it was understandable that the individuals under suspicion would soon enough begin pointing fingers at each other.

Birgit said, "He also includes records that he has managed to come by, showing amounts of money leaving the bank account of"—she fingered through the papers to find what she was looking for— "Taymullah Azhar and he speculates that they *might* have entered the account of Signor Di Massimo once his own business with Signor Azhar was concluded. He encourages you to seek this information about Signor Di Massimo's bank yourself. He points out that while he has no way of knowing what this exchange of money was for, it bears looking into since it suggests that long after his own business with Signor Di Massimo was concluded, Signor Azhar hired him on his own to do something. It was probably to kidnap his daughter, eh?, although he doesn't say that directly in the report. He says that his own business with Di Massimo ended last December within a few weeks of hiring, and he assures you that all the documents he's attaching will support that fact. As will, he says, Di Massimo's bank records if you are able to obtain them." She handed the report and its appended documents to Salvatore, who returned them to the envelope. She said, "Interesting that he mentions them twice, those banking records of Di Massimo, no? Have you looked at his bank records, Salvatore? You can do that, can't you?"

He crossed his arms and leaned back against the bench, stretching his legs with a wince. He said, "*Certo*. And Di Massimo was paid by this man as he says. But he tells a different story altogether, as you would expect."

"But if the bank records that this London man sends and the telephone records and all his invoices and receipts—"

"Untrustworthy as a *puttana*'s claim of love, *cara*. There are too many ways to manipulate information, and the London man believes I do not know this. I suspect that this man would like to engage me in chasing down all of his nonsense"—Salvatore nodded at the report between them—"because that will keep me busy and away from the truth and because, to him, I'm an Italian fool who drinks too much wine and does not know when someone is leading me by my nose like an ass."

"You're talking nonsense. What do you mean?"

"I mean that Signor Doughty wishes the door to shut upon this investigation, with Michelangelo behind it and no one else. Or, perhaps, with Michelangelo and the professor behind it. But in either case, with himself uninvolved."

"That may well be the truth, no?"

"It may be."

"And even if it is not, even if this London man Doughty directed Signor Di Massimo in the matter of the kidnapping . . . What can you do to him from Lucca? How do you extradite on such speculation? And how do you prove anything anyway?"

"He assumes in this"—Salvatore indicated the report—"that I have not earlier looked into Michelangelo Di Massimo's banking records, Birgit. He assumes I have no copy of them. He assumes I would not compare them to what he sends me now. And he does not know that I have this." He took from his jacket pocket the copy of the card he'd received from Captain Mirenda. He handed it to her.

She read it, frowned, and handed it back. "What is this *khushi*?"

"The name he calls her."

"Who?"

"The child's father." And he explained the rest: how it went from Squali to the child and how she had kept it beneath a mattress at Villa Rivelli. Squali, he told her, may have dreamed up the card, but he had certainly not dreamed up *khushi*. Whoever had written it knew the child's pet name. And that was a narrow field of people indeed.

"Is this his handwriting?" Birgit asked.

"Squali's?"

"Her papà's."

"I have little enough to compare to it—just the documents and written remarks at his *pensione* and I am no expert in the matter of handwriting, of course—but it looks the same to me and when I show it to the professor, I expect his face will tell me the truth. Very few people lie well. I think he will be among those who cannot. Beyond that, it is clear that his daughter believed he wrote it." Salvatore explained how the card had been used.

Birgit, however, made a very good point, saying, "Would she know her papà's handwriting, though? Think of Bianca. Would she know yours? What have you ever written to her other than 'Love from Papà' on a birthday card?"

He inclined his head to indicate that she had a good point.

"And if it is her papà's writing, does this not show that the London detective is telling the truth? Her papà writes the card and hands it over—or posts it—to Michelangelo Di Massimo, who takes it from there, hiring Squali to take the child from the *mercato* because he himself does not wish to be implicated in a public abduction."

"All of this is true," he said. "But at the moment, you see, it is no longer the abduction of the child that interests me." He shifted his position on the bench so that he could gaze upon his ex-wife. Despite their differences and the regrettable alacrity with which her lust for him had faded away, Birgit had a good mind and clear vision. So he asked her the question he'd come to ask. "The investigation into the kidnapping is, of course, no longer mine to direct. By rights, I should pass along this copy of the card to Nicodemo Triglia, *vero*? And yet if I do, all matters pertaining to Taymullah Azhar will be taken from me. You see this, no?"

"What 'matters' will be taken from you?" she asked shrewdly.

He told her of the means of Angelina Upman's death. He said, "Murder is a larger question than kidnapping. Keeping Nicodemo and—let us face the truth squarely—Piero Fanucci occupied with Michelangelo Di Massimo as their culprit allows me access to the child's father that I would not have if Nicodemo and Piero knew about this card."

"Ah. That alters the situation. I see." She wiped her hands together as if dismissing every qualm he had about the nature of what he was obliquely suggesting. She said, "I say keep the copy of the card and let Piero Fanucci sink in his own stew."

"But to let Michelangelo Di Massimo take all the blame for the kidnapping of the child . . . ," he murmured.

"You do not know when this card reached Italy in the first place. You do not even know who sent it. It could be years old and written for another matter entirely—the little girl's keepsake of her father, *per esempio*—or it could be something someone came across and saw how it could be used . . . Anything is possible, *caro*," she said. And then she quickly altered the endearment to "Salvatore" as colour flooded her cheeks. "And anyway isn't it time that Piero was taught his lesson? I suggest you allow him to trumpet to the newspapers as much as he would like: 'Di Massimo's our man! We have the evidence! Put the *stronzo* on trial!' And then, of course, a copy of this card sent on the sly to Di Massimo's attorney . . . ? You owe Piero nothing. And, as you say, murder is a larger issue than abduction." She smiled at him. "I tell you: Do your worst, Salvatore. Solve this murder *and* the abduction and send Fanucci directly to hell."

He smiled in turn and winced just a bit at the pain. "You see? This is why I fell in love with you," he told her.

"Had it only lasted" was her reply.

LUCCA
TUSCANY

Back in his office, at the centre of his desk, Salvatore found a stack of photographs along with a note from the resourceful Ottavia Schwartz. She had managed to have them printed on the sly, and they featured everyone who had attended the funeral and the burial of Angelina Upman.

"Bruno was there, Salvatore."

He looked up. She'd seen him and slipped into his office, closing the door behind her. She blanched at the sight of his face. She said shrewdly, "*Il drago?*" and made a colourful suggestion as to what *il Pubblico Ministero* could do to himself. Then she joined Salvatore at the desk and pointed out Daniele Bruno, with his bulbous ears, standing among a group of men consoling Lorenzo Mura. Ottavia unearthed another picture of him, head bent to Lorenzo as they spoke by the gravesite. But the import of this? Salvatore asked her. How could it mean anything more than all of the other mourners who spoke to Lorenzo Mura that day? Like Mura, Bruno was on the city's *squadra di calcio*. Was Ottavia suggesting that he alone of the team members had gone to the funeral of Lorenzo Mura's beloved?

That had not been the case, of course. The other team members had been there. So had the parents of the children whom Lorenzo Mura coached in private sessions. So had other individuals from the community. So had the Mura and the Upman families.

It was this last group upon whom Salvatore focused. He brought a magnifying glass from his desk drawer and he gazed upon the face of Angelina Upman's sister. He'd never seen twins who bore such a remarkable likeness to each other. There was usually something—some tiny detail—that differentiated them, but in the case of Bathsheba Ward, he could not tell what it was. She might have been Angelina Upman sprung to life once more. It was quite astounding, he thought.

VICTORIA
LONDON

The fact that the wife of one Daniele Bruno was a flight attendant on the regular route between Pisa and London turned out to be a non-starter, as Lynley had thought it might when he checked into it for Salvatore Lo Bianco. She flew into and out of Gatwick several times a day, but that was an end to it. She never had cause to spend the night. She would do, on the off chance that an extreme flight delay resulted in aircraft being held overnight. But when that occurred—which it had not done in the past twelve months—she stayed with the rest of the flight crew at an airport hotel and left the next morning.

Lynley reported all this to Salvatore, who agreed that the matter of Daniele Bruno was turning into an unmistakable dead end. He'd seen all the photos of the funeral, he said. Bruno was there, *certo*, but so was everyone else. "I think he has nothing to do with nothing," Salvatore said in English.

Lynley didn't point out that the double negative resulted in Daniele Bruno being guilty of *something*, if only of being part of a fantasy from the fractured mind of a drug addict. For they had only the word of Carlo Casparia that Bruno had met Lorenzo Mura alone at the football practice field in the first place. And this word had come after being held without a solicitor's involvement, after days of interrupted sleep and very little food. Daniele Bruno was a nonstarter, he reckoned, just like his wife.

But there had to be someone, somewhere, with access to something . . .

They both knew who that someone probably was.

St. James's arrival at New Scotland Yard added little to the mix they had. Lynley met his friend in Reception, and they spoke to each other over morning coffee on the fourth floor.

It had been easy enough for St. James to visit Azhar's lab. By virtue of his university background and his reputation as a forensic scientist and expert witness, he had colleagues everywhere. A few phone calls had made a walkthrough of the lab a simple thing to arrange. The excuse was meeting the distinguished professor of microbiology Taymullah Azhar. Since he wasn't there, the offer made by one of Azhar's two research technicians to show St. James round the lab was accepted with gratitude. They were fellow scientists after all, were they not?

The lab was extensive and impressive, St. James told Lynley, but for all intents and purposes the subject of study was indeed various strains of *Streptococcus*. The focus had to do with mutations of these strains, and the equipment in the lab supported this work.

"From what I could see, it appears to be a fairly straightforward operation," St. James said.

"Meaning?"

"Meaning what's there is what one would expect in a lab of its type: fume cupboards, centrifuge, autoclave, refrigerators for storing DNA, sequencers for the DNA data, freezers for bacterial isolates, incubators for bacterial cultures, computers . . . There appear to be two main areas of study going on: the *Streptococcus* that causes necrotising fasciitis—"

"Which is?"

St. James added a packet of sugar to his coffee and stirred it. "Flesh-eating bacteria syndrome," he said.

"Good God."

"The other is the S*treptococcus* that causes pneumonia, sepsis, and meningitis. They're both serious strains, obviously, but the second one—it's called *Streptococcus agalactiae*—crosses the blood-brain barrier and can be deadly."

Lynley thought about this. He said, "Is there a chance someone in the lab could be studying *E. coli* on the sly?"

"I suppose anything's possible, Tommy, but to know for certain you'd need a mole inside the place. Some of the equipment could be used for *E. coli* cultures, obviously. But the broths for growing each of them would be different, as would the incubators. *Strep* requires a carbon dioxide incubator. *E. coli* doesn't."

"Could there be more than one kind in the lab?"

"More than one kind of incubator? Certainly. At least a dozen people work in the place. One of them may have something brewing that deals with *E. coli*."

"Without Azhar's knowledge?"

"I doubt it would be without his knowledge unless someone has a nefarious reason for studying it."

They exchanged a long look. St. James finally said, "Ah. It's a tricky thing, isn't it?"

"It is indeed."

"He's a friend of Barbara's, isn't he? Certainly, she could have some insight here, Tommy. Perhaps if she were to go to the lab herself and do a bit of delving on a pretext having to do with Azhar . . . ?"

"That's not on, I'm afraid."

"Can you get a search warrant, then?"

"If it comes to it, yes."

St. James examined Lynley's expression for a moment before he said, "But you hope it doesn't come to that, I take it?"

"I'm not at all sure what I hope any longer" was Lynley's reply.

VICTORIA
LONDON

He would have liked to talk to Barbara about what he'd learned from St. James. She'd been for years his go-to person when he wanted to toss round ideas in the course of an investigation. But it was unlikely that she would say anything, do anything, or admit to anything that might endanger Taymullah Azhar. So he was left to do his thinking alone.

It had been an excellent means of eliminating Angelina Upman. Once the small matter of no one else's having been affected by the bacteria had been dealt with in one way or another, the road was clear to declaring her death an unfortunate result of food contamination by a virulent strain of bacteria that generally—if detected soon enough—killed no one. Complications from her pregnancy had prevented the doctors from realising what they were dealing with. As did Angelina's own reluctance to stay in hospital once she finally took herself there. As did the fact that no one else who shared meals with her and no one else in Tuscany, for that matter, turned up in hospital with the same symptoms.

Someone must have seen how everything was going to play out, Lynley thought. That suggested Lorenzo Mura, but as to *why* he would wish to harm the woman who was carrying his child, the woman he loved and fully intended to marry . . . Unless, of course, all of his devotion was a front for something else.

He thought back over every encounter he'd had with the man. He could see the many ways in which Lorenzo had had the opportunity to mix the bacteria into Angelina's food—the man was, after all, solicitous of her condition because of the pregnancy—but he couldn't come up with how he'd got the stuff in the first place . . . until he remembered the man he'd seen at the *fattoria* when he'd first called there.

What had Lynley seen? A thick envelope handed from this unnamed man to Lorenzo Mura. What had Lorenzo declared? It was payment for one of the donkey foals he raised on the premises.

But what if that man had brought something other than money? Any possibility was one worth pursuing. Lynley picked up the phone and rang Salvatore Lo Bianco.

He had much to tell him anyway: He began with St. James's visit to Taymullah Azhar's lab, and he ended with the mystery man handing over an envelope to Lorenzo Mura at Fattoria di Santa Zita.

"Mura claimed it was cash for one of his foals. I thought nothing of it at the time, but if there's actually no *E. coli* in Taymullah Azhar's laboratory in London—"

"There is no *E. coli* now," Salvatore replied. "But he would, of course, have no need of it now, would he, *Ispettore*?"

"I see that. He'd have had to be rid of whatever was left—if indeed there was any left—when he returned to London, having already managed to get Angelina to ingest whatever he'd taken to Italy. But here's something else to consider, Salvatore. What if Angelina was not the intended victim?"

"Who, then?" Salvatore asked.

"Perhaps Azhar?"

"How was he to ingest this *E. coli*?"

"If Mura gave him something . . . ?"

"That he gave no one else? How would that have looked, my friend? 'Eat this *panino*, signore, because you look hungry'? Or 'Try this especial *salsa di pomodoro* on your pasta'? And how did he put his hands on *E. coli*? And *if* he put his hands on it, how would he poison the professor but have no one else affected?"

"I think we must find the man with the donkeys," Lynley said.

"Who does what? Brew *E. coli* in his bathtub? Notice it crawling round the droppings of a cow or two? My friend, you try to bend what you've seen to fit what you hope. You forget Berlin."

"What about it?"

"The conference that our microbiologist attended there. What was to prevent someone passing along to him a bit of this bacteria at the conference?"

"That was in April. She died weeks later."

"*Sì*, but he has a lab, does he not? He keeps it there . . . however it is kept: warm, cold, boiling, freezing. I do not know. He labels it as something, I do not know what. But as you say, he is the head of this lab so no one is likely to bother anything labelled with the professor's own writing. When it comes time to use it, he takes it with him to Italy."

"But this presupposes he knew everything from the first: that Hadiyyah would be kidnapped, that Angelina would come in search of her, that he himself would go to Italy . . . If he'd been wrong about anything—especially about any move made by any of the principals—the plan would have crumbled."

"As it has done, *no*?"

Lynley had to admit there was truth in this. He asked Salvatore what was next, although he had a feeling he already knew.

"I will pay a call upon the good professor. And in the meantime, I will have officers look into the work of all the people who attended that April conference in Berlin."

LUCCA
ITALY

Salvatore decided not to have Taymullah Azhar come to the *questura*. He knew how quickly word would filter back to Piero Fanucci that he had done this. And while a conversation with the London professor had not been forbidden to him, he wanted any reports of what he did to go nowhere until he had more information. Once he'd directed Ottavia and Giorgio to look into the attendees at the Berlin conference, he set off for the *anfiteatro*. On his way, he phoned the London professor and told him in his very bad English to phone his *avvocato*.

They were waiting for him in the breakfast room of the *pensione* when Salvatore arrived. He asked where the child was. Had she gone back to Scuola Dante Alighieri?

She had not, he was told. After all, Azhar was anticipating a quick end to whatever matter had caused Salvatore to request his passport. Once clarity had been reached in this matter, they would depart as soon as they could. Sending her to school . . . ? This did not seem a reasonable idea since they would be leaving Italy so shortly.

Salvatore suggested two things at that point. The first was that adequate care for Hadiyyah needed to be arranged. The second was that he look closely at what Salvatore was about to show him.

He passed to the professor and his *avvocato* the copy of the card from Villa Rivelli. He watched closely as Azhar's gaze fell upon it. There was nothing on his face. He turned the paper over to see if anything was written on the back of it, which Salvatore well recognised as a stalling tactic that gave him time to develop an explanation.

He said, "And so, *Dottore?*" to Azhar and waited for Aldo Greco's translation of what the London man would say. Aldo shifted his buttocks, grimaced, passed gas, pardoned himself, and took up the document for an examination. He read it and handed it back to Azhar. Before Azhar could speak, Greco asked what this thing was and how Salvatore had come by it.

Salvatore had no problem with revealing either bit of information. It was a copy of a greeting card, he said. It had been found at the location where Hadiyyah Upman had been held after her abduction.

The card itself or the copy? Greco asked shrewdly.

The card, of course, Salvatore told him, which was still in the hands of the *carabinieri* who'd been called to Villa Rivelli by the Mother Superior. In due time the original would be sent to be included with any other gathered evidence.

"Do you recognise this, *Dottore*? It appears to be in your handwriting."

Aldo Greco intervened at once. He said, "A handwriting expert has confirmed that, *Ispettore*? Surely you yourself are no expert in such a matter."

Salvatore said that, *certo*, an expert would be employed by the police if things came to that. He himself was there merely to ascertain the provenance of this greeting card.

"*Con permesso?*" Salvatore concluded. He indicated with a nod at Azhar that he would be delighted to hear the London man's reply should his *avvocato* deem such a thing a reasonable request.

Signor Greco said to Azhar, "Go ahead, *Professore*."

Azhar said that he did not recognise the card or the message upon it. As to the handwriting . . . It looked similar to his own, he said, but handwriting could be copied by someone with the expertise to do so.

"You know, of course, that there are ways to discern a forgery from a real document," Salvatore told him. "There are experts in forgery— forensic experts—who spend all day doing such work. They look for special signs, marks of hesitation that the true writer of something would not make in the course of penning a note. You know this, *sì*?"

"The professor is not an idiot," Greco commented. "He has answered your question, Salvatore."

Salvatore pointed out the word *khushi*. "And this?" he said to Azhar.

Azhar confirmed that it was his pet name for his daughter, something he had called her from the moment of her birth. It meant *happiness*, he explained.

"And this name *khushi* . . . you alone called her that?" And when Azhar confirmed that this was the case, "Just between the two of you?"

Azhar frowned. "I don't . . . What exactly do you mean, Inspector?"

"I mean was this something said in private only?"

Azhar shook his head. "It was not a secret. Anyone who witnessed us together would know that this is what I call her."

"Ah." Salvatore nodded. It was nice to know in advance what direction Aldo Greco would take if things proceeded as he expected them to proceed. He took the copy of the card from Azhar and returned it to the manila envelope in which he'd carried it to the *pensione*. "*Grazie, Professore*," he said.

In a movement that was nearly imperceptible, Azhar blew out a long breath. It was over, the expiration said, whatever "it" had been.

Aldo Greco, however, was not stupid. He said, "What else, Ispettore Lo Bianco?"

Salvatore smiled in acknowledgement of the attorney's wisdom in this situation. He said to Azhar, "Now we speak of Berlin."

"Berlin?"

Salvatore watched him closely as he nodded. "You told me there were many microbiologists in Berlin when you were there for your conference last month, *vero*?"

"What has Berlin to do with anything?" Greco asked as he translated Salvatore's words.

"I think the *professore* knows very well what Berlin has to do with, *Dottore*," Salvatore murmured.

"I do not," Azhar said.

"*Certo*, you do," Salvatore said expansively, his voice quite pleasant. "Berlin is your alibi for the moment of your daughter's abduction, no? You have insisted upon that from the very first, and I will say that everything you claimed about Berlin has proven itself to be God's own truth."

"Then . . . ?" Greco asked with a glance at his watch. Time was of the essence, he was saying. His own time was far too valuable to be spent beating round bushes.

Salvatore said, "Tell me, *Dottore*, about the nature of this conference once again."

"What has this to do with the matter in hand?" Signor Greco demanded. "If, as you say, the professor's alibi has been confirmed for the time of his daughter's kidnapping—"

"*Sì, sì*," Salvatore said. "But now we speak of other things, my friend." And with a look at Azhar, "Now we speak of the death of Angelina Upman."

Azhar was absolute stone. It was as if his mind had begun screaming at once: do nothing, say nothing, wait, wait, wait. And this was
good advice that his mind was giving him, Salvatore acknowledged
silently. But the vein throbbing in his temple was betraying his body's
reaction to the change of subject.

An innocent man would have no such reaction, and Salvatore knew
this. What he also thus knew was that the London professor was well
aware that Angelina Upman's death was far more than the result of
an unfortunate misdiagnosis on the part of her doctors.

He'd very nearly got away with it. Just a few hours more on the
day Salvatore had requested his passport and he'd have been back in
London, from where only the lengthy and complicated process of
extradition could have wrested him, if it managed to wrest him at all.

Greco said abruptly, "Say nothing," to Azhar. Then he turned in
his chair and went on to Salvatore with, "I insist that you explain
yourself, *Ispettore*, before I allow my client to reply. What is this you're
now talking about?"

"I'm talking about murder," Salvatore told him.

VICTORIA
LONDON

Lynley waited until late in the day to speak to Barbara Havers, two
hours after Isabelle Ardery had buttonholed him in her office. She'd
wanted to know how his "sorting out" was going, and who could
blame her? On her watch, an officer under her command had gone
off the rails and was, for all intents and purposes, continuing to do so.
Lynley's brief was to complete the incomplete picture of John Stewart's
reports on Barbara's activities, but he didn't know how to do it without sinking Barbara's entire career.

Part of him was shouting that it bloody well deserved to be sunk.
Her connection to Mitchell Corsico alone was enough to put her back
in uniform. When one took into account everything else—from
withholding information to outright lying about details relevant to a
case—she was finished in police work. He knew this intellectually. It

was emotionally that he couldn't accept that there were consequences involved and that Barbara Havers had to face them. His heart was arguing that she'd had very good reasons for betraying every tenet of their profession and, in time, everyone would accept that.

That was, of course, the lie. Not only would everyone not accept it, it was a form of insanity on his part to expect them to do so. He *himself* couldn't accept what she'd done. He wouldn't, he knew, be in so much turmoil if he wholeheartedly embraced how Barbara had behaved.

He chose the Met's library for his meeting with Barbara. Any other place and they would be seen. At this time of day, so late in the afternoon, it was unlikely that anyone else would be on the thirteenth floor. So he asked her to join him there, and there he waited. She came in reeking of cigarette smoke. She'd had a fag in one of the stairwells, another infraction but it mattered little set beside everything else that had been going on.

They walked to one of the windows. From here, the London Eye dominated the skyline, with each of its capsules crowded with spectators, and the spires of Parliament poked hopefully upward, towards a sky that today was the colour of old pewter. It exactly matched his mood, Lynley thought.

"Been there?" Havers said to him.

For a moment he didn't know what she meant till he glanced at her and saw that she was looking upon the enormous Ferris wheel. He shook his head and told her he hadn't. She nodded, said, "Neither have I. It's the glass cars or whatever they are. I don't think I'd fancy being inside with a crowd of tourists jostling each other to get a snap of Big Ben."

"Ah. Yes."

And then nothing. He turned from the view and took from his jacket pocket the copy of the greeting card that Salvatore Lo Bianco had sent to him. He handed it over to Barbara. She said, "What's—" but her words faded as she read what was on it.

Lynley said to her, "Earlier, you told me that *khushi* was unfamiliar to you. This was found where Hadiyyah was kept hidden. Azhar has confirmed, by the way, that this *khushi* was his pet name for Hadiyyah. You've known the two of them how long, Barbara?"

"Who?" she asked, although she seemed to have some trouble with the word.

"Barbara . . ."

"All right. Two years this month. But you know that, don't you, so why're you asking?"

"Because I find it impossible to believe that in that time you never heard her father call her *khushi*. And yet that's precisely what you asked me to believe. That and other things as well."

"Anyone could have known—"

"Who, exactly?" Lynley felt the first piercings of an anger he'd been holding at bay since this entire miserable affair had begun. "Do you want to argue that Angelina Upman arranged for the kidnapping of her own daughter? Or Lorenzo Mura? Or . . . who else is there who 'might have known,' as you say, that her father called her *khushi*? An unidentified schoolmate, Barbara? A fellow nine-year-old with kidnap on his mind?"

"Bathsheba Ward would have known," Barbara said. "If she posed as Azhar in emails to Hadiyyah, she would have called her *khushi*."

"And then what, for God's sake?"

"And then kidnapped her to hurt Angelina. Or to hurt Azhar. Or to . . . Bloody hell, I don't know."

"And she managed to duplicate his handwriting as well? Is that part of what you wish to argue? I'd like to hear the full story of how it all played out, from the moment that child went missing in Lucca to the moment her mother ended up in a grave."

"He didn't kill her!"

In frustration, Lynley walked away from her. He wanted to take her by the shoulders and shake her. He wanted to put his fist through a wall. He wanted to break one of the thirteenth-floor windows. Anything other than to have to continue this conversation with a woman so deliberately blind to what was before her. "For the love of God," he tried a final time, "Barbara, can't you see—"

"Those tickets to Pakistan," she cut in. He could see that her upper lip had begun to sweat, and he reckoned she had her hands so tightly fisted in order to keep them from shaking. "They tell you that. Because why the bloody hell would Azhar purchase one-way tickets to

Pakistan if he knew Angelina was going to be dead and Hadiyyah would be returned to him permanently?"

"Because he knew very well that when it came down to it, when everything finally met the light of day, you'd be standing there doing exactly what you're doing: refusing to see what's in front of your eyes. And you have to ask yourself why you're doing that, Barbara, why you're throwing away your career on the off chance that the rest of us won't eventually hunt down every single detail that proves Taymullah Azhar was involved in each aspect of what's happened to his daughter and what happened to Angelina Upman."

At that, for a moment, he believed he'd got through to her. He believed that she would make a clean breast of everything she knew and everything she was hiding. She would do it, he thought, because she'd worked at his side for years, because she'd borne witness to what had led to the death of his wife and to what had followed, because she trusted him to have her best interests at heart, because she knew what was demanded of anyone who carried a warrant card and had a place at the Met.

She went back to the window and her fist pounded lightly on its sill. She said, "Those tickets to Pakistan suggest things. I see that, sir. As far as the kidnapping goes, those tickets and when they were bought and the fact that they are one-way only . . . They make things . . . difficult for Azhar. But *you* have to see they also eliminate him as a suspect for Angelina's murder. Because with Angelina dead, he'd have no need to run to Pakistan with Hadiyyah. She'd been given back to him."

"Which was his intention all along. And into Pakistan he could disappear with her if Angelina's death was discovered as not an unfortunate and unexpected termination to a trying time but instead a carefully planned murder."

He saw her swallow. She squinted against sunlight that was not there, to improve her vision which was already perfect. She said, "That's not how it was. That's not how it is."

"You're in love with him. Love causes people—"

"I am not. I. Am. Not."

"Loves causes people," he went determinedly on, "to lose their objectivity. You're not the first person this has happened to, and God knows you won't be the last. I want to help you, Barbara, but without a clean breast of everything on your part—"

"He's *innocent*. She was taken from him, and he tried to find her, and he failed to find her, and then she was kidnapped, and only then did he know where she had been because Angelina showed up, *accusing* him like she always did, hating him like she always did, manipulating and scheming and leaving grief and chaos behind her and . . ." Her voice broke. "He did nothing. He did not do a bloody goddamn thing."

"Barbara. Please."

She shook her head. She swung away from him and left the room.

MARLBOROUGH

WILTSHIRE

They found a location that was central to both of them in Wiltshire, at an inn just east of the town. In a copse of beech trees, it sat well off the road, half-timbered and brick with a sloping, ancient slate roof. In its car park Lynley waited for forty-five minutes until Daidre Trahair managed to get there from Bristol.

By the time she arrived, the car park was crowded, so she left her car in the remaining bay, which was farthest from the inn's front door. He was out of the Healey Elliott and at her car door before she had switched off the ignition. As she glanced up at him, he realised that he had been quite desperate to see her. She was, indeed, the only person he'd even wished to see at the end of his conversation with Barbara Havers.

He said simply, "Thank you," as he and she opened the car door together.

She said as she got out, "Of course, Thomas. It was no trouble at all."

"I expect you've left a commitment behind in Bristol."

She smiled. "The Broads will practise quite well without me tonight."

They hugged. He took in the scent of her hair and the vague and subtle perfume of her skin. He said, "You've not dined, have you?"

And when she shook her head, "Shall we, then? I've no idea what the food will be like, but the atmosphere looks promising."

They entered the place. It was ages old, with a sloping floor of oak and small diamond-paned windows. A panelled dining room opened off Reception. A teetering stairway led to rooms up above. Although the restaurant was nearly full, they had luck. Someone had just cancelled a booking, so if they didn't mind sitting near the fireplace . . . ? No fire at this time of year, however.

Lynley would have sat on one of the stair treads. He looked at Daidre and she nodded at him with a smile. She had a smudge on her spectacles, which he found endearing. Her sandy hair was somewhat in disarray. She'd come on the run. He wanted to thank her again for her kindness, but instead he followed the maitre d' into the dining room.

A drink?

Yes.

Sparkling water?

That as well.

The night's specials?

Indeed.

Menus?

Please.

Then followed the business of ordering. He wasn't hungry, but she was. Doubtless, she'd been wrestling large animals for most of the day. A rhino with piles, a kangaroo with a swollen ankle, a hippo with kidney stones. God knew. So he ordered a meal he would only pick at so that she would feel free to order in a similar fashion. She did so, and the waiter disappeared, and then they were alone with each other. She looked at him expectantly. Obviously, an explanation was in order.

"Terrible day," he said to her. "You're the antidote for it."

"Oh dear."

"To which part?"

"The terrible day part. I'm rather pleased to be its antidote, I think."

"Think but not know?"

She cocked her head at him. She removed her spectacles and cleaned them of their smudges on her linen napkin. She said when she returned them to her nose, "Ah. I can see you now."

"And your reply?"

She fingered her cutlery, straightening it unnecessarily. She was, as he was learning about her, as always carefully considering her answer. "That's just the problem. The think-but-not-know part. At any rate, it's lovely to see you. C'n I help in some way? I mean, with the day?"

He found of a sudden that he didn't want their evening to be about Barbara Havers and what she'd been up to. He found that he wished to let that sleeping dog lie, if only for the hours he had to spend with Daidre. So instead he asked her about the job she'd been offered at London Zoo. Had she reached a decision about transplanting herself, uprooting her life, and abandoning Boadicea's Broads for the Electric Magic?

She said, "A lot depends on what Mark says about the contract. I've not heard from him yet."

"How might Mark feel about your leaving Bristol if you're leaning in that direction?"

"Well, obviously, there are thousands of solicitors in London waiting for someone like me to come along and hire them for the messy bits of life."

"Yes. But that's not what I meant."

Their sparkling water arrived at the table, along with a bottle of wine. The ceremony of opening this, presenting the cork, tasting, and nodding approval was gone through. The wine was poured for both of them before Daidre replied.

"What're you asking, Thomas?"

He rolled the stem of his wineglass in his fingers. "I suppose I'm asking if there's any point to my seeing you . . . aside from our conversations which I do enjoy."

She looked at her wine as she began her answer. It took a moment as she was not glib and did not pretend to be. "When it comes to you, I'm at war with my better judgement."

"Meaning what?"

"That my better judgement has been insisting that my life is better kept in order through devotion to mammals who can't speak. I became a veterinarian for a reason, you see."

He took this in and evaluated it, turning it this way and that for every meaning he could wrest from it. He settled on saying, "But you can't expect to go through life untouched by your fellow man, can you? You can't want that."

Their starters arrived: freshly smoked Irish salmon for her, a Caprese salad for him. It was far too large. What had he been thinking in ordering it?

She said, "Well, that's just it, isn't it? I can want that. Anyone can want it. There's part of me, Tommy—"

"You've just called me Tommy."

"Thomas."

"I prefer the other."

"I know. And please, it was inadvertent. You're not meant to think—"

"Daidre, nothing is inadvertent."

Her head lowered as, perhaps, she took this in. She seemed to be gathering her thoughts. She finally looked up, and her eyes were bright. Candlelight, he thought. It was only the candles. She said, "Let's leave that for another discussion. What I was intending to say is that there's a part of me that always fails within a relationship. Failure myself to thrive, failure to provide what the other person needs to thrive as well. It's always come down to that in the end for me, and it probably always will, if my personal history is anything to go by. There's a part of me that can't be touched, you see, and that means defeat for anyone who tries to get at the heart of who I am."

"Can't or won't?" he asked her.

"What?"

"Be touched. Can't or won't be touched?"

"Can't, I'm afraid. I'm an independent sort. Well, I've had to be, coming into the middle-class world as I did."

She didn't amplify, but she didn't need to. He knew her background because she'd shown it to him: the decrepit caravan from which she and her siblings had been removed by the government from the care of their parents, the fostering system into which they'd been placed, her own adoption and her change of identity. He knew it all, and it didn't matter a whit to him. But that was hardly the point.

She said, "I'll always have that part of me, and that's what keeps me . . . *untouchable*, I suppose, is the word."

"Because your family were travellers?"

"If they'd only *been* travellers, Tommy."

He let the name go.

"At least there's a culture involved with travellers. There's a tradition, a history, families, whatever. We didn't have that. All we had was my father's . . . What do we want to call it? His compulsion? His mad insistence on what he was going to do with his life? That led us to where we ended up. That led us to why we were taken from him and from my mother and from that terrible place . . ." Her eyes grew brighter. She looked away from him at the empty fireplace.

Lynley said quickly, "Daidre. It's perfectly—"

"No, it isn't. It can never be. It's part of who I am and this . . . this untouchable part of me seeks to honour it, I suppose. But it always gets in the way."

He said nothing. He allowed her the moment to regain her composure, sorry that he had pushed her to this point, which was always the point of departure for the two of them even though he would not have it that way.

She looked back at him, her expression fond. "It isn't you, you know. It isn't who you are or how you grew up or what you owe to several hundred years of your family's history. It's me. And the fact that I have no family history at all. At least not one that I'm aware of or was told about. I suspect, on the other hand, that you can recite your forebears back to the time of the Tudors."

"Hardly." He smiled. "The Stuarts, perhaps, but not the Tudors."

"You see," she said. "You *know* the Stuarts. Tommy, there are actually people out there"—she waved her hand vaguely in the direction of the windows, by which she meant the outside world—"who have no idea who the Stuarts are. You do know that, don't you?"

"Daidre, I read history. It's nothing more than that. And you called me Tommy again. I think you've begun to protest too much. And yes, yes, I know it's Hamlet's mother and don't tell me it signifies anything more than people saying 'There's the rub' because you and I both know that it doesn't. And even if it did, what does it matter at the end of the day?"

"It matters to me," she said. "It's what keeps me apart."

"From whom?"

"From everyone. From you. And besides that . . . After what happened to you, you need—no, you deserve—someone who is one hundred percent *there* for you."

He took some wine and thought about this. She worked on her salmon for a moment. He watched her. He finally said, "That hardly sounds healthy. No one actually wants a parasite. I tend to think it's only in films that we get the idea men and women are supposed to find—what do they call it?—soul mates with whom they march into the future, blissfully joined at the hip."

She smiled, it seemed, in spite of herself. "You know what I mean. You deserve someone who is willing and able to be one hundred percent *for* you, open *to* you, accepting *of* you . . . whatever you want to call it. I'm not that person, and I don't think I could be."

Her declaration felt like the thinnest of rapiers. It slid without effort under his skin, barely felt until the bleeding began. "So what are you saying, exactly?"

"I hardly know."

"Why?"

She looked at him. He tried to read whatever he could on her face, but time and circumstance had made her guarded, and he couldn't blame her for the walls she built. She said, "Because you're not an easy man to walk away from, Tommy. So I'm very much aware of the *necessity* of walking away and the marked reluctance I feel about doing so."

He nodded. For a moment they ate as the sounds of the dining room rose and fell around them. Plates were removed. Other plates came. He finally said, "Let's leave it at that, for now."

Later, after a shared pudding of something called chocolate death gateau followed by coffee, they left the place. Nothing had been resolved between them and yet the sense of having moved forward was something that Lynley couldn't ignore. They walked to her car arm in arm, and before she unlocked it and prepared to drive away, she stepped easily and naturally into his arms.

Just as easily, he kissed her. Just as easily, her lips parted to his and the kiss lingered. He felt a tremendous desire for her: partly the animal lust that drove their species, partly spiritual longing that happened when a soul recognised the immortal worth of another soul.

The inn has rooms, he wanted to say. Climb those stairs with me, Daidre, and come to bed.

Instead he said nothing but "Good night, dear friend."

"Good night, dear Tommy" was her reply.

15 MAY

Barbara's mobile rang as she was showering, trying to wash off not only her feeling of dread but also the stench of cigarette smoke. Her nerves had been raw for more than forty-eight hours now, and only one fag after another had done anything to calm them. She'd gone through four packets of Players and as a result her lungs were making her feel like a woman being tried for witchcraft: A huge stone the approximate size of the Isle of Man sat on her chest, demanding a confession of her misdeeds.

When the mobile rang, she leapt from the shower. She grabbed it, it slipped out of her fingers, and she watched in horror as it launched towards the tiled floor, where it lost its battery and whoever had been ringing her. She cursed, grabbed a towel, rescued the mobile, and put it back together. She looked to see who the caller had been. She recognised Mitchell Corsico's number. She rang him back at once, sitting on the loo and dripping water onto the floor.

"What've you got?" she asked.

"Good morning to you too" was his reply. "Or I s'pose I should say *bone jorno*."

"You're in Italy?" she asked. Thank *God*. The next step was moulding the story he would write.

"Let's put it this way: *Il grande formaggio*—that would be Rodney Aronson over in Fleet Street, by the way—wasn't exactly chuffed to cough up the funds to get me here, so my expense account is large enough for one slice of *focaccia* and a cup of espresso each day. I have to sleep on a park bench—praise God there're dozens of them up on the city wall, at least—unless I spring for a hotel room myself. But other than that, yeah, I'm in Italy, Barb."

"And?" she said.

"And the good professor spent part of yesterday at the local nick. They call it a *questura* here, by the way. He was there with his solicitor in the afternoon, and they left for dinner, which made me think things might not be what they seemed. But then he was back with the same bloke in tow, and in they went for another few hours. I tried to have a word with him in the afters, but he wasn't giving."

"What about Hadiyyah?" Barbara asked him anxiously.

"Who?"

"His *daughter*, Mitchell. The one who was kidnapped? Where is she? What's happened to her? He can't have left her all alone for a day in some hotel room while he talked to the cops."

"P'rhaps not. But the way things are looking, Barb, he sure as hell did something and he surer as hell doesn't want to have a chat about it with me. No one has a whisper about *E. coli*, by the way. There's four journalists I've run into—these're Italians as I'm the only Brit mad enough to be here—and they speak good English *and* they haven't heard a word about *E. coli*. So I'm going to lay something out for you here. This *E. coli* business: truth or lie? I mean, I've had a think in the last twenty-four, and it seems to me you're not above sending your best mate Mitchell on a wild-goose chase for your own reasons. You're not doing that, are you? Better reassure me or things won't look good for you."

"Aside from all of that being rubbish on a scone, you've already printed those pictures of me, Mitchell. What else can you do?"

"Print them up with the dates on them this time round, darling. Send them off to your guv and see what happens next. Hey, you and I know you've been working this situation from every wrong angle because you and the professor—"

"Don't bloody go there," she said. It was bad enough she'd had to go there with Lynley. She had no intention of entertaining her supposed love for Azhar as a subject with Mitch Corsico. "The *E. coli* story is solid. I told you that much. I had it from DI Lynley. I was sitting right at his dining room table when he got it *and* he got it directly from Italy from a bloke called Lo Bianco. *Chief Inspector* Salvatore Lo Bianco. He's the cop who—"

"Yeah, yeah. I know who he is. Pulled from the kidnapping case for incompetence, Barb. Did Lynley tell you that? I reckon not, eh? So this Lo Bianco drops a fanciful word about *E. coli* as a bit of you-know-what."

"Revenge for being pulled from the kidnapping case? A way to muddy the waters? Don't be stupid. And the *E. coli* business has nothing to do with the kidnapping anyway. It's a separate issue. The Italians don't want it hitting the press. That's your story so bloody go after it. You can't think Azhar's been questioned for hours because of a kidnapping that everyone knows he had no part in. They have someone under arrest for the kidnapping, for the love of God. Far as I know, they've got two blokes under arrest for it. This is another issue and the last thing the Italians want is for the information to get out. It panics people. No one buys Italian. Their exports get held for testing and the veg rots in port and the fruit goes soft. 'F they pin the *E. coli* business on a single person—which, believe me, they're intent on doing come hell or you-know-what—they don't have to worry. They call it murder and Bob's the rest of it. *That's* your story." So bloody well write it, she thought, so that the Italian press would pick up on it, run with it, and batter the cops till the real source of the *E. coli* was located. Because the one thing she could and would absolutely bet her life on was that Azhar had nothing to do with Angelina Upman's death.

On his end of the call, Mitch Corsico was acting thoughtful. He hadn't got to where he was without being careful with his stories. He might be employed by a deplorable rag that was more suitable for lining rubbish bins than it was for printing valuable information, but he didn't intend to spend his entire career at *The Source*, so he had a reputation for accuracy that he had to maintain. He said, "Seems to me you're not thinking this through. Far 's I can tell, there's not a hint of pasta-eating lads and lasses dropping like flies because of some mass food poisoning over here unless the health officials for the whole eff-ing country're in on a cover-up, which, you ask me, isn't bloody likely. So are you trying to suggest the Upman woman dipped into a plate of steaming *E. coli* on her own?"

"Who knows how high the cover-up goes? For all we know, there *are* other *E. coli* victims and no one is talking about them."

"Bollocks. There'll be laws about that. Reporting a potential epidemic or something. Like when someone shows up in casualty coughing blood and bloody-hell-we've-got-a-case-of-TB-on-our-hands. They don't let that go. They wouldn't let this go."

Barbara jammed her fingers into her wet hair. She looked round for her fags, didn't see them, realised that she hadn't brought them into the bathroom, remembered that she'd had a shower primarily to wash the stench of them off her, and wanted one anyway.

She said, "Mitchell? Will you listen to me? Or at least to yourself? One way or another you've got a story, so why the hell don't you bloody write it?"

"I expect it comes down to my not quite trusting you."

"Christ. What more do I sodding have to tell you?"

"Why you're so hot to have this story hit the paper for a start."

"Because they should be telling their own papers about it and they're not. They're not warning anyone. They're not looking for the source."

"Uh . . . That's where you've got the wrong end of the stick. You and I both know why the professor's been stuck in the *questura*. This conversation's gone back to where it started. He was there yesterday. Chances are very good he'll be there today, and 'f you ask me, there's a pretty good chance they're not talking to him about how he likes the weather in Tuscany and the *farro* soup in Lucca. Come on, Barb. I did a little digging on our good professor: the ins, the outs, and the whereabouts. He was rubbing elbows with his fellow bacteria lovers just last month. Berlin, this was. Now, if I know that—because it wasn't exactly a top secret, eyes-only confab, Barb—the cops know that. They find someone among that crowd who's studying *E. coli* and it's one hell of a very short trip from that information to someone passing along a petri dish of that stuff to Azhar for use on his lover."

"Mitchell. Are you listening to me?"

"Okay. His former lover, if that's where I've gone wrong."

"Stop it," she said. "Have you been listening? This is a story in which the Italian health services and the Italian police—"

"Barb, you're the one not listening. Uncle Mitchell here has colleagues there. Where you are. In London. And those colleagues have sources elsewhere, even in Berlin. And their sources in Berlin have easy access to that conference of bacteria bigwigs. And what do you think they've uncovered for me? In twenty-four hours, Barb, so you can rest bloody well assured that the Italian coppers will be right behind them."

Barbara's throat was so tight that she could barely get the word out. "What?"

"We've got a woman from University of Glasgow who's a major player in the *E. coli* field. We've got a bloke from University of Heidelberg who's right behind her. Both of them have serious operations going in laboratories on their home patches. And both of them were at the conference. You can connect the dots on that one if you want to."

No, Barbara thought. No, no, no.

She said, and she tried to sound determined, "You're heading in the wrong direction. This is a woman who had more than one lover at a time. She had Azhar and another bloke while she was living with Azhar here in London. And then she had Lorenzo Mura as well. Three lovers at once. She left Azhar for Lorenzo Mura and I'm telling you that it's a fairly sure thing she picked up someone over there once the fires burnt low with Mura. That's who she was."

"You're slithering all over the map, Barb. You can't be trying to tell me this bird had a former lover with access to *E. coli* and a current lover with access as well. How d'you expect that ship to get out of port? *And* you're contradicting yourself anyway. This is either a grand Italian cover-up or it's cold-blooded murder, but it isn't both."

She was as out of ideas as she was out of steam. She was reduced to saying the one thing she knew had no chance at all of winning him to her thoughts. She said, "Mitchell, please."

He said pleasantly, "At the end of the day, this is going to be a very big story, so I s'pose I have to thank you, Barb. I give it another twenty-four hours before they arrest him. They call that *indagato* here. The coppers turn their eyes on you as the principal suspect and the news goes out and you're *indagato*. Taking his passport was the first step. That's the second. So you put me on to a very big story, Barb. Rod might even increase my expense account to include a plate of spaghetti Bolognese."

"You'll destroy him if you start speculating about him in the press. You know that, right? You've already done the Love Rat Dad piece. Wasn't that enough? You've got nothing but circumstantial rubbish to build a story on."

"True enough," he said. "But circumstantial rubbish is our bread and butter. You knew that when you brought me on board."

VICTORIA
LONDON

Barbara forced herself to eat. She even went for something with more nutritional validity than her usual fare. In place of a strawberry Pop-Tart, she opted for a soft-boiled egg and brown toast. She gave in to jam, but that was it. She felt virtuous for five minutes until she sicked up the entire mess.

Luckily that happened before she left Chalk Farm for the Met. She was forced to change her tee-shirt and scrub her teeth and mouth three times. But none of that resulted in her being late for work, which she reckoned counted in her favour.

She tried not to smoke en route. She failed. She tried to divert her mind with chat from Radio 4. She failed. Twice she came close to finding herself on the responsibility end of a roadway crash. She self-talked and tried to get her breath even and her heart beating normally. She failed there as well.

She had two fags in the underground car park, the first to still her nerves and the second to build her courage. What she was attempting to come to terms with was having saved Azhar from a kidnapping charge only to have him charged with murder. In the realm of pyrrhic victories, she reckoned she'd just been crowned its bloody empress.

And where was Hadiyyah? What in God's name had been done with Hadiyyah if Azhar was spending hours on the grill in gaol?

She'd rung his mobile: twice before she left her bungalow in Chalk Farm, once on her way to Victoria Street, and a final time in the underground car park. No reply told her he was probably back at the *questura*, as Mitch had predicted. What she couldn't understand was why he had not rung to tell her what was going on.

She couldn't work out what this meant except that he didn't want her to know he was being questioned in the first place. He'd already deceived her about his participation in Hadiyyah's kidnapping. It wasn't inconceivable that he'd not wanted her to know he was being questioned about Angelina's death.

What she didn't want to toss round in her mind was whether she ought to be concluding that he was involved. Instead, she concentrated on Hadiyyah and on the state of fear and confusion the little girl had to be in. Her young life was in shambles. In six short months, she'd gone through more than most children endure in a lifetime. After being snatched from her father and taken to Italy, after being kidnapped and held for days at an obscure location in the Italian Alps, after losing her mother . . . now her father was under suspicion for murder? How was she to navigate this? How was she to navigate it alone?

When Barbara reached her desk, she checked for messages. She saw that she was under the watchful eye of John Stewart as usual, but that couldn't be helped. Finding nothing that gave her a clue about Italy and Azhar, she went to see Detective Superintendent Ardery. There was only one way to move forward, she reckoned, and she was going to need Ardery's blessing to do it.

She rang Azhar's mobile a final time. She even rang the *pensione* where he was staying, only to discover that the woman who picked up the call spoke not a single word of English. She was great with her Italian, though. Once she heard Barbara's voice and *Taymullah Azhar*, she was off like a jackrabbit, flooding the airwaves with a recitation that could have been anything from a recipe for minestrone to a declamation on the state of the world. Who bloody knew? Barbara finally rang off on her and then there was nothing for it but to go in search of Superintendent Ardery.

She thought of taking DI Lynley with her, in the hope that he might be able to soften up the superintendent with a display of careful reasoning. However, not only was Lynley not yet in for the day—why the bloody hell *not*? she wondered—but she also had to admit to herself that she couldn't rely upon him to be in her corner. Too much water had passed under that bridge in the past few weeks.

When Dorothea Harriman turned from her keyboard at the sound of her name, Barbara clocked her expression immediately. Dee's gaze took in the tee-shirt Barbara had quickly donned after sicking up her breakfast, and Barbara could tell that, while Dee might have been mildly amused by its declaration of *Heavily Medicated for Your Safety*, chances were very good that Isabelle Ardery was not going to be. Barbara cursed silently. She'd grabbed the tee-shirt without considering anything other than getting herself to the Met as quickly as she could without splashes of vomit on her chest. She should have read the slogan, she should have selected more wisely, she should have dressed in a suit. Or a skirt. Or something. She had not, and so she was starting out on her saunter into Ardery's territory on one hell of a wrong foot.

Briefly, she considered asking Dee to exchange tops with her. Ludicrous prospect, she decided. Even picturing the young woman decked out in a slogan-bearing tee-shirt was itself an impossibility. So she merely asked if the guv was available. Before Dee could answer, Barbara heard Isabelle Ardery's voice.

"Of course I'm in agreement that they oughtn't come to town by train, alone," she was saying, "but I didn't mean alone, Bob. Is there any reason that Sandra can't accompany them? I'll be at the station. She can hand them over to me and take the return train to Kent. I'll do the same at the end of the visit."

Barbara looked at Dee. Dee mouthed *ex-husband*. The guv was negotiating time with her twin sons, in the custody of the ex for reasons of breathing the fine air of Kent. Or so Ardery claimed when anyone enquired why her children didn't live in London with their mum. Which very few people had the nerve to do. Well, this didn't look like a good time to approach the superintendent, but that couldn't be helped. Barbara lurked outside her superior's office till she heard

Ardery say, "All right. The following weekend, then. I think by now that I've proved myself, don't you? . . . Bob, please don't be unreasonable . . . Will you at least talk to Sandra about this? Or I can do so . . . Yes . . . Very well."

That was it, the conversation's conclusion making it difficult to know which way the wind of Ardery's mood was going to be blowing. But Barbara had no choice, so she went ahead when Dee Harriman gave her the nod. She got a look at Ardery's face as she entered, though, and she reckoned at once that things weren't going to go swimmingly for her.

Ardery sat with her fist clenched to her teeth, giving a living illustration of the term *white-knuckled.* She was definitely white-knuckling something, and Barbara reckoned it was probably rage as the superintendent was taking deep breaths and her eyes were closed. Good moment to decamp, Barbara thought, but Hadiyyah's well-being hung in the balance. So she cleared her throat and said, "Guv? Dee told me you could see me for a minute."

Ardery's eyes opened. She lowered her fist, and Barbara saw that her nails had deeply indented her palms. She reckoned the other woman's blood was pounding. She wished she'd waited for Lynley's tempering influence.

Ardery said, "What is it, Sergeant?" and the tone of her voice indicated that mentioning the overheard phone call would be a very bad idea.

"I need to go to Italy." Barbara winced inwardly at the way it sounded. She'd blurted it out instead of what she'd planned to do, which was to lead Ardery gently through all the facts so that being given leave to go to Italy would be the natural conclusion of the tale she would tell. But that had gone by the wayside as she'd opened her mouth. Urgency demanded an immediate response.

"What?" Ardery said. It wasn't as if she hadn't heard Barbara's announcement, though. It was as if she couldn't believe it and by making Barbara repeat it, she would be forcing her subordinate to hear how ridiculous her expectations were.

Barbara said again, "I need to go to Italy, guv." She added, "To Tuscany. To Lucca. Hadiyyah Upman's been left alone there, her dad's been questioned for the last two days, he has no family he can rely on, and I'm the only person Hadiyyah trusts. After what's happened, I mean."

Ardery listened to this without expression. When Barbara had finished, the superintendent took a manila file from her desk. She laid it out in front of her. Barbara saw something written on its tab, but she couldn't make out what it was. What she *could* make out was the paperwork inside. There was quite a stack of it, and included among it were clippings from newspapers. She thought at first that the guv meant to review what had happened to Hadiyyah or to look up information that would tell her what was going on with Azhar. But she took neither action. Instead, she gazed at Barbara levelly. She said, "That's absolutely out of the question."

Barbara swallowed. She presented the facts. Angelina Upman's unexpected death; *E. coli*; a possible cover-up by the Italian police, the Italian health officials, and the Italian media; Azhar's passport in the possession of the coppers; Azhar's solicitor; daylong interviews at the *questura*; Hadiyyah alone and afraid, kidnapped first, held in the Alps second, mother dead third, father under the cops' microscope for the last two days fourth. Hadiyyah needed to be cared for until this situation was settled. Or she needed to be returned to London in the event—God forbid—that it wasn't settled today. The child had no one in Italy save her father and—

"This isn't a British affair."

Barbara's mouth gaped. "These are British subjects!"

"And there's a system in place that comes to their aid in foreign countries. It's called the embassy."

"The embassy only gave him a list of solicitors. They said that when someone gets into trouble with the law—"

"This is an Italian matter, and the Italians will handle it."

"By doing what? Putting Hadiyyah into care? Swallowing her up into the system? Handing her over to some . . . some . . . some *work-house*?"

"We're not living inside a Charles Dickens novel, Sergeant."

"Orphanage, then. Holding tank. Dormitory. Convent. Guv, she's nine years old. She has no one. Only her dad."

"She has family here in London and they'll be notified. And I expect her mother's lover will be notified as well. The lover will take her in till the family can fetch her."

"They hate her! She's not even a person to them. Guv, for God's sake, she's been through enough."

"You're getting hysterical."

"She *needs* me."

"No one needs you, Sergeant." And then as if she'd seen Barbara recoil as from a blow, "What I mean is that your presence isn't necessary and I won't authorise it. The Italians are well equipped to handle this, and they will do so. Now if that's all, I've work to do and I expect you're in the same position."

"I can't just stand by and—"

"Sergeant, if you wish to argue this matter further, I suggest you have a think first. I also suggest that you begin your think with a few considerations about a gentleman called Mitchell Corsico as well as *The Source* and about what you might be able to learn from past history. Cops have climbed into bed with reporters in the past. The results have been less than pleasant. Not for the reporters, of course. Scandal is their stock in trade. But for the cops? Hear me well, Barbara, because I mean it: I suggest you consider your own recent history and what it has to tell you about your future if you don't sort yourself out at once. Now is there anything further?"

"No," Barbara said. There was no point to additional conversation with the guv. The only point was getting herself to Italy, which she fully intended to do.

SOUTH HACKNEY
LONDON

First, however, there were matters to settle with Bryan Smythe. The last time she'd seen him, she'd given him his marching orders. She hadn't heard from him about having done the work required. She'd phoned him twice with no success. It was time, she reckoned, to jostle his bones with a reminder of what could befall him if she had a word with the appropriate authorities about what he was up to when he sat down daily at his computer.

She found him at home. He was not, however, at work on anything. Instead he was apparently dressing for going out. He'd done something about the dandruff, praise God, because at least for the moment his shoulders were devoid of the flakes of Maldon sea salt that otherwise had sprinkled his shirts when she'd seen him previously. He was also wearing a jacket and tie. The fact that he came to the door with keys in hand suggested that she'd caught him in the nick of time.

She didn't wait to be admitted into his sanctum sanctorum. She said, "I won't be requiring a cuppa this time," and she sauntered past him, through his work area and into the garden once again. She chose another spot this time. Knowing the bloke's habits as she was learning them, she had little doubt that after her last meeting with him in the garden, he'd wired that earlier area for sound.

At the end of all the fine plantings, she spied a garden shed, disguised with a heavy growth of wisteria in such full bloom that she reckoned he fed it with the ground-up remains of the neighbourhood's missing pets. She headed in that direction, and he followed her. "Let me ask in advance," he said to her. "What part of 'you're trespassing on private property' might be too difficult for you to understand?"

"Where are you with making the changes on the tickets to Pakistan?" she demanded.

"You can leave or I can phone the local cops."

"We both know you're not about to do that. What've you done about those tickets?"

"I don't have time to talk about this. I've an employment interview to go to."

" 'Employment interview,' is it? What sort of employment does a bloke with your talents come up with?"

"I've been headhunted by a Chinese firm. For tech security. Which is what I do. Which is what I *have* been doing for the better part of fifteen years. If you must know."

"That's kept you in expensive art in the modern mode, has it?" she asked archly, indicating his house and its collection.

"Let's be straight with each other" was his reply. "You've done your best to destroy the better part of my career—"

"Such as it was, although it's a bit like hearing a cat burglar complaining because someone's had the bollocks to put a security system on their house. But do go ahead."

"So I owe you nothing. And nothing is what I have to offer you." He glanced at his watch. "Now if there's nothing more . . . and traffic being what it is . . ."

"You're bluffing, Bryan. I'm holding a better hand than you are, or have you forgotten that? Now what's been done about those Pakistan tickets?"

"I told you there was no way to get into SO12's system, and there's no way to get into SO12's system. Surely you're capable of understanding that."

"What I'm also capable of understanding is there are other blokes exactly like you out there in cyberland, and you know each other bloody well. And don't tell me there's no one out there who could hop, skip, and jump their way into SO12's system because on a daily basis these blokes hack into everything from the Ministry of Defence to Inland Revenue to the Royals' social calendars. So if you haven't found someone to do the job, it's because you haven't asked someone to do the job. And in your position, that's risky, Bryan. I'm holding your backups. I could sink you in a minute. Have you forgotten that?"

He shook his head, not an I've-not-forgotten movement but one that signalled disbelief. He said, "You can do what you like, but I think, if you do, you'll find out soon enough that all of us are cooking in the same pot just now. And that would be largely due to you."

"What the hell's that supposed to mean?"

"First of all, you've been bloody stupid to think that Dwayne intends to take the fall for anything. Second of all, if some records can be altered—superficially or otherwise—others can be altered as well. So what I'm suggesting is that you might want to have a think about that one. And when you've finished your thinking, you can get on to third of all. Which is, you stupid cow, that you've been found out. What's known is every movement you've made, I suspect, but especially the movement that led you to my front door."

He turned on his heel at that and headed through the sumptuous spring garden and back towards his house.

She followed him, saying, "What's that supposed to mean besides an idle threat?"

He swung back to her. "It means I had a visit from the Met. Do I need to say more? Because you and I know there's only one way that could have happened and I'm looking at her."

"I didn't grass you up," she told him.

He barked a laugh. "I'm not saying you did. You were followed here, you bloody fool. You've probably been followed since you first got involved in this mess, and you've been turned in to the higher-ups. Now, do I escort you to the door or do I strong-arm you? I'm happy to do either, but in any case, I've an interview to get to and whatever business you and I had, believe me, it's finished."

LUCCA
TUSCANY

In his entire career, Salvatore Lo Bianco had never withheld evidence in the course of an investigation. The very idea was anathema to him. Yet that was the position he found himself in, so he invented a reason for this that he could live with, which was simplicity itself as well as actually being true: He needed to find a forensic handwriting specialist to compare the words on the greeting card that had been given to Hadiyyah to the remarks Taymullah Azhar had made on the comment card at Pensione Giardino. While that was being done, he decided, there was no real reason to make the existence of this piece of possible evidence known to anyone.

Prior to leaving for Piazza Grande, Salvatore had a word with the resourceful Ottavia Schwartz. Along with Giorgio Simione, she was continuing to make progress—albeit tedious progress—on the matter of the attendees at the Berlin conference. The fact that they were an international group made things difficult but not impossible. She showed him the list of names they'd ticked off the list, their specialities accounted for. She and Giorgio had not come up with anyone who was doing research on *E. coli*, she told him, but there were many names left, and she had confidence that among the remaining scientists, she would find someone significant.

Salvatore left the *questura*. He took with him the most recent information that the London private detective had sent to Lucca. Accompanying this were the earlier records of Michelangelo's bank account that he'd unearthed. His intention was to use both sets of these documents to play Piero Fanucci like a mandolin.

Il Pubblico Ministero was in, the man's secretary confirmed upon Salvatore's arrival at Palazzo Ducale. She disappeared into Fanucci's office and returned momentarily with the word that *certo, il magistrato* would not only see him but would wish him to know that he always had time for his old friend Salvatore Lo Bianco. She gave this news to Salvatore expressionlessly since years of working for Piero had allowed her to master the art of delivering information without irony.

Piero was waiting for him behind his impressive desk. It was scattered with papers and manila filing folders thick and dog-eared, heavy with grave and important contents. It wasn't Salvatore's intention to add to this collection. What he'd brought into the room with him, he intended to remove. As he would remove himself once Piero's cooperation was secured.

Il Pubblico Ministero said nothing about Salvatore's appearance. His face was still bruised but improving daily. Soon all evidence of their encounter in the botanical gardens would be gone, but Salvatore was glad that his skin was still marred. In this situation, he hoped that a reminder of their encounter would be helpful.

He said, "Piero, it appears that you have been right all along in the approach you have taken. I wish you to know that I see it now."

Fanucci's eyes narrowed. They moved from Salvatore's face to the folders he had in his hand. He didn't say anything, but he nodded brusquely and indicated with a wave of his six-fingered hand that Salvatore could continue.

Salvatore presented him with the first folder. This contained all of the information that Dwayne Doughty had sent to Lucca from London: receipts, statements, and reports. Since they suggested a landscape of guilt that tied Taymullah Azhar to Michelangelo Di Massimo and pinned culpability on both men for the kidnapping of Hadiyyah Upman, it looked, superficially of course, as if Salvatore was mocking the *magistrato* with his affirmation of the correctness of Piero's approach. Piero—nobody's fool when it came to matters touching upon himself—flared his nostrils. He said, *"Che cos'è?"* and waited for elucidation.

Elucidation came in the form of the earlier material Salvatore had gleaned. This comprised the bank statements and phone records of the dead Roberto Squali and the same of Michelangelo Di Massimo. Set alongside the new material provided by Signor Doughty, it was only too apparent that the London private investigator, for reasons unknown and of his own, was manipulating information to make it appear that Taymullah Azhar had arranged for Di Massimo to kidnap his daughter. See how the money travels from Signor Azhar's account to Di Massimo's to Squali's? For the earlier documents showed a Doughty–Di Massimo–Squali path, and these were documents he—Salvatore—had obtained soon into the investigation. While these most recent documents sent from London, Piero . . . ? They have been amended to alter one's perception of guilt.

"This man Signor Doughty is involved to his armpits," Salvatore told the magistrate. "Michelangelo Di Massimo has been telling the truth. It was a plan from London all along, engineered by this private investigator and carried out by Michelangelo and Roberto Squali."

"And why have you not given this material to Nicodemo?" Piero asked. His voice was meditative, and Salvatore hoped this meant he was taking the information on board.

He said, "Indeed I will, Piero, but I first wanted to apologise to you. Holding Carlo Casparia as long as you have done . . . ? This built in Michelangelo a false assurance that all was well and he was safe from discovery. Had you released Carlo as I was insisting, chances are that Michelangelo would have fled the area once Roberto's body was found. He would have known we were hours from making a connection between himself and Roberto Squali, but because you had Carlo named as principal suspect, he thought he was safe."

Fanucci nodded. He still didn't look entirely convinced by Salvatore's performance, so Salvatore repeated his apology as he gathered the material from the *magistrato*'s desk. He said, "This I will give to

Nicodemo now. So that he—and you—can put a period to the investigation."

"The extradition of Doughty," Piero murmured. "This will not be an easy business."

"But you will manage it, no?" Salvatore said. "You are more than a match for the British legal system, my friend."

"*Vedremo*," Fanucci said with a shrug.

Salvatore smiled. *Certo*, he thought, they certainly would see. And in the meantime, Taymullah Azhar was off the *magistrato*'s radar. Out of sight and out of mind, which made him available in every possible way to Salvatore. Which was what he wanted.

VICTORIA
LONDON

Lynley knew he couldn't put off a meeting with Isabelle. He was out of time. He could attempt to avoid her for a few more days of "I'm on it, guv, but there's one more thing . . ." But as she was not a fool, she wouldn't accept that. So he was down to outright lying to her about what Barbara was up to since the only information John Stewart had been able to provide was where she'd been and not what she'd done there, or he could tell Isabelle the truth.

He regretted knowing a single thing about what Barbara Havers had been doing. He'd given her warning, but that had amounted to nothing. She hadn't backed away from the mad course she was travelling because she was driven by love. But while the expression "love is blind" had applications to overlooking the faults of another person, it had no application to the responsibilities held—and sworn to—by a member of the police force when it came to a crime.

Yet . . . hadn't he wished to protect his own brother several years in the past when Peter's proclivity for involving himself with unsavoury sorts from the underbelly of London's drug culture had resulted in his being suspected of murder? Yes. He had wished so. No matter the evidence to the contrary, he had refused to believe that Peter was involved, and as things turned out, he wasn't. So that could indeed be the case just now between Barbara Havers and Taymullah Azhar. Except they wouldn't learn if Azhar was indeed innocent of all things should she suppress evidence, would they? Which was what it had come down to with Peter. Only by forcing Peter through the process of being a suspect had he been entirely cleared. It had nearly destroyed his own relationship with Peter to keep his hands off what was going on, but he had done so. And this was what Barbara needed to do.

Lynley chose not to wait like a coward for Isabelle to call him to account. When he saw her coming towards him in the corridor, he inclined his head towards her office. Did she have a moment? Yes, she did.

She closed the door. She put distance between them by means of her desk. He accepted this as a declaration of the difference in their positions. He drew a chair up, and he told her what he knew.

He didn't spare her any of the details he'd managed to uncover about Dwayne Doughty, Bryan Smythe, Taymullah Azhar, the kidnapping of Hadiyyah Upman, the death of Angelina Upman, and Barbara Havers. Isabelle listened. She didn't make notes and she didn't ask questions. It was only when he got to the plane tickets to Pakistan and Barbara's knowledge of them that she gave any reaction at all. And then, her reaction was to go pale.

She said only, "And you're certain of the dates? The purchase date and the flight date, Tommy?" Before he could reply, she went on. "Never mind. Of course you're certain. John Stewart wouldn't have known about those tickets, of course. If Barbara discovered them in-house—through SO12—he'd have no reason to wonder what she was doing in talking to those blokes. She hadn't left the building, after all. She might even just have phoned up SO12 and called in a favour from someone, mightn't she?"

"It's possible," he said. "And as she was working on a case, more or less, they wouldn't question her needing to know something from them, especially since they'd already cleared Azhar of all terrorist concerns."

"What a bloody mess." Isabelle sat there thoughtfully, looking not at him but not at anything else either. Her eyes seemed fixed on something in the distance. He reckoned what she was looking at was her own future. She said, "She's met with the reporter again."

"Corsico?"

"They met in Leicester Square. He's in Italy now, so we can assume he's on Barbara's business."

"How do you know? Not the Leicester Square part, but the rest?"

She nodded towards the closed door, towards what lay beyond it in the building. "John, of course. He's not given up. He has her leaking information to the press, disobeying direct orders, conducting her own mini-investigation on matters occurring in another country. Where's that place along the river, Tommy, the spot that pirates got hanged and the tide washed over them?"

"Execution Dock?" he said. "There's probably more legend to that than reality."

"No matter. That's where John would like to see her. Figuratively or otherwise. He won't stop till it happens."

Lynley could sense the despair that the superintendent was feeling. He felt it himself but in far less measure. She'd managed to hold DI Stewart at bay by telling him she was taking on board every detail that he provided her. But if she didn't act upon those details soon, he would go above her head to the assistant commissioner. Sir David Hillier wouldn't look with kindness upon the facts as presented by Stewart. When he turned from those facts to assign to someone responsibility for how they were handled, that person was going to be Isabelle herself. She had to act and soon.

He said, "Where's Barbara now?"

"She's asked to go to Italy. I denied the request. I told her to get back to work. I've still not received her final report on this Dwayne Doughty person, whatever that report is going to look like. Obviously, I can't put her back on John's team and Philip Hale doesn't need her at the moment. Did you not see her when you came in?"

He shook his head.

"Has she not phoned you?"

"She hasn't," he said.

Isabelle was thoughtful for a moment before she asked, "Has she a passport, Tommy?"

"I have no idea."

"God. What a cock-up." She looked at him as she reached for the phone. She punched in a number and waited for an answer. When it came she said, "Judi, I need to arrange a word with Sir David. Is he in today?" Hillier's secretary said something on her end of the line, and in a moment Isabelle looked at the diary on her desk. "I'll be up then," she told the other woman. She thanked her, rang off, and stared at the phone.

Lynley said, "There's more than one way to end this, Isabelle."

"Don't, for God's sake, tell me how to do my job," she replied.

CHALK FARM
LONDON

Who the higher-ups were that Bryan Smythe was referring to, Barbara didn't know. But when she left his house in South Hackney and strode to her car at the end of the street, she learned. Where before she'd been too caught up in her plans, her next steps, and her machinations to be both aware and wary, now she had her eyes open for anything out of place, and she saw it easily enough.

Clive Cratty, newly minted as a detective constable and eager to prove himself to his immediate supervisor, tried to dodge out of sight behind a white Ford Transit some ten houses along the terrace on the opposite side of the street. But Barbara clocked him and she instantly knew that John Stewart had placed someone on her tail.

She was furious about this, but she had no time to deal with Stewart or his minions. He was going to do what he was going to do. She had to get herself to Italy.

Her passport was at home, she needed to throw a few things into a duffel, and she needed a ticket. For this last, she could phone and beg the mercy of an airline, or she could grab her things, head to one of the airports, and hope for the best.

Since it was still working hours, there was plenty of parking when she reached her home. Even the driveway of the big house was empty, so she made use of it and charged to the back of the old villa to her bungalow. She hustled inside, threw her shoulder bag on what went for the kitchen table, and began to tear her clean knickers from a line above the sink. She balled them up, then turned to go to the wardrobe.

That was when she saw Lynley sitting in the armchair next to her daybed. She shrieked and dropped her knickers to the floor.

"Bloody goddamn hell!" she cried. "How'd you get in?"

He held up the extra key to her front door. "You need to be more creative with your emergency key," he said. "That is, if you don't want to come home sometime and find someone less friendly than I sitting here waiting for you."

She gathered her thoughts and her wits along with her knickers, which she scooped from the floor. She said, "I reckoned that under the doormat was too obvious to be obvious. Who would really expect to find a key there?"

"I don't think your everyday housebreaker goes in for reverse psychology, Barbara."

"You obviously didn't." She kept her voice light as she crossed the room.

"Isabelle knows everything," he said. "Smythe, Doughty, what you were up to, what they were up to, intimate talks between you and Mitchell Corsico. Everything, Barbara. She rang Hillier before I left her office. She made an appointment to see him. She knows about the tickets to Pakistan as well, so she's ending this. There was nothing I could do to stop her. I'm sorry."

Barbara opened the wardrobe. Stuffed high on a shelf was her duffel, and she pulled this out. She grabbed up clothing without much thought as to the Italian climate, the appropriateness of her choices, or anything else save the haste she needed to employ to get out of England and into Italy as soon as she could. She could feel Lynley watching her, and she waited for him to tell her she was giving in to a foolhardy madness.

But all he said was, "Don't do this. Listen to me. Everything you've attempted in this business of Hadiyyah's kidnapping and Angelina's death has fallen apart. Smythe has admitted it all to me."

"There was nothing for that bloke to admit." But she didn't feel as confident as she tried to sound.

"Barbara." Lynley rose from the chair. He was quite a tall man, over six feet by several inches, and he seemed in that moment to fill the room.

She tried to ignore him but that was impossible. Still, she continued her chaotic packing. She went to the bathroom and grabbed up everything she thought she might need, from shampoo to deodorant and all points in between. She had no sponge bag for these goodies, so she wrapped them in a well-used hand towel and tried to get by Lynley and back into the other room where the duffel awaited her.

He was in the doorway, however. He said again, "Don't do this. Smythe talked to me and he'll talk to others. He's admitted eliminating some pieces of evidence entirely and doctoring other pieces of evidence. He's told me about the documents he's created. He's told me about the calls you paid upon him. He's given up Doughty as well as the woman. He's finished, Barbara, and his only hope is going to be emigration in advance of a lengthy and complicated police investigation that will land him in gaol for God knows how many years. That's how it is. What you have to ask yourself is which side you'd like to be on in what's investigated."

Barbara pushed past him. "You don't understand. You've never understood."

"What I understand is that you want to protect Azhar. But what you must understand is that whatever Smythe has done, it can only be done in the most superficial way. Do you see that?"

"I don't know what you mean." She shoved the toweled items into the duffel and looked round the room distractedly. He was making it impossible to think. What else did she need? Her passport, of course. That eternally unused document, which had always been intended to mark a change of direction in her life. Something new, exciting, different, edgy. Sunbathing on a Greek island beach, walking along the Great Wall of China, going nose to nose with a tortoise in the Galápagos. Who the bloody hell *cared* as long as it was different from the dismal life she led now?

Lynley said, "Then you need to hear the truth. To do what he does, Smythe has to know people who know people who know people. That's how it works. Someone inside whatever institution he wants to hack into slips him a password or slips someone else a password who then slips it to him. Things get doctored but not in the Gordian knot of backup systems that the institution employs. All of this gets sorted out. Arrests are made. People then talk, and all along the truth itself is buried in a backup system that no one can crack without a court order. That backup system shows everything. And you and I both know what that everything is."

She swung round to face him. "He didn't do anything! You know that as well as I do. Someone wants him to take a fall. Doughty wants him to go down for a kidnapping that he himself arranged, and someone else wants him to go down for murder."

"For God's sake, Barbara, who?"

"I don't know! Don't you see that's why I have to go over there? Maybe it's Lorenzo Mura. Maybe it's Castro, her earlier lover. Or her own dad, for disappointing his dreams. Or her sister, who's hated her forever. I don't bloody *know*. But what I do know is that none of us is going to turn over a stone and find the truth if we're all sitting in London trying to do everything by the sodding book."

She dashed to the table next to the daybed. In its only drawer she kept her passport. She pulled the drawer open and flipped its contents onto the bed. The passport was gone.

That did it for her. Something she couldn't begin to identify broke inside of her, and she flung herself across the room upon Lynley. She shrieked, "Give it to me! Goddamn you to hell, give me my passport!" And to her horror, she began to cry. She sounded like a madwoman, she knew, but there was nothing left inside of her that could possibly explain to her longtime partner why she was doing what she was doing, so like a fishwife out of a Victorian novel, she cursed him and then she beat on his chest. He caught her arms and he shouted her name, but he *wouldn't* stop her, she swore to herself. If she had to kill him to get to Italy, that was what she was going to do.

"You have a life beyond this!" she cried. "I have nothing. Do you understand? *Will* you understand?"

"Barbara, for the love of God—"

"Whatever you think will happen, it doesn't matter to me. Do you get that? What matters is *her*. I'm not leaving Hadiyyah in the hands of the Italian authorities if something happens to Azhar. I won't do that and I don't care about anything else."

She was left sobbing. He let go of her arms. He watched her and she felt the humiliation sweep through her. That he, of all people, should see her like this. Reduced in this way to the disintegrating substance of what comprised her: loneliness that he had never known, misery that he had seldom felt, a future stretching out in front of her that contained her job and nothing else. She hated him in that moment for what he'd brought her to. Her anger finally superseded her tears.

He reached into his jacket pocket and brought out her passport. He handed it to her. She snatched it from him and grabbed her duffel.

"Lock up when you leave" were her final words to him.

16 MAY

S alvatore Lo Bianco inspected his face in the bathroom mirror. The bruises were yellowing up nicely. He looked less beaten up and more like he was recovering from a bout with jaundice. In a matter of days, he would be able to see Bianca and Marco once again. This was good as his mamma was not happy about being denied the company of her favourite *nipoti*.

He went to his car when he left the tower. It was a brisk walk in the fine spring air, and he stopped for *caffè* and a pastry on his way. He ate and drank quickly. He bought a copy of *Prima Voce* from the news vendor in Piazza dei Cocomeri. He glanced at its headline and its cover story. So far, he saw, Piero Fanucci hadn't let the *E. coli* cat out of the bag.

Relieved, he drove to Fattoria di Santa Zita, beneath an azure sky whose cloudlessness promised a day of heat on the alluvial plain where Lucca lay. Above in the hills, the trees offered great banks of shade that would keep the temperatures more pleasant, and along the dusty lane onto Lorenzo Mura's property, the tree branches formed a pleasing, leafy tunnel. When he emerged from it, he parked near Mura's winery. He heard voices from within the ancient stone structure. He ducked beneath the arbour's drapery of wisteria and entered the shadowy place, where the scent of fermentation was like a fine perfume that tinctured the air.

Lorenzo Mura and a younger foreign-looking man were beyond the tasting room and inside the bottling room. They were examining a sheaf of labels, prefatory to placing them on two or three score bottles. *Chianti Santa Zita*, the labels announced, but Mura didn't seem pleased with the look of them. He was frowning as he spoke. The younger man was nodding.

Salvatore cleared his throat. They looked up. Did the port wine birthmark that marred Mura's otherwise handsome face grow darker? It looked so to Salvatore.

" '*Giorno*," he said. He'd heard them talking and followed the sound of their voices, he explained. He hoped that he wasn't interfering.

Of course, he was interfering, but Lorenzo Mura didn't say that. Instead he spoke again to the younger man, whose pale skin and fair hair marked him as either English or, more likely, a Scandinavian who, like so many of his fellows, spoke Italian along with another two or three useful languages. The younger man—no name given and none required, Salvatore thought—listened and disappeared into the winery's depths. For his part, Mura gestured to an open bottle near the labelling machine. *Vorrebbe del vino?* Hardly, Salvatore thought. It was far too early in the day for him to sip Chianti, appreciatively or otherwise. But *grazie mille*, all the same.

Lorenzo apparently felt no such compunction about the hour. He'd been imbibing and so had his assistant. Two glasses stood nearby, still half-filled with wine. He picked up one of them and drained it. Then he said dully, "She's dead. Our child dies with her. You do nothing. Why do you come?"

"Signor Mura," Salvatore said, "we would have these things move quickly but they can only move as fast as the process itself allows."

"And this means . . . ? What?"

"This means that a case must be built. One builds it first and then moves to finish it with an arrest afterwards."

"She dies, she's buried, and nothing happens," Mura said. "And from this you tell me a 'case' is being built. I come to you directly when she dies. I tell you this is no natural death. But you send me away. So why are you here?"

"I come to ask if you will allow Hadiyyah Upman to reside with you here at the *fattoria* until other arrangements can be made with her family in London."

Mura's head jerked. "What does this mean?"

"That I am in the midst of building a case. And when I have built it—which I must do with care—I will take the next step and I will not hesitate. But arrangements need to be made in advance and I have come to you in order to make them."

Mura studied his face as if trying to sift for truth or lie. Who could blame him? Salvatore thought. Nine times out of ten in the country and particularly in Tuscany hadn't it happened that an arrest was made first and then facts were pounded into shape to fit the case afterwards? This was especially the situation when a public minister like Piero Fanucci had a range of vision that was limited to a single suspect from the moment it was decided that a crime had occurred. Mura would know that, and he would wonder why no one was arresting anyone for anything in the matter of the deaths of his lover and their child.

Salvatore said to Mura, "The *fact* of murder has to be established in a death such as that of your Angelina. This has been made more difficult because she was ill in the weeks leading up to her death. We now know what caused her to die—"

Mura took a step towards him, reaching out. Salvatore held up a hand to stop him.

"—but this is something we are not speaking of yet."

"He did this. I knew it."

"Time will tell."

"How much time?"

"This is something we cannot know. But we move forward, keeping what we learn close to our hearts. Still, that I have come to ask you about arrangements of the care of Hadiyyah . . . I would hope that this tells you how near to the end we are."

"He came to us, he built her trust, and when he had it . . . *somehow* he did this. You know it."

"We are speaking today, the professor and I. We have already spoken and we will also speak tomorrow. Nothing, Signor Mura, is being left unturned or going unnoticed. I assure you of that." Salvatore inclined his head towards the door. He said in an altogether different tone, "You raise *asini*, no? This I have learned from the London detective. Will you show them to me?"

Mura's face grew cloudy. "For what reason?"

Salvatore smiled. "For the reason of purchase. I have two children who would love such an animal to keep as a pet in the countryside where I have a small cottage. They *are* pets, *vero?*, these animals you breed? Or if they are not, they are gentle enough to become pets, no?"

"*Certo*," Lorenzo Mura said.

LUCCA
TUSCANY

In the end, Salvatore had accomplished his mission. The sight of Lorenzo Mura's donkeys in the olive orchard had prompted his request to talk to someone who had bought one of the docile-seeming creatures most recently so that he could reassure himself that they were gentle enough to be his children's pet at the family's nonexistent cottage in the country. Mura had given him the name of his most recent customer, and Salvatore had taken matters from there.

A call upon the man had eliminated him as a possible source of the *E. coli* that had killed Angelina Upman. Not because there would have been no bacteria on his farmland near Valpromaro but because he confirmed during their conversation that he had indeed recently purchased a foal from Signor Mura and that he had paid in cash so as to allow Signor Mura to avoid one of the myriad ways in which Italians were taxed. He gave the date of his purchase of the animal, which coincided perfectly with the presence of the man that Ispettore Lynley had reported passing an envelope of something to Mura at the *fattoria*.

When he returned to the *questura*, it was to gather more information from Ottavia Schwartz and Giorgio Simione, still slogging their way through the congregation of scientists who'd met in Berlin in April. They'd located a scientist from the University of Glasgow who studied *E. coli*, Ottavia reported. It was likely that there would be others if the *ispettore* wished them to continue.

He did, he told her. He wasn't about to go Fanucci's route. He wanted to know it all, inside and out, before he made his next move. To Salvatore, *indagato* meant more than just naming a suspect. *Indagato* meant that the investigators were certain they had their man.

PISA

TUSCANY

In the end, it turned out that flying into Pisa was the easiest. Barbara could have flown into one of the regional airports, utilising one of the many budget airlines that appeared to pop up every month or so, but she wanted the peace of mind that came with a brand-name airline unlikely to lose her limited baggage and an airport labelled with the word *international*.

When she landed in Italy, she was assaulted by the foreign experience. People shouted at one another incomprehensibly, signs made announcements in a language she couldn't read, and—once she worked her way through customs and baggage claim—scores of tour guides awaited their charges, while jostling crowds appeared to be bargaining with illegal taxi drivers offering quick trips to the Leaning Tower.

Luckily, she didn't need to do anything other than look for her ride to Lucca, and he was as easy to spot as an albino chimpanzee at the zoo. Despite being in Italy—the veritable home of *la moda*—Mitchell Corsico was garbed as usual. He'd eschewed the fringed jacket—probably because of the heat—but the rest of him was vintage Wild West. For her part, Barbara had set aside slogan-bearing tee-shirts in favour of tank tops, anticipating exactly what she found the moment they stepped from the arrivals hall: blistering heat.

Mitch was on his mobile when Barbara glimpsed him among the hordes. He continued on his mobile as he led her to his hire car. Barbara caught only snatches of his conversation as she hauled her duffel along behind him. It was mostly along the lines of "Yeah . . . Yeah . . . The interview's coming . . . Hey, it's in the diary, Rod. What more can I say?" When he ended the call, he said, "Lard arse," in apparent reference to his editor. At that point, they'd reached the side of a Lancia, and Barbara was sweating profusely.

She squinted in the bright sunlight and muttered, "What's the sodding temperature in this place?"

Mitchell gave her a look. "Get a grip, Barb. It's not even summer."

Their route to Lucca consisted of a terrifying drive on the *autostrada*, where speed limits appeared to be mere suggestions that the Italian drivers chose to ignore. Corsico seemed to be in his element. Any faster, Barbara reckoned, and they'd be airborne.

As he drove, he informed her that the first story had run in *The Source* that morning, in case she hadn't had time to pick up a copy at the airport. He'd moulded it, he said, along lines that would generate a dozen follow-up stories. He hoped she appreciated that, by the way.

"What's that mean, exactly?" Barbara asked him. "What sort of follow-up stories're we talking about? How'd you write the first one?"

He glanced at her. Someone passed them in a blur of silver. He increased the Lancia's speed and wove round a lorry. Barbara increased her grip on the side of her seat. He said, "The usual format, Barb. 'This *E. coli* situation is either a cover-up by the Italians to avoid tanking their economy while the source is being searched out among all the products they sell, or it's a deliberate poisoning by a suspect unnamed . . . with an upcoming charge of murder in sight. Stay tuned.'"

"As long as you keep away from Azhar."

He looked at her, his expression disbelieving. "I'm on a story. If he's part of it, he's part of it, and I'm putting him into it. Let's get something straight, you and me, now we're working hand in hand: You don't climb into bed with a journalist and expect him not to want to feed the beast."

"You're mixing your metaphors," she informed him. "I'd think that's a very bad thing for a writer. Or am I stretching things to actually call you a writer? And who said we're working hand in hand?"

"We're on the same side."

"Doesn't sound like that to me."

"We both want to get to the truth. And anyway, like I said, Azhar's name's already come up."

"I made it bloody well clear—"

"You can't be thinking Rod Aronson would let me hang round Lucca on the strength of some pregnant Englishwoman keeling over in Tuscany. The UK reader needs a hell of a bigger hook than that."

"And what? Azhar's become the hook? Goddamn it, Mitchell—"

"He's part of the story, like it or not, darling. For all I know, he probably *is* the story. Bloody hell, Barb, you should be glad I'm not going after the kid."

She grabbed his arm, digging her fingers into it. "You stay away from Hadiyyah."

He shook her off. "Quit interfering with the driver. We get in a crash and *we're* the next story. And anyway, all I've done so far is go the route of 'By the way, our good professor of microbiology is assisting the police with their enquiries, and we all know what that means, don't we? Wink, wink. Nudge, nudge.' Rod wants an interview with the bloke. You're going to be my route to that."

"I've given you what you're getting from me," she told him. "Azhar's not on the table. I've told you that from the very first."

"Look. I thought you wanted me here to get to the truth."

"So get to the truth," she said. "It doesn't have anything to do with Azhar."

LUCCA
TUSCANY

The outskirts of Lucca made it seem like any other overdeveloped place in any other country in the world. Aside from the fact that the street signs and advertisements were in Italian, everything else was fairly standard. The streets held apartment buildings, inexpensive hotels, tourist restaurants, takeaway food shops, assorted boutiques, and pizzerias. There was a great deal of traffic and congestion. Women with pushchairs took up too much room on the pavements, and adolescents who should have been in school were instead hanging about engaged in the three activities common to adolescents nearly everywhere: texting, smoking, and chatting away on mobile phones. Their hairstyles were different—far more elaborate and excessively gelled—

but other than that they were the same. It was only when the centre of the town was reached that Lucca suddenly became unique.

Barbara had never seen anything like its wall, encircling the oldest part of the town like a medieval rampart. She'd been to York, but this was different, from the enormous grassed-in ditch that lay before it and could at one time have done duty as a moat, to the roadway atop it. Mitch Corsico drove them round it on a shady boulevard whose purpose seemed to be to show the wall to its best advantage. Half of the way round, however, he made a quarter circle in a huge piazza and turned into a short length of roadway that took them beneath and through one of the wall's huge gates.

Here, there was another piazza. Here, they vied with tourist buses debouching elderly people in Bermuda shorts, sun hats, sandals, and black socks. Near a shop hiring bicycles, they found a parking bay. Mitch climbed out of the car with "It's this way," and he left her to wrestle with her duffel once more.

She thought she'd packed light, but as she struggled to keep up with him, Barbara gave serious thought to dumping everything in the nearest wheelie bin. There was no wheelie bin in sight, though, so she was left heaving and dragging the thing as Mitchell led her out of the piazza, past a church—"First of hundreds, believe me"—and into a throng of people who appeared to comprise tourists, students, housewives, and nuns. Lots of nuns.

Thankfully, she wasn't in Mitch's wake for long on this narrow thoroughfare. Ahead of her, she saw him make a turn into another street, and when she finally got there, it was to find him leaning against the wall of a car's-width tunnel. This tunnel, she saw, led into yet another large piazza upon which a merciless sun was blazing.

She thought he was taking a rest in the shade or perhaps even waiting to offer her help. Instead, when she reached him with her heart pounding and sweat dribbling into her eyes, he said, "Don't travel much, eh? Basic rule, Barb. One change of clothes."

He ducked through the tunnel, then, and into the piazza. It was circular, she saw, and Mitch told her it was the town's ancient amphitheatre. Shops, cafés, and habitations formed its perimeter. In the bright light of the day, Barbara wanted to head for the nearest shade to buy something very cold and very wet. In fact, that was what she thought they'd come to do until the journalist pointed to a mass of cacti and succulents displayed in neat ranks in front of a building and told her that was Azhar's *pensione.*

"Time to pay up with the interview," he said. And when she was about to protest, he played the best card last and with considerable skill: "I'm making the rules, Barb, and maybe you need to think about that. I c'n just leave you here to sort out who speaks English and can help you out. Or *you* c'n be a bit more cooperative. Before you make up your mind on that one, though, I'd like to point out that the coppers here don't speak our lingo. On the other hand, loads of the journalists do and I'm happy to give you an introduction to one or two of them. But 'f you ask for that, you owe me. Azhar is how you're going to pay."

Barbara said, "No deal. I reckon I can make myself clear to anyone I want to talk to."

Mitch smiled. He nodded towards the *pensione* in question. "If that's how you want to hang the laundry," he said.

That should have told her, of course. But Barbara wasn't ready for Mitchell Corsico to be dictating the terms of their working relationship in Italy. So she marched across the piazza with her duffel weighing down her shoulder, and she rang the bell outside of Pensione Giardino. Its windows were shuttered against the heat, as were all of the windows in the piazza save one at which a housewife was hanging pink bedsheets on a line that extended across the front of her apartment. Every place else looked deserted, and Barbara was at the point of concluding this same thing about the *pensione* when its front door opened and a dark-haired pregnant woman with a winsome-looking child on her hip gazed out at Barbara.

At first, all seemed well. She noted Barbara's duffel, smiled, and beckoned her inside. She led her into a dimly lit—and, praise God, cooler—corridor, where, on a narrow table, a candle flickered at the feet of a statue of the Virgin and a door opened into what looked like a breakfast room. She gestured that Barbara was meant to place her duffel on the tiled floor, and from a drawer in the table, she brought out a card that looked like something one was meant to fill out in order to stay in the *pensione*. Fine and dandy, Barbara thought, taking the card and the offered Biro. Sod you, Mitchell. There wasn't going to be a problem at all.

She filled the card out and handed it over, and when the woman said, "*E il Suo passaporto, signora?*" Barbara handed it over as well. She was a little concerned when the woman walked off with it, but she didn't take it far—just to a buffet inside the breakfast room—and when she rattled off a few sentences in an incomprehensible lingo that Barbara reckoned was Italian, it seemed as if what she was saying was something along the lines of needing the passport for a bit of time in order to do something with it, which Barbara could only hope was not sell it on the black market.

The woman then said, "*Mi segua, signora,*" with a smile, and hoisted her child higher on her hip. She headed towards a stairway and began to climb, and Barbara reckoned she was meant to follow. This was all well and good, but there were questions she needed to ask before she got herself established in this place. So she said, "Hang on just a minute, okay?" and when the woman turned to her with a quizzical expression, she went on with, "Taymullah Azhar is still here, right? With his daughter? Little girl about this tall with long dark hair? First thing I need to do—well, aside from having a wash—is to speak to Azhar about Hadiyyah. That's the little girl's name. But you probably know that, right?"

What these remarks did was unleash in the woman a veritable flood. She came back down the stairs firing on all linguistic cylinders. None of them, however, were distinguishable to Barbara.

Immediately morphing into the metaphorical deer illuminated by an oncoming car's headlights, Barbara stared at the woman. All she could pick out from the inundation of language was *non, non, non.* From this, she worked out that neither Azhar nor Hadiyyah was in the *pensione*. Whether they were permanently gone she couldn't tell.

Whatever her recitation meant, the woman was agitated enough to prompt Barbara to dig her mobile phone from her bag and hold it up, if only to silence her. She punched in Azhar's number but got no joy from that once again. Wherever he was, he still wasn't answering.

The woman said, "*Mi segua, mi segua, signora. Vuole una camera, sì?*"

She pointed up the stairs, from which Barbara took it that *camera* meant *room* in Italian and not an instrument of photography. She nodded and heaved her duffel off the floor. She trudged behind her hostess up two flights of stairs.

The room was clean and simple. Not an en suite, but what would one expect in a *pensione*? She got herself established in shorter order than she had previously intended—a cool shower would obviously have to wait—and she scrolled through her mobile's address book to find the phone number of Aldo Greco.

Luckily, his secretary's English was as good as Greco's. The solicitor wasn't in his office at present, Barbara was told, but if she left her number . . .

Barbara explained. She was trying to locate Taymullah Azhar, she said. She was a friend from London now here in Lucca, and she had come because for the past two days she'd been unable to reach Azhar by phone. She was dead concerned about him and, more to the point, about Hadiyyah, his daughter, and—

"Ah," the secretary said. "Let me have Signor Greco phone you at once."

Barbara wasn't sure what *at once* meant when it came to Italy, so after she gave her number and rang off, she began to pace the room. She opened the shutters on the windows, then the windows themselves. Across the piazza, she saw Mitch Corsico seated at a café table beneath an umbrella, enjoying a drink of some kind. He seemed perfectly relaxed and perfectly content. He knew something, she reckoned, and he was waiting for her to learn it for herself.

This she did in short order. Her mobile rang and she snatched it up, barking into it. It was Greco.

Taymullah Azhar had been arrested, he told her, for the crime of murder. He'd been at the *questura* for the past two days, in and out and off and on, with the arrest coming at half past nine this morning.

God in heaven, Barbara thought. "Where's Hadiyyah?" she demanded. "What's happened to Hadiyyah?"

In answer, Aldo Greco said that he would meet her at his office in forty-five minutes.

LUCCA
TUSCANY

She had no choice. She had to take Corsico. He knew his way round Lucca, and even if she set off without him, he would only follow her. So when she left Pensione Giardino, she crossed the piazza to him, sat, picked up his glass, and drained it. The drink was something very sweet poured over two cubes of ice. *Limoncello* and soda, he said. "Go easy with that, Barb."

Advice given too late. It hit her directly between the eyes. Her vision felt impaired by a sudden haze. She said, "Bloody hell. No wonder the *vita* is so *dolce* in this country. *That's* what they do for elevenses?"

"'Course not," he said. "They're easier about life, but they're not insane. I take it you got the word about Azhar?"

She felt her eyes narrow. "You *knew*?"

He lifted his shoulders in mock regret.

"Goddamn it, I thought we were working together."

"So did I," he said. "But then . . . when it came down to it . . . on the matter of interviews . . ."

"Christ. All right. So where's Hadiyyah, then? Do you know that as well?"

He shook his head. "But it's not like there're dozens of possibilities. They've got rules to follow, and I expect none of them say nine-year-olds are left on their own to book themselves into the Ritz when their daddies get charged with murder. We need to find her, though. The sooner the better as I've a deadline to meet."

Barbara flinched at the callous nature of the remark. Hadiyyah was nothing to Corsico, just another angle to the story he planned to write. She got to her feet, experienced a moment of dizziness from the drink, and waited for it to pass. She scored a handful of crisps from a basket on the table and said, "We're heading to Via San Giorgio. Know where that is?"

He threw some coins into the otherwise empty ashtray and got to his feet. "Not far," he told her. "This is Lucca."

LUCCA

TUSCANY

Aldo Greco turned out to be a courtly-looking man along the lines of his fellow Lucchese Giacomo Puccini but without the moustache. He had the same soulful eyes and the same thick dark hair touched at the temples with silver strands. His olive skin bore not a single crease. He could have been anywhere between twenty-five and fifty. He looked like a film star.

Barbara could tell he thought that she and Mitch Corsico were a very odd match, but he was too polite to make any comment aside from *Piacere*—whatever the hell that meant—when she introduced herself and her companion to the solicitor.

Greco asked them to sit and offered them refreshments. Barbara demurred. Mitch said a coffee wouldn't go down half bad. Greco nodded and asked his secretary to see to this, which she did efficiently. Mitchell was presented with a thimble of liquid so black it might have been used motor oil. He was apparently familiar with this, Barbara thought, because he put a sugar cube between his teeth and tossed the mess back.

Greco was guarded with them once they'd covered the bases of general courtesy. He had no real idea who Barbara was, after all. She could have been anyone—to whit, she could have been a journalist—claiming to know Azhar. Azhar had not mentioned her to the solicitor, and this presented a problem for Greco, who was bound by ethics and probably otherwise loath to give out even the most superficial detail associated with his client's arrest.

She showed him her police ID. This impressed him only marginally. She mentioned DI Lynley, who'd preceded her to town as liaison officer in the matter of Hadiyyah's kidnapping, but this achieved a solemn nod and nothing else. She finally remembered that tucked inside her purse was a school photo of Hadiyyah that the little girl had given to her at the start of Michaelmas term back in London. On the back of it she'd written Barbara's name, *Friends 4ever*, her own name, and a line of *x*'s and *o*'s. Barbara said, "When I heard that Azhar was in and out of the *questura*, I knew I had to come because Hadiyyah has no relatives in Italy. And her mum's family in England . . . Well, Angelina was estranged from them. What I was thinking is that if anything more happened . . . I mean, she's been through hell, hasn't she?"

Greco examined the photo Barbara had handed him. He didn't look convinced till she hit upon her mobile phone. Upon it, she found an old message from Azhar, thankfully undeleted. She handed the mobile over to the solicitor, who listened and finally seemed convinced enough of her friendship with the man to give her the barest of details.

She would understand, would she not?, that his client had not authorised him to speak to her and therefore certain limits had to apply to what he said. Yes, yes, Barbara told him, and she prayed that Corsico had the good sense not to pull a reporter's notebook from the pocket of his trousers and start scribbling in it.

First, Greco told her, Hadiyyah had been returned to Fattoria di Santa Zita, the home of Lorenzo Mura, where she had been living with her mother prior to her mother's death. This was not a permanent arrangement, naturally. Her relatives in London had been notified by Mura of the child's father's arrest. Were they on their way to fetch her? Barbara asked. If that was the case, she told herself, time was of the essence, for if the Upmans got their hands on Hadiyyah, they would make sure, purely out of spite, that Azhar never saw her again.

"This I do not know," Greco said. "The police made the arrangements to deliver her to Signor Mura. I did not."

"Azhar wouldn't have given the coppers the name of any Upman to fetch Hadiyyah," Barbara told the solicitor. "He would have given them my name."

Greco looked thoughtful as he nodded. "This could be the case, *certo*," he said. "But the police would want a blood relative of the little girl to come for her, as there is no evidence that the professor is actually her father. You see the difficulty in fulfilling whatever desires he might have in the matter, no?"

What Barbara saw was that she needed to know where Fattoria di Santa Zita was. She glanced at Mitchell. He had his reporter's face on: perfectly blank. She knew this meant he was committing everything to memory. There might be a benefit to having him on her team.

She said, "What's the evidence against him? There has to be evidence. I mean, if someone's come up with the charge of murder, they have to list the evidence, don't they?"

"In due course," Greco said. He steepled his fingers in front of his chest and used them a bit as a pointer as he explained to her how the justice system worked in Italy. Thus far, Taymullah Azhar was *indagato*, his name entered into the judicial records as a suspect. He'd been served with the paperwork that indicated this—"We call this *avviso di garanzia*," Greco said—and the details of the charges had yet to be revealed. They would be in time, *certo*, but for the moment an order of *segreto investigativo* prevented their revelation. At this point, only carefully placed leaks in the newspapers were providing information.

Barbara listened to this and at the end of it said, "But you must know something, Mr. Greco."

"As of now, I know only that there is concern about a conference that the professor attended in April. There is also concern about his profession. At this conference were microbiologists from around the world—"

"I know about the conference."

"Then you will see how it looks that Professore Azhar attended. And then, shortly thereafter his child's mother died from an organism that could have been obtained—"

"No one can think Azhar traipsed round Europe with a petri dish of *E. coli* hidden in his armpit."

"Please?" Greco looked confused.

"The armpit bit," Mitchell Corsico murmured.

Barbara said, "Sorry. What I mean is that the entire scenario—how this was supposed to play out?—it's stupid. Not to mention so unlikely that . . . Look. I need to get in to talk to this copper. Lo Bianco. That's who it is, right? You c'n arrange for me to see him, can't you? I work with DI Lynley in London, and Lo Bianco will know his name. He doesn't need to know I'm a family friend. Just tell him I work with Lynley."

"I can make a phone call," Greco told her. "But he speaks virtually no English."

"No problem," Barbara said. "You c'n go with me, can't you?"

"*Sì, sì,*" he said. "I could do this. But you must consider that Ispettore Lo Bianco is not likely to speak to you frankly if I am present. And I assume you wish him to speak frankly, no?"

"Right. Of course. But, bloody hell, doesn't he *have* to tell you—"

"Things are different here, signora—" He stopped and corrected himself with "*Scusi.* Sergeant. Things are different here when an investigation is ongoing."

"But when there's an arrest . . ."

"It is much the same."

"Bloody hell, Mr. Greco, this is *circumstantial* evidence. Azhar went to a conference, and someone died a month later of a microorganism that he himself doesn't even study."

"Someone who had taken his child from him died. Someone who had hidden that child's whereabouts for many months. This, as you know, does not look good."

And it would look worse, Barbara reckoned, if Azhar's part in Hadiyyah's kidnapping became known. She said, "You can't convict someone on circumstantial evidence."

Greco looked astonished. "On the contrary, Sergeant. Here, people are convicted for much less every day."

LUCCA
TUSCANY

It was without surprise that Salvatore Lo Bianco received the news that another representative from New Scotland Yard had appeared in Lucca. He had expected someone from London to show up once he'd arrested Taymullah Azhar. The word would have gone out to the British embassy via Aldo Greco, and the information would have filtered inevitably from the British embassy to the Metropolitan police. This was doubly the case because, once the arrest had been made, an English child was left without an English carer. Someone had to deal with that as she was no relation of Lorenzo Mura's and Mura was merely sheltering her until other arrangements could be made. So to have a police presence from England on hand did not surprise him.

He merely hadn't expected that person to appear at the *questura* so quickly.

It wasn't DI Lynley, which was unfortunate. Not only had Salvatore liked the Englishman, it had also been convenient that Lynley spoke quite decent Italian. Indeed, he found it decidedly odd that the Metropolitan police would send someone to Lucca who didn't speak Italian. But when Aldo Greco rang him and gave him her name and her details—including her lack of Italian—he agreed to see her. Greco assured him that the officer would bring a translator with her. Her companion—an English cowboy, Greco said—apparently had several contacts in the town, and one of them would see to it that Sergeant Havers was accompanied by a native speaker.

Salvatore hadn't thought much about what an English woman detective might look like, so he wasn't prepared for the woman who came into his office some two hours after the phone call from Greco. When he saw her, he reflected on the fact that, perhaps, he'd been too influenced over the years by British television dramas dubbed into Italian. He'd anticipated, perhaps, someone along the lines of one distinguished and titled actress or another, a little hard round the edges but otherwise leggy, fashionably put together, and attractive. What walked into his office, however, was the antithesis of all this, save for the hard-round-the-edges part. She was short, stout, and garbed in desperately wrinkled beige linen trousers, red trainers, and a partially untucked navy-blue tank top that hung from her plump shoulders. Her hair looked as if she'd put herself into the hands of her gardener who'd done double duty while trimming the hedges outside of her house. Her skin was beautiful—the British were served well by their damp climate, he thought—but it was shiny with perspiration.

Accompanied by a bookish-looking woman with very large spectacles and very gelled hair, the English detective strode across the office to his desk with so much confidence and so much un-Italian disregard for her personal appearance that, grudgingly, he had to admire her. She held out a hand, which he discovered was damp. "DS Barbara Havers," she said. "You don't speak English. Right. Well. This is Marcella Lapaglia, and I'll be square with you: Marcella's the partner of a bloke called Andrea Roselli. He's a journalist from Pisa, but she's not going to give him any information unless you say it's fine by you. She's here to translate, and I'm paying her for it, and luckily she needs the money more than she needs Andrea's approval at the moment."

Salvatore listened to this stream of babble and caught a word here and there. Marcella did a rapid translation. Salvatore didn't like it one bit that this other woman was the lover of Andrea Roselli, and when he said this directly, Marcella told the English detective. They went back and forth a bit until he said, *"Come? Come?"* impatiently and Marcella paused to translate for him.

"She's a professional translator" were the English detective's words via Marcella. "She knows how fast her career goes down the toilet if she spreads information she's not meant to spread."

"This had better be the case," Salvatore said directly to Marcella.

"Certamente," she told him evenly.

"I work with DI Lynley in London," DS Barbara Havers told him. "So I'm fairly well in the loop of what's been happening over here. Mostly I'm here to deal with the kid—the professor's daughter—and it'll help me do that if I know exactly what you've got on Azhar and how likely it is that he'll go to trial at some point. She's going to have questions—Hadiyyah, the kid—and I'll need to work out what to tell her. You c'n help me with that. What d'you have on Azhar—the professor—if you don't mind my asking? I mean, I know he's going down for murder—Mr. Greco told me—and I know about his job back in London and the conference in Berlin he attended and what Hadiyyah's mother died of, as well. But . . . well, let's be honest, Inspector Lo Bianco, far as I know at the moment unless you've got more than you're saying, what you've got on him seems iffy at best, hardly the stuff on which arrests are made and charges drawn. So it seems to me, with your approval, I c'n tell Hadiyyah her dad's going to be home soon enough. That is, like I say, unless there's something here I don't know about yet."

Salvatore heard the translation of all this, but he kept his gaze fixed on the detective sergeant, who kept *her* gaze fixed on him as well. Most people, he thought, would drop their eyes at some point or at least shift them to take in the details of his office, such as they were. All she did was finger the dirty shoelace on her red trainer, whose encased foot she held casually on one of her knees. When Marcella had reported all of the sergeant's words, Salvatore said carefully, "The investigation is still ongoing. And, as you must know, Sergeant, things are done differently here in Italy."

"What I know is you've got less than circumstantial evidence. You've got a string of coincidences that make me wonder why Professor Azhar's behind bars at all. But let's not go there for the moment. I'm going to want to see him. You'll need to arrange that."

The order made Salvatore prickly. Really, she was rather incredible, making such a request, considering she was in Italy for the purpose of seeing to the welfare of Hadiyyah Upman. "For what reason do you ask to see him?" he enquired.

"Because he's Hadiyyah Upman's father, and Hadiyyah's going to want to know where he is, how he is, and what's going on. That's only natural, as I expect you know."

"His fatherhood is something unproven," Salvatore pointed out. He was glad to see that his comment made her bristle once she heard Marcella's translation of it.

"Right. Yes. Well. Whatever. You score a point on that one, don't you. But a blood test will sort everything out soon enough. Look, for his part, he's going to want to know where she is and what's happening to her, and I want to be able to tell him that. Now you and I know that you c'n arrange it. I'd like you to do so." She waited while Marcella translated. He was about to reply when she added, "You c'n think of it all as a merciful concession. Because . . . well, let me be frank. You do look like a merciful sort of bloke." Before he could reply to this astonishing remark, she looked round and said, "D'you smoke, by the way, Inspector? Because I could do with a fag but I don't want to offend."

Salvatore emptied the ashtray he kept on his desk and handed it to her. She said, "Ta," and began to dig round in a massive shoulder bag she'd set on the floor. She muttered and damned this and bloody helled that—these words he knew—and finally he reached in his jacket for his own cigarettes and handed them to her. "*Ecco*," he said. To which she replied, "See? I said you looked like a merciful bloke." And then she smiled. He was taken aback. She was, as an object of femininity, quite appalling, but she had an extraordinarily lovely smile and, unlike what he'd come to think of as the English predilection for doing nothing to improve the state of their dentition, she also seemed to care about her teeth, which were very straight, very white, and very nice. Before he knew what he was doing, he smiled back. She handed the cigarettes back to him, he took one, offered one to Marcella, and they all lit up.

She said, "C'n I be honest with you, Chief Inspector Lo Bianco?"

"Salvatore," he said. And when she looked surprised, he said in English, "Not so long," and he smiled.

"Barbara, then," she replied. "It's shorter as well." She inhaled in a masculine fashion and seemed to let the smoke settle into her blood before she said, "So c'n I be honest, Salvatore?" And when he nodded at Marcella's translation, "From what I c'n tell, you're building a case against Taymullah Azhar. But c'n you put *E. coli* into his hands?"

"The conference in Berlin—"

"I know about Berlin. So he was at a conference? What difference does it make?"

"None at all till you look into the conference and discover that he was on a panel along with a scientist from Heidelberg. Friedrich von Lohmann, he's called, this man. There, at the university in Heidelberg, he studies *E. coli* in a laboratory."

Barbara Havers nodded, her eyes narrowing behind the smoke from her cigarette. "All right," she said. "The panel bit? I didn't know that. But 'f you ask me, it's just coincidence. You lot can't go into court with that, can you?"

"Someone has gone to Germany to interview this man," Salvatore told her. "And you and I know that it would not be impossible at a conference of this kind for one scientist to ask another for a strain of bacteria to look at for some reason."

"Like asking to see his vacation snaps?" she asked with a laugh.

"No," he said. "But it would not be difficult for him to create a reason that he needed this bacteria, would it: the project of a graduate student whose work he is supervising, his own shift in interest perhaps. These are merely two examples he could have used with the Heidelberg man."

"But bloody hell, Inspector . . . I mean, Salvatore, you *can't* think these blokes carry samples round with them! What d'you have? Azhar giving Mr. Heidelberg—What was his name again?"

"Von Lohmann."

"Right. Okay. So d'you see Azhar giving von Lohmann the word in Berlin and von Lohmann fishing the *E. coli* out of his suitcase?"

Salvatore felt himself growing hot. She was either deliberately misunderstanding his words, or Marcella was not translating them correctly. He said, "Of course I do not mean Professor von Lohmann had the *E. coli* with him. But the seed of Professor Azhar's interest was planted at that conference and once Hadiyyah was kidnapped by means of the London detective, then further plans were laid."

Marcella's translation arrested the sergeant's cigarette on its way to her mouth. She said, "What're you saying, exactly?"

He said, "I'm saying that what I have in my possession is proof from London that the kidnapping of Hadiyyah Upman was engineered there, not here. This detective in London who sends me the information? He would like me to think that a man called Michelangelo Di Massimo developed the scheme in Pisa, with the solitary assistance of Taymullah Azhar."

"Hang on right there. There's no bloody way—"

"But I have documents here that prove otherwise. Many records that—compared to the earlier records which I also have—have been altered. My point is this. Things are not simple and I am not stupid. Professor Azhar has been charged with murder. But I suspect this is not all he will be charged with."

The sergeant twirled her cigarette, using her thumb and her index and middle fingers in a way that suggested she'd smoked for decades. She held her cigarette like a man, as well. Salvatore wondered vaguely if she was a lesbian. Then he wondered if he was stereotyping lesbians. Then he wondered why he was wondering anything at all about the curious detective.

She said, "Want to share what's taking your head in that direction? It's a bloody strange one, you ask me."

Salvatore was careful with what he told her. He had banking information that contradicted earlier banking information, he explained.

This information made things look as if someone somewhere was fixing evidence.

She said, "Sounds like nothing's traceable to Professor Azhar, far as I can tell."

"It's true that a forensic computer specialist will have to sort through it all to follow the trails. But this can be done, and it will be, eventually."

"'Eventually'?" She thought about this, drawing her heavy eyebrows together. "Ah. You're not on that case any longer, are you? Someone gave me that info."

He waited while Marcella struggled with *info*. When she had it straightened out in her mind and the translation came, he said, "Murder is, I think you will agree, a more pressing issue to be dealt with now that the child is safe and several arrests have been made for her kidnapping. Everything will happen in due time. It is how we do things in Italy."

She crushed out her cigarette. She did this vigorously, however, and some of the ashes spilled onto her trousers. She tried to rub them off, which made things worse. She said, "Bloody hell" and "Oh well," which she followed with, "As to seeing Azhar. I'd like a few words with him. You c'n arrange that, right?"

He nodded. He would do that for her, he decided, as it was only right that the professor see the police liaison from his own country. But he had a feeling that this Sergeant Havers knew more about Taymullah Azhar than she was telling him. He reckoned Lynley would be able to help him out with the questions he had about this strange woman.

VICTORIA
LONDON

The truth of the matter was that Lynley not only didn't know if anything could save Barbara Havers, but he also didn't know if he wanted to go to the effort even to forestall what was looking more and more like the inevitable conclusion to this business.

He told himself initially that the maddening woman didn't really belong in police work anyway. She couldn't cope with authority. She had a chip on her shoulder the size of a military tank. She had appalling personal habits. She was often dazzlingly unprofessional and not only in her manner of dress. She had a good mind, but half the time she didn't use it. And half of the half when she did use her mind, it led her completely astray. As it had done now.

And yet. When she was on, she was on and she gave the job her life's blood. She was fearless when it came to challenging an opinion with which she didn't agree, and she never put the possibility of promotion ahead of her commitment to a case. She might argue and she might bite into a theory that she believed in like a pit bull with its jaws locked on a piece of meat. But her ability to confront the sorts of people she shouldn't begin to be *able* to confront set her apart from every other officer he'd worked with. She didn't pull a forelock in anyone's presence. That was the sort of officer one wanted on one's team.

And then, there was the not small matter of her having saved his life. That act of hers would always hang between them. She never brought it up and he knew she never would. But he also knew he would never forget it.

So he ended up deciding that he had no real choice. He had to give it a go and try to save the bloody woman from herself. The only way he saw to do this was to prove she was right about everything regarding Angelina Upman's death.

It would be tough going, and he brought Winston Nkata in on the process. Nkata would check into everyone associated with Angelina Upman in London: their whereabouts during the time of her illness and death in Tuscany as well as their associates in London and the unlikely possibility of their getting their hands on *E. coli*. He was to start with Esteban Castro—Angelina's erstwhile lover—and he was to include the man's wife, along with Angelina's own relatives: Bathsheba Ward and her parents and Hugo Ward as well. No matter what name he came up with, Lynley told him, he was to follow that name and to look for connections. In the meantime, he himself would head to Azhar's lab at University College in order to double-check St. James's work.

Winston looked doubtful about the entire procedure, but he said he would get on it. "But you don' think any of this lot's involved, do you?" he asked. "Seems to me the *E. coli* bit's asking for a specialist."

"Or someone who knows a specialist," Lynley told him. He sighed and added, "God knows, Winston. We're flying in the dark by our trouser seats."

Nkata smiled. "You sound like Barb."

"God forbid," Lynley said. He went on his way. He was in the car heading to Bloomsbury when Salvatore Lo Bianco rang him from Lucca. The inspector's opening remark of "Who is this extraordinary woman that Scotland Yard has sent over, *Ispettore*?" did nothing to assure him that Barbara was at least behaving herself in Italy. There was a small mercy in the fact that Lo Bianco did not wait for an immediate answer. Instead he gave Lynley the information he needed to fashion a response that didn't condemn Barbara at once.

"She is odd for a liaison officer," Salvatore told him, "as she speaks no Italian. Why did they not send you again?"

Lynley went with the liaison officer part. Unfortunately, he'd not been available this time round, he explained. He wasn't, in fact, in the loop as to what Sergeant Havers was doing in Tuscany. Could Salvatore bring him into the picture?

Thus he learned that Havers was presenting herself as having been sent to Italy to deal with Hadiyyah Upman's situation. Thus he also learned that Taymullah Azhar not only was *indagato* but also was being held in prison while under investigation for murder. Things were moving rapidly.

Salvatore told him about the conflict between the information he'd received from London and his own information. On the one hand, he said, he was in possession of an early set of Michelangelo Di Massimo's bank records, and on the other hand, London had sent him masses of data that, upon examination and comparison to Michelangelo's bank records a second, later time, showed that someone had doctored the Pisan's account.

"They've got someone over here hacking into accounts and creating documents," Lynley told him. "Everything is suspect at this point, Salvatore. Your best course is to have a computer expert at your end work out how they're diddling with things. We could, naturally, try for a court order here to get the banks and the phone companies to delve into their backup systems in order to get our hands on the original records. But that will take time, and it's iffy anyway."

"Why, my friend?"

"An Italian crime would be the reason for our request for a court order. Frankly, that would be difficult to get a judge to move on. I think it might be easier to break one of the principals over here. I've spoken to one of them—a bloke called Bryan Smythe. I can speak to the other, Doughty, if you'd like."

He would welcome that, Salvatore told him. Now as to this unusual officer from the Met . . . ?

"She's a good cop," Lynley said truthfully.

"She wishes access to the professor." Lo Bianco explained Havers's reasoning behind her request.

"It makes sense," Lynley said, "unless it's your wish to increase the pressure on Azhar by keeping him in the dark about his daughter: where she is, how she is, and what she's doing."

Lo Bianco was silent for a moment. He finally said, "It would be useful, *sì*. But while a confession based on pressure would be acceptable in some quarters—"

"To *il Pubblico Ministero*, you mean," Lynley said.

"It is how he operates, *vero*. And while he would accept a confession that grew from a man's desperation, I feel . . . somewhat reluctant. I cannot say why."

Probably because of Havers, Lynley thought. She had a way of skittering between bullying people and manoeuvring people that he occasionally admired. He said nothing but made understanding noises at his end.

Lo Bianco said, "There is something . . . When she spoke to me, there is a feeling I had."

"What sort of feeling?"

"She comes as a liaison officer to see to the welfare of the child, but she asks many questions and offers opinions about the case against Taymullah Azhar."

"Ah," Lynley said. "That's standard procedure for Barbara Havers,

Salvatore. There isn't a topic on earth that she wouldn't have an opinion about."

"I see. This helps me, my friend. Because her questions and her com-
ments were suggesting to me more than merely professional interest."

Dangerous ground, Lynley thought. He said untruthfully, "I'm not
sure what you mean."

"Nor am I, exactly. But there is an intensity about her . . . She
wanted to argue certain points relating to the professor's arrest. Coincidences, she called them. Circumstantial evidence at best, she said.
Now, it is not that her declarations have influenced me, my friend.
But I find the intensity of her interest unusual in someone who is here
in Italy only to see to the care of a child."

This was the juncture at which, Lynley knew, he ought to be telling Salvatore Lo Bianco about Barbara's relationship with Azhar and
his daughter, not to mention about the unauthorised nature of her
jaunt to Italy. But he understood that, if he did so, the Italian would
prevent her access to the Pakistani man. It was likely that he also
would deny her any contact with Hadiyyah. That seemed unfair,
especially to a child who was no doubt feeling both frightened and
abandoned. So he told Lo Bianco that Barbara's intensity of interest
in the case he was building probably had to do with her inquisitive
nature. He'd worked with Barbara many times, he reported to the
Italian. Her habit of arguing, playing devil's advocate, seeking other
routes, looking at matters from all directions . . . ? This was merely
who she was as an officer of the Met.

In a shift of topic, he quickly went on to tell Salvatore that he
would pay a call upon Dwayne Doughty. "Perhaps I can sew up one
part of the kidnapping investigation, at least," he said.

"Piero Fanucci will not like anything that detracts from how he
sees that case," Salvatore told him.

"Why do I expect that will give you a lot of pleasure?" Lynley
asked.

Salvatore laughed. They rang off. Lynley continued on his way to
Bloomsbury.

At Taymullah Azhar's laboratory, he showed his identification to
a white-coated research technician who introduced himself with the

bicultural name of Bhaskar Goldbloom, clearly the offspring of a Hindi mother and a Jewish father. The technician had been seated at a computer when Lynley entered the lab, one of eight people who were at present working in the complex of rooms. None of the researchers had been informed about the arrest in Italy of their laboratory's leading professor, Lynley found. He brought Goldbloom slowly into the picture by means of introducing the reason for his unexpected call at the lab.

He would like, he told the research technician, to be shown everything in the lab. He would need the identification and the stated purpose of every item. He would need to know and to see all the strains of bacteria both in storage and undergoing experimentation.

Bhaskar Goldbloom didn't embrace the idea of a detailed tour. Instead, he pointed out pleasantly that, as far as he knew, Detective Inspector Lynley would need a search warrant for that sort of thing.

Lynley was prepared for this response. It was, after all, reasonable and wise. He pointed out to Goldbloom that he could indeed go through channels in order to obtain the appropriate warrant, but his assumption had been that no member of Azhar's lab would really want a team of policemen to come inside and mess things about. "Which," he added, "I'd like to assure you they'd have no compunction at all about doing."

Goldbloom thought this one over. He said, at the end of his thinking, that he would need to phone Professor Azhar to obtain his permission. And this was the point at which Lynley informed Goldbloom and, through him, everyone else of Azhar's perilous situation in Italy: under arrest for a murder by means of a bacteria and currently unavailable by phone.

This changed the complexion of things at once. Goldbloom said he would cooperate with Lynley. He added, "How many hours do you have, Inspector?" in a sardonic tone. "Because this is going to take a while."

SOLLICCIANO

TUSCANY

When the phone call came through from Chief Inspector Lo Bianco, Barbara Havers and Mitchell Corsico were cooling their heels at a pavement table outside of a café in Corso Giuseppe Garibaldi where, at the moment, an outdoor market was offering a dazzling variety of foodstuffs from several dozen colourful stalls. They were imbibing the national beverage of Italy, a viscous liquid that was dubbed coffee—or at least *caffè*—but which only three cubes of sugar and a dousing with milk made remotely drinkable. Mitch had insisted that Barbara at least try the stuff. "If you're going to be in Italy, for God's sake, you c'n at least get behind the culture, Barb" was the way he had put it. She'd groused but cooperated. Once she'd had a shot of the mixture, she reckoned she'd be awake for the next eight days.

When her mobile rang, giving her the news that Lo Bianco had arranged things so that she could see Azhar, she gave Mitchell Corsico the thumbs-up. He said, "Yes!" but he was less than pleased when she told him that she alone had been given access to the prisoner. Mitchell called foul, and she couldn't blame him. He needed a story for *The Source*, he needed it fast, and Azhar was the story.

She said to him, "Mitchell, Azhar's yours the moment we spring him. The exclusive interview, the picture, Hadiyyah sitting on his lap and looking winsome, the whole plate of ravioli. It's yours, but it can't happen till we get him out of there."

"Look, you got me over here with a tale of—"

"Everything I've told you has been true, yes? You don't see anyone coming after your neck for spreading lies, do you? So have some patience. We get him out of prison, and he's going to be grateful. Grateful, he's going to give you an interview."

Corsico didn't like the set-up, but he could hardly complain. Barbara's position as a police officer had got her inside to see Lo Bianco in the first place. He knew this and had to live with it. Just as she had to live with whatever he came up with as story material at the end of the day.

Azhar was being held at a prison, the customary lodging place for someone who'd been charged with murder. It was miles from Lucca, which necessitated another terrifying race on the *autostrada*, but they made good time and Lo Bianco had phoned ahead with instructions. It was not visiting hours. It was not a visiting day. But the police had access when they wanted access. In very short order once they arrived at the place, Barbara was ushered into a private interview room which, she suspected, was not generally used when family members came calling upon the incarcerated. She'd left behind her bag and everything in it in Reception. She was searched and wanded. She was thoroughly questioned and summarily photographed.

Now in the centre of the room, she sat at its only table. This was fastened to the floor, as were its accompanying chairs. There was a large and grisly-looking crucifix fitted onto the wall, and Barbara wondered if this constituted a means of eavesdropping on what went on in the room. Microphones and cameras were so tiny now that one of the nails in Jesus's feet and one of the thorns in his crown could easily contain them.

She rolled her thumbs along the pads of her fingers and wished for a cigarette. A sign on the wall opposite the dying Jesus seemed to forbid smoking, however. She couldn't read the Italian but the large circle containing a cigarette with a red slash through it was universal.

After a minute or two, she got to her feet and began to pace. She gnawed on her thumbnail and wondered what was taking so long. When the door finally opened after a quarter of an hour, she half expected someone to come in and tell her the gaff was blown and her presence in Italy had not been confirmed—let alone sanctioned—by the London police. But when she swung round to face the door, it was Azhar who entered ahead of a guard.

In an instant Barbara realised two facts about her neighbour from London. First, she had never seen him unshaven, which he now was. Second, she had never seen him when he was not garbed in a crisp white dress shirt. Sleeves neatly rolled up in summer, sleeves rolled down and cuffs buttoned in winter, sometimes with a necktie, sometimes with a jacket, sometimes with a pullover, accompanying jeans or trousers . . . It was always the dress shirt, as definite to him as the way he signed his name.

Now, though, he wore prison garb. It was a boiler suit. It was a hideous shade of green. In combination with his unshaven face, with the dark patches of skin beneath his eyes, with his hollow expression of defeat, the sight of him made Barbara's eyes prickle.

He was, she could tell, horrified to see her. He stopped just inside the door, so quickly that the guard accompanying him stumbled and then barked, "*Avanti, avanti,*" which Barbara took to mean Azhar was to get his arse inside. When he'd cleared the doorway, the guard stepped within and closed the door. Barbara gave a silent curse when she saw this, but she understood. She was not his solicitor, so she could claim no privilege.

Azhar spoke first. He did not sit. "You should not have come, Barbara," he said futilely.

She said, "Sit," and gestured to a chair. She told him the lie she had prepared. "This isn't about you. I've been sent by the Met because of Hadiyyah."

That, at least, prompted him to do as she said. He dropped into a chair and clasped his hands on the table. They were slender hands, lovely hands for a man. She'd always thought so, but now what she thought was that those hands would not serve him well in prison.

She said to him quietly, very nearly in a whisper, "And how could I not have come, Azhar, once I heard about this?" She gestured to the room, to the prison.

He matched the barely audible tone she employed. "You have done too much already to try to help me. There is no help for what has happened now."

"Oh, really? Why's that? Did you actually do what they think you've done? Did you manage to get Angelina to down a dose of *E. coli*? What did you put it in, her morning oatmeal?"

"Of course not," he said.

"Then, believe me, there's help. But it's time for you to start being straight with me. From A to Z. A's the kidnapping, so let's start there. I need to know everything."

"I've told you everything."

She shook her head bleakly. "That's where you go wrong every time. You went wrong in December and you've gone wrong ever since. Why can't you see that if you're still lying about the kidnapping—"

"What do you mean? There's nothing that I—"

"You wrote her a card, Azhar. Something for her kidnapper to hand to her so she would know for certain you were behind the snatching. You had him call her *khushi* and then give her a card, and in that card you told her to go with the man because he would bring her to you. Does this sound familiar?" She didn't wait for an answer. She hissed, "Now, when in hell're you going to stop lying to me? And *how* in hell d'you expect me to help you if you won't start telling me the truth? About *everything*. DI Lynley gave me a copy of that card, by the way. And you can wager everything you've ever owned that the Lucca coppers are having the handwriting verified by an expert even as we speak. What the bloody hell were you thinking? Why did you take that risk?"

His reply was nearly inaudible. "I had to make sure she went with him. I told him to call her *khushi*, but how could I know that would be enough? I was desperate, Barbara. Can you not understand that? I had not seen my child in five months. What if she hadn't gone with someone who merely called her *khushi*? What if instead she had told Angelina that a stranger had approached her in the market, trying to lure her beyond the walls? Angelina would have made it impossible for *anyone* to get near her after that. Hadiyyah would have been lost to me forever."

"Well, that's been taken care of, hasn't it?"

He looked at her in horror. "I did not—"

"Do you see how it looks? How everything looks? You hire a detective to find her, then you kidnap her, then you come over here playing at Concerned Dad, *and* you've got tickets to Pakistan. Hadiyyah gets found, hugs and kisses all round, and in very short order Angelina dies. And what she dies of is a microorganism and you're a bloody microbiologist. Are you following me? This is how a case is built, Azhar. And if you don't start being straight with me about what you know and what you've done and how you've done it, then I can't help you and, more important, I can't help Hadiyyah. Full stop."

"I did not," he murmured brokenly.

"Yeah? Well, someone bloody did," she whispered fiercely. "Lo Bianco's onto a bloke passing you a petri dish of *E. coli* when you were in Berlin. Or posting it to you afterwards. Someone called von Lohmann, from Heidelberg. Meantime, *The Source* has dug up a woman from Glasgow who studies *E. coli* and who was *also* at this bloody conference. You were on a panel with the Heidelberg bloke, and for all I know you played hide-the-salami with the Glasgow woman when the sun went down, all the better to get her ready to hand over a vial of bacteria when you needed it."

He flinched. He said nothing. His eyes were pained.

She sighed and said, "Sorry. *Sorry.* But you have to see how things look and how they're going to look when all the pieces get put together. So if there's anything—and I mean anything at all—that you haven't told me, now's the time."

At least he didn't respond at once. This, Barbara thought, was a good sign because it meant he was thinking instead of just reacting. She needed that from him. Thinking and remembering both. *And,* she knew, he would pass along the information she'd given him so that his solicitor might have the information as to how Lo Bianco was building his case. So all wasn't lost, and she needed very much to keep things that way.

He said, "There is nothing more. You know it all now."

"Have you any message for Hadiyyah, then? She's where I intend to head next."

He shook his head. He said, "She must not know," and he lifted his fingers in a tired gesture that spoke of his whereabouts and his state of mind.

"Then I won't tell her," Barbara said. "Let's hope Mura has the same intention."

FATTORIA DI SANTA ZITA
TUSCANY

Mitchell Corsico had a map to assist with the location of Fattoria di Santa Zita. He even knew who Santa Zita was. During his downtime in Lucca—which, as he put it, there had been a hell of a lot of—he'd seen the highlights of the town, and Santa Zita's corpse was one of them, encased in a glass coffin in the church of San Frediano, up on an altar, kitted out in her maid's clothes, he reported. Just the stuff to enhance every kid's nightmares. God only knew why Lorenzo Mura's property was named after her.

Barbara had already decided that she couldn't take Corsico with her to Lorenzo Mura's home. She hadn't the first clue what was going to happen when she showed her mug at his place, and she didn't want a journalist there to exploit what went down. She thought at first that leaving Mitchell behind would be a problem, but this didn't turn out to be the case. From their excursion to the prison, he had to devise a story to send to his editor and he had limited time in which to do it. He'd remain in Lucca while she went to the *fattoria*, he told her, but he would expect a report from her, and it had better be a full one.

Right, Barbara told him. Whatever you say, Mitch.

On their way back from the prison, she cooperatively fed the journalist what details she could from her visit with Azhar, going heavy on the atmosphere of the place, on Azhar's physical and emotional condition, and on the jeopardy that he faced with regard to the investigation. She went light on everything else, and the kidnapping she didn't bring up at all.

No fool, Corsico didn't take to her limited facts like a baby swallowing a spoonful of honey with the medicine. He jotted down notes, he demanded to know what the circumstances of the circumstantial evidence were, he asked good questions that she did her best to dodge, and at the end he reminded her of their relative positions. If she double-crossed him, she would be sorry, he told her.

"Mitchell, we're in this together," she reminded him.

"Don't forget that" was his parting shot.

Azhar had told Barbara where Fattoria di Santa Zita was, and once she and Mitchell located the place on his map, she set off in his hire car after leaving him on the pavement along Via Borgo Giannotti outside of the city wall. She watched him duck into a café. When he was out of sight, she proceeded up the street, heading for the River Serchio and out of the town.

Fattoria di Santa Zita, she found, was high in the hills and up an unnerving road of hairpin turns and precipitous drops. The countryside here combined forest with agricultural land, and the agricultural land was heavily given to vineyards and olive groves. The *fattoria* was marked with an easily noticeable sign. The reason for this sign she discovered once she made the left turn and headed into the place: She nearly hit a yellow convertible MG on her route, a classic vehicle swervingly operated by a young man whose passenger was intent upon nibbling his neck. Brakes were applied all round, and the driver of the MG yelled out, "Whoops! Sorry about that! Hey, have the oh-seven Sangiovese. We bought a case of it. You can't go wrong. Jesus, Caroline, get your hand out of there!" And with bursts of laughter from him and his companion, he managed to manoeuvre the MG past Barbara's car and hence to the road.

From all this, Barbara reckoned that wine tasting went on at Fattoria di Santa Zita, and she discovered soon enough that she was not wrong. Perhaps a quarter of a mile along the unpaved lane, she came to the driveway into the *fattoria*. Not much farther and she saw an ancient barn with a heavy arbour of wisteria draping lavender flowers towards a scattering of rustic tables and chairs.

The doors to the barn were open, and Barbara parked close by in the space designated for tasters. She crossed the gravel and then the flagstone terrace where the tables stood. It was dim in the barn, so when she went inside, she paused for her eyes to adjust to the change in light.

She expected to see Lorenzo Mura, but she did not. What she saw was a roughly hewn bar set up with wineglasses, a display of the wines ostensibly made on the property, a basket of savoury biscuits, and four wedges of cheese contained beneath a glass dome on a cutting board. The air was so fragrant with the scent of wine that she reckoned she could get tipsy just by breathing deeply. She did so and her mouth watered in anticipation. A glass of wine wouldn't have gone down half bad, and she wouldn't have minded a few pieces of cheese either.

A young man emerged from a cavernous room beyond the tasting area, where Barbara could see three stainless steel vats and row upon row of empty green bottles. He said, "*Buongiorno. Vorrebbe assaggiare del vino?*" and she stared at him uncomprehendingly. Apparently, he read this for what it was because he switched to English, which he spoke with what sounded like a Dutch accent. He said, "English? Would you like to try some Chianti?"

Barbara showed her police identification. She was there to speak to Lorenzo Mura, she said.

"Up at the villa" was his reply. He waved towards the interior of the barn, as if the villa could be accessed from there. He went on to explain how to get to the place. Drive or walk, he told her, it wasn't far. Follow the road, curve past the old farmhouse, go through the gates, and then you'll see it. "He might be on the roof," he told her.

"You work for him, I s'pose?" Barbara said. He looked to be somewhere in his twenties, probably a European student having a spring-through-summer work/study/play in Italy. He said that he did, and when she asked if there were more of his ilk about the property, he said no. He was the only one working on the farm at present, aside from the blokes who were working on the farmhouse and the villa.

"Been here long, then?" she asked.

He'd arrived only the week before, he told her. She scratched him from her list of potential suspects.

She went by foot the rest of the way to the villa. She noted the size of the operation that Lorenzo Mura had going at the *fattoria*. Not only did vineyards fall down a hillside overlooking a rather stupendous view of mountain villages, more vineyards in the distance, and other farms, but olive groves promised a source of income from oil, and cattle grazing near a stream far below suggested beef products as well.

An old farmhouse was under renovation, and so, it seemed, was the villa when she finally came to it. It sat at the top of a sloping lawn, and scaffolding covered the sides of it. On the roof swarmed half a dozen men. They were in the process of removing its tiles, which they were tossing to the ground three floors below them. This was a noisy business, accompanied by enormous clouds of dust as well as a great deal of shouting in Italian. Over the shouting music played at a volume sufficient for most of Tuscany to hear quite easily. It was old rock 'n' roll sung in English: Chuck Berry was asking Maybellene why she couldn't be true.

One of the workers clocked her approach, for which she was grateful since she didn't think she'd be capable of outshouting Chuck. This man waved and disappeared from view for a moment. Into his place stepped Lorenzo Mura.

He stood, backlit by the afternoon sun, arms akimbo, as Barbara approached the villa. She wondered if he would recognise her from their meeting in London the previous month. Apparently he did because he descended the rickety scaffolding quickly and, in her opinion, with insufficient care. By the time she reached the area in front of the building's great loggia, he was coming round the side of the place and his expression didn't indicate that the red carpet was about to be unrolled.

He spoke first, saying, "Why are you here?"

She took a moment before she replied. He looked about as bad as Azhar, she thought. Sleepless nights, too much daytime labour, insufficient food, forcing himself to move forward through every day, grief . . . These would take the stuffing out of any man. But so would a bout with *E. coli*, she thought. He looked shaky, and his colour was pasty. The port wine stain on his face appeared deeply purple.

She said to him, "Have you been ill, Mr. Mura?"

"My woman and our child are in a *cimitero* five days," he said. "How you think me to look?"

"I'm sorry," she said. "For what's happened, I'm sorry."

"There is no sorry for this," he replied. "What want you here?"

"I've come for Hadiyyah," she told him. "It's her father's wish that—"

He swiped the air with a chopping motion of his hand that stopped her words. He said, "Do *not*. There are things we not know. One of them is Hadiyyah's father. Angelina said Azhar but me she tells it can be another." And taking a moment to register the expression on Barbara's face at this bit of news, he added, "You did not know. It is among many things you do not know. Taymullah Azhar was not the . . ." He looked for the word. He settled on "the solo man when he and Angelina first become lovers."

"I know Angelina slept round like a ten-quid tart, but I expect that's not exactly where you'd like this conversation to head. Past actions tend to indicate future actions, if you know what I mean, Mr. Mura."

Colour swept his face.

Barbara said, "So that knife cuts in both directions, doesn't it? You hooked yourself up with a woman with a colourful past, and for all we know till the day she died she had a colourful present as well. Now, I expect you'd like Azhar to doubt Hadiyyah is his, and I expect Angelina would've liked that also, all the better to keep her from him. But you and I both know what a DNA test can prove and, believe me, I c'n arrange for one as fast as you can ring up your solicitor and try to stop me. Are we clear on this?"

"He wants Hadiyyah, he comes for her himself. When he's able to come, *certo*. Meantime—"

"In the meantime, you have a British subject in your digs, and I'm here to collect her."

"I telephone her grandparents to come for her."

"And her grandparents are going to do what? Cooperate with that idea? Fly over, scoop her up in their arms, and take her home to a bedroom they've just redecorated in her honour? That's not bloody likely. Believe me, Lorenzo, they'd never even seen Hadiyyah before Angelina died, if they saw her then. Did they come to the funeral? Yes? It was probably to dance on Angelina's grave, that's how much of a nothing she was to them once she got herself involved with Azhar. They'd've seen her death as her finally receiving what she deserved for getting herself pregnant by a Pakistani Muslim in the first place. I'd like to see Hadiyyah now."

Mura's face had darkened to nearly the colour of his port wine birthmark during Barbara's speech. But he seemed unwilling to argue further. After all, he had work to do on the crumbling villa, and his hanging on to Hadiyyah was only intended to thrust the sword deeper into Azhar's chest, as was handing her over to her grandparents.

Barbara said to Mura, "So . . . are you and I finished here, Mr. Mura?"

Mura's expression indicated that he would have liked to spit on her shoes, but instead he turned and headed into the villa. He didn't go up one of the curving stairways to the loggia, though. Instead, he ducked beneath a mass of honeysuckle that arched over a weathered door at ground level. Barbara followed him.

She was surprised at the condition of the place, considering Angelina Upman had lived within it. The villa was decrepit, a relic from the distant past, and when she saw its wreck of a kitchen—so dimly lit that its higher calling clearly was to be turned into a dungeon—she reflected on how Angelina's first move upon returning to Azhar the previous year had been to redecorate his flat to her own standards. She'd not bothered with that here. Nor, it seemed, had she bothered to clean the place. Dust, grime, cobwebs, and mould appeared to define it.

Barbara followed Lorenzo Mura through several rooms, all of which seemed part of the kitchen. Eventually, they climbed a stone stairway and emerged into some kind of huge reception room with enormous glass doors opened onto the loggia. This room was, like the kitchen below, dimly lit. Unlike the kitchen, it was relatively grime free. Its walls and ceiling were heavily frescoed, but these decorations were hard to make out after their exposure to several hundred years of candle smoke.

In this room, Lorenzo called Hadiyyah's name. Barbara yelled, "Hey, kiddo, look who's come calling!" In reply, footsteps clattered along some kind of corridor up above them. They came storming in Barbara's direction, and a small body hurtled into the room and, more important, into Barbara's arms.

Hadiyyah said the best thing possible. "Where's my dad?" she cried. "Barbara, I want my *dad*!"

Barbara cast Lorenzo Mura a look that said, *So he's not her father, eh?*, but she spoke to Hadiyyah. "And your dad wants you. He's not here just now, and he's not in Lucca, but he's sent me for you. Want to come along, or are you happier staying with Lorenzo? He tells me your granddad and grandma're coming to fetch you. You c'n wait for them, if that's what you'd like to do."

"I want to be with Dad," she said. "I want to go home. I want to go with *you*."

"Right. Well. We can make that happen. Your dad's got a few things he's sorting out, but you c'n stay with me till he's finished up. Let's get you packed. Want me to help you?"

"Yes," she said. "*Yes*. Help me. Do." She tugged at Barbara's hand. She dragged her in the direction from which she'd come.

Barbara followed her, but not without a glance at Mura. He was watching them steadily, his face expressionless. Before she and Hadiyyah were out of the room, he'd turned on his heel and left them to it.

Upstairs, Barbara saw that at least Hadiyyah's bedroom had been made pleasant and modern. It even had a small colour television, and on this television Angelina Upman and Taymullah Azhar were speaking into the camera together. There was a voice-over in Italian, but Barbara recognised the location of the filming: They sat under the wisteria arbour in front of the winery in the company of the ugliest man Barbara had ever seen, his face covered with warts as if a witch had cursed him.

"Mummy" was Hadiyyah's explanation of what she was watching. She said it softly, a single word that exposed the pain and confusion in which the little girl doubtless found herself. She crossed the room to the television and fiddled with the player beneath it. From this she brought out a DVD. She said, "I like to watch Mummy," in a very small voice. "She's talking about me. She and Dad are talking. Lorenzo gave it to me. I like to watch Mummy and Dad together."

The wish of every child whose parents are at odds, Barbara thought.

BOW
LONDON

It was quite late in the day, but Lynley took a chance that Doughty would still be at his place of employment. His time in Azhar's lab had uncovered a detail that might prove crucial to Salvatore's investigation into Angelina Upman's death, and his hope was that a bit of chivvying the detective would go some distance to garner his cooperation in the matter of Hadiyyah's kidnapping. For Doughty faced considerable jeopardy. He'd had Bryan Smythe lay trails in all directions to stymie the Italian police, but some earlier trails led directly back to his own door. Fighting extradition to Italy to face charges of kidnapping—among other charges—was going to prove costly for Mr. Doughty. Lynley was betting that Doughty didn't want to go through that.

A teenage girl was in Doughty's office when Lynley got there. She turned out to be the detective's niece, having a work experience day for an assignment from her comprehensive. She *could* have chosen to spend a workday with one of her parents, she revealed to Lynley, but her mum was a San sister and her dad was an estate agent and a day with either of them was destined to be b-o-r-i-n-g. *That* was before she knew that a day with Uncle Dwayne would be even worse. *She* thought he carried a gun and engaged in shoot-outs and fist-fights with villains in assorted alleys replete with wooden crates and wheelie bins. Turned out he occupied his time sitting outside a William Hill betting shop where some excessively stupid husband of an even more excessively stupid and jealous wife was spending hours and days making useless wagers instead of having an affair, which was what his wife thought and which, mind you, would've been a lot more interesting.

"Ah" was Lynley's response to all this. "And is Mr. Doughty about?"

"Next door," she said obscurely. "With Em."

Em, Lynley thought. This was a name that had not yet come up. He nodded thanks to the girl, who returned—with a mighty sigh— to the typing she'd been doing. He went next door.

Doughty was in conversation with an attractive, male-dressed woman. It didn't appear intense as Doughty was casually leaning against the sill of a window overlooking the Roman Road and Em was facing him in a desk chair, one mannishly clad foot on a computer table. She swung in her chair when Doughty said, "Who are you?" to Lynley.

Lynley showed his identification and introduced himself. He noted the lack of recognition in Doughty's expression. He also noted Em's guarded look. From this he reckoned Bryan Smythe had not revealed to either of them that he had had a recent visit from New Scotland Yard. This could make things easier, Lynley thought.

He began with the purpose of his late-afternoon call. He was, he told him, there to talk to the private investigator about his interactions with a woman called Barbara Havers.

Doughty replied with "My cases are confidential, Inspector."

"Until the CPS becomes involved," Lynley noted.

"What, exactly, are you talking about?"

"An internal police investigation," Lynley told him, "into the activities of Detective Sergeant Barbara Havers. I'm assuming that you knew she was a Met officer when you met her, but perhaps you didn't.

In any case, you can cooperate with me now or wait for the court order for your records. I'd suggest cooperation as it's less messy that way, but it's up to you."

Doughty remained without expression. Em—who turned out to be called in full Emily Cass—glanced at her fingernails and brushed her right hand over her left as if unnecessarily ridding it of dust. Was the name familiar to either of them? Lynley enquired politely when they said nothing. He repeated it: Barbara Havers.

Doughty, he discovered, was a fairly quick thinker. He said to Em Cass, "Barbara Havers. Emily, could she be the woman who came to see us last winter? She was only here twice, but if you could check . . ."

To which Em Cass said to him cautiously, "Are you sure about the name? D'you have a time period? C'n you refresh . . . ?"—also a wise response.

He said, "Two people came to see us about a little girl whose mum had disappeared with her. A Muslim man and a rather dishevelled woman. I think the woman might have been called Something Havers. This would have been late in the year. November? December? You should have it in our files." He nodded at her computer.

She played along, and after a moment perusing her computer's monitor, she said, "I've got it here. You're right, Dwayne . . . Taymullah Azhar was his name. A woman called Barbara Havers came with him." She mispronounced Azhar's name. Nice touch, Lynley thought.

Doughty corrected the pronunciation and carried on with the performance. "They did come about his daughter, as I recall. It was her mum who'd snatched her, yes?"

More reading of the monitor and Lynley allowed this. It was rather fascinating to see how they were going to play the situation, so he let them have as much rope as they wanted. After a moment, she said, "Yes. We traced them to Italy—to Pisa, as it happens—but that was as far as we went. This was last December. It says here that you advised the man—Mr. Azhar—to find an Italian detective who could assist. Or an English detective who spoke Italian. Whichever worked for them."

"She'd gone into Pisa airport, hadn't she? The mum?"

"That's what it says."

He looked intensely thoughtful for a moment while Lynley waited patiently for more, saying nothing but also giving no sign that he intended to leave them any time soon. Doughty said, "But did we . . . Em, luv, did we find a detective to recommend to them? Seems to me that we may have done."

She did some scrolling, did some squinting at the screen, did some glancing in Doughty's direction for a bit of unspoken direction from him, and did some nodding. "*Mass*, it says here. Is that the name, Dwayne? An abbreviation perhaps?"

"I'd have to check." And to Lynley, "If you wouldn't mind coming with me . . . ? I've got more records in my own office."

"Let's all go, shall we?" Lynley said affably.

A glance was exchanged between the other two. Doughty said, "Yes, why not?" and led the way.

His niece was packing up for her departure, a procedure that appeared to involve a magnifying mirror and a massive amount of cosmetics. Doughty made much of bidding her a fond farewell: hugs, kisses, and "best to Mum, darling," and once she left them, he smiled and said, "Kids," to no one's agreement or reply.

He then said to Lynley, "I've got hard copies of some of my cases, so I might have something . . . One plans to write one's memoirs at some point . . . Memorable cases and the like, if you know what I mean."

"Certainly," Lynley said. "It worked quite well for Dr. Watson, didn't it?"

Doughty did not look amused. He opened a filing drawer and riffled through it. He said, "Here. I think we're in luck," and he brought out a slim manila folder.

He flipped from one page to another of the documents within. He pulled on his lower lip and frowned. He said, "Fairly interesting."

"Indeed?" Lynley queried.

"Something apparently got the wind up for me. Couldn't tell you now what it was, but I did a little looking into the woman—"

"Barbara Havers, you mean?" Lynley clarified.

"Turns out that, over time, some money passed from the Pakistani man to her and from her to Italy, to one Michelangelo Di Massimo."

"I think that was the name, Dwayne," Em Cass said. "That's the Italian detective."

Doughty glanced up from his paperwork, saying to Lynley, "It appears that a series of payments flowed from Azhar to Havers to this Di Massimo, so my guess is that she and the Pakistani employed him for quite some time."

"Extraordinary that you should know that, Mr. Doughty," Lynley pointed out.

"I'm merely deducing because of the payments."

"Actually, I'm not talking about Di Massimo's employment. I'm talking about the payments themselves, money moving from Azhar to Barbara Havers to Di Massimo. Extraordinary work on your part, in the true sense of the word. May I ask how you uncovered this information?"

Doughty waved the question aside. "Sorry. Trade secret. Perhaps of larger interest to Scotland Yard might be the fact that payments were made at all. What I can tell you about these two individuals—and this Barbara Havers in particular since she appears to be at the centre of your interest—is that they came to see me in the winter. I gave them what small help I could, I suggested they find an Italian detective, and the rest . . . Well, it is what it is."

"And you saw these two people—Taymullah Azhar and Barbara Havers—how many times?"

He looked at Em Cass. "Was it twice, Em? Once when they came for help in locating the child and once when I had the facts to present to them. Yes?"

"As far as I know, that was it," she confirmed.

"So you wouldn't know, it seems," Lynley said, "that Barbara Havers has for quite some time been followed by another detective from the Met."

Silence on their part. Clearly, they hadn't considered this possibility. Lynley waited, a pleasant expression on his face. They said nothing. This being the case, he removed from the breast pocket of his jacket his reading glasses and from an interior pocket, he took out a set of documents that he'd folded and placed there. He unfolded them and began to read John Stewart's report aloud to the private investigator and his cohort. John had been thorough, in keeping with his compulsive nature and with his animosity towards Barbara Havers. So he had dates, and he had times, and he had places. Lynley read them all.

When he was finished, he glanced up at Doughty and Em Cass, over the top of his glasses. He said, "It tends to come down to trust in the end, Mr. Doughty. Trust always trumps money on the wrong side of the law."

Doughty said, "All right. Agreed. She came to see me more than once evidently. Which, obviously, is why I decided to look into her."

"Indeed. But I'm not talking about your trusting Barbara Havers. I'm talking about anyone trusting Di Massimo. Had he not subcontracted Hadiyyah's kidnapping out to a bloke called Roberto Squali, had Squali not been photographed by a tourist, had he not driven an expensive convertible far too quickly up a mountain road, had he and Di Massimo not been in contact by mobile phone . . . Indeed, had the investigation in Italy not been handled by Salvatore Lo Bianco, who appears to be a shinier coin in the collection plate than the magistrate who heads the case, everything might have gone along the way you intended it to go. But those phone calls piqued Lo Bianco's interest, and he followed the trail of them rather more quickly than you—at this end—apparently anticipated. So what he ended up with is a set of records far different from those you later provided him. And, Barbara Havers aside for the moment, that's quite an interesting development in the kidnapping investigation."

Silence. Lynley let it go on. Outside, down in the Roman Road, two men argued loudly in a foreign tongue. A dog barked and a dustbin's lid clanged against the receptacle. But in the office, there was nothing.

Lynley said, "What I'm assuming is that, in the manner of similar shady characters, all of you have been double- and triple-crossing each other. One person gets a leg up on the other, then that person raises the ante and so on. Now, I'm not going to involve myself in any further questioning at the moment, as the hour is late and I'd like to get home, as I expect you would as well. But before you go, I'd like you to reflect on your neck, Ms. Cass's neck, and the neck of your colleague Mr. Smythe. While you're doing this reflecting, I'd like you to consider that Inspector Lo Bianco will be employing a forensic technology expert to follow all the diddling you've been doing with everyone's records, and the Metropolitan police will be doing the same thing. Computers, as I expect you know, leave trails of cookie crumbs along the paths they take. To the average soul—like me, for example—these trails are impossible to find. To the expert in modern computer technology, this sort of work is a piece of cake. Or cookie, if you will."

He gave Doughty time to look at the material Lo Bianco had sent him. Doughty did so and, as the man could read, he was fully capable of interpreting the message on the wall.

17 MAY

P rior to going to bed, Dwayne Doughty had been able to hold things together in front of his wife because he didn't want to worry her nor did he want to watch her China-blue eyes fill with tears at the thought of their having to flee the country one step ahead of a police enquiry. He rued the day he'd ever got involved in the Italian mess, and the effort to hide from his wife his ruing from the time he arrived home to the time he went to bed resulted in what felt like a very sharp knitting needle piercing his head.

Candace knew something was wrong. She wasn't stupid. But he managed to fend off her questions with the stock answer of "just a bit of a head-scratcher at work, luv," which she accepted for the evening but wasn't likely to accept into the following day. He needed either to perfect his acting skill—a doubtful prospect when it came to facing off with Can—or he needed to work out a solution to his little problem.

He rose at half past three. In the kitchen of their semidetached, he quietly made a pot of coffee, which he began to drink, sitting at the table and mostly staring at nothing as he turned over various possibilities. He had worked his way through an entire package of fig bars—always his favourite, since childhood—but had got not much further than a mild case of heartburn and a more serious case of dietary guilt.

There had to be possibilities for him at this point, he thought, for the simple reason that there always were if one took the time and had the patience to develop them. No way in hell was he going to flush his line of employment, the years he'd spent coaxing it out of nothing, and his whole life down the loo. He'd never let anything defeat him in the past, and he sure as bloody hell wasn't going to be defeated now. Especially was he not going to be defeated by a Scotland Yard detective with a posh public school voice and a Savile Row suit that fairly screamed, *Carefully worn by a faithful retainer for two years before being donned by me.* Absolutely no way was that ever going to happen. But unless something *did* happen to prevent it, he was a few short days away from a knock on his office door that doubtless would herald the advent of some serious difficulties in his future.

It was his own fault. From the first and with Em Cass's insistence, he'd twigged that the woman was a cop, but that hadn't stopped him. He'd agreed to help the professor find his kid—Christ but he had to harden his soft heart or it would finish him off in this line of work— and now look where that had led. He'd spent the past twenty years of his postmilitary life working his arse down to nothing—like his father before him—in order to take the family and its name another step up from the coal mines of Wigan. He had two kids who'd collected respectable university degrees, and he swore that *their* children—when they had them—would do the same from Oxford or Cambridge. He wasn't about to miss that due to having to flee the country or because of the need to spend a stretch of time playing some sweaty yob's wife behind prison bars . . . so what in God's name was he going to do to avoid either prospect?

Another cup of coffee. Another four fig bars. This took him to thoughts of his associates and how much blame he could possibly assign them. He'd always been a careful man, so there was no direct link from him to all the manoeuvring and the tinkering that had gone on. Aside from the one time in Emily's sumptuous flat in Wapping and—all right—once in Emily's office, he never himself actually discussed business with Bryan Smythe, so the truth was that he could throw up his hands in shock and despair and throw Em to the legal wolves. She, after all, had passed along his verbal instructions to

Smythe. How difficult would it be to establish that every idea skittering to every lawless act had come from her? But the question was:
Could he really do that to Em after the years in which they'd worked
together?

He knew the answer to that before he even got to the end of the
question. He had history with Em. He also had history with Bryan.
So together they had to climb out of this pit. It was his curse that he
was such an ethical bloke.

The second hour into his brooding about the problem had gained
him only the insight that he might be able to use this bloke Lynley's
potential attachment to DS Barbara Havers in some way to benefit
himself, much as he'd used *her* obvious attachment to the Pakistani
professor to keep her in order. The difficulty with this was that he
couldn't work his mind round to believing there *was* an attachment
between the detective sergeant and the posh inspector. So he was left
with a nut needing to be cracked and having ninety minutes more in
which to crack it before Can's alarm went off and she staggered into
the kitchen completely unamused at his having devoured all the fig bars.

The thought of Can's displeasure with regard to the fig bars stirred
Dwayne to hide the evidence. He needed to make another pot of
coffee, so he roused himself from the kitchen table and crumpled the
wrapping of the sinful biscuits. He couldn't put this in the rubbish.
His wife would find it and a lecture about his nutritional habits would
ensue. So he grabbed up a folded newspaper from the stool by the
kitchen door, where others of its ilk waited for recycling, and he unfolded it on the draining board. He would, he decided, dump the
coffee grounds on this and hide the fig bar wrapping beneath them.
He was supposed to recycle the grounds as well—or was it compost
the grounds? He could never remember all the terminology for what
one did with one's rubbish these days—but allowance could be made
this once for not putting the grounds to use for a higher purpose.

He took them from the coffeemaker. He spread the fig bar wrapping neatly onto the unfolded newspaper, and he was just about to
dump the coffee grounds on top of this when his hand was stayed in
best biblical fashion. There before him beneath the fig wrapping lay
the answer. Or at least part of it. For he'd opened the newspaper to a

story whose elements he well recognised: Italy, an Englishwoman's death, a possible cover-up, and stay tuned for more. He shoved the fig bar wrapping to one side and read, and the names leapt out at him. The problem was that he'd opened the paper to the middle of the story, and one paragraph into it the floodgates of his ability to plan and devise and ultimately triumph opened . . . but he needed the rest of the story.

He wasn't a praying man, but he did pray that Candace hadn't used the front of the paper to discard last night's leftover chili con carne into. He rooted through the stack of recycling aspirants, and he found what he was looking for. This was a name, a reporter's name. And there it was beneath the page-one headline: Mitchell Corsico. It sounded Italian to Dwayne, but Italian or not, obviously the bloke spoke English. And since he spoke English, he was the answer. He was the plan.

For Dwayne Doughty, aside from heartburn and caffeine nerves strung out like wires for a tightrope walker, all was finally well.

LUCCA
TUSCANY

What Barbara hadn't anticipated was Hadiyyah's desire to be with her father. She'd been so anxious to get her away from Lorenzo Mura and to protect her from whatever might occur should her foul grandparents show up to fetch her that there had been nothing else on her mind but scooping her up and dashing back to Lucca with her.

That had been enough at first. They'd had dinner in Lucca, at a multinational restaurant/cafeteria in Via Malcontenti, where upon the walls hung placemats decorated by past clientele extolling the virtues of the pizzas, the goulash, and the hummus in various languages. They'd had gelato afterwards, from a vendor near the main tourist office in Piazzale Giuseppe Verdi. Then they'd walked up from that office to a section of the ancient wall among the Italians enjoying their evening stroll. When at last they'd returned to Pensione Giardino, Hadiyyah had been more than ready just to sleep in the second bed in Barbara's room.

Bullets were not dodged for long, though. The first was from Corsico, who rang at half past seven in the morning wanting the next story for his editor, which, he told her, needed to be along the lines of *English Child's Agony with Dad in Prison*. He said he'd be happy to make it all up—"par for the course, Barb"—if Barbara just produced the kid for a picture looking soulfully out of the window of the *pensione*. "Missing her dad and all that rubbish, you know what I mean," he said. Barbara foisted him off with the information that Hadiyyah was still asleep and she would ring him when the child awakened. But that put her into contact with the second bullet, which was Hadiyyah's desire to see her father.

That, Barbara knew, was the last thing Azhar would ever want: his beloved child getting an eyeful of him in prison garb, sitting alongside the other inmates on visiting day. She wasn't about to do that to either of them, so she told Hadiyyah that her dad was helping Inspector Lo Bianco look into a few things about her mummy's death. He was out of town just then, she explained to the child, and he wanted her to remain in Barbara's care. This was true so if she had to expand on the story at a later time, she could do so without having to retrace her steps. She didn't like keeping the full truth from Hadiyyah, but she didn't see any other course.

What she knew was that she had to make some sort of arrangement to keep Hadiyyah out of the hands of the Upmans. The investigation into Angelina's death was never going to lead to Azhar, but until the Italians saw things that way, he was going to stay in prison, giving the Upmans the ability to claim her if they chose to do so. She had to make Hadiyyah unavailable to them, and the best way to do that was to get her out of Italy and in a location where she couldn't be found.

It didn't take her long to come up with that location. She needed Lynley, though, in order to arrange it. So she suggested to Hadiyyah that they ask Signora Vallera if she could, perhaps, watch television in the family section of the *pensione* while Barbara made a few pressing phone calls, and when Hadiyyah said with an anxious but eager crumpling of her forehead, "Could I watch the film of Mummy, Barbara?" Barbara snatched at the idea as the best possible plan. It would soothe the little girl at the same time as it would occupy her. She said, "Let's see if we c'n sort out a DVD player, then," and she hoped Hadiyyah's Italian was good enough to do so.

It was. In short order she and the Vallera toddler were side by side on a sofa watching Angelina Upman and Taymullah Azhar speak to the camera, and Barbara was back in the breakfast room, ringing Inspector Lynley's mobile.

Before he could say anything other than "Isabelle's had an appointment with Hillier, Barbara," she cut in.

"I've got Hadiyyah. I need to get her back to London. Mura's rung Angelina's parents to fetch her, and in advance of that, we need to—"

He cut in irritably with "Barbara, do you ever listen to me? *Did* you hear me? I've no idea what they talked about, but whatever it is, it's probably not good."

"What you still don't understand is that Hadiyyah is what matters," she said. "I've got my police ID, so I can get her a ticket back to London, but you need to meet her at the other end."

"And what?" he asked.

"And then you've got to hide her."

"Tell me I'm not hearing you correctly as I think you might have just said I must hide her."

"Sir, it would only be for as long as it takes me to get Azhar out of gaol. I need to rattle a few doorknobs over here. I need to shake a few skeletons. You and I know that if the Upmans get their hands on Hadiyyah, they're going to make it impossible for Azhar to get her back."

"You and I," Lynley said, "know nothing of the sort."

"Please, sir," she said. "I'll beg if I have to. I need your help. She c'n stay with you, can't she? Charlie can mind her. He'll love her to bits. And she'll love him."

"And when he has an audition, is he to take her with him or perhaps give her an assignment in the house? Something along the lines of polishing the silver, perhaps?"

"He can take her with him. She'd enjoy it. Or he c'n pop her over to Simon and Deborah. Deborah's dad can mind her or Deborah herself can. She's mad about kids. You know she is. Please, sir."

He was silent. She prayed. But when he responded, it was not to say anything that lifted her spirits.

"I've been to his lab, Barbara."

Her stomach was liquid. "Whose lab?"

"There's another connection, one that existed between Azhar and Italy far in advance of Hadiyyah's kidnapping and Angelina's death. You're going to need to come to terms with this, and you're going to need to prepare Hadiyyah to do the same."

"What?" She forced the word out. In the other room, she could hear the voice-over on the film of Angelina and Azhar, and she could hear Hadiyyah's chatter in Italian either to Signora Vallera or to her daughter.

Lynley said, "He has incubators, Barbara. Two sets of them, in fact. One set comes from here, from Birmingham. The other set comes from Italy."

"And?" she demanded, although her incredulity was forced. "He may have a bloody pair of Italian shoes as well, Inspector, but it's rubbish to think that has anything to do with Angelina dying over here. Italian incubators have nothing to do with anything anyway, and you know it. Christ, what if he has Italian olive oil in his kitchen cupboard? How 'bout a bag of imported pasta? What about cheese? He might like Parmesan."

"Are you quite finished? May I continue?" When she said nothing more, he did so. "Italian incubators in and of themselves mean nothing. But if you have incubators you also have the conditions under which the incubators are tested by the company that makes them, to make certain they do the job for which they were designed. Can we agree on that?"

She was silent for a moment, thinking about this. There was a heaviness within her that she couldn't ignore. "S'pose," she finally said.

"Right. And what better way to test those incubators, Barbara, than with the different kinds of bacteria they're meant to grow?"

She rallied. "Oh, please. That's completely ridiculous. So what did he do? Drop by the company over here and say, 'Afternoon, you lot. How 'bout handing over some truly virulent *E. coli* for a little romp on top of someone's pizza? Just to see, mind you, if the incubators really work?'"

"I think you know what I'm saying, Barbara."

"I bloody well don't."

"I'm saying there's another link. And you can't afford to ignore a link."

"And what, exactly, do you intend to do with this information?"

"It has to go to Chief Inspector Lo Bianco. What he then decides to do with it—"

"Oh, for God's bloody sake. What's the matter with you? You've lost the plot. And when did you become such a sodding prig? Who turned you, eh? Has to be *Isabelle*."

He was silent. She reckoned he was counting to ten. She knew she'd crossed over a line with the mention of Superintendent Ardery, but she was beyond social niceties at this point. He finally said, "Let's not venture in that direction."

She said, "No, no. Let's stick to what we know for sure. What *I* know is that you're not about to help me. Chuck Hadiyyah out with the bathwater and let her swim in it as best she can. That's your game, isn't it? You'll do your duty. Or whatever you do, you'll *call* it your duty. You'll sigh and say, 'It is what it is,' or some rubbish like that and meantime lives hang in the balance but what do you care because one of those lives isn't yours." She waited for him to reply to this and when he did not, she went on. "Well. Right, then. I won't ask you to hold back information for a day or two. That wouldn't be doing your *duty*, would it?"

"For the love of God, Barbara."

"It has nothing to do with God. Or with love. It has to do with what's right."

She cut off the call. She found her eyes were stinging. She found her palms were wet. Christ, she thought, she had to get herself *sorted*. She went to the breakfast room, downed a glass of orange juice still on the sideboard, sardonically thought, Whoops! Must be careful. Someone could've put *E. coli* in there. And she wanted to weep. But she had to think and what she thought first was that she would ring Simon and Deborah St. James. She would ask them. Or p'rhaps Winston. He lived with his parents, right? They could mind Hadiyyah, couldn't they? Or a girlfriend of his could do the minding. He had to have dozens. Or Mrs. Silver back in Chalk Farm who minded Hadiy-yah during school holidays. Except of course Chalk Farm would be the first place anyone would look for her, inside one of the other flats in the converted Edwardian house.

Something, something, something, she thought. She herself could take the child back to London, but that left Azhar to his fate and she couldn't have that. No matter what anyone said or anyone believed, she knew the truth of who the man was.

She went in search of Hadiyyah. For now she would keep the little girl with her. It was the best she could do. Come hell or what-ever, she had no intention of allowing her to fall into the hands of the Upmans.

Hadiyyah was still in the family area. Signora Vallera had joined her to watch the DVD, which looked to Barbara as if it was on its third or fourth time through the interview.

She sat in a straight-backed chair to watch along with the others as Angelina Upman and Taymullah Azhar talked about their missing child. The camera showed Angelina's exhausted face. The camera showed Azhar. The camera dollied back to show where they sat at the table beneath the arbour in the company of the man with the wart-infested face. He talked with such velocity and such passion that it was difficult to notice anything save him. The other two people, the table, the background . . . it all faded away as the man spat and roared.

Which, Barbara realised with a bolt of understanding, was why the film had played on television, had been given to Hadiyyah, had been watched and watched without a single person involved seeing what was in front of them the entire time.

"Oh my God," she murmured.

She felt dazed and her mind began to spin as she tried to come up with a next step and then another and then a third, all of which could evolve into a plan. Lynley, she knew, would not help her now. That left only one possibility.

LUCCA
TUSCANY

Thus, Mitchell Corsico was the proverbial port in the storm that was brewing. He'd been in Italy long enough to acquire the sort of sources Barbara needed now, but she knew he was going to want a deal. He wouldn't hand anything over to her unless he had his picture of Hadiyyah. So she rang his mobile and she prepared herself for a round of bargaining with the bloke.

"Where are you?" she asked him. "We need to talk."

"Your lucky day," he told her. He was just outside in the piazza at that very moment, enjoying a *caffè* and a brioche as he waited for Barb to come to her senses in the matter of Hadiyyah Upman. He'd been working on the story, by the way. It was a real tearjerker. Rodney Aronson was going to love it. Page one guaranteed.

Barbara said sourly, "You're the confident one, aren't you?"

"In this business, you'd better be confident. 'Sides, one gets to know the scent of desperation."

"Whose?"

"Oh, I wager you know."

She told him to stay where he was as she was coming out to meet him. She found him as promised: beneath an umbrella at a café table across from the *pensione*. He'd finished his coffee and pastry, and he was busily tapping away at his laptop. His remark of "Christ, I'm brilliant" as she reached him told her he was working on his Hadiyyah story.

She took from her bag the school photo of Hadiyyah that she had showed Aldo Greco on the previous day. She laid it on the table, but she didn't sit.

Mitch looked at the photo and then at her. "And this is . . . ?"

"What you want."

"Uh . . . no." He pushed it back to her and went on typing. "If I'm manufacturing horse dung here"—with a gesture at his laptop—"for the delectation of the great UK public, then something about the tale has to be genuine and what that something is going to be is a picture of the kid here in Italy."

"Mitch, listen—"

"*You* listen, Barb. F'r all Rod knows I'm here having the holiday of a lifetime although God knows why I'd choose Lucca to have it in since its after-dinner nightlife consists of hundreds of Italians on bikes, in trainers, or with pushchairs circling the town on that wall like crows contemplating fresh roadkill. But he doesn't know that, does he? Far as he's concerned, Lucca's Italy's answer to Miami Beach. I need something that shows him I'm hot on the trail of whatever. Now, from what I can tell, you need to *be* hot on the trail of whatever, so let's cooperate with each other. We'll start with a picture of the kid— showing she's in goddamn Italy, by the way—and we'll go from there."

Barbara could see that further argument would get her nowhere. She took back the photo of Hadiyyah and struck the deal. She'd get him that picture herself as there was no way in hell she ever wanted it getting back to Azhar that she'd allowed a tabloid journalist to photograph his daughter. She'd pose Hadiyyah at the window of the breakfast room, which looked out on the piazza. She'd photograph the front of the building so that Mitchell's editor would be able to see that his ace reporter was indeed in Italy with his nose to the grindstone. He could then edit the size of the picture any way he wanted to. Her guarantee was that Hadiyyah would look soulful in spades.

Corsico wasn't thrilled to bits with this plan, but he handed over his digital camera. Barbara took it from him and told him what she wanted in exchange for the picture, which was a conversation with one of his new Italian journalist mates, one with access to the television news.

"Why?" Corsico asked her warily.

"Just *do* it, Mitchell." She strode back across the piazza.

LUCCA
TUSCANY

When Salvatore took the phone call from DI Lynley, he saw at once that the connection suggested by the London man had more than one application. DARBA Italia, Lynley had told him, was the manufacturer of two of the incubators in the laboratory of Professor Taymullah Azhar, creating a heretofore unknown link between the microbiologist and Italy that needed exploration. Salvatore agreed with this, but the very idea of manufacturers of incubators prompted him to think in larger terms than a single company. At an international conference of microbiologists, surely manufacturers of the equipment they used showed up to demonstrate their wares in the hope of sales, no?

So he gave Ottavia Schwartz new direction under the topic of Investigating the Berlin Conference. She had two new assignments, he told her. Had manufacturers of laboratory equipment been present at the conference? If so, who were they and what individuals—by name—had represented them in Berlin?

"What are we looking for?" Ottavia asked, not unreasonably.

When Salvatore said that he wasn't entirely sure, she sighed, muttered, but got on with it.

He went to Giorgio Simione next. "DARBA Italia," he said to him. "I want to know everything about it."

"What is it?" Giorgio asked.

"I have no idea. That's why I want to know everything."

Salvatore was heading back to his office, then, when he saw Detective Sergeant Barbara Havers just entering the lobby of the *questura*. She was not accompanied by translator Marcella Lapaglia on this day, however. She was alone.

Salvatore went to her. She was, he noted, garbed not dissimilarly from the previous day. The clothes themselves were different, but their dishevelled nature was unchanged. Her tank top was, at least, tucked in. But as this emphasised the wine-barrel shape of her body, she might have been better advised to wear it untucked.

When she saw him, she began speaking, at a volume and with exaggerated movements that attempted to clarify what she was trying to tell him. In spite of himself, he had to smile. She was as earnest as he'd ever seen anyone. It took some fortitude to attempt to make oneself understood in a country where one was a stranger and didn't speak the language. In her place, he wondered if he'd be able to do the same.

She pointed to herself. "I," she said, "want you"—pointing at him—"to watch"—pointing to her eyeballs—"this"—pointing to the screen of a laptop that she was holding.

"Ah. You want I must to watch something," he said in his terrible English. Then, "*Che cos'è? E perché? Mi dispiace, ma sono molto occupato stamattina.*"

"Bloody goddamn," the woman muttered to herself. "What'd he just say?"

She went through the pointing and speaking routine a second time. Salvatore realised it would be quicker to watch whatever she wanted him to watch than it would be to find someone who could translate what he already understood. So he gestured that she was to follow him to his office. On the way he asked Ottavia to find the usual translator on the chance that what the English detective wanted him to see was going to prompt him to ask her questions. Barring that individual's availability, he told her, find someone else. But not Birgit. *Chiaro?*

Ottavia raised an eyebrow at the Birgit part, but she nodded. She shot a look at the detective sergeant that managed to convey an Italian woman's incredulity that a member of the same gender would wander about thus garbed, but then she went about her business. She would find someone and she would do it quickly.

Salvatore ushered the detective sergeant into his office. He said politely, "*Un caffè?*" to which Sergeant Havers went on at some length. Among her words, Salvatore caught one: *time.* Ah, he thought. She was telling him they did not have time. Bah, Salvatore thought. There was always time for *caffè.*

He went to make it after gesturing her into a seat. When he returned to his office, she'd set up her laptop in the middle of his desk and she was standing at the ready. She'd lit a cigarette, which she looked at, gestured to, and said, "Hope it's *buono* with you." Salvatore smiled, nodded, and opened a window. He indicated the *caffè* he'd brought her. She put two sugar cubes into it, but during the course of their meeting, she never took a sip.

As he stirred his own *caffè,* she said, "Ready?" with lifted eyebrows. She pointed to the laptop and smiled encouragingly. He shrugged his acceptance. She left-clicked on the laptop and gestured Salvatore over to join her at the desk.

She said, "Right. Well, watch *this*, Salvatore," from which he presumed she meant *guardi*, so that was what he did. In short order he found himself viewing the interview of Angelina Upman and Taymullah Azhar that had appeared on the television news. It contained their appeal for the safety of their child and their appeal for her return. It also contained Piero Fanucci's frothing rant about bringing the malefactor to justice one way or the other. Salvatore cooperatively watched the sequence, but he gained absolutely nothing from it. When it was over, he looked at Barbara Havers, frowning. She pointed upward with a finger and said, "Wait," and she directed him to watch the screen where the film continued.

The sequence comprised conversation that was mostly inaudible during which people removed their microphones. Salvatore didn't see what any of this had to do with anything. Then Lorenzo Mura appeared with a tray. On it were an array of wineglasses and plates that he began to hand out to the film crew. He then set a plate and a glass in front of Fanucci, gave the same to the reporter, and then to Taymullah Azhar. To Angelina he gave only a plate.

Barbara Havers froze the picture at that moment. She pointed to the screen and said with excitement in her voice, "There's your *E. coli*, Salvatore. It's right there in the glass he gave to Azhar."

Salvatore heard "*E. coli*." From where she was directing his attention—her finger pointing to the glass sitting in front of the professor—he understood what she meant. He was less clear when she went on, her voice so rapid that only individual names were clear to him. She said, "He intended Azhar, not Angelina, to drink the wine with the *E. coli* in it. But he didn't know that Azhar's a Muslim. He has one vice that he shouldn't have—he smokes—but he doesn't drink. And he does the whole Muslim bit from A to Z otherwise. The hajj, the fasting, the almsgiving, whatever. But he *doesn't* drink. He probably never has. Angelina knew that, so she took the wine from him. Here, watch." And she showed the next sequence of the film. In it, Angelina took the wine meant for Azhar and Barbara Havers said with a wink at him, "Just like bloody *Hamlet*, eh, mate? Mura tried to stop her from drinking it, but she thought he was just worried because she was pregnant. So what the hell was he supposed to do? I expect he could've leapt over the table and dashed the glass out of her hand. But it all happened too fast. She just knocked the vino back. And then? That's what you want to ask, eh? Well, he could've made her sick it up, I s'pose, or he could've thrown himself on her mercy and told the truth, but he was never completely sure of her, was he? No bloke ever was. She loved 'em and she left 'em and sometimes she had three of 'em at once and that's just who she was. It's what, I expect, made her different from her sister and God knows they wanted to be different from each other. But let's suppose he goes ahead and tells her what he's done—sorry, darling, but you've just knocked back a glass of deadly bacteria—and *then* what? How does she view him then, eh?"

Nearly all of which Salvatore did not follow. So he was more than grateful when Ottavia appeared with the *questura*'s translator, a multilingual and distractingly buxom thirtyish woman showing so much cleavage—*Dio*, was it eight inches?—that he momentarily forgot her name. Then it came to him: Giuditta Something. She asked how she could be of assistance.

She and Barbara Havers spoke at some length. After an equally lengthy translation from Giuditta, Salvatore asked only two questions. Both were crucial to building a case if, indeed, a case even could be built on something that seemed so speculative. How? he wanted to know. And why?

Barbara Havers went with the why first: Why would Lorenzo Mura want to kill this man Taymullah Azhar? Good question, Salvatore. He, after all, had won Azhar's woman. He had taken her from the Pakistani man. She lived with him in Italy, far from London. He had made her pregnant. They were to marry. What was the point?

"But who could ever be sure of Angelina Upman?" was the Englishwoman's explanation. "She'd messed about with Esteban Castro while she was with Azhar. She'd left them both for Lorenzo Mura. Anyone could see there was still a bond between Azhar and her, and beyond that, they shared Hadiyyah. Once Azhar appeared on the scene, he was going to be a permanent fixture in their lives. She might have decided to return to him. Who the hell *ever* knew what she would do?"

"But ridding their lives of Azhar would not have made his own position with Angelina secure," Salvatore pointed out.

Barbara listened to the translation, then said, "Sure, but he wasn't thinking like that. He wasn't looking at the big picture of If Not Azhar, Then Who Else Might She Leave Me For? He just wanted Azhar gone and he was doing it the best way he knew: make him good and ill and hope he keels over and there's an end to the problem. Salvatore, when people are jealous, they don't think straight. They just want the object of their jealousy gone. Or ruined. Or devastated. Or what*ever*. But what did Lorenzo Mura have? The return of the rejected lover, Hadiyyah's dad back in Hadiyyah's life, Hadiyyah's dad back in *Angelina's* life."

"Men survive that sort of thing all the time."

"But those men aren't entangled with Angelina."

Salvatore considered this. It was plausible, he thought. But it was only *plausible*. There still existed the biggest sticking point: the *E. coli* itself. If what the sergeant was saying was true, how had Lorenzo come to put his hands upon it? And not just *E. coli* but a deadly strain of it.

He spoke to the detective sergeant about this: about the *how* of the *E. coli*'s acquisition. She listened but could offer him no advice. They—along with Giuditta—meditated in silence upon this thorny issue. Then Giorgio Simione came into Salvatore's office.

For a moment, Salvatore blinked at him in absolute incomprehension. He'd given him an assignment, but he couldn't recall what it was, even when Giorgio said helpfully, "DARBA, *Ispettore*."

Salvatore said, "*Come?*" and repeated the word. When Giorgio said, "DARBA Italia," Salvatore recalled.

"It's here in Lucca," Giorgio told him. "It's on the route to Montecatini."

LUCCA
TUSCANY

Mitchell Corsico had to be dealt with first. He'd done her an enormous favour in getting the entire, unedited television news film via one of the contacts he'd made with the Italian journalists. He was going to want the payoff for this, and he was going to need to pass along a juicy and otherwise significant detail to the Italian who'd helped him in the first place. Quid pro quo and all that. So Barbara had to tell him something, and she had to make sure it was something good.

When she understood from the translator that Salvatore's intention was an unannounced call upon DARBA Italia, she fully intended to accompany him there. But she couldn't have Mitch Corsico tagging along with them. She and Salvatore needed time to pin down their information. What they didn't need was any of it leaking to the press.

She'd left him in the café down the street from the *questura*, across the road from the railway station, and the last thing she'd needed was Salvatore Lo Bianco putting his hooded gaze upon the UK's version of the Lone Ranger sans mask. Because of the distance and the crowds of people milling about, she knew she'd be able to make her escape from the *questura* without Mitchell becoming wise to her whereabouts. But if he discovered she'd done this, there would be hell to pay.

She had to use half-truths. While Salvatore went for a vehicle in the car park next to the *questura*, she rang Corsico.

"We've got a potential source for the *E. coli*," she told him. "I'm heading there now."

"Hang the hell on. You and I had an agreement. I'm not letting you—"

"You'll get the story, Mitch, and you'll get it first. But 'f you show up now and want to play tagalong, Salvatore's going to want to know who you are. And believe me, that'll be tough to explain. He trusts me, and we need to keep things that way. He finds I'm leaking to the press, we're done for."

"It's *Salvatore* now? What the hell's going on?"

"Oh for God's bloody sake. He's a colleague. We're heading for a place called DARBA Italia, and that's all I know just now. It's here in Lucca, and 'f you ask me, it's the source of the *E. coli* and that's where Lorenzo Mura got it."

"If it's here in Lucca, it could also be where the professor got it," Corsico pointed out. "He was here in April looking for the kid. All he had to do was waltz over to this place and make the buy."

"Oh, too right. Are you trying to tell me that Azhar—a man who speaks no Italian, by the way—swanned over to DARBA Italia with euros in hand and said, 'How much for a test tube of the worst bacteria you lot have going? I'll need something I don't grow in my own lab, so all forms of *Strep* are off the table.' And then what, Mitch? One of their salesmen tap-danced into the place where they keep this stuff—Quality Control, maybe?—and nicked a little bacteria without anyone noticing? Don't be a fool. This stuff is going to be controlled. It can take out an entire population, for the love of God."

"So why the hell are you going there? Because what you just said—save not speaking Italian—applies to Lorenzo Mura as well. And while we're talking about this whole bloody mess, how the hell do you know they have *E. coli* in the first place?"

"I *don't* know. That's why we're paying them a visit."

"And?"

"And what?"

"I'm sitting here waiting for a story, Barb."

"You've got your piece on Hadiyyah. Go with that."

"Rod's not chuffed. He says page five. He says Professor Falsely Imprisoned is the only path to page one. Thing is, of course, from what you just told me it sounds like the *falsely* part of the headline might not be needed."

"I've told you how—"

"I got you the television film. What's the payoff for me?"

Salvatore Lo Bianco pulled to the kerb and leaned over to push open the passenger door. Barbara said, "It's coming. I swear I'll keep you in the loop. I've given you DARBA Italia. Ask your Italian journalist mates to take things from there."

"And give them the story ahead of me? Come on, Barb—"

"It's the best I can do." She ended the call and got into the car. She nodded to Salvatore and said, "Let's go."

"*Andiamo*," he told her with a smile.

"Back at you, mate," she replied.

VICTORIA

LONDON

Isabelle Ardery's meeting with the assistant commissioner had lasted two hours. Lynley had this information from the most reliable source: David Hillier's secretary. It didn't come to him directly, though. The conduit was the redoubtable Dorothea Harriman. Dorothea cultivated sources of information the way farmers cultivate crops. She had informants within the Met, the Home Office, and the Houses of Parliament. So she knew from Judi MacIntosh the length of the meeting between Hillier and Ardery and she knew it had been tense. She also knew that present at the meeting had been two blokes from CIB. She didn't know their names—"I did try, Detective Inspector Lynley"— but the only details she had managed to unearth were that the blokes had come from one of the two arms of the Complaints Investigation Bureau, and that arm was CIB1. Lynley received this titbit with a frisson of apprehension. CIB1 dealt with internal complaints. CIB1 dealt with internal discipline.

The superintendent didn't offer to share the content of her meeting. Lynley tried to learn something useful from her, but her quick and firm "Don't let's go there, Tommy" told him that things were in motion and the nature of those things was as serious as he'd earlier concluded they might be when she'd phoned Hillier and asked for a meeting.

So he was deeply thoughtful when he took a surprising and welcome phone call from Daidre Trahair. She'd come to town to look for a flat, she told him. Would he like to meet her for lunch in Marylebone?

He said, "You've taken the job? That's brilliant, Daidre."

"They've a silverback gorilla that's quite won my heart," she said. "It's love on my part, but I can't say how he feels just yet."

"Time will tell."

"It always does, doesn't it?"

They met in Marylebone High Street, where he found her waiting inside a tiny restaurant at a very small table tucked into a corner. He knew his face lit up when she raised her head from studying the menu and saw him. She smiled in return and lifted a hand in hello.

He kissed her and thought how completely normal it felt to be doing so. He said, "Have Boadicea's Broads gone into permanent mourning?"

She said, "Let's say that my stock isn't very high with them at the moment."

"The Electric Magic, on the other hand, must be breaking out the bubbly."

"One can only hope."

He sat and gazed at her. "It's very good to see you. I needed a tonic, and it seems you're it."

She cocked her head, examined him, and said, "I must say it. You're a tonic as well."

"For . . . ?"

"The grim process of looking at flats. Until I sell up in Bristol, I'm beginning to think I'll be sleeping upright in someone's broom closet."

"There are solutions to that," he told her.

"I wasn't hinting at your spare room."

"Ah. My loss."

"Not entirely, Tommy."

At that, he felt his heart pound harder a few times, but he said nothing. Instead he smiled, took up the menu, asked what she was having, and gave their orders to a waiter hovering nearby expectantly. He asked her how long she was in town. She said four days and this was the third. He asked her why she hadn't phoned sooner. She said the business of finding a flat, of meeting people at the zoo, of seeing what was needed to organise her offices and labs, of speaking with the various keepers about problems they were encountering with the animals . . . It had all taken up so much of her time. But how lovely it was to see him now.

This, he thought, would have to suffice. Perhaps it was enough to feel how engaged he became in her presence, as the rest of the day faded into insignificance.

Unfortunately, that engagement in her presence did not last long. As their starters were set before them, his mobile rang. He glanced at it and saw, heart sinking, that it was Havers. He said to Daidre, "I'm sorry. I'll have to take this call."

"I need your help" was Havers's first remark.

"You need more than what I can provide. Isabelle's had a meeting with two blokes from CIB."

"That doesn't matter."

"Have you entirely lost your mind?"

"I know you're cheesed off. But Salvatore and I are onto something over here, and what I need from you is a piece of information. One little piece of information, Inspector."

"Coming from which side of the law?"

"It's completely legitimate."

"Unlike virtually everything else you've done."

"All right. Agreed. I get it, sir. You need to scourge me and the only thing wanting is a pillar. We c'n see to that when I get back. Meantime, like I said, I just need one piece of information."

"Which is what, exactly?" He glanced at Daidre. She'd tucked into her starter. He rolled his eyes expressively.

"The Upmans are on their way to Italy. They're coming to fetch Hadiyyah. I need to prevent that. If they get their mitts on her, they'll keep her from Azhar."

"Barbara, if you're heading in the direction of my intercepting—"

"I know you can't stop them, sir. I just need to know if they're on their way *now* to fetch Hadiyyah. I need to know what flight they're on and which of them is coming. It would also help to know the airport. It might be the parents coming—they're called Ruth-Jane and Humphrey—or it might be Bathsheba Ward, the sister. If you ring the airlines and check the flight manifests . . . You know you can do this. Or you can get SO12 to do it. That's it. That's all I need. And it's not for my own sake. It's not even for Azhar's. It's for Hadiyyah's sake. Please."

He sighed. He knew Havers would not relent. He said, "Winston's checking into everyone here associated with Angelina Upman, Barbara. He's looking for any connection that might point from here to Italy among people she knew. So far, there's nothing."

"And there won't be, sir. Mura's our man. He intended Azhar to ingest the *E. coli.* Salvatore and I are heading to a place called DARBA Italia to prove it."

"That's the incubator company from Azhar's lab, Barbara. Surely, you can see how this points to—"

"Right. I can see it. And for the record, Salvatore's made the same point."

"Salvatore? How exactly are you managing to communicate with him?"

"Lots of hand gestures. Plus he smokes, so I think we've bonded. Look, sir, will you sort out the Upmans-on-their-way-to-Italy situation? Will you have SO12 do it? One piece of information. That's it. Full stop. And it's not for me. It's for—"

"Hadiyyah. Yes, yes. I've received your point."

"So . . . ?"

"I'll see what I can do."

He rang off then and looked for a moment not at Daidre but at the wall, where a stylish photograph of cliffs and the sea put him in mind of Cornwall. Daidre, apparently seeing the direction of his gaze, said, "Considering an escape?"

He glanced back at her and thought about the question. He finally said, "From some things, yes. From others, no." And he reached across the small table for her hand.

LUCCA
TUSCANY

In the best of all worlds, Barbara thought, Lynley would somehow manage to stop the Upmans before they reached the airport or, at least, before they boarded the plane to Italy. But she didn't live in the best of all worlds, so she reckoned they were on their way, whoever was coming. What was available to her was the knowledge of their whereabouts and her ability to dodge them when they reached Lucca. They would go first to Fattoria di Santa Zita, where they would presume Hadiyyah was still in residence with Lorenzo Mura. He would tell them she'd been fetched by Barbara. He might reckon Barbara was staying where Azhar had stayed. But he might not.

In any case, she had only a limited amount of time to get Hadiyyah out of the Pensione Giardino and into a hideaway somewhere. And before she did that, she needed to see what Salvatore managed to uncover at DARBA Italia.

It didn't take long to reach the manufacturing concern. They did a quarter's circumnavigation along the boulevard that skirted Lucca's wall, and then they took a sharp right and headed out of the town. DARBA Italia was some three miles along the road, tucked off a neatly paved driveway and posted with an elaborate metal sign above double glass doors. There were very few trees in the immediate vicinity and lots of asphalt in the car park, so the heat was intense and it rose in visible waves from the ground. Barbara hustled after Salvatore to get inside the place, praying for air conditioning.

Naturally, she couldn't follow a word of the Italian that passed between Salvatore and the receptionist, who was a gloriously hand-some Mediterranean youth of about twenty-two: olive skin, masses of wavy hair, lips like a Renaissance putto, and teeth so white they looked painted. Salvatore showed his police ID, gestured to Barbara, and spoke at great length. The receptionist listened, shot a glance at Barbara that dismissed her as quickly as it acknowledged her presence, nodded, said *sì* and *no* and *forse* and *un attimo*, of which only *sì* and *no* were remotely recognisable. Then he picked up his phone and punched in a number. He turned his back, spoke in a hushed voice, and made some sort of arrangement, since his next action was to rise from his chair and tell them they were to follow him. At least, that was what Barbara worked out from his words since Salvatore trailed him into the bowels of the building.

Things happened far too quickly for Barbara's liking after that. The receptionist took them to a conference room where a mahogany table in the centre was accompanied by ten leather chairs. He said something to Salvatore about the *direttore*, which she took to mean that the managing director of DARBA Italia was the person they were going to see. That person showed up perhaps five minutes into their wait. He was beautifully suited and equally well mannered but clearly curious about the police showing up on his professional doorstep.

She caught only his name: Antonio Bruno. She waited for more.

There was very little. Salvatore spoke, and she strained to pick up *E. coli* from among the flood of Italian that came from him. But nothing in Antonio Bruno's expression indicated he was listening to a tale of anyone's death by any substance that DARBA Italia might have provided. After an exchange of seven minutes' length, the managing director nodded and left them.

She said to Salvatore, "What? What's he doing? What'd you tell him?" although she knew it was useless to expect an answer. But her need to know overrode her ability to reason. She said, "Do they have *E. coli*? Do they know Lorenzo Mura? This has nothing to do with Azhar, does it?"

To this, Salvatore smiled regretfully and said, "*Non La capisco.*" Barbara reckoned she knew what that meant.

The return of Antonio Bruno didn't clarify anything. He came back to the conference room with a manila envelope, which he handed over to Salvatore. Salvatore thanked him and headed for the door. He said, "*Andiamo, Barbara,*" and to Antonio Bruno with a courtly little bow, "*Grazie mille, Signor Bruno.*"

Barbara waited till they were outside to say, "That's *it*? What's going on? Why're we leaving? What'd he give you?"

From all of this, Salvatore seemed to understand the last question, for he handed over the manila envelope, and Barbara opened it. Inside was only a list of employees, organised by each of the company's departments. Names, addresses, and telephone numbers. There were plenty of them, dozens. Her heart sank when she saw them. She knew, then, that Salvatore Lo Bianco was engaged in the slog of an investigation: He would look into each person listed among the employees of DARBA Italia. But that would take days upon days to accomplish, and they didn't have days before the Upmans arrived.

Barbara needed results and she needed them now. She began to consider how best to get them.

LUCCA

TUSCANY

For the first time, Salvatore Lo Bianco thought that the woman from London might actually be correct. He could tell when she began a passionate discourse that she had no idea why they were leaving DARBA Italia so abruptly and he certainly didn't have the English to tell her. But he managed *"Pazienza, Barbara,"* and it appeared that she understood. Nothing happened quickly in Italy, he wanted to tell her, save the rapidity with which people spoke the language and the speed with which they drove their cars. Everything else was a case of *piano, piano.*

She was tumbling through words he did not understand. "We don't have the time, Salvatore. Hadiyyah's family . . . The Upmans . . . These people . . . If you only understood what they intend to do. They hate Azhar. They've always hated him. See, he wouldn't marry her once he got her pregnant and anyway the fact that he got her pregnant and he's a Pakistani and they're . . . God, they're like something out of the Raj, if you know what I mean. What I'm trying to say is if we—I mean you—have to go through every single one of those names on this list"—she waved the manila folder at him—"by the time we do that, Hadiyyah will be lost to him, to Azhar."

He recognised, naturally, the repetition of names: Hadiyyah, the Upmans, and Azhar. He recognised, also, her agitation. But all he could say was *"Andiamo, Barbara,"* with a gesture at the car that was steaming in the day's heat.

She followed him, but she didn't give up talking despite the many times he said with much regret, *"Non La capisco."* He did wish that he spoke her language better—at least enough to tell her not to worry—but when he said, *"Non si deve preoccupare,"* he could tell she didn't understand. They were like two inhabitants of Babel.

He started the car and they were on their way back to the *questura* when her mobile rang. When she said into it, "Inspector? Thank God," he reckoned it was Lynley ringing her. From her earlier call to the London detective, he knew she'd asked him about the Upmans. He hoped for her sake that Thomas Lynley had discovered something that would relieve her anxiety.

That was not the case. She cried out like a wounded animal, saying, "Bloody hell, no! *Florence?* That's not far from here, is it? Let me send her to you. Please, sir. I'm begging. They'll find her. I know it. Mura will tell them I took her and they'll look for me and how the hell hard will it be for them to find me, eh? They'll take her away and I won't be able to stop them and it'll destroy Azhar. It'll kill him, Inspector, and he's been through enough and you know it, you *know* it."

Salvatore glanced at her. It was odd, he thought, her passion for this case. He'd never encountered a fellow cop with such a fierce determination to prove anything.

She was saying, "Salvatore took us to DARBA Italia like I said. But all he did was get us in to see the managing director and that was it. He picked up a bloody list of employees but he didn't ask a single question about *E. coli* and there's no time to go at things this way. Everything hangs in the balance. You know this, sir. Hadiyyah, Azhar, everyone's at risk here."

She listened to something Lynley was saying. Salvatore glanced at her. He saw tears sparkling on the tips of her eyelashes. Her fist pounded lightly on her knee.

She handed him the mobile phone, finally, saying unnecessarily, "It's Inspector Lynley."

Lynley's first words were said on a sigh. *"Ciao, Salvatore. Che cosa succede?"*

But instead of telling the London man about their visit to DARBA Italia, Salvatore sought some clarification. He said, "Something tells me, my friend, that you have not been completely honest with me about this woman Barbara and her relationship to the professor and his daughter. Why is this, Tommaso?"

Lynley said nothing for a moment. Salvatore wondered where he was: at work, at home, out questioning someone? The London man finally said, *"Mi dispiace, Salvatore."* He went on to explain that Taymullah Azhar and his daughter Hadiyyah were neighbours of Barbara Havers, in London. He said that she was quite fond of them both.

Salvatore narrowed his eyes. "What means this *fond*?"

"She's close to them."

"Are they lovers, Barbara and the professor?"

"Good God, no. It isn't that. She's jumped off into some deep water, Salvatore, and I should have told you when she showed up over there, when you first rang me about her."

"What has she done? To be in this deep water, I mean."

"What hasn't she done?" Lynley said. "Just now she's gone to Italy without leave from the Met to do so. She's determined to save Azhar in order to save Hadiyyah. That's it in a nutshell."

Salvatore glanced at Barbara Havers. She was watching him, a fist pressed to her mouth, her eyes—such a nice blue they were—fixed on him like a frightened animal. He said to Lynley, "Her greater interest is the child, you are saying?"

"Yes and no," Lynley told him.

"Meaning what, Tommaso?"

"Meaning that she's telling herself her greater interest is the child. As to the reality? That I don't know. To be honest, my fear is that she's blinded herself."

"Ah. Mine is that she sees things too clearly."

"Meaning?"

"She may have proved me as lacking as Piero Fanucci when it comes to seeing the truth, my friend. I have spoken to the managing director of DARBA Italia. He is called Antonio Bruno."

"Good God. Is he indeed?"

"He is indeed. I'm on my way to discuss this with Ottavia Schwartz. If I hand this phone back to Barbara Havers, will you tell her please that things are well in hand?"

"I will do. But, Salvatore, Hadiyyah's grandparents have landed in Florence. They'll be on their way to Lucca to fetch her. The child doesn't know them. But she does know Barbara."

"Ah," Salvatore said. "I see."

LUCCA
TUSCANY

All he said to her was "Barbara, you can trust Salvatore," but she wasn't prepared to trust a soul. What she needed to know was how long it might take for the Upmans to get from Florence to Lucca.

Would they come by train? Would they hire a car? Would they arrange for an Italian driver? No matter how they did it, she needed to get to the *pensione* in Piazza Anfiteatro in advance of them, so she told Salvatore to take her there. She told him in English, but he seemed to understand from *pensione*, *Piazza Anfiteatro*, and the repetition of Hadiyyah's name.

Once inside the *pensione* itself, she took a few breaths. It was essential, she thought, not to panic Hadiyyah. It was also essential to work out where the bloody hell she was going to take her. Out of Lucca seemed best, some obscure hotel on the edge of town. She'd seen plenty of them on her route in from the airport as well as on her route to and from DARBA Italia. She'd have to rely on Mitch Corsico to help her out with this manoeuvre, though. She didn't want to do it as she was loath to give him access to Hadiyyah, but there wasn't much choice.

She ran up the stairs. Signora Vallera, she saw, was cleaning one of the bedrooms. She said, "Hadiyyah?" to the woman, who gestured to the bedroom that Barbara and the child were sharing. Inside, Hadiyyah was sitting at the small table by the window. She looked completely forlorn. Barbara's determination hardened. She *would* get both Hadiyyah and her father back to London.

"Hey, kiddo," she said as brightly as she could. "We're going to need a change of scenery, you and me. Are you up for that?"

"You were gone a long time," Hadiyyah told her. "I didn't know where you went. Why didn't you tell me where you were going? Barbara, where's my dad? Why doesn't he come? 'Cause it's like . . ." Her lips trembled. She finally said, "Barbara, did something happen to my dad?"

"God, no. Absolutely not. Like I said, kiddo, and I cross my heart on this one, he's gone out of Lucca on some business for Inspector Lo Bianco. I came over from London because he asked me to, to make sure you didn't worry about where he went." It was, even without a stretch, the basic truth about what was going on.

"C'n we meet him somewhere, then?"

"Absolutely. Just not quite yet. Just now, we need to pack our things and skedaddle."

"Why? 'Cause if we leave, how'll Dad find us?"

Barbara dug out her mobile and held it up. "Won't be a problem," she said.

She wasn't as confident as she sounded. She'd hoped the trip out to DARBA Italia would have put the nails in someone's coffin. But it hadn't done, and now she was faced with the big What Next? Corsico was going to have to be appeased, and in the meantime she was going to have to find a place for herself and Hadiyyah that would allow her access to what was going on with the case at the same time as it protected them from the tabloid journalist's discovery as well as the discovery of Hadiyyah's maternal grandparents. She thought about all this as she gathered up her things and shoved them higgledy-piggledy into her duffel. After making sure that Hadiyyah was packed up as well, she clattered down the stairs with the little girl following. At the foot of them, she found Salvatore waiting.

Her first thought was that he intended to stop her. But she soon discovered that she was wrong. Instead, he negotiated payment with Signora Vallera, picked up Hadiyyah's suitcase and Barbara's duffel, and nodded towards the door. He said, "*Seguitemi, Barbara e Hadiyyah,*" and he walked outside. He didn't take them to his car, however. Instead, he headed out of the amphitheatre on foot and wound his way through the narrow medieval streets. These led into the occasional unexpected piazza ruled over by one of the city's ubiquitous churches, past shuttered buildings where the occasional opened double doors gave glimpses of hidden courtyards and gardens, and along the fronts of businesses just reopening after the day's break for lunch and rest.

Barbara knew there was no point in asking where they were going, and it was some way along the route before it occurred to her that Hadiyyah's youthful Italian would probably serve the purpose perfectly. She was about to ask the little girl to make the enquiry of Salvatore Lo Bianco, when he stopped at a narrow structure many floors tall and set down the duffel and the suitcase.

He said to them, "*Torre Lo Bianco,*" and fished in his pocket to produce a key ring. Barbara got the Lo Bianco part, but it wasn't until he opened the door with the key and called out, "*Mamma? Mamma, ci sei?*" that she twigged this was his mother's home. Before she could clarify this or protest or say anything at all, an elderly woman with well-coiffed grey hair appeared from an inner room. She wore a heavy apron over a black linen dress, she was drying her hands on a towel, and she was saying, "Salvatore," in greeting and then in a different tone, "*Chi sono?*" as her dark eyes took in Barbara first and then Hadiyyah, partially hidden behind her. She smiled at Hadiyyah, which Barbara took for a good sign. She said, "*Che bambina carina,*" and bending to put her hands on her knees, "*Dimmi, come ti chiami?*"

"Hadiyyah," Hadiyyah said, and when the woman said, "*Ah! Parli italiano?*" Hadiyyah nodded. Her "*un po'*" produced another smile from the woman.

"*Ma la donna, no,*" Salvatore told her. "*Parla solo inglese.*"

"*Hadiyyah può tradurre, no?*" Salvatore's mother replied. She spied the duffel and the suitcase, which Salvatore had left on the doorstep. "*Allora, sono ospiti?*" she said to her son. And when he nodded, she held out her hand to Hadiyyah. She said, "*Vieni, Hadiyyah. Faremo della pasta insieme. D'accordo?*" She began to lead Hadiyyah farther into the house.

Barbara said, "Hang on. What's going on, Hadiyyah?"

Hadiyyah said, "We're staying here with Salvatore's mum."

"Ah. As to the rest?"

"She's going to show me how to make pasta."

Barbara said to Salvatore, "Ta. I mean *grazie*. I c'n at least say *grazie*."

He said, "*Niente,*" and went on a bit, gesturing towards a stone stairway that climbed up what was clearly a tower as well as being the family home.

Barbara said to Hadiyyah, "What's he saying, kiddo?"

Hadiyyah said over her shoulder to Barbara, "He lives here, too."

LUCCA
TUSCANY

In the way of all things Italian, they had to eat first. Barbara wanted to deal at once with the list of employees Salvatore had brought with him from DARBA Italia, but he seemed as intent upon having a meal as his mother was intent upon serving one. He did make a phone call, however, speaking to someone called Ottavia. Barbara heard DARBA Italia mentioned and then the name Antonio Bruno several times. From this she took hope that someone at the *questura* was checking into something. This made her doubly eager to get out of Torre Lo Bianco, but she learned that no one put Salvatore and his mamma off their food. It was simple enough: roasted red and yellow peppers, cheese, several kinds of meat, bread, and olives, along with red wine and, afterwards, more Italian coffee and a plate of biscuits.

Then Salvatore's mamma began bringing forth the ingredients for Hadiyyah's experience in homemade pasta, and Salvatore and Barbara left the tower. Once outside, she saw that the building was indeed a bona fide tower. There were others in the town whose shape she'd clocked without really taking in what they were as they'd long ago been converted to shops and other businesses that disguised their original purpose. This one, though, was unmistakable, a perfect square soaring into the air, with some kind of greenery draping over the edges of the roof.

Salvatore led the way back to the car. In very short order, they returned to the *questura*. He parked, said, "*Venga, Barbara,*" and Barbara congratulated herself on her budding understanding of the language. She went with him.

They didn't get far. Mitchell Corsico was leaning against a wall directly across the street from the *questura*, and he did not look like a happy cowpoke. Barbara saw him the same moment that he saw her. He came in their direction. She walked more quickly, in the hope of getting into the building before he reached them, but he wasn't about to be played for a fool a second time. He cut her off, which in effect cut Salvatore off as well.

"Just what the bloody hell is going on?" he demanded hotly. "D'you know how long I've been waiting for you? And why aren't you answering your mobile? I've rung you four times."

Salvatore looked from her to Mitchell Corsico. His solemn gaze took in the journalist's Stetson, the Western shirt, the bolo tie, the jeans, the boots. He seemed confused, and who could blame him? This bloke was either dressed for a costume party or he was an evacuee from the American Wild West via time machine.

Salvatore frowned. He said, "*Chi è, Barbara?*"

She ignored him for the moment, saying to Mitch as pleasantly as she could, "You're going to cock things up if you don't leave immediately."

"I don't think so," he said. "The leaving part, I mean. I don't think I'll be leaving. Not without a story."

"I gave you a story. And you've had your bloody picture of Hadiyyah." Barbara shot a glance at Salvatore. For the first time she was thankful that he spoke practically no English. No one would conclude that Mitchell Corsico—dressed as he was—was a journalist. She needed to keep things that way.

Corsico said, "That pony isn't about to gallop. Rod wasn't chuffed by the winsome photo. He's running the story but only because it's our lucky day and no politician got caught in a car behind King's Cross Station last night."

"There's nothing more, Mitch. Not just now. And there's not going to *be* more if my companion here"—she didn't dare use Salvatore's name and clue him in that he was part of the discussion—"works out who you are and what your living is."

Mitch grabbed her arm. "Are you threatening me? I'm not playing games with you."

Salvatore said quickly, "*Ha bisogno d'aiuto, Barbara?*" And he clutched onto Corsico's hand tightly. "*Chi è quest'uomo? Il Suo amante?*"

"What the bloody hell . . . ?" Corsico said. He winced at the strength of Salvatore's grip.

"I don't know what he's saying," Barbara said. "But my guess is that if you don't back away, you're going to find yourself in the nick."

"I *helped* you," he said tersely. "I got you the bloody television film.

I want what you know and you're double-crossing me and there's no way in hell—"

Salvatore twisted Mitch's hand sharply away from Barbara's arm, bending the fingers back so far that Corsico yelped. He said, "Jesus. Call Spartacus off, all right?" He took a step back, massaged his fingers, and glared at her.

She said quietly, "Look, Mitchell. All I know is we went to a place where they make equipment for scientists. He talked to the managing director there for less than five minutes, and a list of employees is what we came up with. He's carrying the list in that envelope he's holding. And that's all I know."

"Am I supposed to get a story out of that?"

"Christ, I'm telling you what I know. When there's a story, I'll give it to you but there isn't a story yet. Now you've got to leave and I've got to think of some bloody way to explain who you are because, believe me, once he and I"—with a jerk of her head at Salvatore— "walk into the *questura*, he's going to fetch a translator and give me a proper grilling and *if* he twigs that you're a you-know-what, we are cooked. Both of us. Do you understand what happens then? No breaking story at all, and how's your mate Rodney going to feel about that?"

Finally, Mitchell Corsico hesitated. His gaze flicked to Salvatore, who was watching with an expression that combined distrust with calculation. Barbara didn't know what the Italian was thinking, but *whatever* he was thinking, his face seemed to support what she was claiming. Corsico said to Barbara in an altered tone, "Barb, this better not be bollocks."

"Would I be that stupid?"

"Oh, I expect you would." But he backed off, showing upheld empty hands to Salvatore. He said to Barbara, "You answer your mobile when I ring you, mate."

"If I can, I will."

He turned on his booted heel and left them, striding towards the café near the railway station. Barbara knew he'd wait there for some sort of word. He owed his editor a Big Story in exchange for this jaunt to Italy, and he wasn't going to rest until he had one.

LUCCA
TUSCANY

Salvatore watched the cowboy walk off, his long strides made seemingly longer by the straight-legged jeans and the boots he wore. They made an odd couple, this man and Barbara Havers, Salvatore thought. But the nature of attraction had always been something of a mystery to him. He could understand why the cowboy might be attracted to Barbara Havers with her expressive face and fine blue eyes. He couldn't, on the other hand, understand at all what would attract Barbara Havers to him. This would be the Englishman who had first accompanied her to see Aldo Greco, however. The *avvocato* had spoken of him, using the term *her English companion* or something very like. Salvatore wondered what that term really meant.

Bah, he thought. He had no time for these considerations, and of what import were they? He had work to do, and it wasn't for him to work out the details of a couple's interaction on the street. Enough that the cowboy had taken himself elsewhere so that he could put Barbara Havers into the picture of what was going on.

He knew she was confused. Everything that had happened at DARBA Italia was a source of anxiety for her. She'd expected him to make a clear move that would take them in the direction she wanted to go: an arrest of someone who was not Taymullah Azhar. He was doing that, but he lacked the words to tell her that things were moving along.

Ottavia Schwartz had seen to that. While he was helping Barbara move Hadiyyah and her belongings from the *pensione* to his mamma's house, while he and Barbara and the child had been eating their little meal with his mamma, Ottavia had been fulfilling his orders. In a police car, she'd gone with Giorgio Simione to DARBA Italia. She'd returned to the *questura* with the director of marketing. He was waiting for them now in an interview room, where he'd been—Salvatore consulted his watch—for the last one hundred minutes. A few more wouldn't hurt.

He took Barbara Havers to his office. He pointed to a chair in front of his desk, and he pulled another over and joined her there. He swept a few articles on the desk to one side, and he laid out the list of employees provided to him by the managing director of DARBA Italia.

She said, "Right. But what's this doing to help us sort out—"

"*Aspetti,*" he told her. He pulled from a pen and pencil holder a highlighting marker. He used it to draw her attention to the name of every department head on the list of employees. Bernardo. Roberto. Daniele. Alessandro. Antonio. She frowned at the highlighted names and said, "So? I mean, I see that these blokes run the show and yeah, okay, their last names are all the same so they must be related, but I don't get why we aren't—"

He used a red pen to draw a square round the first initial of each name. Then he wrote them out on a sticky pad. Then he unscrambled them into DARBA. "*Fratelli,*" he said, to which she said, "Brother." This word he knew and he said, holding up his hand to illustrate what he meant: "*Sì. Sono fratelli. Con i nomi del padre e dei nonni e zii. Ma aspetti un attimo, Barbara.*"

He went to the other side of his desk, where upon a corner lay a stack of files comprising some of the materials he'd amassed on the death of Angelina Upman. From these he pulled out the photographs from the Englishwoman's funeral and burial. He leafed through them quickly and found the two he wanted.

These he placed on top of the list of employees. "Daniele Bruno," he told Barbara Havers.

Those fine blue eyes widened as they took in the pictures. In one of them Daniele Bruno was speaking earnestly to Lorenzo Mura, one hand on his shoulder and their heads bent together. In the other, he was merely a member of the *squadra di calcio* who had attended the funeral to show their support to a fellow player. Barbara Havers gazed at these pictures, then she set them to one side. As Salvatore had assumed she would, she took up the employee list and found Daniele Bruno's name. He was the director of marketing. Like his brothers, he doubtless came and went from his family's business with no one wondering where he was going or why.

"Yes, yes, yes!" Barbara Havers cried. She soared to her feet. "You're a bloody genius, Salvatore! You found the link! This is it! This is how!" And she grabbed his face and kissed him squarely on the mouth.

She seemed as startled as he was that she had done this because an instant afterwards, she backed away. She said, "Christ. Sorry, mate. *Sorry*, Salvatore. But thank you, thank you. What d'we do next?"

He recognised *sorry* but nothing else. He said, "*Venga*," and indicated the door.

LUCCA
TUSCANY

Daniele Bruno was stowed in the interview room closest to Salvatore's office. During the time he'd been waiting, he'd managed to fill the space with enough cigarette smoke to asphyxiate a cow.

Salvatore said, "*Basta!*" as he and Barbara Havers entered. He strode to the table and removed from it a packet of cigarettes and an overfull ashtray. He placed them outside the door. Then he opened a tiny window high on the wall, which did little to remove the fug of smoke but at least acted as mild reassurance that their respiration could continue for a few more minutes without one of them keeling over.

Bruno was in a corner of the room. He seemed to have been pacing the place. He began jabbering about wanting his lawyer the moment Salvatore and Barbara entered. Salvatore saw from the Englishwoman's face that she hadn't the first idea what Daniele Bruno was saying.

He considered the request for an *avvocato*. The presence of a lawyer could actually help them, he decided. But first Signor Bruno needed to be a little more shaken than he was.

"DARBA Italia, signore," he said to Bruno. He motioned to a chair and sat himself. Barbara Havers did likewise and her gaze went from him to Daniele Bruno to him again. He heard her swallow and he wanted to reassure her. Everything, my friend, is well in hand, he would have said.

Bruno made his request for his lawyer again. He stated that Salvatore could not hold him. He demanded to be allowed to go. Salvatore told him that this would happen soon. He wasn't under arrest, after all. At least not yet.

Bruno's eyes danced in his face. He took in Barbara Havers and clearly wondered who she was and why she was there. Barbara Havers helpfully added to his paranoia by taking a notebook and a pencil from her capacious shoulder bag. She settled into her chair, rested her right ankle on her left knee in a way that would have made an Italian woman pray for her sartorial salvation, and jotted down something, a perfect nonexpression expression on her face. Bruno demanded to know who she was. *"Non importa"* was Salvatore's reply. Except . . . Well . . . She was here on a matter of murder, signore.

Bruno said nothing although his gaze skittered from Salvatore to Barbara to Salvatore. Interesting that he did not ask the victim, Salvatore thought.

"Tell me about your employment with DARBA Italia," Salvatore said to Bruno in a friendly fashion. "This is a company your family owns, no?" And when Bruno gave a head jerk of a nod, Salvatore said, "For which you, Daniele, are director of marketing, no?" A shrug in reply. Bruno's fingers suggested he wanted to light another cigarette. That was good, Salvatore thought. Anxiety was always useful. "This company manufactures equipments that are used in medicine and in scientific research, I understand." Another nod. A glance at Barbara. She was busily writing something, although God alone knew what since she wouldn't have the first clue what he was asking the other man. "And I would suppose that whatever is sold must also be tested to ensure its quality." Bruno licked his lips. "This is true, yes?" Salvatore asked. "There is testing, yes? Because I see from my list of employees—your brother Antonio gave this to us just"—he looked at his watch elaborately—"some three hours ago—that you have a quality control department that your brother Alessandro heads. Would Alessandro tell me that his job is to oversee the testing of the equipments you make at DARBA Italia, signore? Should I call him to ask him this question or do you know the answer yourself?"

Bruno seemed to evaluate all possibilities attendant to giving a verbal reply. His jug ears reddened, like overlarge rose petals attached to his skull. He finally affirmed that the products made by DARBA Italia were indeed tested by the department overseen by Alessandro Bruno. But when Salvatore asked him how they were tested, he claimed that he did not know.

"Then we will use our imaginations," Salvatore told him. "Let us start first with your incubators. DARBA Italia makes incubators, no? I mean the sort of equipments used to grow things inside. Things that need a steady temperature and a sterile environment. DARBA Italia makes these, no?"

Here Bruno asked once again for his *avvocato* to be summoned. Salvatore said, "But why is there this need, my friend? Let me bring you a *caffè* instead. Or some water? A San Pellegrino perhaps? Or a Coca-Cola? Perhaps a glass of milk? You were given lunch, no? A *panino* from the lunch trolley would have been correct . . . You want nothing? Not even a *caffè*?"

Next to him, Barbara stirred on her chair. He heard her murmur, "*Venga, venga,*" and he stopped his lips from curving into a smile at her use of his language, however she meant it.

"No?" he said to Bruno. "So we proceed for now. It is only information we need from you, signore. There is, as I told you, a small matter of murder."

"*Non ho fatto niente,*" Daniele Bruno said.

"*Certo,*" Salvatore assured him. No one, after all, was accusing him of doing anything. His answers to their questions were all that was sought. Certainly, he could answer questions about DARBA Italia, no?

Daniele didn't ask why he—of all the brothers Bruno—had been brought to the *questura* to answer questions. It was always the small mistakes like these, Salvatore thought, that ultimately gave away the game.

"Let us suppose a bacteria is used to test the worth of an incubator. This is a possibility, no?" And when Bruno nodded, Salvatore said, "So this bacteria would be right there in Alessandro's quality control department." Bruno nodded. He glanced at Barbara. "I see," Salvatore said. He made a great show of thinking about this. He got up, walked from one side of the room to the other. Then he opened the door and called out for Ottavia Schwartz. Could she bring him, he asked, all of the materials from his desktop, *per favore*, as he seemed to have left them behind. He closed the door and returned to the table. He sat, thought, nodded as if reaching a profound conclusion, and said, "A family business, no? This DARBA Italia."

Sì, he had already confirmed this. It was a family business. His great-grandfather Antonio Bruno had started it in the day when medical equipment was confined to centrifuges and microscopes. His grandfather Alessandro Bruno had expanded it. His father Roberto had made it the jewel in his paternal crown, the inheritance of the brothers Bruno.

"Providing employment for all of you," Salvatore said. "*Va bene, Daniele.* How nice this must be. To work among the members of your family. To see them daily. To stop by with an invitation to dinner. To chat about the nieces and nephews. This must be a very welcome kind of work."

Daniele said this was so. Family, after all, was everything.

"I have two sisters. I know what you mean," Salvatore told him. "*La famiglia è tutto.* You talk often with these brothers of yours? At home, at work, over *caffè*, over *vino*." When Daniele said again this was so, Salvatore said, "At work and at play, eh? The brothers Bruno, everyone knows you at DARBA Italia. Everyone sees you and calls you by name."

Daniele said that this was the case, but he pointed out that the company was not large and that most employees knew everyone there.

"*Certo, certo,*" Salvatore said. "You come, you go, they call out, 'Ciao, Daniele. *Come stanno Sua moglie e i Suoi figli?*' And you do the same. They are used to you. You are used to them. You are . . . Let us say you are a fixture there, like a piece of medical equipment yourself. You pop in to talk to Antonio one day, to Bernardo another, to Alessandro a third. On some days you pop in to talk to every one of your brothers."

He loved his brothers, Daniele asserted. He did not think there was a crime in this.

"No, no," Salvatore told him. "Love for one's brothers . . . this is a gift."

The door opened. All of them turned as Ottavia Schwartz came into the room. She passed the requested manila folders to Salvatore. She nodded, shot a glance at Daniele Bruno and another at Barbara Havers—particularly at her shoes—and left them. With much ceremony Salvatore set the folders on the table, but he did not open them. Bruno's gaze flicked to them and then away.

"*Allora*," Salvatore said expansively, "another question if you please. Back to this testing we were speaking of. I would assume that dangerous substances—of the sort that cause illness, death, disease?—are kept under close watch at DARBA Italia. Under lock and key perhaps? But safely away from anyone who might use them for mischief. Would that be true, my friend?" Bruno nodded. "And in order to test these equipments you make, I would assume more than one dangerous substance is used, eh? Because incubators . . . they differ, no? Some are used for this, some are used for that, and you at DARBA Italia make them all."

Bruno's gaze went to the folders again. He couldn't control it, nerves not allowing him this small amount of discipline. He was, after all, not a bad man, Salvatore reasoned. He'd done something stupid, but stupidity was not a crime.

"Alessandro knows all these bacteria that are part of the testing of the equipments, *vero*? And you have no need to answer this, Signor Bruno, because my colleague has already ascertained this. He named all the bacteria for her. He was curious, naturally, about our questions. He said there are many controls in place that guard these substances so that they cannot be abused. Do you know what he means by that, signore? Me, I think it means that employees cannot put their hands upon these substances. Nor would they want to, eh? They are too dangerous, what is contained in the testing area. Exposed to them, someone could fall ill. At the extreme, someone could even die."

Bruno's forehead had begun to shine, and his lips had begun to dry. Salvatore imagined how thirsty he must be. Once again he offered something to drink. Bruno shook his head, one shake like a tremor seizing his brain.

"But one of the Bruno brothers . . . He comes and goes, and if he carefully takes some of the more dangerous bacteria, there is no one to notice. Perhaps he does it after hours. Perhaps early in the morning. And even if he is seen in Alessandro Bruno's department, no one thinks about it because he is often there. The brothers live in and out of each other's pockets, eh? So no one would think about his appearance in a place where he does not belong because he does belong there, because he belongs everywhere, because that is how things are at

DARBA Italia. So for him to take this bacteria—and let us say his choice was . . . well, let us say *E. coli*—no one would notice. And he would be wise and not take all of it. And since it is in the incubator to reproduce itself, no?, whatever he takes will soon enough be replaced."

Bruno lifted a hand to his mouth and squeezed his lips between thumb and fingers.

Salvatore said, "It was meant to look like a natural death. Indeed, he could not be sure death would even be the consequence although he was willing to try nearly anything, I expect. When there is so much hate—"

"He did not hate her," Bruno said. "He loved her. She was . . . She did not die as you think she died. She had not been well. There were such difficulties with her pregnancy. She had been in hospital. She had been—"

"And yet the autopsy does not lie, signore. And a single terrible case like this one . . . ? A single case of *E. coli* does not happen, unless of course, it is deliberate."

"He loved her! I did not know . . ."

"No? What did he tell you he needed this bacteria for?"

Bruno said, "You have proof of nothing. And I say nothing more to you."

"This is, of course, your choice." Salvatore opened the folders he'd asked for. He showed Daniele Bruno the photos of himself in earnest conversation with Lorenzo Mura. He showed him the autopsy report. He showed him the pictures of Angelina's dead body. He said, "You must ask yourself if a woman who carries a child should die a painful death for any reason."

"He loved her," Daniele Bruno repeated. "And this—what you have—is evidence of nothing."

"Just circumstances, *sì*. This I know," Salvatore said. "Without a confession from someone, all I can lay before the *magistrato* is a set of circumstances that look suspicious but prove nothing. And yet, the *magistrato* is not a man who quails in the face of mere circumstances. You may not know this about Piero Fanucci, but you will."

"I want my lawyer here," Daniele Bruno said. "I say nothing more to you without my lawyer."

Which, as it happened, was fine with Salvatore. He had Daniele Bruno where he wanted him. For the first time Piero Fanucci's reputation for prosecuting based on virtually no evidence was actually a boon.

LUCCA
TUSCANY

Daniele Bruno's solicitor spoke English. He spoke, in fact, exactly like an American and with an American accent as well. He was called Rocco Garibaldi, and he'd learned the language from watching old American films. He'd only been in the US once, he told Barbara, laying over in Los Angeles for two days en route to Australia. He'd gone to Hollywood, he'd seen the imprints in cement of the hands and feet of long-dead movie stars, he'd read the names on the Walk of Fame . . . But mostly he had practised his language in order to see how well he'd done learning it.

Perfectly well, Barbara reckoned. The man sounded like a mixture of Henry Fonda and Humphrey Bogart. Obviously, he favoured the old black-and-whites.

After an interminable exchange of Italian between Garibaldi and Lo Bianco in the reception area of the *questura*, they all decamped to Lo Bianco's office. Salvatore indicated that Barbara was to accompany them and she did so, although she hadn't the first clue what was going on and Rocco Garibaldi, his perfect English notwithstanding, did not enlighten her. Once inside the office, the unimaginable happened in very short order. Salvatore showed Bruno's lawyer the television film, followed by the list of employees from DARBA Italia, followed by what appeared to be a report that she highly suspected was the autopsy information from Angelina Upman's death. What else could it be since Garibaldi read it, frowning and nodding meditatively?

All of this Barbara watched in a welter of nerves. She'd never seen a cop play his hand in this manner. She said, "Chief Inspector . . ." quietly and in appeal, then, "Salvatore . . ." then, "Chief Inspector," although she didn't know how the hell she could stop him aside from physically backing him into a corner, tying him to his desk chair, and gagging him.

She hadn't the first clue about what had passed between Salvatore and Bruno in the interview room. She'd picked out various words among the Italian being flung about, but she hadn't been able to put together much. She'd heard *DARBA Italia* over and over, as well as *E. coli* and the word *incubatrice*. She'd seen Daniele Bruno's growing agitation, so she had some hopes that Salvatore was putting the thumbscrews to him. But throughout the interview, Salvatore had looked like a man in need of an afternoon siesta. The bloke was casual to the point of virtual unconsciousness. Something had to be going on beneath those hooded eyes of his, Barbara thought, but she had no idea what it was.

At the end of his reading, Garibaldi spoke again to Salvatore. This time, he brought Barbara into their conversation by saying, "I am asking the *ispettore* to allow me to see my client, Detective Sergeant Havers." This, Barbara thought, was what a UK solicitor would have done in the first place, and just when she'd got to the point of accepting that things were different in Italy when it came to police work, they became more different still.

Salvatore made no move to take Garibaldi to his client in the interview room. Instead, he had Daniele Bruno brought to them. This was irregular but she was willing to wait to see how things would proceed from there. She got no comfort at all when within less than five minutes Garibaldi gave a formal little from-the-waist dip to Salvatore, said, "*Grazie mille,*" put his hand on Bruno's arm, and led him from the premises. It happened so quickly that she didn't have time to react other than to swing round to Salvatore and cry, "What the bloody hell?" to which he smiled and gave that Italian shrug of his.

She cried, "Why did you let him *go*? Why did you show him that TV film? Why did you tell him about DARBA Italia? Why did you give him . . . Oh, I know he would've got to see everything eventually, at least I think he would've because God knows I haven't a clue what goes in this country, but for God's sake you could have pretended . . . you could have suggested . . . But now he knows your hand—which, let's face it, is bloody empty—and all he has to do is to tell Bruno to keep his mug plugged from now till the end of time because all we have is supposition anyway and unless you blokes practise some very strange form of justice over here *no* one is going to gaol based on supposition, and that includes Daniele Bruno. Oh, bloody hell why don't you speak English, Salvatore?"

To all of this Salvatore nodded sympathetically. For a moment, Barbara thought he actually understood, if not from her words then from her tone. But then, maddeningly, he said, "*Aspetti, Barbara.*" And with a smile, "*Vorrebbe un caffè?*"

"No, I do not want a cup of bloody coffee!" she fairly shouted at him.

He smiled at this. "*Lei capisce!*" he cried. "*Va bene!*"

To which she said with sagging shoulders, "Just tell me why you let him go, for God's sake. All he has to do is ring up Lorenzo Mura and we're cooked. You see that, don't you?"

He gazed at her, as if some kind of understanding would come from a close reading of her eyes. She found herself getting hot under his scrutiny. Finally, she said, "Oh, sod it," and dug her packet of Players from her shoulder bag. She took one of the fags and offered the packet to him.

"Sod . . . it," he repeated softly.

Their cigarettes lit, he nodded towards the window of his office. She thought he intended them to blow the smoke from it into the afternoon air. But instead he said, "*Guardi,*" and he indicated the pavement below them. There she saw Garibaldi and Bruno had emerged from the *questura* and were strolling along without a care.

"And this is supposed to reassure me?" she demanded.

He said, "*Un attimo, Barbara.*" And then, "*Eccolo.*" She followed the direction of his hooded gaze to see a man in an orange baseball cap following some thirty yards behind them. "Giorgio Simione," Salvatore murmured. "*Giorgio mi dirà dovunque andranno.*"

Barbara felt only a small measure of relief at the sight of Giorgio following the other two men since all they needed to do was get into a car and that was that when it came to Bruno disappearing or getting in touch with Lorenzo Mura. But Salvatore seemed absolutely and preternaturally bloody *assured* of everything going along according to some sort of inner plan he had. Barbara finally decided there was nothing for it but to trust the man, although she hated to do so.

They spent a half hour waiting. Salvatore made a few unintelligible phone calls: one to mamma, another to someone called Birgit, and a third to someone called Cinzia. Real ladies' man, she reckoned. It probably had to do with those hooded eyes of his.

When Rocco Garibaldi appeared at the doorway to Salvatore's office, Barbara was both relieved and surprised. He came alone, which caused her some serious consternation, but this time when he spoke to Salvatore, he showed some degree of mercy by telling Barbara what he was saying.

His client Daniele Bruno was back in the interview room. He was now ready and willing to tell Ispettore Lo Bianco everything he knew about this matter under investigation because he was deeply grieved by the death of an innocent woman who was carrying a child. That he now wished to speak had nothing at all to do with any fear he had for his own neck, and he had insisted that Garibaldi make this clear to the *polizia*. He would tell everything he knew and everything he had done because what he did not know at any time was how Lorenzo Mura intended to use the *E. coli* that he gave to him. As long as Ispettore Lo Bianco could promise to be satisfied on this one point, they could proceed. But it would be information in exchange for release: total immunity for Signor Bruno.

Salvatore appeared to think about this at great length, as far as Barbara could tell. He jotted a few notes on a legal pad, and he paced to the window where he made a phone call from his mobile in a very hushed voice. For all Barbara could tell he was ringing somewhere for takeaway Chinese, and when he at last finished the call, she had a suspicion she wasn't far from the truth.

More Italian ensued during which she caught *E. coli* mentioned and the word *magistrato* dozens of times. So was Lorenzo Mura's name. So was Bruno's and Angelina Upman's.

From this, all Barbara could work out was that a deal was being reached. Garibaldi said to her, "We have an understanding, Detective Sergeant," at which point he stood and shook Lo Bianco's hand. But what the understanding was remained a mystery until Salvatore made yet another phone call, followed by their return to the interview room where Daniele Bruno sat expressionlessly at the table, clearly waiting to hear about whatever deal had been struck between Garibaldi and Lo Bianco.

The deal became apparent very soon. A knock on the door heralded a police technician, and he carried with him a large plastic container of equipment, which turned out to be of an electronic nature. This he began to unpack upon the table as the rest of them watched.

He began a lengthy explanation to Bruno of what comprised all the items on the table, but in this instance, Barbara required no translation. She recognised them well enough along with the deal that Lo Bianco and Garibaldi had worked out.

Daniele Bruno would tell them everything. That much was certain. But he would also meet with Lorenzo Mura, and when he did so, he would wear a wire.

LUCCA
TUSCANY

The clatter of feet on a stone floor and cries of "Papà! Papà!" greeted them when they returned to Torre Lo Bianco that evening. A little girl was running from the direction of the kitchen, and she was followed by a boy not much older, and both of them were followed by Hadiyyah. The little girl—whom Salvatore called Bianca—began chattering excitedly, and it came to Barbara that she was speaking about her. She concluded whatever she was saying by speaking to Barbara directly with "*Mi piacciono le Sue scarpe rosse,*" to which Salvatore fondly told her that "*La signora non parla italiano, Bianca.*"

Bianca giggled, covered her mouth with her hands, and said to Barbara, "I like the shoes red of you."

Hadiyyah laughed at this and corrected her with "No! It's 'I like your red shoes,'" after which she said to Barbara, "Her mummy speaks English, but sometimes Bianca mixes the words up 'cause she *also* speaks Swedish."

"No problem, kiddo," Barbara told her. "Her English is bloody good compared to my Italian." And to Salvatore she added, "That's right, eh?"

He smiled and said, "*Certo,*" and gestured her towards the kitchen. There he greeted his mother who was in the midst of making dinner.

It looked as if she was expecting a horde of foot soldiers. There were large trays of drying pasta on the worktops, a huge vat bubbling with sauce on the stove, the aroma of some kind of roasting meat coming from the oven, an enormous salad standing in the middle of the table, and green beans sitting in a large stone sink. Salvatore kissed his mother hello, saying, "*Buonasera, Mamma,*" which she waved off with a scowl. But the look she cast him was one of fondness, and she said to Barbara, "*Spero che abbia fame.*" She nodded at the food.

Barbara thought, *Fame?* Famous? No. That couldn't be right. Then she twigged. *Famished.* She said, "Too bloody right."

Salvatore repeated, "'Too bloody right,'" and then to his mother, "*Sì, Barbara ha fame. E anch'io, Mamma.*"

Mamma nodded vigorously. All was right with her world, it seemed, as long as anyone entering her kitchen was hungry.

Salvatore took Barbara's arm then and indicated she should come with him. The children stayed behind with Mamma in the kitchen as Barbara followed Salvatore up the stairs, where a sitting room comprised the floor above them. At one side of the room, an old sideboard tilted on the uneven stone floor. There, Salvatore poured himself a drink: Campari and soda. He offered Barbara the same.

She was strictly an ale or lager girl, but that didn't appear to be on offer. So she went for the Campari and soda and hoped for the best.

He indicated the stairs and began to climb. She followed as before. On the next floor was his mamma's bedroom along with a bathroom making a bulbous extension out from the ancient tower. The next floor held his own room, the floor above it the room she shared with Hadiyyah. It came to Barbara at this point that she and Hadiyyah were sharing the room belonging to Salvatore's two children, and she said to him, "Sod it, Salvatore. We're sleeping in your kids' room, aren't we? Where does that leave them?" He nodded and smiled at this. He said, "Sod it, *sì*," and continued upward. She said, "It would help if you spoke better English, mate," and he said, "English, *sì*," and still he climbed.

They came out at last upon a rooftop. Here Salvatore said, "*Il mio posto preferito, Barbara,*" and indicated with a sweeping gesture the entirety of the place. It was a rooftop garden with a tree at its centre, surrounded on all sides by an ancient stone bench and shrubbery. At the edge of the roof, a parapet ran along all four sides of the tower, and to this parapet Salvatore walked, his drink in his hand. Barbara joined him there.

The sun was setting, and it cast a golden glow upon the rooftops of Lucca. He pointed out various areas to her, various buildings that he quietly identified by name as he turned her here and there. She understood not a thing he said, only that he spoke of his love for this place. And there was, she admitted, a lot to love. From the top of the tower, she could see the twisted, cobbled medieval streets of the town, the hidden gardens that were barely visible, the ovoid shape of the repurposed amphitheatre, the dozens of churches that dominated the individual tiny neighbourhoods. And always the wall, the amazing wall. In the evening, with a cool breeze now blowing across the great alluvial plain, it was, she had to admit it, like a slice of paradise.

She said to him, "It's gorgeous. I've never even been out of the UK, and I never thought I'd ever be standing in Italy. But I'll say this: If someone or something drags one out of one's local chippy and into a foreign country, Lucca's not a bad spot to end up." She hoisted her glass to him and to the place. "Bloody beautiful," she said.

He said, "Bloody right."

She chuckled at this. "*Bene*, mate. I think you could learn to speak the lingo without that much trouble."

"Sod it," he said happily.

She laughed.

18 MAY

The ringing of her mobile phone awakened Barbara. She grabbed it up quickly and glanced at the other bed in the room. Hadiyyah was sleeping peacefully, her hair tumbling on the pillow around her. Barbara gave a look at the incoming number and sighed.

"Mitchell," she said by way of greeting.

"Why're you whispering?" was his hello.

"Because I don't want to wake Ḥadiyyah, and what the bloody hell time is it?"

"Early."

"I twigged."

"I knew you were quick. Get outside. We've things to discuss."

"Where the hell are you?"

"Where I always am: across the piazza at the café, which, by the way, is not yet open and I could do with a coffee. So if Signora Vallera wouldn't be crushed by the thought of your stealing out into the dawn with a cup for me—"

"We're not in the *pensione*, Mitchell."

"*What?* Barb, if you've scarpered, there's going to be hell—"

"Untwist them. We're still in Lucca. But really, you can't think I'd still be at the *pensione* with Hadiyyah's grandparents about to show their mugs in town."

"Well, they're here. Tucked up in the San Luca Palace Hotel, by the way."

"How d'you know?"

"It's my job to know. Fact is, it's my job to know all sorts of things, which is one of the many reasons I suggest you trot over here to the piazza . . . No, better yet. I need a coffee. I'll meet you in Piazza del Carmine in twenty minutes. That should give you enough time to perform your morning toilette."

"Mitchell, I have no clue where Piazza whatever-you-called-it is."

"Del Carmine, Barb. And isn't that why you're a cop? To suss things out? Well, do a little sussing."

"And if I don't wish to accommodate you?"

"Then I just hit send."

Barbara felt the grip of pain in her stomach. She said, "All right."

"Wise decision." He ended the call.

She dressed in a hurry. She looked at the time. Not even six in the morning but there was mercy in that. No one in Torre Lo Bianco appeared to be stirring.

Shoes in hand, she began a slow descent of the stairs. She worried that there might be something complicated about getting out of the tower, but it turned out to be a straightforward affair. Major key in the lock, but it rotated without a sound. She was out in the narrow street soon enough, wondering what direction she should take to find Piazza del Carmine.

She set off arbitrarily, just seeking another human presence in the cool early morning. She found it in the persons of an unshaven father-and-son duo trundling two large wooden carts of vegetables along a narrow path between a church and a walled garden. She said to them, lifting her shoulders quizzically and looking hopeful, "Piazza del Carmine?"

They looked at each other. "*Mi segua*," the older one of them said. He gave the jerk of the head that Barbara was beginning to recognise as the Italian nonverbal for *come along with me*. She followed them. She wished she'd thought of breadcrumbs to find her way back to the tower at the end of whatever happened with Mitch Corsico, but there was no help for that now.

It wasn't long before she found herself in the assigned meeting place, a less-than-scenic piazza that accommodated a disreputable-looking restaurant, an unopened supermarket, and a large mildewed white building of indeterminate age with *Mercato Centrale* across the front of it. This was where Barbara's companions were themselves heading and after tossing "Piazza del Carmine," over his shoulder, the younger of the men trundled his cart of vegetable boxes inside the place, followed by his companion, followed by Barbara.

She found Mitch Corsico without any trouble. She just tracked the scent of coffee to the far side of the space and there he was, leaning on a narrow counter built into a wall, a few feet away from an enterprising African adolescent selling takeaway coffee from a shopping trolley.

Corsico saluted her with his cardboard cup, saying, "I knew you had the right stuff."

She scowled and went for some coffee herself. It teetered just north of utterly undrinkable, but times were desperate. She took it to where Corsico was standing, after throwing a few coins into the African's palm and hoping they would do.

"And . . . ?" she said to Corsico.

"And the question is why didn't you phone?"

Barbara thought for a moment, wondering how far she could push this. She said, "Look, Mitchell. When there's something to phone you about, I'll phone you."

He evaluated the expression on her face, but he didn't go for it, fondly shaking his head at her. "Doesn't work that way," he said and slurped his coffee. He turned his laptop so that she could see the screen. *Grieving Parents of Dead Mum Speak of Abandonment and Loss* was his title of the piece. She didn't need to read far into it to see that he'd scored an interview with the Upmans. They'd employed their hatchets on Azhar: as a father and as the man who'd "ruined" their daughter like a villain from a Thomas Hardy novel.

"How the hell did you get them to talk?" she asked him, the only thing she could think of as her mind raced with possible ways to appease him.

"Had a chinwag with Lorenzo at the *fattoria* yesterday. They showed up while I was there."

"Lucky," she said.

"It had nothing to do with luck. So where did Lo Bianco stow you?"

She narrowed her eyes in response but said nothing.

He took this on board. He gave a martyred sigh. He said, "You shouldn't have let him settle your account with Signora Vallera. She gets up early, by the way. A knock on the door and there she was, and *dove* means *where* in their lingo. *Ispettore* was clear enough to me. And where you and I come from, one and one still make two. What I expect at this point is that the Upmans will be seriously chuffed to know the inspector pulled you and Hadiyyah out of the *pensione*. But I also expect you'd rather I didn't trot over to the San Luca Palace Hotel and interrupt their brekkers to give them the word." He fiddled with the keys on his laptop, and Barbara saw him access his email, although she didn't have a clue how he'd done it from this location. A few manoeuvres and he'd attached the Grieving Parents story to a message to his editor and his finger was hovering one click away from send. "Now, do we still have a deal or do we not, mate? Because as I've tried to explain to you ad nauseam, I've got to keep the beast fed or it's going to eat me."

"All right, all right," she told him. "Yes, it was *E. coli*. Yes, it was intended for murder or at least for a very serious illness. I c'n confirm it came from that place I told you about: DARBA Italia. They make and test medical equipment, including incubators of the sort that breed bacteria for laboratories to study. One of the bacteria they have on site is *E. coli*, and it was handed over to Mura. The bloke who did it—"

"Name, Barb."

"Not yet, Mitch."

He pointed a warning finger at her. "That's not how we're going to play this."

"Forget it, Mitchell. He's agreed to wear a wire, and if I give you his name and you use it, the entire investigation goes straight to hell."

"You can trust me," he said.

"I trust you like I trust my hair to stop growing."

"I won't use the name till you say the word."

"Not going to happen and that's how it is. You write your story.

You leave blanks or whatever else you want to leave where the names should go. Once we have what we need from the wire, I give you the names and then you hit send. That's how it has to be because there's too much on the line."

He thought about this for a moment, slurping his coffee another time. Around them Mercato Centrale was starting to heat up with activity as more vendors arrived and organised themselves in something of a ring round the place. The coffee-selling business began to be brisk.

Corsico finally said, "Problem is . . . I don't trust you not to go sour on me. I think some kind of guarantee . . ."

She nodded at his laptop and said, "You've got your guarantee right there. I don't do what you want when you want it, you just hit send."

"Send this, you mean?" He clicked and the story was on its way to his editor. "Whoops," he said solemnly. "There it goes, Barb."

"And there goes our deal," she told him.

"I don't think so."

"No? Why not?"

"Because of this." He did a bit more expert manoeuvring and revealed another story he'd been writing. This one's proposed headline was *Dad Was Behind It*, and when Barbara read through it quickly, her teeth seemed to grind of their own volition.

He'd got to Doughty. Or Doughty had got to him. Or perhaps it was Emily Cass or Bryan Smythe, but she reckoned on Doughty. He'd given Mitch Corsico line and level, A to Z, the whole bleeding alpha to omega on Azhar, on Barbara, on Hadiyyah's disappearance, and on her subsequent kidnapping in Italy. He'd given him names and dates and places. He had, in effect, pointed a loaded gun at Azhar. He'd also put an end to her career.

Barbara discovered that one couldn't actually think when one's heart was leaping about like a wounded kangaroo. She raised her eyes from the laptop's screen and simply had nothing to say other than, "You can't do this."

Mitch said, "Alas and alack," in a tone so speciously solemn that she wanted to punch him. Then this tone altered and the words were stone. He glanced at his watch. "Midday should do it, don't you think?"

She said, "Noon? What're you talking about?" although she had a fairly good idea.

"I'm talking about how much time you have before this baby rockets off into cyberspace, Barb."

"I can't guarantee—"

He waggled a finger at her. "But I can," he said.

LUCCA
TUSCANY

Barbara named it a miracle that she found her way back to Torre Lo Bianco, although she didn't do it without several wrong turns. But as things developed, the tower was well known to the citizens of Lucca because of its rooftop garden, and it seemed that many of them used it as some sort of landmark. Everyone she asked knew where it was, although the directions to get there—always in Italian—seemed more complicated each time she enquired about them. It took her an hour to locate it. By the time she arrived, everyone in the tower was in the kitchen.

Salvatore was at his coffee, Hadiyyah was at a mug of hot chocolate, and Mamma was at a stack of what looked like demented tarot cards, which she was laying out in front of Hadiyyah. Barbara looked at these as a way of avoiding Salvatore's speculative gaze. Mamma was presenting one that depicted a robe-clad woman holding a tray that contained a pair of eyeballs, presumably hers if the blood on her face was anything to go by. Above this, other cards had been arranged: a bloke being crucified upside down, another chained to a pillar and sprouting arrows, a youngish man in a vat with a fire lit beneath it.

Barbara said, "Bloody hell! What's going on?"

Hadiyyah said happily, "*Nonna* is teaching me 'bout the saints."

"Could she possibly choose less bloody ones?"

"I don't think there are any," Hadiyyah confided. "At least not so far. *Nonna* says that what's brilliant is you c'n always tell who the saint is by what's going on in the picture 'cause it shows what happened to them. See, this is St. Peter on the upside-down cross, and this is St. Sebastian with the arrows and *this*"—she tapped the young man in the vat—"is St. John the 'Vangelist 'cause nothing they did to him killed him and look how God up here is sending gold rain down to put out the fire."

"*Guarda, guarda,*" Mamma said to Hadiyyah, tapping yet another card, on which a young woman tied to a stake was being consumed by eager flames.

"St. Joan of Arc," Barbara said.

Mamma looked delighted. "*Brava, Barbara!*" she cried.

"How'd you know?" asked Hadiyyah, equally delighted.

"Because us Brits killed her," Barbara said. And since there was no further way to avoid it, she smiled at Salvatore and said, "Morning."

He said, "'*Giorno, Barbara.*" He'd already risen politely, and he indicated an Italian coffeemaker that sat on a burner of the old stove. On the worktop next to this, an array of breakfast foods was spread out. Barbara said, "Cake for breakfast?" to him. "I could start liking this place."

Hadiyyah said, "It's a breakfast *torta*, Barbara."

Mamma said, "*Una torta, sì. Va bene, Hadiyyah,*" and she smoothed her hand fondly on Hadiyyah's hair. To her son she said, "*Una bambina dolce*" to which Salvatore said, "*Sì, sì,*" but he seemed preoccupied.

When he presented Barbara with her coffee, he said something which Hadiyyah translated as, "Salvatore wants to know where you were," as she was presented with another saint's card, which Mamma announced as a depiction of San Rocco.

Barbara made walking motions with her fingers against the tabletop. "Out for a morning walk," she told him.

"*Ho fatto una passeggiata,*" Hadiyyah said. "That's how you say it."

"Right. *Oh fat-o una passa*—whatever."

"Ah. *E dov'è andata?*"

"An' where did you go?" Hadiyyah translated.

"I got bloody well lost. Tell him I'm lucky I didn't end up in Pisa."

When Hadiyyah passed this along to Salvatore, the inspector smiled. But Barbara could see it didn't touch his eyes, and she steeled herself for whatever was coming next. This turned out to be Salvatore's mobile, which chimed. He looked at it and said, "Ispettore Lynley."

She pressed a finger to her lips, asking Salvatore in this way to keep mum on her whereabouts. He nodded cooperatively.

He said with a smile, *"Pronto, Tommaso,"* into the mobile. But after a moment, his face altered. He glanced at Barbara, and he left the room.

VICTORIA
LONDON

Not having heard from Barbara Havers felt to Lynley distinctly like a case of no news being good news, although he knew how unlikely this was. So he was unsurprised when the relative ease he was feeling ended shortly after his arrival at work. Winston Nkata related that there was no connection to Italy that he could find among Angelina Upman's family and associates aside from the fact that her parents were evidently now in Lucca, and shortly thereafter DI John Stewart accosted him in the corridor and handed over a copy of *The Source.*

On page one of the tabloid was a very large and extremely soulful picture of Hadiyyah Upman gazing out of a window, below which were arrayed a large collection of highly recognisable succulents. The picture was accompanied by a story headlined *When Will She Come Home?* This story was attached to the by-line *Mitchell Corsico.* In combination with the photo, this revealed the absolute worst. For there was only one way that Mitchell Corsico could have worked out where Hadiyyah had been stowed by Barbara Havers. Lynley knew this, and so did Stewart.

The other DI made this point clear when he said, "What's it to be, Tommy? Do I give this to the guv or do you? If you want my opinion on the subject, she's been in bed with *The Source* God only knows how long. Years, probably. She's been on the take as a snout and now she's finished."

Lynley said, "You carry your aversions too openly, John. I'd advise you to back off."

Stewart's lips formed a sneer that was as amused as it was all-knowing. "Would you indeed?" he said. "Right. Well, I suppose you would." He glanced in the direction of Isabelle Ardery's office to indicate the subject of his next point. "She's met with CIB1, Tommy. The word's out on that."

Lynley said calmly, "Then obviously your sources are far better than mine." Tapping the tabloid against his palm, he concluded with "May I keep this, John?"

"Many more where that came from, mate. Just in case it doesn't end up on . . . on *Isabelle's* desk." He winked and sauntered off, his step quite jaunty. They were down to the last set, and he was determined to win the match.

Lynley watched him go. He gazed at the tabloid's page-one story once he was alone. It was vintage material from *The Source*: The good guys wore white. The bad guys wore black. No one wore grey. In this case, both Taymullah Azhar and Lorenzo Mura were the bad guys for reasons having to do with the death of Angelina Upman (Azhar) and with keeping Hadiyyah from her father (Mura). Of course, since Azhar was in prison at the moment, put there by Inspector Salvatore Lo Bianco (white), who was in charge of the investigation into the death of Angelina Upman, the child had to be domiciled somewhere and the villa in which she had lived with her mother and Mura (pictures on page three) had seemed reasonable until other arrangements could be made. But hers was now the face of sadness, abandonment, and the desperate need to recover from the crimes that had been committed against her, and nothing was being done about that. She was now alone and in the hands of a foreign government (very black), and *when* was the Foreign Secretary (white but moving towards black very quickly) going to step in and demand that the child be returned to London where she belonged?

Much space was taken up with the recap of what had happened to Hadiyyah since the previous November. Interestingly, though, there was no mention of anyone from New Scotland Yard being sent there to liaise for the troubled child.

That, Lynley knew, was a telling detail. The tale it told was one of collusion between the journalist who had written the story and Barbara Havers. For if he named her, he named his source, and he wasn't fool enough to do that. Yet Barbara was the only way he could have located Hadiyyah. And only through Barbara's cooperation could he ever have managed to get a picture of the child.

This article, Lynley knew, put the lie to everything Barbara Havers had said about her interactions with Corsico. She wouldn't be the first cop to have been exposed as on the take from a tabloid. In recent years, cops on the take had become just another part of the landscape of what was a growing national scandal involving the gutter press. But in combination with every other black mark against her, this was going to finish her.

He went to Isabelle's office. The fact that she'd requested CIB1's involvement was an indication of her confidence in the case she was building against Barbara. But there had to be a chance that this tabloid article could be painted another way.

He tossed his copy of *The Source* into the nearest rubbish bin. He knew this was only a temporary measure since, as John Stewart had pointed out, there were more available just up the street. A few steps over to St. James's Park Station and any one of half a dozen or more tabloids could be purchased. Stewart had probably already popped out to buy one. He'd see to it that Isabelle was apprised of the page-one story, and he'd do it soon.

Isabelle's office door stood open, but she wasn't inside. Dorothea Harriman, however, was. She was in the midst of arranging a stack of files on the superintendent's desk. When she saw Lynley, she said merely, "Tower Block."

"How long?"

"It's just gone an hour."

"Did he phone her or did she phone him?"

"Neither. It was a scheduled meeting."

"CIB1?"

Harriman looked regretful.

"Blast," he said. "Did she take anything with her?"

"She had a tabloid," Dorothea said.

Lynley nodded and headed back to his office. There he placed his call to Salvatore Lo Bianco. If Barbara had indeed gone bad, then he owed it to his Italian colleague to warn him.

When Lo Bianco answered, he was still at home. Chattering in Italian was going on in the background. This faded as Salvatore stepped out of the room to speak to Lynley.

The Italian brought Lynley up-to-date on everything: his call upon DARBA Italia, his discoveries there, his subsequent interviews with

Daniele Bruno, the *E. coli* connection between Bruno and Lorenzo Mura. "We have an agreement, his lawyer and I. He will wear a wire," Salvatore told him. "In this way I believe we will have a resolution this very day."

Lynley said, "And the child? She's with Barbara Havers?"

"She is well and she is with Barbara."

"Salvatore, tell me. This is an odd sort of question, but can you tell me . . . is Barbara in Lucca alone?"

"How do you mean?"

"Have you seen her in the company of anyone?"

"I know she has been in the company of Aldo Greco. He is the lawyer of Taymullah Azhar."

"I'm speaking of an Englishman," Lynley said. "He might be dressed like a cowboy, actually."

There was a pause before Salvatore chuckled. "A strange question, my friend," he said. "Why do you ask this, Tommaso?"

"Because he's a tabloid journalist from London and he's written a story that indicates to me he's there in Lucca."

"But why would Barbara be in the company of a tabloid journalist?" Salvatore asked, not unreasonably. "And what is this tabloid?"

"It's called *The Source*," Lynley said, and at that point he found that he could go no further with the information. He couldn't bring himself to tell Salvatore about the picture of Hadiyyah at the window of Pensione Giardino, and more than that, he couldn't bring himself to tell Salvatore what this meant. Obviously, the Italian could seek out a copy of *The Source* himself, either online or from a *giornalaio* selling UK tabloids for purchase by English speakers. If Salvatore did that, he could put together the pieces, but chances were still that he might put them together in an order that didn't make Barbara look bad. So Lynley said, "He's called Mitchell Corsico. Barbara's acquainted with him, as are the rest of us here in London. If she hasn't seen him, you might warn Barbara of his presence when you next see her."

Salvatore didn't ask why Lynley simply didn't ring Barbara and pass on the information. He said instead, "And he looks like a cowboy?"

"He wears a cowboy kit. I've no idea why."

Salvatore chuckled another time. "I shall pass this information to

Barbara when I meet with her today. But I myself have not seen such a person as this. A cowboy in Lucca? No, no. I would remember had I seen him."

LUCCA
TUSCANY

Barbara tried not to feel as if she were carrying a ticking time bomb in her shoulder bag. She tried to act as if everything were business-as-usual and the business was getting Daniele Bruno set up with a wire. But as she and Salvatore set off for the *questura*, she could think only of the hands of the clock, moving relentlessly in the direction of midday and Mitchell Corsico's hitting send.

She could hardly protest when Salvatore suggested they walk to his office, and in other circumstances she might actually have enjoyed the stroll. For the day was fine, church bells were still ringing all over town, shops were just coming to life, the fragrance of pastries was in the air, and the cafés were serving morning espressos to people head-ing out for the day. Students and workers passed on bicycles, and the *blinging* of their bells acted as punctuation to the greetings that the riders tossed at one another. It was like being in the middle of a bloody Italian film, Barbara thought. She half expected someone to yell, "Cut and print."

Salvatore seemed changed. His mood of morning good cheer had altered to one of studied solemnity. Since Lynley had phoned him, Barbara reckoned it had to do with whatever the London DI had related. But with Salvatore's limited English and her own nonexistent Italian, there was no way for her to discover exactly what it was that Lynley had said. She could have rung him and asked him directly, but she had a feeling that would not serve her well. So as they walked, she cast worried gazes in Salvatore's direction.

When they reached the *questura*, she was relieved to see that a white van was parked just at the entrance. That it was not only unmolested but also blocking traffic heading in the direction of the train station suggested that it was not a delivery transport for some product despite the unintelligible Italian scrolled artfully along its side. Barbara reckoned this was going to be the means of picking up whatever Daniele Bruno was able to transmit via the wire he would wear, and when Salvatore slapped his hand against the back door of the vehicle, she saw that she was not incorrect.

A uniformed officer opened the door, headphones on head. He and Salvatore exchanged a few words, at the conclusion of which Salvatore said, "*Va bene,*" and proceeded into the *questura.*

Daniele Bruno and his solicitor were waiting. More intense and incomprehensible Italian was exchanged. Rocco Garibaldi graciously translated the high points for Barbara: His client wished to know how he was supposed to cajole Lorenzo Mura into admitting his guilt.

It seemed to Barbara that more was going on with Bruno than the man's merely wanting a little bout of how-to from Salvatore. The man was sweating profusely—enough to make her think he was probably going to short out the wire they put on him—and he looked struck by half a dozen fears growing from more than his ability to act whatever part Salvatore wished him to play. She said to Signor Garibaldi, "What else?"

Garibaldi said, "It is a matter of family." He spoke at length to Salvatore as Daniele Bruno listened anxiously. Salvatore looked interested and then spoke at length in return to Garibaldi. Barbara wanted to bang their heads together. Time was passing, they needed to get the ball rolling, and *she* needed to know what the bloody hell was going on.

It turned out, according to Garibaldi, that Bruno's main concern was not that he might end up being tossed into a gaol cell. It seemed he would welcome that rather than have his brothers discover what he had done. For his brothers would report to their father. Their father would, perforce, inform their mamma. And in short order, their mamma would lay down the law of a punishment that appeared to consist of Bruno, his wife, and their children no longer being welcome for a Sunday lunch experienced with aunts, uncles, cousins, nieces, nephews, and a cast of what sounded like hundreds. Reassurances were thus desperately required, but Salvatore either could not or would not give them. Salvatore's refusal to calm Bruno's fears had to be discussed from every angle. It took a teeth-gnashing half hour before they could move on.

Bruno then became insistent that Salvatore understand what had occurred with Lorenzo Mura. Lorenzo had told him that he required the *E. coli* to perform some tests associated with his vineyard, and Daniele Bruno had believed him when he'd claimed the impossibility of coming by the *E. coli* in any other way. Lorenzo said it was to do with the wine, Bruno said. Right, Barbara thought. Like how fast do I need to have Azhar tossing this back in a glass of wine in order to make certain the bacteria was still viable?

Finally, all points of discussion were exhausted. They decamped to one of the interview rooms, where Bruno stripped off his shirt, exposing an impressive chest. A technician joined them and another lengthy conversation ensued. Garibaldi told Barbara that his client was being informed exactly how the wire would work.

Barbara found herself caring less and less about the minutiae of the discussion as she cared more and more about how much time it all was taking. She wondered where Mitchell Corsico was and what means she could employ to keep him from sending off to London his story about Azhar if noon rolled round and she hadn't delivered names and places to him. She could ring him and give him a pack of lies, she reckoned, but Mitchell wouldn't take that in his stride when the real facts became known.

The door opened to the interview room as the final touches were being put to wiring up Daniele Bruno. A woman whom Barbara recognised as Ottavia Schwartz entered and spoke to Salvatore.

Barbara heard *Upman* being said by the policewoman. She cried, "What's going on?" but she received no answer as Salvatore abruptly left the room.

Rocco Garibaldi filled her in. The parents of Angelina Upman were in Reception, demanding to speak with Chief Inspector Lo Bianco. They were insisting that something be done about the disappearance of their granddaughter from Fattoria di Santa Zita. Apparently, she had left in the company of an Englishwoman, Garibaldi said. The Upmans were there to declare her missing.

LUCCA
TUSCANY

Since it was made clear to Salvatore that the Upmans had no Italian, a translator was going to be required. Ottavia Schwartz—with her normal high degree of competence—had put out the call for one, but it took more than twenty minutes for her to arrive in Salvatore's office. In the meantime, the Upmans had been left to cool their heels in Reception. They were not happy to be kept waiting, a fact that Signor Upman's appearance made clear, although, at first, Salvatore thought the Englishman's white-to-the-lips face presaged illness brought on by the flight to Italy. This turned out not to be the case. The pale complexion came from the man's fury, which he was only too happy to share with Salvatore.

Introductions had barely been made by Giuditta Di Fazio when Signor Upman launched into a diatribe. Giuditta had impressive skills in languages, but even she was hard-pressed to keep up with the man's words.

"Is this how you incompetent layabouts deal with people who've come to report a missing child?" Upman demanded. "First she is kidnapped. Then her mother is murdered by her father. Then she goes missing from the only home she's known in this infernal country. What is it going to take for someone to handle this bloody situation? Do I need to bring in the British ambassador? Because, believe me, I *will* do that. I have the ability. I have the connections. I want this child found and I want her found now. And do not bloody wait for the translation from Miss Big Tits over there because you know exactly why I'm here and what I want."

While Giuditta put Signor Upman's words into Italian, his wife kept her gaze on the floor. She clutched her handbag. She murmured only, "Darling, darling," when her husband launched into his second harangue.

"Someone who doesn't even speak English is in charge of investigating crimes against British nationals? Incredible. English . . . the most widely spoken language in the world . . . and you don't speak it? God in heaven—"

"*Please*, Humphrey." From her tone, it was clear that she was embarrassed by her husband and not cowed by the man. She said to Salvatore, "Forgive my husband. He's unused to travel and he was . . ." She appeared to seek an excuse and settled upon "He was unable to eat a proper breakfast. We've come for our granddaughter Hadiyyah, to take her home to England until whatever is going on here is resolved. We went to Fattoria di Santa Zita first, but Lorenzo told us she left in the company of an Englishwoman. She's called Barbara, but he can't recall her surname, just that he previously met her with Taymullah Azhar. From what he said . . . I believe she came with Azhar to see us last year, looking for Angelina. We ask only—"

Upman swung on his wife. "You think grovelling will get you what you want? You listen to me. You were desperate to dash over here and now we've dashed over here and now you get to bloody shut up and let me handle things."

Mrs. Upman's face flushed with anger. She said to him, "You're not getting us closer to Hadiyyah."

"Oh, I'll get you close to Hadiyyah soon enough."

Through all of this, Giuditta Di Fazio murmured, making the conversation clear for Salvatore. He narrowed his eyes at the Englishman and wondered if a little time alone in one of the interview rooms might cool him off. He said to Giuditta, "Tell them their journey has been premature. As we are now learning, Hadiyyah's father is innocent in everything pertaining to the death of her mother. More than that, I cannot say, but the professor will be released from custody within a few hours. He would, of course, not be pleased to learn that, during his detainment, his child was handed off to people who came in off the street to claim her. This is not the way we do things in Italy."

Upman's face went rigid. " 'Came in off the street'? How dare you! Are you suggesting we hopped on a plane and came here out of the blue to . . . to do what? Kidnap a child who is by all rights *ours*?"

"I do not suggest you mean to kidnap her as you yourself have indicated that you only wish to take her to England until this matter is resolved. I tell you in return that it has been resolved as far as Professore Azhar is concerned. So while you have been very good-hearted to come to Italy—may I assume that Signor Mura sent for you?—I tell you now that the trip was not necessary. The *professore* is innocent in all ways related to my investigation into the death of the mother of Hadiyyah. He will be released this very day."

"And *I*," Upman said, "do not mean to suggest that I care about that Paki's guilt or innocence."

His wife said his name sharply, placing her hand on his arm.

He shook her off and swung on her. "You bloody shut up, for God's sake." And to Salvatore, "Now you have a choice. You either tell me where that brat of Angelina's gone off to, or you face an international incident that's going to singe your eyebrows right off your face."

Salvatore sought to control his temper, although he knew his face was reflecting what he felt. English people, he'd thought, were supposed to be calm, supposed to be reserved, supposed to be rational. Of course, there were always the football hooligans, whose reputations preceded them wherever they went, but this man did not have the appearance of a football hooligan. What was wrong with him? A medical condition eating away at his brain and his manners simultaneously? He said, "I understand you well, signore. But I have no knowledge of where this Englishwoman . . . What did you call her?"

"Barbara," Mrs. Upman said. "I can't recall her surname and neither can Lorenzo but surely someone must know where she is. People have to register when they stay at hotels. Our own passports were taken and our identities noted, so it can't be impossible to find her."

"*Sì, sì,*" Salvatore said. "She can be found. But only if her surname is known. A Christian name only? This is not enough. I have no knowledge of where this woman Barbara might be. Nor have I knowledge of why she has taken Hadiyyah from Signor Mura. He did not report this to me or to my colleagues, and as that is the case—"

"She's done it because the Paki told her to do it," Mr. Upman snapped. "She does everything she does because of the Paki. You can bet she's been spreading her legs for him since Angelina left him last year. He's the sort who doesn't let grass grow, and just because she's an ugly cow, it doesn't mean—"

"*Basta!*" Salvatore declared. "I have no knowledge of this woman. File a missing person's report and have done with it. We are finished here."

He left the office, his blood on the boil. He stopped for a *caffè* on his way back to Daniele Bruno. It wasn't likely that espresso would do much to settle his nerves—quite the contrary—but he wanted a moment to think and he couldn't come up with another way to achieve this.

At this second instance of lying to someone about Barbara Havers, Salvatore had to pause. And then he had to ask himself why he was pausing when any man exhibiting rational behaviour would at this juncture toss her out of the *questura* on her ear. For she was clearly trouble incarnate, which he didn't need to be associated with, since he was already himself navigating very difficult political waters. So then he had to ask himself what he was doing, hiding this woman in his own home while claiming not to know where she was. And he also had to ask himself why in his conversation with DI Lynley, he had claimed ignorance of her association with a cowboy journalist whom he—Salvatore Lo Bianco—had seen with his very own eyes. In addition to this, there was now her intimacy with Taymullah Azhar to consider. Upman was a madman, *certo*, but hadn't Salvatore seen from the very first that there was something more than neighbourly concern in Barbara's journey from London?

So he couldn't trust her. But he wanted to trust her. And he didn't know what this meant.

Salvatore downed the rest of his *caffè*. He headed back in the direction of the interview room where Daniele Bruno waited with his solicitor. He was rounding the corner to reach this room when before him, he saw its door open. Barbara Havers emerged and there was something in her manner . . .

Salvatore stepped back to hide himself. When he looked again, she was entering the ladies' *bagno*. She was also removing a mobile phone from her bag.

LUCCA
TUSCANY

Her insides were jangling as the minutes stretched into half an hour and then three-quarters. Although Daniele Bruno was fully wired, when the wire was tested as they waited for the return of Salvatore, it was discovered that the unit placed upon Bruno was faulty and another had to be fetched. Barbara watched the clock, saw the minutes draining away at what seemed like double the normal pace, and knew she was going to have to do something.

Mitchell Corsico wasn't going to wait. He had a story that was hotter than any he'd previously filed. Unless she could get him a better one, he was going to send it to London no matter how many people it harmed. She had to stop him or to reason with him or to threaten him or to . . . to do *something* and she didn't know what. But ringing him was a first step, so three-quarters of an hour into their wait for Salvatore's return, she excused herself and headed for the ladies'.

She ducked inside and looked into each of the three stalls before locking herself into the last one and ringing the London journalist. She said, "Things are taking longer than I thought."

He said laconically, "Oh, too right, Barb."

"I'm not lying to you, and I'm not stalling. The damn Upmans showed up here and—"

"I saw them."

"Bloody hell, Mitchell. Where are you? You've got to stay out of sight. Salvatore's already got a scent about you—"

"It's your job to do something about that."

"Oh, for God's sake. Listen to me. We've got this bloke set up with a wire."

"Name?"

"I've already told you I can't give you a name. If this first try doesn't get an admission from Mura, then we'll need another go at him. Just now it's one bloke's word against the other bloke's word and there's no case that can be built out of that."

"No good, Barb. I have a story needing to be sent to Rodney."

"You'll get the story as soon as I have it. Listen to me, Mitchell. You can be there for Azhar's release. You c'n get a shot of him being reunited with Hadiyyah. You'll have the whole thing exclusively. But you have to wait."

"I have other things exclusively as well," he pointed out.

"You use that and we're finished, Mitchell."

"I use it, darling, and so are you. So you have to ask yourself if that's the way you want this to play out."

"Of *course* it isn't. Whatever else you think, I'm not a bleeding fool."

"I'm chuffed to hear that, so you'll understand that, while I personally would love to give you all the time God ever invented to produce the names, the dates, the whatevers and whoevers, in my line of work, time counts for something. Deadlines, Barb. That's what they're called. I have them, you don't."

She thought furiously. She knew the disaster that would befall not only her but also Azhar if Mitchell Corsico sent off the story he'd crafted from what Dwayne Doughty had given him: Her next job—and only if she happened to be extremely lucky—would probably be sweeping the gutters in Southend-on-Sea while Azhar's future would consist of facing kidnapping charges or, if he somehow managed to get home before those charges hit the light of day in this country, spending the next few years fighting extradition to Italy.

"Listen to me, Mitchell," she said. "I'll give you everything that I can. There'll be a transcript of what goes down between the bloke we have wired and Lorenzo Mura. I'll put my hands on that and send it your way. You'll have your Italian journalist mate do the translation—"

"And give *him* the exclusive? Not bloody likely."

"Okay, you'll have someone else do the translation . . . Aldo Greco, Azhar's solicitor . . . and then you'll have the story."

"Fine. Excellent. Brilliant."

Barbara thought, Thank God.

But then he added, "Just as long as I have it by noon."

He rang off on her crying out his name. She cursed him soundly. She thought about throwing her mobile phone into the loo. Instead, she left the stall she'd been occupying.

She opened the door and walked directly into Salvatore.

LUCCA
TUSCANY

Salvatore couldn't lie to himself about the nature of the phone call that Barbara Havers had just made. He'd heard her say *Mitchell* and he'd noted the urgency in her tone. Even had that not been the case, the expression on her face would have told him that trusting her had been an error. He reflected briefly on why he felt so afflicted by this betrayal. He decided it was because she was a guest in his home, because she was a fellow cop, and because he'd only just protected her from the loathsome Upmans. He thought, ridiculously, that she owed him something.

She began to babble, regardless of the fact that he couldn't understand a word she was saying. He could see that she was trying to explain and that she was asking him to find someone who could translate her words for him. He recognised *bloody, bleeding, sodding,* and *hell,* and whatever she said was also peppered with *Azhar* and *Hadiyyah* and references to London. When he nodded at her mobile and said quietly, *"Parlava a un giornalista, nevvero?,"* he could see that she perfectly understood what he meant. She said, "Yes, yes, all right, it was a journalist but you've got to try to understand because he has information from a bloke in London and it can sink me and it can sink Azhar and Azhar will end up losing everything including Hadiyyah and you need to see for the love of God that he can't lose Hadiyyah because if he does then he loses everything and why why why don't you speak English because we could talk this out and I could make you see because I can tell from your face that this is something personal to you like I've stabbed you straight in the heart and bloody hell Salvatore bloody bloody bleeding hell."

None of which he understood as it all came out, to him, as one very long word. He nodded to the door of the ladies' *bagno* and said, *"Mi segua,"* and she followed him back to the interview room where Daniele Bruno was waiting for what came next.

He opened this door, but instead of walking inside, he told Bruno and his *avvocato* that he had to deal with one small matter before they could proceed. This small matter was taking Barbara Havers to a second interview room, where he asked her to sit by indicating a chair on one side of the table.

"*Il Suo telefonino, Barbara,*" he said to her. To make sure she understood, he took out his own mobile and pointed to it. She said, "What? Why?" which was clear to him. He merely repeated his request and she handed it over. He could tell she thought he was going to use it to hit a redial on the number she'd rung, but he had no intention of doing that. He knew whom she'd phoned. But as he lived and breathed, she wasn't going to phone him again. He slipped her mobile into his pocket. She gave a cry that needed no translation. He said to her, "*Mi dispiace, Barbara. Deve aspettare qui, in questura adesso.*" For he had no idea how she might betray him further. There was no other choice he could see but to detain her in the interview room while the next part of their little drama played out.

She said, "No! No! You've got to understand. Salvatore, I had to. He didn't give me a choice. If I didn't cooperate . . . You don't know what he's holding you don't know what I've done you don't know how ruined this is going to make me and make Azhar and if that happens then Hadiyyah's going to end up with those wretched people and I know how they are and what they think and how they feel which is that they don't even care about her and they sure as bloody hell don't want her round them and there is no one else because Azhar's family . . . please, please, *please.*"

"*Mi dispiace,*" he repeated. He was indeed sorry. He left her locked carefully in the room.

He returned to Bruno and Rocco Garibaldi. After a negotiated glass of wine to still his nerves, Bruno made the phone call to Lorenzo Mura from a telephone set up to tape their exchange. It was very simple. Bruno said tersely that they needed to meet. The police had been to DARBA Italia. Things were heating up.

Lorenzo Mura was hesitant. Daniele Bruno was insistent. They agreed to meet at the location that Salvatore had decided upon, its having the best possibility for an unobstructed view of their encounter as well as an unrestricted taping of their words. The Parco Fluviale in one hour, at the *campo* where Mura held his soccer clinics. Mura agreed to this and promised to be there. He sounded a little irritated but not suspicious.

Rocco Garibaldi attended them. He and Salvatore rode in the white delivery van, which, Salvatore explained to him, would be parked at the outdoor café some one hundred metres from the field Mura used. At this time of year, on a fine day such as this, the café would be crowded. Its car park would be filled. A van such as theirs would go unnoticed. Anyone who saw it would merely conclude that its driver had stopped for refreshments.

Daniele Bruno would, of course, drive his own car and leave it in the small parking area beside the *campo*. He would get out of it and wait at one of the two picnic tables beneath the trees. He would remain visible to Salvatore at all times, walking into the parking area once Lorenzo Mura arrived. Thus he would be monitored from the café. Binoculars would be fixed on him lest he decide to do something in silence to warn the other man that he was wired for sound.

As Salvatore and his companions had a far shorter distance to drive to reach the Parco Fluviale, they were there within fifteen minutes. Bruno was put into position, the white van was established in such a way that Bruno remained well within sight, and then, after testing the quality of sound from the wire, they waited the forty minutes that remained.

Mura didn't show. An additional ten minutes past the appointed hour ticked by. Bruno stood from the picnic table and began to pace. With earphones on, Salvatore could hear his "*Merda, merda*" with perfect clarity.

Another ten minutes. Bruno declared that the other man was clearly not coming. Salvatore rang his mobile and said, No, my friend. They would continue to wait. At the half-hour point, Lorenzo Mura showed up.

He spoke first as he got out of his car. "What is it that we must talk about that cannot be talked about on the phone?" He sounded sharp, aggrieved. He was not yet worried about the conversation.

Bruno's response followed the instructions he'd been given. "We must speak of Angelina and how she died, Lorenzo."

"What is it you're talking about?"

"The *E. coli* and how you meant to use it. And what you told me the use would be. I believe you lied to me, Lorenzo. There was no experiment with wine and the vineyards that you had in mind."

"And this is why you asked me to meet you here?" Lorenzo demanded. "What is it that you think, my friend? And why are you so nervous, Daniele? You sweat like a pig in the heat." He glanced round the area and for an instant seemed to look directly into Salvatore's binoculars. But it was impossible that Mura could have seen anything other than a white van parked among many other vehicles some distance away from where he himself stood.

"The police have been to DARBA Italia," Bruno told him.

Lorenzo glanced at him sharply. "You have told me this. What is your point?"

And now the lie they had all agreed upon. Salvatore prayed that Bruno could carry it off: "Someone saw me take the *E. coli*," he said. "It was nothing to him at first. He wasn't even sure what he saw. He thought nothing at all until the story about Angelina's death appeared in *Prima Voce*. And even then he thought little enough till the police showed up."

Lorenzo said nothing at first. Salvatore watched his face through the binoculars. He lit a cigarette, his eyes narrowing from the smoke of it. He picked a bit of tobacco from his tongue. He said, "Daniele, what is this that you speak of?"

"You know what I speak of. This *E. coli*, the particular strain of it . . . The police are asking serious questions. If Angelina is dead because of *E. coli*, if they found it still within her body . . . Lorenzo, what did you do with the bacteria I gave you?"

Salvatore held his breath. So much hung on Mura's reply. The man finally said, "And this is why I come to meet you all the way from the *fattoria*? To tell you what I did with a bit of bacteria? I flushed it down the toilet, Daniele. It was not useful to me as I thought it would be . . . an experiment with bacteria and wine . . . so I flushed it away."

"Then how did Angelina die with *E. coli* in her system, Lorenzo? This is what the police want no one to know. This *E. coli* is what killed Angelina. It is what they are withholding from her murderer."

"What are you saying?" Lorenzo demanded. "I did not kill her. She carried my child. She was to be my wife. If her death was *E. coli* . . . You know as I do that this is everywhere, this bacteria, Daniele."

"Some *E. coli* is everywhere. But not this *E. coli*. Lorenzo, hear me. The police have been to DARBA Italia—"

"You tell me this already."

"They speak to Antonio, they speak to Alessandro. They have made a connection and they will want to speak to me soon and I do not know what to tell them, Lorenzo. If I tell them that I gave the *E. coli* to you—"

"You must not!"

"But I *did* give it to you, and if I am to lie on your behalf, I must know—"

"You need to know nothing! They can prove nothing. Who saw you give it to me? No one. Who saw what I did with it? No one."

"I do not wish to be arrested for what I did, my friend. I have a wife. I have children. My family is everything to me."

"As mine would have been. As it *could* have been had he not shown up. You talk of family while mine has been destroyed, just as he planned it."

"Who?"

"The Muslim. The father of Angelina's daughter. He came to Italy. He intended to have her back. I could see this: the loss of her, the loss of my child because she left me as she had left others and this is something . . ." Lorenzo's voice cracked.

Daniele Bruno said, "It was for him, no? The *E. coli*, Lorenzo. It was for the Muslim. To do what? To make him ill? To kill him? What?"

"I do not know." Lorenzo began to cry. "Just to be rid of him so that she would not look at him, she would not call him by a pet name, she would not allow him to touch her or to care for her while I stood by and had to watch this . . . this *thing* between them." He stumbled towards the picnic tables. He fell onto one of the benches and sobbed into his hands.

"*Va bene,*" Salvatore said, removing his headphones within the white van. He radioed the police cars that waited for his word, farther along the road and deep into the Parco Fluviale. "*Adesso andiamo,*" he told them. They had enough. It was time to bring Lorenzo Mura to justice.

LUCCA
TUSCANY

He lifted his head the moment he heard the scrape of tyres on the gravel of the parking area. He saw the police cars, and he didn't wait to catch sight of the white van trundling along Via della Scogliera from the direction of the café. He knew in an instant what had happened. He ran.

He was very fast. A football player, he had remarkable speed and equal endurance. He took off across the *campo* where he coached his soccer pupils, and before Salvatore was out of the van, he had crossed the field with four uniformed officers in pursuit.

He quickly disappeared into the trees at the far side of the field. He was heading southwest, and on the other side of those trees, Salvatore knew, a steep berm rose, its side heavily grown with grass in this springtime month, with a walking path along its top.

His officers were no match for the man's speed. They were going to lose him in very short order. But this was of no import to Salvatore. Once he saw the direction that Mura was taking, he had a very good idea where the man was heading.

He said, "*Basta*," more to himself than to anyone else. He turned away, nodded at Daniele Bruno for a job well done, and left him in the hands of his *avvocato* and the officers within the white van who had taped his words. They would transport him to the *questura* and to his release. Meantime, Salvatore would take care of Mura.

He commandeered one of the police cars. He headed along Via della Scogliera, northeast along the River Serchio. The river sparkled in the sun of the afternoon. He lowered the window and enjoyed the breeze.

At the entrance to the park, he headed back towards the centre of Lucca. But he did not go as far as the *viale* circumambient to the ancient wall. Instead, he chose to skirt the neighbourhood of Borgo Giannotti on its north side, coursing down a street where luxurious garden trees sheltered houses hidden behind tall walls. He was held up for two minutes along this route by a large *camion carico* attempting to manoeuvre into position so as to deliver its load of furniture to the

occupants of a newly purchased house. Several impatient drivers behind him applied their car horns to the frustration of having to wait,
but he felt no need to do so. When he set off again, he passed Palazetto
dello Sport and the large playing field of Campo CONI. At last he
reached his destination: the *cimitero comunale*.

There were cars and bicycles in the main car park, but there was no
indication of a burial going on within the tall and silent walls of the
cemetery on this day. The gates were open as always, and Salvatore entered them respectfully. He crossed himself at the feet of the guano- and
weather-streaked bronze Jesus and Mary. A solemn mausoleum rose behind them forbiddingly, but the statues themselves bore faces at peace.

He paced along the gravel path, where the scent of flowers was a
mixed perfume in the air and the sun cast brilliant light upon the
marble slabs that topped the gravesites. Across the large quadrangle
that he was walking through, tombstones rose as quiet witnesses to
his progress towards Lorenzo Mura.

He was where Salvatore had concluded he would be: at the grave
of Angelina Upman. He had thrown himself across the patch of dirt
that would remain unmarked until her own marble slab covered the
site of her burial. In the dry, warm dust that stood in place of this
marker, Lorenzo Mura wept.

Salvatore allowed him this time to mourn, and he did not approach
him for some minutes. The man's agony was a terrible thing to behold,
but Salvatore beheld it. It was a reminder to him of the price of love and
he asked himself if he ever wanted to feel such attachment to a woman
again.

Finally, when Mura's worst weeping had passed, he went to the man.
He bent and took his arm in a grip that was firm but was not fierce.

"*Venga, signore*," he said to Lorenzo, and Lorenzo rose without
protest or question or fight.

Salvatore walked him out of the cemetery and eased him into the
car for the short drive to the *questura*.

LUCCA
TUSCANY

At first, she banged on the door like a bad actress in an even worse television drama. The first time, Ottavia Schwartz came to see if she was in danger or in urgent need of something, and she tried to explain, tried to bully her way past the policewoman, tried to beg, tried to flee. But Ottavia spoke no English, and even if she had done, it was clear she'd had her orders from Salvatore. As had everyone else, it seemed, for no one came in answer to her shouts once Ottavia had again secured the door against her.

All she needed was a mobile phone. She tried to make this understandable to Ottavia by mimicking, by saying *telefonino* when she finally remembered the word she'd heard used, by begging, by telling her that all she required was the ability to make one simple brief phone call . . . But she achieved nothing.

She was left with watching the time pass. She watched it on a wall clock. She saw it on the inexpensive watch she wore. With the passage of the deadline that Mitchell Corsico had given her, she tried to tell herself that the journalist had only been bluffing. But she knew the story he had was far too huge. It was page-one material and Mitchell wanted to reestablish his place on page one. Every tabloid reporter worth his salt wanted this: a by-line that melted the nerves of anyone whose activities suggested that a reputation-demolishing exposé was in order in the inimitable style of *The Source*. She'd known that when she'd got involved with the bloke.

So she paced. She had her cigarettes, and she smoked. Someone brought her a *panino* which she did not eat and a bottle of water which she did not drink. Once a female officer escorted her to the loo. And that was all.

Hours had passed by the time she was released. Salvatore was the one to fetch her. In those hours, much had happened. Lorenzo Mura had been brought to the *questura*, he had been questioned, he had been processed, and all the details had been taken care of.

"*Mi dispiace*," Salvatore told her. His eyes were indescribably sad.

Barbara said, "Yeah. Me too," and when he handed her her mobile phone, she said, "D'you mind if I . . . ?"

"*Vada, Barbara, vada,*" he told her.

He left her. He closed the door, but he didn't lock it. She wondered if the room was wired, figured it was, and stepped out into the corridor. She rang Mitchell Corsico.

It was, of course, too late. Mitch said, "Sorry, Barb, but a bloke's got to do what a bloke's—"

She ended the call without listening to the rest. She trudged to Salvatore's office. He was on the phone with someone called Piero, but when he saw Barbara, he rang off. He stood.

She said, throat tight, "I wish I could make you understand. I didn't have a choice, see? Because of Hadiyyah. And now . . . things're going to be worse because of what comes next and I still don't have a choice. Not really. Not in the ways that are the most important. And you're not going to understand the way it comes down, Salvatore. You're going to think once again that I'm betraying you and I s'pose I will be, but what else is there to do? A story—a big one—is going to hit a major tabloid tomorrow morning. It's going to be about Azhar, about me, about what was planned and who planned it, about hiring certain people to snatch Hadiyyah, about money exchanging hands and records altered and all of this is very bad. Your tabloids are going to pick up on it, and even if they don't, DI Lynley is going to ring you and tell you the truth. And you see, I can't let that happen although I've already failed to stop the tabloid story from being sent in." She cleared her throat mightily and said through lips that felt as if they would bleed, "And I'm so sorry because you are one very decent bloke."

Salvatore listened carefully. She could see the care he was taking to try to sort it all out. But it seemed to her that the only things he picked up on were names: Azhar and Hadiyyah. He spoke about Lorenzo Mura in reply, about Azhar, about Angelina. From this she reckoned he was telling her that Mura had confessed to what she herself had suspected: that Azhar was intended to drink that wine with the *E. coli* in it. She nodded as he said to her, "*Aveva ragione, Barbara Havers. Aveva proprio ragione.*"

From this, she supposed he was telling her that she had been right all along. It certainly gave her not a moment's pleasure.

19 MAY

Barbara rose before half past five. She dressed and sat on the edge of her bed. She watched Hadiyyah sleeping, innocent of the knowledge of the change that now had to come to her life.

One did not orchestrate an international kidnapping and simply walk away from that kidnapping's fallout. Within a few hours, Azhar was going to be free to return to London with his child, but once the full story came out, the hell that would follow would ruin him financially, personally, and professionally. Interpol would see to that. Italian prosecution would see to that. Extradition would see to that. A London investigation would see to that. And the Upman family would see to that.

What Barbara knew she had to do was to get to work on the problem and do it quickly. She had little enough time to see to things properly, and she needed Aldo Greco to help her.

She'd rung him late on the previous day. She told him what she needed. He'd already been informed of Lorenzo Mura's arrest and of Azhar's being in the clear of all charges related to the death of Angelina Upman, so when she suggested that it was imperative to little Hadiyyah's mental and psychological state—"The kid's been through the emotional wringer, eh?" was how she put it—that she be reunited with her father quickly, he was on board at once.

Unfortunately, he explained, he had to be in court in the morning. But he would ring Ispetorre Lo Bianco immediately and make the appropriate arrangements.

She said, "C'n you ask him . . . I'd like to . . . Well, he and I are a bit on the outs—"

"*Come?* The 'outs'?"

"We've had a difference of opinion. It's a language thing. I've had a bloody hard time making myself understood. But I'd like to be able to speak to Azhar before he sees Hadiyyah. Everything that's gone on? It's rattled her, and he needs to know before he sees her, to prepare himself, eh? He doesn't speak Italian either, so Salvatore can't tell him and as you've got to be in court . . ."

"Ah, *capisco*. This I will handle as well."

Which he had done in short order, clearly a man who had no back burner on the cooktop of his professional life. Within thirty minutes, it had all been arranged. Azhar would be ready for release in the morning, Salvatore would himself drive to the prison to fetch him, he would take Barbara along with him, and Barbara would be given the time to speak to Azhar privately so as to prepare him for his daughter's state.

Hadiyyah's state, of course, was perfectly fine. There was much about what had occurred that she did not yet understand, and there would be much for her to process in the time to come. But like so many children, she was in and of the moment in which she lived. Salvatore's mother had been a boon in the care of her. As long as Hadiyyah liked to learn Italian cooking and was quick about memorising the scores of Catholic saints whose holy cards Signora Lo Bianco presented to her, all was well.

Barbara went out for a walk. She rang Mitchell Corsico. She had hopes he'd had second thoughts, hanging on to the idea of the reunion story—*Father and Kidnapped Daughter Together at Last!*—as bigger than the one he'd written with Dwayne Doughty's information. But even as she gave thought to the hope, she knew it was an unreasonable one. International kidnapping scandals would always trump tender reunions between fathers and their children. Combine that scandal with Barbara's own participation in the crimes that had gone down . . . One couldn't have hopes.

Once again Mitchell said, "Sorry, Barb. What could I do? But listen, you need to look at the story. You won't be able to score a copy of the paper here in Lucca 'less you find a newsagent with English papers. But if you look online—"

Once again, she ended the call, cutting him off midsentence. She'd learned all that she needed to learn. The project now was to get to Azhar.

She could tell that Salvatore no longer trusted her, but as a man with a daughter Hadiyyah's age, he was going to want to do what was right for the child. Barbara didn't know what Aldo Greco said to the Chief Inspector, but whatever it had been, it worked. Before they each went off to their respective bedrooms in Torre Lo Bianco on the previous evening, he'd set the time for their departure to fetch Azhar back to Lucca, and he was as good as his word when it came to her accompanying him.

They were silent on the route, for what else could they be in a situation in which neither of them spoke the other's language. Barbara could tell she'd dealt a real blow to the Italian, and more than anything she wanted him to understand why she'd done as she had done.

He saw her as on the take, no doubt. Anyone would. Police all over the world were dirty—not all of them, of course, but there were enough—and he would have little reason to think she was anything other than an inside source for the worst tabloid in London. That this wasn't the case . . . How could she explain? Really, who would believe her in any language? She said to him again, "I bloody wish you spoke decent English, Salvatore. You think I betrayed you, but it wasn't *meant* as betrayal and it wasn't intended as a personal blow to you. Truth is . . . I bloody like you, mate. And now . . . with what happens next . . . ? That's not going to be a personal blow either. But it'll look like it. It'll sodding look like I used you only to betray you again. I won't mean it that way. Believe me, I won't. God, I hope you'll be able to understand someday. I mean, I c'n tell I've lost your trust and whatever good opinion you might've had about me and believe me I c'n see it in your face when you look at me. And I'm so bloody sorry about that, but I didn't have a choice. I've never had a choice. At least not one that I could ever see."

He glanced at her as he drove. They were on the *autostrada* and traffic was heavy with commuters, with lorries, and with tourist coaches heading to their next glorious Tuscan destination. He said her name in a very kind tone which, for a moment, made her think she had his forgiveness and his understanding. But then he said, "*Mi dispiace ma non capisco. E comunque . . . parla inglese troppo velocemente.*"

She had enough Italian at this point to understand that much. She'd heard it from him often enough. She said, "*Mi dispiace* as well, mate." She turned to the window and watched the Italian scenery whizzing by: leafy vineyards, wonderful old farms, orchards of olive trees climbing hillsides, mountain villages in the distance, all of it crowned with a cloudless azure sky. Paradise, she thought. And then she added wryly, Lost.

Arrangements had been made in advance at the prison where Azhar was being held. He was ready when they arrived, not a prisoner in a boiler suit any longer but a gentleman scientist in his white shirt and trousers, released into the company of the policeman who had investigated him and the policewoman who was his most determined friend. Ispettore Lo Bianco kept a respectful distance as Barbara and Azhar greeted each other.

She spoke to the Pakistani man quietly, walking him ahead of Salvatore, linking her arm with his in a manner that would demonstrate warm friendship, leaning towards him, saying, "Listen, Azhar. It's not how it looks, this thing. I mean your being released. It's not how it looks."

He looked at her quickly, his dark eyes confused.

She said, "It's not over." Quickly, she told him about Corsico's story, which would be in *The Source* that morning. Doughty, she told him, had given Corsico everything in order to save his own neck. Names, dates, places, money exchanging hands, Internet hacking, the entire enchilada of information. She'd tried to stop the bloody journalist from writing the story, she said. She'd begged. She'd pleaded. She'd reasoned. And she'd failed.

Azhar said, "What does this mean?"

"You know. Azhar. You *know*. The Italian journalists are going to pick up on the story sometime today. Once they do, there'll be a bloody big hue and cry. Someone is going to pursue the facts, and if it isn't Salvatore, it'll be some other detective who gets assigned. You'll be detained again and I've burnt too many bridges with Salvatore to be able to help you."

"But at the end of the day . . . Barbara, they will see how little choice I had once Angelina left London and hid Hadiyyah from me. They will show compassion. They will—"

"Listen to me." She tightened her grip on his arm. "The Upmans are here in Lucca. They went to the *questura* yesterday and they're bloody well going to go there today. They want Hadiyyah turned over to them. Salvatore held them off, but once the kidnapping story hits the papers here . . . And that's supposing the Upmans haven't already been rung up by Bathsheba from London telling them about the story in *The Source*, at which point, believe me, they'll demand Hadiyyah because what kind of dad kidnaps his own kid and stows her in a convent with a madwoman who thinks she's a nun, eh?"

"I did not intend—"

"D'you think they care what you intended? They hate you, mate, and you and I know it and they'll go for custody of her just *because* they hate you, and they'll bloody get it. Who cares that she means nothing to them? It's you they're after."

He was silent. Barbara glanced at Salvatore, who was speaking into his mobile, still a respectful distance from them. She knew how little time they had. Their conversation had already gone on too long for a woman who was only supposed to be passing along information about the state of her friend's beloved child.

She said, "You can't go back to London. And you can't stay here. You're cooked either way."

His lips barely moved as he said, "What then do I do?"

"Again, Azhar, I think you know. You've not got a choice." She waited for him to take this in, and she saw on his face that he had done so, for he blinked hard and she thought she saw on his lashes the brilliance of unshed tears. She said, although she felt as if the pain of doing so might actually drive a sword through her heart, "You still have family there, Azhar. They'll welcome her. They'll welcome you. She speaks the language. Or at least she's been learning it. You've seen to that."

"She won't understand," he said in an agonised voice. "How can I do this to her after what she has been through?"

"You don't have a choice. And you'll be there for her. You'll ease her way. You'll see to it her life there is an extraordinary one. And she'll adjust, Azhar. She'll have aunts and uncles. She'll have cousins. It will be okay."

"How can I—"

Barbara cut in, choosing to interpret the rest of his question in the only way possible now. She said, "Salvatore has your passports, probably locked away in the *questura*. He'll hand them over, and you and Hadiyyah and I will head to the airport. Fond farewells to him and all the rest. He may take us there, but he won't stay to see where we go or even if we depart. I'll go to London. You'll go . . . wherever you can go to get a flight to Lahore. Just *out* of Italy. Paris? Frankfurt? Stockholm? It doesn't matter as long as it's not London. You'll do what you have to do at this point because it's the only thing left. And you know it, Azhar. You bloody know it."

He looked at her. She saw his dark eyes fill with tears. He said, "And you, Barbara? What about you?"

"Me?" She tried to sound lighthearted. "I'll face the music back in London. I've done it before, and I'll survive. Facing the music is what I do best."

LUCCA
TUSCANY

First was Torre Lo Bianco, where Hadiyyah leapt into her father's arms and buried her face in his neck. He held her close. She said, "Barbara told me you were helping Salvatore. Did you help him a lot? What did you *do*?"

Azhar cleared his throat roughly. He smoothed back wisps of her hair and said with a smile, "Many, many things did I do. But it is time for us to go now, *khushi*. Can you thank the signora and Inspector Lo Bianco for taking such good care of you while I was away?"

She did so. She hugged Salvatore's mamma, who kissed her, got teary, and called her *bella bambina*, and she hugged Salvatore who said "*Niente, niente*" as she thanked him. She asked them both to tell Bianca and Marco *arrivederci*, and she said to Barbara, "D'you get to come home as well?"

Barbara told her that indeed she did, and in very short order, they'd taken their bags to where Salvatore had left his car and they were on their way to the *questura*. At every moment, Barbara looked for some sign that Mitch Corsico's page-one story had somehow broken in Italy. She also looked for the Upmans on every street corner and behind every bush as they coursed the route along the *viale* outside the town wall.

At the *questura*, things moved rapidly and Barbara was immensely grateful for this. Passports were returned to Azhar, Hadiyyah was left in the company of Ottavia Schwartz, and the buxom translator was called in so that Azhar might hear Salvatore's explanation of how Angelina Upman had come to die of ingesting a devastating strain of *E. coli*. He covered his mouth with his hand as he listened, and the pain in his eyes was evident. He pointed out that, had he been the one to drink the affected wine, it was likely he would have survived the subsequent illness. But because it had been Angelina who'd drunk it, Angelina who was already unwell with her pregnancy, things had been misinterpreted by her doctors until it was far too late. "I wished her no ill," he concluded. "I would have you know that, Inspector."

"Plenty of ill was wished towards you, Azhar," Barbara put in. "And I wager you wouldn't have gone to hospital had you got ill. You would've thought you'd picked up a bug: on the flight, in the water, whatever, eh? You'd've got over the first bout with this stuff, but then the next step would've been a worse bout and losing your kidneys and probably dying as well. Lorenzo might not have known all that, but it wasn't important to him. Making you suffer was what he had in mind, with the hope that making you suffer would lead to making you gone from Angelina's life."

Salvatore listened to the translation of all this. Barbara cast a look in his direction, saw once again the solemnity of his expression, but also read the great kindness in his eyes. She knew that there was one more thing that had to be said in advance of Corsico's damning kidnapping story breaking in the Italian papers.

She said to Azhar, "C'n you give me a moment with . . ." And she nodded in Salvatore's direction.

He said of course, that he would go to Hadiyyah, that they would be waiting, and he left her alone with Salvatore and the translator to whom Barbara said, "Please tell him I'm sorry. Tell him, please, it was nothing personal, anything I did. It wasn't meant as a betrayal or as using him or anything like that, although I bloody well know it looked that way. Tell him . . . See, I have this London journalist on my back— he's the cowboy bloke Salvatore saw?—and he was here to help me help Azhar. See, Azhar's my neighbour back in London and when Angelina took Hadiyyah from him, he was . . . Salvatore, he was so broken. And I *couldn't* leave him like that, broken. Hadiyyah's really all he has left in England in the way of family so I had to help him. And all of this . . . everything that's gone on? Can you tell him it was all part of helping Azhar? That's all, really. Because, see, this journalist has another story that he's running and . . . that's all that I can say, really. That's all. That and I hope he understands."

Salvatore listened to the translation, which came nearly as rapidly as Barbara herself was speaking. He didn't look at the translator, though. He remained as he had been before, with his gaze on Barbara's face.

At the end, there was silence. Barbara found that she couldn't blame him for not replying and, indeed, that she didn't actually want him to reply. For he was going to want to hunt her down and strangle her when he finally discovered what her next move had been, so to have his forgiveness in advance of betraying him another time . . . ? She didn't know how she could contend with that anyway.

She said, "So I'll say thanks and good-bye. We c'n take a taxi to the airport or—"

Salvatore interrupted. He spoke quietly and with what sounded like either kindness or resignation. She waited until he had finished and then said to the translator, "What?"

"The *ispettore* says that it has been a pleasure to know you," the translator replied.

"He said more than that. He went on a bit. What else did he say?"

"He said that he will arrange your transport to the airport."

She nodded. But then she felt compelled to add, "That's it, then?"

The translator looked at Salvatore and then back at Barbara. A soft smile curved her lips. "No. Ispettore Lo Bianco has said that any man on earth would find himself lucky to have had in his life such a friend as you."

Barbara wasn't prepared. She felt the claw of emotion at her throat. She finally was able to say, "Ta. Thank you. *Grazie*, Salvatore. *Grazie* and *ciao*."

"*Niente*," Salvatore said. "*Arrivederci, Barbara Havers*."

LUCCA
TUSCANY

Salvatore waited, patiently as always, in the anteroom of Piero Fanucci's office. This time, though, it was not because Piero was forcing him to wait or because someone was being berated by *il Pubblico Ministero* inside his inner sanctum. Rather, it was because Piero had not yet returned from his lunch. He'd taken it later than usual, Salvatore had discovered, because of a lengthy meeting with three *avvocati* representing the family of Carlo Casparia. They had come on the not small matter of false arrest, false imprisonment, interrogations without an *avvocato* present, coerced confessions, and dragging the family name through the mud. Unless these issues were resolved to the satisfaction of *la famiglia Casparia*, *il Pubblico Ministero* was going to face an investigation into his investigation and have no doubt about that.

Il drago had evidently done his usual bit upon hearing this unveiled threat. He'd breathed the roaring flames of *segreto investigativo* at the placid lawyers. He was under no obligation to tell them anything, he declared. Judicial secrecy ruled the day, not their pitiful claims on behalf of the Casparias.

At this, the *avvocati* were not impressed. If that was how he wished to proceed, they informed the *magistrato*, so be it. They left the rest of their remarks hanging in the air. He would be hearing again from them soon.

All of this Salvatore had from Piero's secretary. She'd been present to take notes, which she was more than happy to share with him. It was her intention to outlive Piero in her position as secretary. Her hope had long been that outliving Piero meant watching him be summarily dismissed from his job. That looked highly probable now.

Salvatore evaluated all the information as he waited. He put it onto the scales in which he had been weighing his next move since the departure of Barbara Havers and her London neighbours. He had felt unaccountably sad to see the dishevelled British woman depart. He knew he should have remained furious at her, but he'd found that fury was not among the feelings he had. Instead, he'd felt compelled to take her part. So when the Upmans arrived at the *questura* later that morning, he'd dealt with them by not dealing with them at all. Their granddaughter was with her father, he told them through the translator. As far as he knew, they both were now gone from Italy. He could be of no help to the signore and the signora. He could not assist them in wresting Hadiyyah from the custody of her father. "*Mi dispiace e ciao*," he said to them. If they cared to know more—especially in regards to their daughter Angelina—they might wish to speak to Aldo Greco, whose English was superb. Or, if they had no wish to learn the truth about Angelina's death, then they, too, could return to London. There, and not here, they could take up the matter of who would have custody of little Hadiyyah.

Signor Upman's subsequent mouth-frothing had done little to move Salvatore. He left the man standing alongside his wife in Reception, where Salvatore had met them.

Then had come the phone call from the *telegiornalista* who had supplied Barbara Havers and the cowboy from London with the film taken on the day that Lorenzo Mura had placed the tainted glass of wine in front of Taymullah Azhar. This man spoke of a story breaking this very morning in a London *giornale*, one that had come to him firsthand from the reporter whose work it was in a tabloid called *The Source*. It involved the careful plan to kidnap Hadiyyah, one that had her father as its engineer. Names, dates, exchanges of money, alibis created, individuals hired . . . Was Ispettore Lo Bianco going to pursue this? the *telegiornalista* enquired.

Purtroppo, no had been Salvatore's reply. For surely the *telegiornalista* knew that the kidnapping case had been handed over to Nicodemo Triglia some weeks ago? So Salvatore had no place in any pursuit of this new information.

Did he know, then, where Taymullah Azhar and his daughter had gone? For the *telegiornalista* had learned that Azhar had been released from the prison where he'd been held, released into the care of Salvatore Lo Bianco and the English detective who'd accompanied him. Barbara Havers was her name. Where had Ispettore Lo Bianco taken them?

Here, of course, Salvatore had said. The *professore* had collected his passport and had departed, as was his right.

Departed? For where?

"*Non lo so,*" Salvatore had told him. For he had been most careful about this. Wherever they were going, he did not wish to know. Their fate was out of his hands now, and he intended to keep it that way.

When at last Piero Fanucci returned from *pranzo,* he appeared to be fully recovered from whatever concerns he might have had during his conversation with the Casparia family's team of *avvocati.* Salvatore gave idle thought to the idea that a half liter of wine probably had gone far to allay those concerns, but he nonetheless welcomed Piero's expansive greeting and he followed the *magistrato* into his office.

He was there to speak only about the death of Angelina Upman and the guilt of Lorenzo Mura. In the interview room at the *questura,* Mura had confessed brokenly to everything. With Daniele Bruno's assistance and his willingness to testify at whatever trial would follow the events associated with his meeting with Mura at the Parco Fluviale, it seemed to Salvatore that the investigation was now complete. Mura did not intend his woman to die, he explained to the *magistrato.* He did not intend her even to drink the wine that contained the bacteria. He'd meant it for the Pakistani man who'd come to assist in the search for their child. He had not known that, as a Muslim, Taymullah Azhar did not drink wine.

Piero said at the conclusion of Salvatore's remarks, "It is all circumstantial, what you give to me, no?"

It was, of course. But the circumstances were damning, Salvatore said. "Still, I leave it to you and to your wisdom, *Magistrato*, to decide how you wish to prosecute Signor Mura. You have been right about so many things, and I trust whatever decision you make once you have familiarised yourself with all the reports." These were in the folders that Salvatore carried. He handed them over, and Piero Fanucci placed them on the stack of other folders waiting for his perusal. Salvatore added, "The Mura family . . ."

"What of them?"

"They have hired an *avvocato* from Rome. It is my understanding that he will wish to strike a bargain with you."

"Bah," Piero said dismissively. "Romans."

Salvatore made a formal little bow, just an inclination of the head to indicate his acceptance of Piero's opinion of any lawyer who might come from Rome, that centre and hotbed of political scandal. He said farewell, then, and turned to leave. "Salvatore," Piero said, which stopped him. He waited politely while Piero gathered his thoughts. He was unsurprised when the other man said, "Our little spat in the Orto Botanico . . . I deeply regret my loss of control, Topo."

"These things happen when passions run high," Salvatore told him. "I assure you that, on my part, it is all forgotten."

"On mine as well, then. *Ci vediamo?*"

"*Ci vediamo, d'accordo,*" Salvatore agreed.

He left the office. A brief *passeggiata* was in order, he decided, so he took a little detour instead of heading directly to the *questura*. He wandered in the opposite direction, telling himself the day and the exercise would do him good. That his exercise took him to Piazza dei Cocomeri was of no import. That in the piazza was a very large newspaper kiosk was purely coincidental. That the *giornalaio* sold newspapers in English, French, and German as well as Italian was merely an intriguing discovery. He did not yet have that day's edition of *The Source*, however. The British newspapers generally arrived by late afternoon, flown over to Pisa and transported from the airport. If the *ispettore* wished a copy to be held for him, this could be easily arranged.

Salvatore said yes, he would like a copy of that particular paper. He handed over his money, nodded at the *giornalaio*, and went on his way. *Certo*, he could have used the Internet to see that morning's edition of the tabloid. But he'd always liked the feeling of an actual newspaper beneath his fingers. And if he had no English sufficient to read what was in the pages of this tabloid, what did it matter? He could find someone to translate it for him. Eventually, he decided, he would do so.

VICTORIA
LONDON

Isabelle Ardery's third meeting with the assistant commissioner took place at three o'clock. Lynley learned about it in the usual way. Prior to that meeting, Dorothea Harriman informed him sotto voce, there had been a flurry of phone calls from CIB1, followed by a lengthy encounter in Isabelle's office with one of the deputy assistant commissioners. To Lynley's question of which one of the DACs had met with Ardery, Dorothea lowered her voice even more. It was the one in charge of police personnel management, she told him. She'd tried to sort out what was going on, but all she could report was that Detective Superintendent Ardery had asked for a copy of the Police Act yesterday afternoon.

Lynley heard all this with a sinking heart. Sacking a policeman or -woman was an inordinately difficult manoeuvre. It wasn't a matter of saying, "Right, you're gone. Clear out your desk" because from a remark such as that, a lawsuit would follow as the night the day. So Isabelle had been necessarily careful in building her case, and although it pained him to know this, Lynley found that he couldn't blame her.

He rang Barbara's mobile. If nothing else, he could at least prepare her for what was to befall her when she returned to London. But he got no answer, and so he left a simple message for her to ring him at once. Then, after five minutes of waiting, he rang Salvatore Lo Bianco.

He was trying to get in contact with Sergeant Havers, he told the Italian man. Was she with him? Did he know where she was? She wasn't answering her mobile and—

"I suspect she is on an airplane," Salvatore told him. "She left Lucca at midday with the *professore* and little Hadiyyah."

"Returning to London?"

"Where else, my friend?" Salvatore said. "We are at a conclusion here. To the *magistrato* I gave my report this afternoon."

"What will he be pursuing, Salvatore?"

"To this, I confess I do not know. The case of Signora Upman's death ends with Signor Mura. As to the kidnapping of little Hadiyyah . . . ? That was taken from me long ago, as we both know. It, too, is in the hands of the *magistrato*. And Piero . . . ? Ah, Piero goes his own way in things. I have learned not to attempt to direct him."

That was the extent of Salvatore's information. Lynley had the distinct feeling that there was more going on than Salvatore was willing to say via phone. But whatever it was, it was going to have to stay in Italy until such a time that Lynley travelled to Lucca again.

A phone call from Dorothea Harriman supervened upon his conversation with Salvatore Lo Bianco. DI John Stewart was in conference with the detective superintendent now. He had taken a copy of a tabloid into the meeting, Detective Inspector Lynley. Harriman thought it was *The Source*, but she couldn't be sure.

Lynley rang Barbara Havers another time. Another time, it was her voice mail he heard. Just a surly "This is Havers. Leave a message," in an impatient tone. He told her to ring him as soon as possible. He added, "Salvatore tells me you're on a flight to London. We do need to talk before you come in to the Met, Barbara." More than that, he wouldn't say. But he hoped she sensed the urgency in his tone.

For an hour afterwards, he was weak-stomached. He recognised this not only as completely unlike him but also as an indication of how little he could do at this point to stop the concrete ball from rolling down the ice slope on which it had been perched. When his desk phone rang at last, he snatched it up.

"Barbara," he said.

"Me." It was Dorothea. "Coast is clear. Detective Inspector Stewart has just left her office. He's looking grim."

"With triumph?"

"Couldn't say, Detective Inspector Lynley. Raised voices for a moment or two in there, but that was it. She's alone now. I thought you might like to know."

He went to Isabelle at once. On his way, he met John Stewart in the corridor. As Harriman had indicated earlier, the other DI carried a tabloid with him. He had it rolled into a tube, and when Lynley nodded at him and began to pass by, Stewart stopped him. It was a sharp move in which he slapped the rolled tabloid against Lynley's chest. He moved in far too close, and when he spoke, Lynley could smell the acrid scent of his breath. He felt rising in himself the inclination to shove the other man against the wall by means of his hand on Stewart's throat, but he quelled this inclination and said, "Is there a problem, John?"

Stewart's voice was a hiss. "You think you were discreet, the two of you. You think no one knew you were fucking her, don't you? We're going to see about that one, you and I. This isn't over, Tommy."

Lynley felt his muscles go so tight that the only release for the energy that made them that way would have been to throw Stewart to the floor and throttle him. But there was too much at stake here, and the truth of the matter was that he hadn't the slightest idea what was actually going on. So he said, "I beg your pardon?"

"That's right, mate," Stewart sneered. "You go all public school on me. That's just what I would expect of you. Now get out of my way or—"

"John, I believe you're in *my* way," Lynley said quietly. He took the tabloid from the other man's hand, where still it pressed against his own chest. "Thank you for this, however. A little light reading over dinner tonight."

"You piece of shit. The two of you. The three of you. All of you directly up to the top." This said, Stewart pushed past him.

Lynley went on his way, but as he did so, he opened the tabloid to see the front page. Mitchell Corsico's by-line was no surprise. Neither was the headline *Kidnap Dad Behind It All*. He didn't need to read the article to see that he had been outplayed by Dwayne Doughty. The private investigator was a master, he realised, the mouse who could wrest the cheese from the trap without even coming close to the neck snap that would kill him.

When he got to Dorothea Harriman, he nodded at Isabelle's closed door. She said she would check and she spoke into her phone. Would the detective superintendent be available to see Detective Inspector Lynley? she enquired. She listened for a moment and then told Lynley to give his superior five minutes.

The five minutes that passed stretched to ten and then fifteen before Isabelle opened her office door. She said, "Come in, Tommy. Close the door behind you," and when he'd done so, she gave a tremendous sigh. She gestured to her mobile and said, "It shouldn't take such an effort to plan a holiday to the Highlands. Bob wants to argue that it's 'out of the country' and as he has custody, et cetera, et cetera. Is it any wonder I took to drink?" And when he shot her a look, she said, "I'm joking, Tommy."

She went to her desk and dropped into her chair. Uncharacteristically, she removed her simple necklace, dropped it on the desk, and rubbed the back of her neck. "Pinched nerve," she told him. "Stress, I think. Well, it's been a rough time."

"I saw John in the corridor."

"Ah. Well. He was taken aback. Who can blame him? He wasn't to know he was being looked into, but honestly, what else could the man have been expecting?"

Lynley watched her. Her face was nothing if not completely what it ought to be. He said, "I'm not sure I understand."

She continued to see to the tight muscles in her neck. "I wasn't sure how it would work out, of course, once I assigned her to him and then reassigned her elsewhere, but I did think his antipathy towards both of us would do him in, which of course it did. She ran him on a merry chase all over London, and he ran after her. Doubtless there's some fox-hunting metaphor that a man of your background might come up with—"

"I don't hunt," he told her. "Well, once, but once was quite enough for me."

"Hmm. Yes. I suppose that's in order, isn't it? I daresay you've always been a traitor to your class." She smiled at him. "How are you, Tommy?" she asked. "You've seemed . . . lighter these days. Have you met someone?"

"Isabelle, what's going on, exactly? Hillier, CIB1, the DAC from police personnel management . . ."

"John Stewart's been transferred, Tommy," she said. "I thought you understood what I was talking about." She returned her necklace to her neck and rebuttoned her blouse. She said, "Barbara's brief was to suss him out. She would misuse her time left, right, and centre, and we would see if he misused his authority by setting up an unauthorised investigation of her. Of course, that's exactly what he did as his reports to me proved from the very first. Naturally, ridding ourselves of the man entirely is a virtual impossibility, but CIB1, Hillier, and personnel management came to believe that a spate in Sheffield might be just the ticket for John. To learn how to operate effectively within the confines of a hierarchy, I mean."

The release he felt was enormous. So was the gratitude. He said, "Isabelle . . ."

She said, "At any rate, Barbara played her part well. One would almost believe she was seriously out of order. Wouldn't you say?"

"Why?" he said quietly. "Isabelle, *why*? With so much at risk for you . . ."

She looked at him quizzically. "You're confusing me, Tommy. I'm not at all sure what you're talking about. At any rate, it's not important, I suppose. The crux of the matter is that John's been dealt with. The coast is clear, as they say, for Barbara's return and for a private celebration for a job well done."

He saw that she was not going to relent. She would have this her way or not at all. He said, "I don't know what to . . . Isabelle, thank you. I want to say that you won't regret this, but God knows that's not likely."

She regarded him evenly for a very long moment. For a flash he saw in her face the woman whose body he'd so enjoyed in bed. Then that woman was gone and, he reckoned, she was gone forever. Her next words made this so.

"It's guv, Tommy," she told him quietly. "Or it's ma'am. Or it's superintendent. It's not Isabelle, though. I hope we're clear on that."

20 MAY

She hadn't returned a single call from Lynley. What the fallout was going to be was something she didn't want to know just yet. So when she'd returned, she'd dragged herself into her bungalow and dumped the contents of her duffel onto the floor. She'd looked at the dismal collection of dirty clothing, and she'd decided that the next step was to lug it all to the launderette. She'd done so, sitting inside the place with its saunalike temperature and its unmistakable odour of mildew. She'd washed and she'd dried and then she'd folded. When it could no longer be avoided, she'd returned home.

The aloneness of the place seeped inside her skin. Given, she'd been alone for years, but it had been an alone she'd managed to deny through work, through the obligatory visits to her mother's care home, where the poor woman's mind was being taken from her by the tablespoonful, and through the unexpected but always welcome interactions with her neighbours. Those neighbours she didn't want to think about, but when she passed by their flat with its closed and curtained French windows, it was impossible to think of anything else.

It hadn't been a wrenching parting at the Pisa airport. That was the stuff of films. Instead, it had been something of a rush in which Azhar acquired tickets for, as things turned out, a flight to Zurich, from where he would begin the process of getting himself and Hadiyyah to Pakistan. This flight was soon to depart, and Barbara worried that, in these days of international terrorists, he would be denied a ticket by virtue of being Muslim, dark-skinned, and seeking to go one way only. But perhaps it was the presence of his charming daughter, clearly thrilled at the idea of a holiday in Switzerland with Dad, that obviated the need for further questions. His documents were in order and so were Hadiyyah's and that, it seemed, was all that would be required. Meantime, Barbara was arranging her own return to London. Soon enough—far too soon—they were on the other side of passport control and ready to part.

Barbara said, "Well, right. That's it," and she gave Hadiyyah a one-armed hug. She said to her with a heartiness that she made every attempt to seem real, "Bring me a kilo of Swiss chocolate, kiddo. What else do they have for souvenirs? Swiss Army knives, I reckon."

"Watches!" Hadiyyah cried. "D'you want a watch as well?"

"Only if it's dead pricey." And then she looked at Azhar. There was nothing to say, and certainly nothing that could be said in front of the little girl. So she said to him with a smile that felt like a rictus, "What an adventure it's been, eh?"

He said, "Thank you, Barbara. For what's gone. For what comes."

Unable to speak past the stricture in her throat, she gave him a jaunty salute instead. She managed a "Later, then, mate." He nodded and that was it.

She had the key to his flat. Upon her return from the launderette, when there was nothing more for her to do inside her own bungalow, she walked to the front of the villa and across the lawn and let herself inside the place, empty of him, empty of Hadiyyah, but somehow bearing the echo of them both. She wandered its rooms and ended up in the one Azhar had shared with Angelina Upman. Her belongings were gone, of course, but his were not. In the clothes cupboard everything hung neatly: the trousers, the shirts, the jackets, the neckties. On the floor were shoes, arranged in a row. On the shelf were scarves and gloves for winter. On the back of the door were ties. She fingered the jackets and she held them to her face. She could smell him on them.

She spent an hour in the sitting room that Angelina had so carefully redone. She touched surfaces of furniture, she looked at pictures on the walls, she fingered books on shelves. At last she sat and did nothing at all.

Finally, she knew, there was nothing for it. She'd gone to bed. At that point, she'd had eight calls from Lynley on her mobile and two more on her landline. Each time, as soon as she heard his well-bred baritone, she deleted the message at once. Soon enough, she would face the music she'd so jauntily claimed herself perfectly capable of facing. But not yet.

She slept better than she expected. She readied herself for work with more than her usual brand of care. She actually managed to put together something that a charitable fashionista might brand an ensemble . . . of sorts. At least, she eschewed elastic or drawstring waistbands in favour of a zipper and belt loops, although she certainly did not possess a belt. She also let slogan-bearing tee-shirts sit by the sartorial wayside. Her fingers *did* pause at *This is my clone. I'm actually somewhere else having a much better time*, but she concluded that—while true—the sentiment was largely inappropriate for work.

When she could avoid it no longer, she headed out for Victoria Street in the fine May weather. Passing beneath the profusely blossoming limbs of the ornamental cherry trees, she decided on the Underground instead of her car, and she made her way over to Chalk Farm Road. This would allow her to stop at her local newsagent. She needed to know the worst in advance of having to deal with her superiors' reaction to it.

Inside the place, it was airless as usual, its temperature a nod to the proprietor's homeland. It was a shop just marginally wider than a corridor, with one wall devoted to magazines, broadsheets, and tabloids and the other to every kind of sweet and savoury known to humanity. What she wanted, though, was not going to be among what was on offer that morning. So she worked her way past three uniformed schoolgirls in earnest discussion of the health benefits of pretzels over crisps and a woman with a toddler attempting to escape his pushchair. At the till she asked Mr. Mudali if he had any remaining copies of yesterday's edition of *The Source*. He responded with the assurance that indeed he had. He brought forth a bundled square of what had not sold from among the newspapers on the previous day. It was a simple matter to hand over *The Source*—she was lucky, he said, as there was only one left—and although he refused to take money for a day-old newspaper, she pressed it on him anyway. She also purchased a packet of Players and one of Juicy Fruit before she left the place.

She didn't open *The Source* until she was on the Northern Line, where most unusually, she actually was able to secure a seat among the commuters heading for central London. For a moment she hoped against all reason that Mitchell had not made good his threat, but a simple glance at *Kidnap Dad Behind It All* told the tale.

Her very soul felt heavy. She folded the paper without reading the story. Then, two stops farther along, she reckoned she needed to prepare herself. The many phone calls from Lynley that she'd ignored spoke of the Met's knowledge of her participation in everything concerning Hadiyyah's kidnapping. No matter that she had not known of Azhar's plan. She was complicit from the moment she'd involved Mitchell Corsico in manipulating New Scotland Yard into sending Lynley to Italy in the first place. Perhaps, she thought, she could come up with some sort of defence. The only way to do it was going to be to forearm herself through reading Mitch's story.

So she unfolded the paper and did so. It was damning, of course. Names, dates, places, exchanges of cash . . . the whole rotten business. There was only one thing missing from the article. Nowhere in it was she herself mentioned.

Mitchell had deleted every reference to her before he'd sent the piece to his editor. She had no idea if this was mercy or a Machiavellian preparation for worse to come. There were, she knew, two ways to find out. She could wait for the future to unfold or she could ring the journalist himself. She chose the latter when she reached St. James's Park Station. Walking along Broadway in the direction of the heavily secured front entrance to the Met, she rang the man on his mobile.

He was, she found, still in Italy, hot on every part of the *E. coli* story and the arrest of Lorenzo Mura. Had Barbara seen his piece this morning? he asked. It was another front-pager and he was dining out on the information he was supplying his cohorts in Italy who, alas, did not have his sources. By which, of course, he meant Barbara herself.

She said, "You changed the story."

He said, "Eh?"

"The one you showed me. The one you were holding over me. The one . . . Mitchell, you took out my name."

"Oh. Right. Well, what can I say? Old times' sake, Barb. That and the goose."

"I'm not the goose, there are no eggs, and we have no old times," she told him.

He laughed outright at this. "But we will, Barb. Believe me. We will."

She rang off. She passed a rubbish bin and tossed the day-old edition of *The Source* on top of a half-eaten takeaway egg salad croissant and a banana peel. She followed the line of people going through the Yard's enhanced security system. She was safe from one kind of judgement, she reckoned. But she certainly wasn't safe from others.

Winston Nkata was the one to tell her. Odd for him, she would think later, since Winston wasn't given to gossip. But that something big was going on was evident the moment she stepped out of the lift. Three detective constables were earnestly talking at the black detective while a buzz of conversation in the air spoke of changes having nothing to do with a new case developing and a team beginning to work upon it. This was something different, so Barbara approached her fellow detective sergeant. There, in short order, the news broke over her. John Stewart was gone, and someone would soon be promoted to replace him. It was that or bring in a different DI. The DCs present round Winston's desk were telling him he was all but poised to be the man of the hour. They had no ethnic DI under Ardery's command. "Go for it, mate" was how they put it.

Nkata, ever the gentleman like his mentor Lynley, would make no move without Barbara's blessing, and he asked her, "Have a word, Barb?" in order to get it. After all, she'd been a DS far longer than he, and just as they had no ethnic DI under the command of Isabelle Ardery, so also had they no female DI.

Nkata took her to the stairwell for a natter. He descended two steps to mitigate the great difference in their heights. What he had to say needed to come from an equal and height was a metaphor for this, she supposed.

He said, "Took the exam a while back. I di'n't talk about it cos . . . Seemed like I would jinx it, eh? I passed, though, but I got to say it: You been a sergeant for a long time, Barb. I'm not goin for this if you want it."

Barbara found this oddly charming, that Winston would defer to her when the likelihood of her even keeping her job at this point was more remote than the moon. Besides, it had to be said that Winston Nkata would always be the better choice to lead a team of coppers. He played by the rules. She did not. At the end of the day, that was a critical difference.

"Do it," she told him.

"You sure, Barb?"

"Never more than now."

He flashed his brilliant smile.

Then she went on, heading for the superintendent's office to learn her fate. For she'd been spared by Mitchell Corsico, but her sins were still great nonetheless. Away without leave was among the worst of them. There was a price to pay, and she would pay it.

BELSIZE PARK
LONDON

Lynley found a parking space midway down the street, in front of the long line of terrace houses. It was in an area undergoing gentrification. The house in question, alas, had not been touched by this particular brand of architectural magic. He wondered—as he always did when it came to areas in transition—about the safety of this part of town. But then what was the point of such wondering when his own wife had been gunned down on the front steps of their house in a pricey neighbourhood unknown for anything other than a house alarm accidentally blaring when an owner stumbled home too inebriated to think about disarming it?

He grabbed up what he had brought with him to Belsize Park: a bottle of champagne and two long-stemmed flutes. He got out of the car, locked it, hoped for the best as he always did when he parked the Healey Elliott in the street, and climbed the front steps to a shallow porch where the Victorian tiles that lined it had, gratifyingly, remained unmolested.

He was a little late. A conversation with Barbara Havers had resulted in his offer to drive her home. Since driving her home put him in the area to which he was going anyway, it seemed the reasonable thing to do. But traffic had been bad.

She'd spent ninety minutes in Isabelle Ardery's office. She'd emerged, according to that most reliable source Dorothea Harriman, white-faced and seeming . . . Was it humbled? chastened? humiliated? surprised? stunned by her good fortune? Dee didn't know. But she could tell, Detective Inspector Lynley, that no voices were raised during the colloquy that Detective Superintendent Ardery had with Detective Sergeant Havers. She'd overheard the detective superintendent say, "Sit down, Barbara, because this is going to take a while," before the door closed. But that was it.

Barbara reported very little to him. Other than "She did it for you," she didn't appear to wish to talk about it. But his "I assure you, she didn't" prompted further discussion between them because what he wanted to know was why she had refused to take his calls when his calls were meant to prepare her for what was going on at the Yard.

She said, "Guess I didn't want to know. Guess I didn't trust you, sir. Guess I don't trust anyone, not even myself. Not really."

She was silent after that and, knowing her as he did, he could tell she wanted to light a cigarette. He also knew she wouldn't do so in the Healey Elliott. So he used her nerves to press a point. "You've been saved in any number of ways. I saw Corsico's article about the kidnapping."

"Right," she said. "Well, that's Corsico for you. He goes his own way."

"For a price. Barbara, what do you owe him?"

She looked at him. He noted how drawn her face was . . . She looked broken, he thought, and he knew this had everything to do with Taymullah Azhar. She claimed they'd parted at the airport in Pisa. He wanted a few days with Hadiyyah, she said. Just the two of them, she said, to recover from everything that had happened in Italy. That was all she knew, she claimed.

As far as Mitchell Corsico was concerned, she reckoned he'd raise his Stetson-covered head when next he wanted a hot bit of information. She would, of course, be his contact of choice. She would hold him off. What else could she do? Of course, she went on, she could apply for a transfer. Mitchell would hardly want her as a source if she changed her circumstances so as to become gainfully employed in . . . say . . . Berwick-upon-Tweed. If it came to that, that's what she would do, she told him. Isabelle knew that. Indeed, the paperwork that was necessary to requesting a transfer had already been filled out, signed, sealed, and placed carefully away in the superintendent's desk.

"So she's got me by the nipple hairs, and don't I know I deserve it?" Barbara said.

He couldn't deny the truth of this statement. Still, he watched her trudge up the driveway in the direction of her bungalow, and he regretted the disconsolate set of her shoulders. He wished for her a different sort of life. He did not know how she was going to achieve it.

When he rang the appropriate buzzer next to the door, indicating Flat One, Daidre came personally to open it. Flat One was just to the right of the entry. She smiled, said, "Terrible traffic?" and he sighed, "London," and kissed her.

She led him inside Flat One and shut the door behind him. He heard the *snick* of the lock and was reassured by this. Then he told himself that Daidre Trahair could take care of herself very well, thank you. Truth to tell, though, when he saw what her accommodation was, he had his doubts.

It was a terrible place, with a shotgun arrangement of rooms, each more horrible than the one preceding it. They began in the sitting room, which was painted the pink of a newborn's tongue with a radiator done up in a less-than-compelling shade of blue. The floor was hardwood that had sometime in the past been painted lavender. There was no furniture, and he couldn't help thinking that was for the best.

A corridor ran the length of the place, narrow and sided by the walled-up stairway that had once made the building a family home. Off of this opened a single bedroom wallpapered in stripes of the bright vintage associated with the 1960s, Carnaby Street, and the heavy use of psychedelic drugs. The room would have no need of curtains upon its single window. It was painted over. Red had been the choice.

The next room contained the toilet, a washbowl, and the tub. The tub looked like a host for every sort of deadly bug. The window here was painted blue.

The kitchen came last, such as it was. There was room for a table and chairs, but neither a cooker nor a refrigerator stood in place. One knew it was a kitchen by virtue of a large sink. That there were no taps was merely a compelling detail.

Beyond the kitchen was, as Daidre explained to him, the finest feature which made the flat a true must-have. This was the garden, accessible only to her. When she had it cleared of the rubbish, the weeds, and especially the cooker and the refrigerator that lay on their sides with broom blooming through their cracks and crannies, it would be lovely. Didn't he think so?

He turned to her. "Daidre . . . darling . . ." He stopped himself. Then he couldn't keep from saying, "What on earth are you thinking? You can't live here."

She laughed. "I'm very handy, Tommy. It's all cosmetic . . . well, aside from the kitchen plumbing, which will require someone with more expertise than I have. But other than that, one must look at the bones of a place."

"I'm thinking osteoporosis."

She laughed again. "I like a challenge. You know that."

"You haven't bought it," he said. And then hopefully, "Have you?"

"Can't, I'm afraid. Not until my place sells in Bristol. But I *do* have an option. I'm quite happy about that. A freehold, as well. And that's nothing to sniff at, is it?"

"Ah. Indeed not," he said.

"You're less than wildly enthusiastic," she said. "But you must consider its benefits."

"I'm all ears and ready to embrace them as they are spoken."

"Right." She took his arm and they strolled back towards the sitting room, although in the narrow corridor this was something of a careful manoeuvre. "Number one is that it's not terribly far from the zoo. I can bicycle there in a quarter hour. No need for transport. I could even sell my car. Which I won't, of course, but the point is that I needn't deal with traffic to get to work. That and the benefit of the exercise as well. It's actually . . . well, it's heavenly, Tommy."

"I'd no idea you were a cyclist," he said mildly. "Roller derby, tournament darts, cycling . . . You're full of surprises. Is there more I should know?"

"Yoga, running, and skiing," she said. "Trekking as well, but not as often as I would like."

"I'm humbled," he said. "If I walk to the corner for a newspaper, I feel virtuous."

"I know you're lying," she told him. "I can see it in your eyes."

He smiled, then. He held up the bottle of champagne he carried. He said, "I'd thought . . . Well, I have to say I expected something . . . a bit different. Sitting on a sofa, perhaps. Or in a pleasant garden. Or even sprawled on a tasteful Persian rug. But in any case, christening the place and welcoming you to London and . . . I daresay, whatever followed."

Her lips curved. "I don't see why we can't do that anyway. I am, as you know, quite a simple girl at heart."

"Requiring what?" he asked. "I mean, of course, for the christening."

"Requiring, as it happens, only you."

BELGRAVIA
LONDON

It was just past midnight when he arrived home. He felt filled with emotions that would take time to sort through. There was, for the first time, a rightness about the life he was leading. Something fragile and previously broken was being reconstructed one extremely careful piece at a time.

The house was dark. Denton had, as always, left a single light burning at the foot of the stairs. He switched it off and climbed upward in the darkness. He made his way to his room, where he felt for the wall and flipped on the light. He stood for a moment, considering all of it: the great mahogany bed, the chest of drawers, the two vast wardrobes. In silence, he crossed to the embroidered stool that stood in front of the dressing table. Across the glass-topped surface of this, Helen's perfumes and jars still stood untouched as she had left them on the last day of her life.

He picked up her brush. Still it held a few strands of her chestnut hair. For less than a year he'd been able to watch her as she'd brushed it at the end of the day, just a few strokes as she chatted to him. *Tommy darling, we've had an invitation to a dinner that—may I be honest?—will be nothing short of the soporific that the world of science has been seeking for decades. Can we come up with an artful excuse? Or do you wish for torture? I can go either way, as it happens. You know my facility for looking fascinated while my brain atrophies. But I have my doubts about your ability to dissemble so well. So . . . what shall I do?* And then she'd turn, come to the bed, join him, and allow him to mess the hair she'd only just brushed. Whether they went to the dinner or not made little difference to him, as long as she was there.

"Ah, Helen," he whispered. "Helen."

He closed his fingers over the hairbrush. He carried it to his chest of drawers. He opened the top one and, deep at the back, he placed the brush like the relic it had become. He closed the drawer carefully upon its contents.

Upstairs, Charlie Denton was asleep as Lynley had expected. He knew that he could leave things until the morning, but he felt that this was the moment and he did have some fear that it wouldn't come again. So he went to Denton's bed and touched his shoulder. He said his name, and the younger man was instantly awake.

Denton said quite unusually, "Your brother . . . ?" for the fact of Peter Lynley's addictions and his battles with them was something they did not generally discuss. But wakened so suddenly, what else would he think? Only that something terrible had occurred to a member of his family.

Lynley said, "No, no. Everything's fine, Charlie. But I wanted to . . ." How to go on? he wondered.

Denton sat up. He turned on the light on his bedside table. He reached for his glasses and put them on. Awake now and back in the character he so assiduously played, he said, "D'you require something, sir? I've left dinner in the fridge for reheating and—"

Lynley smiled. "His lordship requires nothing at all," he said. "Just your help tomorrow, as it happens. I want to pack Helen's things in the morning. Can you sort out what we need to do this?"

"In a tick," Denton said. And when Lynley thanked him and headed for the door, "Are you sure about it, sir?"

Lynley paused, turned, and considered the question. "No," he admitted. "I'm not at all sure. But there's no real certainty about anything, is there?"

ACKNOWLEDGEMENTS

I'm indebted to some wonderful people who helped me with this novel, not only in the United States and in Great Britain, but also in Italy.

In the UK, Detective Superintendent John Sweeney of New Scotland Yard set me on the correct course towards understanding exactly what happens when a British national is kidnapped in a foreign country, as well as what happens when a British national is murdered abroad. It's a complicated process that involves the British embassy, the Italian police, the victim's local police from the individual's hometown in England, and New Scotland Yard, and I've attempted to make it a process that the reader is able to follow easily in this novel, and I hope I have been somewhat successful in that endeavour. The indefatigable and always resourceful Swati Gamble assisted in this, making initial arrangements for me and tracking down bits and pieces of information as I needed them. Private Investigator Jason Woodcock was essential to my understanding of what private investigators can and cannot do in the UK. He also was terrific when it came to the art of blagging, and it must be said that he bears absolutely no resemblance to Dwayne Doughty in this novel. Fellow writer John Follain weighed in via email with information about the labyrinthine nature of Italian policing, and his book *Death in Perugia: The Definitive Account of the Meredith Kercher Case* gave me additional assistance. Douglas Preston and Mario Spezi's extraordinary book *The Monster of Florence* was a great help to me in sorting out the part played by the public magistrate in a criminal investigation, and Candace Dempsey's *Murder in Italy* as well as Nina Burleigh's *The Fatal Gift of Beauty* were also extremely helpful.

With this novel, I bid a very fond farewell to my longtime UK editor at Hodder, Sue Fletcher, who retired in December 2012, and I begin my thanks to my new editor, Nick Sayers, with the hope that I'll be continuing to thank him for any number of years. It's also high time for me to thank Karen Geary, Martin Nield, and Tim Hely-Hutchinson for all they do to promote my books in the UK.

In Italy, Maria Lucrezia Felice started me out in Lucca with a detailed tour that took me into churches, piazzas, parks, and shops in order to familiarise me with the medieval centre of the town. She was also helpful in Pisa at the Field of Miracles, and together she and I attempted to work through the parts played by the *Polizia di Stato*, the *Arma dei Carabinieri*, the *Polizia Penitenziaria*, the *Polizia Municipale*, and the *Vigili Urbani* when it comes to an investigation. Giovanna Tronci's home in the hills above Lucca—Fabbrica di San Martino—was the model for my Fattoria di Santa Zita, and I am most grateful for the tour she and her partner gave me of the house itself as well as of the property. A chance encounter with Don Whitley on the train from Milan to Padua gave me the one thing I was desperate for—the source of the *E. coli*—and I am grateful that he was my seatmate for that journey, willing to let me pick his brain about his business in West Yorkshire. Finally, Fiorella Marchitelli was my amiable and lovely Italian tutor in Florence while I studied the language in Scuola Michelangelo.

In the US, Shannon Manning, PhD, of Michigan State University, was my go-to source for all things relating to *E. coli*, which she studies in her lab. She fielded phone calls and sent me photographs, and it has to be said that without Shannon's participation, there probably would not have been a book called *Just One Evil Act* in the first place. Josette Hendrix and the Northwest Language Academy started me off on my long and ongoing journey to learn Italian, Judith Dankanics has willingly practised the language with me for several years now, and for this novel native speaker Fiorella Coleman kindly went over every single Italian word or phrase to make sure I wasn't making any ghastly errors. This same service was also supplied by two excellent copy editors: Mary

Beth Constant and Anna Jardine. If there are any linguistic errors remaining at this point, they are my own.

Also in the US, I'm grateful to my assistant, Charlene Coe, who maintains good cheer and a gracious presence in my life no matter what request I throw at her; to my husband, Tom McCabe, who puts up with my long hours of disappearance into my study; to my goddaughter Audra Bardsley, who was my initial companion-in-arms in Lucca and who is always willing to go on a girl-trip no matter where it takes us; and to my supportive friends and fellow writers here on Whidbey Island and elsewhere. They always believe I can do it, and they never tire of telling me so: Gay Hartell, Ira Toibin, Don McQuinn, Mona Reardon, Lynn Willeford, Nancy Horan, Jane Hamilton, Karen Joy Fowler, and Gail Tsukiyama. There are probably others that I am forgetting in this moment of writing, but their omission is unintentional.

Finally, I must thank my literary agent, Robert Gottlieb, for steering the ship; my extraordinary Dutton team of Brian Tart, Christine Ball, Jamie McDonald, and Liza Cassidy; and above all I must thank Susan Berner, who has been my cold reader for an incredible twenty-five years. This book is dedicated to her, for that reason and for many others.

Elizabeth George
WHIDBEY ISLAND, WASHINGTON